UNEXPECTED GRACE

In Loving Memory of Anita Morreale and Franka Slattery

Unexpected Grace

RUTH PORTER

Photographs by the author

Ruth Porter

BAR NOTHING BOOKS

Montpelier, Vermont

Published in the United States by
Bar Nothing Books
100 State Street
Suite 351, Capitol Plaza, Box 3
Montpelier, Vermont 05602
802 223-7086
info@barnothingbooks.com
SAN 256-615X

Designed by Glenn Suokko
Typeset in Adobe Garamond Pro
Printed in Canada

978-0-9769422-7-6 (hardback) 0-9769422-7-5

978-0-9769422-8-3 (softback) 0-9769422-8-3

FIRST EDITION

Library of Congress Control Number: 2017900012

MAJOR CHARACTERS

Monika Adler
Her daughter, Alyssa Adler Bradshaw
Alyssa's husband, Richard Bradshaw

Alyssa and Richard's daughters
Sonia
Sonia's husband, Brian
Sonia's son, Jack
Alix (Alexandra)
Alix's boyfriend, Reuben

The Martel Family
Sam Martel
Sam's wife, Bonnie

Sam and Bonnie's children
Marnie (Marlene)
Marnie's boyfriend, Steve Louzone
Marnie's former husband, Ray
Marnie's son, Danny

Junior Martel
Junior's wife, Alma
Junior and Alma's two daughters

Night Time at Noon

by Ceres Porter

It's noon,
But inside our house
It is night time.
My mother is on the couch,
Curtains pulled shut
Behind her,
Refusing the sunlight.
She is mourning;
Her sister is dead.

But my eyes have been captured
By the thin ray of light
Coming from beneath the door.
The most beautiful thing, I think
I've ever seen.
Illuminated dust particles
Hang in the hazy, golden air.
And my mother is crying;
Her sister is dead.

CHAPTER I

Monday, April 19, 2010
West Severance, Vermont

Alyssa stopped walking and looked down at the trail. There was the little arrow Richard had made out of pebbles to mark the place where they could look down on the brook and the ravens' nest in one of the trees along it. There were four eggs in the nest when they found it a few weeks ago. That was when Richard marked the spot with pebbles. Alyssa thought it was like Hansel in the fairy tale.

She stepped carefully around the arrow and looked over the edge of the ravine. One of the adult birds was circling overhead, saying *quork, quork, quork,* but it didn't seem too upset.

At first, she was so excited that she couldn't be sure what she was seeing. When she finally got Richard's binoculars adjusted for her eyes, she saw it was true. The eggs had hatched. There was a moving mound of naked pink in the nest. It was more than two. She couldn't decide whether there were three or four babies.

Then the mother bird flew down and landed on the edge of the nest. While she perched there, she made one low call, and the baby birds opened their mouths and started to cry and beg for food, their heads waving on their skinny necks, their open mouths and throats bright red. Alyssa was sure she could make out three separate heads.

The mother bird stuck her beak in two baby mouths and flew away without feeding the third. Maybe she had fed that one before, because they all three got quiet when she left.

Alyssa watched for a few more minutes and then started down the trail for home. The stream below was wild with spring runoff. It made so much noise boiling over the rocks that it was impossible to hear much else. Now, late in the afternoon, the air had ice in it. It would be warmer in the yard. She probably should have stayed there. She had hardly started raking out the flowerbeds when she dropped the rake and went up the trail into the woods to check on the ravens' nest.

Alyssa tried to hurry, but the trail was steep and slippery with patches of old snow, and she wasn't as sure-footed as she had been when she was young. Once she had to stop for a fit of coughing left over from when she had the flu. She didn't know what time it was either, because she had taken off her watch before she started raking. Richard thought he would be back from town around four-thirty, but that probably meant five. It couldn't be five yet, but it might be after four, and she hadn't planned what she was going to do about dinner.

The first glimpse of the house was the best. All wood and glass, it sat exactly right on the land. They had left so many trees when they built it that they couldn't see the road or the Martels' house and barn next door. It could be as far away from anything as the ravens' nest.

She put away the rake and walked down the driveway to the mailbox. Under the trees, the first bloodroot flowers were standing above last year's dead leaves. Sam Martel was getting his mail. His big German shepherd was beside him. If she had noticed him in time, she might have waited until he wasn't there, but she couldn't turn around after he saw her.

"Hello, Sam. How are you?"

"Well, I ain't dead yet. I can say that much. How about yourself?"

"I'm fine. Wasn't it lovely today? Everything is being reborn. I took a walk...." She stopped in confusion. She tried to cover the pause with a cough. She had almost said something about the ravens' nest.

Sam was flipping through his mail and didn't notice. "Junk. That's all the mail is any more. Junk and bills. What a load of crap." He was a big man, and he had a deep voice. His hair was very dark, and he had one of those old-fashioned, handlebar mustaches. Alyssa was a little afraid of him, although Richard said she was silly.

Down the road behind Sam, Alyssa could see a red pickup coming toward them. "I bet that's Richard right there," she said. "It must be later than I thought."

The truck pulled up beside them and stopped. Richard put down the window. "Hello," he said. "What am I missing?"

"Nothing. We were just getting our mail."

"How're you doin, Sam?"

"Can't complain. And yourself?"

"Fine," Richard said. "Just fine. We made it through another winter, I guess."

"We ain't done yet. Not for another couple a weeks or so."

"I know," Richard said. "You can't ever be sure of the weather in Vermont. Still, I can't help getting hopeful this time of year. It's something just to see the ground again."

Sam nodded, but he was looking down at his mail.

"Come on, Alyssa. I'll give you a ride up to the house."

"That's okay. I'll be right up. I haven't even got the mail yet. You go on."

So Richard drove off, and she got their mail out of the box and followed. Sam was right. There wasn't anything interesting. Sam and his dog were partway to the barn by the time she turned around. She called a good-bye and followed Richard to the house.

When she opened the door, he was putting wood in the stove. He looked up. "It's freezing inside," he said. "The fire's just about out."

"I was thinking how warm it was in here. But I've been outside for hours. I guess that's why."

Richard shut the door of the stove and stood over it, rubbing his hands together. "I hope that's going to go." Just then, the stove roared as the new wood caught, and Richard smiled. "That sounds like it," he said, still rubbing his hands together. "I hope your day was nicer than mine."

Alyssa sat down in the chair by the stove to take off her muddy boots. One of her regrets was that when they built the house, they hadn't built a mudroom. Someone coming in stepped directly from the deck into the main living area. It was beautiful, but they were always tracking in snow and leaves and mud. "I've had a glorious day. The sun was so warm. Spring is really here. Everything feels alive again. I started to rake out the flower beds."

"I wish I had been here."

"I wish you had too, because—and this is the best part—I went up to the ravens' nest."

"Are they born?"

Alyssa nodded. "Three, I think. I saw the mother feeding them."

"I wonder what happened to the other one."

"Maybe the egg wasn't any good, or maybe the other baby was there, and I didn't see it. Come up with me tomorrow and look."

"Okay. Now, what's for dinner? I'm starving."

"I don't know. I've been outdoors all afternoon, and I haven't planned anything. What would you like?"

"What have you got? It needs to be hot, and it needs to be quick."

"I should have started something for dinner before I went outside. Oh, I know. I have some spaghetti sauce in the freezer. That won't take long. How does spaghetti sound?"

"Great, if there's a lot of it. I'm really hungry."

"There's plenty, I think. I'll get started right away."

It wasn't that much later when they sat down to dinner. The light was just beginning to change outside. Alyssa lit the candles on the table anyway. Later on, the little golden lights would be reflected over and over in the glass of the living room. The stove was ticking with all the heat, and the room was very warm. It felt so safe and cozy, so tucked in, to sit in their own beautiful room and know the coming dark and the ice were just on the other side of the glass.

As they sat down, Richard said, "I wonder if there are any phone messages."

"I forgot to check."

"I did too. I'll do it now."

"It could wait."

"It won't take a minute. I'll be right back." When he sat down again, he said, "There was only one. For you. From Dr. McCormack's office. You're supposed to call them."

"It's too late now." She didn't say that she was glad it would have to wait.

"What's it about?"

"It can't be anything much. I was just there for a checkup. I'll call them tomorrow."

"What did Dr. McCormack say about your cough?"

"Not much. He thought I ought to be over it by now."

"I think so too. Did he give you something for it?"

"No."

"You should have asked him for something."

"I didn't want to. It's only a cough, for God sakes. Let's not talk about it."

"Okay. Forget it. Tell me more about the ravens. I wish you had waited for me."

"Let's go up there tomorrow. Maybe you'll be able to tell whether there are three or four of them."

"Did you take the binoculars?"

"Yes."

"Did you put them back in the case?"

"Yes," she said, but she wasn't sure. What had she done with them when she went to the mailbox? She'd been drunk on spring and new birth, and she hadn't even thought about Richard's binoculars. She just hoped she had set them down some place safe and that she could find them before Richard did.

"When I was getting our mail, and Sam was there, I was so full of the ravens being born that I almost told him about them. I stopped myself just in time."

"That was lucky."

"I know. Suppose he thought they would hurt his sheep? He might go up there and destroy the nest or something."

"We've seen him butcher animals."

Alyssa shuddered. "I haven't, and I don't want to either. I don't think I could be polite to him if I saw him kill an animal."

Richard sighed. "If you meant that, you wouldn't eat meat."

"But Richard, really. I know I've said this before, but you don't pay any attention. I love to cook. That's why. I don't know why you won't believe me."

Richard looked up at the ceiling and said, "All right. I give up."

That hurt Alyssa's feelings, and she almost said so, but they had been over the same ground many times before, and they always ended up in the same place. Both of them ate in silence after that. Alyssa was thinking up arguments, which she didn't say out loud, and she supposed Richard was doing the same thing.

After dinner Richard helped her carry the dirty dishes to the sink. Then he went to his study to check his e-mail, and she began to wash the dishes. She thought about Richard's binoculars several times while she was cleaning up, and then she didn't think of them again until much later. Richard was still upstairs. She could hear the water running, so she knew he was taking a shower. She could go out and look for them without him noticing anything.

She opened the glass door and stepped out onto the deck. Here, on the other side of the thin sheet of glass was a different world. She stepped away from the door and looked up. Beyond the light from the house, the sky was black as velvet, with the stars pricked out and sparkling, some in the clear night sky, and some caught in the bare branches of the trees. There was a crescent-shaped moon in the west. It was completely still, except for the sound of the brook overflowing with spring runoff. The night was huge, a cathedral of icy purity.

Alyssa was aware of her own insignificance. She was even pleased by it. And then she looked down, and there on the railing by the steps were Richard's binoculars. It was as though they had just been set down there by a generous universe. How else to explain why she hadn't seen them before in such a conspicuous spot, or else why Richard hadn't?

She said, "Thank you," in a small voice and picked them up. They were cold, and so was she. She hurried indoors to put them away. It was a magic moment, but one she couldn't share with Richard. She knew it would go all wrong if she tried. Better to keep it to herself.

When Alyssa got up the next morning, it was just beginning to get light. The sky outside was electric blue, the way it is just before dawn when it's going to be a nice day. The stove was still warm, but the fire was out. She got paper and kindling and made a new fire. When it was going, she put a few small logs from the woodbox on it and went into the kitchen to make coffee.

While she waited for the coffee to brew, she stood over the woodstove, trying to catch what heat there was and watching the light grow stronger in the pure, cold morning. She coughed a few times, but she always had a cough in the morning in the winter. The air in the house was so dry.

After a while, she poured a cup of coffee for Richard and carried it up the spiral stairs. He loved to have coffee before he got out of bed. Her bare feet made a small metallic sound on every step. The iron was so cold it stung. Richard was proud of that iron staircase, and Alyssa had to admit it was beautiful. But when Sonia came with her child, it was a nuisance. She remembered how Jack managed to get around the barricade even though he was only one and just beginning to walk. She and Sonia had been talking and cooking dinner. They didn't notice Jack until he was six or seven steps up, standing, holding on to the railing, but swaying back and forth. Sonia managed to get to him before he fell, but it was a near thing. He could have been badly hurt if he'd tumbled down those stairs.

From the upstairs hall, she could look down on the living room filled with golden April light. The glass front of the woodstove glowed orange from the fire inside. She went into their room and set Richard's coffee down on his side of the bed. She could see a little bit of his hair. All the rest of him was buried under the tumbled bedclothes.

"Richard, wake up. It's a beautiful day."

He groaned and stayed under the covers. "What time is it?"

"A little before six, I think. I brought you some coffee."

He groaned again.

Alyssa went to the window at the end of the room and threw back the drapes. Even though their window looked north, clear light poured into the room.

Richard turned over, pushed back the covers, and hoisted himself onto the pillows, until he was almost sitting up. "It's going to be a good day."

"I told you. Let's go up to the nest."

"I bet it's cold out."

"We could wait til later, but I don't want to. It won't be that cold."

Richard took a sip of his coffee. "Oh, that's good," he said. "Where's yours?"

"I'm going down to stoke the stove. I'll get some then. The fire was out."

"So it's cold inside too. I think I'll stay right here." He grinned at her. She knew he didn't mean it. He was awake now. She went downstairs.

She was standing by the stove, drinking her coffee, when Richard came clanking down the spiral stairs. He had his clothes on, but he hadn't combed his hair. It stuck out in every direction. He went into the kitchen for more coffee and then came over to the stove. "You're not even dressed," he said.

"I know. I'm going right now. I'll be back in a minute." She started up the stairs. She hoped Richard hadn't realized that in the last few years she had tried to arrange things so that he didn't see her without her clothes on. If he had noticed, he would have tried to tell her that she didn't need to do that. He would have said something flowery, something she couldn't really believe, about how he thought she was more beautiful now than she had been when she was young. All she knew was that she was pretty sure Richard had been faithful to her for a long time now, and that those old days of lying and sneaking around were safely in the past. It wasn't as if he had ever done much. It was long ago, and maybe it had nothing to do with looks, but she didn't want to take any chances.

In a few minutes she was back in the kitchen. "Come on," she said. "Let's go up to the nest now. I want you to see it."

When they got partway up the trail, the ravens noticed them. They could hear first one and then both of the parent birds saying, *quork, quork, quork.* A few minutes later, they could see the dark shadow as one bird flew over just above the treetops.

"Hey," Richard said. "Don't worry. It's just the neighbors."

"The Martels are neighbors too, and they might need to worry about them."

"They probably know. In fact, they probably recognize us. Crows can recognize faces, supposedly."

Alyssa said, "I could feel that yesterday. They seemed to know me and to know I didn't mean to harm them. It made me feel great, like I was somebody important."

When they got to the place in the trail where Richard had made the arrow out of pebbles, one parent bird was sitting in a tree near the nest, a place where it could watch both the nest and the trail above it. The other bird was circling in the sky, making small questioning noises. Alyssa thought of that one as the mother bird, asking her mate if everything was going to be all right.

She stood behind Richard while he studied the nest through the binoculars. She was eager to know what he thought, but she knew he wouldn't like it if she interrupted him.

Finally, he lowered the binoculars and turned around. "You're right," he said. "There are three of them. I can't get a good look into the bottom of the nest. Maybe the other egg is there. There are definitely three live ones. Do you want to look?"

Alyssa took the binoculars and looked at the mass of pink moving in the nest. Every once in a while she could distinctly see a yellow beak. "It was much easier yesterday, when the mother was feeding them." She handed the binoculars back to Richard. "Do you want to stay and watch for a while? Maybe they'll get used to us and come in with some food."

Richard crouched down on the trail, and Alyssa backed up a little into the trees. They waited like that for a while, but nothing more happened.

Richard said, "I think the birds have more patience than the humans do. They're waiting for us to leave."

"I'm ready. My feet are getting cold. Maybe if we come up every day, they'll get used to us and go about their normal business while we're here."

So they started down the trail. Richard went first. Alyssa liked to go more slowly and look at things. At first the roaring brook was far below them, and there was a steep drop beside the trail. But as they went down, the difference leveled out. When they got to the waterfall, the trail ran beside the water. They walked around the pool where they swam in the summer. The ice was out now, and the water looked dark and cold. Beyond the pool the trail went up again, under the large, old hemlocks, past the cabin.

Alyssa said, "I can't believe we ever lived there. It's so gloomy under these trees."

"It's different in the summer. You want shade then. We bought it for summers, remember."

"You stayed in it almost the whole winter after you lost your job."

"That was different. I came to nurse my wounds. Maybe I even wanted to hide in the darkness, in the woods. And later on, you lived there too."

By now they were coming out into the yard, and their house stood before them with the sun glinting off the glass.

Alyssa hurried a few steps until they were walking side by side. "Well, I'm glad the way it all happened, because otherwise we wouldn't live in this beautiful place."

Richard took her hand. She could feel his fingers through both of their gloves. "You didn't always feel that way."

"I do now. Let's never leave. Let's stay here for the rest of our lives."

"That suits me. I love it here." He gave her hand a squeeze and then dropped it to open the door.

CHAPTER 2

Richard had set up his laptop so he could work on the sofa in the upstairs hall. It was one of his favorite spots. It was filled with light from the windows in the living room below, and it was the warmest place in the house when the woodstove was going.

He was just about to check his e-mail when he heard a noise downstairs. He set the computer off his lap and went to the railing and looked over. Someone was on the deck knocking on the glass door. The legs and feet looked like Sam Martel's, but that was all Richard could see from that angle.

He went down the spiral stairs in his sock feet and slid open the glass door. It was Sam. His big, black dog was right behind him.

Richard said, "Come on in."

"I can't. Thanks, but I got my barn clothes on."

"That's okay. It doesn't matter."

But Sam shook his head.

Richard didn't want to step outdoors in his sock feet, so he couldn't close the door. He started to ask Sam what he wanted, but he was silenced by the troubled look on Sam's face. "Are you okay, man?" was what he said instead.

Sam nodded yes, but his face was crumpling. He looked about to cry.

Richard didn't know what to do or where to look. Sam always seemed to have everything together. The only emotion he ever showed Richard was irritation at the stupidity of other people. And Richard didn't know him all that well, even though they had lived next door to each other for more than twenty years. If Sam did begin to cry, what would he do? If he put an arm around Sam to comfort him, it could be misinterpreted. It could be worse than doing nothing. Richard stood there in the open door with his arms dangling, feeling embarrassed and mean-spirited.

Sam turned his back for a minute and blew his nose. When he turned toward Richard again, his face had smoothed out some, but he still didn't look directly at Richard. "Sorry about that. I need to talk to you."

"Oh sure, sure." Richard's mind was stumbling over all kinds of crazy ideas. "Come inside."

"No, I can't, and Alyssa...." Sam looked past him into the room.

"She's not here. She's gone to town."

"I'm on my way to my barn to do chores. That's where Bonnie thinks I am now. Could you come over there, do you think?" He looked doubtfully down at Richard's sock feet.

"Oh sure. I'll be glad to. I just have to turn off my computer and get my boots and a jacket."

"I'll see you then," Sam said. "Come on, Colt." He walked off with the dog beside him.

In a few minutes Richard followed them. He was still puzzling over what it could be about. He didn't even think of leaving Alyssa a note until he was halfway to Sam's barn, and then he decided not to take the time to go back.

He opened the barn door and went inside. The entryway was dark and cluttered. There were bits of old harness hanging on the walls and rusty pieces of machinery on the floor. Everything was dusty and draped with cobwebs. He went out into the main part of the barn, a long, low-ceilinged room filled with dusty light from the windows along both sides. Sam's dog gave a short bark when he saw Richard standing in the doorway. He came over and sniffed Richard's legs.

Richard hadn't been in Sam's barn many times over the years, but he remembered the surprise of stepping into that bright room after the first dark one. In Dan Martel's time, it was the milking parlor for a small herd of Jerseys. Richard remembered how those cows stood facing the windows. When he walked in there the first time with Alyssa and the two girls right on his heels, Dan Martel stood up from somewhere and came toward them down the center aisle between the rows of cows. That was in the summer of 1978. They were in Vermont on a camping vacation when they saw Dan Martel's handwritten sign saying he had a cabin and ten acres for sale. They ended up buying the property, a thin strip of woods along a wild, cascading brook.

Richard stood at the end of the center aisle, thinking about Dan Martel and how much the barn had changed since his time. Sam only had one small Jersey cow. She stood in her stanchion at the near end of the row. Beyond her, Sam had taken out stanchions and boarded over some of the windows to make pens for his sheep and pigs.

Richard was just about to walk down the aisle for a closer look into the pens when he saw Sam at the far end with a bale of hay in each hand. The sheep must have seen him too because they all began to baa and stick their heads over the gates. Richard was going to say something to Sam, but there was too much noise.

Sam stopped part of the way down the aisle to break open the bales and hand out hay to the sheep pens. Things got quieter. Sam carried some of the hay down to the little cow. Then he straightened up and looked at Richard. "Thank you very much for comin'," he said formally.

"Of course. But I don't know...."

Sam said, "They let me go." He turned around and slapped the little cow on the rump. He must have hit her hard because she jumped forward, rattling her stanchion.

It took Richard a moment before he realized what Sam was saying.

"Oh man," he said. "I'm truly sorry. I thought you wanted help with something in the barn."

Sam turned around and looked at him. "I could of handled that." He wiped his nose on his sleeve. "But I don't know how to keep Bonnie from findin out."

"You'll have to tell her."

"I can't do that. You don't know her. You don't know how she'd carry on."

"You haven't got a choice. I mean, if you could hide it, you might want to try, but there's no way you could pull it off, and if you try, you'll make the whole thing worse."

"If she finds out, it'll be awful. She'll cry and carry on. I need to...."

"Do you want me to tell her?"

Sam looked directly at him for the first time. "Oh my God, no. That would be even worse. That ain't why I wanted you here. Don't even think it. I hope she didn't see you when you came in. She's in the house, you know."

Just then the cow slowly raised her tail and let out some manure. Sam got a manure fork and picked it up and threw it into the gutter, away from where they were standing.

Richard began to get impatient. He didn't know what he was doing there, and he didn't see how he could leave. Alyssa could get home any time now, and he hadn't left her a note. He said, "Think about it, Sam. You don't have a choice."

"You don't know what I'm tryin to deal with here."

"Well, yes I do, as a matter of fact. I remember when it happened to me."

"You?"

"Yeah. I got laid off in 1989, I think it was, from my job in Stamford."

"You did?"

"That was how we ended up in Vermont. Of course I remember the feeling. I felt like I wanted to crawl in a hole and die."

Sam made a choking noise and nodded his head.

"It was just after Thanksgiving. We had bought the land and the cabin from your dad for a vacation spot about ten years before. I didn't want to see anyone, so I came up and stayed in the cabin where I could be alone. I felt like a wounded animal."

"That's how I was when I got home from 'Nam. That's why I built that cabin in the first place. That was a tough time for me. I'm not sure I can go through that again. If you think it's goin to be that bad...."

"Don't go by me. I don't know. I was just remembering what it felt like when it happened to me. Maybe it won't be like that for you. What are you going to do?"

"What can I do? I'll have to find another job."

"Okay. That makes sense."

"It's a awful bad time to be lookin."

"You can't help that. How long until you're all done?"

"Just this week. That's all they're goin to give me. I'm all done Friday." He choked a little and went out into the anteroom. The dog was lying on some hay and watching everything.

When Sam came back with the milk pail, Richard said, "You'll be eligible for unemployment. Right?"

"I guess so." He sat down on a milking stool beside the cow and began to wash off her bag. After a minute, Richard could hear the steady, rhythmic sound of the milk hitting the side of the pail. He'd always wanted to learn how to milk. It really looked easy. He thought he would ask Sam to show him how, but not today. He said, "I could loan you some money to get you by until you start to collect unemployment."

Sam swiveled around so that he was looking up at Richard with his head still against the flank of the little cow. "Thanks," he said. "We'll be okay...for a while anyhow. Bonnie's workin, and we've got some savins too. It ain't the money exactly."

"I know what you mean. A job kind of gets you out there. Somehow you have time on your hands without it."

Sam was still milking. The sound of the milk hitting the pail changed slowly as the pail filled. "I could use more time. I've had to turn people away, people that wanted me to do their butcherin. I have more jobs than I can get to."

"There you go," Richard said. "It could be good."

Sam stood up and handed the pail to Richard. "Stand back a little. I've got to let her loose."

Richard stepped aside. The little cow backed out of her stanchion and walked sedately down the aisle between the pens.

Sam said, "I always thought I might go out on my own with a little meat processin business." He went after the little cow. Richard set the pail down and followed them.

Over his shoulder Sam said, "I thought I would be the one to choose the time. That's all."

At the back of the big room there was a trough with water running through it. They stood waiting, while the little cow drank.

"Spring ain't the right time to start a butcherin business."

"Who knows? It might give you a chance to get it all organized before you get too busy. This might be the push you've been waiting for."

Sam reached out for Richard's hand and shook it. "I've always said you were a good neighbor. Thanks for helpin me sort this out."

On the way down the aisle Richard lagged behind and stopped at a pen with two large pigs in it. He was thinking about how crowded their quarters were when Sam came back from putting the little cow in her stanchion.

"Them two have been needin to be butchered for quite a while. I guess I'll have some time to catch up now." He took a stick that was leaning against the pen and began to scratch the pigs' backs, first one and then the other. Each pig curved its back up against the pressure of the stick and grunted with pleasure. "Would you like some pork? I could give you a real good price. These pigs are goin to be good eatin."

"Thanks," Richard said. "I'll have to ask Alyssa. And I probably better get back over there, if you're all right. Let me know if there's anything I can help you with. What are you going to do about Bonnie?"

"I'm goin to try to tell her. I don't know if I can, that's all."

"Sure you can. Just do it fast, and then it'll be over with."

"I'll try."

"Good man."

Alyssa was in the kitchen when he walked in. It was very warm inside, and the radio was on loud. Alyssa leaned over the counter. "Where were you, Richard? I looked for you everywhere. I even went part of the way up to the ravens' nest."

"I was over at Martels'."

"What? Oh, wait a minute." She turned off the radio.

"I said I was at Martels', in the barn."

"You were? I never would have thought of looking there."

He took off his jacket and boots and put them away. "Sam came over and got me. He asked me to come to the barn."

"What was wrong?"

"I thought he needed help with something heavy or broken, or maybe with a hurt animal. But it wasn't anything like that."

Alyssa was listening with interest. She reached behind her and turned off the stove without looking at it.

At first he didn't want to tell her. He had felt close to Sam and as though he had helped him, and Alyssa was outside that. Also, she didn't really like Sam that much. He intimidated her with his blustery manner. But she was waiting to hear, so he blurted it out. "Sam got laid off."

"Really? Poor Sam. Was he upset?"

"Of course. It's a tough thing. For a few minutes there, I thought he might begin to cry."

"God. That doesn't sound like Sam. I'm really sorry."

"I think he was feeling a bit better when I left."

"What was his job anyway?"

"I didn't like to ask. I thought I remembered that he worked in the granite sheds, but I don't remember what he did there, if I ever knew."

"Why did he tell you? I mean, we've never had that much to do with the Martels."

"He wanted someone to talk to. He was trying to figure out how to keep Bonnie from finding out."

Alyssa opened her mouth to say something, but he went on. "I think I convinced him that was impossible."

"Crazy, that's what it is."

Richard stood with his back to the fire. He had to move forward every few minutes when his clothes got too hot, but the heat felt nice. "I can understand it. It feels shameful to be laid off, even if it is one of those times when a whole bunch of people get laid off together, like the way it happened to me. It still feels like someone is saying they don't want you, they don't need you, what you were doing wasn't useful to them. That hurts. Of course he doesn't want Bonnie to know. I remember how hard it was for me to tell you when it happened to me."

"But, Richard, didn't you think I'd be sympathetic?"

"Yes, I knew you would be. And I'm sure Bonnie will be too. I guess I didn't want your pity. I wanted your respect. I wanted to look good for you. Sam's afraid Bonnie will cry and carry on."

"Do you think I ought to call over there?"

"No. Let's let Sam handle it his way."

"I'd better get back to my cooking."

"It smells great. What are we having?"

Alyssa turned the stove back on. There were lots of sputtering noises. "Pork chops and mashed potatoes and peas. I hope you're hungry. I found some really nice chops at the co-op grocery. They were quite cheap."

"Pork," Richard said, almost to himself. "That's funny."

"Why?"

"I mean, it's strange. I was looking at two big pigs Sam has in a pen in his barn. He said he was going to butcher them and that he would give me a good price on the meat. He said it was going to be very tasty."

"What price did he say?"

"I don't know. I felt uncomfortable standing right there in front of them, scratching their backs and talking about eating them."

"They couldn't understand."

"I know, but it still felt creepy."

"I wonder how much he's going to charge."

"Are you interested then? I didn't think you would be. I thought you'd be horrified."

"I am. But we've got to eat, and it would be nice to help Sam."

She turned around to adjust the meat in the pan, and he stood there by the woodstove, watching her and thinking how after all the years they had been together, she could still surprise him. He could still be entirely wrong when he thought he knew what she was thinking.

"Okay," he said. "I'll ask Sam tomorrow what he wants for some of that pork."

"Good."

"I'll ask him if he'll cut it up for us. It'll be a good excuse to go over and see how he's doing."

She didn't answer. Maybe she didn't hear. He watched her moving around between the stove and the counter. Her cheeks were flushed and her dark hair curled around her face. When she was absorbed like that, she looked young, the way she had long ago. He wondered, as he always did, about her hair. His got duller and grayer all the time. It had never been anything but an in-between color at best. But hers stayed dark and bright. If she did anything to it, she was very discreet. He'd never caught her at it.

CHAPTER 3

When Sam went into the kitchen, he was surprised to find it empty. On the way from the barn he argued with himself about telling Bonnie he had lost his job. Part of him thought he should say something right away, but another part of him thought he ought to wait until dinner was over at least. Then he pictured himself sitting across the table from her, and he wondered what he would say if he wasn't telling her, and he could see how nervous he would get. She would be sure to notice. Thinking about it like that made him realize that Richard was right. He hadn't pictured to himself what it would be like not to tell. Picturing it, he saw that he would have to tell, and the sooner the better. By the time he got to the house, he had decided.

So he opened the door and walked in, already saying, "Bonnie, I got to tell you somethin." And he said it to the empty kitchen. She wasn't there. There was something cooking in the oven. He could hear it hissing. It smelled good. He washed his hands in the kitchen sink, a thing Bonnie didn't like him to do, and looked in the oven. A casserole dish of macaroni and cheese was bubbling in there. It looked ready to eat.

He closed the oven and straightened up just as Bonnie walked in, swaying a little from side to side, the way she always did. "It looks good," he said. "Is that what we're havin?"

She smiled at him. "I hope you're hungry. There's cake for dessert too."

"I'm plenty hungry," he said. "Shall I set the table?"

"Fix us a couple of trays so we can sit out by the TV. I want to put my feet up. My legs have been botherin me all day."

"I'm sorry," he said. He got out two trays and put plates and silverware on them. "Couldn't you leave early?"

"No. It was really busy. I couldn't even sit down hardly."

Sam didn't say anything. He couldn't help comparing it to his own situation. And more, as long as she was the only one with a job, she wouldn't be able to take time off, no matter how much her legs bothered her.

He hurried into the TV room and moved the big footstool over so that it was in front of her seat on the couch. Then he took all the pillows and plumped them up around her place.

When he looked up, Bonnie was standing in the doorway with her tray in her hands. "I fixed your plate," she said. "There's bread if you want it. I gave you some salad and macaroni. *What* are you doin?"

"Just makin you comfortable. Is there any beer?"

"I think there's one in there. There's plenty of Diet Pepsi anyways."

When he came back with his food, Bonnie was sitting down. Her feet were up on the footstool, and Minnie was lying beside it. She said, "Oh good, you found a beer."

"Yes," he said, hoping it would give him some courage. He had missed the chance to tell her right away. "It's the last one."

"I'll get more tomorrow."

He sat down, and they began to eat. Bonnie shifted her weight around and groaned a little.

Sam jumped up. "Can I move the footstool to a better place for you?"

"Sam, what's goin on?"

"Nothin. I'm just worried about you." He sat down again.

"You're actin so weird. You're makin me nervous."

"The macaroni is good tonight."

"Uh huh. You done somethin you don't want me to know about."

"Well, no…I mean…it wasn't me." He put down his tray and jumped up again.

"See. I knew it."

"No, Bonnie, you got it wrong."

"Well, tell me then."

"We could wait til we're done eatin. I could tell you after."

"No. Tell me now." She set the tray to one side and sat back against the pillows. "Come up here, Minnie. Come sit on my lap."

Minnie stood there, looking up. She could do it, but it was hard. Sam picked her up and set her on Bonnie's lap. Then he began to walk around the room. Every time he looked at Bonnie, she was watching him. He took in a breath and said, "They laid me off." It wasn't the way he meant to tell her.

"Oh," she said, and then she was quiet. She sat looking down at Minnie.

"Now, Bonnie, don't get upset."

"I'm not. I'm just thinkin. You act like it was your fault. Was it?"

"No, of course not. I wasn't the only one. They laid off a whole bunch of guys."

She sat there, looking down at her hands, playing with Minnie's white curls.

"See," he said. "I knew you'd be upset."

"I just wanted to make sure it wasn't your fault. You could of got in a fight with somebody or somethin.'

"Well, I didn't."

"I'm glad of that. I don't worry about the job. You'll get another job."

"That's what Richard said."

"Richard? Richard Bradshaw? How come he knew about it when I didn't?"

"He came over to the barn while I was doin chores, so I told him."

"Oh."

"You know what he said? He said this might turn out to be a good thing. It might be the push I been needin to get this butcherin business started. I mean, I'll have more time."

She nodded. "More time, but less money," she said, still looking down at her hands. "How long before you're all through?"

"Just this week."

"My. They really spring it on you, don't they?"

"We'll make out, Bonnie. Don't you worry."

"I know. I won't. I know you'll find another job. You're a good worker. Now, finish eatin. I want some cake."

On Saturday Bonnie was sitting at the table drinking her coffee when he came in from doing the morning chores. Colt was right behind him, practically stepping on his heels.

Bonnie said, "Junior called. Him and Alma will be out here before eight."

"Richard said he would be over too, but I don't know how much he can do. He wants to help, but he don't know nothin about killin a pig."

Bonnie nodded. She was wearing her pink fuzzy bathrobe that made her look like a big stuffed animal. "Get yourself some coffee, Sam. I put your breakfast in the oven to keep warm."

He went into the bathroom in his sock feet to wash up. Colt didn't follow him, the way he usually did. He stayed right by the door.

When Sam got back to the kitchen, Bonnie said, "It's about time them pigs got done. We're almost out of bacon."

"I know it. I just ain't had a chance." He got his plate out of the oven and sat down at the table. Minnie moved over so that she was sitting by his chair, staring up at him. She quivered all over when he looked down at her. "Bonnie, this little dog of yours is hungry. Didn't you give her breakfast?"

"You know I did. She's tryin to make you feel bad so you'll give her some more."

"Look at Colt. He knows we're goin to do somethin, and he don't want to miss out on it. If anyone opens that door, he's goin to be the first one through. He's a pretty smart boy, ain't he?"

"I guess. What did Junior say when you told him you got laid off?"

"Not much. I think he said he was sorry about it. What *could* he say? And anyway, he never says much."

"You want me to get you some more coffee or some more breakfast?"

"No. I want to get goin."

"It's only seven thirty. They won't be on time anyhow."

"I got some stuff to do before Junior gets here. I have to clean out that tub and set it up. I ain't used it since last fall. I got a lot to do before I can even start the water."

"Junior can help."

"I know. But it's goin to be tight if we do both them pigs today."

"We'll get 'em done. Let me get you some more coffee." She pushed off the table and stood up.

"No, honey," he said. "Thanks, but I need to move."

"Okay," she said. "I guess there's no help for it. I'd better get movin too. I can see this is goin to be a hard-drivin day." She smiled at him and left the room. He could hear Minnie's little feet clicking on the linoleum as she followed. Bonnie needed to clip her claws again.

He put his dishes in the sink, got his boots and jacket, and went out with Colt.

By the time Junior and Alma drove up, he had the bathtub scrubbed out. He had dragged it across the driveway in front of the barn and blocked it up with rocks. The hose was hooked to the waterline in the barn, and he was filling the tub while he set up the propane heater.

Junior came over. "How're you doin, Pop?"

"All right. I'm hopin we'll have time for both them pigs."

"I got all day and so doesn't Alma."

"Good." He started the heater and straightened up.

Junior took off his feedstore cap, smoothed his hair down, and put the cap back on. Junior was big and solid and square, like his mother. Beyond Junior, Sam could see Richard coming toward them from his house. Over the roar of the heater, he said, "Richard's goin to buy a side of this pork."

Richard came up to them and said hello. "It's been a long time, Junior."

"Ain't that the truth."

"I tried to get Alyssa to come over and watch, but she didn't want to."

Sam and Junior nodded. Sam put his hand in the water. It was already lukewarm, and the tub was still filling. "We better get that pig," he said. "Come on, Colt." He caught the look of surprise on Richard's face. "He knows what to do. He's a big help sometimes."

Junior and Richard followed him into the barn. He turned off the water, and they all went back to where the pigs were penned. For a minute they stood by the pen, looking in. The pigs were excited. They thought they were finally going to get the breakfast that got skipped this morning.

"Which one do you want, Richard?"

"I don't know."

"We're goin to do 'em both today. It ain't goin to make no difference to them."

It won't make any difference to me either, I guess."

"I think that one in the back there might dress out five or ten pounds heavier, but they're both goin to be good eatin. What do you say, Junior?"

"It don't matter to me neither."

Sam looked over at Richard. "I'm payin Junior in meat for his work and Alma's."

Junior climbed into the pen and blocked one of the pigs in a corner. Sam opened the gate. He had a bucket of feed. He showed it to the other pig and backed through the gate. "Richard, you and Colt stand in the aisle so he won't go the wrong way."

The pig came cautiously forward and stopped halfway through the gate. While he was hesitating, Junior turned around and gave him a slap on the rump, and the pig jumped forward far enough so that Junior could push the gate shut behind him.

The pig came slowly down the passage, grunting and snuffling at the floor and digging his nose into corners. Sometimes he moved forward, tempted by the bucket of grain Sam held in front of him. Once he stopped to eat something he found, smacking his lips over it. He couldn't go back the way he came since Richard and Junior and Colt were blocking his retreat.

When they got to Daisy in her stanchion, the pig turned toward her, and she swung out a little sideways with a back foot and kicked him. He squealed and turned around and ran toward his pen. Junior blocked him. Junior tried to get a bucket over his head, but the pig turned again and went back toward the cow, although this time he went by her, staying out of range of her feet.

"All right," Sam said. He opened the door and went out, shaking the bucket of grain and saying, "Here pig, pig, pig." He walked across the dark entry room, what his dad used to call the milkroom, and opened the outside door. It was going to be another clear, cool day, just the right weather for this work. He could hear the pig grunting behind him.

He walked out to the driveway and poured a pile of grain onto the ground and stepped back saying, "Here pig, pig," again.

The pig stopped in the open door and sniffed the air and grunted. He looked over his shoulder at Junior right behind him. He couldn't go back. He stepped out into the spring sunlight and hesitated. But then he ran forward to the pile of food and started eating greedily, grunting and smacking his lips.

Sam edged toward his gun, which he had left propped against the barn. He was eager to get it done. He aimed at the pig's forehead. Just then the pig paused in his eating and looked up, curious about what Sam was doing. That made the bullet go in a little low, but it was still good enough to drop the pig where he stood. His feet twitched a little, as though he was trying to run away, and then he was still.

Sam took out his hunting knife and cut the pig's throat. Richard and Junior were standing in the open doorway watching. "Come here, you guys, and help me turn him around, so he'll bleed downhill."

Junior came out and grabbed the back feet. Sam got the front. They spun the pig around, while Richard tried to help by pushing on the shoulders.

"There," Sam said. "That ought to do it." They all stood around the dead pig, looking at it. It was the first chance Sam had to feel sorry. The pig was friendly. He hadn't wanted much, and now he was dead, after a short life in a small pen. Now he was nothing but meat. Sam gave him a little kick in the belly with the toe of his boot and went to check the water temperature. It was almost hot enough, but it would be a while before the pig was bled out, so he turned down the heater and went to get the shovels and the scraper and the ropes.

When he came back, he leaned the shovels against a tree and threw the ropes down onto the driveway. Richard and Junior stood over the pig, talking. Junior was talking a lot, and that wasn't what he usually did, but Richard was asking questions, and Junior liked Richard.

Sam arranged the ropes beside the pig's body so they could slide them underneath. Then he ran his hand through the water. It was hot enough. He turned off the heater. "All right, Junior," he said. "Let's get this thing roped up. It's bled out enough."

They made two big loops of rope, one behind the front legs and the other in front of the back legs. Then they took the ends of the ropes and got on the other side of the tub so they could slide the pig's body up the car ramps and into the water.

"Easy now," Sam said, but he didn't need to. Junior knew what to do. They let the pig down into the hot water without much of a splash.

Richard hovered around trying to help, but they had it under control, and there wasn't a place for him on the ropes. When he saw how they slid the pig up the side of the tub, he said, "Hey, that's pretty cool."

Junior grinned at him. "One of Pop's little inventions to use them car ramps. They work good, don't they?"

Then Junior got on the other side of the tub with two of the rope ends, and they rolled the pig around in the water. Water sloshed over the sides of the tub. The pig's skin got pink and clean, and the water got dirty.

Sam pulled on a clump of hair to test it. "Not yet," he said. He saw Richard watching. "When we get it just right, the hair'll start to slip. It gets real loose. That's when we pull him out. If we wait too long, it'll set up again."

Richard nodded. "I'd like to help," he said.

"There'll be plenty for everybody when we start scrapin. We'll show you what to do."

After a few minutes, he tried the hair again. This time it came out easily. "Okay," he said. "Let's get it out."

Sam and Junior both pulled on the ropes. The water boiled and splashed. Junior grunted with the effort. After a few heaves, they flopped the carcass up onto the ramp. There was a big splash of water. Richard jumped back.

They let the pig slide slowly down the ramps to the ground and pulled it out onto the driveway away from the tub. Then they threw off the ropes. There were bright pink lines around the pig's body where the ropes had worn the hair off.

Sam pulled out a clump of bristles. "Good," he said. "It feels good." He got the shovels for Junior and Richard and took the hog scraper for himself.

He showed Richard what to do, and then left Junior and Richard to work on the body while he did the head with the hog scraper. He could see that Richard was trying to copy what Junior did. After a while they rolled the pig over and worked on the other side.

When they thought they'd cleaned off all the bristles, Sam looked it over. "Of course I know I'll find some places we missed. You always do." He said it as though he was saying it to both of them, but he was really talking to Richard because he thought Richard would mind him looking over his work. Junior wouldn't think anything of it.

He found a few places that needed more work. "Okay," he said. "I guess that does it. I'll bring the tractor around, Junior. The single-tree's layin over there by the tree."

By the time he got back, they had the pig's back legs hitched to the singletree. Sam lowered the bucket of the tractor, Junior hooked the singletree on to it, and Sam raised the bucket until the pig was off the ground. He drove the tractor around the side of the barn and left it running while he got off. They gutted the pig there and left the guts in a steaming pile on the ground. Sam drove the pig back to the bathtub. Junior cut it into two sides with the meat saw. They washed it off, and Sam drove it over to the basement door. He and Junior hung one side in the cooler and put the other on the butchering table. Then he called up the stairs to tell Bonnie and Alma it was ready for them. It was only twenty to eleven, and they were ready to start on the second pig.

CHAPTER 4

The odd thing was that Alyssa had to stop on the steps of the doctor's office and look around the parking lot for her car. She had no memory of where she had left it, and she always remembered things like that. It wasn't a big parking lot either. Her brain didn't seem to be working properly. She couldn't seem to make sense out of what the doctor said. That was the one thing that made her believe that there might be something in it. But it was crazy. She felt fine. There was nothing wrong with her except a cough, and she always had a little cough in the winter. Everybody did.

It was hot inside the car. She put the windows down and sat there for a minute. The cool outside air came in, smelling of earth and water. Spring was the time to be thinking of new birth, growing things, and hope, not disease and death. Everyone else was happily living their lives, and she might be facing a sentence of death. It didn't make sense.

And she really felt fine, not like when she had the flu. If Dr. McCormack had told her then that she had a spot on her lung, she would have believed it, but not now. He was probably being cautious and thorough. Still, she might have to have the tests he recommended, even a biopsy, even if it seemed silly.

She would have to tell Richard if she wanted his opinion, and it would be easy for him to say she ought to have the tests, even if some of them were painful. She felt very alone. She decided she wouldn't tell anyone. There was no sense in getting everyone upset about nothing. She would get all the tests, including the biopsy if she had to. Then when the whole thing was resolved, as she felt pretty sure it would be, she could talk about the incident in the past tense, almost as a joke, because she was sure it was nothing to worry about. She was so healthy, after all. After the tests, she would have something concrete to tell everybody, including Richard.

All during dinner she thought about not telling, about how the knowledge of what the doctor said was hers alone. It wasn't that she wanted to keep it away from Richard exactly. They weren't fighting at all. They were getting along very well. But the fact that the news was a secret made it less important somehow. It was a game she was playing, a maneuver, and she didn't have to think about what it could mean. If Richard knew, he would want to discuss it, and she would have to think about all the details.

She thought she was satisfied with her decision, but while they were cleaning up after dinner, Richard said, "Alyssa, are you mad at me?"

She was putting dishes in the sink. She didn't turn around to look at him. She just said, "No, not a bit, why?"

"It feels like it."

"I don't know what you're talking about." She started the water and put in some soap and stood watching as the water swirled over the dirty plates and into the glasses, and the soapsuds bubbled up.

"Well, like now. You won't talk."

She put her hand into the water, but it was too hot. "Ouch," she said, and then, crossly, because her hand was hurting, "What do you want me to say?"

"See. I knew you were mad. I just don't know what it's about."

Alyssa didn't say a word. She put both hands into the soapy water, even though it was still too hot, and she washed dishes and put them into the other sink. Richard came over and began to rinse them standing beside her. She was looking down at the dishes, hoping that her hair, falling past her cheek, would keep him from seeing the tears.

They stood side by side, working silently, but Alyssa kept feeling that Richard was fuming in the silence. She looked around at him, and that was when he saw that she was crying.

"Oh, Alyssa, what's the matter?"

"Nothing. The water's too hot. That's all."

"What?" He looked bewildered. He pushed the faucet her way. "Here. Put some cold in it. Is that really what's making you cry?"

"Yes…. No…. I don't know."

"Is it something I did?"

"No."

"What then? There must be something wrong." He turned off the water, even though there were more dishes to do. "Tell me."

"If I tell you, you'll think I'm worried, and I'm really not."

"Alyssa, what are you talking about?"

"If I say anything, you'll get the wrong idea. You'll make it into something bigger than it is."

"Try me."

"Well…."

"Come on, Alyssa. Let's sit down by the fire. I'll finish up the dishes later. I want to know what this is about." He led her over to the spot on the couch where she always sat in the evenings and took the rocking chair by the woodstove for himself.

He was being so sweet that she had to tell him. "I don't think I was really crying. It was because the water was burning my hands, and I wasn't going to say anything about what the doctor said because…."

"The doctor? Oh, that's right. I forgot you had an appointment today. So that's what's the matter."

"Richard, see, I knew you'd get it all wrong. Nothing's the matter."

Richard stood up and opened the door of the stove. He poked up the fire and put on another log.

Alyssa could see that he was trying. When he sat down again, carefully not looking at her, she said, "Dr. McCormack wants me to have some tests, including a biopsy." She couldn't help shuddering a little as she said the word.

"Where?" Richard said, still looking at the floor.

"I don't know. In the hospital, I guess. It sounds horrible."

"No, I mean, where on you? What makes him think you need these tests?"

"He said he saw something on the X-ray. Remember when I had to go have an X-ray the other day?"

Richard nodded. He looked too serious.

"Dr. McCormack said he saw something that looked like a spot on one of my lungs. But he said it was much too soon to know anything. Don't look so worried, Richard. I knew you'd make too much of it. That's why I wasn't going to say anything, and honestly, it wasn't what I was crying about—if you could even call it crying."

Richard came over and sat beside her and put his arm around her, and that was comforting.

She snuggled against him. It felt warm and cozy. "I didn't want you to worry when there wasn't anything to worry about. I'm sure it'll be fine."

They sat close together without saying anything for a while. Alyssa could feel herself slipping toward sleep.

Then Richard said, "Aren't you going to call your mother?"

Alyssa was suddenly awake again. "There's no sense in telling her until there's something to tell." But she knew she had already lost the argument.

"You know she's going to want to know."

"Oh, damn it. I knew I shouldn't have told you."

"And the girls. What about them?"

"I'll have to tell them if I tell Mom. You know the first thing she'll do is call them up. I just can't do it tonight. I'm not awake enough. I would say it wrong and scare her. I'll have to call her tomorrow." She thought for a minute. "If you really think I have to tell her before I get the tests done. It would be so much easier then. I could tell her that I had to have these tests, but they came back and said I was fine, and she didn't need to worry."

She could feel Richard's arm tighten a little across her shoulder. She said, "Richard, you know it's going to be all right. I've got a strong feeling about it."

He patted her shoulder and stood up. "I'm sure you're right, but you still need to tell Monika and the girls. Think how you'd feel if Alix or Sonia had to have a biopsy and didn't tell you until the results came back. You'd be so upset."

"But I don't overreact the way she does."

"You look tired, Alyssa. Call her in the morning. That'll be better for her too. She'll hear you better. Why don't you go up to bed, and I'll finish the dishes and do the fire and come up."

She looked at him standing there in front of her and felt a rush of love for him. He still looked the way he did when they met so many years ago. It was because he was so thin—all his friends had gotten wide and dumpy. "You don't have to take care of me. I'm not sick, you know."

"It's not that. You just look like you would like to be in bed right now."

"Well, it's true. I would. It's the crying, I guess. That always makes me tired, but really, Richard, I was crying because I burned my hand."

"I know that. Now go on, and I'll be up soon."

"Okay," she said meekly, and she went because it would feel so wonderful to be in bed, but she felt a twinge of fear as she went up the stairs. Did Richard believe her when she said it was going to be all right? Because if he thought something was wrong, it made the possibility much more real. That might be why she had thought of not telling him in the first place. And it felt funny to have him taking care of her. She was always the caretaker, ministering to his sports injuries and putting him to bed when he hurt himself. To have it go the other way felt strange.

She was all curled up under the comforter in a warm nest of bedding and nearly asleep when she heard Richard coming up the stairs. After a little while, she felt the covers rise up. A wave of cold air poured into her warm nest. Richard snuggled up close to her and put his arms around her. She groaned a little to tell him that she didn't want to wake up.

The next morning, after Richard left for town, Alyssa paced around the house, thinking of all the things she wanted to do, things she might start before she called. She knew she was making it into something bigger than it was. They talked almost every day, but telling her mother what the doctor said was going to be tricky.

She allowed herself another cup of coffee, as a bribe to be good. It was cold outside and raining. She sat by the woodstove and dialed the phone.

She counted four rings before Mom picked up. She sounded weak and distant when she said hello.

"Mom, how are you?"

"Is this Alyssa? Oh, I guess I'm all right. I've been kind of lame. It's my knee, as usual. But I'm okay."

"You don't sound it. I'm sorry."

"It's really okay. I don't want to complain. Sonia's coming over today after school to bring me some groceries so I don't have to go out. She's so good to me." There was a pause. "Well, they both are. I'm very lucky."

"You're very good to them too, Mom, you know."

"So how are you, Alyssa? Is your snow gone yet?"

"Oh yes, it's gone. It's raining here now. They say it might turn to snow, but I don't believe it. Is the sun shining down there?"

"No. It's raining here too."

"So," Alyssa thought, "here goes." Out loud, she said, "I'm fine, but I have to have a few tests."

"What? What did you say? What kind of tests?"

"It's nothing much. I think it's fine. I feel fine. The doctor just wants to check on...."

"On what?"

"Oh, it's just that I had an X-ray because I was coughing, and he saw something he wants to check out. That's all."

"Oh, Alyssa."

"It's nothing, Mom. I feel fine. I just wanted to let you know."

"But…."

"It's too soon to worry. I'll let you know. I'm sure it will be fine."

"Have you told Alix and Sonia?"

"You tell them."

"I will if you want me to."

"But be sure to tell them it's nothing, just routine tests."

"You promise you'll tell me?"

"Mom, I just *did* tell you. That's proof, isn't it?"

"Yes…. I guess so."

"Tell Alix and Sonia that I didn't want to bother them because I knew it was nothing."

"Okay."

After she hung up, Alyssa sat there by the fire, thinking about the conversation. At least she hadn't had to mention that one of the tests was a biopsy.

CHAPTER 5

Monika had looked out the window so many times already, starting long before she could possibly have expected Sonia. When she finally saw Sonia's big silver station wagon turning in the drive, she almost didn't believe it. She hurried to the door and out onto the little back porch. It was damp and cold.

Sonia got out of the car and took a big stretch. Then she came around the car to Monika's side to get Jack out. "You don't need to come out in the wet, Nana. I can get your groceries."

"Oh, Sonia, I'm so glad you're here. I've been worrying all day."

"About me?"

"No, about your mother. She said not to worry. That's what I'm worried about."

Sonia was leaning into the car, undoing the buckles on Jack's car seat. She straightened up and looked at Monika, laughing. "You're worrying because she told you not to?"

"No, Sonia, don't laugh. This is serious."

Sonia stuck her head back into the car and finished undoing Jack's car seat. She lifted him out and stood him on the ground beside the car. Then she looked at Monika. "What is, Nana? I don't know anything about it."

"Your mother called me up this morning to say she had to have some tests, but not to worry."

"Did she talk to Alix? She didn't talk to me. Why didn't she call us?"

"She said she didn't want to worry you, that I should tell you about it, and tell you there was nothing to worry about."

By this time, Jack was partway up the stairs onto the porch.

Sonia said, "Jack, stay on the porch and wait for us."

Jack kept walking up the steps, across the porch, and into the kitchen.

Sonia looked at Monika and shrugged. "I'll get your groceries and bring them in, Nana."

Monika followed Jack into the kitchen. By the time she got there, he had pushed a kitchen chair over to the cupboard where she kept the cookies. "Wait for Mommy to get here, Jack. She has to say if you can have a cookie."

Jack looked at her solemnly and then climbed onto the chair.

Sonia came in with a bag of groceries. "I got everything on your list except…Jack, what are you doing?"

"He wants a cookie, Sonia. Is that okay?"

"I guess so…but just one, Jack."

By this time Jack was standing on the countertop. Sonia set down the bag of groceries and scooped him up with one arm. She opened the cupboard and handed him a cookie. Then she kissed him and set him on the floor. "I couldn't get you any plain bagels. They were all out. I got you some raisin ones. You used to like those."

"That's fine." She was so glad to see Sonia after worrying all day. "You always know what I like." She felt like hugging her.

Sonia smiled at her and turned around to unload the bag of groceries.

"I'm probably being silly about your mother. I mean, if it was anything, I'm sure she would have called you girls. But there was something about the way she said not to worry that got me worrying."

39

"You worry too much, Nana, and being all alone here all day makes it worse. How's your knee, anyway?"

"My knee?" She felt embarrassed. "To tell you the truth, I haven't thought about it much today. I should have done my own grocery shopping and saved you the trip."

"That might have kept you from worrying so much."

"Still, I'm awfully glad to see you." The groceries were all out of the bag. They put them away as they talked. Monika found the sales receipt and went to get her purse.

When she came back, Sonia was down on her knees, brushing the crumbs from Jack's cookie into a pile. Jack was standing beside her, watching.

"Don't worry, Sonia. I can do that later. But if you call your mother, can you let me know what you think...if you think she sounds all right or not?"

Sonia stood up and dumped a handful of crumbs into the sink. "Of course, but I don't know anything yet. There are all kinds of tests. What are these for?" She looked at Monika, and then she hurried on. "These probably aren't anything to worry about. I expect she's right about that."

"It's because she was coughing a lot. The doctor did an X-ray, and now he wants to do more."

"I don't like that. Why does he want to do more?"

Monika felt a clutch in her stomach. She was just going to say something about it when they both noticed that Jack wasn't there. She said, "Where's Jack?"

Sonia moved. She caught him partway up the stairs and carried him, kicking and protesting, back into the kitchen. "You can't go up there, Jackie. We have to go home. Daddy will be home soon. Don't you want to see Daddy?"

Jack stopped kicking and allowed himself to be stood up on the floor.

Monika said, "I wish they hadn't gone to Vermont. I don't see why they had to do that."

"You've forgotten how miserable Dad was when he lost his job. I was a teenager, but I remember what a blow it was to him. I guess that was the first time I realized that my parents weren't invincible."

"Yes, I remember, but he could have found another job here."

"They're very happy there. Mom loves that house and all the gardens she's made."

"I just wish they weren't so far away, that's all."

Sonia put her arms around her and kissed her cheek. "Oh Nan, it could've been so much worse. Suppose he'd found a job in California."

Jack climbed on a chair by the table.

"If they still lived in Stamford, we would probably know if something was wrong with your mother. You can't tell over the phone. You can't be sure she'd tell us either."

"I know."

"Richard's no use. I love him and all, but he might not notice if something was wrong with her."

Sonia laughed. She lifted Jack down from the chair and set him on the floor again. "If you're a good boy, maybe Nana will let you come over tomorrow." Sonia looked up at her. "I'll call you in the morning, and see what you think. I'm not working tomorrow, so we can do it any way you like." She gave her a quick hug and started for the door. "Come on, Jack. We have to go."

Monika didn't even have a chance to hug her back. "Wait," she said. "I haven't paid you for the groceries. I have the sales slip right here."

"I can get it tomorrow. Brian has a meeting tonight. I have to have supper early, and I'm already late. Come on, Jack. You can walk like a big boy. You'll see Nana tomorrow."

They went down the steps, while Monika watched from the doorway. She hated to see them go. It had been such a nice diversion, a swirl of activity that kept her worries at bay. She watched Sonia put Jack in his car seat. Then Sonia turned around and started up the porch stairs again.

Monika stepped out onto the porch. "What's wrong?"

"Nothing, Nana, but I just had a great idea." She was breathless. "Let's go up and visit them. We can see firsthand how she's doing." Sonia's face was full of eager excitement.

"Well, I…."

"It could be such a fun trip. We haven't been up there for ages. You could see how her gardens are doing."

"We'll have to ask them if they want us to come…."

"Oh Nana, you know they would, especially Mom. They haven't seen Jack for so long. I'll call them tonight." She ran back to the car, blew a kiss and drove away.

Monika stood there on the porch thinking for a while. After a little thought she began to like the idea, and after some more thought, she realized that it was the only possible way to settle the worry.

CHAPTER 6

Sam came in from doing the morning chores, while Bonnie was putting breakfast on the table. He set down the pail of milk and went back into the mudroom to take off his barn clothes. When he went back into the kitchen he said, "It must be a foot deep out there at least. I didn't think it would keep snowin all night. It's a regular winter blizzard. And it ain't over yet."

"Has the plow been by?"

"Not that I could see. Nothin's movin anywheres. I guess we're in for it this time."

"It sounds worse than I thought."

"I don't think you can make it in there, Bonnie. You ain't even got snow tires on your car."

"Sit down to your breakfast, Sam. I'll call Janine and tell her."

Sam washed up and sat down to the eggs and bacon and biscuits. He could hear Bonnie talking on the phone. After a few minutes she came in and sat down across the table from him. Minnie clicked along behind her and lay down by her chair. "Well, I got to go in after all. Do you think you could get me there, Sam?"

"Sure. I'll take you in the truck. We'll get through in that. But why?"

"A couple of the girls have already called in to say they can't make it. Janine's desperate."

"When do you want to go?"

"Let's have our breakfast. We can go as soon as I get ready. Okay?"

"It might could be a slow trip."

"It's crazy, ain't it? I mean, it's May."

They left about half an hour later. The plow hadn't been by yet. There was no one on the road all the way in except for an occasional plow truck. The snow was swirling and blowing around. There was no visibility. The whole world was reduced to streams of white outside the windows. Inside the cab, with country music on the radio and the heater blowing hot, he and Bonnie were in a cocoon, alone in the world.

It was a slow trip, but they got there. Bonnie looked at her watch. "This is great, Sam. I ain't even late. Thank you. I'll call you later, hon." She opened the door and slid down from the high seat. Then she slammed the door and was gone.

Sam drove home, trying to decide how he would spend the day. All the spring jobs he had been working on—fencing for the sheep and planting the garden—all those spring jobs he had been so busy with a few days ago had to be put on hold because of the sudden return of winter. It wouldn't last long. It couldn't, not in May, but there was nothing he could do about it now. He decided to go out and put the plow back on his truck and plow the drive. If it was going to be winter, he might as well act like it.

He couldn't find his warm gloves, and the zipper was broken on his winter jacket. He didn't want to go back to winter. It wasn't fair. The trouble was that there wasn't anyone to be mad at. It wasn't anyone's fault. His clothes might be ripped and used, but the wild creatures had it worse than he did. All the birds were back and lots of trees had blossoms on them. It was a matter of life and death for them. That didn't make him feel better exactly, but it did stop him from feeling so sorry for himself. He might as well get over it and plow the drive.

It took more than an hour to get the plow on. And he hated to undo all his work. He had it all greased and ready for next year, put away around the side of the barn and covered with a tarp. After he got it on the truck, he had to reconnect all the hydraulics and fill the reservoir. That took longer than it did to get the driveway cleared. But he got into the rhythm of it—the roar of the engine going forward and backward. The snow was wet and heavy, but still he got enough cleared so Bonnie's little car could make it out. He didn't need to push the snow back very far. This was sure to be the last storm of the year. And he laughed to himself, because if they did have another one even later in the spring, he wouldn't have to worry, because he would be already gone, on the way to Florida. If this was what they called 'global warming', he was going south.

When he finished his plowing, he drove over to Richard's place. He left the truck running and knocked on the glass doors on the deck. It had been only a couple of weeks since he was there before, upset because they were laying him off. He hoped it would be Richard who answered the door, and it was.

"Hey, Sam. You were right."

"What about?"

"You predicted this snow a few weeks ago."

"I did? That's weird. It took *me* by surprise."

"The other day at the mailbox you said we still had some more winter left to go."

"Oh, right. Well, you never know. You don't want to get too confident."

"I'm sure you didn't come over to brag about your prediction."

"No. I forgot I said that. I wondered if you wanted to be plowed out. I put my plow back on."

"I wasn't going to bother, but since you're here with the plow on and all...yes, we have family coming from Connecticut on Friday."

"Okay, I'll be glad to do it."

"Thanks. I'm hoping the snow will be gone by then. It's got to melt fast this time of year. But if any is left, these down country relatives will freak out." He grinned at Sam. "I'm really talking about Alyssa's mother. She's a nice lady, but she's in her eighties, and stuff upsets her, unexpected stuff, like going back to winter when you thought it was already spring."

"I got you," Sam said. "I can't change the season around here, but I can tidy things up a little bit."

When Sam was all done and about to drive away, Richard came out on the deck and waved to him. Sam stopped the truck, and Richard came over to it. He had two twenties in his hand.

Sam said, "Forget it, man. This ain't business. I'm just bein a neighbor."

"Take it, Sam. Every little bit counts, and I know you're going through a rough patch. Thanks for being a good neighbor. I'm sure it'll even out."

So what could he do but take the money? "I appreciate it," he said. "Thanks."

Sam went back home. It would be a while before Bonnie was done work. He turned on the TV to see if they had any news about the weather. There was a lot about the oil spill in the Gulf and how it was a lot worse than anyone thought. He saw a video of them getting boats ready to try to contain the spill with booms.

Bonnie called a little earlier than he expected. He left right away to pick her up. The roads were better than they had been in the morning, but it was still snowing.

He parked in front of the restaurant, and a few minutes later, Bonnie came out. "Hi Sam," she said. "You put the plow back on. You been out plowin all day?"

"No. I only did ours and Richard's. I figured you might want your car tomorrow."

"That's good. I will. Did you see any weather reports?"

"The snow's supposed to quit tonight."

"I hope it does."

"They're goin to try to contain that oil spill by puttin big logs around it in the water. That ain't goin to do no good. They ought to shut if off. That's what they ought to do."

"They can't, I guess."

"It's a pipe, ain't it? Why don't they plug the pipe?"

"I don't know, Sam. I guess they would if they could."

"Well, you wouldn't think they'd start in to somethin like that without knowin how to shut it off."

"Did they say this storm was goin to end tonight?"

"That's what the TV said."

"That's good. Janine wants me to come in again tomorrow."

"How was it today?" They were driving out of town now. You couldn't see very far ahead, but the roads were pretty good, and they could make decent time.

"It was okay. We heard there was trees down all over the place. Everyone was losin their power. Did we?"

"I don't think so. If it was out, it wasn't off for long. I didn't even notice, but then I wasn't in the house that much. Were you busy at work?"

"It was a funny kind of a day. For starters, we were short-handed because a couple of girls couldn't get in, but at first it looked like the customers weren't goin to get in either, and it seemed like it wouldn't matter. But then, all of a sudden around noon, it got real jammed up with all the guys that were out fixin the electric lines and the phone lines and the ones that were plowin everybody out. After that it got quiet again. And that was good, because we were really run ragged there for a while."

"When we get home, you can sit down and put your feet up, and I'll take care of you."

"That's sweet of you, Sam, but I'm okay. It ended up not bein a bad day. I ain't that tired, and you got chores."

They rode on through the winter landscape. Sam said, "It seems funny, don't it? I mean, it looks like a whole different place than it was a few days ago. It's like we got picked up and moved some place else."

Bonnie smiled. "It'll get back to normal in a few days."

"I hope so. It's confusin. I don't know what to do—plow snow or plant the garden."

"That's funny. You can't plant seeds in the snow drifts."

Later on, after Sam had finished the chores, and they had had supper and cleaned up, they turned on the television. It was still snowing outside, but it had slowed down a lot. They were waiting for the weather report when Bonnie said, "I was thinking I'd go to the bank tomorrow or Friday and move $500 over to the checkin, so we could keep up with our budget like we would of if you'd got your paycheck. What do you think about that?"

"I hate you to do it. That's what I think about it."

"I won't then, Sam, if that's the way you feel."

"Wait a minute. Let's see what he says about the weather." So neither of them said anything, and Sam tried to pay attention to what the weatherman was saying. He was standing in front of his big map and talking about things like fronts and systems that Sam wouldn't have wanted to understand even if he wasn't having trouble paying attention.

The man got done talking. Sam said, "He did say it was goin to clear off, didn't he? I get all mixed up when he starts in on all this front stuff."

"Yes, he said the snow was goin to stop around dark, and it was goin to be a lot warmer tomorrow." She reached across the couch and patted Sam on the leg. "I won't get that money out if you don't want me to."

"It ain't goin to last if we take $500 out every week."

"We won't have to when your unemployment kicks in. When is that?"

"They said it would start about ten days after I filed for it, and I did that last Friday."

"So maybe we'll only have to take money out the one time then."

"I'll believe that when I see it."

"We got all the regular bills to pay. They ain't goin to wait for the unemployment check to get here."

"Okay, Bonnie. I guess we don't want to get behind and have it all piled up on us, but let's just do it the one time."

"Sure, Sam. It's goin to be fine." She patted him on the leg again.

"Thank you, Bonnie. I know it is." But he didn't, really. Anything could happen. He might find another job, or he might be able to make enough butchering and cutting and wrapping meat, but he might not too. There was just no telling. It made him uncomfortable to think about it. He said, "They've got company comin over to Richard's this weekend."

"Who is it?"

"He said they were comin from Connecticut. That would be Alyssa's mother, and I think maybe she's comin with one of the girls and her family. I ain't sure."

"The snow'll surprise them."

"I plowed 'em out for that very reason. Richard thought they might could freak out over the snow."

"Did he pay you?"

"Yes, he did. Richard's okay. He gave me two twenties."

"See, Sam. We'll make out. You're a real good worker, you know."

"Thanks, Bonnie. You're the best."

CHAPTER 7

Richard watched Alyssa put down the phone. She said, "That was Sonia."

He could feel her looking at him, but he didn't say anything. They were sitting by the woodstove. It was a wintry night outside.

Alyssa coughed and said, "Don't you want to hear what she called about?"

"If you want to tell me."

"She was just making certain that we wanted her to come up on the weekend with Mom…and Brian and Jack, of course."

"I thought it was all settled."

Alyssa coughed again. Her cough was still bad. He flinched when he heard it.

Then she said, "Do you think they're coming because I told Mom about those stupid tests?"

Richard sighed. "I don't know. What did Sonia say about it?"

"She didn't say anything."

"Did you ask her?"

"No, how could I? I don't even know if Mom told her."

"Do they know we're having a blizzard up here?"

"I don't know. Maybe I should call back and tell them not to come."

He said, "Why don't you wait and see? I think it's going to melt really fast. It isn't still winter, even if it looks like it is, and Sam has plowed the driveway."

"Will you get out the crib tomorrow? If they don't come this weekend, they'll come soon, and we'll need it for Jack."

"What about Alix and her boyfriend? Aren't they going to come?"

"Sonia's been trying to talk Alix into it, but she doesn't think she can."

"That's too bad."

"Maybe they'll come on a different weekend. That would really be nicer for me. If they were all here at the same time, I'd be so busy feeding everybody, I wouldn't have much time to spend with anyone."

Later on, when they went upstairs and she started to open the bedroom windows, the way she always did, he said, "Let's leave them shut tonight."

"But why?" She looked around at him. "You always want them open, and the storm's almost over."

"Yes, I know. But I think it makes your cough worse."

"It doesn't matter. It'll get better on its own time, I guess."

"Let's try leaving the windows shut to give you a chance to get over it."

"Well...okay."

"It would be good if it was better when your mother got here. You know it'll freak her out if she hears you coughing all the time."

"That's true," she said.

"Besides, you might keep me awake with your coughing."

"Oh Richard, that's silly. Nothing ever keeps you awake." But she was smiling. "And I thought you were worrying about me."

On Friday night at eight-thirty, Sonia and her family and Monika still hadn't arrived. Alyssa got everything ready for them and then fidgeted around, looking out the door and arranging and rearranging things. Finally, Richard had to ask her what she was so nervous about.

"I don't know. I didn't even know I *was* nervous." She sat down and picked up the book she was reading.

Richard watched. She kept moving around, looking up from the book to stare outside. They had a fire going in the stove. When she jumped up to put on more wood, Richard wanted to say she was going to make it too hot, but he didn't want her to be more self-conscious.

When the car finally drove in, Alyssa was the one who heard it first. She looked out the glass door. "They're here," she said and went out without waiting for him.

He shut his book and caught up with her by the driveway, waiting for everyone to get out of the car. There was some snow left, mostly in the shaded places, but there were also small mounds along the drive, left over from where Sam had pushed the snow when he plowed the other day. Brian was driving, and Sonia was in the back seat with Jack.

Monika opened the door before Richard could get there to do it. She stood up slowly, holding on to the open door to support herself. Alyssa hugged her, patting her on the back. "I'm so glad you're here, Mom. Did you have a good trip?"

"It was long."

Richard went around to the driver's side of the car and shook hands with Brian. "We had to stop for refreshments for Jack. Sorry we're so late. I don't believe it. You guys still have snow?"

"We had a big storm on Wednesday, but even a lot of snow won't last this time of year," Richard said. He was looking into the back, where Sonia was getting Jack out of his car seat. "Hello Jack. How are you?"

"Okay," Jack said. "What's that noise?"

Richard listened for a minute. "It's the water in the brook, running over the rocks. It's called the Roaring Branch. Isn't that a good name for it? I'll take you to see it in the morning."

"Why can't we go now? I'm not sleepy any more."

"It's too dark. You couldn't see anything."

Alyssa said, "Come inside, Jack. I've got some cookies and cocoa for you."

That did it. They all walked toward the glass doors, slowly, so Monika wouldn't be left behind. When Richard saw how much trouble she had going up the steps to the deck, he resolved privately to spend more time working out. He didn't want that to happen to him. When he opened the door to the living room, a wall of warm air met them.

Sonia supported Monika into the room and walked her over to the chair by the fire. "Sit here, Nana. It's warm by the stove."

Monika sat down heavily. She groaned a little. "It's good to be here at last, even if it is still winter," she said.

Jack was right behind them. Sonia saw him and took him closer to the stove to warn him that it was hot. Richard, standing in the doorway with Brian, was touched to see how Sonia tried to make everyone comfortable. It reminded him of Alyssa.

And Alyssa was bustling around the kitchen getting the cocoa ready. She leaned across the counter. "Mom, can I bring you some cocoa?"

"I'm afraid it would keep me up. I'd like to go to bed soon, if that's all right."

"Of course it is. I know what. I'll make you some chamomile tea. That'll help you sleep."

"That would be nice." Monika leaned back in the chair and closed her eyes.

Richard decided to go get the suitcases. He opened the door and stepped out. It was a relief to get into the cold air outdoors.

Brian came out too, holding Jack's hand. "Let's find something for you to carry, Jackie." He opened the trunk and set everything on the ground behind the car. There were a lot of bags and a crib for Jack.

He showed Richard which ones were Monika's, and Richard took them to her room and came back to help with the other stuff. Brian had moved everything up to the deck by the time he got back.

"Grampa," Jack said. "Let's go look at the water now. Daddy said I could go if you would take me."

"It's dark. I don't think you could see anything."

"I don't care. I just want to go. Daddy said we could."

"Well," Richard said, stalling for time, until he thought about how hot it was in the house and how nice a walk in the dark would be. "Don't you want some cocoa and cookies?"

"No. I want to walk with you."

Richard melted—a little boy who would rather be outdoors than have a cookie was just what he had always wished for. "Brian, we're going to take a look at the brook. Do you want to come?"

"I'll get these things inside, and then I'll catch up with you. Do you want a flashlight? There's one in the car."

"We'll be okay. The moon will be up soon, and our eyes will get used to the dark. Won't they, Jack?"

For answer Jack reached up and took his hand.

"Shall we go see the place where the water goes over the rocks down by the road? Or do you want to see the pool where the fish live?"

"I want to see the fish, Grampa. Will we see some?"

"We might." They were walking across the yard. It was a black and silver night. The moon was just coming up. "It's going to be dark under the trees. Maybe we should have brought your dad's flashlight."

"Do bears live here?"

"Let me carry you, Jack. I know the way to the pool."

"Okay, Grampa."

Richard hoisted Jack up to sit on his hip. "If there was a bear around here, he'd run away when he heard us coming."

"Really?"

"Yes, really. The bears that live around here are scared of people."

The trail went uphill under the hemlocks. There was still snow under the trees. Richard navigated more by the feel of his feet than by what he could see, but he didn't want to hesitate, because Jack might think he was afraid.

"Sometimes you can hear the splash when a fish jumps. Listen for it."

"Okay." Jack was holding on tight. "Look," he said. "There's a little house over there."

"That's the cabin where we used to live."

"Did Mommy live there?"

"When she was a little girl. We came here for vacations, and that's where we stayed, and then your grandmother and I lived there for a while, until we built our house."

"Can we go inside?"

"Tomorrow. Here's the path down to the pool." He stood Jack on his own feet.

The path sloped to an open place beside the water. There was more light now that they were in the open. The pool lay still and silver before them, a smooth surface wrinkled on the far side where the water came over the falls. Richard held Jack's hand, and they stood side by side. A fish jumped. Richard could feel Jack's hand tighten in his.

"What was that noise, Grampa?"

"That was a fish. Let's come back and catch him tomorrow."

"Really?"

"Maybe we can't, but we can try." Up by the cabin, there was a light. "We're down here, Brian."

"Hurry, Daddy. There's a fish."

The light moved closer.

Jack ran up the path. "There's a big fish, Daddy. We heard him jump. Grampa and I are going to catch him tomorrow."

"Okay. We can have him for lunch."

Brian stopped beside Richard. They were both smiling, the good will felt more than seen.

Jack was standing by the water's edge. There was a patter of little splashes.

"What was that?"

"I threw some stones in the water, Grampa."

"Oh."

"I'm making the fish jump."

Richard started to say that fish didn't jump because they were startled. They jumped to catch insects. But there was plenty of time for Jack to learn, and he liked Jack's enterprising spirit. He watched him go up the path to get another handful of pebbles.

Jack threw them in the water and stood there, quite still, waiting to see what would happen next. After a minute, he turned to look at his father and Richard. "Grampa, how can we catch the fish? What can we catch him *with*?"

"We'll use a fishing line with a worm on it. That works pretty well."

"But where can we get the fishing line?"

Richard looked at Brian, but he couldn't read his expression. "Well, Jack, this was going to be a surprise, but I'll tell you. I got you a little fishing rod."

"Really? Where is it?"

"It's at the house right now, waiting for you."

"Let's go get it."

"We have to wait until tomorrow. We can go fishing as soon as you wake up."

Brian laughed. "That might be pretty early. Isn't that nice of Grampa, Jack?"

"Yes, and I'll catch the big fish and give it to him."

Brian switched on his flashlight, and by common consent they walked back toward the house. Partway along the trail, Richard felt Jack's little hand take hold of his.

Brian said, "We've been wondering how Alyssa is. Monika is worried."

"She's fine," Richard said. "She has a cough, but it's left over from when she had the flu or something early in the spring."

"Monika thought…."

"She's always worrying about something, isn't she? Haven't you noticed that about her?"

Richard could hear the laughter in Brian's voice when he said, "Well, that's certainly true, but…."

"Alyssa has to have some tests, but I think the doctor's just covering himself. He doesn't want anyone to come back later and say he missed something. She seems in good shape to me."

"I thought she had to have an X-ray."

"She did. That's what started the whole thing. The doc thinks he saw something on the X-ray. He wants to check it out. He's probably just cranking the meter."

Ahead of them the lights from the house were streaming out into the yard.

Richard said, "It's probably my fault Monika is worried. Alyssa wasn't going to say anything until after she got the results of the tests back, so she could tell her mother there was no problem. I thought Monika and the girls would want to know. And I always think it's good for old people to be kept in the flow of things. It's good if they have something to worry about."

They were going up the steps to the deck now. Jack let go of Richard's hand and pushed through the door ahead of them.

Richard looked at Brian. "But maybe we have to make an exception for Monika. She seems to find plenty to worry about by herself."

They looked at each other, grinning.

"Oh," Richard said, "I forgot to tell you that you didn't need Jack's crib. I set up our old crib in your room."

"Thanks, I saw that. I put Jack's back in the car."

They went inside together with Richard thinking that he didn't know Brian very well, but he would like to.

In the early morning Alyssa brought him his coffee in bed, the way she always did, but he got up anyway and started to get dressed.

"Aren't you going to drink your coffee?"

"I'll bring it downstairs with me. I don't want them all to think I take advantage of you."

"That's silly, Richard. They've seen me bring you coffee in bed before."

"I know."

"Nobody's up yet anyway."

"I'll be down in a couple of minutes."

When he walked into the living room, Alyssa was sitting at the table, reading the Sentinel. She looked up at him and smiled. "Do you want some of the paper?"

"No," he said and held up his Kindle so she could see it. "I've got the Times." He hadn't had his Kindle very long. It was still a surprise and a delight to him that he could sit in his Vermont country home and read the New York Times first thing every morning

Brian came into the room about twenty minutes later. He was carrying Jack, and Jack was carrying his new fishing rod. Brian was sleepy and disheveled. Jack was in his pajamas.

Alyssa looked up and saw them standing in the doorway. "Come sit down, Brian. I'll bring you some coffee."

"I was planning to go back to bed, but it looks so peaceful out here. I guess I'll stay up." He walked down the steps and set Jack on one of the chairs by the table. "Stay here, Jackie. I'll go get your clothes."

"Get me some fishing clothes."

Richard said, "We'll have to dig worms first of all."

"Okay, Grampa. Can I take my fishing rod out of the package now?"

"Let's do it together," Richard said, charmed by Jack's serious expression.

Brian came back with the clothes. He picked Jack up without warning and carried him over to the couch, where he sat down with Jack on his lap. Richard watched the boy's face, thinking how startled he must have been to feel himself suddenly whisked into the air and moved away from what he was doing. But Jack's face showed nothing. He seemed to take it in stride. It probably happened to him all the time. Richard supposed he had done that to his children too.

He attached the reel to Jack's fishing rod and threaded the line through the eyebolts. He did everything but tie on the hook. It would be safer to do that later. He stood the rod up against the table.

When Jack was dressed, he walked over to the table and stood silently looking at the fishing rod, until Alyssa put a bowl of cereal and a glass of milk down in front of him. Jack climbed into his chair and began to eat in a trance of obedience. Between each bite, he looked at the fishing rod beside him.

Richard was glad for the moment in Wheeler's store when he happened to see the fishing rods for sale. If he hadn't had to wait in line, he might not have noticed that there were some small ones. That was what made him think of buying one for Jack.

He took his empty coffee cup to the sink. "Finish your breakfast, Jack, and meet me outside on the deck. I'm going to get my fishing rod and a shovel so we can dig some worms."

By the time he got back from the garage, Jack was standing at the top of the steps. He said, "Good man. Let's go get those worms." Jack followed him around to the compost bin. "This is the best place to find worms. Alyssa, I mean Grandma, won't mind if we take some."

Richard propped his fishing rod against the side of the bin. Jack did the same with his rod. It was warmer than yesterday, and the air was full of the smell of earth and water.

After a few shovelfuls of dirt, Richard turned one up with two worms in it. "Get them, Jack. Put them in the can before they get away."

But Jack just stood there, crouched a little, looking at the worms that were trying to burrow their way under the dirt. His fingers twitched.

Richard put the first worm in the can and told Jack to hold out his hand. He set the second worm on Jack's palm and watched the internal conflict as Jack struggled not to jerk his hand away. Bravery won. Jack dropped the worm into the can.

"We need a few more, and then we can go." He turned over shovelfuls of dirt, and Jack pounced. After a few minutes they had at least a dozen worms in the can.

Richard showed Jack how to carry his fishing rod over his shoulder, and they walked up the trail side by side in the early morning light. The snow was mostly gone. There were only scraps in the hollows under the trees. It was going to be warm enough to sit out on the deck in the middle of the day. Even Monika would find it comfortable.

Before they got close to the water, Richard stopped and whispered to Jack that it was time to put a hook and a worm on his line. They were going to try to sneak up on the fish.

Jack said, "Maybe the fish are still asleep."

The water was still and quiet. Little threads of mist rose from it. There was no wind, and the air smelled sweetly of moss and growing things.

Richard handed Jack his fishing rod with a worm on the hook. "Toss the worm out as far as you can. Let it sink, and then slowly reel it in. You want the fish to think it's their regular food."

But Jack was impatient to be fishing and didn't hear. He stood at the water's edge, flipping the worm into the water by swinging his rod, and then pulling it out again. He was having fun with the idea of fishing. It must have been a kind of waterboarding experience for the worm, but Richard didn't even want to think about that. He told himself that a person had to draw the line somewhere, and the worm was lucky, because he probably wasn't going to be eaten, since Jack had very little chance of actually catching anything.

Richard was beginning to wonder how much longer it would be before Jack got sick of the game, when the rod jerked down and pulled Jack toward the water. Richard grabbed the back of Jack's jacket with one hand and the rod with the other. "Hold on," he said. "You've got something."

"I can do it myself, Grampa. You can let go."

Richard did let go, even though he wondered which of them, Jack or the fish, was the stronger.

His hands were itching to take the line, but he managed not to do it. "Can you reel him in?"

Jack reached for the reel, but only for a second. He had to keep both hands on the rod to keep it from getting jerked away.

The fish was racing around the pool. Once it jumped out of the water, but Jack held on. Once the fish would have pulled him into the water if Richard hadn't grabbed him as he was being jerked forward.

After a while, the fish began to get tired. Jack developed his own method of shortening the fishing line by turning and running away from the water.

Richard helped by gathering in some of the line, and at last the fish lay gasping on the bank. Jack stood over it, panting. Richard looked at the combatants. The next step was up to him and was one of the reasons why he didn't go fishing very often. What's the point of trying to do something, if you are going to be sorry when you succeed? He picked up a rock and hit the fish on the head to stun it.

Jack said, "Grampa, don't. What are you doing to my fish?"

"Do you want to put him back in the water?"

"No. He's mine. I want to show him to Mommy and Daddy."

"Then we have to kill him and clean him."

Jack looked horrified. "Let's keep him just like this."

"He has to be in the water, or he'll die. We could put him back in the water and let him swim away. Do you want to do that?"

"No, because then he would be gone."

Richard saw the fish beginning to move. If he didn't hurry, he would have to stun him all over again. "What's it to be, Jack? We can clean him and eat him, or we can put him back in the water."

Jack looked frantically from Richard to the fish and back again. "I don't want to put him back in the water...."

"Okay," Richard said. "We'll eat him then."

He hit the fish again and moved the limp body onto a flat rock by the edge of the water. He got out his knife and cut through the backbone, around the gills, and down the belly. He worked fast because he didn't want to do it at all, and because he didn't want to turn Jack against fishing and the killing involved. He didn't want Jack to notice the paradox that lay at the heart of it.

"Mommy and Daddy are going to be so surprised when they see what a big fish you caught all by yourself," he said, trying to take Jack's mind off what he was doing and hating himself for tempting Jack into this situation that had no simple outcome. He tried to do it smoothly so Jack would learn from his example. He only meant to please his grandson, to buy a little boy something to have fun with, and it came trailing life and death in its wake.

Jack watched intently. His eyes and mouth were round circles of surprise. Richard could feel the grimace on his own face. When he finished with the knife, he laid it aside and asked Jack if he would like to be the one to pull out the guts. Jack's eyes and mouth opened a little wider, and he shook his head.

So Richard did it himself. He threw the guts into the bushes away from the pool and washed the fish off in the water. When it was clean, he handed it to Jack. "Let's go show it to Mommy."

They started for the house slowly. Jack held the fish high most of the time, but once in a while, he let it down so the tail dragged in the dirt of the path, or else he stepped on it. Richard carried the two rods and the can of worms. He wanted to take the fish too, but Jack wouldn't hear of it. So he tried to assist by raising the fish when Jack let it sink toward the ground.

When they got to the house, Richard leaned the two rods against the deck and dumped the can of worms into the flowerbed. By then Jack was on the deck, standing in front of the glass door, holding up the fish so everyone inside could see it.

By the time Richard got the door open, Sonia and Alyssa were on the other side, and Monika was watching from the table.

"I caught him all by myself," Jack said. "Grampa helped me when he was already caught."

Sonia kissed him on top of the heard. "Oh, Jack," she said. "He's wonderful."

"I want to keep him forever, but Grampa says we have to eat him."

"Let's take pictures of him. You can keep the pictures and eat him too."

Richard got himself another cup of coffee and sat down at the table with Monika. He tried to start a conversation, but her answers were perfunctory. She wasn't paying attention to him or to the drama of the fish.

Alyssa sat down beside him. "Mom's really worried. She picked up the wrong bottle of medicine when she packed her things at home, and now she doesn't have the cortisone she's supposed to take every day for her knees."

Richard looked at Monika, who was tapping her spoon nervously on the table. He couldn't tell whether she heard what Alyssa said or not. "What is she planning to do? Maybe it's all right to skip a couple of days?"

Alyssa was the one who answered. "You know you're not supposed to miss a dose of cortisone, and she already missed one yesterday. She has a call in to the doctor in Stamford. He'll tell her what to do."

"I can go in to the drugstore."

Alyssa put her hand on his arm in a way that made him feel very glad he offered. "Thanks, Richard. Let's see what the doctor thinks she ought to do. How do you think I ought to cook this fish?"

Just then Monika's cell phone rang. She listened to the voice on the other end for a few minutes and then asked for the name of a pharmacy in Severance. When Richard said that the Severance Pharmacy was the best, she told the doctor and spoke for a few minutes and hung up. "He says I'm very lucky. He has a good friend who practices in Severance. His name is Jim Brooks. Do you know him?"

Both of them shook their heads.

"Well, it doesn't matter. Dr. Joyner's going to call him and ask him to call in a prescription for me, and I can pick it up. So I'll only miss one day."

"I can pick it up for you, Monika," Richard said. He turned to Alyssa. "If you need anything for lunch I can get that too."

Alyssa stood up. "There are a few things. I'll make a list."

Monika said, "I'd like to ride in with you, Richard. It will only take me a few minutes to get ready."

"Fine," Richard said. "We want to get back in time to enjoy the fish."

CHAPTER 8

Richard was already in the car when Monika finished getting ready. She hurried outside and down the steps as fast as she could, conscious of how halting and lame she looked.

"Sorry to keep you waiting, " she said, as she got into the car beside him.

"That's okay. It wasn't long."

"I thought you had a pickup truck."

"This is Alyssa's car. I thought you'd be more comfortable in it."

"That's considerate of you. Thank you." They were out on the road now. "Do the same people live next door?"

"You mean the Martels? Yes, they're still there. Dan died fifteen or twenty years ago, but Sam and Bonnie are still there. They moved in when Dan got sick. They took care of him."

"Oh," Monika said. She couldn't remember exactly what she had asked. She was wondering for the thousandth time how she came to pick up the wrong bottle of pills. She thought she had a pretty good system for telling the bottles apart, but this mistake had made her question herself. She might have taken the wrong pills before and never noticed. "I remember when he got sick," she said. She hoped she was saying something that made sense. Would Richard think the long pause was strange?

She looked at his profile, wondering why Alyssa had chosen him, and remembering at the same time how Alyssa had pined like a schoolgirl when he went to Vermont and she and the girls stayed in Stamford. She remembered the gangly boy he was when they married. He looked quite distinguished now. It was interesting how people changed over time.

That thought brought her right to the brink of the deep pool of sadness that she always carried in her heart. What kind of a man would Aaron have been if he had had a chance to become a man? She would never know. She remembered how Alyssa used to take such motherly care of him when they were little. She sighed. Richard looked around at her and back at the road again. She didn't know of anything to say. She must not think of Aaron any more now. There would always be a deep well of sadness in her heart, but she didn't have to dip into it.

"It's much warmer today," she said, looking out the window. How far behind everything was. Up here, the leaves were just starting to unfurl, and there weren't that many flowers. There were only the very early bulbs, the daffodils and tulips. Poor Alyssa. It would be weeks before there was the profusion there was at home. And then the winter came so early, and everything died again, while Stamford was still beautiful.

"Yes, it's quite warm. The radio says there might be rain this evening."

They were going through Severance now. "Thank you for taking me to the drugstore. It was stupid of me to pick up the wrong bottle like that."

He looked at her. Did he look puzzled about how it had happened? She hoped he wasn't wondering if there was something wrong with her eyes.

"I was in too much of a hurry when I packed. I always make mistakes when I try to hurry."

"I know how that goes." He smiled. "Look, I'm going to let you off at the pharmacy and go get some groceries for Alyssa. There's a bench on the sidewalk in front. You can wait there. I'll be back soon."

"Fine."

"I don't think I'll be much longer than you are."

"That's okay. It doesn't matter. I'll be fine."

When she got out of the car, she had a moment of confusion. She realized that she was expecting to see one of those big chain drugstores. But the Severance Pharmacy was a small shop in the middle of a row of storefronts on what had to be the main street of Severance.

A bell jangled as she opened the door. It was like drugstores used to be when she was young. The floor was wooden and creaked with every step she took. The pharmacist was waiting for her behind the prescription counter at the back.

She was relieved. She had been worrying that she wouldn't be able to manage a large unfamiliar store with her eyes the way they were. She paid for her prescription and a bottle of water and went out to sit on the bench and take her pill.

After that, she felt better about everything. She sat on the bench and watched the people and cars going by. When she saw what she thought might be Alyssa's car, she stood up and watched. The car pulled into a parking place down the street. She saw Richard get out, and she walked toward him, smiling because she had managed what she needed to do. Once upon a time she wouldn't have doubted her ability to do something so small and simple. Age and infirmity had made her doubt herself, and that very doubt had made her even more unsure.

When they were both in the car again, Richard said, "Did you get the medicine?"

"Yes, thank you."

"Let's go home then. I got Alyssa's groceries."

Neither of them said anything after that for most of the trip, until Monika realized she was letting an opportunity slip away. She wanted to know what Richard thought, and here was her chance to ask him. "Richard, how do you think Alyssa is doing? Do you think anything is wrong? Doesn't it worry you that the doctor wants to do all these tests?"

He glanced around at her then. "Oh no, Monika. I don't think you should worry. Doesn't she look healthy and fit?"

"Well, yes, that's certainly true." She couldn't say that she was having trouble getting a good look at anything these days. She didn't want them all to worry and to tell her she should stop driving. She was managing to do that on her own, and when her eyes got over whatever it was, she could go back to the way things used to be.

"I like her doctor, but I think he's trying to make sure he covers himself." He paused. "And that's good. We want him to be thorough, but he's putting us all through a lot of worry for nothing."

"I don't like that."

"No, I don't either. Alyssa is bearing the brunt of it, and she's being great about it. *She's* not worrying. She would know if something was wrong."

"Suppose she does know and is keeping it to herself." She did not go on to say, "That's what I would do."

"I'm sure she'd tell *me*." He looked around at her again. "And, Monika, I give you my word, if she tells me anything like that, I'll let you know. All right?"

"Yes, Richard. That's good of you. I would like to know. And until then, I'll try not to worry."

"Look at it from the doctor's point of view—if he doesn't order these tests, and something is discovered later, he wouldn't have been doing his job, and actually, we might be able to sue him. He has to think of that."

"I see," she said, but she was thinking of what he said about discovering something later. She had almost been reassured until he said that. Still, she was a worrier, and she knew it. She needed to put that aside and enjoy her time here with Alyssa. At her age, any time she saw someone she loved, it could be for the last time. Even at eighty-four, she was in good health and able to be independent, but that could all change tomorrow, or later today. She needed to remember that and not waste her time in worry. "Thank you, Richard. You've made me feel much better about Alyssa. I'll count on you to tell me when it's time to start worrying."

"All right, Monika. I'll take that very seriously. You can trust me to let you know." He looked around at her again, and this time he smiled. "But I'm sure I won't need to. It'll be just fine."

The next morning Monika was sitting at the table having a cup of coffee. It was a beautiful spring morning, clear and bright. Alyssa was the only one still indoors. She was reading the Sunday Sentinel at the other end of the table. She looked up. "Don't you want some of the paper, Mom?"

"Maybe in a little while. I like looking out the window. It's going to be a nice day, isn't it?"

Just then Sonia and Jack came in.

Alyssa said, "What's Brian doing?"

"He's with Daddy," Sonia said. "They're getting out the old canoe, the one Daddy made."

"Do they need help? He had it up in the rafters of the garage for the winter."

"No, I don't think so. They almost had it down when we came in."

"Good. He's been talking about getting it out for a while now. I'm glad Brian's here to help him."

"This is the first time Brian has actually seen it. Of course, he's been hearing stories about it ever since he met me."

Alyssa said, "Jack, I'm surprised they didn't want you to help them."

Sonia answered for Jack. "They asked him, but I'm going to take him over to the Martels' barn to see the animals. It's our last chance to do that before we leave."

"Are you going to call them?"

"I don't think so. I saw Sam Martel going into the barn a little while ago. I thought I'd just walk in. Will you come with me, Mom?"

"Oh, I don't know."

"Please. I think I'm still sort of scared of him. I guess it's left over from when we were little. He always seemed so big and so angry, and he had that huge mustache. Does he still?"

"Yes, he's just the same. I know how you feel."

"Really? I thought it was just me."

"No. I'm scared of him too, even though I know it's silly."

"So now you have to come with me, Mom. We can be scared together."

Alyssa said, "I'll come and protect you if my mother will come and protect me. Will you, Mom?"

"Come with us, Nana. We can all be brave together."

Monika thought about it. "Okay, I'll come and protect everybody. How's that?"

Sonia said, "Oh good. Let's go. Come on, Jack."

"I have to get my jacket," Monika said. She stood slowly, holding on to the table for support. Her legs always ached and felt weak when she first stood up.

"I'll get it for you, Nana. Do you want the dark red one?"

"Yes, that's the one. Thank you."

Sonia hurried down to Monika's room and was back before Monika was even solidly on her feet. Then she and Jack started for the Martels' barn, leaving Alyssa and Monika to come at Monika's slow speed. Alyssa slowed herself down on purpose. She hadn't got to old age where everything was a hesitation, and a doubt. It was nice of her to wait. Monika said so.

"Of course, Mom. I want to spend this time with you. I'll be sad when you leave."

When they got to the bottom of the steps, Alyssa slipped her arm through Monika's and squeezed a little. Monika was glad to feel how strong she was. Surely, she must be well. She felt well. If something was wrong, couldn't she, her own mother, sense it through their linked arms?

She stopped for a minute to ask. "Alyssa, are you feeling well? You're not worried about yourself, are you?"

"Oh no, Mom. I'm fine. There would be some sign of sickness if something was wrong."

"But these tests?"

They were walking again now, on a path through the trees and bushes that lined the edge of the property. Alyssa had let go of her arm and was walking ahead. Monika couldn't see her face.

"I think Richard is right about the tests. I have to do them, but I don't think they will show anything."

"I'm glad to hear you say that."

Alyssa took her arm again. "Don't worry. I would tell you if I thought something was wrong."

"I couldn't bear to lose you, Alyssa. You're all I have left."

"Don't be silly, Mom. You have Alix and Sonia and Sonia's family, and lots of friends, and…I could go on and on."

"No one matters to me the way you do, Alyssa. Just stay strong."

"I will, Mom, I promise." She squeezed Monika's arm again.

By then they had caught up to Sonia and Jack, who were waiting for them outside the door to the barn.

"Go on in, Sonia. You didn't need to wait for us."

"You go first, Mom, and ask him if it's all right if we come in."

"All right," she said, and she walked in boldly, without hesitation.

Sonia looked at Monika, and they both laughed. They thought Alyssa would come right back, but she didn't. Jack began to get restless. He started picking up pebbles in the driveway and throwing them. After a few minutes, he started to throw them at the wall of the barn. Sonia took his hands and shook them until he dropped all the pebbles. She said, "Come on, Nana. Let's go in and see what's happened to Mom."

They went inside. There was no light in the first room, a small room crowded with farming equipment. Sonia and Jack went ahead. Monika followed, groping in the dark, waiting for her eyes to adjust.

The next room was better. It was large. Dusty light came through dirty windows. There was a sour smell of manure. Small pens lined both sides of a central aisle. Alyssa was standing outside a pen while Sam Martel stood inside, leaning on his shovel. Monika walked toward them. Snuffling and grunting sounds were coming out of the pen. Monika looked over the fence. There were a lot of piglets around Sam Martel's feet. The smell was appalling.

Jack climbed up the fence and reached his hand in. The piglets crowded over to sniff and maybe to bite it. The others were talking to each other and didn't notice. Monika wanted to snatch Jack back out of danger, but she was afraid Sonia and Alyssa wouldn't like it. She watched, ready to jump forward at the last minute. The piglets smacked their horrid little mouths and crowded around, but Jack didn't realize he was in danger.

Sam Martel said, "I had a hard time finding piglets this year, and the prices people wanted…well, it's crazy."

Alyssa and Sonia nodded politely, and still no one noticed Jack.

"That's why I bought so many. I think I'll keep a couple over for brood sows."

At last Sonia looked down. "Jack, what are you doing? Keep your hands out of the pen. They could bite you."

Monika was glad to see Jack pull his hand back, but she had to think that if they were going to bite, they would have done it already. She didn't say anything.

Sam handed Jack a stick. "Here. Scratch their backs. They like that."

Sonia said, "Where are all your other animals? I thought you had more than this."

"I put the sheep out yesterday for the first time. I only have the one cow right now. She's out back with the sheep. I had a couple of big pigs I butchered last weekend."

Alyssa noticed Monika just then. "Are you okay, Mom? You look tired."

"I'm okay." She didn't want Alyssa to suggest that she start back ahead of the others. It would be so much easier to make that walk with Alyssa's helping arm. She did hope they wouldn't be much longer. It was hard for her to see in the dim light, and there was nowhere to sit down. She had agreed to come because she thought she ought to get some exercise before the long trip back, but this was enough.

Alyssa said, "We bought one of Sam's pigs."

"What? A pig? Where is it?"

Sam and Alyssa looked at each other and smiled. Sam said, "It's going in their freezer when I get it all packaged."

Monika said, "Oh." She tried to look as though that was a normal and a good thing to have done. She hoped they couldn't tell that she was a little shocked. Of course she knew that Richard wasn't Jewish, and anyway, it wasn't as though any of them were practicing Jews, but the idea of eating those creatures, especially after you had seen and smelled how dirty they were…well, she wouldn't say anything, but she felt a little horrified. She was glad Alyssa hadn't served any pork dishes over the weekend.

Sam said, "I'm sorry there aren't more animals for your little boy to see. There's chickens out back, would he like to see them?"

"He'd love it. Wouldn't you, Jack?"

Jack nodded and kept on scratching the piglets with the stick. They fought with each other to get in the best position. The piglet who was getting a back rub arched his back and grunted with pleasure.

Sam climbed over the fence and walked with Alyssa and Sonia toward the back of the barn. Jack followed slowly, and Monika came last. She hoped no one noticed the way she was shuffling. She couldn't see enough, and she didn't want to put her feet down wrong and fall.

She could hear water running somewhere. She followed them down a ramp into a smaller, darker room. When she finally caught up with the others outside, Sam was taking Jack into the chicken house.

Alyssa took her arm. "We'll go home in a minute, Mom. This is so nice for Jack."

"I'm all right. Don't worry about me."

There was a startled commotion, and Sam said something to Jack.

Sonia said, "Alix and I used to love to come over and try to catch the chickens. I'm sure it was bad for them, but it was so much fun."

"Maybe that's why Sam used to be angry."

"I don't remember if he ever caught us. They were gone a lot, even in the summer."

Alyssa said, "You girls always wanted to play with Junior and Marnie."

"I wonder where they are now."

"I think Marnie's moved away, but Junior's still around."

"We could ask Sam."

"You do it, Sonia."

Just then Jack came out carrying an egg. "Look, Nana. He gave this to me. A chicken made it this morning. I'm going to eat it for lunch."

Sam stepped out of the chicken house and closed the door behind him.

Monika hoped no one would start a conversation with him about his children. Jack was eager to get his egg back to the house, a tricky business, since he wouldn't let anyone help him carry it.

Monika thought she wouldn't mind spending the afternoon sitting in the car after all the walking she had done. She hoped they could leave after lunch. It would be good to get back home where she could really rest, back to her own routine and her own animals. She hoped her cats were all right. Still, she was glad she had come to see how Alyssa was doing. Nothing could reassure her the way being with Alyssa could do.

CHAPTER 9

Sam had just poured himself another cup of coffee, even though he wasn't sure he wanted it. He was standing by the table with the coffeepot in his hand when Bonnie came into the kitchen in her pink uniform. She walked slowly, tilting her head to the side to put on an earring.

"Do you want some coffee, honey? There's still some left in the pot."

"I shouldn't, but yes. I'd love some. Pour me just a little." She finished putting on the earring and sank into her seat. "What're you gonna do today?"

He set the coffeepot by the sink and sat down across the table from her before he answered. "I don't know. I ain't got a thing lined up for today. There's a couple more butcherin jobs, but nothin today."

"That don't matter, Sam. It won't hurt to take a day off."

Sam sipped his coffee. It tasted burned. He should have skipped it. "There's nothin new comin in. After I get caught up with these jobs, that'll be it."

Bonnie was bent over, tying her shoe. She hauled herself up, holding on to the table. Her face was red with the effort. "Judy's got the shoes I want. They're slip-ons. I wouldn't have to go through this every day."

"Why don't you get some?"

"I think I will. Maybe when I get paid this week."

"But, honey…." he said, and then he stopped, because he wasn't sure what he meant to say. Should he point out that there was still plenty of money for shoes in the bank? Because how long would it last if he didn't find some work?

Before he could say any more, Bonnie jumped up. "Oh Lord, look at the time. I have to go." She grabbed her jacket and her pocketbook and opened the door. Then she looked back at Sam, sitting at the table, surrounded by dirty dishes. "I'll see you later. I'm sorry I didn't have time to clean up."

"I'll do it," Sam said. "It's the least I can do."

She closed the door. He didn't know whether she heard him or not. He sat there, feeling miserable, until after a while the quiet started to get to him. He thought about turning on the radio, or maybe the television set. That would be company. He stood up and started to move the dirty dishes to the sink. He could scrub down the whole kitchen and surprise her. He filled the sink with soapy water and put some of the breakfast dishes in it.

Then he decided to call Junior. To his surprise, Junior answered the phone on the second ring.

"Hey, what're you doin home this time of day? You ain't sick, are you?"

"Naw. I'm fine. Why'd you call if you didn't think I was home?"

"I don't know. Somethin to do, I guess. Why are you home?"

"They shut down today. Nobody went in. I don't know what it's about. All I know is we don't get no pay."

"So join the club."

"What're you doin today, Dad? You want some help?"

"I ain't got nothin today. I wish I did."

"Hey," Junior said. "I know what. Let's go fishin. We ain't done that in a while."

"Well, okay. Let's do."

"We could go up to the pool behind Richard's. I almost asked him about it the other day."

"I don't want to go there."

"Why not? He wouldn't care. We could ask him to go with us."

"It wouldn't make no difference."

"I bet there's lots more fish in there than there used to be when you used to fish there all the time."

"I don't care, Junior. I ain't goin to fish there. And that's it. I don't want to talk about it."

"All right," Junior said. "Don't mind me. Where shall we go then?"

"What about we could go up Gooseneck Brook until we get to the pond, and maybe we could fish off of the dam up there?"

"We could do that. I got a few flies we could try."

"I'm goin to get some worms, and then I'll be over to pick you up."

"I'll be ready."

Later on while they were riding in the pickup, with Colt standing proudly in the back, Junior said, "Ma had to work today?"

"Yeah."

"So didn't Alma."

Sam glanced around at him, but Junior was looking straight ahead. Sam didn't say anything.

After a while, Junior said, "I used to fish in that pool all the time when I was a kid. It never bothered me that it didn't belong to us no more."

Sam shut his mouth a little tighter and didn't say a word.

"Course, I didn't fish there when they was stayin in the cabin, but they didn't come up that much in them days. Marnie and I used to sneak over to go swimmin too." He didn't look around. He could have been talking to himself. "It never seemed like such a big deal to me."

"You could of got in a lot of trouble."

"We never did. You and Ma didn't even know."

"God damn it, Junior. It was different for you. Dad sold that land before you were born. You never knew nothin else. For me, that pool and the brook and the woods around it—that was the most important place in the world. That's why I built my cabin there when I came home from 'Nam." He looked over at Junior, but Junior was looking straight ahead, and his face was blank. It wasn't like any of it was new information. "And then Dad went and sold it without even tellin me."

"He needed the money to pay Gram's hospital bills."

"That's what he said." Then they were both quiet. Sam didn't want to talk about it. He didn't even want to think about it. It just made him feel bad, and angry at Dad, and there was no point in that now that Dad was gone. He *did* need the money to pay the hospital bills for Ma's cancer. But it was more than that too, because Dad was mad. He felt like Sam didn't help when he should have. He felt abandoned by him. He never noticed that Sam had his own life to live.

But Sam didn't want to get into all that with Junior. It just made him feel sad. There was no sense thinking about it. So he turned on the radio, and they rode along listening to Willie Nelson.

When Sam pulled to a stop in front of the store in East Severance, Junior looked at him with a question on his face.

"I won't be a minute. I'm just gettin myself some coffee. You want somethin?"

"I'll come with you. I could use some Pepsi."

Sam told Colt to stay, and he and Junior went up the steps. There was no one inside but the girl behind the counter. She looked up and smiled and then looked back down at the game she was playing. The store was quiet except for the creak of the wooden floor and the electronic beeps from the girl's game.

Junior was already at the counter when Sam got there with his coffee. Sam started to say he'd pay for Junior's purchases too, but he stopped himself. Junior was the one with a job, after all. He didn't say anything, and he hated himself for his silence.

When they got to the truck, Sam put his coffee in the cup holder and peeled Colt's Slim Jim. Colt waited for it eagerly.

Junior said, "Them things ain't good for dogs."

"It's meat. How can that hurt him?"

Junior didn't say anything. He tossed his new fishing lure onto the dashboard and opened his Pepsi and took a long drink.

As they drove away, Sam said, "That stuff's bad for people."

"So's coffee and cigarettes."

"That stuff's worse. You and your ma. It'll make you fat."

"It's too late for that, Pop."

Sam couldn't argue with that. He fiddled with the radio dial a little. Junior picked up his new lure and looked at it.

Sam said, "What the hell is that thing?"

"It's a daredevil. I have good luck with 'em."

"There ain't nothin that lives around here that's red and white stripes. It don't look like fish food to me."

"Well, you ain't a fish. The fish always go for daredevils."

"Fish are lookin for food, not entertainment."

"Okay, Pop. You might could be right. We'll find out, won't we?" He looked around. "We're just about to put it to the test, ain't we?"

Sam could feel Junior looking at him, but he didn't say anything, and he didn't turn his head.

"We could even put a little money on which one of us is goin to catch the most fish."

Sam looked at Junior then. He was annoyed. "I can't go around spendin money like that when I ain't even got a job. I can't use up your ma's salary foolin around. She works hard for her money. Her feet hurt her all the time."

"I'm sorry, Pop. I didn't mean nothin. Forget about it. Okay?"

Sam said okay, but he was sore for a while. Everything seemed to be hitting him wrong. He was worried, of course, but it wasn't Junior's fault. He needed to get a grip on himself.

This could be a good day. The sun was shining. The leaves were coming out on the trees. Last week's crazy snowstorm was history. For the first time in who knows how many years, he had enough time to do all the spring work, preparing the garden, getting all the fences ready, cleaning up from winter. It usually made him crazy to try to work it all in, and this year he would have time to do a good job on all of it. He just had to keep a positive attitude. After a while he was able to say, "Okay, Junior. We don't need a bet to put it to the test. We're just about to find out. We'll let the fish decide."

Sam parked the truck at the picnic area on Gooseneck Brook, and they both got out. He slapped his thigh and said, "Come on, boy," and Colt jumped out of the back.

There was the sound of the water everywhere. Sam went over to the stream. Close to the water, a layer of pure, cold air was rising. It smelled sweet and clean.

He walked back to the truck. Junior already had his waders on. He was sitting at the picnic table, rigging his fishing rod.

"I'll go up two or three pools and come down toward you. How's that sound?"

Junior looked up at him. "Sounds great to me, Pop. But I don't want to take advantage of you. You're goin to do more walkin, and that means less fishin."

"That's okay. We can trade off later." He leaned against the picnic table and started to put on his waders.

Junior was tying on the thing he bought at the store.

"What're you gonna do when a fish takes that thing?"

"I got more of 'em. Don't worry about it, Pop."

"I ain't. You're the one who needs to worry." He picked up his basket and his fishing rod and whistled to Colt. "I'll see you up there."

"You could go partway and then head for the dam. The water's runnin good. It'll clear fast. You'd just be puttin 'em on notice that somethin tasty was comin later."

"Don't get too cocky there, Junior. We ain't got started yet."

Junior said, "Okay there, Pop."

Sam started to walk away, but when he had gone a few steps, he looked back. Junior had a can of WD-40 sitting on the picnic table beside him. Sam watched as Junior picked up his new lure and sprayed it with WD-40. He couldn't help it. He said, "What the hell are you doin now?"

Junior actually grinned at him. "It's my secret weapon, Pop. The fish love it."

Sam said, "Well, Jesus Christ. I don't believe it. That's the craziest thing I ever saw."

"Okay, Pop. The fish'll decide for us."

Sam didn't say anything after that. He turned around and started walking up the brook, but he stayed well away from the water. He didn't want the fish to know he was there. Colt stayed back too. Colt was one in a million. He knew what Sam was planning to do, just like a person would. Better really, because he didn't have to have the plan explained to him. He just knew what it was.

Sam was glad to get away by himself. He felt soothed and peaceful walking along with the sun on his back and the noise of the water rushing over the rocks from one pool to the next. Sometimes it sounded like people talking, only he couldn't quite catch what they said. Whenever the voices were quieter, he would slip a little closer to see if the water was flowing through a pool. He wanted to get an idea of the likely places to try on the way downstream. The blackflies were getting bad, but they ought to make the fishing better.

He had been walking part of the time on the road, and he was hot and dusty. He had been remembering what Junior was like when he was a little kid, but now he began to get nervous, thinking how he was just walking, and Junior was down there already catching fish.

He gave a low whistle to Colt to tell him they were changing direction and went over to the water. He got out a worm and rigged up his fishing rod and stepped into the water above a little waterfall. Below was a quiet pool that ought to have some fish in it. He felt around with his feet and turned over a couple of rocks. After the loose dirt washed down into the pool, the fish watching there would think it was normal for a worm to float down to them. He put two sinkers on his line at a short distance from the worm and let it go in the waterfall. His plan was that the sinkers would lodge first. Farther into the pool the worm would be stopped by the line, but to the fish, it would look like a worm washed downstream by a bank cave-in.

From where Sam stood, he couldn't really see into the pool, and he didn't want to move for fear the fish would notice him and get suspicious. He waited. Nothing. He reeled in the line and tried again. Nothing. It was a deep pool with a few big rocks in it, the perfect spot for a trout to hang out. Certainly there were fish in that pool. He didn't want to hurry on and miss them.

He tried twice more, and then he reeled in the line and stepped up onto the bank. Colt was nosing around in the woods. When he saw Sam step out of the stream, he came over to see if they were leaving.

Sam pulled a few leaves off a nearby bush and threw them into the pool. They floated downstream undisturbed. He turned over a rock and found three insects and a worm. One by one he threw the insects into the pool below the waterfall where the water was calm and smooth. There was no action when he threw in the first insect and only a dimple on the water when he threw in the second. But with the third insect, there was a splash. Something big took it even before it hit the water.

"Oho," Sam said. "I knew you were in there."

Now his whole world narrowed to the waterfall and the pool and the hidden fish, the icy breath of the stream, its gurgling conversation as it flowed past rocks and over the falls, the sun on his back and shoulders and sparkling off the water into his eyes, and even the blackflies swarming around his head and landing on his face and neck. That was the whole world, and it was beautiful. The only thing that could make it better would be if he could catch that fish.

He put a second worm on his hook and stepped into the water again. He tried the worms several times. He knew that fish was there. But the only thing it wanted to eat was a fly. Junior would come along any minute, and that fish would fall for Junior's bait. On the edge of his mind, there was an uneasy feeling that Junior was somewhere down below catching a lot of fish.

Sam was just starting to reel in his line, when bam, the line went taut and began to unspool as the fish took it to the far end of the pool. Then he came back with Sam frantically trying to reel in the extra line. Just as suddenly the line went slack. Sam reeled it in. The hook was there, but the worms were gone.

It was time to try somewhere else. That fish was too badly spooked to think of eating anything for a while. Sam didn't care if there were other fish in the pool. They would probably be scared too. He gave a low whistle to let Colt know he was moving and waded right through the pool and into the rocky rapids below it. He hoped he gave that fish a bad fright and scared him all over again when he waded past, stirring up the bottom and splashing as he went.

He tried the next pool, but even throwing insects into the water got no reaction. Maybe that fish was master of several pools. He was big enough. Dogs controlled their territory to make sure they would have enough food. But were fish like that? Fish might be more like chickens. A big chicken would snatch a prize away from another and gobble it down before any other chicken could take it, but no chicken ever tried to defend a piece of ground.

After a while Sam could see Junior in the distance coming toward him. Junior was still too far away for Sam to be able to tell if he had any fish in his pouch. He watched Junior casting and dipping his rod, reeling in and casting again. He thought for a minute that he was going to have to watch Junior reel in a fish right in front of him, but if Junior hooked one, it got away. Sam stepped out of the water and sat on the bank, waiting. Colt came and joined him. They watched Junior work his way toward them.

When he got close, he climbed up the bank and sat down heavily on the ground. "How'd you do?"

"I worked a big one, but he spat out the hook. How about you?"

"I thought we was goin to have to measure fish to see who was ahead. I got three, but they're all pretty small."

"You're ahead then. I ain't got nothin yet."

They sat there for a minute. Then Junior said, "Where'd you hook that big one?" He said it in a low voice, like he didn't care whether Sam told him or not.

And Sam almost didn't tell him. He really didn't want Junior to get that fish. Then he thought he might as well tell him and let him waste his time on a fish that was too scared to bite. He hated himself for that thought too. Finally, playing for time, he said, "Did you throw yours back?"

"Naw," Junior said. "I've got 'em in my pouch. You want to see 'em?"

Junior's pouch was an old ammo bag from the army-navy store. Sam always felt a twinge of discomfort when he looked at it. It reminded him of when he was in Vietnam. "That's okay. You see those willows up there, where the stream makes a dogleg to the left? That's where that pool is at. Let's get goin."

"I'm ready. Do you want to go upstream? That's your best shot, and it looks like the daredevils is ahead of the worms right now."

"If I go upstream, where're you gonna go?"

"I'll walk up to the dam and come down. Okay?"

"All right. Let's see how that works."

Junior heaved himself up onto his feet. "Good luck, then."

Sam just grunted. His peaceful mood had evaporated.

"And, Pop," Junior said, looking down at him, "I'm just kiddin about this contest thing."

Sam grunted again, but when Junior held out his hand, Sam took it, and Junior pulled him up onto his feet. He couldn't say it out loud, but he loved Junior right then, even if he was catching more fish. More fish, hell, he was catching the only fish.

Sam picked up his basket, put the strap over his shoulder, and started up the stream. He thought about having another go at that fish and decided not to waste his time. There were lots of other fish. It wasn't a question of finding fish, it was a question of finding something that would tempt them to feed. And he was going to have to work hard just to even the score.

He took a worm out of his basket and threaded it carefully on the small hook. Then he walked upstream until he got to a new pool. He went all the way up like that, trying pools, sometimes throwing things in to test the water, sometimes turning over rocks to make his worms look more natural.

He got a few small nibbles, but nothing to get serious about. He met Junior a little way below the dam, and they walked up to it together. Junior hadn't had any luck either. They stood on the dam and fished side by side for a while. Sam even caught a respectably sized fish. That went a long way toward making the score even, and he felt better.

They would have stayed longer, except that they were both hungry, and the fish weren't biting any more. Junior said, "Hey, Pop, I'm all done. Why don't I walk down and get the truck? I'll come back and pick you up."

Sam wondered what Junior was thinking. That he was too old or too weak to walk down the hill? "No, he said. "I'm ready to quit too. I'll walk down with you."

They packed up and started down the road together. Colt trotted ahead with his tail up in a plume. Junior said, "We might could get some lunch and have time to come back."

"They never bite in the middle of the day anyhow."

"What time does Ma get home?"

"About four if she don't stop on her way through town. She don't work the dinner shift no more. It's too hard on her legs."

"I know the feelin," Junior said.

"Both of you ought to lose a little weight."

"It ain't a easy thing to do."

"If you got the weight off, everythin else you did would be easier."

They were both quiet. Then Junior said, "Hey, ain't them the trees by the pool where you hooked the big one?"

"I think so."

"I might just go over and see if he'd like to try a daredevil."

"He was particular to start with, and since then he's had a bad scare," Sam said. He hated the idea of Junior catching that fish, and he hated himself for hating it.

"I think I'll have a try. I could meet you at the truck if you wanted to go on."

"I'll wait for you." Sam knew he'd just think about it all the way to the truck. "You gonna try that dumb red and white thing?"

"Sure. Let's see if maybe that's what he's been waitin for."

Sam sat on the bank with Colt beside him. Colt's fur was hot to the touch where the sun had been on it. At first, Sam was sure he wanted Junior to fail, but as he sat there watching while Junior made the daredevil dance around in some strange pattern of his own, Sam began to get excited, hoping Junior would win the prize. He loved Junior, even though it was embarrassing. It wasn't something he could ever say to anyone, since grown men weren't supposed to feel that way. But he did, and when Junior gave up and climbed out of the pool, Sam was genuinely disappointed.

They walked the rest of the way to the truck in friendly silence. The blackflies were terrible while they were taking off their waders and putting away their gear. They went back to the store for some sandwiches and a couple of Slim Jims for Colt. By then it was too late to go back to the stream. Junior wanted to get home before his kids got out of school.

"Listen, Pop, I think this contest is a draw. I have more fish, but yours is the biggest."

Sam thought that himself, but he still hated it when Junior said it. It felt like Junior was trying to keep him from finding out what everyone else already knew, that he was worthless, a has-been, that he couldn't cut it any more. "Don't coddle me. I ain't a baby. You won fair and square. You got three to my one. It ain't much of a haul, but you got it. I'm just glad we didn't have no money ridin on it."

Junior grinned at him.

Sam went on. "And I guess that stupid red toy is the real winner. What do you call that thing?"

"A daredevil."

"Well, don't hold your breath or nothin, but I might ought to get me a couple. If that's what the stupid fish want, I guess I'd better use 'em."

Junior grinned even wider. "Way to go, Pop."

Sam pretended to be mad, but he really wasn't. Before they got to Junior's house, they were both laughing.

CHAPTER 10

This was the first time Alyssa had ever been in Dr. McCormack's office. All the other times over the years she had been in his examining room, where she sat on a thing that was a cross between a bed and a table.

It was like going to a lawyer. She sat beside his desk. He wasn't going to examine her. And it wasn't exactly an appointment either. It was strange, and it made her nervous, and because of that she kept needing to cough.

"So, Alyssa, I asked you to come in because I want you to know everything I can tell you so you can make the best possible decisions for yourself. I saw Jack Girard over the weekend, and I asked him a few questions. Of course, I know it's too soon. We don't really know anything yet. But he's an oncologist, and we can get him more involved later, if we want to."

On Dr. McCormack's desk was a row of framed photographs, angled so he could look at them while he worked. Sitting where she was, it was hard for Alyssa to tell who they were. Long-ago pictures of his wife? His children? They must be grown-ups with their own children by now. He was talking about another doctor, but she missed the point. She just knew that he liked this other doctor. She smiled and nodded so he would see that she agreed.

"Jack Girard says they have made so much progress with this disease recently, that it isn't at all the same thing as it used to be. I didn't know that. It isn't my field, and I don't keep up the way he does. That's why I wanted...."

Alyssa could see his framed diplomas on the paneled wall behind his head. Why did doctors do that? Did they think their patients wouldn't trust them without those pieces of paper? Now he was standing up, so she stood too. She should have been paying more attention.

He held out his hand, and she took it, and he held hers and patted it while he talked. It was all very strange. "Stop by Marta's desk so she can make appointments for you for the MRI and the CT scan. I hope they can be done tomorrow. You can do that, can't you?"

She nodded, even though she couldn't remember what she had planned for tomorrow. He ushered her out to the receptionist's desk with his hand in the small of her back.

She agreed with everything they said to her, and then finally, she was able to leave. Outside, the air seemed unbearably sweet. It was warm, and birds were singing everywhere. She had planned to stop at the grocery store, but she decided not to. She didn't want to waste any of her precious freedom, and she had to come back tomorrow morning.

The next morning she was at the hospital at eight o'clock. She felt numb and cold. Polite, efficient people, who didn't care about her but pretended they did, ushered her from room to room down sterile, windowless halls. In both the tests, she had to lie absolutely still on a stretcher and be fed into a large machine like a tunnel. She was told to try not to breathe. The CT machine whirred and clicked as it circled around her. She had to concentrate all her energy on trying not to cough. She was sure she was going to cough and ruin whatever pictures they were hoping to get, and then everyone would be angry.

No one stayed in the room. She wished she had said yes when Richard offered to come with her. She had said it wasn't necessary because she wanted him to think she was brave.

The next day was nice again. She knew she ought to be inside cleaning the upstairs or doing the laundry, but she decided to give herself the whole day as a present. And feeling delighted with her own wickedness, she was outside by ten o'clock working on the flowerbeds around the deck. By one she had the side toward the garage weeded and dug out, ready for new flowers. It was the shortest side, but she had the whole, long afternoon for the other side. She was having a wonderful time.

She stopped for lunch, just long enough to take off her boots and wash her hands and get some bread and cheese and a glass of water. She took the food out to the deck and sat on the steps. She was too dirty to sit down inside.

After a short time, she got back to work. The sun was heavy on her back. The dirt smelled rich and fertile. She could hear the water splashing against the rocks in the brook. Flies buzzed around her head. The birds were singing in all the trees around the yard. They were still in that exciting state of mating and nest building before the babies came along. After that, they would have to buckle down to the difficult task of getting enough food to keep the babies fed, and they wouldn't have time for gay spring songs. Being in the windowless hospital began to seem like a distant bad dream. The wheelbarrow filled up with the sod she cut out and the weeds she pulled. Time disappeared.

After a while the newness was over. In the beginning the work seemed different and fun and not that hard, and she plunged in, confident that it wouldn't take that long. But that part was behind her now. She had gone about a third of the length of the longest flowerbed. A good distance stretched behind her, too much of a commitment to think of quitting. And a daunting distance stretched out ahead. She could be more realistic now. She knew how hard it was and how slowly she was moving forward.

She sat in the dirt under the hot sun thinking about the job, and then she jumped up and started up the trail into the woods. She didn't decide to take a break, she just started up the trail, and then, when she was already under way, she decided to check on the ravens' nest.

She went up the trail slowly, savoring how much had changed since the last time she was there. Everything was getting green. The leaves were unfurling on the trees. The water was still high, roaring down the hill, drowning out other sounds. The woods smelled of water and moss and dead leaves. She was filled with happiness.

She stopped at the remains of Richard's arrow. Now that the leaves were coming out, it was much harder to see the nest through the trees. She should have brought Richard's binoculars. She sat down on the trail, hoping that if she were still and patient, she would see something.

After a while she was rewarded. There was a jostling, and one of the baby birds hopped up onto the edge of the nest. It was covered with feathers that were scraggly and unkempt. It was at least twice as big as it had been before. After standing there for a minute, it hopped down inside again. Alyssa could see a lot of movement. Other babies must be in there. When nothing else happened, she stood up and went back down the trail, feeling refreshed.

The work was different now. It stretched out ahead, but somehow that didn't matter. She worked steadily without noticing how much she had done or how much was left to do. The sun wasn't so hot any more. Big gray clouds were piling up in the sky. When she went into the house to go to the bathroom, she was amazed to see that it was after four o'clock. She checked the phone messages. Dr. McCormack's office wanted her to call. It was tempting to put it off, but she would just have to stop again to do it later.

Marta answered the phone at the doctor's office. When Alyssa told her who she was, Marta sounded excited. She said, "Oh, I was afraid you wouldn't get my message in time. We got lucky. There was a cancellation, so I grabbed it for you."

Alyssa tried to sound grateful.

Marta hardly noticed. "It's first thing tomorrow morning. Eight o'clock. They want you there at seven-thirty."

"What's this for?"

"I'm sorry. I thought you knew. Dr. McCormack thinks you need a biopsy."

"He does?" Suddenly she wanted to sit down, but she was too dirty. She went out on the deck and sat on the steps. From there she could see her work.

"If you can't do tomorrow morning, I can make you another one. It's just that Dr. McCormack wanted it to be soon. And I knew he would be so pleased, you see. He never thought I could get you one this soon."

"Okay. I'll do it." As soon as she said the words, she was sorry. Marta gave her a few instructions and said goodbye.

Alyssa went out to the garden and tried to get back to that lovely place she was in before, in the sunlight and the dirt, full of the sounds of the birds and the rushing water. She sat there, but it was no good any more. There was an ominous dark wing of cloud across the sky. She couldn't stop thinking about tomorrow. It spoiled everything. There must be something about the results of the other tests that worried Dr. McCormack, although no one said so. Maybe she should call Mom and tell her, but she didn't know anything except that she had to have a stupid biopsy. There wasn't really anything to tell, and Mom was sure to have lots of questions.

She sat in the dirt wondering what to do, and getting more and more tense. Her last scrap of time was disappearing. Even if she could work until dark today, she couldn't finish, and now tomorrow was gone, and what would come next? She coughed. It turned into a fit of coughing that she couldn't stop. It was getting cold. She hadn't coughed this much all day. If they would just leave her alone, she'd be fine. She didn't know what any of it meant. If she was going to find out something really life changing, wouldn't there be a terrible, stunning moment when someone said it to her? Wouldn't there be a before and an after? Instead, no one had said anything, and there was just this confusion. She didn't know whether to be worried or not. She didn't know how to act. Something was going on. Something had changed. But no one had even mentioned that something was wrong, so she didn't want to act worried or scared.

She stood up and brushed the worst of the dirt off her pants. She could go inside and call Mom and then come back and put away the tools unless there was some time left to work. It was getting very windy. She dialed Mom's number angrily, irritated that she had to call to tell her that there was nothing to tell, hoping that she'd get the answering machine and could leave a quick message and have it over with.

Mom answered the phone.

"It's Alyssa, Mom. How are you?"

"Okay. Just the usual complaints. How are you?"

"I'm fine. I've been working outside all day. I'm extending the flower gardens by the deck, the way you said to."

"You don't have to do it just because I said to."

"I know that. It's a really good idea. It's going to look great when I finish."

"What are you planning to put there?"

"Flowers that will bloom all summer, the way you said. I guess annuals this year anyway. I don't know about next year."

"Anything you put there will look nice. Have you had any of those tests yet?"

"I had two of them yesterday. But I don't know anything about them except that they want me to go in for a biopsy tomorrow morning. I was hoping I wouldn't have to do that. And it's so soon."

"At least you'll get it over with."

"That's no good. I was hoping I wouldn't have to do it at all, and for all I know they will just say I have to have something else done."

"It's not so bad, Alyssa. Did they tell you how long it was going to take?"

"Nobody told me anything except that I have to be there at seven-thirty tomorrow morning."

"Well, it can't last that long, and then you'll be home and you can get back to the garden."

"But what if I have to stay in the hospital?" She could feel the tears beginning to pool up behind her eyes. "What if I'm too weak to work in the garden?" Now her voice was beginning to tremble.

"It's not so bad, Alyssa."

"It's not so bad for you. It's easy for you to talk," she said angrily. She was really crying now. Everything seemed so awful.

"I'm sorry, sweetie. I wish I could do it myself, so you didn't have to."

The unexpected generosity of that statement fortified Alyssa as nothing else could have. "I'm sorry too, Mom. I didn't mean to dump it on you. I wasn't expecting to get this call so soon." She choked on a sob. "And they haven't even told me what it means."

"They'll probably tell you more tomorrow."

"So I don't know why I bothered you because I don't really have anything to tell you."

"I'm glad you did. I wish I could help you. Do you want me to come up?"

"No, that would be silly. Anyway, you were just here."

"That doesn't matter."

"Anyway, you couldn't get here. It's too long a drive for you all by yourself."

"I could come on the train."

"No, Mom, really. I don't want you to do that."

"Well, all right. But try not to get so unhappy about it. It'll be over soon. And I could come up, you know."

"Thanks. I'll be fine. I'm sorry if I've worried you."

"I'll call you tomorrow to see how it went."

"Okay."

"Shall I tell Alix and Sonia?"

"I guess so. Tell them I'll talk to both of them when it's over."

"Okay, sweetie."

She managed to get off the phone before she started crying again. She stood there, trying to decide whether to go back to the garden or not. But she didn't feel like it any more. The sun was gone, and it was getting cold. It looked like a thunderstorm was coming. Her face felt swollen from crying.

She picked up the tools and put everything away, angry that she didn't finish and that she wouldn't be able to finish. It had been such a nice day, and now it was spoiled.

She took a shower and put on clean clothes, and that made a difference, even though her head was still stopped up. As she went down the back stairs, she could hear Richard's voice. He was home, and he was on the phone. It was raining hard outside.

Just as she got to the kitchen, he hung up. He was standing by the glass door to the deck. He turned and looked at her. "That was your mother. She says she's coming up on the train tomorrow, and she wants me to meet her."

"I told her not to do that."

"What's this all about? I'm missing something."

"I'm sorry, Richard. I haven't had a chance to tell you. I have to have a biopsy tomorrow."

"What did they say about it?"

"Hardly anything. I really don't know much, except that I have to be there at seven-thirty in the morning."

"Dr. McCormack didn't say why?"

"I didn't even talk to him. His nurse said that was what he wanted me to do."

"It doesn't make sense." Now he was pacing back and forth from the woodstove to the glass door. "And how did your mother get into it?"

"I called her up to tell her—not that I knew anything—because I didn't want her to say later on that I should have told her."

"I'll make us a fire in just a minute. It's kind of cold in here." He sat down at the table, looking puzzled.

Alyssa went down the steps and sat across the table from him. "It's been beautiful all day. Maybe when the thunderstorm is over, it will be clear again."

"I still don't understand why your mother is coming up. She was just here."

"I'm going to call her and tell her not to come. I got upset on the phone, and I guess I upset her. It's just because I don't want to have to waste my whole day at the hospital." She reached across the table and took his hand. "I want to show you what I've been doing all day. It's going to be so pretty. And I didn't get a chance to finish it, and now I won't get to work on it tomorrow." She could feel herself choking up again. "But, of course, if Mom was here, I'd have to take care of her too, and I'd have even less time to work on the garden." She was crying again now. It was ridiculous.

She got up and went to the glass door. "I want to show you. Maybe the rain will end before it gets too dark to see it." She opened the door, but it was cold and damp, and she shivered and closed the door again.

Richard noticed and took her hand. "Do you want to go out and get some dinner so you don't have to cook?"

"That would be nice," she said. "Where would we go?"

"There's that new place down by the river in Severance. We could go there. We've been saying we wanted to check it out."

"Okay, let's do that."

"I'll make a fire while you change your clothes. He stopped and looked at her. "If you want to, that is. You could go like that. You look fine."

"You could make the fire when we get home. I always worry about leaving it."

"Then it'll be cold in here. I'll make a really small one, and we can build it up later."

"Okay. I'll change then. I think I'll wear my new red dress just for fun." She waited a minute to see what he would say, but he was already balling up newspaper for the fire and didn't hear her.

A little later she came back into the room in her new dress and her best high-heeled boots.

Richard was just shutting the firebox door. He looked around at her and then straightened up, still looking. "Very, very nice," he said. "Do you think I'm okay? You won't be embarrassed to be seen with me, will you?"

"Oh Richard, don't be silly. You look fine. You look like you always do." Suddenly, a horrible thought stopped her. She looked into his face, across the room, trying to read there if he would tell her the truth. "Richard, why are you being so extra nice to me? Do you think I'm going to die tomorrow or something?"

That got such a reaction that she knew her question must have surprised him. He gave a kind of snort of laughter and crossed the room to grab her by the shoulders. He looked into her eyes. "No, I don't think any such a thing. Of course I don't." Then he hugged her. "I know you're dreading tomorrow, and I thought…."

"I'm sorry, Richard. That was a dumb question. Okay? I just got scared for a minute." Her face was pressed against his chest so the words came out muffled. She could smell the fresh, outdoor smell of his shirt and underneath that, the sharp smell of his sweat. "If you ever thought that, you'd tell me, wouldn't you?"

He pushed her away a little, holding on to her shoulders. "Of course, I'd tell you. I'm sorry you have to spend part of the day in the hospital tomorrow, but that doesn't mean I think there's something wrong."

"You don't, really?"

"Alyssa, look at you." He pulled her close to him again. "You're in great shape. If something was wrong with you, it would show."

She started to say something about the cough, but a cough wasn't something wrong with you. It was your body's mechanism for clearing your air passages.

"You look beautiful. In fact, you look too nice to waste on just me. Let's go."

The restaurant was named the Riverview. It was a casual place. Alyssa didn't need to have changed her clothes, but she was glad she had made the effort to look nice for Richard.

They got a table on the long glassed-in porch looking over the river. The only light came from the candles on the tables and the last bit of daylight left in the sky. The thunderstorm was over, and the sky was clear again. In the dim light Richard looked the way he had years ago. Alyssa just hoped she looked that way to him. She said, "Do you remember our first date?"

"Of course I do. I took you for a ride in my canoe. I wanted to impress you."

"Your canoe impressed me, that and the way you knew so much about paddling."

"I'd spent an awful lot of time in that canoe. Mom thought I was crazy to bring my canoe. She made me put an old bedspread on the roof so it wouldn't scratch her car. I was afraid you would notice how dumb it looked."

"I don't remember that at all."

"Mom was wrong. Taking that canoe was one of the smartest things I ever did. You wouldn't have gone with me if I hadn't offered you a canoe ride."

"I don't know. I might have. I don't know what made me take off for the whole day like that. I was supposed to be studying for exams."

"I'm glad you did."

"Me too, especially since I didn't fail anything."

Richard said, "Remember how they teased us? They all said they wanted to go with us, and somebody said, 'Is that like showing Alyssa your etchings?' There was that awful moment when I thought I was going to have to ask Joey to come with us, and then I looked at you, and I knew I wasn't going to miss my chance."

"I remember you said, 'Come on, Alyssa,' and I just followed you. I didn't even have to think about it."

The light was almost gone outside, but there were a few bright places where the water caught and held the reflections of street and car lights. The moon was in the last quarter and would be up later.

"The river looks beautiful."

Alyssa said, "You haven't ever canoed this stretch of the river."

"There are so many great places to go. I never thought of going through the middle of Severance."

"It might be fun canoeing through people's backyards—it would be like the way it is on the train."

Richard smiled at her. "Will you come with me? We could go this summer."

"Sure," she said, but she was still back in the day they met. "I couldn't believe how beautiful your canoe was. And then you said you had made it! I remember thinking that you must have been teasing me, that nobody could actually make something like that."

"It took a long time. You can do anything if you have enough time."

"Well, I couldn't have. And you did it when you were in high school."

"It was pretty much all I did."

"That was a wonderful day, Richard."

"I know. I had dreamed about going back to Candlewood Lake all the time I was in Germany. But I never dreamed you into the picture."

Their food arrived. Richard had ordered a steak, the way he always did, but for once his lack of imagination about food didn't even irritate her. Part of her was still back when they first ate together, when they didn't even know what each other liked. She said, "I've been on so many canoe trips with you over the years, you would think they would all merge together in my mind, but somehow that day stands out so clearly. Is it that way for you too?"

"I think so. How's your dinner? This steak isn't very good."

"It's okay, but ordinary."

"That's what I think about mine."

"The view over the river makes up for a lot."

"Yes, but you can't eat it," Richard said. He reached out and took her hand across the table. "Do you want me to come with you tomorrow?"

She couldn't think what he meant for a minute. "No. I'll be fine. I forgot all about it." She squeezed his hand. "Thanks for giving me such a lovely evening."

"It's been nice for me too."

Later on, driving home, Alyssa said, "Remember when we were out on Candlewood, and I asked you to show me how to paddle, and you came up behind me when I didn't know you were there, and I was so surprised?"

"You jumped so high, you almost tipped us over. I should have told you I was coming."

"Everything about that day has stayed so clear in my mind."

"That's because it was your first canoe ride."

"Or maybe my first day with you. Tomorrow when I'm waiting for them to do things to me, I'm going to pretend to be back in that day."

On the way into town the next morning, she remembered that idea and hoped she would be able to concentrate well enough when the biopsy was actually happening

When she got to the hospital, they told her where to go. She walked down a long corridor, feeling cold and grim, and then, instead of telling her to wait, they hurried her along to a hospital bed where she had to lie for a long time, halfway between being awake and being asleep, while uncomfortable things were being done.

Once she had a coughing fit that she couldn't stop, and a cross technician asked her if she smoked. She said she quit years ago. She was proud of that, but he just grunted and left the room. She was the center of the nurses and the doctor, and yet they ignored her. There was something that felt like it was going to choke her going down her throat, but when she reached out to push it away, she found that her hands were tied down.

It felt as though it would be like that forever, but it wasn't. After a while, she was alone in the room. After more time, when she was more awake, a nurse came in and told her she could leave. That was when she found out that she was supposed to ask someone to drive her home.

She had to wait in the waiting room until Richard could get there. When she saw him, she tried to stand up, but she had to sit down again. He came over and sat down beside her. "Are you okay?"

"I think so. I just felt dizzy. I didn't know it would be like this afterwards. I'm so glad I don't have to drive myself home."

"I'm sorry I didn't come with you this morning. I should have. They should have told you to bring someone with you."

"Maybe they did, and I didn't pay attention. Let's go home." She leaned heavily on him as they went out to the car. "What about your truck?" It was the first time she had thought of it.

"We'll have to get it later."

"We could leave my car."

"No, you'll be more comfortable, and anyway, I'm going to need it later to pick up your mother at the train station."

"Oh God, I forgot about that." Richard opened the door for her, and she sank into the seat, grateful to be there. "At least the biopsy is over."

"Was it bad?"

"I don't think so. I can't remember. They gave me something that made me sleepy, and then they stuck something down my throat. That part was bad, but I don't know how long it lasted."

"How do you feel now?"

"Tired and shaky, but okay. I don't hurt any place."

"Are you hungry?"

"Not a bit. I think I want to lie down for a while when I get home. What time is it anyway?"

"A little after eleven. I'm going to take you home and help you get to bed, and then I'm going to come back in to the grocery store. You'll be okay by yourself, won't you?"

She didn't even argue with him about it because they would need some groceries if Mom was coming. She just nodded a yes, which he probably didn't see, and fell asleep in the car.

She woke up at home with Richard helping her out of the car and up the stairs to the bedroom. He got her partly undressed and under the covers. When he started to shut the curtains, she woke up enough to ask him not to. It was raining outside, and the light was pale and gray. Everything was warm and soft, and the biopsy was over. She drifted away on a sea of comfortable feelings.

CHAPTER II

Monika had the seat all to herself until Springfield. She was very comfortable. Her bag was under her feet, and her basket of snacks was beside her. It passed the time to be nibbling on something. Her book was laid open on her lap, but it was a ruse. It was hard enough to read at home, with the light just right. Here on the train, with the light from the window flickering, and the train lurching and jiggling, it was impossible to read at all. Still, no one would think she was having trouble with her vision when they saw an open book on her lap.

At Springfield a young person got on and asked if the seat was taken. Monika had to say no and move her stuff, but she was sorry to give up the space.

At first she thought it was a young boy whose voice hadn't changed yet, but then she realized it was a young woman in mannish, nondescript clothes. As near as Monika could tell with her poor vision, since she didn't want to be obvious about it, the young woman was in her twenties with short, cropped hair.

They rode along in silence for a while. Monika thought about raising her book, but she looked out the window instead. She could feel the girl looking her over with curiosity. Finally the girl said, "Where are you headin?"

"Severance," Monika said. "I'm going to visit my daughter for a few days."

"I'm goin home. My dad is sick."

"That's too bad. What's the matter with him?"

"They don't know, but he's in a lot of pain. He hasn't been able to work for a while now."

"I'm sorry," Monika said. "Where is your home?" She was hoping it wouldn't be Severance or north of Severance.

"Windsor. Well, they don't live right in Windsor, but that's where I get off. My dad used to work in the Windsor prison."

"Oh."

"That was a long time ago. It ain't a prison no more."

"Oh."

"They have a farm up near Hartland."

"Oh."

"Except that for a while now he ain't been able to do any kind of work. I was down there in Springfield, but I got laid off four months ago. I've been hopin they would call us back in again, but it don't look like they're goin to."

"I'm sorry," Monika said again. Windsor must be only a few hours away.

"Where's your daughter live at?"

"Severance. Well, like your family, she lives out in the country in West Severance."

"That's cool. Is she married?"

"Yes. She has grown-up children, and one of them has a child, so I'm a great-grandmother." She didn't want to talk about why she was going to visit Alyssa. She hoped the girl wouldn't ask.

They were quiet for a while after that. Monika looked out the window, but it wasn't comfortable anymore. They crossed the border into Vermont. Soon afterward the train stopped in Brattleboro. The basket was jammed onto Monika's lap on top of her open book. Her handbag was pushed down into the seat between them. She was starting to get stiff, but there wasn't any room to change positions.

She said, "Would you like something to eat? I have some snacks in there." She handed the basket to the girl. That made things a little more comfortable. She was able to close her book and put it and her handbag on the dirty floor with the suitcase, and after that she could shift her legs a little.

The girl was digging around inside the basket. She brought out a box of crackers and a bag of raisins. Monika wasn't sure what else she was going to pull out, but she didn't care. It felt so nice to change positions.

"There are some apples and pears in there, I think."

"Oh, thanks. This is great. I didn't realize how hungry I was." She was talking with her mouth full. "I was goin to get something at the snack bar, but it's so expensive."

"I guess they don't have a dining car on this train."

"Oh no, they haven't had one for years, just the snack bar. And the food is awful."

"It used to be so nice to have dinner on the train, tablecloths and waiters. The food was good, and you could watch the scenery out the window while you ate."

"I've never done that. It must have been a long time ago."

"It was. You could travel in style in those days. Now everyone has to travel like a peasant. I'm glad I brought my basket of food."

"Me too. You don't mind if I eat more, do you?"

"No. Go ahead." Monika was a little horrified by how hungry the girl was, and she was so thin too.

Monika looked out the window at the Vermont countryside, the woods, and two-lane country roads, the little villages and scattered houses. The train went up beside the Connecticut River, beautiful and still, like a shining ribbon laid across the land.

"We're goin to be at Windsor soon. I'm so pleased to make your acquaintance."

Monika looked at her. She was holding out her hand. Monika took it.

"My name's Dawn. Dawn Ravinsky."

"Ravenous Ravinsky," Monika thought, but she didn't say it out loud. Instead, she said, "Monika Adler. It's nice to meet you."

"Same here. I'll have to tell my folks about you, comin all the way from wherever you started."

"Stamford."

"Comin all the way from Stamford at your age to visit your daughter. I'm always askin my mom and dad to come visit me, but my mom would be too scared to try it, and my dad's too sick to go anywhere."

After the train left the Windsor station, Monika relaxed into the seat and spread out a bit. She put her handbag and her book up on the seat beside her and looked into the basket. There was one apple left. The cores of the other apples and the pears were gone. Monica had no idea what happened to them. Maybe she ate them too, and the stems and the seeds. There was one cracker left in the box of crackers and one raisin left in the bag of raisins. Monika felt annoyed, but the poor girl was obviously very hungry.

After a while the conductor came by and took the stub of her ticket. He said they would be in Severance in a few minutes. A few people began to stand up.

Monika stood too and picked up her things. With her basket in one hand and her suitcase in the other, she bumbled forward, slowly and clumsily, bumping into the backs of the seats as she passed. She was afraid Richard wouldn't be there, or that he would be there and she wouldn't recognize him because of her poor vision.

She climbed down the steps with the conductor holding out his hands to catch her if she fell. Monika felt like saying, "I'm not *that* old. I'm not just going to topple over." But at the same time, the steps were steep and her legs felt weak and stiff. She really might fall.

There was a little group of people on the platform, a blur of white circles. Richard reached out and took her bag out of her hand.

"Oh, there you are," she said. She was relieved. That worry was over. "How is Alyssa?"

"Mom, I'm right here. You can see for yourself."

That was embarrassing. She couldn't say she didn't see Alyssa, since

Alyssa was right there in front of her. Only blindness or mental incapacity could explain why she hadn't seen her. She could only hurry past her mistake. "Oh, there you are," she said, and hugged her. "How do you feel?"

"Fine. I told you it would be okay."

"It's over then?"

"It lasted for a few hours this morning. I slept a lot this afternoon, and I'm fine now."

Monika could feel a slight undercurrent in what Alyssa said. The unspoken words were, "See. Everything is normal. You didn't need to come all this way."

Richard said, "If this is all of your luggage, we can go to the car." As they walked, he said, "We have to go by the hospital, if you don't mind. I had to leave my truck up there this morning, and I might need it tomorrow."

"I don't mind."

"Are you hungry?"

"Not very. I brought some snacks with me on the train, but a very hungry young woman ate most of them."

"Oh, Mom." Alyssa squeezed her arm. "You always let people take advantage of you."

"It was all right. I had enough, and she was very thin." A cold rain was falling. She had traveled backward in time to an earlier season.

Alyssa squeezed her arm again. "We could go out to dinner somewhere before we go home."

"That's not necessary. It's late. I'm tired, and you must be too."

"I'm fine. I slept all afternoon. But it is late. Richard got some groceries today, so there's plenty to eat at home."

"That would be the nicest."

"I think so too."

The next morning Monika felt rested and ready to work. When she got to the kitchen, it was warm. The fire was flickering behind the glass door of the stove. At the table Alyssa was reading the newspaper, and Richard was reading his Kindle. Monika hated to interrupt them, even though she wanted to be part of the cozy scene. She dreaded having to pretend to be reading.

Alyssa looked up and saw her standing there and stood up quickly. "Good morning, Mom. I'll get you some coffee."

"Don't get up, Alyssa, please. I know where everything is. Let me bring you some coffee."

"No thanks, Mom," Alyssa said, sitting down again.

"Richard?"

"What?' Richard looked up. He had missed everything they had said. Monika held up the coffeepot, and he said, "No thanks. I'm fine."

Monika poured some for herself and fixed it with milk, the way she liked it. Then she stood at the top of the steps, looking down at them as they sat at the table below her. They were both reading again. Monika was reluctant to go down the steps with a full cup of hot coffee in her hand and no railing to hold on to.

Standing at the top of the steps she said, "I'd like to help you with the new garden, Alyssa. It looks like a nice day outside." She thought for a minute. "Actually, I'm free all day. I'm going to work on it, unless you don't want me to. It would be fun if we could work together, but I can do it alone, if you're busy."

"I'm not. I'd love that, Mom."

"Okay," Monika said with satisfaction. "Let's get a lot done, and then I think I'll go home tomorrow morning."

"That isn't much of a visit, Mom."

"It's enough. I wanted to see you with my own eyes." She felt an uncomfortable twinge saying those words. "I wanted to make sure you were all right, and I've done that. There's nothing wrong with you. I don't need to worry, so my mission has been accomplished. Now I want to have some fun."

Alyssa's face lit with a big smile when she heard that. Monika was glad she had said it. Alyssa was pleased with her, and that was lovely.

It had looked so nice through the windows, but when they went out, there was a cold wind blowing. It felt much more wintery than it looked. Monika resisted a wish to go back inside. Resolutely, she said, "Your new garden looks wonderful. You've done so much. Later on, we can go to a greenhouse and pick out some plants. The sooner you get something planted, the sooner you'll have flowers here."

"I don't know what I'm going to put in."

"We can look around. What you want is something that will bloom after your daffodils and irises are finished, something for the middle of the summer, and something not too tall."

They worked companionably for a while without saying anything. Monika was filled with love. The strength of the feeling on this bright morning must come at least partly from relief. She dug through the dirt that Alyssa had cut the sod from. It was very cold out. Her hands even in the gardening gloves were numb with it. No, she always felt full of love for Alyssa, for Alyssa as she was now, and for the Alyssa of long ago.

She said, "Remember how you took Aaron into his classroom on his first day of school to introduce him to his teacher?"

"He was so scared—all those kids bigger than he was."

"Then you took him to your classroom to show him where you were going to be."

"I wanted him to know I was there if he needed me."

"You were a good big sister."

Alyssa didn't say anything. She spaded up some more sod, shook out the clumps, and put them in the wheelbarrow.

Monika tried to see if Alyssa was feeling sad about Aaron, but she didn't want to look at her too openly, and her eyes kept her from being able to see much.

After a few minutes, Alyssa said, "Remember when we were going on some trip, and we stopped by the road at a roadside stop, and Aaron and I got lost in the woods?"

"I don't remember that."

"There were picnic tables. You were setting out our lunch, and Daddy was looking at a map. I don't remember where we were or where we were going. But Aaron needed to pee, and you told me to take him back into the trees. He was two, or maybe three, and trying to go without diapers. It must have been warm weather, because I don't remember that we had coats on. The sun was shining through the trees. I wonder where we were going."

"I can't remember." Monika was digging through the dirt, combing it through her fingers to get all the roots out. But she was picturing them all as a young family on an outing together. They were all together then.

Alyssa said, "We walked a little way into the trees, and then I looked back and there you were, busy laying out our lunch, and Daddy was sitting in the driver's seat of the car with his feet on the ground and the map held up so I couldn't see his face, and I thought we had better go a little farther away, because if we could see you, you could see us. I don't know why we cared, except that you told us to go back in the trees out of sight to take a pee. I guess we were trying to do what you said."

"I wonder what trip it was. There's no one to ask any more. Maybe we were going to visit Papa and Mama. We'll never know now, and someday when you and I are gone, the whole story will disappear. And who will remember Aaron then?"

"Oh Mom. Don't. You sound so sad."

"That's because it is sad. It's all gone, or what's not gone will be soon."

For a while neither of them said any more. Little bits and pieces of those long-ago days flickered in Monika's head, pictures of Aaron and Alyssa and what they were like as children. She could almost remember that day they got lost in the woods.

Alyssa said, "When we had both peed and I had fixed our clothes, I looked around. I couldn't see anything but trees surrounding us. I couldn't remember which direction we had come from. I asked Aaron, but he didn't know either."

"You could have called to us, you know. We were right there."

"I know that now, but I didn't then. Little kids think such odd thoughts sometimes. I thought I could take care of both of us. I told Aaron not to be afraid, that I would find our way back to our parents just the way Hansel and Gretel did. That was a mistake, because it made Aaron think there might be a witch in the woods. He got really scared and started to cry. I had just gotten us started walking—I think we were walking in the wrong direction—when we heard you calling, and in just a minute, you were there. It was like magic."

"I must have heard Aaron crying. You were never very far away. I'm sure I would have remembered it if you were."

"It seemed like miles. I can still remember that feeling of looking around…forest in every direction. Nothing to show us which way to go. I knew exactly what it felt like to Hansel and Gretel."

"You always took such good care of Aaron, just the way Gretel took care of Hansel."

"How lovely those days were when Aaron and Daddy were still with us, and we were a family."

"And now we are the only ones left." She almost said that soon she would be gone too, and Alyssa would be absolutely alone. But she didn't say it, luckily, because in a minute she saw it from a different angle. "No, that's not true. We have Alix and Sonia and Sonia's family." She paused. "And Richard also," she said as an afterthought. It hadn't always been easy to get along with Richard. But Alyssa smiled down at her, and she was glad she said it.

They stopped in the middle of the morning for breakfast. Richard was gone to town, so it was just the two of them. It felt lovely to go into the warm house. She sat at the table and watched while Alyssa put wood on the fire and cooked them some eggs. She moved with efficiency and grace. Monika took delight in watching her and didn't even feel guilty for not helping.

They left the dishes in the sink when they went back to work. In the middle of the afternoon, Alyssa suggested that they take a break and walk up the trail by the brook to see what was happening at the ravens' nest, but Monika didn't think she could walk that far. By that time all she wanted was to sit by the warm stove and rest.

They finished the job about four in the afternoon. After they had put the tools away and dumped the last wheelbarrow load of sod into the compost pile, they went into the house.

Alyssa said, "What shall we do now?"

Monika held her hands over the stove to warm them. It felt so nice to be finished with the job. "I'll do whatever you would like to do."

"You look tired, Mom. I'll build up the fire and make us each a cup of tea."

"That suits me fine."

They sat facing each other across the table. Monika put her hands around her mug of tea. It was hot and that loosened her fingers. They had been clumsy and stiff all day, digging in the cold dirt. The fire ticked pleasantly behind her. "This is awfully nice," she said.

"Yes. It's nice to have that job finished. I wonder what I ought to plant there."

"Almost anything will look pretty, even if it doesn't flower."

"But what?"

"Go to a nursery and look around. Find what you like the look of. You'll find something."

"Why don't you stay another day, Mom? We could do it together. I've had such a good time today." Then she was overtaken by a fit of coughing.

Monika cringed at the sound of it. Alyssa was doubled over trying to get her breath. It was a few minutes before Monika could say anything. "I hope you're not getting sick, a cold or the flu."

"Oh no. It's left over from when I was sick in March. It's nothing."

"I don't want to leave if you're getting sick, but I really need to get back home."

Alyssa cleared her throat and took a drink of her tea. Then she looked at Monika in such a loving way. "We've had an awfully good time together today, Mom. Or at least I have." Her voice was husky from all the coughing.

"Me too."

"We could go get some plants tomorrow."

"It's tempting to think of spending another day here, another day with you." She thought about how Alyssa might be appealing to her motherly instincts by coughing so much. But no, Alyssa was fine. She looked fine, and she had just had lots of tests. Monika thought of her distant home. It had its own siren song. "I didn't leave things in very good order. I hurried up here because I was worried about you."

"Well, you don't need to worry, but we could have fun. Think about it, Mom."

"I'll be thinking about it all the way home, but there will be lots of other chances for us to spend time together." She paused. "I mean, even though I'm eighty-four, I think I will be here for quite a while longer. I don't have anything wrong with me."

"I know, Mom. I think so too." She got up and came around the table to Monika and put her arms around her. "We'll have lots more days like today. Thank you."

CHAPTER 12

Richard was in the garage, putting the second coat of spar varnish on the outside of his canoe. It was a spring ritual that he loved. He still had the inside to do, and then he could put her in the water. All winter he had been planning where he would go this year.

"Richard, so you're in here. I couldn't find you. I've been calling, but you didn't answer."

He looked up. Alyssa was standing in the doorway. "I've been right here. I'm sorry I didn't hear you."

"You look half asleep. The fumes aren't getting to you, are they?"

"No, I don't think so. Doing this job always brings back memories. I was somewhere in the past. That's why I didn't hear you."

Alyssa went partway up the stairs and sat down on a step. The cuffs of her blue jeans were full of garden dirt, and she was sitting directly above the open can of varnish.

When Richard dipped his brush in the can the next time, he pushed the can across the stair, so that she wasn't sitting right over it.

"What were you thinking about?"

"I was remembering that trip John Ingersoll and I took down the Connecticut after we graduated from high school."

"When your canoe was new."

"That's right. That was the first trip I took it on. Mom and Dad drove us up to the Canadian border. They stayed in a motel, and we camped in the campground near Canaan. We cooked supper for them and breakfast the next morning, and then we started down the Connecticut, and they went home. You've heard this a thousand times."

Alyssa started to say something, but it was overtaken by a series of coughs. She doubled over her knees. Richard was glad he had been able to move his varnish without her noticing. When she got her breath back, she said, "I know, but I always wonder. That must have been awful hard for your parents."

Richard thought for a minute. "It was Dad's idea to give us that trip for a graduation present. They gave us money and supplies. John's parents did too."

"But they must have been worried about you."

"I suppose they were. I never asked them."

"Would we have let Alix and Sonia do something like that?"

"They're girls. That's different."

"I don't think we'd have let them do such a trip, even if they were boys."

"Maybe not. We were gone almost three weeks."

"See what I mean? And there were no cell phones and no way to get in touch with you."

"We called home every few days. When we went into a town for supplies, we would find a pay phone and call home."

"You should write it all down, Richard, while you can still remember it."

"There's no danger of me forgetting. It has always stayed so vividly in my mind." He made a few final passes with the brush. "There, the outside is ready for summer." He put the lid on the can of varnish and tapped it into place. He wrapped the brush in a plastic bag, so he wouldn't have to clean it.

Alyssa had another coughing fit.

Richard said, "I wish you'd hear from Dr. McCormack. It's been almost a week since you had that biopsy. I thought he was in such a hurry."

Alyssa stood up. "I really came to ask you if you wanted to take a walk."

"Sure. Do you want to go up the brook to the ravens' nest? We haven't been up there for a while."

"Let's do that."

They left right away. Richard didn't even bother to wash the varnish off his hands. They went by the cabin and the pool where they swam and fished.

Alyssa said, "You haven't been fishing for a while."

"No. Not since Jack was here."

"That fish was delicious."

Richard laughed. "Yes, it was. I should try for another one."

"We could have fish for dinner."

"I have to catch one first."

They went on up the trail. Every once in a while, Alyssa had to stop to cough.

Richard stopped beside her, but he didn't know what else to do. "I wish you'd get over this thing," he said. "Maybe when the warm weather really settles in, it will clear it out of you."

"Maybe," she said.

The leaves were starting to unfurl on all the trees. There was a haze of delicate green over the woods. The little breeze was full of the smells of warm earth and water.

They didn't need any arrows made of pebbles to show them where the nest was. Ravens were calling and flying back and forth. When they got close, they could see that one of the babies was out of the nest, perched on a branch, like a kid at the end of a diving board, too scared to jump or to go back. The parents were flying around, scolding and calling instructions.

Richard didn't dare look away, afraid he would miss what happened next. He hoped the kid would try it. If he opened his wings, he could glide down slowly, even if he couldn't fly.

After a little while, the bird hopped along the branch, and then, with an extra large jump, flapping his wings, he landed awkwardly on the rim of the nest.

Alyssa said, "Thank goodness he's safe."

The parent birds must have thought so too, because they calmed down. One lighted on the branch of a nearby tree, and the other flew off in a large circle.

"He could have made it."

"You don't know that, Richard."

"Well, he has to try it sometime."

"His parents were telling him not to."

"You don't *know* that."

"That's what it sounded like. You didn't like it when our girls disobeyed you."

"Yes," Richard said. "You're right. It made me angry. But I can see now that it was a good thing."

The bird was hunkered down in the nest with the others. Even without binoculars, Richard thought he could see disappointment on the bird's face. But how could you tell what a bird was thinking?

Alyssa doubled up with another cough. Richard patted her on the back, but he felt helpless.

"I thought you were so much better lately. Do you want to sit down for a minute?"

"No, I'm fine," she said smiling, but she was gasping for breath too, and trying not to let it show.

Richard could tell she didn't want him to notice, and that made him feel even more helpless.

After the coughing fit passed, they went down the trail.

Later in the afternoon, Richard went up to the pool with his fly rod. He tried all around the edges of the pool. He tried flies, and then he turned over some rocks and tried worms. But nothing worked. It didn't matter. The warm sunlight coming through the trees and the sound of the water as it went over the little waterfall was soothing. He sat on the ground just glad to be there.

He was picking up little pebbles and bits of stick, throwing them into the water to see the tiny splashes, when suddenly there was a swirl and a strike. So there were fish in there after all. It made him laugh. Sometimes, it was only when you stopped trying for a thing that you would be given it. And sometimes that was when you no longer cared. He got up and went down the trail to tell Alyssa that they would have to think of something else for dinner.

Much later in the evening, when the dishes were done and they were sitting by the woodstove reading, Richard said, "I think we ought to buy a new tent."

"You do?"

"Yes, I do. It's getting so I have to patch the patches. If we're going to take some trips to Maine or maybe Canada this summer...and I hope we are...we're going to need a new tent."

"Well, that's okay, Richard. Whatever you think. Are they expensive?"

"No, not very. A couple hundred dollars could get us a pretty good one."

"Why don't we do it then? If we need it so much."

"I've found some online I could show you."

"Okay."

He stood up to go get his computer.

"Do you think we're going to be taking a lot of trips this summer?"

"I hope so." He had one hand on the stair railing, ready to go up.

"Richard, I want to tell you something."

"Okay, sure, but don't worry. We'll get the tent you want us to get."

"All right, but what I want to tell you doesn't have anything to do with what tent we buy."

"Okay, sure," he said again, still standing at the foot of the stairs. "What is it?"

"It's this," she paused, looking down at the book on her lap.

He wanted to tell her to either hurry up or wait a minute while he went upstairs for his laptop. He was just about to say he would be back in a minute when she said, "I did hear from Dr. McCormack's office."

"Oh," he said, surprised. "What did they say about it?"

"It wasn't they. It was Dr. McCormack himself. He left a message on the answering machine."

Richard's first thought was that probably meant bad news. He walked over to the woodstove and stood with his back to it, looking at Alyssa. He tried to tell himself that it could be good news too. Dr. McCormack might want to give her the good news in person. But he didn't say any of that. All he said out loud was, "What did he say?"

"Not much, but enough for me to know it was bad news." She was sitting on the couch with her legs tucked up beside her. She looked at him. "He said I should call back right away so I could make an appointment to see that doctor who's a friend of his. I can't remember his name."

Her eyes were big and dark with fear. Richard wanted to reassure her, but he didn't know enough yet. "What did he say when you called back?"

Her eyes dropped away to her lap. "I didn't."

"What?"

"I didn't call him back."

"You didn't? Alyssa, when did he call you?"

"Last Friday."

"*Last week*? Why didn't you call him back? Why didn't you tell me?"

"I don't know."

He looked at her hard. He could feel himself getting unreasonably angry. "You've known about this for almost a week, and you never told me?"

"Richard, don't." Her eyes were full of tears. "I needed some time to think about it. I wanted to decide what I wanted to do."

"But I could *help* you."

"Please don't get mad. I want to know what you think I ought to do, but I wanted to know what *I* thought, all by myself, first. Doesn't that make sense?"

"No, it really doesn't, and anyway, you don't have much choice about what you do." He wished he could keep the hard edge out of his voice. He knew she could hear it, and he knew it made her cringe. "What else can you do at this point? You have to call him, don't you?"

"No, I don't." She looked away from him again. "That's what I have been thinking...how I could just do nothing about it and see what happens."

"Alyssa, that's *crazy*."

"Maybe they're wrong. They don't always know. And sometimes these things go away by themselves. That's what I've been thinking anyway."

Richard walked across the room to the stairs and back to the stove again. He could feel himself getting tighter and tighter. "You don't even know what you're talking about here. You don't know if this is something really serious, or something the doctors know they can fix. You have to find that out first. You should have made that call right away." He stopped in his tracks. That wasn't what he meant, or rather, it was exactly what he meant, but not what he wanted to say to her.

He knew what she ought to do. And he was sure he was right, but he didn't want to make her feel worse than she already did. She had just suffered a grievous wound. She had just learned that something monstrous might be growing inside, something that might choke and strangle her. That was a horrifying thought. Maybe she didn't see it as clearly as he did. He hoped she didn't. He needed to be careful. He didn't want her to know what he was thinking.

He sat down in his chair again. Neither of them spoke. The sound of the fire clicking inside the stove was loud in the silence of the room. Richard thought of several possible things to say, but he discarded them one by one and said nothing.

Alyssa sat curled up on the couch, looking down at the closed book on her lap. He could feel her waiting for what he would say next. He took a breath in as though he was going to say something, and she looked up. Her eyes were big. When he saw that, he didn't know what to say any more. He felt so sorry. He knew it could be long and hard and painful. He could help her, but the pain would be all hers to bear.

Finally, after a long, naked minute, while they looked at each other, he said, "I'll help you all I can. You know that, don't you, Alyssa?"

"Yes, I do know that. Thank you, Richard."

"You have to fight. You know that too, don't you?"

She looked down at her lap, and when she spoke, it was even quieter than before. "I'm not sure yet. I want to think about it."

"I don't know what you could be thinking. You can't just sit here and wait to die." His voice was louder than he intended it to be. He stood up and opened the door of the woodstove. He poked at the fire with the poker. Sparks flew around. He got a log out of the wood box and threw it onto the fire and closed the door. Alyssa still hadn't said anything. "I'm sorry, Alyssa. I don't want to rush you. You should know what you think before you make any decisions." He wanted to go on to say that when she had thought it over, she would see that he was right, that there was only one thing she could do. But he managed to stop himself in time.

She looked up at him and smiled a little, and he thought how he loved her, how he wanted to take care of her, to protect her from this pain. She was a creature as fragile and delicate as glass that had been put in his keeping. He couldn't fail her. And then he had to wonder about his own motives. Was he so sure he knew what she ought to do? That was the course that was right for him. He could fight with her and for her. She would get better, and he wouldn't lose her. She would be saved, and it would be his doing, and everyone would notice what good care he had taken of her. He was horrified, but only for an instant, because right away he told himself that the important point, the bottom line, was that she would be alive. So his motives didn't really matter, because they both wanted the same thing, and he was going to make it happen.

He wanted to say something to end the silence, but there wasn't anything else for him to say. All he could do was wait to see if she was going to speak. But Alyssa didn't move. She sat quietly, looking at her hands in her lap. She seemed unaware of his presence.

Finally, Richard went upstairs and got his laptop. He had bookmarked the site, so it was easy to find the tent he thought they ought to buy. He sat down beside her on the couch to show her. "Look at this one," he said. "It's plenty big enough, but it's light, and it only costs $269. What do you think?"

He was wrenching her mind away from her own troubles; he could feel that that was what he was doing. He didn't know whether it was the right thing to do or not.

She leaned in close to see the computer screen, and then she looked at him and smiled a weak smile. "That looks really nice, Richard. Why don't you order that one?"

"Do you want to look around and see if there's one you like better?"

She smiled again, a smile of great sadness, as though she was far away. He wanted to say, "Alyssa, nothing has changed. Don't *do* this." But he said nothing. If she had asked him what he meant, he wouldn't have been able to tell her. He felt as though he was standing on the bank of a river, watching her as she was swept away by the rushing water. She reached her arm out to him. He could almost grab her hand, but then she slipped farther away so that he was unable to reach her to save her, no matter what he did.

She said, "Let's have the tent you picked. Do you think we'll use it a lot this summer?"

"I hope so. I always plan more trips than we get to, but if I didn't, we would probably take even fewer. We need to be ready."

"Yes," she said. "I think you're right. Let's think of some wonderful new places to go this year."

"Let's do," Richard said. "I'll order the tent tomorrow." He stood up and closed the computer. He walked over to set it on the table and then came back to her and reached out to pull her up beside him, so he could put his arms around her. She was so important to him that she seemed larger than she was. He always forgot how small and finely made she was. All his anger had disappeared. He felt full of tenderness. "Let's go to bed, Alyssa. You must be tired."

"I am," she said, burrowing her face into the front of his shirt so that her words came out muffled. "But you must be too."

"I am, but I want to hold you in my arms while you fall asleep, the way I used to do with the girls when they were small."

She reached up to put her arms around his neck. "I'd like that," she said.

He felt strong and full of love. He wanted to say, "We can beat this thing together. Let me help you fight it," but he had the wisdom not to say it. He said, "I love you," instead.

In the morning Richard asked her if she wanted him to stay to give her moral support until she had made the call.

She gave him a kiss and said, "I'm tempted to have your company. You are being so sweet to me, but go on. I want to do a few things. I'm probably going to make the call this morning, but I need to think about it for a while by myself."

She got up from the table where they were both sitting and took her coffee cup up the steps to the kitchen to fill it. "Do you want me to bring you some?"

"Thanks, but no. I have plenty."

She leaned over the counter and looked down at him. "I'm really glad I told you, Richard. You said some things I hadn't thought of, and I thank you. It was helpful to hear what you had to say." She got her coffee and went back to the table.

He wanted to say something more, to give her other arguments. He opened his mouth, and then he turned away and looked out the window.

Did she notice that he caught himself just in time? He couldn't tell. She wasn't looking at him, but she said, "Thanks, Richard. I really appreciate you giving me some space to make up my own mind."

He got up. When he went past her, he kissed the top of her head. "I guess I'll go on then. I'll call you later to see if you need anything from town."

CHAPTER 13

After Bonnie left, Sam piled the dirty dishes in the sink and went outside. It was warm. There was a light, drizzly rain falling. Everything smelled washed and fresh.

He pulled his pickup under the hayloft door and went into the barn. Colt followed him as far as the stairs to the hayloft, but they were too steep. He waited at the bottom.

The loft was almost empty now. There were a few broken bales and a small pile of good ones at the far end. There were less than fifty bales left. It was a good idea to clean out the old hay before he started putting in the new, but being so close to having none made him uneasy.

Shafts of light came through cracks in the board walls. As he walked across the floor, dust motes danced up into the light. He grabbed a bale in each hand and took them to the hayloft door and threw them down into the bed of the pickup below. He went back for two more. Four bales ought to be enough. He latched the door and went down.

He pushed the bales around to make room in the back for Colt. Colt always wanted to ride, no matter how short the distance was.

They drove across the road and stopped by the garden fence. Sam threw the bales into the garden and went in himself. The loose soil clumped up on his boots. But he was glad of the rain. At least it kept most of the blackflies away, and they had been awful lately.

Colt jumped down and turned around a few times, and then with a groan, he settled himself into the grass by the garden gate. He could tell they were going to be staying for a while.

Sam worked steadily, shaking out the flakes and spreading the hay evenly so there was a good thick cover on the ground where he meant to put the onions and carrots and beets.

While he was working, he heard a car honk, one quick burst of sound. He looked up in time to wave. Richard was driving by in Alyssa's car. She was riding in the passenger seat. Something was strange. Sam remembered what he hadn't really registered before, that they drove by the same way yesterday when he was working in the garden. Something was going on. He hoped they weren't planning to sell the place. That would be awful. He and Bonnie could never afford to buy that land back now that there was a house built on it.

It took all four bales to make two patches of ground mulched for the onions and carrots and some beets for Bonnie to pickle. By the time he had the rows opened up, it was almost eleven o'clock, and he had to quit so he would have time to change out of his wet clothes and load up his truck with the butchering equipment. He'd told Cookson he would be out at his farm by one.

He managed to change and get the truck loaded by twelve-fifteen, and that ought to be plenty of time if he didn't get lost on the way. He'd been to Cookson's once before, but that was a couple of years ago.

He opened the door to the cab and told Colt to load. The backend was full of equipment. Then he got in and put his sandwich and a Diet Pepsi down on the dashboard, so he could eat lunch on the way, and they took off for Cookson's farm up in the hills east of Severance.

When he pulled into the driveway, even though he was only fifteen minutes late, Cookson was standing there looking down the road.

"Sorry," he said out the window. "I took a wrong turn back there a ways." He got out of the truck.

"He's around back," Cookson said. "I'll show you."

The house and barn were attached, one long building lying across the end of the drive. Sam followed Cookson around back. Behind the building, the hill sloped up from a little muddy yard. The runoff must have been awful when the snow first began to melt. Even now, halfway through May, the yard was a mud soup. The Jersey steer stood in the middle, knee deep in the muck. His pelt was matted and caked with manure.

Sam said, "How wild is that steer? I don't want to drop him in that mud. Hell, we might could lose him in there."

"It ain't that bad. You should of seen it a few weeks ago."

"I bet," Sam said. "Can you lead him outa there?"

"Sure. Where'd you want him?"

"It'll be easier if I can get my truck up close." He thought a minute. Cookson was a small guy, almost as wide as he was tall. He didn't look like he would be much good at lifting, but then, short guys could fool you sometimes. "Can you bring him round in front?"

"I'll have to get some grain." He went into the barn and came out with a bucket. "I had to unplug the fence too." He untangled the spider web of spliced and re-spliced wires and threw them back.

The steer stood watching until Cookson shook the bucket so that the grain rattled around. Then the steer stood up a little straighter and began to walk slowly toward the opening in the fence. Every time he put his foot down, there was a sucking sound, and then a pop as he pulled it out.

Cookson walked around the barn and poured the grain onto the ground in a pile behind Sam's truck. The steer lumbered over and began to eat.

Colt was sitting in the cab of the truck watching the steer through the window. Sam patted him and got his rifle out of the gun rack behind the seat. He loaded it and went back behind the truck and stood there while the steer ate.

Cookson said, "What're you waitin for? Why don't you do it?" He was shifting his weight from foot to foot.

Sam thought about how he liked that steer a whole lot better than he liked Cookson, and yet he was going to do what Cookson told him to do, and he was going to kill the steer. "Might as well let the poor bastard enjoy his last meal. You ain't in that big a hurry, are you?"

"No, I guess not." His little eyes were darting all around. "But what if he gets away?"

"He ain't goin nowhere. Not while there's grain left. Why would he?" Sam looked hard at Cookson. "And besides, he wouldn't get very far. I ain't goin to miss."

"If you're sure...."

They stood there waiting, listening to the steer's teeth grinding the grain. When the pile was gone, he looked up at Sam, his jaws still moving. And Sam was suddenly angry. The stupid animal didn't even know he was as good as dead. He raised his rifle and put the bullet right between his eyes. The steer folded slowly, down to his knees, and then the rest of the way down, so he was lying on his side. His legs twitched, as though he was just now thinking of running away when it was already too late.

Sam set up his big tripod by the backend of his truck. He got out his heavy-duty extension cord and asked Cookson to plug it in. When the steer stopped twitching, Sam hooked the back legs onto the old singletree he used for a spreader and hoisted the carcass up the tripod with his come-along. It was a Jersey steer and not very big. Sam was able to get him well off the ground.

Cookson just stood there without offering to help. Sam figured when he needed a hand, he wouldn't ask, he would just tell Cookson what to do. He cut off the steer's head and started on the skinning while the steer bled out. Cookson brought him a bucket of hot water from the house.

When he finished the skinning, he washed the hide off with Cookson's hose and spread it out on the grass. It was dirty with caked manure, but maybe that wouldn't lower the price. He hadn't nicked it many times when he was skinning it out.

He cleaned his hands and the knife before he started his saw.

"That's a nice little saw you got there," Cookson said.

"I like it." He was starting the big cut from the groin to the throat, and he needed to pay attention.

"How come you use an electric saw?"

Sam didn't answer until he had finished the cut. Then he shut off the saw. "It makes a lot finer of a cut. I got more control, I guess. It don't waste so much meat."

"Looks like you might have to worry about cuttin your own electric cord."

"Well, yeah. I done that when I first got it. I guess it taught me my lesson. I ain't done it since."

Cookson smiled a little at that, and Sam liked him even less.

He cut out the guts and the organs and pushed the whole mass out of the body cavity onto the ground. "What do you think about all this oil they're spillin in the Gulf? It's a shame, ain't it?"

"Somebody ought to pay for cleanin up that mess, and I guess it'll be us, like always."

"Ain't that the truth." Sam cut out the heart and the liver and washed them off in some of the hot water. He put them in his clean bucket and did the same thing with the lungs and kidneys. "What do you want out of these organ meats here?" he asked Cookson.

"I don't want none of that stuff. My wife wouldn't cook it. You can throw it out."

Sam happened to look up just then. Colt sat silently watching out the window of the truck. Sam knew who would be glad to get all he didn't want himself, so he didn't say any more. He put the lid on the bucket and set it in the back of the truck.

"Did you hear the new plan they got for stoppin that oil leak?" he said. He was hosing out the hanging carcass while he talked. "They're goin to shoot golf balls and old tires down into the pipe. Ain't that the dumbest thing you ever heard? Either they've got to be morons, or they don't really want to stop that leak. That's all I can figure out about it."

He picked up his saw and made the cut all the way down one side of the backbone. Then he cut each piece again, dropping the forequarters onto the tarp he had spread below the tripod. He turned off the saw and stepped back. A neat job. Cookson stood there watching, but Sam couldn't tell whether he appreciated how nicely the job was being done. Sam realized he wasn't thinking about the steer anymore, and he supposed Cookson wasn't either. It was just meat now.

Cookson was still standing in the same spot with his mouth open, watching while Sam tried to wrestle one of the forequarters up into the truck.

Sam said, "Hey, man, give me a hand, will you?"

Cookson was a help, even though Sam hated to admit it even to himself. He needed Cookson more on the front quarters than on the back. He was able to swing the back quarters over the tailgate before he let them down into the truck. When the meat was loaded, he hosed off the tarp and covered the meat and laid the hide on top to keep the tarp from blowing off on the ride home.

He loaded the tripod and the rest of his equipment. Then he washed his hands and poured what was left of the warm water over his boots. He was all done.

"Well, I guess that does it," he said. He went around to the door of the truck and stood there without opening it. Colt was looking at him across the seat, patient and polite. He thought he ought to try to have as good manners as Colt had. He opened the door and got in the truck. "You can pay me all at once, when I get your meat packaged for you." He started the engine. "It's got to hang for a while. It's goin to be a couple, three weeks before it's ready."

"That's okay," Cookson said. "I'm just glad to be done with the damn thing."

"I'll call you when it's ready," he said, as he drove off.

The first thing he had to do when he got home was unload the meat into the cooler. He drove around back to the hatchway and backed up as close as he could get. He opened the doors and set his little four-wheeled cart in place so that he could drop the quarters right out of the truck and into the cart. He was proud of the way he had set it up. He could do the whole thing alone, and he didn't even have much lifting to do.

He dropped the quarters into the cart and rolled them one at a time into the basement. It was easy enough to hang them on hooks, using the come-along he'd set up for the purpose. Then he could push them along the track into the cooler he'd built. When they were all unloaded, he set the bucket of organ meat on the floor below them and closed the door. There was a heavy, chunking sound as the insulated door closed tight. Hearing that sound always gave him a feeling of satisfaction, the satisfaction of a job well done.

He got back in the truck and went up the hill behind the barn with Colt riding shotgun beside him. Things were greening up nicely. When he got to his animal dump, he backed up until his tailgate was hanging over the place where he always dumped the guts and dead animals.

There were no birds around when he got out, but before he had rolled the gut barrel back to the tailgate, a big raven flew over. It was so low that he could hear the leathery creak of its wings. He dumped the barrel and looked around, but the bird was gone. He rolled the empty barrel to the front of the truck bed and got in the cab. As he was driving down the hill, he looked in the rearview mirror. There were two ravens circling the dump. They looked ready to land on the pile of guts.

Sam was pretty sure they had a nest up there somewhere. He really ought to find it and get rid of them. They were scavengers. And he had heard that they would peck the eyes out of newborn lambs. He had never seen such a thing himself, but it was a good idea to get rid of them before they did anything like that.

His gun was in the rack behind him, but he didn't have the right shells. He wasn't going to hit a bird, even a big bird, with a rifle bullet. They were smart birds, and it would just make them more wary. He didn't feel like going all the way down to the house to get his shotgun and some birdshot.

When he got down the hill, he parked beside the barn so he could unload the tools and the tripod. Bonnie's little car was parked in front. He was glad he had decided not to go up to the dump again.

He went into the house.

Bonnie was in the kitchen. She was still wearing her pink waitress uniform. Sam told her there was fresh liver in the cooler. She said she would cook them some for dinner, so he went down to get it while she changed.

Later on, after Sam had finished doing the chores, and they were eating supper, he said, "Somethin's goin on over to Richard and Alyssa's. I seen them drive by a couple, three times when I was workin in the garden these last few days."

"There ain't nothing strange about that."

"Every time, he's been drivin her car, and she's been right beside him in the passenger seat."

"That don't seem strange to me."

"Well, maybe it's not. Still, I got a feelin somethin's goin on. I've been wonderin if they were about to sell their place maybe. It's been botherin me. We couldn't never buy that land back now there's a house on it, unless we won the lottery or somethin."

"We don't need that land. It ain't good for nothin anyways. That's why your dad sold it in the first place. It's just the brook and a strip of stony ground."

"What about the pool? Suppose they sold to someone who put 'No Trespassing' signs all over the place?"

"That wouldn't kill us, Sam. We got plenty without that."

"You don't understand any more than Junior does. I always thought I could buy it back some day, that pool and my cabin. Dad never should of sold it."

"He needed the money for your ma's hospital bills."

"That's what Junior says." He was getting more and more sure that Richard must be planning to sell out, and there wasn't going to be anything he could do about it.

Bonnie said, "That liver was real good, and it'd be even better if we had some bacon to put with it."

"The new pork ought to be ready to smoke pretty soon." He sat there for a minute thinking about getting up to clear off the table.

And then it came to him. "I know what I'm goin to do," he said. "I'll take some liver over to Richard and Alyssa. We've got more than enough. Maybe they'll have somethin to say about what's goin on."

"Do you think they'll want it? Some people don't...."

"You mean like Cookson. He said to throw it out."

"Yes, like Cookson. We don't really know what they like, even after all the years of livin nearby."

"Well, it won't hurt to ask, and anyhow it's a good excuse."

"Okay. You go on then. I can clean up here."

"Thanks, Bonnie." He got a bowl and went down to the cooler where he cut a couple of nice-looking lobes off the liver. "I won't be gone long," he said, as he went through the kitchen. "Come on, Colt."

He knocked on the glass door on Richard's deck.

Richard opened the door. "Hello, Sam. Come on in."

"No, that's okay. I got Colt here with me. I was just wonderin if you and Alyssa might like some fresh beef liver." He held out the bowl so Richard could see it.

Richard said, "That looks great. Let me see what Alyssa says. She used to make really good liver paté." He took the bowl and went inside, leaving the door open.

Alyssa was in the kitchen. Sam could see them talking, and then Alyssa took the bowl and looked around at him and smiled and waved.

In a minute Richard was back at the door. "Thanks, Sam. I'll bring you and Bonnie some of the paté when she gets it made. Wait until I get my shoes and a jacket, and I'll walk over with you."

"Okay," Sam said. "We'll be down in your yard." He walked around the side of the deck. They had expanded the flowerbeds. Bonnie would love to have some flower gardens like these, but she was always too busy. Maybe he would make some for her this summer.

Richard came down the steps, putting on his jacket. "You must be doing some butchering business. The liver wasn't from your beef, was it?"

"Nah. I butchered a little Jersey steer for a guy this afternoon. He wants me to cut and wrap it too. I get good money for that part."

"Can I pay you for the liver?"

"No, man. That's between neighbors. I got it free anyways. The guy didn't want it."

"We haven't paid you for the pork either."

"Don't worry. You haven't got your meat yet. I know you're good for it. Hell, you can't even get away." Saying that reminded him again that he wondered what was going on.

And as though Richard was reading his mind, he said, "I have something I want to tell you about." Richard was walking behind him on the path through the trees that separated their properties. As usual, Colt was leading the way.

Sam thought, "Oh no. Here it comes. I knew they were sellin out."

Richard stopped walking at the edge of Sam's drive. Sam turned to face him. Richard said, "I hope this turns out to be nothing, but I wanted you to know about it anyway." He paused and took a breath. He was looking at Sam. "Alyssa has a tumor on her left lung. The doctors are confident they can operate and take care of it...."

"Oh man," Sam said. "That's a bummer."

"I'm making it sound worse than it is. The docs are very hopeful."

"I knew somethin was up," Sam said. "I've been seein you drive by." Privately, he couldn't help but think that at least they weren't selling their place, but he felt like an asshole for even thinking such a thing. At the same time, he thought of his mother and her battle with cancer.

"We've been on the road a lot lately. Poor Alyssa has had to have so many tests. It has been something almost every day."

Sam had gone far away thinking about Ma. He was confused for a minute. He had to jerk his mind back to the present. "What can I do?" was what he finally managed to bring out.

"Oh thanks. If there's anything, I know I can call on you. You're a good neighbor. But it's going to be fine."

Sam nodded, remembering bleakly that Ma thought exactly that at first.

"Once she's had her operation, things will start to improve. These docs are right on top of it. They're going to get her surgery done next week if they possibly can, and if not that soon, then definitely the week after. It's really good the way they're pushing it along."

"How's Alyssa holdin up?"

"She's good. She's positive most of the time. She might get worried once in a while, but usually she's quite upbeat."

"I saw her at the mailbox not that long ago. She didn't look sick then."

"That's the thing. She really doesn't have any symptoms, except for a cough she can't seem to get rid of."

"Tell her we wish her luck."

"I will later on. Right now I'm not going to tell her that I told you because she doesn't want people to know—not until after the operation anyhow."

"I won't say nothin."

"Thanks. I wanted you to know about it. I guess maybe she doesn't want anybody to feel sorry for her."

"Maybe. Well, I probably won't see her, so it won't be a problem. Let me know if there's anything I can do for you...or for her."

"Thanks, Sam. I will, and I'll let you know how the operation goes too."

Sam patted him on the shoulder and said, "Good luck, man." Then he walked toward the house. Colt was already standing at the door.

He wondered whether to say anything to Bonnie about it, and he guessed he would if she asked, but otherwise not. He didn't like to think about it. It made him think about Ma and those awful, dark days when she got weaker every time he saw her. He and Bonnie were married and living in town by then, so he couldn't get out to see her as often as he meant to. But even years before, when he came home from 'Nam, she wasn't that well. That was why he built his cabin, so he would have a place to go when the nightmares got bad. He'd wake up in the night shouting, dreaming he was back in Vietnam. His shouting woke everybody, including Ma, and she needed her sleep. He used to take a sleeping bag up to the pool to get away. That's what gave him the idea of building the cabin. He moved in when all he had was a dirt floor and the frame of a building, not even a roof. But at least he didn't bother anybody when he had nightmares.

Bonnie wasn't in the kitchen. He didn't need to say anything to her. The kitchen was all cleaned up, and he heard the TV going, so he went down the hall and joined Bonnie on the couch. She was watching the news.

Sam sat down beside her, and she smiled at him. "Did they want the liver?"

"Yes. They liked it. Alyssa's goin to make us some liver paté."

"What's that?"

"I don't know, but I guess we'll find out."

She smiled at him again. "This tube they're puttin in that broken oil pipe seems to be workin."

"Oh yeah. Is that what they're doin now? That sounds better than shootin the pipe full of golf balls and old tires and junk. I don't know where these people get their ideas from."

"This is a better one. They put a pipe down in the broken one, and it's suckin up the oil. They pipe it up to a ship and haul it away. That makes sense, don't it?"

"Why didn't they do that in the first place?"

"I don't know, Sam. They must of had a reason."

He thought about it, and he thought about Alyssa, counting on some guy in a suit to know what was wrong and fix it. Those guys never got laid off. They always had lots of money and cars and clothes. Ma believed her doctors too, and look where it got her. He didn't want to think about it. It made him too angry, and then the sadness would come pouring in.

CHAPTER 14

Alyssa was sitting on the deck with Richard. It was the end of the day, but still warm out. There was no wind. They were lying stretched out in their deck chairs so they could look up into the luminous night sky, which wasn't really black at all, but an incredible, midnight blue. The moon was rising.

Richard said, "It's the full moon tonight."

"Oh, that's right. What's the name of this one?"

"The Milk Moon."

"I thought this was the Flower Moon."

"That's June."

"The Milk Moon. I guess they call it that because all the animal mothers are giving birth, and they have milk for their babies."

"Maybe."

Neither of them said anything for a while. The peepers got louder and louder, almost drowning out the roar of the brook. There were the deeper voices of a few frogs too, but the frogs hadn't really gotten into full chorus yet, the way they would later in the summer. A dog barked in the distance. Maybe it was Sam's. And there was an owl far away answered by one a little closer.

Richard said, "You need to tell your mom that they have scheduled your operation for Monday."

"I already did. In fact, I called all of them, Sonia and Alix too. Aren't you proud of me?"

Richard reached across to her without taking his eyes off the moon-lit sky. He took her hand and squeezed it. "I think you're the best. What did they say?"

"They want you to call them when it's over and tell them how it went. They all said that. I thought Mom was going to want to come up for the weekend, but she didn't say anything about it. I guess she's been here so often lately that she doesn't want to make the trip again. I don't really know. I was surprised that she didn't say anything about it, and Alix and Sonia didn't either."

"Umm."

After a while, she said, "I look at the sky and all the stars and other worlds and think of all the eons of time and all the people who have lived and loved and died, and my troubles seem so small. I'm just one tiny grain of sand. When I look at it that way, it doesn't really matter what happens next week."

Richard squeezed her hand again. "It does to me."

"I know. It does to me too. Of course. But when I think of all the people who have felt that way, in all the world, in all of history...."

Richard didn't say anything.

"I guess it could be depressing to think of it that way, but it isn't. It's comforting. I have so much company."

Richard squeezed her hand again, so she knew he heard what she said.

After a while she shivered, and then she coughed. Once she started, she couldn't stop. She hunched over with the effort, and she had to pull her hand away from Richard's.

"Oh damn," he said. "Let's go inside. I don't think this night air is good for you."

"You sound like someone from the nineteenth century." She smiled at him, trying not to cough. Her voice was harsh and raspy. "It's so beautiful out tonight. The color of the sky…. I wish I had a dress that color…with spangles down the front like stars." She coughed again.

Richard stood up. "Come on. Next time the moon is full, you'll be over the operation, and you'll probably have your strength back. We can stay out here all night long, and you won't cough at all."

She stood. "You make it sound so simple." For a minute, she was reassured, but then a sliver of doubt crept in, and she felt less confident.

"By Monday the moon will be past the full stage. You don't think it's unlucky to have this operation on the waning moon, do you?"

Richard had started toward the door. He turned back in surprise. "What?"

"I was just wondering if the operation was going to be on a good day for it…by the phase of the moon, I mean. I tried to look it up. My horoscope said it wasn't a good day to start something new." She stood up, facing him. "I just wondered…what you thought."

"Now *you* sound like the nineteenth century. You know you don't believe in that stuff."

"I know. I just thought…."

"It's silly."

"It doesn't hurt anything. I know it doesn't do any good, but…."

"It's voodoo. It has nothing to do with real life."

"I know, Richard." She hadn't been coughing for the last few minutes. But now it shook her again. When she was able to speak, she said, "Of course I don't believe it, but I was just thinking it would be nice if the stars were aligned in my favor. There *is* magic and mystery in the world. It's all around us." She managed to get it out before she had to cough again.

Richard came back the few steps and took her hand again and led her inside. "This operation isn't magic…it's science, and that's better than magic. It doesn't matter where the moon and stars are. It matters who your doctors are, and you have good ones. Don't worry. *They* are aligned in your favor, and that's what counts. It's going to be fine. I know it is."

The next morning, after Richard left for town, she went upstairs looking for her book of fairy tales, the one she read over and over when she was a child, the one Alix and Sonia always wanted her to read to them. Alyssa wasn't sure which fairy tale she wanted, or why she wanted to read a child's story right now. She felt a little embarrassed by it. At the same time, she was looking for something, and she felt she could find it there.

She sat on the floor, flipping through the book, reading pieces of stories, but she couldn't find the right one, the one that was calling her. She put the book into the bag she was going to take to the hospital. She was planning to take her makeup and some jewelry and her prettiest nightgown. Maybe she could avoid the horrible hospital johnnies. It was hard to know what to pack. It wasn't like packing for a trip. She didn't know how long she would have to stay or what she would feel like after the operation was over.

She put the bag back on the floor of the closet and went downstairs. It was as warm as summer outside, but fresh and clean, full of delicate scents, not overblown and rank with plant growth and insect life, the way it would be in July. The early spring flowers were past, and the irises and peonies and roses were just beginning. Birds called. There were already more shades of green than a person could count.

She should be planting the vegetable garden. This was the weekend all the old-timers planted their gardens. Maybe Richard would help her tomorrow. Sunday was Memorial Day, and Monday was a holiday too. She wondered why they were going to do her operation on a holiday.

She sat on the deck for a while, but then she felt like doing something. She didn't want to work. She wanted to savor the sweetness of the morning. She had to go away in a few days, and she didn't know how long she would be gone or what she would feel like when she got back. She decided to take a walk up the brook. There was no way of knowing how long it would be before she felt like going up there again.

At first she thought she would see what was going on at the ravens' nest, but she had been there recently, so she knew they were gone, and the nest was deserted. She decided to take the brook trail part of the way and then switch over to Sam's road, which led to the pasture at the top of the hill. It had been a long time since she had been up there.

When she got on Sam's road, she noticed his tire tracks right away. Sam must have driven up recently. Alyssa felt pleased with herself for noticing. The tracks went down the road to his dump. She followed.

When she stepped into the clearing, two ravens lifted heavily into the trees. All around was a smell of rot. Great clouds of flies were circling and buzzing over a large mound of something pink and purplish. The air was so thick with the smell of death that it was hard to breathe.

Alyssa stepped back through the trees, gagging. She hurried to the main road and along it to Sam's hilltop pasture. When she got there, she sat down under the old thorn tree. The view was spectacular. Row after row of blue mountains, getting paler with distance. The air was sweet, full of the scent of new grass and flowers, but the thick smell of rot and death was still in her nose. Why had she gone down Sam's dump road? She knew it was there. It was a place she and Richard were always careful to avoid. She sat under the tree, resolving not to let that small incident spoil her beautiful day.

After a while, she thought she would go back down the hill, but not along Sam's road this time. So she cut through the woods to the brook and walked down the trail. Where the path went down beside the water, she stopped and sat on a rock. She couldn't hear anything but the noise of the stream running over the rocks. Everything here was cool and clean. The air was full of misty spray. Toward the sun, there were little rainbows over the water. The world was fresh and beautiful again, newly minted for her enjoyment.

When Richard got home, he asked her what she had been doing.

"Nothing. I took a long walk up the brook."

"Was it nice?"

"Oh yes. I sat under the big hawthorn tree in Sam's pasture at the top of the hill."

"Were his sheep up there?"

"I didn't see them. Come to think of it, I didn't cross any fences either."

"Maybe he hasn't moved them up there yet."

"The grass is quite tall."

"I'm glad you had a nice day."

"Yes. It was nice. I came down along the brook." She didn't mention Sam's dump because she couldn't explain why she had gone there. She didn't like to think about it.

"I should have stayed home. My day was boring, and I didn't even get much done."

They were sitting side by side on the steps to the deck. Alyssa reached out and patted his shoulder. "I'm sorry," she said.

"I ought to go in tomorrow to finish up, but I'm not going to. I'm planning to spend the day with you."

"Oh good. I hope you'll help me in the garden."

"Don't you want to do something fun on your last...."

She looked at him. She wanted to ask him what he meant. What did he think was going to happen?

But before she could say anything, he hurried on. "That's not what I meant. You know this operation is going to go fine. I was going to suggest a canoe ride because I thought it might be a while before you felt like going out again."

He looked around at her, and she tried to smile.

"Honestly, that's all I meant."

Alyssa stood up and walked down the steps. "I was hoping to get the vegetable garden planted before I go. That's what I should have been doing today." She reached out a hand to him. "Walk over with me, and let's take a look at it."

"Okay, if that's what you want to do...."

He stood up, and they walked down the drive to where the garden plot lay between the brook and the driveway.

"If we don't get our plants in pretty soon, we won't get anything later, and when I come home, I don't know how long it'll be before I can do the work."

"You'll have to take it easy at first. That's for sure."

They stood together looking at the plot of bare ground Sam had turned over for them, the way he always did.

"It's all ready to be planted," Alyssa said. "I should have done it days ago. I shouldn't have spent so much of my time on the flowers."

"But just think, Alyssa, when you come home from the hospital and are recovering, it's going to be so nice to sit on the deck and look out at all your flower gardens just booming away."

"It's probably going to drive me crazy not to be able to get out there to weed them."

"I hope not," Richard said, as they walked back to the house. "I don't want to have to chase you around trying to make you be quiet."

By the middle of Sunday afternoon, they had most of the garden planted. Alyssa was sitting on the steps to the deck, thinking how she hated to leave, when Richard came and sat down beside her.

"Are you all packed, Alyssa?"

"I just have to put in a few last-minute things, and I have to change clothes and get all the garden dirt off."

"I keep thinking I smell smoke. Do you smell it?"

"No, but my head is stopped up. I'm not sure I could smell anything." She didn't tell him that she'd been crying.

"Maybe Sam's burning something."

"I heard on the radio that there are forest fires in Canada. Do you suppose the smoke could come so far?"

"It's happened before. Remember that year that the sky was all brownish from fires in Canada?"

"It's kind of funny, overcast weather today, isn't it?"

"That must be what I smell."

"I think so too." She sighed. "I wish I didn't have to go."

Richard patted her shoulder. "You'll be back home so soon, and it will be over, and that will be a relief."

"I know it. I'm sorry to be such a baby when you're being so nice to me."

She stood up to go and get ready. She couldn't stop the crying, and she didn't want him to see.

"Oh Alyssa. Don't cry." He stood up beside her and put his arms around her.

"Don't," she said. I'll get you all dirty."

He laughed. "Don't worry. I'm as dirty as you are."

That made her smile a little.

He said, "It's going to be all right. I promise."

"I know. I didn't mean to do this. I meant to be happy all day today. I'm sorry."

"Just think, in a few days you'll be back home." He hugged her and patted her on the back. "You'll be sitting on the steps in the sunshine, just like you were a few minutes ago. You'll remember this, and you'll wonder what all the fuss was about."

"Oh, Richard, I love you." She hugged him back. "You always know what to say to make me feel better. I'll go get ready."

"Okay. I have to clean up too. We might as well get it over with. We have to be there before four, don't we?"

"Yes. That's what they said. I don't know why."

They drove to the hospital in Alyssa's car with Richard driving. Neither of them said anything. To Alyssa, even on this dry, overcast day, the world was incredibly lovely. She felt as though she was leaving it, and her heart was breaking. She couldn't say it out loud, because she knew she was being absurd. She didn't want Richard to get annoyed by her. It was only for a few days, and it would all be here just the same when she came home. It wouldn't even have time to change before she was back again.

In the lobby of the hospital there were signs saying that everyone had to go first to the billing office.

"It figures," Richard said. "Thank God we've got great insurance."

They did what they were told. Alyssa gave the woman in the office the same information she had given them many times before. They always asked for it over again.

Then the woman called for someone to take Alyssa upstairs. A stocky young man in the blue clothes of a hospital orderly appeared in the doorway.

Alyssa stood and followed him down the hall. When they got to the lobby, Richard hesitated. They all stopped walking.

Richard said, "Maybe I should go now, Alyssa, and let you get settled."

It was so sudden. It caught Alyssa by surprise. She didn't know what to say. She just looked at him. With all her heart, she wanted him not to go.

He must have seen the pleading in her face because he said, "I don't have to leave now. I could come with you, if it's all right." He looked at the orderly.

The man said, "Oh sure. There's no reason to leave. You can help her get settled in her room."

Alyssa smiled with relief. As long as Richard was still with her, the operation was not happening yet. It was still somewhere in the future.

Richard took her hand while they were going up in the elevator.

The man looked at them. "You people from around here?" His hair was dark. He was overweight, and the light glinted off his glasses. Alyssa guessed he was about the same age as Alix and Sonia.

Richard said, "We're from West Severance."

"Oh. It's pretty country out that way." He looked at Alyssa. "What are you here for?"

Alyssa opened her mouth to speak, but before she could do so, Richard said, "She has a small tumor on one of her lungs. They're going to take it out."

Alyssa was grateful for the 'small.'

By then the elevator doors were open. Richard and Alyssa followed the man down the hall to a room with two beds in it. Alyssa went to the one by the window. The other bed was neat and clearly unoccupied.

"Well, here you are folks." He turned to Richard. "You can stay if you want to. They'll tell you when you have to leave."

Alyssa sat down on the edge of the bed.

The orderly reached out to shake her hand. "Goodbye," he said. "And good luck. It'll go just fine."

After he left, she said, "Richard, did you hear what he said? That was so nice of him. He didn't have to say that."

"Damn it, Alyssa. What difference does it make what he says? He doesn't know anything about you." He walked over to the window and stood there looking out.

Alyssa sat on the edge of the bed and said nothing. Richard had been so nice to her, and now they were miles apart, and each of them was alone. She wanted to hold on to the orderly's kind words, but she couldn't say so to Richard.

After a while a nurse came into the room. Her footsteps were loud and squeaky in the quiet room. She set a hospital gown on the foot of the bed. "Here you go, Ms. Bradshaw. You can just get into this."

Alyssa said, "Thank you, but I brought my own nightgown." She looked at the ugly cotton with its faded print and suppressed a shudder.

The nurse stood looking down at her. "Well, all right. You can wear your own gown tonight, but tomorrow morning before they get you ready for the surgery, you have to be in this one."

"Oh," Alyssa said.

"Don't worry. You won't care tomorrow. You'll have other things on your mind."

"Oh," Alyssa said again.

"Don't unpack anything unless you need it tonight. We'll be moving you to a different room after your surgery."

Alyssa managed not to say 'oh' this time.

"You need to give us your jewelry to keep safe at the nurses' station."

Richard walked over to stand beside the bed.

The nurse looked at him. "Or else you could take it home for her. It wouldn't be safe to leave it unattended in her room."

Richard said, "I'll take it home." He looked at Alyssa. "Unless you would rather let the nurse keep it for you."

"No," Alyssa said. "Take it home for me, please."

She sat on the edge of the bed and took off her earrings and bracelet and her rings. They made a glittery mound on the bedclothes.

"What's that around your neck?"

She reached up to touch the little crystal star that her mother gave her for Christmas when she was thirteen. She planned to pretend she forgot it was there. It wasn't valuable. She could take it off later and put it in her overnight bag, and she would have it with her for good luck. She didn't want to tell Richard that she needed a good luck charm, so she said, "Oh, I forgot." She took the star off and added it to the pile of jewelry.

Richard pulled off a long strip of toilet paper and brought it over to the bed. He wrapped up each piece of jewelry, including the little star. Then he put each wad of toilet paper deep into his pocket. "There," he said. "Everything should be safe. I'll put it away when I get home."

"There's a little more in my bag," Alyssa said. "Can you fit this in your pocket?" She took out a pouch with a pair of earrings she was planning to wear when she was able to leave the hospital.

"I think so," Richard said. He stuffed the pouch into his pocket and sat in the chair beside her bed. She leaned back against the pillows. There wasn't much to say.

A young girl came in with Alyssa's dinner on a tray. She cleared off the nightstand on the other side of the bed and set the tray there. She smiled shyly and left. The smell of the food drifted around the room.

"Are you hungry Alyssa?"

"I was before the dinner arrived. Now I'm not so sure. It smells like cardboard."

Richard gave a little snort of laughter. "I'm sorry. Maybe it will taste better than it smells."

"I doubt it. It's funny, isn't it? You would think people in a hospital would need good food more than anything, and yet the food is always horrible."

Richard laughed again. After a while, he said, "I'm hungry anyway. I think I'll go down to the cafeteria and get something for myself."

"Can I come? I really, really want to."

Richard looked worried. "They probably wouldn't like it."

"I could sneak out with you. We wouldn't have to tell them," she said. She didn't want him to leave her. She hated the smell of the food, and she didn't want to be in that room, in that hospital bed.

"Alyssa, I think you'd better stay here. I'll bring you back something nice." He stood and gave her a quick kiss on top of her head and left without looking back.

She sat on the bed with tears running down her cheeks and dropping into her lap. She didn't even raise a hand to wipe them away. After a while she looked at the food. It was fish and mashed potatoes. On the tray around the plate were little dishes of salad and dessert. She picked at the fish with a fork. It didn't look any better than it smelled.

She closed the door and got undressed and packed her clothes away neatly in the overnight bag. Then she opened the door again so she could watch for Richard. She got under the covers and tried to read the book of fairy tales, but she couldn't pay attention. Every time someone walked by in the hall, she looked up, hoping it was Richard.

It was a long time before he came. "I hurried as much as I could," he said. "And you didn't miss much. The food down there wasn't any good either. Here." He held out a paper plate.

"Oh, Richard, thank you. I couldn't eat any of what they brought me." She took the paper cover off the plate, and there was a mixture of stir-fried vegetables.

"It looked better than other things they had for sale," Richard said.

"It looks good. And I am hungry. What did you have?"

"The same thing." He sat down in the chair beside the bed. "Now I wish I had brought my dinner up here too. We could have eaten together."

"I'm glad you're here now. I missed you. I wish you could stay all night."

"I don't think they'd let me. And anyway, tomorrow morning they will be getting you ready for the operation."

"They won't do it early. The operation isn't until eleven."

"I'm sure they wouldn't let me stay. There's a reason they wanted you here the night before."

She looked into his eyes. "You could ask. Please. I wouldn't be scared if you were here."

Richard resisted, but she kept looking into his face, and after a minute, he said, "All right. I'll go see what they say." He stood and walked to the door.

When he got there, he turned back to look at her, and she blew him a kiss.

"But don't get your hopes up, Alyssa, because I know they'll say no."

"Don't be negative. Think 'yes' while you're asking them."

He nodded and left.

Alyssa finished the food he brought, but she was still hungry. She looked at the uneaten dinner and shuddered a little. She didn't feel like reading fairy tales, so she just sat with her hands folded in her lap, waiting for Richard to return.

He wasn't gone long. As he came into the room, he was saying, "I'm sorry, Alyssa."

Her heart sank. "Did you tell them that the other bed is empty?"

"Yes, I did. They said it didn't make any difference, that those were the rules."

"I think it's mean. It wouldn't hurt anybody, and it would make me feel so much better."

"I know. They told me I had to leave at the end of visiting hours, and the worst of it is that they'll be watching now to make sure I go."

Alyssa sat back against the pillows and ducked her head a little so that her hair swung partway across her face. Her lip was trembling. "It's okay, Richard. It'll be much nicer for you to sleep in your own bed."

Richard took her hand and squeezed it. "You know I'd stay if I could."

She nodded.

"Don't think about it. The night will be over so soon. You'll be asleep. You won't even notice, and then the operation will be over, and it will be steady improvement after that."

She nodded again, and they sat together in silence. Alyssa knew she was being childish, but she couldn't manage to fake a cheery attitude. Richard would see through it in an instant. She sat there dreading the time when he would leave her. She was feeling very sorry for herself.

And of course visiting hours did end. There was an announcement over the loudspeaker in the hall. Richard jumped up. Alyssa thought bitterly that he had been waiting until he could go.

He kissed her on top of the head. "I'll be back first thing in the morning. Maybe they'll let me see you then." He kissed her again. "But if not, I'll be here until they do let me see you. I love you."

She nodded her head. She couldn't say anything because her lip was trembling.

Richard stopped in the doorway to look back at her. Then he turned and walked away. She tried to hear his footsteps going down the hall, but there were too many other noises.

A nurse stuck her head around the door and said, "Okay, hon, I see he's gone. I was just going to make sure he knew his time was up."

"Thank you," Alyssa said, as coldly as she could.

The nurse disappeared, and she was alone and abandoned. She knew she shouldn't feel that way, that it wasn't even true, but she couldn't help it. She had the long night to get through, and she didn't want tomorrow to come.

CHAPTER 15

It was a little before eleven in the morning. Richard was just raising the cup to take a sip of his coffee as he walked through the door into the surgery waiting room. Monika was sitting right there looking toward the door. Alix was on one side of her, and Sonia was on the other. Richard was so surprised that the cup wobbled, and hot coffee went over his hand and down the front of his shirt. "Monika," he said.

By then Alix and Sonia were on him. Sonia was hugging him, and Alix ran past them to the bathroom to get some paper towels. She was back in an instant, wiping his chest and hand and then the puddle on the floor.

"Why didn't you tell me you were coming?"

"We wanted to surprise you," Sonia said.

"We decided at the last minute," Alix said.

"How is she?" Monika said. She was the only one sitting down.

"They wouldn't let me see her this morning. I hope she's all right. Last night she looked so small and frightened. I hated to leave her."

"Poor Mom."

"I know. It was all I could do to go last night. I wish we could tell her you were here. Where did you stay last night?"

The cleanup was finished. Richard sat down beside Monika and took a drink of what was left in his coffee cup. It wasn't very good.

Alix said, "We left a little after four this morning."

"Really?"

Sonia said, "Don't worry, Dad. We were careful. We took turns driving."

"Well, you made it. You can get a good rest tonight."

"No, Dad. We have to go back. This was a crazy trip, but we all wanted to be here for Mom. Do you think they'll they let us see her after the operation?"

"Unless…." He started to say they would, unless something went wrong, but he didn't want to suggest that in front of Monika.

They had the waiting room to themselves. They talked a little off and on, but there were long periods of silence. Richard couldn't sit still. He longed for the operation to be over so he could be sure Alyssa would be all right. He tried to glance at the others without them noticing. They had to be feeling the same way.

After a while Alix and Sonia left to go to the cafeteria, and Richard stayed with Monika. Monika had a book on her lap, but she made no move to open it and read. Richard couldn't help feeling that it would be rude if he got out his Kindle. He had been trying to read the New York Times all morning between interruptions.

"Richard, do you think we'll have to wait much longer? Did they tell you how long it was going to take?"

Richard turned in his seat so he could see her face. She was sitting very straight and not looking in his direction. He could see she was making a tremendous effort to keep her fears to herself. He felt a rush of sympathy for her. "They couldn't say for sure, because they couldn't know what they would find. They said at the very best, it would be an hour or two, and it has only been an hour so far. We couldn't expect to know anything this soon."

"Yes, of course. I'm sorry. I can't help being nervous."

"I don't blame you. I am too."

"And we have to go back to Stamford today."

"Can't you stay over just for one night?"

"I wish we could. It makes the trip so hard…not for me, but for Sonia and Alix, but they say they have to do it this way."

"I'll talk to them."

She looked at him then and smiled. "You do that, but I don't believe you'll get anywhere. They both said it was the only way they could manage it."

"They're good girls, aren't they?" he said with pride.

"Yes," she said. "We're lucky." And then, without a pause, "Do you think Alyssa is going to be all right?"

"I'm sure of it," he said. "Don't worry." He felt like putting his arm around her shoulders. She was trying so hard. It made him like her.

Alix and Sonia came back with a picnic breakfast for everyone. They were pleased with themselves. They moved some tables and chairs around and laid out bagels and coffee. They even had some tea for Monika.

Richard didn't really want anything, but they had made such an effort. He wanted to please them by participating in their party, so he pretended to be hungry.

Later, when two worried middle-aged women came in to wait, they sat deferentially in a corner of the room. The waiting room belonged to Alyssa's family. Richard wanted to say something to the women to make them more comfortable, but he didn't know how to begin. Sonia offered them some bagels, but they shook their heads and stayed in their corner, bickering quietly with each other.

Alix and Sonia were bubbling over with good cheer, and Monika was trying hard to keep her nerves to herself. Richard kept glancing at the clock. One o'clock went by and one-thirty and then two. It was almost two-thirty when a man in green, blood-splattered hospital scrubs stopped in the doorway and said Richard's name. He wasn't a doctor Richard had ever seen before.

Richard stood and walked forward, holding out his hand. "I'm Richard Bradshaw. Do you have news for me?"

The man introduced himself as Alyssa's surgeon, and they shook hands. The man made a few references to the weather.

Richard felt an overwhelming impatience. He had to stop himself from saying, "Come on, man. Out with it." Behind him he could feel the others waiting with held breath.

"She's fine. Your wife came through the operation fine."

Richard could feel them all relax a little.

"It took longer than we thought it would. We decided to go ahead and take out the whole lobe of lung. Otherwise, we might have had to go in again. This way we feel confident that we got it taken care of. She should be just fine."

Richard said, "That's wonderful news." He turned around to look at the others to make sure they heard, and they were all smiling.

Richard turned back to the doctor. "When do you think we could see her? This is her mother and her daughters. They live in Stamford, Connecticut, and they have to drive back there today. They'd like to see her before they go."

"I'll find out for you. I think it should be possible when she has stabilized. I don't know exactly when that will be, but I'll get someone to come and tell you. You might have to go in to see her one or two at a time."

"That would be fine." Richard looked around at the others and happened to notice the two women in the corner. They were listening intently. Richard felt sorry for them. They were still in that restless, worried state. He was thankful that his suspense was over.

The man left. Richard sat down again. The breakfast party was different now. "Oh thank God, thank God," Richard said under his breath. She was going to be all right. Anything else was almost unimaginable.

Later on a nurse came to the waiting room to say that they could go two at a time to see Alyssa. Richard went first with Monika. They had to follow the nurse for a long way down crowded, fluorescent hallways.

Richard could see that it was a struggle for Monika. He took her arm, and she looked up at him, smiling her thanks. He would have liked to suggest getting her a wheelchair, but he didn't want to embarrass her, and he was afraid it might confuse or frighten Alyssa.

Finally they got to Alyssa's room. It was only a cubicle, and all the space was filled with monitors. Alyssa lay on a narrow bed, looking very small and pale and insignificant in the crowd of machines.

The nurse walked them to the bedside and then left. Richard ran after her to ask for a chair for Monika. The nurse seemed surprised, but she went off to see what she could do, and in a few minutes she came back pushing a chair, which she put close to Alyssa's head. Monika sank into it with a sigh.

Alyssa opened her eyes several times, but she shut them again almost immediately. She didn't seem conscious that they were with her. There were tubes in her nose and more tubes in her mouth. Her lips were crusted with dried blood, and there was a thin trail of it that ran across one cheek down to her chin. Richard longed to wash it away, but he didn't dare disturb her. She looked so fragile, like a small and delicate alabaster statue. He took her hand. It lay cool and limp in his, and after a minute he put it gently back by her side on the bedclothes.

He looked across her sleeping body at Monika. He could see that she was feeling the same way he was. They were both hoping for some sign, some acknowledgment from Alyssa.

The nurse appeared in the doorway, motioning that it was time for them to leave. Monika saw her and stood up slowly, holding on to the bed for support.

Richard said, "Alyssa, can you hear us?"

Alyssa's eyelids fluttered, but she didn't open her eyes.

"We have to go now, but I will be back soon. Your mother is here to see you, and the girls are coming in also. The doctor says you are going to be just fine." He put his hand lightly on her forehead, brushing back the damp strands of hair. Her eyelids fluttered again.

Neither Richard nor Monika spoke as they followed the nurse down the hall to the waiting room. But after the nurse left with the girls, Richard said, "I guess she looked pretty well, considering."

Monika nodded. She was biting her lip, trying to stay calm. "She looked so frail…as though a breath of wind could carry her off."

Richard patted her on the shoulder. "Don't worry so much. Alyssa has always been a lot tougher than she looks. Remember what the doctor said."

It was almost three-thirty by the time the girls got back to the waiting room. Richard offered to take them all out for an early dinner before they left, but they thought they ought to start for home. Richard knew they were right. He went down to the car with them. Alix and Sonia were excited by their visit to see Alyssa. They thought she looked much better than they had expected. They were both sure she had been conscious enough to know they were there, and they were elated by the knowledge. It made their whole trip worthwhile. Richard thought the girls were too optimistic, but he didn't say anything.

For a while they stood in the parking lot. Richard wanted them to stay with him, and at the same time he wanted them to go.

Alix said, "That's strange. I keep thinking I smell smoke."

Then they all began to notice the smoke in the air.

"Alyssa and I have been noticing it for days. There are forest fires in Canada. I think that's why it's so cloudy. The clouds look kind of brownish too."

Monika was already sitting in the front seat of the car with the door open so she could be part of the conversation. Now she said, "Richard, why do you suppose they decided to do the operation on a holiday?"

"I really don't know. Maybe they're extra busy, and this was the only time they could do it."

Sonia said, "It's lucky for me and Alix. We might not have been able to get away if it wasn't a long weekend."

Richard said, "I'm glad it happened the way it did."

They left soon after that. Richard watched the car drive away and started back inside. He felt suddenly tired and alone. At Alyssa's room, he got a shock. The room was empty. No lights were flashing. All the monitors were dark and silent. The narrow bed was empty, neatly made up, as though Alyssa had never been in it.

At first Richard thought he must have been wrong about where she was, but the cubicles on both sides had patients in them, and neither of those people was Alyssa.

He was standing in the hall, trying to decide what to do next when the same nurse who had escorted them came walking down the hall. She said, "If you're looking for your wife, they've moved her back to her room." She looked at her chart and found the number of Alyssa's room for him.

A little while later, Richard walked into the room in a different part of the hospital. Alyssa lay there asleep. Her face was clean. She was pale, but she looked like herself again.

Richard felt as though he were coming home. He sat down beside her bed and got out his Kindle. It was very quiet. There was someone in the other bed, but the curtain was drawn between the two beds.

Richard sat reading for a long time. Someone brought Alyssa's dinner on a tray. That made him realize that she had only been in the hospital for twenty-four hours. So much had happened that yesterday seemed long ago.

When Richard looked up later, Alyssa's eyes were open. "Richard," she said. "What's happened? I feel as though I have been asleep forever."

"The operation is over. It went fine. They're positive they got all the cancer." He saw her flinch a little when he said 'cancer.'

"I had the strangest dream." She paused for a minute. "Well, I had lots of dreams, but there was one that was so amazingly real." She smiled. "I dreamed that Alix and Sonia were standing beside my bed looking down at me, saying that they loved me. It was such a beautiful dream."

"But it wasn't a dream."

"What?" She lifted her head off the pillow and propped herself up on her elbow so she could see him better. "Oooh," she said. "It hurts."

"Lie back down. Maybe it's too soon to be moving around."

She sank back onto the pillow. "But what did you say about the dream not being real?"

"I said it wasn't a dream. They were here. Alix and Sonia were standing beside your bed after the operation. You must have woken up enough to know they were there. They thought you saw them."

"Really?" She was smiling. "Where are they now?"

"They had to go back. They left about three hours ago."

"It was so lovely. I opened my eyes and saw them standing there."

"Your mother came too. She and I went in to see you first. You almost opened your eyes a couple of times, but I guess you didn't wake up enough to know she was there."

"I wish I had."

"They'll be back soon."

She was still smiling when she fell asleep again.

Richard stayed until the visiting hours were over, and then he went home. He was very hungry, but he wanted his own food, made by Alyssa, not by anyone else.

CHAPTER 16

Sam was washing the breakfast dishes when Bonnie came in from work. He meant to have them finished before she got there, but he still had a lot left to do.

Bonnie hung up her jacket and sat down at the kitchen table. "Don't worry about them dishes, Sam. I can get 'em later. How was your day?"

"I spent most of it tryin to fix that leak in the waterline in the barn. I think I finally got it, but it took a lot longer than it should have." He said this over his shoulder while he kept on washing.

"Alma and Junior are playin at the Country Club tonight. A couple of the girls were talkin about it at work."

"Junior didn't say nothin to me about playin when I talked to him the other day."

"He probably didn't want us to feel like we had to go."

"I don't think he'd feel that way."

"Maybe he just forgot."

Sam shut off the water and turned around to look at her. "Do you want to go?"

"Sure."

"I don't want to if you're real tired or your legs are botherin you."

"No. I'm good. It was a quiet day. If we had leftovers for dinner, I could lay down for a while before we went."

"That would suit me. I got chores to do too."

Bonnie said, "We got plenty of time. There ain't any sense in gettin there before nine o'clock."

"Well, listen, Bonnie. Are you sure you want to go out after workin on your feet all day?"

"Sam, I *said* I did. We ain't gone out in I don't know when." She was sitting at the table with her shoes off, massaging her feet.

"It costs money to go out."

"We've got money, not a whole lot, but enough."

"You do, you mean." He sat down across the table from her.

"Oh, come on, Sam. If you was workin, and I was home, you'd say the money belonged to both of us."

"That would be different."

"I don't see why."

"Because you're a woman, for one thing."

"That's a silly reason. We share what we got. It don't matter who earned it. I would of been real mad if you'd ever said I couldn't have some money because you'd earned it, and it was yours." She smiled at him. "You never did that though. You never even thought of it, did you?"

Sam was indignant. "No, of course not."

"See what I mean? But it don't make no difference this time, because I want to go see Junior and Alma play."

They got to the Country Club a little before nine. It was already pretty crowded. They found an empty booth, but it was way in the back where they couldn't see the bandstand. Bonnie sat down, and Sam went to the bar to get their drinks. The jukebox was playing, and the bandstand was dark when he went by.

When he finally got a beer for himself and a Diet Pepsi for Bonnie and was on the way back, the bandstand was lit with spotlights. Junior and the other guys were there with their instruments. Junior didn't see him, and he didn't stop, because his hands were full and it was tricky maneuvering through the crowd. He sat down and told Bonnie that he saw Junior and the band setting up. They sat there nursing their drinks and looking around. It was too noisy to talk, even before Junior began to play.

After a little while they heard the band start up and a lot of clapping when Alma began to sing. Sam took a drink of his beer and leaned back in his seat. Whenever he heard Alma singing, he knew exactly why Junior married her. She modeled herself on Patsy Cline, and like Patsy Cline, her voice was cracked and broken by all the pain she had suffered. It made Sam want to do anything he could to comfort her and protect her. He could see a little of what Junior must feel. Out at the farm, helping with the butchering or canning, Alma was just another big woman. But on stage she was like one of those old paintings. She was beautiful, and so was her voice.

When the song ended, Sam said, "I'm goin to walk down toward the front so I can see 'em. Want to come?"

Bonnie nodded.

They left their drinks on the table, walked around the edge of the dance floor, and stood with the crowd watching the band. Alma was out in front. She was wearing a bright pink tank top. Her arms were bare. The flower tattoos on her round shoulders were plainly visible.

Junior saw them standing there. He smiled and raised his guitar high for a minute. Sam turned to Bonnie, but she hadn't seen anything, and Sam thought he could have been mistaken.

At the end of the song, after the applause died down, Junior said, "I just saw we have some real special guests. My folks are in the audience. Hey, it's great to have you here tonight." He said something to Alma, and then he started to play 'Sweet Dreams.'

In her husky speaking voice, Alma said, "We'd like to do this one for Sam and Bonnie Martel. It's their song." Then she began to sing in that way that was like Patsy Cline. She didn't move around much or throw open her arms. She just stood there, singing and looking out into the audience with a sad smile, like she was telling you privately about the bad stuff that had happened to her.

Sam caught Bonnie's hand. He mouthed the words, "I love you. Let's dance."

Bonnie tried to pull away at first, but Sam wouldn't let her go. "Come on sweetheart. It's our song."

She stopped resisting and followed him onto the dance floor. When he put his arms around her and started to dance, the people along the edge of the dance floor began to clap. He wanted to pull back a little and take a bow. He loved to show off his dancing. But he didn't because he could feel Bonnie cringing. They used to have a great time dancing together before she got so self-conscious about her weight. So he just relaxed into being close to her while he let the music wash over him.

Gradually, the dance floor filled up, and Bonnie got more comfortable, so that Sam was able to get her to join with him in a few fancy steps. They ended the song with a twirl.

Junior said, "Way to go Ma and Pop." And then Sam was able to take his bow, while everyone laughed and clapped. "Don't they make a beautiful couple? My Ma and Pop! Ain't they somethin?"

Bonnie smiled a quick, shy smile at Junior. Then she said, "Come on Sam," and headed back to their table to sit down. Sam couldn't get her to go out on the dance floor again until much later, when it was crowded enough so no one could see her.

While they were dancing, Sam noticed a guy who kept hanging around the bandstand. He was alone and just standing there in front of Alma. At the end of the song, he clapped in a clumsy way and asked Alma if he could buy her a drink. He was speaking very loud and slurring his words.

Sam said, "That guy's too drunk to be there."

Alma was calm about it. She just smiled and shook her head, trying to ignore him. Sam and Bonnie were halfway back to their seats when they heard the commotion behind them. They turned around to watch.

Junior was in it now. He was trying to get the guy to leave Alma alone. The drunk shouted at Junior, saying he was just trying to be a nice guy and to show his appreciation for Alma's singing.

It was when he began to shove Junior that Sam dropped Bonnie's hand and headed for the bandstand. The band started to play another song without Junior, and Alma tried to join in, even though she had backed out of the way and wasn't near her microphone.

Sam didn't look back at Bonnie because he knew she would be telling him not to get in the middle of it, and that was just what he was eager to do.

Junior was trying to take his guitar off with the drunk pushing him backwards into the drum set.

Sam was filled with righteous anger. He didn't even know how much he had been spoiling for a fight. He had to be part of it. He wanted to hurt someone—he wanted to hurt that drunk. No one could stop him at that point, not even Bonnie. If she had held on to his arm and cried, begging him to stay out of it, he couldn't have stopped himself. He would have shaken loose from her clinging hands and gone without looking back. So he was very glad that all she did was tell him not to go. In the noisy bar, it was easy to act as though he hadn't heard her.

He pushed through the crowd until he was standing beside the drunk. It wasn't a guy he knew, although his face looked familiar.

The band was still trying to play. Sam looked at Alma. He saw that when she recognized him, a look of fear came onto her face, but by then, he was too far in to change direction.

He looked at Junior, and Junior said, "Whoa, Pop. I got it." Still, he thought he could tell that Junior wanted him there for backup.

Sam tried to grab the guy by the arm, but he jerked free and tried to push Junior again.

Sam said, "Okay buddy, it's time for you to hit the road." He grabbed the guy's arm again, and with his other hand, he took a hold on the back of the guy's shirt.

The man felt loose and wobbly. Sam started walking him across the dance floor toward the bar and the front. He looked back over his shoulder. Junior was picking up his guitar. He was grinning. That made Sam feel great. He couldn't remember when he'd felt so good about himself.

The drunk's feet kept twisting around, like he wanted to go back to Junior, but he had to keep walking the way Sam was steering him.

When they got to the edge of the dance floor, someone started to clap, and everyone joined in. The drummer did a roll on his drums, and Junior said, "That's my dad. Thank you, Pop."

Sam was flying high. He didn't know what he would do when he got to the door, but he knew nothing could stop him now.

The drunk guy turned one way and then the other, trying to go back to the bandstand, but he had to keep going the way Sam was pushing him.

When they started into the front room, the bartender was watching, and as they walked past the booths, everyone sitting in them turned to look. The conversations stopped. Junior's band was playing in the back room, and Alma was singing, but in the front it was quiet.

Sam walked the guy out the door, and conscious that everyone behind him was paying attention, he said, "Go on home now. You've had enough excitement for one night." Then he turned around and walked back through the room without looking around to see what the drunk was doing behind him.

No one said anything. Sam resisted the urge to dust off his hands the way they did in the old cowboy movies. A couple of people at the bar turned around on their stools to shake hands with him. Everyone in the booths was smiling. But when he got to the back room, no one was paying attention any more. Even Junior didn't notice when he walked past. He was disappointed by that.

He slipped into his seat in the back booth. Bonnie was sipping her Pepsi. He took a drink of his beer. She was watching him over the rim of her glass, but she didn't say anything.

Finally, Sam said, "That guy ain't goin to bother Alma no more tonight."

Bonnie still didn't say anything.

"Aw, come on, Bonnie. Don't be mad." He stood up and reached his hand out toward her. "Come dance with me, sweetheart."

She put her glass down and stood up slowly. When she was standing beside him, she looked at him hard and said, "Just the one, and then we're goin, okay?"

He put his arm around her soft shoulders. "You're the boss, sweetheart." He was still feeling cocky. He almost hoped somebody else would need him to get tough. It had been a long time since he'd been in a fight. He wouldn't start anything, but if something came up... he felt ready. He put everything into his dancing, all his best steps, so that Bonnie was out of breath and laughing when the song ended.

They were back in their seats, finishing their drinks, when Marnie showed up. Sam was facing toward the back, so he didn't see her coming. He saw Bonnie look up with a smile, and then Marnie slid into the seat beside him. She leaned against him for a minute and said, "Way to go, Pop. We saw you get that guy out of Alma's face. You did a great job."

"Thanks, honey. It's nice to see you." He couldn't help a quick look at Bonnie.

Bonnie said, "It was a dumb thing to do. It could of turned into a bad fight."

"I know, Ma. I had to keep a real tight grip on Steve, or he would have been in it too, and he's on probation."

Sam wanted out of the conversation. He said, "Let me out, Marnie. I'll go get you somethin. What're you drinkin tonight?"

Marnie stood up so he could get out. She was almost as tall as he was, and her hair was just as dark. Junior was like Bonnie, but Marnie took after him. "I can't, Pop. I'm drivin. You know how careful you got to be these days."

"Let me get you a Pepsi then. I'm goin to get myself a beer."

"No thanks, Pop. I gotta get back. Sally and Bud are with us too."

Sam looked down at Bonnie. "Can I get you another Pepsi, sweetheart?"

Bonnie shook her head no. He could tell it meant she didn't want him to have another beer.

Marnie sat back down. Sam stood there. He had wanted to get away from Bonnie's criticism, but he didn't want to leave Marnie. *She* liked the way he took care of that drunk.

"Why don't you and Steve stay over with us? You could go home tomorrow."

"We can't, Ma. Sally and Bud have a babysitter."

Bonnie said, "Oh, I forgot about them." She reached across the table and took Marnie's hand. "Are you doin okay, honey? You look tired."

"I'm okay, Ma. Things at work, and Steve...I got a lot of worries right now, but I'm okay."

"I hope so." She looked up at Sam, a quick look.

Sam wasn't sure what she meant by the look. Maybe she wanted to talk to Marnie without him around. He said, "Well, I guess I'll go get that beer." He looked down at Marnie, sitting in his seat. She did look tired, or maybe a little old, even though her hair was still as black as ever. He said, "Why don't you come up and see us sometime soon. Bring Steve if you have to."

She smiled up at him, and he left. If he stayed, he might be tempted to say more about Steve, and it wouldn't be complimentary. He went to the bathroom and got himself a beer, and when he got back to the table, she was gone.

Sam sat and drank his beer. Bonnie was silent. Finally he said, "Did Marnie have any more to say after I left?"

Bonnie shook her head no and sat watching him until he finished the beer, and then she said, "Okay, it's time to go while we still can."

Sam started to say, "What's that supposed to mean?" But he snapped his mouth shut and said nothing. He could feel all the fight energy filling him up inside again, and he didn't want to let it spill out on Bonnie. Except for trying to stop him from getting rid of the drunk, she'd been a pretty good sport.

He started for the door, feeling kind of shaky. Bonnie grabbed his hand. When they got in front of the bandstand, Sam tried to put his arms around her for one more dance, but she shook him off and kept on pulling him toward the front door. She only looked back once to wave to Junior and Alma.

Junior called out, "Goodnight, Ma and Pop," as they were going through the door.

In the front room, everyone looked around at them. Sam tried to walk straight. He tried not to resist going where Bonnie was steering them. He didn't want to be a repeat performance of the guy he had shoved out the door a while ago. It was a similar situation, and some of the people in those booths had been there all evening.

Outside, the fresh night air, with its smells of damp earth and growing things, revived him. "You can let go of me now, Bonnie. I ain't goin to run back inside from here."

"I know," she said, but she kept a grip on his hand while they walked down the street.

"Did Marnie say any more after I left? I thought you gave me a look to tell me you girls had somethin private to discuss."

"I didn't give you a look, and she didn't have any more to say. She's worried about her job. They're talkin about layoffs."

Sam snorted at that.

"And you know Steve."

"Yeah, I know that s.o.b. I wish I didn't. Marnie's much too good for that bastard."

Sam was looking for his truck and didn't even see her car. He opened up his mouth to say, "Hey, where's my truck?" But just in time he remembered that she was the one who drove in. He shut his mouth, hoping she hadn't noticed anything.

She got into the driver's seat. When Sam got in, she was digging around in her pocketbook for the car keys. He wanted to say, "Why don't women ever put their keys away where they can find them again?" He resisted saying that too.

When they were on the road, going toward West Severance, Bonnie said, "Put your seatbelt on, Sam."

"I don't need it."

"Yes, you do."

He started to tell her not to boss him around like she was his mother or something, but then he decided not to. He put the seatbelt on. They were skating along the edge of a fight anyhow, and he didn't want to make it worse. He was still hoping to continue the party at home where Bonnie could have a few beers with him.

They rode in silence for a few minutes, and then Bonnie said, "Junior is a grown man. He can handle his own situations without his dad steppin in to bail him out."

Sam thought, "I knew this was comin. I just *knew* it." Out loud he said, "You ought to be proud of me. I didn't get in a fight."

"I know, but...."

"I felt like doin a lot more to that guy than I did."

She didn't have anything to say to that.

"You heard Junior. He was glad I showed that drunk the door. He thanked me in front of everybody."

"Yes, but, Sam, it could of gotten out of hand. You could of ended up in a real fight."

Sam didn't say that was what he was hoping for, but he thought it. Out loud he said, "I could of handled it."

"That's just what I was afraid of. You're always so ready to get in a fight. You always want to mix it up."

"Don't treat me that way, Bonnie. I ain't some little kid on the playground, you know."

"I know, Sam, and that's just what bothers me. You ain't some little kid. You're a grown-up. You're even a grandfather, for God's sakes. And you don't act like it."

"Bonnie," he said. "Don't say no more. That's enough out of you."

Then they were both quiet. All Sam's good feelings about himself and how he had handled the drunk had leaked away. Bonnie was behaving like such a bitch that he didn't even care if there was any beer at home.

He was so mad at being treated like a child that he thought he would go straight to bed without even looking to see if there was beer in the refrigerator, but when they were going through the kitchen door, Bonnie bumped into him hard with her shoulder, and he had to grab the door frame to keep from going down. For some reason, that made both of them start to laugh.

"Did you do that on purpose?"

She said, "I ain't tellin." And that made them both laugh even harder. Bonnie was always that way. Their fights almost never lasted. That was the great thing about Bonnie—she never could remember to stay mad for very long.

CHAPTER 17

It was a little after noon when Sam finished raking and went back to the house to get some lunch. The first thing he did was to turn the television on loud, so he could hear the weather from the kitchen. Colt gave him a disgusted look and lay down by the door with a sigh.

The sun was still shining, but clouds were beginning to pile up in the west. Sam knew he had taken a chance by cutting hay when he did. He was glad now that he had hedged his bets by only cutting half the field. It was always tricky. There was always the possibility of losing. He could cut too soon and have the hay spoiled by rain. Or he could wait for perfect conditions and wait so long that he lost his chance for a good second cut.

The weather report confirmed his worries. A front was coming through. Ahead of it was a line of thunderstorms with the possibility of heavy downpours. There was nothing Sam could do about it except to work fast.

Last year he had a job and money coming in. Hay had gotten expensive, and they couldn't stretch Bonnie's pay far enough to cover the expenses they had now.

Sam made himself a baloney and cheese sandwich and got out a can of Bonnie's Diet Pepsi. When he went into the other room to turn off the television, Colt stood up.

Sam picked up his own lunch and grabbed a couple of dog biscuits. They went across the road to the hay field where the baler was parked. The hay wagon was already hitched on behind.

The baler was almost ready. Sam wanted to make a few minor adjustments and grease a couple of spots, and then he could begin. There were a lot more clouds than before, and they were darker too. He needed to hurry. If Bonnie got home in time to drive the truck to pick up the bales that wouldn't fit in the wagon, and if there weren't any major breakdowns, it might be possible to get it under cover before the storm hit.

Colt had found himself a shady spot under the trees on the edge of the field. Sam finished his sandwich and the work on the baler and went to get the tractor. Colt flapped his tail lazily a few times as Sam walked by.

He backed the tractor into position in front of the baler. He had to get down to hitch the baler on, and then he got back on the tractor and started the baler.

He went slowly at first, but gradually, as he saw it was working the way it should, he boosted it up to full power. The engine roared, and the baler pounded. Sam was in the middle of it, and he loved it. He didn't want to wear those hearing protectors, even though Bonnie complained that he couldn't hear anything she said.

He headed into the field and started down the first windrow under a mountainous tower of gray cloud. It was going to be a close race, but everything was working. He made several rounds without a hitch. He didn't even break a bale.

After four rounds, the unstacked mound of bales in the wagon was so big that bales were being kicked out through the broken board on the side. Even if he had remembered to fix that board, he would have had to stop to stack the load.

He looked out across the field. He had probably baled about a third of the cut hay. The sun was gone. He put the tractor in idle and climbed out of the cab and stood for a minute before he moved into the wagon. His legs were stiff. There was no wind. It felt as though the world was holding its breath, waiting to see whether Sam or the rain was going to get there first.

He climbed onto the load and burrowed his way through the bales to the back of the wagon. At first he had to move bales away just so he could put them back again, but little by little the stack grew until he had all the bales packed tightly into a wall across the back of the wagon. Now the ones he hadn't baled yet would have room to land in front of the stack.

He jumped down and tried to wipe off his face with his handkerchief, but he couldn't make a difference in the dirt and sweat and hay chaff. He itched everywhere. But the sun was shining again, and now there was a breeze blowing the cloud towers across the sky. The storm was playing cat and mouse with him.

He climbed into the cab and got the tractor in gear. He put the power to her and engaged the baler, and they were back in business again. He hadn't gone far when he happened to look back past the baler and wagon to see a pickup at the far end of the field. When he got another chance to look in that direction, he saw that it was his own pickup, and there were two people, one driving, and one throwing on the bales that had missed the wagon. When he got to the other side of the field, he saw that it was Marnie driving, and Steve was throwing the bales on. Marnie grinned at him, and he gave her a thumbs-up. He tried to include Steve, even though he didn't like him much.

When he went by them on the next round, Marnie jumped out and came running over. Sam stopped and cut back on the gas so he could hear her.

She climbed up the steps and stuck her head in the cab. "Hi Pop. I told you I'd be up to see you soon."

"That's great, honey. But how did you know I had hay to pick up?"

"I didn't. I had a day off, so we decided to come see you and Ma. Where's she at, anyways?"

"She had to work. Somebody was sick. She should be home soon. I hope you can stay awhile."

She nodded and smiled at him.

"That's good, because I got plenty of work for you and Steve."

"Right, Pop. We ain't leavin until it's in the barn. But we got to hurry." She gestured up at the clouds. "We're goin to have to make more than one load. You want it in the regular place, don't you?"

"This is the first of it. Start the stack wherever you like. It should be just about empty up there." He looked down at her. Most of her hair was stuffed up under a cap, but strands hung down by her face. "I'm glad you're here, Marnie," he said. That was a lot for him to say. He gave the tractor some gas to cover his embarrassment.

Marnie reached out toward him, and then she turned and ran back to the pickup. Sam watched the truck start down the row, and then he started moving himself.

After a while he saw the loaded pickup drive out of the field and across the road. When he had gotten all he could on the wagon, he drove over to where he parked the machinery and took the wagon off. When the pickup came back to the field, there was someone else there, but Sam couldn't tell who it was.

He baled the rest of the windrows while they did another pickup load. Then he parked the tractor and baler by the wagon and went to help them get the last bales. The weather was really bad now. The wind smelled of water, and the sky was dark gray. Now that the tractor was shut off, Sam could even hear a little distant thunder.

It was Richard helping Steve throw bales on the truck. When Sam came up, Richard pointed toward the clouds and said, "I thought you guys could use a hand."

"You're right about that," Sam said. He climbed into the backend of the truck and started stacking the load, while Marnie drove slowly between two windrows and Richard and Steve threw bales on from each side.

Steve grinned at him. The tattoos on his bare arms were shiny with sweat and stuck with hay chaff. "We might could make it," he said.

"It's lucky for me that you guys came along."

169

"That's Marnie. I just do what she tells me to." He grinned again.

When the last bale was on, Sam jumped down and went over to talk to Marnie. "I'll bring the wagon over while you're unloadin this here. We're goin to beat this rain, thanks to you."

Just then a big gust of wind came up. "We ain't done yet, Pop." She shouted past him to Steve and Richard. "You guys want a ride?"

Steve said, "Naw, we'll walk over." And Marnie sped off out of the field and across the road.

Sam walked with Steve and Richard to the edge of the field. They walked with the loose-jointed ease of people who have been doing hard work and moving around a lot.

When Sam got to the tractor, he started it up and unhitched the baler. He stopped just long enough to put the cover on the baler, and then he hitched the wagon behind the tractor again and headed for the barn. He thought he felt the first drops as he was climbing into the cab. There were splashes on the windshield.

When Sam went by the house, he saw Bonnie's little car in the driveway. A red Toyota pickup was just pulling in. Sam couldn't see who was driving, but he didn't stop to get a better look. He drove around the barn and up the hill to the ramp that led into the hay bay. They were going to have to bring out the truck before he could get the wagon in. He hoped they were hurrying. He drove up the road above the ramp until the wagon was lined up to back in. He got off the tractor and chocked the wheels of the wagon before he unhitched it.

Just then Marnie drove the empty pickup out of the barn and down the hill.

Steve came over. "What can I do?" he said. "We got the pickup unloaded and out of your way."

"Good," said Sam. "I'm going to turn the tractor around. Then you can hitch the wagon on to the front end. The pin's right there on the wagon tongue. You'll see where it goes."

"Okay," Steve said, but he looked confused.

"It's a lot easier to go up the ramp this way. It ain't so likely to jack-knife on you."

"Okay," Steve said again. "I believe you." He held his hand out, palm up. It was really raining now.

Sam turned the tractor around and eased it down to where Steve was standing, holding the wagon tongue in one hand and the pin in the other, watching until he could get the hitch on the wagon lined up with the one on the tractor. Sam could see how jumpy Steve was about the rain. He was trying to hurry and go slowly and calmly at the same time.

Marnie was walking up the hill. Some guy was with her, but Sam didn't have time to see who it was. Steve was motioning to him to back up, but just as he put it in reverse, Steve dropped in the pin and stood up grinning and backing up out of the way and motioning to Sam to go forward.

Sam started up the ramp slowly to keep the wagon straight. He was thinking how much help Steve had been today. He almost didn't want to say even to himself how Steve was an okay guy and all, but that combination of tough guy swagger and jumpiness could get on your nerves really fast. He wondered how Marnie was able to put up with it.

When the wagon was all the way under the roof, Marnie shouted, "Way to go, Pop." She and Steve and the other guy came up the ramp behind the tractor.

Sam shut it off and climbed out of the cab. The rain was drumming loudly on the tin roof of the barn. It was Joe Tripaneer from work, standing beside the tractor with Marnie and Steve. Sam said, "Hey Joe. This is a surprise. What're you doin out here, man?"

"Just a little social visit. I been wonderin how you was makin it." He had a six-pack of Bud Lite under his arm, and he twisted a little sideways so Sam could get a look at it. "I see you been workin hard and cuttin it close."

Sam said, "This is my daughter Marlene and her friend Steve. I wouldn't have made it at all if it wasn't for them. But I think we did. I don't think it had time to get wet." He looked at Marnie and Steve when he said the part about the hay getting wet.

Sam had forgotten all about Richard being there until he came out of the hay bay and past the wagon to join them. Sam introduced him to Joe, and Richard took off his work glove to shake hands.

Marnie said, "Maybe we ought to put these ones on their sides. That's how Steve and Richard and I done with the other ones."

"If we left 'em on the wagon, the wet places would be right on top. They'd be the ones to dry out first."

Sam looked at Steve when he heard that. He knew Steve was dying to get at Joe's beer. He said, "They'll dry out better in the open. Come on. It won't take long. Marnie's up for it, ain't you girl?"

Marnie grinned and said, "What d'you say, Steve?" She looked at the others. "Steve's done most of the heavy liftin so far."

Joe set his beer down on the steps of the tractor. "I can help. I ain't done nothin yet."

Marnie climbed up on the load and started throwing bales down, but she couldn't keep ahead of four of them, even though they had to carry the bales back to the stack in the hay bay.

A little while later Sam saw that Richard was up on the stack throwing off bales and laughing with Marnie. Steve was carrying two bales to the stack and didn't notice. "Hell," Sam thought. "If he was that worried about Marnie, he'd be up on that stack with her himself."

Richard was standing near the step of the wagon, reaching for a bale, when one came flying and knocked him backwards. Marnie was up on the top of the stack and laughing. She said, "I'm sorry, Richard. Are you okay?" She didn't look sorry.

Richard stood up. "That's all right," he said. "I'd better watch what I'm doing." He was laughing too.

Sam happened to catch the look of triumph on Steve's face. He looked like he thought he'd done it himself.

They went on moving the hay back to the growing rows of bales along the wall under the eaves. The stack on the wagon was getting smaller.

Sam had just put down a couple of bales when he heard Marnie scream. He hurried back to the wagon. She was nowhere in sight. Richard was climbing up the pile of bales, apologizing as he went. He pulled her up out of a hole in the hay and helped her stand up.

Marnie said, "You sure fooled me. I wasn't watchin out at all."

"I really didn't mean to hit you that hard."

Joe said, "Well, Marlene, it's always the ones you don't look out for. Them's the ones that clobber ya."

"I won't forget again. You better watch your back, Richard. We still got some hay up here."

Richard was smiling at her. "I'm planning to keep my back to the wall from now on."

Sam turned to pick up a bale, and that's when he happened to notice Steve. All Sam could think was how the comic books would draw Steve, with his own personal thundercloud above his head, raindrops coming down, and a bolt of lightning stuck through the cloud like a feather in a cap.

Sam picked up the bales without saying anything. It was Steve's problem, not his. On the way back to the wagon, he saw Joe going the other way. Joe grinned and shrugged as they passed each other.

They had just finished unloading, and they were all brushing themselves off, when Bonnie came up the ramp past the tractor, carrying two grocery bags. She had on a shirt of Sam's and one of his old feedstore hats.

"The work's all done, Ma."

Bonnie set the grocery bags down on the empty wagon bed. "I know," she said. "I thought you'd be ready for some snacks."

"Is it still rainin?"

"Yes. It's comin down hard. It looks like it's goin to keep on for a while. Did the hay get wet?"

Sam said, "Not enough to matter."

"Boy, Sam, you sure cut it close."

"I didn't mean to. And I wouldn't have beat it if it wasn't for Marnie and Steve."

"You got some of your Diet Pepsi there, Ma?"

"Of course." She rummaged in the bag and pulled one out and handed it to Marnie.

Joe got his six-pack from the step of the tractor. "Wouldn't you rather have a beer?" He held the six-pack out toward Marnie.

"Oh thanks, but I got to drive home later."

Joe opened a beer for himself and offered one to Sam. Sam took it, and opened it, and took a long drink. It was still cold enough, and it was just what he wanted.

Joe said, "I don't worry. The cops ain't never on the dirt roads. I just stick to dirt when I've had a few."

Marnie said, "We got to go all the way to Randolph. I better not chance it."

"I'll take one of them. I ain't drivin."

Joe held out the six-pack, and Steve took one. He was practically licking his lips. He sat down beside Marnie on the bed of the wagon.

Sam said, "What about you, Richard? Don't you want a beer?"

Joe held out the beer, and Richard took one and sat down. Sam was afraid he would sit beside Marnie, and he almost did, but then he must have thought the better of it, because he went to Bonnie's end of the wagon and sat down beside the big bowl of potato chips. There was dirt and hay chaff everywhere, but no one noticed.

"So Joe, what's the occasion?" Sam said. "You ain't been out this way before, or at least, I can't recall it."

"I thought I'd just see how you were doin. I'm startin my new job on Monday, and I ain't goin to have so much time to get around and see people."

"New job? Where?" Sam was trying his best to sound pleased about it.

"I'm goin with Mitchum Springs 'n Weldin. I'll be back in the shop there."

"That sounds good."

"It ain't the best job in the world, but at least it's work. I know some of the guys back there. They say it's an okay place to work at."

"Well, like you say, it's work. And you're lucky to have found somethin."

Joe took a long pull on his beer. "It wasn't just luck. I was out there lookin every day."

Sam said, "I've been out there too, but not every day."

"You been workin around the home place, Pop. Like this here today. That makes you feel like you already done a day's work, even though you ain't gettin paid for it. Steve does that same way. He fixes the sink or somethin, and then he feels like he's got a job." She smiled at Steve. "Ain't that right, honey?"

Sam didn't see what happened next because he was taking a swig of his beer, but he heard Marnie say, "Ow! Don't do that, Steve. It hurts."

Steve smiled a little and chugged down the rest of his beer.

Sam could feel himself getting tight all over. He looked at Bonnie and thought he saw that she was thinking what he was thinking.

Joe said, "I bet I worked harder tryin to get that job than I ever worked when I had one. Now I'm lookin forward to a well-earned rest."

Sam tried to laugh as hard as everyone else.

"Don't worry, Pop. Your turn will come. The first thing you have to do is to decide whether you really want to work out on a job."

Bonnie pushed the bowl of chips in their direction. "That's exactly what I keep tellin him, Marnie."

Richard said, "How's the butchering going, Sam? You had quite a few customers a little while ago."

"I'm all caught up now, and there ain't nothing ahead of me. I might get some business when people have their chickens raised. Maybe the second part of July. That's a ways off though."

There was silence for a moment, except for the rain coming down hard on the tin roof. They were sitting and standing around in a wide circle. Joe was on the step of the wagon with his six-pack on the wagon bed beside him. Sam could see how Steve kept glancing at it. There were only two beers left.

"I hope this rain cools things off. It's early for it to be so hot."

"What's the weather goin to be for the next few days, Sam?"

"I don't know. I was concentratin on today. I didn't even look ahead."

Bonnie said, "How's Alyssa, Richard?"

"I think she's getting her strength back. She gets tired awfully easily, and that frustrates her."

Bonnie looked over at Joe. "Richard's wife had to have a operation a couple, three weeks ago."

"Poor Alyssa," Marnie said. "Please tell her I'd like to come visit her the next time I'm at Ma and Pop's."

"I'm sure she'd like that." He smiled at her. "Well, we both would."

"I ain't been to your house since I was a teenager. I don't think so anyways."

Richard was about to say something, but before he could get a word out, Marnie swung around and slapped Steve hard on the shoulder. "Don't do that, Steve. I told you it hurts."

"It was just a joke. Why can't you take a joke?"

"It's not funny. That's why. It hurts. Don't do it again. I mean it." She was rubbing her upper arm and trying to twist around so she could see the spot.

"Oh you're such a baby. It's not even red. Get over yourself for God's sakes." He looked around at Sam as though he thought Sam would be on his side, as though they both knew how ridiculous women could be sometimes.

But Sam was jiggling his bottle to make the last of the beer slosh around. He looked at the bottle and carefully avoided Steve's eyes.

When he couldn't get any reaction out of Sam, Steve picked up Joe's six-pack and looked questioningly at Joe.

"Sure," Joe said. "Help yourself." Sam could tell he didn't want to give the beer to Steve. "Long as your lady friend don't mind. You might could ask her."

Steve twisted off the beer cap without looking in Marnie's direction.

Marnie said, "That's all right. Maybe it'll put him in a better mood for the trip home."

Sam couldn't even look at Bonnie. He knew she was steaming.

Later on they talked about it. They were sitting in front of the TV, but it was just a place to sit and be comfortable. They weren't watching anything. They didn't even have the sound on.

"Don't you hate that?" Bonnie said.

"What?" Sam opened his eyes slowly. He thought she must be talking about something on the TV.

"The way he treats her. Don't you hate it? If he pinches her right in front of her ma and pop, what does he do to her when they're alone?"

"You can't know. Maybe he's nice to her when they're alone."

"Sam, for God's sakes. I saw your face. You were just as mad as I was."

"Yeah, that's true, but I was just sayin…."

"Well, don't say nothin good about Steve. I don't want to hear it."

"Okay, Bonnie. Keep your cool. There ain't a thing we can do about it."

"I wish she was still a little girl, so we could boss her around. We could tell her she wasn't allowed to go near Steve."

That made Sam laugh. Marnie was never easy to order around, even when she was a toddler, and the idea of telling her what to do now was ridiculous.

"Don't laugh at me, Sam. I wasn't serious. I was just wishin."

"I wish we could get her away from him too. But we got to wait it out. We got no choice."

"Are you hungry, Sam? You ain't had much to eat today. I'll fix you somethin."

Sam leaned his head back and shut his eyes again. "No thanks. It feels like too much work to chew. I'm goin to sit here and relax. It feels so good to be all done."

"Okay. If you change your mind, I'll get you somethin."

"Thanks, Bonnie." He reached his hand over and patted her soft thigh. "I'll help you clean up the kitchen in a few minutes."

"It's all done. I did it when you were doin your chores."

"Good girl. And there ain't no sense in worryin about Marnie." He spoke without opening his eyes or raising his head. "She's a big girl. She can take care of herself. One of these days that bastard will go a little too far, and she'll be all done."

"I just hope he don't hurt her in the process."

"There ain't nothin we can do about that. Maybe he'll get another DUI, and they'll lock him up. We can hope, anyhow."

"She's such a beautiful person. Why does she want to stay with a no-good like Steve?"

"It don't make no sense. It's just the way it is." He sat up and smiled at her. "Look at you and me, sweetheart. I bet there's people in your family sayin that about you."

"That's not true, Sam. You know my folks like you."

"Yeah, at least I don't pinch you." He heaved himself to his feet. "I'm goin to take a shower and go to bed. What about you?"

"I'll be along in a minute. You get started. I won't be long. I'm tired too."

CHAPTER 18

When Alyssa woke up, it was still dark outside. Lately she had been spending a lot of time asleep, glad to not be awake and in pain. Because of that, she often woke up during the night. But this was different. She felt really awake and alive. Even without looking at the clock, she could feel that the night was ending, and she wanted to get up to see the dawn.

The amazing thing was that she didn't hurt anywhere. Even the incisions between her ribs had almost healed. She slid out from under the covers carefully, so that Richard wouldn't notice. He might think something was wrong. Her clothes were piled on a chair near the foot of the bed. She scooped them up and tiptoed out of the room. She dressed in the bathroom and went downstairs without turning on any lights. When she got to the living room, she could see the wall of darkness outside the glass door.

She opened it and stepped onto the deck. Standing there, she could make out the darker shapes of trees against the sky. It was very quiet, but there was a tension in the stillness, as though the world was holding its breath, waiting for the arrival of the light. The only sound was the gurgle and splash of the water in the brook as it hurried around the rocks on its way down the hill.

Alyssa stood, listening to the silence, while the first rosy gray crept into the sky above the trees, and the first birds began to sing, shy and uncertain at first, but gradually gaining confidence from each other and the growing light.

Alyssa stepped back through the door so she could see the illuminated face of the clock over the stove. It was a little before five, too early to wake Richard up with a cup of coffee.

She went back out onto the deck. The light was stronger now. She could see the flowerbeds, and the driveway, and the grass stretching out toward the trees. There were lots of birds singing. The robins were making as much noise as they could. The air smelled spicy and of cedar, of trees and earth and water.

She decided to go just as far as the edge of the lawn so she could see how high the brook was. The water level was probably very different than the last time she had looked. That was weeks ago. She had been so preoccupied with her own insides that she hadn't noticed much around her. The spring runoff had been over for a while. It would be interesting to see.

She put on her sneakers. When she got down into the dewy grass, her feet immediately got wet. She would have gone back for her boots, but she was only going a little way for a quick peek. It wasn't worth bothering about wet feet for such a short stretch.

The brook was lower. All sorts of interesting rocks were sticking above the water. She forgot about Richard, forgot she was only going to take a quick look and go back, forgot about her wet feet and the chilliness of the morning.

She went down the bank to get a closer look at the new, smaller stream. For the first time this year, it was possible to walk across on stones that stuck out of the water. She had to try it, even though it wouldn't have mattered if she had slipped in, since her feet couldn't get any wetter than they already were. But it was a contest to see if she could stay on the rocks.

Once on the other side, it made sense to go up the stream to see what had happened to the little pool that was a miniature version of the pool by the cabin, complete with its own tiny waterfall. It was lower, but there were still fish in it, tiny fish that darted away to hide when the shadow of her head appeared on the water. She lay down on a big rock and was completely still. A few at a time the fish ventured out into the middle of the pool. Then she moved her head, and they all darted back under the rocks. When she moved, little points of sunlight shifted on the sandy floor of the pool.

She went farther upstream to see if it would be possible for the little fish to get to the big pool. Sometimes she climbed over the rocks. Sometimes she walked on one side of the stream and sometimes on the other, but wherever she was, she was always discovering something new to look at just ahead.

Then with surprise, she saw the big pool in front of her. The sun was higher and stronger. The birds were quieter. They had gotten over their first excitement of the dawn. Just as Alyssa got to the water's edge, a fish jumped out in the middle. The ripples spread in shimmering circles, one outside the other toward the bank.

Alyssa sat down in the grass. She felt wonderful. She didn't hurt anywhere. She lay back luxuriously. The sun was high enough now so that it poured over her like a warm blanket. Maybe she fell asleep. All of a sudden, there was a whirring and a quacking. A pair of ducks circled the pool and then splashed down into the middle of the water.

Alyssa raised up on one elbow to watch them through the grass. They circled each other, quacking in conversation. Then the male climbed up the bank quite close to her. He began to groom himself, pulling and poking at his feathers. When he shook himself, droplets of water flew in every direction. Alyssa could smell his fishy scent. The sunlight sparked on the iridescent green feathers of his neck. He turned his head almost all the way around so that he could smooth the feathers of his back.

Alyssa was sure he knew she was there, so she didn't try to be quiet or hidden. After all, when the ducks flew in, they had flown right over her. So she was surprised when she raised up above the grass to watch him preening, and he gave a squawk of terror and scrambled into the air. His mate flew after him. They spiraled up and disappeared over the trees.

Alyssa sat up. She suddenly realized she had lost all sense of time. The sun was higher in the sky than she thought. She jumped to her feet and started for home, hoping she was mistaken and that it wasn't as late as it seemed. Maybe Richard was enjoying a nice late sleep and hadn't noticed she was gone.

But that wasn't the case. When she got to the turn in the path where she could see the house, she could see Richard on the deck, walking back and forth.

After a minute, he saw her too. He jumped down the steps and came hurrying across the grass, already talking. "Where were you? Are you all right? I was so worried. I thought you might have had to go to the hospital while I was asleep, but your car is still in the garage. What were you doing?"

Alyssa put her arms around him. She was laughing, pleased that he was so upset. "I'm sorry. I only meant to go out for a few minutes. I went to see if the water had gone down."

"In the brook? I walked over there, but you weren't there."

"I was there. It was so beautiful that I went up to the pool. There were fish in the little pool, and...oh, Richard, there were ducks, mallards, and it was so funny...." She stopped. He didn't look like he wanted to hear about it. She decided to tell him later. "What time is it, anyway?"

"It must be after eight by now."

"Really? God, I'm sorry. I had no idea it was so late. I must have lost all track of time. I left just as it was getting light, a little after five."

"I couldn't figure it out. I was so afraid."

"I shouldn't have gone. I'm so sorry." She thought a minute. "But I'm glad too. I've had such a lovely time." She reached out to him, and they walked up the steps and into the house with their arms around each other. "I don't know what happened. I guess it was because I woke up this morning feeling like myself again. I didn't hurt anywhere, and I wasn't even thinking about operations and pills and pain. That was why I was wondering how full the brook was. I haven't thought about anything like that for a long time. And when I got over there, I kept seeing something up ahead that I wanted to look at more closely. I wish you had gone with me. You would have loved it." But even as she said the words, she realized she wasn't telling the truth. If Richard had been with her, no matter how well they were getting along with each other, it would have changed the whole thing.

"Have you had any coffee this morning, Alyssa?"

"Oh you poor thing," she said, because the real question was would she make some now. "I'll start a pot right away. You could have had some without me. You must have had to make your own coffee quite a lot lately with me in the hospital or asleep so much."

"I could have. I didn't think of it. I was too worried about you. And then Hank called up. I thought it might be you, so I answered it without even checking to see who it was."

"Is everything okay with them? Nothing's wrong, is it?"

"No. He was just calling to say hello. But, Alyssa, I told him about your operation. I hope you don't mind. I know you didn't want me to say anything before."

"It's okay. It's different now."

"He was asking about you, and I felt like I had to say something. I mean, we aren't that close, but he *is* my brother. I couldn't exactly say there wasn't any news with you."

"It's fine. When I was scared, before the operation, I didn't want to have to talk about it, especially to people I don't talk to that often. I know you guys are very different, but he's your only near relative now. I think you ought to make more of an effort to be friends with him, so I'm glad you told him. What did he say?"

"He was very sympathetic. He said to give you his love. He said he was glad you were going to be all right. He sounded like he really meant it."

"That's nice. You should go and visit them. It isn't that far. No, we both should go. I'll go with you. We haven't been there since your mom died. Let's go this summer, as soon as I get my strength back."

"If you want to. I know it's a lot closer than Stamford, but somehow it seems much farther away."

"That's because we've always stayed in better touch with my family, but we should work on that. Here's your coffee, at last. Let's go sit outside."

CHAPTER 19

Monika opened the oven door and slid the coffee cake in on the middle shelf. It seemed awfully hot in there, but it was an oven. It was supposed to be hot. She set the timer for twenty minutes so she wouldn't forget to check on it. She even got out the magnifying glass to make sure she had set the timer correctly.

Alix had to be in town for something connected with her work. She and Sonia were planning to meet for coffee here around two o'clock. It was only ten in the morning now, but Monika wanted everything to be nice, and things took so long with her eyes the way they were. She hadn't been able to see the recipe for coffee cake, and it was a long time since she had made it, but she was pretty sure she remembered it correctly. It was already starting to smell good.

Monika had been thinking about the Christmas Aaron got his new bike. Alyssa was so happy for him that she almost forgot about her own gifts. There were some wonderful snapshots of that Christmas in one of the photo albums. Monika thought she remembered which one.

She went to the bookcase in the living room where she kept all the albums and got out the two green ones and the blue one. She hadn't looked at any of them for a long time. At first she sat down with them at the dining room table, but she couldn't see enough, so after a few minutes she moved to the kitchen, where the light was better.

She had found the right album and even the picture she remembered, and she was straining to see it when the bell went off. For a minute she couldn't think what it was for. Half of her was back in the old days when the children were small and they all were a family. It was hard to know what she saw in the picture with her blurry vision and what she remembered was there.

Then she came back to the present. The bell was about the coffee cake. She stood up. She had to hold on to the table for a minute until her legs straightened. That was when she noticed the smell of burning. She forgot about her stiffness and made a jump for the stove. When she opened the oven door, a cloud of black smoke boiled out. She peered through the smoke into the oven. The coffee cake was ruined.

She put on her oven mitts and pulled out the pan. The coffee cake was a black, crusted mass. She carried it outside, down the porch steps, and around the corner of the house, where she set it down in the grass out of sight. She didn't want the girls to know. She had probably ruined the pan too.

She opened all the kitchen windows. Maybe the smell would be gone before they arrived. It was when she reached to turn off the oven that she realized that she had misread the dial and turned the oven up much too high.

She sat down at the table and pushed the photo albums aside. All her plans were spoiled. The girls would be understanding and even sympathetic. But if they knew why she had burned up the cake, they would try to convince her to go to the eye doctor. Maybe he could do something so that she could see a little more. But what she wanted wasn't so simple. She didn't want it just to be better. She wanted it to be the way it used to be long ago. Everything was being taken away from her bit by bit. She sat among the old photographs and cried.

After a few minutes, she wiped her eyes and blew her nose. It wasn't getting her anywhere, and the girls would be arriving soon. She took off her apron and got her handbag and the market basket. She could get something that would do at Joe's Market, but she would have to walk. She didn't trust herself to drive even in the neighborhood these days.

She walked slowly so she could do it without a cane. If she tapped along the street, everyone in the neighborhood would know she was going blind. As she walked, she decided to lay all the coffee things out on the front porch table. They could sit there, far away from the smell of burned cake. It was cloudy, and it might rain later, but it was always nice on the porch. The weather was odd today, rain and then sun and then rain again.

The smell of the flowers was always so strong before the rain. Since she had been gardening less, she had been enjoying the flowers even more. She didn't worry so much about the improvements she wanted to make in the gardens, and that left her more time to appreciate what was already there. She would have to remember to stick the pan with the burned coffee cake back underneath the bushes, in case the girls felt like walking around to look at the flowers.

Mr. Sweeney's grandson was behind the cash register when she went inside the market. She said hello and walked down the aisle of baked goods. She hoped he wouldn't notice how she had to peer at the packages to see what was inside. She held a package of little cakes up to the light. It looked like the right kind of pastry. She didn't care how good it tasted, as long as the girls didn't wonder why she chose something strange. She bought some cream for the coffee as well as the little cakes and walked back home again with her basket on her arm.

Sonia arrived a little before two. She said she came early to see if Monika needed some help, but by that time, Monika had everything ready. When Alix arrived, they all went out onto the porch. The girls exclaimed over the wisteria vines, saying they were even more beautiful than last year.

They all sat down, and then Sonia jumped up again to serve

everyone, exclaiming over the little cakes and the coffee, until Monika began to wonder if Sonia suspected something wasn't right.

Sonia set two cups of coffee on the little table in front of the sofa where Monika was sitting beside Alix. She passed around the plate of little cakes and then sat down with her own coffee in the chair beside Alix.

Monika took up a cake and bit into it. It tasted like cardboard.

Sonia said, "Oh Nan, real cream. Did you get it just for us?"

"Of course. I know how you like it."

"Thank you, Nana." She poured some into her coffee and took a sip. "Your coffee is the best."

"The cream helps."

"Where did you get these sweet little cakes? They look delicious."

"I got them at Joe's, and they aren't as good as they look."

Alix had been sitting quietly between them. She hadn't even picked up her coffee cup.

Sonia always noticed what everyone was doing. "Did you get your work done before you came over here, Alix?"

Alix shifted around on the sofa. Monika could feel it through the cushions.

She leaned back and said, "No, I didn't." There was a silence, and then she said, "I mean it's different than that."

They were both listening hard now.

Alix said, "I mean, I have something that I need to tell both of you." She reached out for Monika's hand where it lay between them on the seat.

"Oh God," Monika said. Her heart was pounding. "It's bad news, isn't it?"

Alix said, "Oh Nana. I didn't mean to scare you. Sonia, give me your hand too. It's good news. Really it is."

"Tell us quick then. You're scaring Nana."

"Okay, it's this."

Monika took a deep breath and leaned her head back against the back of the couch. She hoped she was ready. She looked at Alix.

"Okay, so this is my news." She smiled at each of them in turn.

"I'm pregnant. That's the news. I wanted to tell you both in person, so I made up the excuse of having to come to Stamford on business. I really took a day off."

They sat there holding hands. Even the usually talkative Sonia was silent.

Then Alix squeezed Monika's hand and said, "Say something, Nana. Don't you think it's good news?"

Monika squeezed back. "Oh yes, it's wonderful news. I was scared for a minute. I thought it might be something horrible, like the news about your mother. I'm so glad it's not." She knew what she was saying wasn't adequate. She would have to count on Sonia for that, at least until her heart could get quiet again.

Sonia was jumping up to hug her sister. "I've been wishing to hear this news for years. I had no idea you were even thinking of it."

"I haven't been for long. It was when Mom got sick in the spring...." She turned to look at Monika. "But, Nana, don't think this means I think she's not going to be all right. I know she will be fine. It isn't that."

Monika smiled. She hoped they wouldn't see that it was a smile full of sadness. She was thinking, "The moving finger writes and having writ moves on," because her baby, her Alyssa, might be all right, and with all Monika's heart she hoped she was, but she would never be the same again. It was a new baby's turn now. She couldn't say any of this, and she didn't want to spoil Alix and Sonia's happy moment. It *was* their turn now. She didn't want them to notice, and they didn't. They were busy bubbling away to each other about what was going to happen, about baby clothes and baby furniture. And Sonia was so pleased to be the old hand, the experienced one, even though she was the youngest. All her helping instincts were coming out.

Monika sat there smiling, trying to look glad, in case anyone noticed. And after a little while, Sonia said, "Nana doesn't want to hear any more about baby clothes. We've got plenty of time to get ready too. Why did you get the photo albums out, Nana?"

"I was thinking about some old pictures and remembering what happened the Christmas Aaron got a new bike and your mother was so excited about it that she forgot her own Christmas presents. I was looking for photographs of that day. I was remembering it."

"Have you talked to Mom recently?" Alix asked.

"Yesterday, or maybe it was the day before. She sounded like her old self again."

"I know," Sonia said. "I thought that too. Isn't it amazing?"

"I think they caught it very early."

Alix said, "I've got to call her and tell her about the baby. I was just waiting until I had told you two."

Monika was wondering why she didn't tell her mother first, when Alix went on. "And I didn't want to tell her my happy news when she was feeling sick and trying to get her strength back."

Sonia said, "It might help her recovery to hear such good news. I know she will be so glad about it."

Monika was thinking how she loved Alix. Alix didn't say much, but Monika could tell that she had the same thought she herself was having—that the future belonged to the new generations, and their portion was the past. Monika reached out and patted Alix on the shoulder. "I'm so happy about your news, " she said. And this was the first time she really meant it. "Do you want to call your mom right now? I'll get my phone. It would make her a part of our party."

Alix was still thinking about it when Sonia ran off into the house to get the phone. Sonia handed her the phone, and she had no choice. Sonia and Monika watched while Alix made the call. They could tell that it was going to the message machine.

Alix hung up and looked at them. "I didn't want to leave it on the messages," she said. "I'll try again later." She looked at Monika, and then she said, "Maybe they're outside, taking a walk or something."

Monika said, "I was looking for the snapshot of your mom and Aaron from the Christmas when Aaron got his new bike."

Sonia said, "I remember that picture. You do too, Alix."

Alix shook her head.

"I'll find it, and then you'll remember."

Monika said, "I found it this morning. It's in one of the green ones. Look in the middle."

Sonia sat down beside Alix and started flipping through the pages. She found the picture and tilted the album so Alix could see. "Mom looks so proud of herself."

"She was," Monika said. "She bought the headlight for the new bike with her own money."

"She's pointing to it," Alix said.

"I think she cared more about Aaron getting the new bike than she did about her own gifts that Christmas. She was always such a generous person." There was a little pause, and Monika realized she was talking about Alyssa in the past tense. "Oh, that's not what I meant," she said. "She *is* such a generous person." But the words she had said were still hanging in the air. They couldn't be unsaid.

"Who took that picture, Nana?"

"It must have been Harry. He was always taking pictures." She leaned closer to the page. "There I am in the background."

Sonia laughed. "That's not you, Nana. That's the frame of the door."

"Oh of course," Monika said, sitting back. "I can't really see the picture from this angle. I thought I remembered I was in it." She didn't dare look at either of them. "I must have been thinking of some other photograph."

Alix said, "Let's go out in the garden and look at Nana's flowers."

But Sonia was flipping through the back pages of the album. "Wait a minute. I want to find that picture of Nana when she was working as a welder during the war. It's in here somewhere."

"Don't look at that. It was just a joke, and it wasn't very funny."

"But I love it, Nana. I always used to look at it when I was little."

"My friend, Mary Catherine, and I wanted to get jobs like that. All the girls wanted to be Rosie the Riveter, but they didn't have any shipyards in Stamford. We would have had to go to New Jersey, and our parents wouldn't let us. We took those pictures of ourselves for a joke."

"Come on," Alix said, pushing the book onto Sonia's lap and standing up. "Let's go see Nana's flowers." She walked down the steps.

Sonia shut the book and hurried to catch up. Monika was glad they didn't wait for her, because it took a few minutes of straightening and standing before her legs were strong enough to work properly. She always said her joints were rusty, and she had to work them a while to break up the rust.

When she got to the bottom of the porch steps, Alix and Sonia were walking around the side of the house toward the back. They were deep in conversation with each other. Suddenly they both stopped, looking down at the grass in front of their feet. That was when Monika remembered the burned coffee cake. She meant to stuff it back under the bushes out of sight, but when she got home from Joe's Market, she forgot. She walked up to them.

Sonia said, "What's this, Nana?" She sounded like a school teacher.

"It's a cake. I let it get too cooked. I meant to throw it out, but I forgot." She was afraid they could tell that she was trying to give as little information as she could.

"But, Nana...." Sonia was frowning.

"Come on," Monika said, walking past them. "Wait til you see my peonies."

They followed her past the burned pan, even though Sonia was clearly bothered by it. She was inches away from putting the pieces together enough to see that Monika was having some kind of trouble.

They walked along the peony beds with the girls exclaiming politely. The heavy perfume filled the damp air. When they got to the bench that Harry had made so long ago, Monika sat down, and the girls walked on past the gardens and the mowed lawn into the little overgrown field with its bleached dead grass that Monica didn't even pretend to keep up with any more. The old apple still struggled along, even though one of its main branches lay on the ground. All Harry's other fruit trees had died and disappeared, one by one.

Monika watched the girls walk as far as the apple and sit down together on the fallen branch. They bent their heads toward each other as they talked. Monika could see them more clearly now that they were in the distance. She hoped their conversation was about babies and not about her and what was wrong with her. But it probably wasn't about her. It was egotistical of her to think they would pay that much attention to her infirmities. In fact, she had been surprised that she had managed to keep her failing eyesight a secret for so long.

All day the weather had been like early spring, rain and then sun and then rain again. It was sunny now. It warmed her back and the top of her head. It caressed her and filled her with well-being. She felt like one of her cats, purring in the sun.

After a while, she saw them get up and start to walk toward her. She stood so that she would have a little time to get ready to walk. Didn't they notice that she had trouble walking? They might not want to call attention to it. She couldn't ask of course. "Have you noticed how much trouble I have getting around these days? I can't drive because my eyes are failing, and I can't walk because my legs are failing." But she couldn't say that, could she? It would be to give in to it. And maybe they hadn't noticed that she was struggling. It wasn't much compared to what other people her age had to deal with, and those were the ones who were still alive to struggle.

When the girls got to her, each of them took one of her arms, and they all three walked back to the house together. It felt very nice to be so sweetly supported.

Sonia said, "We both have to get going, but we want to clean up the dishes for you first."

"You don't need to do that. I've got plenty of time. You girls go along."

"But, Nana...."

"No. I won't hear of it. I'll pick up slowly and think about the visit and Alix's news."

Alix said, "Sonia and I are going to try to get up to Vermont sometime soon. Would you go with us, Nana? You haven't been there since Mom's operation, have you?"

"No. I didn't want to go until she got her strength back. I don't want to make extra work for her, but if you girls were there too...."

Alix said, "I'll ask Dad what he thinks about us coming up soon. We could stay at a Bed and Breakfast. That would make it easier for her."

"I'd love to see her." Monika paused, thinking about it. "She says she's getting her strength back, and I think I could believe it if I could see her and hug her."

They were near the house and the cars now. Monika hugged each of them in turn. "Now get going, girls." She pushed them toward their cars.

After they left, she went in through the kitchen and out to the front porch, where she started picking up, feeling happy and sad at the same time. As she put away the coffee things, she decided that she really had to go to the eye doctor. She couldn't put it off any longer. It was foolish to hope it was temporary and would fix itself. And there might even be reason to suppose that there was something the doctor could do.

CHAPTER 20

"Oh God," Richard said. "There goes the phone. Let's pretend we didn't hear it." There were sitting on the deck. It was a beautiful summer night, clear and still warm, with stars everywhere. There was a glow on the eastern horizon. The moon was a few days past full. It would rise soon and dim the stars.

"There it goes again. It might be important."

"They'll leave a message. That's what we have a message machine for."

"I can't do it," Alyssa said, jumping up. "Suppose something happened to Mom or one of the girls." She went inside.

Richard could hear her talking to someone, but he couldn't tell who it was. He lay there looking up into the dome of the sky. He didn't need to know who it was. She would come out and tell him soon enough, too soon, really. He concentrated on trying to float up into the air, up among the sparkling stars.

Alyssa came out. "That was Sonia," she said. "I'm glad I answered it."

Richard could feel himself plop down in his chair. So much for his interplanetary trip.

"She and Alix were wondering if I felt strong enough for visitors. They're hoping Mom will come too."

"When?"

"They were talking about next weekend."

"How do you feel about it?"

"I know they want to see how I'm doing…back from the dead and all that. And I am…getting back to normal, I mean." She leaned back in the chair and didn't say any more. Richard looked over at her, lying with her eyes closed. Her profile was dark and enigmatic against the glow along the horizon. Then her eyes popped open. "We don't have anything planned for this weekend, do we?"

Richard sighed. "Well, I did. I've been waiting until you seemed strong enough, and then I was going to take you for a day trip—maybe to the Green River Reservoir. I know how much you love it there. I was thinking we could go this weekend."

"Oh Richard, how lovely. I didn't know you were planning a trip for me." She sat up and looked over at him. "I'll tell them not to come." She paused. "Only I don't want them to think we're trying to hide something."

"We don't have to take this canoe trip."

"But I want to. Maybe I should just tell them that I want to spend the time with you."

"Why don't we go tomorrow? The canoe's all ready. Then we'll be sure nothing will interfere."

"Oh let's. And I'll call Sonia and tell her they should come this weekend."

"Unless you think it would be too much for you."

"No. I think it will be good for me. I need to push myself a bit." She jumped up, full of energy, and went inside to make the call.

Richard lay back in his chair, thinking. He had made a list of all Alyssa's favorite foods. This picnic was going to be a celebration of the fact that she had stepped into death's path and then danced lightly away before he could grab her and take her to his dark lair.

When she came back, Richard said, "You know I would have done both those phone calls for you if you had wanted me to."

"I know, but I'm so much better. We don't need to pamper me any more. Of course, I've still got to get through the chemo. I don't know what that's going to be like."

"I'll help you. Maybe it won't be so bad. We can get you some weed too. That's supposed to help."

She was lying back in her chair now with her face turned toward the stars. She giggled a little. "It'll be like old times."

"We never did that much."

"No, that's true. But it was fun. Are we really going to take a canoe trip tomorrow?"

"That's up to you. Are you well enough? I was just waiting for that."

"I think so. I think it would help me get well again. I want to, and if we don't go soon, something might get in the way, like them all coming to visit this weekend."

"Yes, let's go before they come. We don't want anything to get in the way. I didn't check tomorrow's weather, but looking at the sky, I think it will be fine. The canoe's all ready. We can get something for lunch on the way."

"Bread and cheese is all we need. Can we go to the Green River Reservoir?"

"We'll go wherever you say. This is your trip."

"No, it should be for both of us, a celebration of things getting back to normal again."

"Let's get an early start. I'll put the canoe on the truck first thing, and we can stop for some food along the way, maybe in Morrisville. We can have a picnic on that island with the big rock."

"You're the best, Richard. I love you."

They went to bed then, with Richard thinking how strangely things evolve in life. Here they were in such a loving place, but they had to go through some very dark times to get there. He resolved right then not to let their relationship slide backwards into the hostility they used to feel so often in the old days before Alyssa got sick.

The next morning Richard had the canoe loaded at first light. The eastern sky went through a series of transparent colors, gray, shading to pink and then to blue, as the moon was setting. The radio was right. It was going to be an incredible summer day. Richard had slid out of bed without waking her. He wanted the canoe on the truck before she knew he was loading it. He didn't want her to spend her strength at the beginning of the trip by trying to help.

When he got back to the kitchen, Alyssa was just coming down the stairs. "Why didn't you wake me when you got up? I could have helped you with the canoe."

"I didn't need any help. My one-man system works great. It's loaded already."

"I could have made you some coffee anyway."

"Do it now, and we can take it with us. Let's get going."

Alyssa started the coffee and went to finish getting dressed. When the coffee was ready, and she still wasn't back, Richard went upstairs looking for her.

She was standing in the bathroom with the door open.

"The coffee's ready. What about you?"

"I'll be there in just a minute. I have to do my makeup."

"Makeup? You don't need any makeup. You look fine, and anyway, no one's going to see you."

She was standing in front of the mirror with her hands raised and her head tilted, about to put on one of her earrings. She looked at him thoughtfully. "You are."

"I am what?"

"You are going to see me."

"Oh yeah, true...but I always like the way you look."

She finished the earring. "That's because I always try to look nice for you." She picked up her makeup pencil and turned to look in the mirror. "I'll be right down."

Richard didn't know what else to say, so he left.

She came downstairs about five minutes later. She was wearing perfume. It made no sense when they were going for a canoe ride, but Richard felt pleased by it anyway. She was making that effort for him.

He got his binoculars and a hat, and they went out to the truck, carrying their cups of coffee. It was still early, not yet seven, but the light was getting strong. There were robins singing, and farther away, the water in the brook was splashing over the rocks.

They drove past a little country store on the edge of Severance where Alyssa thought they could get something for lunch, but Richard convinced her there would be better places to stop in Morrisville. He didn't say it, but he was hoping to find a larger store, one with more options.

By the time they got to Morrisville, the supermarket was open. Richard pulled into the parking lot. "I'll run in, and you can wait here, Alyssa. I'll be right back."

He was expecting her to say she wanted to come with him, but she didn't. She just said, "Okay," meekly. He hurried away before she had a chance to change her mind. He grabbed everything on his list as fast as he could.

When he got back to the truck, he found her sitting just as he had left her. For a minute he wondered if she was all right, but he didn't like to say anything. It might make her worry about herself. He would have a good chance to watch her today. He felt sure he would be able to tell.

"I got us some lunch," he said. He set a bag on the seat beside him and started the truck. "And I got us some bagels for now." He moved the bag a little closer to her. "Are you hungry?"

"Where are the other groceries?" she asked as she looked in the bag.

"I put them in the back, but you know what? I forgot to get butter. Shall I go back?"

"It's okay. I don't mind eating them without butter if you don't."

So he didn't go back. They drove the rest of the way eating bagels dipped in the dregs of their coffee.

When they got to the Green River Reservoir, there were only two cars in the parking lot, and no one was around. As they got out of the truck, Richard said, "I guess we have to try to find a park ranger."

"Why?"

"It's a state park now, and we're supposed to pay a fee. They just started charging at the beginning of July. I saw a notice about it."

Alyssa said, "We could pay them on the way back if they're around." She looked at him. She was grinning. "And maybe we won't see them then either."

Richard was taking the bungee cords off the canoe. He grinned back. "Alyssa, you are so bad."

"Why what do you mean? We tried to find someone to pay, but there wasn't anyone around."

"You're right. It's only a few dollars anyway. We're here because we know how it used to be when hardly anyone knew about this place and there were no rules." He slid the canoe out of the truck to the ground, and they half-carried, half-dragged it to the water's edge.

They loaded everything into the canoe, and Alyssa got in the bow, while Richard pushed off and jumped in himself. The canoe glided out past the end of the point.

The water was a smooth reflection of the sky, pale blue with little wisps of clouds floating in the blue above and the blue below. It was so quiet that they could hear the water going over the dam a quarter of a mile away.

Every so often a little whiff of Alyssa's perfume would drift back to Richard, mingled with the fresh, sharp smells of the water and the evergreens along the shores.

Alyssa's shirt was pink and gauzy. It fluttered and rippled as she stroked with her paddle. It was a bright spot of color against all the blues and greens.

Suddenly across the stillness came the long, quavering cry of a loon. Alyssa turned around to smile at him. They both sat still and silent, waiting to hear it call again. But it didn't, and after a minute of waiting, they began to paddle once more.

What did the call mean? And why did it come just as they were setting out onto the lake?

CHAPTER 21

When she heard the loon, Alyssa turned around to look at Richard. He had stopped with his paddle raised and dripping. He smiled at her with a look of love. She had turned around to thank him for bringing her to this beautiful spot, but she didn't need to say the words. She could tell he understood her. Her heart overflowed with the joy of being alive in a beautiful place with someone she loved. She turned back to her paddling.

Richard was doing most of it, and he didn't need her help. She was only paddling because she wanted to be part of it. She took a few strokes on the left and then lifted the paddle across to the other side. When she shifted the paddle from one side to the other, crystal drops rained down on her legs. The first few times, she tried to keep from getting wet, but after that she forgot to care.

Richard said, "What's that close to the far shore?" He put down his paddle and took up his binoculars. "It's the loon. Oh, it's beautiful."

He handed the binoculars to Alyssa and started paddling again. "I'll see if I can get us a little closer."

Alyssa watched the loon as they moved toward him. She thought of it as a male, a proud father guarding a female with eggs. At first he didn't pay any attention to the approaching canoe. Then he stood up on the water, flapping his wings. Richard stopped paddling to watch, entranced. When the loon came down onto the water again, he circled around so he could see them better, and he began to swim toward them.

Alyssa handed the binoculars to Richard. "Look at him," she said. "I don't think he wants us to come any closer. Maybe he has a mate sitting on a nest."

"We could go and see," Richard said without lowering the binoculars.

"No. I don't want to. The mother might abandon her eggs. That would be awful."

"Whatever you say. You're the boss." He turned the boat back toward the shore of the island, and Alyssa, who was watching to see what the loon would do, felt justified when she saw the bird turn away from them and begin gliding smoothly through the water toward the far shore. "Maybe I will be able to see the mate if he has one." She scanned along the shoreline, but she couldn't see anything, and after a few minutes she lost sight of the loon too. What had looked like a smooth shore must have had a hidden bay, so that the loon swam around a point and out of sight.

An airplane went over very slowly, very high, droning like a large insect. Down at the north end of the lake where the water divided into smaller channels, there was a noisy group of ducks. Alyssa looked at them through the binoculars. There was one duck a little apart from the others. Behind her was a long string of tiny dots of ducklings in a row.

Alyssa was just holding out the binoculars so that Richard could see the ducklings, when he said, "Oh great. We're in luck. No one is here." He turned the canoe toward the island and the big rock.

"Are we going to have lunch here?"

"If you want to."

"I do. I know it's early for lunch, but I'm hungry."

They beached the canoe, and Alyssa climbed up the rock. Richard handed her the bag of groceries and the cushions from the boat.

"This bag is so heavy. What did you get, Richard?"

Richard was pulling the canoe up past the edge of the little beach. "Don't look," he said. "It's a surprise."

"You got a bottle of wine."

"You'll find out. Do you want to have lunch now?"

"Definitely. I want to see what you got us."

The rock was already warm from the sun. Alyssa set everything down and sat herself on the cooler part where the trees hung over and the rock was in shadow."

Richard climbed up and sat down beside her. He looked at his watch. "It's only ten-thirty—too early for lunch."

"Oh no, it's not. It's time for lunch when you're hungry, and I'm hungry now."

Little waves splashed against the beach. A rowboat went by with two grown-ups and a child in it. The woman waved at them, and they waved back.

Richard started to take things out of the bag one by one, setting them down on the rock.

Alyssa knew she wasn't supposed to watch, so she lay back with her head on one of the boat cushions. Little, bright sparkles of light came through the dark branches of the fir tree that hung over the rock.

She had almost closed her eyes when she was aware that Richard was putting everything back into the bag. "What are you doing?"

"Just stay there. There's something I need to do before we have lunch."

"What is it?"

"I'll be right back, and then I'll show you."

"Can't I come with you?"

"No. I'll be right back."

Alyssa closed her eyes. She could hear him walking off into the woods. She supposed he was going into the woods to find a place to go to the bathroom.

She must have dozed off, because the next thing she knew, he was climbing up the rock. He sat down beside her and started taking things out of the bag again. She watched through half-closed eyes. He was setting things down behind the bag so she couldn't see them.

He took out a dark green bottle. She sat up. "I saw that you bought some wine," she said. "I mean I could feel the bottle through the bag."

"You'll see." He took out his Swiss Army knife and used the corkscrew to pop out the cork. He poured some and held it out to her in a little cup. Watch out," he said. "It leaks."

She took the cup. "Richard, I don't believe it. It's made of birch bark. Where did it come from?" The little cup was dripping on her legs.

"I forgot to bring any dishes." He poured some for himself into another little cup. They touched the cups together. "Here's to our new life with each other," Richard said. "Better than ever." He took a drink. "Hurry. Before it all leaks away."

Alyssa put the cup up to her lips. Little bubbles burst against her skin. "Is this champagne? Where did you ever get champagne?" She was laughing.

"They had it in the grocery store back there in Morrisville. Who would have thought."

"Pour me some more, Richard. I want to make a toast too." When her cup was full, she held it dripping up to his. "To us," she said. "I love you, Richard. Where did you find the cups?"

"I told you I forgot to bring any dishes. I didn't even think about it until I took the champagne out of the grocery bag. Then I realized we couldn't do a proper toast without glasses."

"You made them?"

"I've always wanted to try it. It was quite easy."

"They're lovely. It doesn't matter if they leak a little. It just means you have to drink it all at once." She drank what was in her cup and set it down on the rock beside her. "Now for some food."

Richard unrolled a big square of birch bark and tried to lay it out on the rock. He had to crack it in a few places to keep it from rolling itself up into a scroll. "That's our plate," he said. He set out several packages of cheese, a box of crackers, and a little can, which he opened. "I got crackers instead of bread. I thought you liked this kind."

"And liver paté? I don't believe it. You got all my favorites." She could feel how pleased he was with the success of his party.

The sun had shifted so they weren't in shadow any more. Its warmth rained down on them.

"How nice it is to be alive on such a beautiful day," Alyssa said with a sigh of pleasure. "I'm full. And think how many millions of people in all of history have felt that way."

"Full?"

"No, silly. Glad to be alive for their brief time in this beautiful world."

"Not always brief."

"I know."

"And some people get a second chance."

"I know that too, Richard, and I'm grateful."

She lay back on the cushion and closed her eyes. The sun was so warm. She wouldn't have thought she could sleep so soundly on the hard surface of the rock, but she must have, because the sun was a lot farther to the west when she woke up. She looked around for Richard. He had picked up the remains of their lunch. Nothing was left on the rock but the cushion she was lying on.

She felt a twinge of panic. Had he left her? She looked over the side of the rock. The canoe was still there, just above the beach. And then she saw Richard through the trees, walking along by the water's edge.

She scrambled down and climbed over rocks along the shore to where he stood. "You could have woken me up, Richard. You've just been waiting for me."

"You looked so peaceful. I hated to wake you. And anyway, there was plenty to explore."

"I guess I'm not as strong as I thought I was."

"You just need time to get your strength back."

She took his hand, and without saying any more, they walked back to the canoe.

"Where's the pillow you were sleeping on? Is it still up on the rock?"

"No. I put it in the boat. There's nothing left up there."

"I guess we should head back then."

"I guess so, but I hate to leave."

"We'll be back—plenty of times."

"I know."

Richard ran the canoe up onto the beach at the parking area, and they unloaded everything. Alyssa backed the pickup down to where the canoe was lying on the shore. She got out of the truck and watched, but she didn't try to help, even though Richard was struggling alone. Richard was proud of his homemade canoe rack and the way it made him able to load his canoe by himself.

He turned the canoe over and raised the bow until it was resting against the back crossbar of the rack. Then he picked up the stern and rolled the canoe forward until the bow was over the cab of the truck.

Alyssa put the food and cushions and paddles into the back of the truck. She was trying not to notice that it was hard for Richard to raise the canoe all by himself. "I thought a park ranger might have come along and left a note about how we haven't paid," she said. "But I looked. There's nothing on the windshield or on the seat."

Richard finished strapping down the canoe. "I guess they didn't notice we were here. That's nice. It's like it used to be."

"Do you want to walk over to the dam? Maybe there's a ranger over there."

"Who's being a law-abiding citizen now? I thought you wanted to dodge them."

"I don't care one way or the other. It's only a few dollars. But I would like to see the waterfall again." She paused. "If you think we have time, that is."

They pulled the truck back into its parking place and followed the trail through the woods to the dam. There was no one there. They stood together watching the water as it poured over the dam.

Alyssa said, "There's so much water."

"We've had a lot of rain lately."

They were silent again. Alyssa thought how human beings were like those drops of water. There were so many, but they would all go over the dam sooner or later. She began to try to watch one drop as it traveled down the vertical face of the falls. Of course, she couldn't pick out an individual drop, but instead of focusing on the flood of water as it streamed, she tried to let her eyes follow a speck of water as it went over the edge and down and away along the river below.

After a few minutes she realized that the whole scene was changed. Instead of a loud and rushing mass of water, when she was able to focus that way, what she saw was peaceful. The world felt different because she was looking at it differently.

She tried to tell Richard about it on the way home, but she couldn't explain it so he could understand. Because of that, it became her private domain, an alternate universe that she could visit just by changing what she focused on. Alyssa thought of other places she could try to see in a new way—the road as it unspooled in front of their car, for instance. She could almost make the road new and different before her eyes, but it was difficult, and she was tired.

Then, not far from the bridge where they turned onto their road, a group of ravens rose into the air before the car and flew down the road in front of them, flapping and twisting in the air, their wings a black shimmer. Richard turned to go across the bridge, and the ravens flew off along the road. Maybe it was a good omen. Alyssa didn't say anything. She didn't want to sound superstitious. She hoped it was their raven family from the nest up the brook.

CHAPTER 22

It was still raining when Sam stepped out on the porch early Saturday morning. It had rained hard during the night, but now it was a light drizzle, just what they needed after the week of hot, dry weather. That dry spell had given him a chance to get the rest of his hay, but now that it was in the barn, Sam was glad to see the rain at last. He took a deep breath, filling his lungs with the clean smell of it.

He walked around the barn and up the hill to the gate. Even before he got there, he could see that Daisy wasn't waiting to come down to be milked like she always was.

He shut the gate behind him and started up the road, expecting every minute to see her coming down. By the time he got to the field near the top, he was really getting puzzled, although he wasn't worried yet. He walked out into the open of the field. The sheep were grazing peacefully. A few raised their heads to stare at him, but most of them didn't even look up. They were busy eating the freshly washed grass, which probably tasted better than it had all week.

He was out in the middle of the field before he saw her lying in a little hollow by the tree line. He walked toward her. "Daisy. Come on, girl. It's milkin time."

He could see her moving around a little, so at first he thought she was just reluctant to get up. But as he got closer, it was obvious that something was wrong.

She was lying on her side with her head downhill. Her belly bulged up more than normal. When he got near her, she threw her head back and looked at him out of the tops of her eyes with her eyeballs rolling a bloodshot white. Her body arched as she kicked at the ground. She had been lying there for quite some time. The grass in a circle around her was torn out and turned to mud. Milk had leaked out of her bag onto the ground, so the mud was a creamy, coffee color.

Sam tried to get her onto her feet. He even dropped down on her back with his knees to make her jump, but she was too far gone in pain and terror to notice. She rolled her great eyes around, looking at him pleadingly, and he hurried away, out of the field and down the hill to call the vet.

Bonnie was in the kitchen. When she saw him, she said, "Where's the milk at?"

"Daisy's down. I'm goin to have to call Doug. It looks pretty bad."

"Oh Sam. And I ain't goin to be here to give you a hand. I got to leave in just a few minutes. I've got Darlene's shift today. You want some breakfast before I go?"

"Naw. I ain't got time to eat anyhow. Is the coffeepot full? That's all I want."

"I'll put you on a fresh pot before I go."

By the time he hung up the phone, Bonnie had come back into the kitchen in her pink uniform. She started making the coffee.

"That's some good news anyhow. Doug ain't too far away, and he's comin right over."

"That's lucky, especially on a Saturday." She turned around. "Your coffee's in the pot. It'll be ready in a couple minutes. And I'll see you later."

Sam went out on the porch to watch her drive away. Colt was lying at the top of the steps. Sam could tell he knew the vet was coming.

No, maybe he didn't know who was coming, but he certainly knew they were waiting for someone.

When the coffee was ready, Sam got a cup and took it out to the porch. He sat down on the railing to drink it. He knew he ought to be doing the other morning chores. The pigs still had to be fed, even though there was no milk to give them. The chickens needed feed and water, and there would be eggs to pick up. But somehow he couldn't make himself go into the barn or around the back where he couldn't see the road.

He went inside to put his empty cup in the sink, and then he went back out to the porch. Colt looked up with interest as a little, dark blue car drove up Richard's driveway. It was early in the day for visitors, but maybe one or both of their girls were up for the weekend.

Sam stood up and sat down a few times. He wondered what was going on with Daisy. She might be better than she was when he saw her. He had seen that happen. It didn't happen very often, but it could. He didn't dare go up to see, because Doug might arrive and find no one around.

Sam got up and went into the kitchen. He thought he could clean up the dishes. But when he turned on the water, he began to wonder if Doug could be driving in, and he had to step out on the porch again to make sure he wasn't. He walked out to the road and looked down it, but no one was coming.

He was just going back inside again to start doing the dishes when he saw Doug's white truck turning in the drive. He saw by the clock that he had only been waiting for fifteen minutes. It felt like hours.

Doug stopped in front of the barn. He was just climbing down from the truck when Sam got over to him.

"She ain't in the barn. I wish she was. She's all the way up in the field at the top of the hill."

"Can I get up there in the truck?"

"Oh sure. There's a road all the way."

"Climb in then."

Sam told Colt to stay, and both he and Doug climbed in Doug's truck.

"Will I need the four-wheel drive?"

"I don't think so," Sam said. "It's a pretty good road. I made it myself."

They had to stop for Sam to open the gate, and then they went the rest of the way with no trouble. Doug stopped where the road turned in to the field.

Sam was just about to say, "What're we stoppin for?" when he realized it was because Doug didn't know where to go. "She was down there by the tree line. She was in a hollow down there." He didn't say that he hoped she had moved.

But she was right where Sam had left her, lying flat out on her side at the bottom of the field with her head stretched out on the downhill side.

Doug said, "Uh-oh."

Sam looked around at him. "What?"

"I'll tell you in a minute. I don't know anything yet, but it doesn't look good."

"I was hopin she might be better."

"Let's see. We don't know anything yet, do we?"

Doug parked the truck near the cow, and they both got out. Doug went around to the back of his truck and opened up a compartment and took out some stuff while Sam waited.

Then he walked over to Daisy's head and leaned down over her, while Sam watched. Daisy didn't move. She didn't appear to realize he was there. He pushed back her eyelid and looked at her eye. Then he raised her lip and looked at her teeth and gums. He grunted and straightened up and looked at Sam.

Sam wanted to ask what the grunt meant, but he managed to keep quiet.

Doug listened to her heart and said, "Hummm." Then he took her temperature. He looked at the thermometer and then at Sam. "I'm going to palpate her, but I'm pretty sure what I'll find. She's got a twisted intestine." He put on a long rubber glove and knelt down behind her so he could put his arm up inside. He stayed there for a few minutes, moving his arm around and grunting with the effort.

Then he stood and took off the long glove.

Sam noticed that it wasn't that dirty. "It's bad, ain't it? I had a pig get that one time. He didn't make it."

"Most of 'em don't."

"Couldn't it untwist itself?"

"It's not very likely. I could give her something, and we could wait a while and see." He looked at Sam. "What do you want to do?"

"If you give her somethin, I won't be able to use the meat."

"This is true."

"And it ain't likely to do any good."

"True."

"That would make her a total loss."

"Here," Doug said. "Let me show you something." He walked over to Daisy's head and lifted up her lip. "See that black line along her gum?"

Sam nodded as though he saw something, but he didn't see a thing, and he didn't really try either, because he knew it was all over. In his mind he had already moved on to how he was going to do it.

"The poison has gone all through her system already. I'm afraid the odds are against her. Her pulse is just about twice what it ought to be, and it's getting weaker by the minute."

Sam straightened. "Okay, Doug," he said. "I really appreciate you comin over so fast. I'll take over from here. We can use the meat if I bleed her out good, can't we?"

"Yes, if I don't give her anything. But do it soon. She's in a lot of pain."

"I'll get right on it. If you'll give me a ride down, I'll get my pickup and what I need."

"Glad to do it, Sam. I'm sorry it didn't have a better outcome."

"I knew when I saw her first thing this morning what was goin to happen."

They were riding down the hill again. Doug stopped at the gate. Sam opened it and went up to Doug's window.

"Aren't you going to close it when I get through?"

"Naw. I'll load my gear and go right back up. You said not to leave her too long."

"Right. Well, I'll see you then."

"Thanks, Doug." He was thinking about the bill. He'd have to pay it, even though the visit did no good, and it would be a lot of money. But he didn't say anything to Doug, because that's just the way it was. And he knew how that went. He'd had a few jobs himself where someone wanted him to put an animal out of its misery, when the person wouldn't get anything out of the deal, not even the meat. He charged for those jobs, just like the butchering ones. He would have lost money otherwise.

After Doug drove away, Sam went into the house to get bullets. Colt was lying on the porch at the top of the steps. When Sam came toward him, he raised his head and thumped his tail on the floor a few times.

When Sam came out again, he said, "Come on, boy. You can go this time."

Colt stood up slowly and stretched to show he didn't care all that much one way or the other. Sam knew that meant Colt's feelings had been hurt because he didn't get to go before.

He followed Sam to the truck, and Sam opened the door and told Colt to get in the cab. Then he loaded the tripod, the come-along, and the gut barrels in the back. He opened the big doors to the basement and got his knives and his meat saw. Finally he was ready to go back to the field.

He climbed in the cab and drove through the gate, but this time he went back and closed it. He didn't know how long he was going to be up there, and he thought the gunshot might spook the sheep. They might just head for the barn in a panic.

When he drove into the field, only a few of the sheep even looked up. He drove across, hoping that Daisy would be better, and knowing his hope was impossible. If she had raised her head when he drove up, it would have been something. But no. In fact, he could see that she was worse. She was laid out so flat and motionless that for a second he thought she might already be dead. She was probably exhausted by the pain and the struggle against it.

He got out of the truck. Colt looked at him with a question in his eyes. "Stay, boy," he said. He took his gun out of the rack and loaded it and walked over to the cow.

Her eyes were open and staring. She seemed not to know he was there. He was glad she wasn't pleading with her eyes any more, begging him to help her, when there was nothing anyone could do.

He stood before her, pointing his rifle at her forehead. Because her head was on the ground, the angles weren't that good. Still, he managed to hit her between the eyes on a diagonal. It was good enough. She gave a jerk and didn't move again.

"Sorry, Daisy," he said. "I hope you know I didn't want to. I wish it hadn't turned out like this." He went back to the truck and ejected the second bullet and put the gun away. He got his knife and slit her throat, so she could bleed out.

While he was waiting for that, he walked over to check on the watering system he had made for the pasture by diverting a small part of the stream, so it would flow through a tub he had set into the ground to make a drinking pool.

He looked back once and saw Colt sitting up straight, watching him out the window. He knew Colt wanted to come with him, but it might scare the sheep. Sam said, "Stay, boy," and walked on to check the water. It was running fine, even though the brook was way down since the last dry spell. That rain last night hadn't helped much.

On the way back, still killing time, he stopped long enough to get a good count on the sheep. Then he walked back to Daisy's body. He was reluctant to begin, but the weather was warm, and he knew he shouldn't delay.

He set up the tripod and come-along and hoisted the carcass up by one leg so he could skin it. Then he cut off the head and the lower legs and hooves. With every step, it became less Daisy and more a piece of meat he needed to work on. When he had to run the saw to cut off the head and legs and later to separate the meat into two sides, the sheep got frightened by the noise and went into a huddle on the far side of the field.

He loaded all the offal, the guts and head and legs, into his waste barrels and pushed them forward in the truck bed until they were right behind the cab. Then he backed the truck up until he could swing each side into the bed. He had to back up again to get them all the way in. He loaded the bucket of organ meat and his saw and the knives and, last of all, the tripod, and then he was ready to go.

There was nothing left of Daisy except a patch of ground where the grass was all dug up and the dirt was wet with blood. Sam was just about to climb in the truck when he thought about the smell of meat and blood on that patch of ground. It could bring predators right in among the sheep. He wondered what to do for a minute, and then he thought about a bag of chemical fertilizer he had in the barn. That bad smell might cover the smell of blood. Anyway, it would help the grass to come back. He decided to bring the bag up and spread it when he came up later to dump the gut barrels. Satisfied with that idea, he drove down the hill with Colt sitting beside him and what was left of Daisy in the back.

He was just putting the truck in reverse so he could back up to the basement entryway, when he happened to look over at the tree line between his place and Richard's. A woman and a child came out of the trees and started walking across the yard toward him. It was Sonia and her little boy, the one who came over to see the animals about a month ago.

Sam didn't move. Maybe they wouldn't notice him sitting there in his truck. They got almost to the door of the barn, and he thought they would go in. But just then, Sonia looked up and saw him. She took the child's hand, and they walked over to Sam's truck.

Sam didn't know whether to stay where he was in the cab so they couldn't see how dirty and bloody his clothes were. Still, if he stayed where he was, they might look in the back and see the sides of bloody meat. But he didn't have time to choose before they were there, looking at him through the window.

"Hello, Sam. How are you?"

"I can't complain," he said, feeling very dirty and uncomfortable.

There was a short silence, and then she said, "What do you think the weather's going to do? We were hoping for a sunny day."

"Tomorrow might be fine."

"We have to go back to Connecticut tomorrow."

"Well, maybe this afternoon...." He looked at the sky. Sometimes it looked as though it might clear, but then the clouds would roll back in again. He didn't want to say so, but they needed the rain. Flatlanders always thought they deserved sunshine on the weekends, no matter how parched things were. "How's your mother comin along?"

"She's getting her strength back."

"That's good news."

"They think they caught it early enough, before it had a chance to spread. They think they were able to get all of it. She's happy about that, of course."

Sam didn't know what to say next. He wanted to move the conversation along so he could get on with his work. He had a lot to do. He had to get the meat in the cooler right away, and he hadn't even done the morning chores.

There was silence again. Then Sonia said, "I was wondering if it would be all right if we went in your barn to see the animals. Jack had such a good time before."

"Sure," Sam said. "Go ahead. There's not much in there right now. The sheep are all out on pasture." He didn't want to discourage them because he wanted to get away. "The pigs are inside. But be careful. They get excited." He didn't say they hadn't been fed, and they would go crazy when they saw someone coming in. He was starting to feel trapped. He definitely didn't feel like sitting around making small talk.

Sonia's little boy had been playing in the tall grass up the hill near the barn, but he came back to stand by her side. He grabbed her hand and pulled on it while she talked. After a minute she looked down at him. "Stop it, Jack."

He pulled her down a little so he could say something to her that Sam couldn't hear.

She said, "Oh," and then, "Well, just be quiet a minute, and we'll go." When she straightened up, Sam could see by her eyes that the little boy had told her about the dead cow in the back of his truck.

Sam waited to see what she would say. He had no reason to feel secretive and ashamed. It was a normal part of life, as well as the way he made his living. There was no reason to feel uncomfortable, and yet he did.

Sonia only said, "Thank you. We'll go see your pigs then. Come on, Jack." She took his hand, and they walked off. The little boy said something, and she jerked his arm impatiently.

After they disappeared into the barn, Sam backed the truck up into the entryway, so he could unload the sides of beef. It was a quick, one-man job because of the track he had built into the ceiling. He could move the big slabs of beef right into the cooler just by pushing them along.

He unloaded the bucket of organ meat and went upstairs to wash his face and hands and grab a clean shirt. When he came out, he saw that Colt was still sitting in the cab of the truck. He let him out, and they went into the barn together.

As soon as he stepped inside, the pigs spotted him. They threw themselves against the fence, snorting and snapping at the air. He got a bucket of grain and climbed in the pen, with them jostling him and each other. They tried to stand on the trough while he picked it up to turn it over. They had dumped their water tub in their excitement. Finally, he got food and water before them, and things got a little quieter, and he had a chance to look around.

There was no sign of Sonia and Jack. Sam supposed he would find them in the chicken house. When he stepped out the back door, he was pleased to see that they had been sensible enough to close the door of the chicken house behind them. But when he went in himself, he saw that they weren't there either. They must have slipped out of the barn to go back to Richard's when he was unloading the meat.

That was good. He still had to dump the gut barrels and do whatever he could to clean up the patch of ground in the sheep pasture. He was glad he didn't have to stand and smile while Jack chased his chickens around their house.

CHAPTER 23

Monika started watching at eight-thirty, even though Sonia wasn't supposed to pick her up until nine. She was dressed and ready, so she took her coffee and went out to the front porch and sat down, watching the street.

The summer morning was rich with the scent of cut grass and flowers. There was a sense of stillness. Everything was hushed, wrapped in a soft blanket of fog. When it burned off later, the day would turn hot and sunny.

A car came along, its tires hissing on the damp pavement. Monika thought it was too early for it to be Sonia, but the car turned in at her driveway.

She went into the house, carrying her empty coffee cup. She locked the front door, put the cup in the sink, picked up her pocketbook, and went out the back door. She was just locking it when Sonia came up the steps.

"I knew you'd be ready, Nana."

"This is nice, Sonia. You're even earlier than we planned."

"I thought we might want a little extra time because of the fog."

They were walking to the car now. "Thank you, dear. You were already leaving extra time to humor me."

"It suits me too, Nana. I don't want to be trying to find the doctor's office at the last minute. I mean, I don't know downtown Hartford all that well."

They got into the car. Monika was glad Sonia didn't seem to notice that she fumbled with the back door before she realized her mistake and went to the front. She said, "Where's Jack? I thought he was going with us."

"I took him to the babysitter. I wanted to be able to hear what the doctor has to say."

"Oh."

"Jack would have made it hard to go into the doctor's office when he examines you, and I'd like to be there, if you don't mind."

"No, of course not."

"Sometimes two heads can be better than one. I hope that's okay."

"Of course."

"Jack has fun at the babysitter's, and this is a nice chance for us to talk."

They drove through town. The light was soft and pearly because of the fog, but it was getting stronger and brighter by the minute.

Sonia said, "I thought we'd go up by the Merritt. It will be beautiful along there this morning."

"I'd like that. We have plenty of time, don't we?"

After a little while, Monika began to notice the trees along the road, and she knew they were on the Merritt Parkway, a road she had always loved for its peaceful scenery. It was strange the way she was able to see better when she was riding in a car—not enough to drive, of course, but enough to know where she was most of the time. The odd thing was that the less she paid attention, the more she could see. When she really needed to be able to see something was when she was most unable to. She was always testing herself to see how bad it was, how little she could see.

"When did you go to Dr. Bronson, Nana? I didn't drive you."

"I think it was about two weeks ago."

"I didn't even know you were having trouble with your eyes."

"That's why I went to Dr. Bronson. I thought I needed new glasses. I thought if he changed my glasses, my eyes would be fine again. It was a big surprise to me when he wanted to send me to the specialist in Hartford."

"What did he tell you was wrong?"

"He didn't say much. He even said he didn't want to worry me until this Dr. Lali in Hartford had a chance to look at my eyes."

"Maybe if I had been with you, I could have asked him some questions."

"It wouldn't have made any difference. He would still have wanted me to go to the specialist. I'm trying to get used to the idea that new glasses might not be the answer."

"Has it been getting worse?"

Monika had to think for a minute to decide how much she wanted Sonia to know. She had been very successful at keeping the secret of her deteriorating eyes. It was hard to let go of it. She sighed. "Yes, I guess it has gotten worse, a little bit, anyway." She looked around at Sonia.

She couldn't see her clearly, but just then, with her dark curls, she looked a lot like Alyssa. Sonia's eyes were on the road, and she didn't look around.

After a few minutes of silence, she said, "How long have you been worrying about your eyes?"

"I don't know. I guess it was about the time we all started worrying about your mother. That was back in the spring. Maybe it was in April that I first started noticing something."

"So long ago as that?"

"I think so."

"And you didn't say anything to anybody?"

"If I had told anyone, it would probably have been you. Don't forget how worried we all were about your mother's operation. I didn't want to complain about my own troubles. They seemed so insignificant."

"But Nana...."

"When the operation was over, and it looked like Alyssa was going to be okay, I made an appointment with Dr. Bronson. I thought it would be simple, but nothing is ever as simple as you think it will be." She sighed again.

"Nana, tell me something. Did you…" she spoke softly and without looking around. "Did you drive yourself there?"

"Of course not," Monika said with a quick laugh. "I wouldn't do that. I took a cab."

"I would have been glad to drive you."

"I know, dear. But, you see, I thought I could get a prescription for some new glasses and be right back where I was, and no one would need to know about it."

"But what difference would that have made?"

"I don't know." Monika looked out the window at the peaceful trees flowing past. "It seemed like everyone had more important things to think about. I didn't want everyone to say I shouldn't drive…I wasn't driving anyway." She looked out the window. She couldn't tell how far along the Merritt they were. "I didn't want to get rid of my car, because I thought that with new glasses, I might be able to drive again, and I was afraid everyone would say I shouldn't."

It was hard to think what her reasons had been. There was just that impulse, strong but irrational, to guard the fact that she had changed, that she was losing ground. "I guess I didn't want you all to feel sorry for me. Maybe you would think I couldn't take care of myself any more. Maybe you would think I couldn't live in my house any longer."

"Oh Nana. I'm sorry. I wish we could have had a conversation about it."

"Maybe. But you know what I would have said. Would you have listened? Wouldn't you all have said that I was getting old, that I didn't know what was good for me any more?"

"I hope not. I hope we would have listened."

Just then there was a rushing noise, and the light got dim. At first Monika felt frightened, but it was the tunnel. She hadn't seen it coming.

The noise stopped, and the light came back. Monika said, "I guess I did to you what I was afraid you would do to me."

"What do you mean?"

"Because I didn't tell you what was going on with my eyes, I prevented you from having an opinion about it. Don't you see how that was a way of not listening to you?"

Sonia laughed. "I do see."

"I think I can do better than that."

"Me too. I'm going to try." They rode on in a warm silence for a few minutes, and then Sonia said, "Was that the reason you didn't come with us last weekend when we went up to Vermont?"

"I don't know."

"Because you didn't want us to notice how much trouble you were having with your eyes?"

"I guess so." She thought for a minute. Was that really the reason she didn't want to see Alyssa? "No," she said. "That wasn't it. I was afraid. That's what it was."

"Afraid? What of?"

"This is hard to talk about, Sonia. I was afraid that I would see that she wasn't all right, and I didn't know if I could handle it. It sounds so stupid when we are talking about the trouble I'm having seeing anything. But that's what it was. I hadn't even said it to myself until you asked me. I wanted you girls to see her first and come home and tell me it was safe to look." After a few more minutes, she went on, "I'm embarrassed to tell you that. It's so cowardly."

Sonia reached out across the seat for her hand. "You didn't need to be afraid to see her, you know. She really looked good. She'll be well soon. I'm sure of it."

"Thank you, Sonia." After a little while, she said, "You wouldn't say that if you didn't truly believe it, just to make me feel better. You wouldn't do that, would you?"

"Of course not. I always tell you the truth." There was a short silence, and then she said, "I try to, anyway."

"Thank you, dear. I should have come with you."

"We'll go up again soon. It'll be nice for you to see that she's well again."

"It'll be even better after I've had my eyes taken care of."

"Saturday morning Jack wanted to see the animals, so we walked over to the Martels'. Sam was there, sitting in his truck. I went up close to ask if we could go in the barn. He was covered with blood, and the back of his truck was full of great chunks of meat. It must have been some poor animal that he had killed and chopped up. Jack saw it and got quite upset."

"How horrible."

"I don't know what he was doing, but he looked like a murderer."

"What did your dad say about it?"

"I didn't get a chance to ask him. I didn't want to say anything in front of Jack. I knew he'd listen."

"Sam Martel butchers animals for people sometimes. I know that."

"I don't think that could have been what he was doing. There was so much blood. It was horrible whatever it was."

The highway had changed a lot in the last little while. Monika thought they must have gotten to the end of the Merritt, and that meant they were getting close to Hartford.

"What time is it, Sonia?"

"Oh, we're fine, Nana. It's only a few minutes after ten, and we're just coming in to Hartford. We have plenty of time to get lost."

"I'm not going to be able to help you much with my eyes the way they are."

"That's all right. I don't think I'll need help. I have the paper of directions the doctor's office sent you. It doesn't look that complicated."

"I hope not."

"Just sit back and enjoy the ride, Nana. I'll get us there."

So that's what Monika tried to do. It was hard to feel relaxed. Their progress after they got off the highway and onto the smaller city streets was jerky, as Sonia tried to drive and read the street signs at the same time. Monika tried hard to keep her anxiety from showing. She willed herself not to shift restlessly in her seat. Anything she did would make Sonia's job more difficult. The more she tried to see out the window, the less she could actually see. They seemed to be wandering around on tree-lined streets. Maybe they would never find it.

The car stopped. Monika looked around at Sonia, but before she could even ask, Sonia said, "We're here. What shall we do? We have half an hour before your appointment, but I haven't seen any coffee shops or restaurants for a while, and I'm not sure how to get back to the ones I did see."

"That's all right. Now that we're here, maybe we ought to stay, or I should anyway." She reached across the seat and patted Sonia on the shoulder. "You could go and find a place to get some coffee, and I could wait in the doctor's office. Then it wouldn't matter how long it took."

"That's all right. I think I'd like to stay with you. We can find a place to get lunch afterwards."

"Okay, dear." Monika opened the door of the car and swung her legs out. They had been in one position for more than an hour. She straightened each one slowly and painfully. The fog was gone, and the sun was beating down. Her skirt stuck to her legs.

By this time Sonia had come around the car and was standing by Monica's open door. Monika said, "I wish I was wearing stockings. I can't remember why I decided not to." She began to pull herself up to standing, holding on to the open door.

"By the time we start home, it will be blazing hot. You'll be glad for bare legs then." She reached down to help pull Monika to her feet.

"I don't need help. Just give me a minute to get my knees working again." Then after balancing herself on top of her legs, she said, "There. I'm okay now. My joints get stiff, but they loosen up when I move."

"That's the spirit, Nana."

Monika took a few slow, wooden steps, and Sonia grabbed her arm.

"I don't need you to support me, Sonia. I can do it. Walk a few steps in front of me, so I can see where to go."

So Sonia did, and they went slowly up the sidewalk to the doctor's door. There were a few steps, but Monika could manage them by supporting herself on the railing.

They walked over to the receptionist's desk in the waiting room with Sonia a few steps ahead. Monika's legs were loosening up now, so she could walk normally and not shuffle along like an old person. The room was full of light. Monika thought she could see several people sitting on chairs, dark silhouettes against the bright glass of the big windows.

Sonia stood aside, and Monika told the receptionist her name and that her appointment wasn't until eleven o'clock. The receptionist handed her a clipboard with a paper on it. Sonia guided her to a seat with her back to the bright wall of glass. She sat there with the clipboard on her lap, dreading the struggle ahead. Sonia was looking at her little telephone and laughing.

Finally, Monika began to fill out the questionnaire. Some of it she could almost see, and some she could guess at. Her writing was slow and clumsy, even though writing was easier than reading.

After a few minutes, Sonia turned off her phone and said, "Why don't I do that for you, Nana? I can ask you anything I don't know."

Monika handed her the clipboard. "Yes, please. I wasn't doing a very good job. You can do it much neater." She was trying to stop being secretive about how little she could see, but the honesty part was slow in coming.

There were two people sitting on the other side of the room. They were blurry, black shapes with the light from the windows behind them, so Monika wasn't sure whether they were men or women, but she knew they were together, because sometimes they leaned toward each other, whispering. She thought they were probably talking about her, about how she wasn't even able to fill out her own forms.

Sonia was still writing. Monika could feel her arm moving as she wrote. She wished she would hurry up. It was embarrassing. Finally, Sonia stood up and took the clipboard back to the receptionist. When she came back, she said, "It's almost eleven. It shouldn't be much longer now."

"That's good. Thank you for filling out that thing. You knew all the answers. You didn't have to ask me anything."

"They didn't want much information. Maybe they got most of it from Dr. Bronson." There was a silence, and then she said, "I didn't realize how bad your eyes were. I guess I thought you could see well enough to read. I'm so sorry."

"I've been having trouble reading for a while now."

"How can you play cards with your friends?"

"I can't. I haven't for a while."

"But you loved to play."

"It wasn't much fun any more. I made mistakes all the time. It got quite uncomfortable." She should have known that little by little it would all come out. She sighed. She might as well tell it. "I told them I didn't want to play over the summer, and that I would probably start up again when fall came. That should give me enough time to straighten out my eye problems, don't you think?"

"I guess so. Did you tell them you were having trouble with your eyesight?"

"No, of course not."

"Not even Mabel?"

"I didn't want any of them to feel sorry for me, not even Mabel. Everyone has their own problems, and nobody can do anything about my eyes but an eye doctor. When I get some new glasses, I think I'll be all right."

"I wish you had someone to talk to. Maybe one of the women in your card group has had the same trouble."

"I don't think so. No one else makes embarrassing mistakes."

"I would have wanted some sympathy from my friends."

"I didn't want to be a burden to anybody. Everyone has problems to deal with. I wouldn't want any of my friends to think they had to help me on top of everything else. When you get old, I think you have a different kind of friendship. Remember what it was like when you were a teenager—you and your best friend told each other everything? You were so close. You thought it would be like that your whole life."

Sonia said, "My friend Karen and I were like that." Just then the nurse appeared in the doorway and called Monika's name. Sonia jumped up and reached out her hand to help.

Monika took it and rose slowly until she felt balanced on top of her legs. She held tight to Sonia's arm to keep her balance. She could feel the people across the room watching her.

They walked down a long hallway, following the gleaming white of the nurse's uniform. Monika wanted to tell Sonia how friendships change when you get older, but she had to concentrate on keeping up.

The nurse stopped and stood beside a doorway to a dim room, motioning them to enter. She sat Monika in a complicated mechanical chair in the middle of the room, and then she left them.

It was dark. Monika said, "Sonia, are you there?"

"Right here, Nana. There's a chair in the corner. Can you see me?"

"No, but stay there. I don't want to be alone."

"I won't leave you. I promise."

They were quiet then, waiting. There was a man's voice out in the hall.

After a few minutes, Sonia said, "Are you all right, Nana?"

"I wish he'd come."

"Me too."

"I'm scared," Monika said. "What's he going to say?"

"It'll be easier when we know what's wrong."

"I hope so."

They were quiet again. They could hear the man's voice, louder now, right outside their room.

He came in. "Good morning, ladies. What a beautiful day, is it not?" He held out his hand to Monika. It was hard to see in the dimness. "My name is Vijay Lali. I am your doctor."

Monika guessed from his accent that he must be from India. He was slight, and he wore glasses. Monika could see a flash of light from the lenses. He wrote on a clipboard he was carrying. How could he manage to write in the dark? That was something Monika would like to learn how to do. But how could she practice, when she couldn't see the results?

"Okay," he said, putting down the clipboard. "Let's see what we can see." He pulled down a big apparatus in front of her face, the thing they always made her look through when she needed new glasses. He asked her to read the letters as he flashed them on the wall. She concentrated as hard as she could, trying to shift her eyes around for a better look, although somehow she knew she wasn't supposed to do that. She couldn't tell how well she was doing. Sometimes he said, "Fine, now try these." Sometimes he said, "Well, what about these then?" One statement seemed more positive, but she couldn't be sure.

After she read, or didn't read, the letters, he said he would see her later and left the room. A nurse came and put drops in her eyes and led them into another waiting room, this time a dimly lit room with no windows. They were the only ones there.

When the nurse was gone, Monika said, "How bad does he think my eyes are? That thing he put in front of my face is what helps them figure out what to give you for new glasses. He clicks those lenses around until he gets the right ones."

"I guess so."

"But, Sonia, it couldn't be too bad if he's going to give me new glasses. That's what I've been saying I needed all along."

Sonia didn't say anything.

"I did okay reading the letters, didn't I?"

"You missed some of them."

"I know that. I had to guess sometimes, but I think I got a lot of them right."

Sonia said nothing. Monika wanted to ask her how many mistakes she made, but she didn't quite dare. If she couldn't see the letters, even with the lens machine, did that mean something else was wrong, maybe even something that couldn't be fixed?

After a while Monika said, "I'm scared of losing my independence."

"Don't worry, Nana. We'll take care of you."

"But I don't want that. Can't you see? After your grandpa died, I had to fight so hard to be able to take care of myself. I'm not going to give that up. I've worked too hard for it. It's just awful to get old."

"Don't, Nana. It's too soon to fret like this. It'll be all right. That's why you came all the way to see this doctor."

"I'll try not to think about it until I hear what he says," she said. But she couldn't help it. They sat there in the dim room with Monika willing herself to appear calm, while inside her thoughts were jumping all over the place. She could keep her body still, but not her mind.

Finally the nurse came in. She looked at Monika's eyes and said they were good. She led them into another dim little room.

The doctor came in and looked into one of her eyes with a little light, moving it around to get different views. He said, "Ummhmmm, now the other one." Then he went back to the first. Monika could feel her heart beating fast.

He stepped back and wrote something down. Then he said, "Okay, dear lady. I can confirm what your Dr. Bronson diagnosed. You definitely have macular degeneration."

Monika said, "Oh." She felt as though someone had hit her. She realized that until then she had believed in the magic of new glasses. Sonia and the doctor were talking, but Monika could only hear in snatches because she was so full of her anxious thoughts. She would never see the bright world again. She would be a blind person—she was a blind person. She heard them talking about treatments and schedules, and she couldn't even concentrate enough to know what they were talking about. She just felt miserable. It was over. She would be something someone had to take care of from now on. Maybe she would have to go to a nursing home and slump in a wheelchair in the hallway all day with her mouth open and drooling.

Sonia stood up and thanked the doctor. He shook hands with both of them and left the room.

Monika had been too busy with her own unhappy thoughts to listen to their conversation. All she knew was that she was going to live in darkness forever. "What's happening, Sonia?" she asked in a low voice, as Sonia took her arm and tried to get her on her feet.

"Let's go. We can go now. I'll tell you all about it in the car."

Outside the sun was blazing. It was painfully bright, even under the trees. Monika's legs were weak from too much sitting. She shuffled down the sidewalk. It seemed like ages before they got to the car. "I'm sorry I'm so slow. I seem to be stiffer than ever."

"Take your time, Nana. We'll get there."

Finally, Monika could flop down onto her seat. Sonia got in and started the car.

"Put your seatbelt on, Nana."

"Oh, I forgot." She was trying to position the paper glasses over her regular ones. "It's so bright out. It hurts my eyes."

"That's because of the drops. It takes a while for them to wear off. The doctor said to keep those dark glasses on for at least an hour."

They were driving through Hartford now. "What's the difference? My eyes are no good any more," Monika said bitterly.

"Don't be discouraged. The doctor said lots of hopeful things."

"He said I had macular degeneration."

"But it isn't the way it used to be. He said that too. It's different now. I'll tell you everything he said. First though, are you hungry? Because we are just about to come to the highway going out of Hartford, and then it will get harder to find a place to stop. What do you want to do?"

"I don't care. Stop if you want to, but don't stop on my account. I'm not hungry."

"Okay. I'll keep going then."

The car was hot, and the light was painfully bright. Monika said, "All this time I thought everything was going to get better. I thought my vision would come back, and I could do the things I loved to do, like playing cards with my friends. I wish I hadn't made you bring me all this way just to hear that that wasn't so."

"But you heard what he said, didn't you?"

"I don't know what I heard. I couldn't really listen when he was talking to you. But I know what happens when you get macular degeneration. There's nothing they can do. I think it was what I was afraid of. Maybe I always knew. It's no use thinking about it."

"Oh Nana, don't. It really isn't as bad as you think. I wish you had heard what he said. They have something new now. It's a shot they give you. It always stops it, and sometimes it even makes it a little better. I told him you would definitely want it, and you know what?"

She turned to look at Monika with a smile of triumph that Monika could plainly see even with her eyes the way they were, even through the dark glasses. "What?" Monika said, meaning what false hope are you going to throw at me now?

"He has an office in Stamford, so we won't use up a whole day when I take you to get the shots, because, of course, I will take you."

"Then why did I have to go all the way up to Hartford today?" Monika said, still feeling suspicious.

"They always do the first appointment in Hartford. That's what he said when I asked that very question. That's their main office. Maybe they have more machines there or something. He didn't say why." She paused for a minute and then went on. "But he did say how important it was to get the shots as soon as possible. You can see that."

"I guess so, if they really stop it from getting worse. I guess that's important." She turned her head toward the bright window beside her. Bitterness rose up like a sour taste in her mouth. "Not that I want my eyes to stay the way they are now."

"But you don't want them to get worse, do you?"

"No, that's true. I don't want them to get worse."

Then they were both quiet. Monika could see enough to see that Sonia wasn't taking the Merritt this time, but she didn't say anything. Maybe Sonia thought the highway would be faster.

After a long silence, Monika said, "Sonia, promise you won't tell your mother about all this."

"But...."

"We don't want to worry her. She has enough to worry about now without this too."

"I won't if you ask me not to. I mean, I have to do what you ask me to do, of course, but we were just saying on the way up to Hartford that it's much better not to have all these secrets."

"I know. But this is different. Your mother would feel she had to do something to take care of me, and I don't want her to feel that way."

"She doesn't need to. I'm going to help you, and we could tell her that."

"I think she would. She's the only child I have...now."

"She told you about her cancer operation. She didn't have to. Do you wish she had kept that a secret? She might have thought you would feel you had to help her."

"I'm so glad she told me. I think I would have worried even more if I thought something might be going on, and I didn't know what it was."

"That's what I was saying on the ride up."

"I guess…but I still…let me think about it for a few minutes, because what would we tell her anyhow?"

"The first thing we'd say is that she doesn't need to worry because it's fine. You're going to get the shots, and things will be different, and we'll see how your eyes are then. I mean, after the shots."

"She's still going to worry."

"Yes, that's true. She'll worry a little."

"If we didn't tell her, she wouldn't worry at all." Sonia opened her mouth to say something, so Monika went on quickly. "I'm just saying. I'm glad she told me about the cancer, so I get your point."

"Look, Nana. I can't tell you what you ought to do. If you want to keep this secret, I won't tell Mom, or Alix, or anyone, except Brian, and I can't help that because I told him I was taking you to the eye doctor this morning. But I won't tell him any more if you tell me not to. I just want to say that I don't think you can have a close relationship with someone if you keep important things secret from them. I know I feel much closer to you since I found out about your eye trouble. Because I think people always can sense when something's not right. And Mom did tell you, and she didn't have to."

"Now I don't know what to do."

"I'm not going to say any more. You have to decide what you want to do about this."

"I thought I knew. I thought it was simple, but you've mixed me up."

"Good. You just tell me if it's all right to tell people, and until you do, I won't say anything to anybody."

They drove into Stamford not long after that. They hadn't stopped anywhere for lunch. Monika suggested stopping in Stamford, but she just said it to be polite. She really wanted to go home, and Sonia knew. Sonia said she thought she would go along and pick up Jack.

When Monika got out of the car, she leaned back in to look at

Sonia. She thanked her for everything, and she meant it most sincerely. Sonia was so good to her. Then she said, "I need to be the one to tell her, and I'll do it. I promise. I'm going to think it out and then call her up, and I'll let you know what she says."

Sonia drove away. Monika was hungry, but she was tired too. She thought she would lie down for a few minutes to think about what she was going to say when she called Alyssa. The next thing she knew it was several hours later, and she was very hungry. And she had forgotten to think about what she was going to say when she called Alyssa.

CHAPTER 24

Alyssa heard the glass door sliding open, and then, after a pause—he must have expected to see her in the kitchen—she heard him say, "Alyssa?"

"I'm up here, Richard."

"Where? I thought you were coming in to start the soup. Are you feeling okay?"

"I'm fine. I was just checking my e-mail." She got up from the couch and leaned over the railing of the balcony so she was looking down at him.

He saw her. "Do you want me to start the soup?"

"No. I'll be right down. I'll just shut the computer off. I have something to tell you."

"Okay. I hope it's not bad."

She put the computer on sleep and clattered down the iron staircase into the kitchen. "No, it's great, or at least *I* think it is. I hope you will too."

"Try me."

"All right." She walked past him, up the steps to the refrigerator to take out the big pot of soup. "I got an e-mail from Margie this morning."

"From who?"

"Oh Richard, you know. Margie Granton. That's who she used to be years ago. She was in the class behind me. You didn't know her. She was only a freshman when you were a senior."

Richard had come up the steps and was leaning on the counter, watching as she spooned the cold soup into a saucepan.

"How hungry are you?" she asked.

"Quite. But that looks like enough. Is it chicken soup?"

"Yes. I made it the other day. But I can't wait to tell you what Margie said."

"How come I don't know anything about her?"

"Because I don't either. I mean, I completely lost touch with her after we got married. But last winter, when we got the high speed internet hookup, I was fooling around on Facebook, and I found her."

She put the saucepan on the stove, turned on the gas, and adjusted the flame. "Facebook is amazing, isn't it? I sent out a friend request, and I heard from her in half an hour. She lives in Colorado now. She has a couple of children, but they're grown up."

"Well, that's nice."

Alyssa gave him a look to see if he was being sarcastic, but she couldn't tell. She stirred the soup. "We e-mailed back and forth a bit, and after a while there didn't seem to be much more to say. Then I got my diagnosis, and I didn't want to tell her about it, so I stopped writing. A couple of weeks ago, I was thinking about her and feeling guilty, so I e-mailed her."

Richard went to the sink to wash his hands. He said, "Go on. I'm listening."

She hated it when people washed their hands in the kitchen sink. She could feel her shoulders getting tight, but she didn't say anything. She told herself she must be almost back to normal if things like that were bothering her again. She was still trying to remember not to take petty stuff seriously, not any more, not the way she used to. "When

I e-mailed Margie, I told her about the cancer, and the operation, and how it seemed like it was going to be okay, although it's kind of soon to tell, and I still have to have some tests, and some radiation, or chemo, and maybe even both."

The soup was bubbling. Alyssa gave it another stir and turned off the fire under the pot. "There," she said. "Let's have some bread and cheese too."

They put everything on the table and sat down across from each other. Richard said, "The soup is good."

"Thank you. It's nice to feel like cooking again."

"Nice for me too. So I keep trying to picture this Margie person. What does she look like?"

"I don't know about now. She used to be okay looking. She had long brown hair and a really pretty smile. She had the kind of figure that's bigger on the bottom than on the top. You said you thought she looked like someone who would get fat when she got old, but you might have said it just so I wouldn't think you liked the way she looked." She watched his face as she said that last bit, but he was spooning up a mouthful of soup, and he didn't look up.

There was a pause, and then, "I said that?"

"Yes, you did. I remembered because I was afraid you might think the same thing about me."

"I don't remember her at all."

"I'll see if I have an old picture of her. I don't know what she looks like now. Maybe she *is* fat."

"So she e-mailed you?"

"That's just what I wanted to tell you about. She didn't answer, and I thought she wasn't going to get in touch with me any more. You know how some people don't want to have anything to do with someone who's sick or dying? How they act like it might be catching or something? How they think if you had been smarter or more careful, you wouldn't have gotten sick? I thought she might be like that. When I didn't hear from her, I thought I probably wasn't going to."

Richard stood up. "I'm going to get some more soup. Shall I fill you up too?"

"No thanks. I've got plenty." When he sat down again, she said, "That's why I was so surprised when I checked my e-mail a little while ago. There was an e-mail from her. She said how glad she was that I was going to be all right, and she invited me to visit her on Cape Cod."

"I thought she lived in Colorado."

"She does, but they have this house in North Truro that they rent in the summer. I mean, they own it and rent it to other people. There's a week between their tenants, and she and Darren—that's her husband—were going to spend the week getting ready for the next renters, but now he can't come, so she invited me instead."

"Well, that's nice. It's awfully short notice. She invited you to come as her cleaning lady."

"No, Richard. That's not fair." She could see by the slight upturn at the corners of his mouth that he was teasing her. "She says there isn't much to do, and I don't need to help if I don't feel like it. And she just found out that Darren couldn't come."

"What about your mom?"

"What about her?"

"I thought you might want to go down to visit her."

"Because of her eyes, you mean? She says she's fine. She says she doesn't need me to do anything, that the only thing that's different is that she has to have these shots in her eyes." She shuddered. "Doesn't it sound gruesome? I don't even *want* to be there for that, and Sonia is going to take her, so that's okay."

"Maybe she would like some comforting. It must be an awful thing to lose your sight."

"She might think I was spying on her, trying to see if she is too old to live on her own. No, I think I ought to wait for a while, and anyway, Richard, I want to do this. I've been thinking while we were having lunch about how much I want to see the ocean again. You don't mind if I go, do you?"

"Of course not, if it's not too hard for you. Do you want me to come with you to do the driving?"

"Oh no. That would be much too much. And anyway, I'm kind

of looking forward to the challenge. I've been thinking about that too—how it will be a sign I'm getting back to normal."

"Okay, then, I think you ought to go. But remember, it's probably a five hour drive. "

"I can stop and get a room if I get too tired, but I don't think I will. I think I'm ready. And you know what? I think she invited me because she felt sorry about the cancer, and she wanted to do something special for me."

"I've been wanting to get us a GPS system. How soon does she want you to come?"

"That's the thing. She's going to get there next Tuesday."

"That's the day after tomorrow. I didn't think it would be that soon."

"But it doesn't matter, does it? I know you have been planning to buy a GPS, but I wouldn't want one anyway. I've got a map, and Margie will send me some directions to her house. That should be plenty. If I had one of those things, I would have to figure out how to use it, and I don't want to. You don't need an excuse. Get the one that's right for your canoe trips. I'll be fine."

It was almost ten o'clock on Tuesday morning when she finally got away. She had to drive through Severance to get to the highway. When she drove down Merchants Row, she noticed a parking place right in front of the art supply store. On an impulse she pulled in and parked.

As soon as she stepped into the store, she spotted a box of watercolors, a big box, full of so many beautiful colors that it was as though a rainbow was held captive inside. She couldn't leave it behind, even though she almost changed her mind when she saw how expensive it was.

But she wanted those magical colors. She chose a large pad of watercolor paper and put both things down on the counter in front of the clerk, a young girl with a sharp, thin face. She looked at what Alyssa was buying and then looked at Alyssa and said, "You want to get a couple of brushes too. The ones they put in those kits are crappy."

Alyssa picked out three brushes, small, medium, and large. She wanted to ask how you could tell a good brush from a bad one, but she was too shy. Her face was burning. She knew the girl could see that she didn't know what she was doing. She paid for her purchases. She had spent more than one hundred dollars before she even got out of Severance.

Later on, as she drove down the highway, she wondered why she had spent so much money on art supplies when she had no plans to do any painting. True, she had always had a fantasy that she might do some art now that she was retired, but she wasn't thinking of doing any right away, so it didn't make sense. There was another strange thing that occurred to her. She realized that she hadn't told Richard that Margie was leaving on Friday, and that she was planning to stay on alone in Margie's house until Sunday. That period of solitude by the ocean was what the trip was all about. But Richard might not understand. He might think she wanted to get away from him, when it didn't have anything to do with him. What she wanted was a few days without the usual interruptions and responsibilities of being at home, a few days where she could think about what she had just been through. If she tried to describe that to Richard, he might get his feelings hurt, and after he had taken such good care of her too.

She thought about that as she drove south. She hadn't said it to herself plainly before the drive. She had just not mentioned the fact that Margie was leaving on Friday. It was a little spooky the way she was doing what she was supposed to do without even knowing what it was. She seemed to be operating on instructions she didn't know about. All the pieces were falling into place without her control. But it was sort of exciting to let the shadowy puppeteer make the decisions.

By the time she got to the Cape, she had seen some glimpses of the ocean, and she was very glad she was making the trip. She drove down Route 6 to North Truro and then followed Margie's directions to Arrowhead Road and a small gray cottage. The car in the drive had Massachusetts plates. That confused her until she realized that Margie would have had to rent a car at the airport. Alyssa pulled into the driveway and got out. She locked her new paint supplies in the trunk, but she left her bag of clothes on the back seat and went up the steps to the front door.

It was about four o'clock. The day was cooling off. The shadows were getting long. She hesitated. It had been so many years. Even if this were the right house, Margie might not recognize her, or she might not recognize Margie. She raised her hand to knock, but then she put it down again. Maybe she shouldn't have come. She raised her hand again, and this time she knocked. A vacuum cleaner was running somewhere inside. She knocked louder. If she knew Margie better, she could have opened the door and shouted to her, but she didn't feel comfortable doing that now.

She was tempted to get back in the car. She could drive to the end of the street and check that it was the right one. She could go farther. But before she could make a move, the vacuum was shut off. She knocked again into the silence, even though she regretted it while she was still knocking.

The door swung open. The person standing there wasn't fat, but she was chunky and square. There were gray curls all over her head. At first Alyssa was sure that she had come to the wrong house, but then she saw that under the gray curls was a version of Margie's face, wider and more weary than the old Margie, but still her face.

She said, "Alyssa, is it really you?" But before Alyssa could answer, she went on. "I thought I heard something, but I convinced myself I was wrong. I was planning to get all the vacuuming done before you got here. The tenants left the place in worse shape than I thought they would. As soon as they figure out that someone else is going to clean up, they start to act like pigs. But come inside." She stepped back from the door. "I'm so glad you're here. And I don't believe it. You look great. You haven't changed a bit. I would have recognized you anywhere."

"You haven't changed either, Margie." Alyssa gave her a quick hug.

"What do you mean?" Margie said, stepping back into the room. "Look at me. I'm much wider than I used to be—and grayer. But that's the way it goes." She gave Alyssa a mischievous smile. "Where's your suitcase? You must have a suitcase."

"I left it in the car. I wasn't sure this was the right house. I'll get it."

Margie's voice followed her down the steps and across the yard. "You didn't have trouble finding it, did you?

"Not at all. Your directions were good. I didn't even get lost once."

When Alyssa got back to the steps with her suitcase, Margie was still standing in the doorway. She said, "Here. Let me take that for you." Alyssa handed her the suitcase.

"Come in. I'll show you around."

The door opened into a small living room. There was a television set. Two shabby couches and a couple of chairs were arranged around it. The stairs started near the door and went up along the wall.

"It used to be nicer," Margie said. "But you can't leave things you care about if you're going to rent it." She spoke over her shoulder as she clumped up the stairs.

Alyssa nodded, but she was behind, and Margie probably didn't see her.

Upstairs there were small rooms on both sides of a narrow hall, which ended at the bathroom. Margie stopped and turned to look at Alyssa. "You can have any room you like. That's my room there, near the bathroom. You could have that one across the hall."

"That would be fine," Alyssa said.

Margie set the suitcase on the bed. "It's convenient if you have to get up in the night. I don't know about you, but I can't make it through the night any more. We're all getting up there in age." She sighed. "Still, I can't believe how great you look, Alyssa. No one would know you've been sick."

"Thank you. I wasn't sick that long. It's all over now. It happened very fast."

Margie hugged her. "I'm glad it's over."

"I lost some weight when I was sick. I'm hoping I won't gain it back again."

"I wish I could lose some. I guess I like to eat too much. And your hair. It looks just the way it always did. You haven't gotten any older."

"Oh Margie, that's simple. I cheat on the color. Everybody does these days. You could too."

"I've thought of it." She sighed. "It seems like a lot of trouble, but when I see how great you look, I think it might be worth it." She gave Alyssa another hug. "I'm going to go downstairs. You get settled and then come find me. We can make up your bed later."

The room was small. There was nothing in it but the bed, like an old-fashioned hospital bed, a straight-backed chair, and a small bureau. Everything was painted white, but the paint was old, dingy, and chipped. Out the window there was a small backyard, a solid board fence, and then another yard and house. Alyssa could hear Margie's vacuum cleaner start up again.

She got out her cell phone and called Richard. He answered on the second ring.

"I expected you to be outdoors," Alyssa said. "I'm here at Margie's."

"I thought I ought to stay near the phone in case you had trouble. Did you? Have trouble, I mean?"

"Not a bit. Thanks for worrying about me."

"I hope you'll have a good time. Tell Margie I said hello, even though I don't remember her. But you don't need to tell her that part."

"I think it's going to be good, but I just got here. I haven't even seen the ocean yet, except out the window of the car."

"Your mom called."

"She did?"

"I didn't know what you told her about this trip, so I said you weren't here and that you'd call her later. I didn't know what else to say. I thought you were going to tell her."

"I meant to. I just forgot. I'll call her tonight. Is she all right?"

"Oh yeah. I asked her about her eyes, but there wasn't anything new. Sonia's going to take her for the shots, but they haven't started yet. You'd better call her. You need to tell her about this trip."

"I will. I promise. I'll do it tonight. I miss you, Richard, and I'm sorry you had to hang around by the phone."

"That's okay. I wanted to be here if you needed me. I hope you'll have a good time."

"I'm sure I will. I'll call you soon."

"I'll leave you a message if there's anything to tell you. Do you know how to get your messages on that phone?"

"No, I don't."

"Never mind. Just keep it turned on so I can call you."

"Okay. Oh, and Richard, I didn't even get lost. Margie's directions were good. I didn't need a GPS."

They said goodbye. Alyssa couldn't hear the vacuum cleaner any more. She went to the window and stood there looking down into the backyard. Right then, she wished Richard was with her. The grass in the yard was scruffy with bald patches where the sand showed through. It was her fault. Richard could have come too.

When she went downstairs, she walked through several small rooms toward the back of the house. She found Margie in the kitchen, washing dishes.

Alyssa stopped in the doorway. "What a nice room," she said. "It's so full of light."

Margie turned off the water. "This is the only room we have changed. We took out a partition to make one big room out of two small ones. We had other things planned, but now we probably won't get to them."

"Why not?"

Margie dried her hands and took a bottle out of the cupboard. "Would you like a glass of wine?"

"I'd love it."

Margie filled two small glasses and handed one to Alyssa. "I'm sorry there aren't any wine glasses. They got broken. Let's sit on the porch, at least, until the mosquitoes drive us back inside. And I'll tell you why we probably won't make any more improvements."

They went out the back door and set their glasses down on the table. Alyssa looked around. The porch ran across the back of the house. It had a wide roof over it. "You must spend all your time out here. It looks so comfortable."

Margie sat down at the table. "Cheers," she said, touching her glass to Alyssa's. "Sit down. Sometimes the mosquitoes can make it bad out here, but most of the time, it's good. I forgot to say we rebuilt the porch when we did the kitchen. We were planning to screen it in, and that would make it even nicer, but now that Mom's gone, we don't come here often enough to make it worthwhile."

"I'm sorry about your mother."

"That's okay. She was sick for a long time. She wasn't going to get better. It happens, you know?"

"Mine is still very much on the scene. She's eighty-four. There's nothing wrong with her except for her eyes. I have to remember to call her tonight."

"That's amazing."

"She's still living in her own house by herself. My dad has been dead for about twenty years now. But she's got macular degeneration, and she can't drive any more. I think pretty soon she's going to have to go into a nursing home, or else start living with us, and I don't know if that will work for any of us. I've been worrying about it."

"What can you do? My mom didn't want to move in with either of my brothers, and she certainly didn't want to go all the way to Colorado where she didn't know anyone."

"I know. And we live way out in the country in Vermont. My mom doesn't really like it, even for a visit. Did you grow up around here?"

"In Fairhaven. It's just off the Cape. After Dad retired, they moved over here to Wellfleet. When our kids were little, Darren and I used to come east and spend a lot of the summer with them. But when Dad died, Mom went into the nursing home, and my brothers sold her house to pay for her care. So we bought this house to spend summers near Mom like we had been doing. Mom's been gone for four years now, and the kids are grown, and no one has time to come east any more. So we've been renting it out."

"That's too bad. It's a nice house."

"It's an awful lot of trouble. If you hire a management company to take care of the tenants and make sure the place is ready when they come, they take almost all the money. I guess we'll wait until houses start selling again, and then we'll probably be able to get a decent price for it—like you say, it is a nice house."

It was about six o'clock now. The shadows of the trees were stretched across the backyard, and the air was cool. "I'm sure you can sell it," Alyssa said.

"It has a lot of potential, I know that." They were both silent for a minute, and then Margie said, "Do you want another glass of wine?" She held the bottle out over Alyssa's glass.

"Just a very little. I guess the trip made me tired."

"Let's have some wine, and then I can get us some soup." She poured a little wine in Alyssa's glass and filled her own. She set down the bottle and took a long drink from her glass. "Unless you would like to go out for dinner somewhere? There are lots of good places around here, especially in Provincetown."

"No thanks," Alyssa said. "Soup sounds like plenty. I'm not that hungry, and it's nice sitting here and talking. We have a lot to catch up on."

"We do, and I've been doing all the talking. Tell me about you and Richard. How many years have you guys been together?"

"I think it's forty-one."

"That's a long time. But I'm not surprised. I only met him once, but I remember how good-looking he was."

"I'll tell him you said so. He'll love it."

"Did he grow up in Connecticut? I know you came from Stamford. I remember that."

"He's from the Adirondacks, a tiny, little town called Ray Brook. Well, it was tiny when he lived there. He was related to almost everybody in town. Later on, after we were married and living in Stamford, the Adirondack Park put its headquarters there, and the town got much bigger. I remember when we got married, we went there so his family could meet me. It was like going back in time to homesteader days or something."

"That must have been scary."

Alyssa hadn't ever thought of it like that, and if it had worried her in the beginning, it had worked out all right. She said, "I don't know. It's always hard to know what you used to think. I guess I must have liked the idea. I mean, the first time I met him, he took me for a canoe ride in a canoe he built himself."

Margie said, "I remember that. It was so romantic." She drained her glass. "Let's put clean sheets on your bed, and then, if you get really tired, it'll be all ready." They both stood up. Margie put their glasses in the sink, and they went upstairs.

As they worked on the bed, Margie kept talking. It was restful in an odd way. The stream of conversation poured past Alyssa, and she didn't have to think of what her contribution would be. She didn't remember that Margie talked a lot when they knew each other before, but that was long ago.

"An early night would be good for me too. I had to get up real early to get to the plane, and I've been moving ever since."

"Let's do your bed too."

"That's a great idea."

"And then I think I'd better call my mother and tell her where I am."

"You can do that while I heat up some soup. It's just from a can, but I got some Portuguese bread from the bakery that's delicious. We always miss it when we're in Colorado."

After the phone call, Alyssa went down to the kitchen again. The table was set in the kitchen. Margie said, "I thought we'd better eat in here because of the mosquitoes. We can move outside later if we want to." She turned off the stove. "Sit down. Everything's ready."

While they were eating, Alyssa talked about the conversation with her mother. "She was really surprised that I wasn't at home, still recovering from the operation. I think she thinks I'm weaker than I am."

"Maybe she was hoping you'd come visit her instead of some old school friend you hadn't seen in more than forty years."

"I know. I need to go see her, especially now that there's something wrong with her eyes. But this trip was for me."

"What did you say was the matter with her eyes? I know you told me, but I forgot."

"It's macular degeneration. I guess that's something that comes on slowly. And she hid it from everybody for quite a while." Alyssa sighed. "She even came up to visit us once on the train, and we thought she needed new glasses or something. It's amazing what you can take for granted, isn't it?"

"That's the way that generation always did things. My parents were the same way—so secretive. That's one of the reasons we decided to spend time here in the summers, and also why we decided to buy this house. I couldn't count on my brothers to know what was going on with Mom."

"I'm the only one my mother has to take care of her. Well, no, that's not true. I have two daughters who live near Stamford. They are very good about keeping an eye on her."

"I thought you had a brother."

"I did, but he was killed in Vietnam."

"I'm sorry. We were lucky. My brothers are both older than I am. They both served their time and got out before Vietnam."

"Richard escaped too, even though he got drafted at the worst of it. He was planning to refuse to go to Vietnam, but he didn't have to, because they sent him to Germany. I met him when he was home on leave. He came to the school to see some of his friends."

"I wish I could remember him better. What did he major in?"

"Math, and then later he switched to business administration."

"I guess that's why. I didn't know anyone at WCSU taking those courses."

"It sounds so geeky, but he isn't like that. What he really cares about is being outdoors, in the woods or on the water."

"But math?"

"He's always been good at it. He got a math scholarship to WCSU. That's why he went there. And he's always been able to find work as an accountant or a business consultant, even when we moved to Vermont. Thank you for the dinner. You're right, the bread is delicious."

After they finished eating, they took the wine bottle and the glasses and went out on the porch. The moon was one day past the full and just rising on one side, while the sun was going down on the other.

There was no wind to keep the mosquitoes at bay, and in the quiet, Alyssa could hear them whining as they came in to attack. She tried not to listen.

Margie said, "I'm going to get us a citronella candle tomorrow. I should have bought one today. I always forget how many insects there are in the East."

"You mean there aren't any mosquitoes in Colorado?"

"Of course there are some. But there aren't as many. I think it's because it's so much drier in the West."

Alyssa didn't say anything. She was thinking that once it was dark out, even with all the moonlight, she could say she thought she would go up to bed. It would be too rude to go to bed when it was still daylight.

Finally, when she thought she was going to end up being even ruder by falling asleep in her chair, she said she thought she would go to bed, but that she would be glad to do the supper dishes first.

Margie wouldn't hear of it. She said she was going to leave them in the sink. They could easily do them in the morning. She said, "You go on up. I'll be there soon. I'm going to have one more glass of wine, and then I'll be up."

CHAPTER 25

It was a little after noon when they got all the sheets and towels washed and dried and folded at the laundromat.

Margie said, "We've done enough housework for a while. How about a short hike? I know a beautiful spot that not very many people go to. It's usually empty when all the beaches are packed.

"I'd love to see it," Alyssa said.

They left the main road and drove down a small side road until they came to a large, paved parking lot. It was almost empty. Margie parked near a gazebo at the far end. No one was in there either.

Alyssa said, "Everyone must be at the beach. It's a good day for it."

"I'm going to lock the car anyway. It would be a bummer if someone stole all our clean laundry."

They walked past the gazebo and into the trees. The sun, which had been pressing down on Alyssa's head with its harsh brightness, was suddenly soft and sweet. Fluttering patches of light and shadow moved across the sandy path. The tree trunks were black, and the tall grasses underneath were green and golden.

Instantly, Alyssa understood that this was what the trip had been leading her toward. Everything had conspired to bring her to this spot. The spicy smell of the plants and the crunch of the dead leaves as they walked along the trail all overwhelmed her. "Oh Margie," was all she could say.

"There's a marker up here where they think the pilgrims first found fresh water. Did you know they stopped here on their way to Plymouth?"

"Why did they leave? I could stay here forever."

"They were here for a few weeks, but they were looking for farmland so they could grow food. The soil isn't very good out here."

"What's this place called?"

"It's the Pilgrim Springs Trail."

They walked through the woods and came to the marker, a stone sitting in a grassy patch.

"The first time I came here, I thought the spring had dried up, but then I found water back in the briers over there. Come. I'll show you."

There was a small wet patch under the bushes. A tiny rivulet flowed away from it into the woods.

"It doesn't look very historical," Alyssa said.

"No, it doesn't, but it's probably the same spring. Maybe it moved, or else they didn't want to put the stone too close. Maybe they wanted the tourists to look at the monument and leave the water alone."

They walked on. The trail went up to a grassy, open highland. "I feel as though I am going back in time to the savannahs of Africa and our ancient ancestors," Alyssa said.

And then she stopped short, because laid out before her was a wide panorama of land and water. In the distance, along the curve of the sandy shore, waves were breaking. "Oh Margie," she said again. "That is the first real look I've had of the ocean for so long."

"Let's go over there. They don't like it when you leave the trail, but they won't know. The only thing we have to watch out for is poison ivy. We'll just be careful not to step in it, that's all."

So they picked their way through the tall grass and bushes and patches of poison ivy until they came to a bluff. They climbed to the top, and there was the ocean, stretching to the horizon beyond the long golden curve of the beach. They went down the bluff and sat side by side in the hot sand, looking at the waves curling along the shore in front of them.

"I've been wishing to see the ocean. It's been a long time since I sat on a beach. It reminds me of Aaron. Mom and Dad used to take us to the seashore every summer." She sighed. "I miss him, even after all these years."

"What happened to him?"

"I don't really know. I know he was in the jungle, but I don't know what happened to him there. Maybe they told Mom, but she wouldn't ever talk about it. Maybe she didn't want them to tell her. She's like that sometimes."

"Darren was in Vietnam before I met him. He won't talk about it either. I know it must have been bad because he still gets nightmares." She thought for a minute. "The odd thing is that it's not getting better. In fact, after all these years I think it's getting worse. I mean, I think he has more nightmares than he used to have. I wonder why, but he won't talk about it."

They didn't look at each other. They sat looking out to sea and patting and smoothing the warm sand with their hands as they talked. It was as though each of them was talking to herself. After a while, they both stopped talking and just sat there in the sand. A little wind came up the beach, bringing the sharp, clean, salty smell of the water.

Margie said, "Let's walk along the beach before we go back."

They walked down by the water on the hard sand, dampened and smoothed and hardened by the waves. There were strings of seaweed and sometimes pebbles, but hardly any shells. Their feet made precise prints that the waves came up and erased.

Alyssa wondered how they would find the place where they came over the bluff, but Margie seemed to know. Alyssa hoped she would be able to recognize the place when she came back later to paint, because this beach was another place she planned to come back to when she was alone with her new paint box. She could get some sticks in the woods to stand in the sand to mark the route. That would work better than Hansel's white pebbles.

The next morning Alyssa planned to help Margie make up the beds and finish getting the house ready for the tenants, but she felt too unwell to get up. Margie was very nice about it. She brought her some tea in bed. Alyssa was grateful and a little embarrassed. She kept meaning to get up, and she kept falling asleep instead. She spent the whole morning like that. By then Margie had the beds all made up with clean sheets, except for her bed and Alyssa's, and she had finished cleaning the rest of the house.

Alyssa got up at lunchtime and thought she was better. They drove to a beach in Provincetown to go swimming. It was a hot day, and the beach was crowded.

They put their towels down in the sand, and Margie started off toward the water. Alyssa said she would be there in a minute. She lay down on her towel. It was so warm and comfortable. She didn't feel like moving. She wasn't sick any more, but she felt so weary. She couldn't seem to move. The next thing she knew, icy drops were falling on her hot skin. She opened her eyes.

Margie stood there, wet and dripping. "Oh, I'm sorry," she said. "The water feels wonderful. It's not cold when you get used to it. Aren't you going to go in?"

"I might not. It's so nice right here."

"Are you sick again?"

"No. I don't think so. Just tired."

"Maybe this trip was a lot for you to handle. Maybe you still haven't recovered from your operation."

"Maybe, but I don't think so. It doesn't feel like that. I just feel too comfortable to move. That's not the way I felt after my operation."

But she still felt tired and weak, so they didn't do much the rest of the day, and they went to bed early. Before they parted for the night, Margie said, "Are you going to be okay Alyssa? I have to leave first thing in the morning, and I hate to leave you not feeling well."

"Don't worry. I'll be fine in the morning, and if I'm not, I can call Richard."

"Okay. Let's see how you are when we get up. I have to leave around nine, but you'll be up, won't you?"

"I'm sure I will. I'll get up specially."

The next morning Alyssa got up early enough to have coffee with Margie before she left. She was feeling stronger, and she was determined not to waste what she considered the reason for the whole trip. She saw Margie off and promised to leave the house ready for the new tenants. She sat on the porch drinking coffee, and then she gathered everything she would need for her excursion to the Pilgrim Springs Trail.

She left her car in the parking lot and got her painting supplies out of the trunk and set off down the woodland trail looking for the perfect spot.

She walked slowly, even though she was excited. She needed to look carefully. The perfect place was waiting up ahead somewhere. But it would be easy to walk by and not realize she was missing the spot she had come all this way to find. She must be vigilant.

There was a vista of black tree trunks, black verticals with the tawny grass spread out horizontally underneath. She stopped and put down all the things she was carrying.

While she was getting out the watercolor pad and opening the box of paint, she saw that a little farther along the trail there was an even better scene. The same dark trees were there, but they were grouped differently. Alyssa moved everything to the new place. She did that three times, and then she told herself she had to stay where she was.

This time she got everything set up, and then she sat there restlessly, looking at the tree trunks and at the blank page before her. She scrubbed around in the black paint with the largest brush until its bristles began to fray. They were sticking out at all angles, as though a little kid had been using the brush. And still there were no marks on the paper.

Finally, she made a series of black lines on the page. She was sitting in the sandy dirt with the pad of paper propped on her pack. She leaned back to get a longer view. It was hateful. She turned to a new sheet of paper. When she had screwed up her courage enough to make some marks, the picture became just like the first one. Little children could have done it better. They would have been quicker at it too.

It was so amateurish. She was close to tears. It didn't help to tell herself that she *was* an amateur. It was impossible. She couldn't do it. She had wasted the money she spent on art supplies. She didn't want them any more. She pictured herself stuffing the box of rainbow colors into a trash can and walking away. She pictured herself dusting off her hands in a cartoon gesture of good riddance.

She decided to go to the ocean beach, not to paint it, but just to be there. She packed up her things and began to walk. She was almost to the end of the trees when she saw a vista of tree trunks that was so much what she was looking for that she actually did a double take. She stopped and put everything down.

She would do this picture, not because she had any hope, but because she had made up her mind to do it. It would be a throwaway. Still, it didn't matter to anyone else whether she painted a picture or not, and it only mattered to her if she let it matter.

She would take it one step at a time, without thinking about the result—one mark and then another and another. She would just put down exactly what she saw.

She had made a mess of the largest brush, so she laid it aside. She was just about to dip the medium-sized brush into the black paint, when she stopped, amazed. How could she have thought the tree trunks were black? There were so many colors, streaks of gold and rose and lavender. Even the darkest shadows were full of color, if she looked at what was there, instead of thinking that she knew. No wonder what she painted before was stupid. She had been painting what she thought, not what she saw.

She began again, not with hope, but with new resolve. She looked and put some paint on the paper, and looked and painted and looked and painted. Time and space and she herself disappeared. The world was reduced to the trees before her and the trees on the page.

She didn't even know how long she worked, starting a new picture when the paint got thick enough so that that the colors began to merge and muddy each other. But suddenly she felt exhausted. She put everything away and went down the trail to the car. She was only half-present. A large part of her was still in the world of the painting.

By the time she got back to Margie's house, she was starving. She had forgotten about the sandwiches she brought with her. It was four o'clock. The day was mostly gone. She let herself into the house and went out on the porch with her sandwiches.

It was lovely and peaceful in the late afternoon light. She ate the sandwiches and then sat there, full and satisfied. Like a cat, all she wanted was to be there, letting the contentment soak into her.

But she did think about the paintings she had done. She wondered what they were like. She had been so busy making them that she hadn't taken the time to look. They were almost certainly no good, childish, amateur work. Still, there was that 'almost', that tiny possibility that they were not quite as awful as the first ones. She was mildly curious and would have gotten up to look if she hadn't been too lazy, too comfortable where she was.

Then after a while she decided that she didn't want to know what they were like. It would ruin the mood of peace and satisfaction. It might even spoil the possibility of being able to do it again. And it didn't matter whether the paintings themselves were any good. She had had such a transcendent time making them. That was what mattered. She decided not to look at them until she was packing up to go home.

She called Richard and went to bed very early.

The next morning she was more methodical than she had been the day before. She felt like a professional. She got breakfast, packed everything she might need, and got to the Pilgrim Springs parking lot at a little after eight o'clock, ready for a good day's work. This time she was going to paint the ocean and the beach.

When she got there, she set down her things and took a walk, looking for the perfect spot to set up. After a short walk in each direction, she decided to stay where she was. The beach was one long golden curve, the same at one point as at another.

She got out the paper and the paints and arranged everything neatly in the sand in front of her. She picked up a brush and looked expectantly out at the water, ready to work. She asked herself what color the water was, and of course it was wonderfully various, like the tree trunks yesterday. She knew that. Still, it was hard to make a mark. Her heart was beating fast, and she was out of breath, she wanted it to happen so much. She walked down the beach and came back with new resolve. But even that wasn't enough. She made a few tentative marks and then stopped again, tense, restless. It was hard to see why she wasn't able to begin, since she was even more ready than she had been yesterday. She took another walk along the beach, not hurrying back this time, but dawdling along the way. She was afraid of what it would be like when she went back to the paint and paper.

Maybe that was enough to chasten her, so that she was able to begin in a worried and fearful state, so that she was able to proceed without hope or expectation, with nothing but desperate determination. Because suddenly she was able to put marks on the page again, deliberately and carefully, so that she could slide into that other world where there was nothing but the scene before her and the scene on the page. Maybe she could only get there by giving up the wish to get there.

She painted until she was so tired that she lay back in the warm sand and slept, and then she woke up and painted some more. She thought of moving to a new place, but there was still so much to explore where she was. A few Jeeps went by with waving people inside, but they hardly broke her concentration.

In the end, it was as good a day as yesterday, although, early on, she wouldn't have believed that it could turn out that way. Whatever power had brought her to this place, that power didn't want her to take it for granted. It wanted her to come to the page in a state of fear and uncertainty.

She needed to know these things, because she had had a wonderful time, and she would make room in her life to spend more days painting. It didn't matter what the paintings were like.

It was the middle of the afternoon when she got back to Margie's, spent but pleased. She finished getting the house ready. She had to take her sheets and Margie's to the laundromat. She got something to eat and cleaned up the kitchen. She called Richard.

"I talked to your mom. She had one of those shots on Friday. She felt bad yesterday, but she's better today."

"I'll call her. And Richard, I'm going to try to start early tomorrow morning, so I should get home in the middle of the afternoon."

"I'll be watching for you."

"You don't need to."

"But I want to."

"Okay. It'll be nice to be home again."

Richard told her to be careful.

The last thing she did was call her mother.

"Oh Alyssa, is that you? I've been wondering where you were. Are you home again?"

"Not yet. I'm leaving first thing in the morning."

"I wish Richard was with you. Why didn't he go too? I wouldn't worry about you if he was there."

"You don't need to worry about me anyway. I'm fine. How are you? What about your eyes?"

"I had a shot on Friday."

"I know. That's what Richard said."

"It hurt a lot…not when they did it, because they numbed my eye with something. But later on it felt like someone punched me in the face, and I couldn't see much for quite a while."

"Oh, Mom, I'm sorry."

"It's better today. I just hope it works."

"The doctor said it would, didn't he?"

"He's cautious. You know how they are. They don't want to get your hopes up."

"I know." Alyssa was afraid she was going to be asked a lot of questions about what she had been doing on the Cape, questions that would not be easy to answer. But her mother was thinking mostly about Alyssa's drive home and the dangers that lay in wait for her along the road. So from Alyssa's point of view the conversation went well.

After it was over, Alyssa sat on the porch with a glass of wine, trying to get up the nerve to get out the watercolor notebook to look at what she had done. She couldn't make up her mind. She was not sure she was ready to face the fact that she could have such a wonderful time doing something that yielded such pathetic results. All she was sure of was that she would find other occasions to waste time painting. She sat on the porch for a long time, listening to the voices and the music from the nearby houses. She felt so peaceful that she didn't even notice the mosquitoes. Finally, she went upstairs to sleep in the bed without sheets.

In the morning she woke up around dawn. The sky outside the window was a soft, pearl gray. She put clean sheets on her bed and Margie's, dressed, and gathered all her things together. She checked each room and went downstairs. It was good of Margie to trust her to leave the place in order.

She was on the road at six-thirty, eager to get home to Richard. The sky was full of clouds. Sometimes the sun would come out and sometimes there were sprinkles of rain. She stopped near Brattleboro for a sandwich. It felt like coming home to be back in Vermont. Everything was so green. The highway was almost empty. It ran by farms and fields and woods.

She called Richard from Severance to see if he needed anything from town. He sounded glad she was back. She was glad too. Vermont hadn't always felt like home, but it did now.

She was tired when she got to the house. It was two-thirty. Richard was on the deck, reading. He looked up. When he saw the car, he threw the book aside and bounded down the steps. He got to the car before she could open the door.

"You're here," he said, smiling. "You must have made good time."

"I did. And I started early too. It's a long way." She got out of the car and straightened up, slowly and stiffly. She walked past him to the trunk for her suitcase. She didn't know what to do about the paints and the watercolor pad. Richard was so happy to see her. It made her feel guilty about the days she had spent alone. She shut the trunk quickly before he had a chance to look in.

They sat on the deck while Alyssa told about her trip. After a little while, she remembered that she needed to call her mother to tell her she was home. She went inside to get the phone. Everything was neatly in its place. The living room looked just the way it did when she left. She made the call and went back outside.

"Everything looks so tidy, Richard. Evidently, you don't need me to help you keep house. I think you do better without me."

"That's not true, and anyway, I don't want to do without you. But tell me how your mom is. That was a very quick phone call."

"I didn't get her. That's why. I left her a message. I talked to her last night."

"I did too." He stood and reached out to her. "Come with me. I want to show you what I've done in the vegetable garden."

They walked across the drive together holding hands.

Richard said, "The peas were ready. I picked a lot of them and put them in the refrigerator. I thought we could have them for dinner."

"Okay." They stood together, looking at the growing plants. "It looks great, Richard. How did you have time to do all the weeding?"

"It didn't take that long."

"Let's walk over to the brook. I feel as though I have been gone for months."

Richard squeezed her hand. "I'm glad it wasn't *that* long."

"I had a good time though, especially after Margie left."

They stood on the bank, looking down at the water. The stream was wide and shallow at that place. The water ran sparkling over rocks, sending up flashes where it caught the sunlight.

"I think it might be a little lower than it was when I left."

"The weather has been dry," Richard said. "Oh, that reminds me. Sam came over to tell us that they're having their Martel reunion next Saturday. I don't know what they'll do if it rains."

"They must have some backup plan."

"He wanted me to be sure to tell you that they'd like us to come."

"I don't know…we don't know any of those Martels except for Sam and Bonnie…and Junior and Marnie, of course."

"Sam was worried about you when he saw you weren't here. He thought you might have had to go back to the hospital. I could tell he was relieved when I said you were visiting a friend on the Cape."

They walked across the yard, still holding hands. Richard said, "Why did you say you had a good time after Margie left?"

"I meant…." She stopped. She had already said more than she was going to. But Richard was so good and so glad to see her. She wanted to tell him everything. She wanted to have that kind of relationship. She took a gulp of air and began. "Margie had to leave Friday morning, but the tenants weren't planning to arrive until today, so she said I could stay on if I wanted to. So I camped out there alone for those two days."

"Really?"

It was her turn to squeeze his hand. She knew she had said it in a confusing way, but she was trying to be open, or she hoped she was. "It was such a strange thing, Richard. I felt like I was supposed to be alone, and that I was programmed by something—I don't even know what—to do it in a certain way." They walked back to the deck and sat on the steps. "Before I even left Severance, I stopped at the art supply store. I bought watercolor paint and paper. I can't tell you why I did that. I didn't plan to, except that I've always thought that when I retired, I would try my hand at painting, or maybe writing. But I didn't think I was going to start right then." She looked at him sitting there beside her, with his puzzlement making little frown lines between his eyes. "Who hasn't had those thoughts?"

"Go on," Richard said. "Does Margie paint?"

"I don't even know. I was too shy to let her know anything about it. But she left on Friday morning, and before that she took me on a hike, and without realizing it, she had shown me exactly what I wanted to paint. I knew exactly where to go after she left."

"I wish I had known you were going to be alone there. I could have come down and kept you company."

Alyssa leaned against him, pressing her shoulder against his. "I know, Richard. I kept wishing you were there, but it was like it was out of my hands. It had to happen the way it did."

"My being there wouldn't have made any difference."

"It would have to me. I kept wishing you were there." She bumped him with her shoulder. "But…and please don't get your feelings hurt, I think I had to be alone, even though I didn't want to be. Maybe I had to be lonely and a little sad for the magic to work."

She stood up. "Come with me. I'm going to get out the pictures I did. I know they are embarrassingly awful." She smiled at him. He looked so solemn. "I hope you won't laugh at me. I had two wonderful days doing them."

They took the things out of the trunk. Alyssa opened the box of paints. "Look, Richard. Isn't this a box of magic? Can you see why I couldn't resist?"

Richard nodded, but he wasn't really looking. He had picked up the watercolor pad, and now he began to open it.

Alyssa put her hand on the pad, closing it again. "No," she said. "Wait. Let's go up on the deck. We can look at it together. I'm kind of nervous about it. I haven't looked at them since I did them. I was going to, and somehow I couldn't do it. That's kind of dumb, isn't it? I mean, I already knew they were no good."

They went up on the deck. Richard set the notebook down on the table and opened to the first painting.

"Oh God," Alyssa said. "I warned you. It's kindergarten work."

Richard didn't say anything. He just turned to the next picture. Alyssa tried to sneak a sideways look at him, but his expression gave nothing away.

He turned another page. This was the first painting of tree trunks, where Alyssa had really begun to see what was in front of her.

"Well now," Richard said. And he turned another page.

After the first two awful attempts, the paintings became different. Alyssa forgot to be embarrassed. She knew the paintings weren't good, of course, but somehow, there was something alive, something real.

Richard turned the pages to the end and then went backward to the beginning again, looking at each one. Then he took a step back.

"Well, Alyssa, I think…no, I don't know what I think. I'm surprised, I guess. I wouldn't have…well, I'm just surprised, that's all."

"Maybe you mean shocked," she said, smiling. But she knew he didn't. There really was something there, and she could tell he saw it too.

CHAPTER 26

Sam threw a log into the pit. The fire was really going good. Sparks swirled up, and flames rose higher than the edge of the hole. Sam took a step back and looked out past the smoke and flames. Danny was on the other side of the road, about to cross. Sam watched him look both ways and then come running over.

"Grammie said I could help you, Gramp. Can I?"

"Sure. I been waitin for ya. Here. Stir the fire so it all gets burnt." He handed Danny the long poker that he used in the sugaring arch.

Danny grabbed the end with both hands and tried to move the other end around in the pit. It took him a little while to figure out how to do it.

Sam watched him struggling. "How old are you now, Danny?"

"Eleven."

"That's what I thought. That's plenty old enough to help me drive the tractor."

"Can I really?"

"Sure. But first we got to get the fire ready."

"What are we doin this for anyhow, Gramp?"

"This is for the barbecue. Don't you remember last year?"

"Oh yeah. It was good. I ate a lot. I had a stomach ache after."

"That was pork. This one's beef. It's goin to be even better."

"Last year there was beans too."

"Right. See that little mound of sand over there? The beans are under there, cookin already."

"Yum."

"Stir that fire around while I put on some more wood."

They worked on the fire until Sam was satisfied that all the wood was burnt down to coals. Then he positioned the two old wheelbarrows on the far side of the pit and started shoveling them full of hot coals.

Danny wanted to help, but Sam wouldn't let him. It was too dangerous. "What would your ma and Grammie do to me if I let you fall in there? You just hold your horses until I say so. You'll have a job in a minute, as soon as I get enough of these coals out."

"Okay, Gramp."

Sam filled both wheelbarrows. "That should do her. Now we got to put the meat in. We're goin to do that with the tractor."

"Is the meat in that big package thing chained to the front of the tractor? Do I get to drive it, like you said?"

"I said you could help me drive it. First we're both goin to drive, and then I'll show you what I want you to do. Okay?"

They climbed onto the tractor. Sam started it and raised the bucket so the meat was dangling off the ground. He went forward until it was swinging over the pit. Then he showed Danny the lever to raise and lower the bucket.

Danny paid attention and looked very serious, but Sam still took the precaution of chocking the wheels in case Danny bumped it into gear. He didn't want Danny to drive into the flaming pit.

It went well. Danny had to raise and lower the meat a few times according to Sam's hand signals while Sam pushed the dangling package into position with the poker. After a few tries, they got it into place.

Sam undid the chains and laid them over the edge of the pit for later. Then he got on the tractor, and together they backed it out of the way.

"Okay, Danny. Now we have to get that hole filled in as fast as we can before the meat catches on fire."

"But, Gramp, it'll still catch on fire even after we fill in the hole."

"It can't burn without it's got some air down there. That's why we fill it up with sand."

Sam dumped the coals out of the wheelbarrow into the pit. He spread them to cover the meat, and then he started shoveling sand on top. When the hole was almost filled, he gave Danny the shovel, so he could do some too.

When they finished filling the pit, Sam set a couple of sheets of roofing tin over the meat hole and another, smaller piece of tin over the bean hole. "I guess we're all done here. Get your beer, and let's sit down for a minute before we go over to help Grammie and your ma."

"It's not a beer, Gramp. It's root beer. Ma wouldn't ever let me have a real beer. You funny guy."

"I'm just sayin," Sam said. "We're havin a party." They sat down at the picnic table.

"How long does it take to cook the meat, Gramp?"

"It goes slow, but we got time. It'll be ready around noon tomorrow."

"It cooks all night?"

"Yup. You wait. It'll be real tasty. You'll see. How're you and your ma gettin along these days?"

"Fine."

"Is that Steve Louzone still around?"

"Yeah, but it's all right. You don't have to worry, Gramp. I can take care of us."

"I wish you didn't have to. If Steve would just get out...he's not around that much, is he?"

"He's home more of the time since his job got over with."

"He doesn't have a job?"

"Well, he's on probation...."

"You can work when you're on probation, for God's sakes. He had one before. What d'ya mean 'the job got over with'?"

"He ain't doin it no more. Maybe…. I think they told him not to come back."

"Marnie should tell him the same thing."

"It's okay, Gramp. He ain't that bad. That's what she says." He took a long drink of his root beer and wiped his mouth with his hand.

"He ain't ever hurt her, hit her or nothin, has he?"

No," Danny said, but he looked so uncomfortable when he said it that Sam knew he was lying.

"Danny, that means yes, don't it? I can tell by the way you're actin."

"It's okay, Gramp. It's really okay." He was squirming on the bench, trying to keep from crying, and that really upset Sam.

"What d'ya mean, okay?" He felt like the top of his head was going to pop off. He tried to keep his voice down. "What do you mean? If he hit her, it's not *okay*. It's never okay to hit a woman. What the hell are you talkin about?"

"I'm just tellin you what she says about it. She says it's okay, and that I shouldn't worry about it. But, Gramp, she also says I ain't supposed to tell anybody. She says if I tell anybody, Steve will find out, and then it'll be much worse. You can't let her know, and anyhow, I didn't tell you—you figured it out."

"Don't worry, Danny."

"I help her with it. I stay around home when he's there, so I can watch what he does."

"God damn it, Danny, I don't want that creep showin you how to treat women. We got to get him outa there."

"We can't. Ma says we can't. It would make it worse. He's already on probation, Gramp. He's goin to mess up one of these days, and then he'll be gone. That's what she says. I'll be glad, even if she ain't."

Sam sat at the picnic table, trying to get calm. He watched his hand squeezing the beer can until it was dented. Then his hand turned the can, so it could push the dents out by putting other dents in. He had to think about his beer can, so he wouldn't picture Marnie trying to deal with that low-life bastard, while Danny, who shouldn't even know about such things, was forced to watch.

Danny took a drink of his root beer. He was a little more in control of himself now. He looked right at Sam. It was a serious, grown-up look. "Gramp, I'll tell you more, but you got to be careful, so Ma and Grammie don't know you know. Okay?"

"I already told you I would be."

"I'm really goin to be in trouble if Ma finds out."

"Don't worry about it. Just tell me."

"One time I heard a thump, and she made this weird noise. I think he hit her in the stomach, and she kind of folded up in a chair. I was in bed, but I went out there. She told me she was okay, and she told me to go back to bed. I think she thought he was goin to hit me too. But he didn't." He stopped talking and sat looking at Sam.

Sam jumped to his feet and started pacing back and forth. He didn't know what to say. He realized that he had known that little creep would hit her sooner or later. Why couldn't she have seen that's what would happen? She ought to have protected Danny, even if she couldn't protect herself.

Danny was waiting for him to say something, but he didn't know what to say. Finally he said, "When did this happen, Danny?"

"Just last week. Maybe something more happened that I don't know about, because she made me go back to bed." He was looking at Sam, studying his face for signs. "He's already on probation. He ain't supposed to drink at all. He could be in big trouble if they find out."

"I don't care about him. What I want to know is this—did she tell him to get out when he hit her?"

"No, she didn't, and now he acts like he's real sorry. That's probably so she won't tell on him."

"Why don't she get him out of there? By God, I could get him out." His poor little girl, his Marnie.

Danny said, "She's all right. You saw her. Don't worry about her, Gramp." He stood up too. "And don't forget you promised."

"What?" Sam said. "Oh yeah, don't worry, Danny. But we got to figure out what to do."

"Come on, Gramp. Let's go over to the house. And I can tell you what to do. Just act like you don't know. Otherwise, you'll get me in a lot of trouble."

"You're the boss man. Let's go." He put his hand on Danny's shoulder, and they walked like that all the way to the house.

When Sam opened the kitchen door, he saw that they had put several tables together to make one long one, which filled the kitchen. There was just room enough left to walk around it. All the counters had been cleared too.

"Wow," Sam said. "I guess you girls are ready for some food to arrive."

Bonnie grinned at him. "Do you think it looks okay? It's pretty tight in here."

Marnie was standing on the other side of the table. "Nobody won't be able to crash the line. There ain't no passin room." She was grinning.

Sam wanted to hug her, the way he used to when she was little, but he could feel Danny beside him, and he didn't dare give anything away.

Marnie said, "Danny, you'd better get to bed. Did you ask Gramp?"

"No. I forgot."

"Do you still want to sleep out in the barn? There's plenty of room upstairs."

"Yes, I do. I just forgot."

Marnie said, "Pop, I was tellin Danny how Junior and I used to sleep in the hayloft when we was kids. He wants to try it. But you don't have to let him."

"It's fine, if he wants to. Danny you'll be all alone. You might get scared."

"I won't."

"Well, okay then. Grammie can get you some blankets."

"I got my sleepin bag. I got a flashlight too. I'll be fine."

"Okay, but if you're scared, you can come in. You can sleep in Junior's room like you always do."

"I won't get scared."

Marnie smiled. "He won't either. He's Mister Iron Man. Right, Danny?"

"Right."

When Bonnie came back into the kitchen, they asked her too. She thought it was okay, but Sam could tell she expected Danny would come inside sometime during the night. There wasn't much left to do to get ready for the reunion, so after Marnie helped Danny carry his stuff up to the hayloft, they all went to bed.

When Sam got up at five-thirty next morning, he made a pot of coffee. When it was ready, he poured himself a cup and stepped out onto the porch to drink it. The mist was thick. Even things as close as the barn were hazy with it. It was still cool, but it was going to be a hot one. Sam took his cigarettes out of his pocket. He shouldn't be carrying them with him all the time. It was too much of a temptation. He felt awful every time he bought a pack, since he was living mostly on Bonnie's money these days. Technically, he didn't try to keep it a secret from her, but he knew she wanted him to quit. She'd been after him about it for a long time. And he really had quit. This was just tapering off. Still, he was glad she was asleep. If he heard her in the kitchen, he could put it out. He set the coffee cup down on the porch railing and lit up. He took a long drag and blew the smoke out into the fog, savoring the taste. It was one of the good ones. He stood there, feeling the mist on his face and wondering if Danny spent the whole night in the loft like he said he was going to do.

Sam put out the cigarette and broke up the butt. He sprinkled the tobacco in the flowerbed and put the paper in his pocket. Then he went to the barn to feed the chickens and the pigs. The pigs made so much noise over their breakfast, that Sam was pretty sure Danny wasn't in the hayloft. He didn't climb up to see. He fed the chickens and was just getting into his pickup to go check on the sheep, when the barn door opened, and Danny came out, blinking and still half-asleep.

He came over to the pickup, where Sam was standing with one foot in the cab and the other still on the ground.

"Where you goin, Gramp? Can I go with you?"

"I'm goin up to the pasture to see do the sheep need anythin. Climb in."

"Did you know Colt was in the back?"

"He likes to go with me."

"Does he always ride in the back?"

"He prefers it. If it's real loaded with my tripods and saws and stuff, he has to ride in the cab."

Sam drove up to the gate behind the barn. "Okay, Danny, my man, get the gate for us. You can close it after I go through. I'll wait for ya."

When Danny was back in the truck, and they were driving up the hill, Sam said, "I thought you might decide to move into the house in the night."

Danny was sitting forward on the edge of the seat, peering over the dashboard. "It's awful foggy, Gramp. Will we be able to find the sheep?"

"It won't be foggy there. It all pools up in the valley. I guess you didn't get scared last night, did ya?"

"Naw. I like it in your barn. Besides, I had Colt with me."

"You did? I wondered where he went. I thought he might of stayed over by the fire pit."

"Naw. He was with me until the early morning."

Sam stopped the truck at the top of the hill where it flattened out. The sun was shining, and the sheep were grazing quietly.

Danny said, "Maybe we should have the reunion up here where it's sunny."

"By the time everybody gets here, it'll be sunny down there too."

"I hope so."

"Don't worry. The sun'll burn the fog off."

They got a good count on the sheep and checked to see that the water was running through the pool where the sheep drank.

"Okay," Sam said. "We're done up here. Let's go down and take a look at the fire pit."

"Can I drive down?"

Sam was climbing into the driver's seat. "You know what?" he said. "The next time we come up here, you can drive up. You're not ready for down yet. Up comes first."

"I don't see what difference it makes."

"More can go wrong a lot faster when you're goin down."

They drove out of the field and across the road to the picnic table and the fire pits.

Sam said, "I guess it's still cookin. We won't know nothin for sure til we open 'em up."

"When do we do that?"

"Probably around noon. We want to let it all cook a while yet. Let's go see what your ma and Grammie have cooked for breakfast. I don't know about you, but I don't want to wait til the family arrives to get somethin to eat."

"Okay, Gramp."

Alma and Junior and their girls showed up a little before eleven, so they could help with last minute preparations. By noon when it was time to open the fire pits, there were a lot of people around ready to help.

They took the beans out first. Junior drove the tractor with Danny on his lap maneuvering the bucket. Sam flipped over the tin, so it was out of the way. Junior brought the tractor in close, and Sam hitched on the chain that was attached to the top bean pot. The tractor raised it slowly. Hot coals poured off it as it rose out of the hole. The tractor backed up, and Danny lowered the bucket until the bean pot was sitting on the ground. They did the same with the second pot of beans. It was a slick operation. Sam was glad a lot of the relatives were watching.

He took off the chains and brushed away the remaining coals and ashes. There was a circle of guys around the pot watching. Sam used a stick to raise the lid slowly. The beans were bubbling. They were cooked to a rich, dark brown. They looked good. Danny wanted to try them right away, but Sam said they had to wait.

They set both pots of beans in the bucket of the tractor, and Junior and Danny drove them over to the kitchen. Meanwhile, Sam and the other guys who were hanging around shoveled the coals and sand back into the bean hole. Sam put the tin on top.

By the time the tractor got back, they had started to uncover the meat pit. Sam and Uncle Jimmy and Tyrone Parker dug out some sand and coals. There were two sets of chains, one for each end of the side of beef. Sam hitched one chain to each end of the tractor bucket. He motioned for them to raise the bucket. Slowly the meat came up, shedding coals, until it was dangling above the pit. Junior drove the tractor over to the picnic table, which Sam had covered with a piece of roofing tin. Junior lowered the meat onto the table.

Everyone crowded around to watch Sam cut into the burlap package. It was the moment of truth. It smelled delicious, but it could be burned up inside the packing. Sam peeled back the last layer. Everyone cheered. It looked great. Sam sliced into it. It was so tender that it flaked apart under the knife. Sam wanted to take a bite to see if it tasted as good as it smelled, but there were too many guys watching. He started filling platters, so they could be carried over to the kitchen. When he had piled up six big plates with the meat, all the guys were gone. He broke off a few bites for himself and began to fold the burlap cover over what was left. It was as tasty as he had hoped it would be.

He met Uncle Jimmy on the porch, coming out of the kitchen with a loaded plate. "Well, Sammy. You done good. This is even better than last year."

Sam smiled.

"I don't think there's nobody else in our family that could put on a reunion like this here. You're goin to be stuck with it forever, if you keep on doin such a good job."

"That's okay," Sam said. "As long as everybody likes it, I'll keep on doin it."

"That's a good sport. Well, get some of your beef before everyone eats it all."

Sam went into the kitchen and got in line behind a couple of teenagers he didn't recognize. Irene Martel, Uncle Jimmy's youngest, was ahead of them. She waved at him.

The table was crammed with casseroles and salads and the platters of barbecued beef. Sam filled his plate. He didn't see anyone from his part of the family. Even Bonnie was somewhere else. He got a can of beer and took his plate outside.

There were groups of people sitting on the grass under the trees in front. There were more groups of people sitting on the hillside behind the house. There were many different groups to choose from, and he knew he would be welcome. But no matter who he sat with, he would be making a statement and maybe even taking a side in a family feud. And the Martel family was a great one for feuds.

Sam sat down on the porch steps by himself and started to eat. He was pleased with the taste of the beef. He thought about what he was going to try next year. A steady stream of people passed by him going in and out. He sat over to the side of the steps so he wouldn't block the flow.

He hadn't been there very long when Junior came by. He was carrying an empty paper plate in each hand. "Hey, Pop. What're you doin here all by your lonesome?"

"Just havin some lunch."

"So why ain't you sittin out there on the grass? There's Leon and Sally and Uncle Jimmy and them."

"Whoever I choose, it might make somebody else mad. You know how easy offended some people can get, and there's that whole thing about Grandma's dishes that's got everybody upset. You know how the Martels can get."

"Well, Pop, come over and sit with Alma and me. You'll be welcome. There ain't nobody goin to think you're takin sides if you do that."

"I might be over when you get your food."

When Junior came out with two loaded plates, Sam followed him over to the hillside by the barn, where Alma was sitting on their blanket.

She looked up and saw him standing there. "Hello, Pop. I hope you're comin to sit with us."

"I will, if you'll have me." He sat down beside her on the blanket. Junior handed her a plate and sat on the other side of her.

Sam said, "How do you think the beef came out?"

"Now you're fishin for compliments," Alma said, turning her sweet smile on him. "What d'you think? I bet everybody's been tellin you what a fabulous cook you are."

"I hope you think so."

"Well, you know I do."

They ate in silence for a few minutes. Then Sam set down his plate and leaned back on his elbows against the slope of the hill. The sky was bright blue. Puffy, white cumulus clouds were beginning to pile up, but they didn't look threatening. Two red-shouldered hawks spiraled up above them, making their short, harsh cries.

"Why do they give themselves away like that?" Sam said. "You'd think they'd catch more if they kept quiet."

"I always thought those cries would send the little critters into a panic, so they'd run for cover, and the hawks could spot 'em when they were movin," Junior said.

"You might could be right about that." Sam watched as the hawks circled, getting higher and farther away to the north, until they were only specks against the clouds.

Alma put her plate down with a sigh. "I wish I had more room. I'd get another helpin, even though I don't need it. But I got to give up, cause I ain't got no place to put it."

Sam said, "The beans come out good, didn't they?"

"Who made 'em?"

"It was two different batches. Irene made one pot. I know that. I disremember who made the other one. Irene brought hers out yesterday morning."

Junior gave a grunt in reply. Sam knew he tried to stay out of family politics. That's what he tried to do himself, so he had to respect it.

Sam stood up. "Well, I guess...." he said.

"Don't rush off, Pop. It's nice here," Alma said.

"Thanks for the invite, but it's probably time to fill up those meat platters again." He leaned over and picked up the empty paper plates. "How about if you two kids give us some music later on?"

"We could do that. Right, Alma?"

"Oh sure. I'd be glad to, Pop. Junior brought his guitar."

"When everybody gets done eatin then."

"Okay, Pop. We'll set up after a while."

Sam walked off toward the kitchen. He was planning to see how much meat was left, but before he could even get to the garbage cans, Joyanne stopped him. If he'd seen her in time, he would have dodged out of her way.

"Hey there, cousin," she shouted, and when he turned around to look, she was bearing down on him, so they ended up at the garbage cans at the same time. "Where you been? I was lookin for ya."

"I been here all day. I was sittin up on the hill with Junior and Alma."

"I ain't seen Junior in I don't know when. How's he doin?"

"He's okay. You'll see him later. Alma's goin to sing."

"That'll be good. It's goin great this year, ain't it?"

"It's all right," Sam said, wondering what she wanted. She hadn't changed that much since high school. He remembered her from then. She wasn't heavy like lots of women in the family, but she looked tired, and that made her looked older than she was. She'd had a lot of things wrong with her, and she'd had to have a lot of surgeries. He said, "How've you been, Joyanne?"

"Not so good. I've had more than my share of health problems. You might have heard about it." She cocked her head, eyeing him a little sideways. It reminded him of a bird.

"I heard you had to have a operation. I can't remember who told me. It might of been Bonnie. She's always hearin stuff at work." He guessed it was safe to pin it on Bonnie."

"So did you hear about Grandma's dishes too?"

"Oh, here we go," Sam thought. Out loud he said, "I might of heard somethin a while ago." He was edging toward the trash barrel, hoping someone would come along and interrupt before she really got going.

"I've always liked you a whole lot, Sam. I want you to know the truth. I wouldn't want to think you heard a bunch of lies about me."

He smiled down at her. "Oh, don't worry. I wouldn't believe bad stuff about you."

She was thin and shaky, and her skin had a kind of grayness to it. Even back in high school she'd looked worn out.

275

He dumped the paper plates and turned around, looking out at all the family groups. Unless someone came along and changed the conversation, he was in for the whole story. And the worst of it was that everyone was going to see her talking to him, and they would all think he was on her side. But he couldn't just walk away. She'd had it tough all her life.

"Grandma always told me those dishes would be mine. I used to spend a lot of time with Grandma back before your ma and dad and you kids started to live here with 'em. And after too…you remember. Grandma used to watch me when Ma was at work. We would get out them dishes and look at 'em, and Grandma would tell me how she wanted me to have 'em after she was gone. She wouldn't of said that if she'd wanted Dawn to have 'em. But Dawn took 'em, and she won't give 'em to me."

Sam edged a little bit away from her. He could see people looking at them. "Why don't you tell Dawn what you just told me? If she knows that's what Grandma said…."

"Oh, I've tried. Believe me I've tried. She won't even talk to me."

"Why don't you go up to her today and explain the whole thing. She's here. I saw her with her boyfriend."

"That's her husband. It's her second. They got married a while back. That's why she wanted to take them dishes all of a sudden."

"I think you should talk to her. It don't do no good to tell me about it."

"Oh Sam, you're just a baby. She won't even look at me. She's over there by the picnic table, but if I go over there, she'll walk off. She don't want to hear it."

"Well, look, Joyanne. I got to go over there and cut some more meat off. I'm goin to tell her she needs to come talk to you."

"Okay, you do that, but it ain't goin to do no good. You wait. You'll see."

Sam patted her on the shoulder, and she gave him a quick hug in return. Then he was able to walk away toward the kitchen. He got two empty platters and didn't have to stop for any conversation. There weren't that many people in the kitchen. There was still plenty of food, but everyone must be getting full. They always had a lot of food left over after one of these reunions. All the Martels prided themselves on that.

Sam went across the road with the empty platters. Dawn was standing near one of the fire pits, smoking a cigarette. It made Sam want one himself, but it was too public a spot for him. Dawn's boyfriend or husband was with her. Sam recognized his face, but he couldn't think of his name. He went up to them.

Dawn said, "Hey there, Sam. Have you met Fred?"

Sam said, "Yeah, how're you doin?" He shifted the plates to one hand, so he could shake hands with him.

Dawn said, "My cousin Sam belongs to the other faction of the family."

Sam opened his mouth to say he wasn't taking sides, but he didn't get a chance.

"I seen you over there talkin to Joyanne. Don't try to deny it. And I know she told you how I stole them dishes."

Sam tried again to speak, but he wasn't quick enough.

Dawn blew out a long stream of smoke and said, "Them dishes has been laying around in Mom's house for years, ever since Grandma died. If Joyanne wanted 'em, she would of come and got 'em long ago. Mom needed the space so she said I might as well take 'em since I had a lot more room at my place."

Sam managed to say, "I told her she ought to come over and talk to you. But I don't think she'll do it."

"I don't care. She knows she don't have no good reasons. That's why she won't never talk to me. She left them dishes at my mother's house for years, and she never said nothin about 'em, and now, when somebody else shows some interest, she suddenly remembers where they're at. If she's got somethin to say, let her come over and say it. I ain't stoppin her. I bet she don't do it though."

She tried to act as though she didn't care, but Sam could see the pain in her face. And Fred must have seen it too, because he put his arm around her.

Sam walked over to the picnic table and started to unwrap the hunk of meat. The more he tried to stay out of the fight, the deeper into it he got. And why should they drag him into it? No one was offering him the damn dishes. He didn't care what happened to them. When he was little and his family was living here at the farm with Grandma, he spent time with her the way Joyanne did. But then later on, when Ma got sick, Grandma had to move to Williamstown to live with Aunt Linda. He didn't see her much after that. He was sorry now, but he was young then, and she was old and sick, and Williamstown was a long way off.

He sliced off enough beef to fill two platters and wrapped the meat up again. He called over to Dawn and Fred to say he was glad to see them, and he started across the road with one full platter in each hand.

When he got to the porch, Steve Louzone was just opening the door for himself. He held it open for Sam. Sam couldn't manage any more than a grunt in acknowledgement. His only thought was that he was going to be feeding the s.o.b. that hurt Marnie. She was in the kitchen. Steve grabbed her in a big embrace, showing off what a great lover boy he was.

Sam managed to set down the platters of meat without throwing them at him. Maybe he didn't want to waste good food on something so worthless. His fists went up as soon as his hands were free. He didn't even see Bonnie. He didn't know she was in the room, until she had a hold of his arm and was pulling him out into the hall.

"Come on, Sam. I want to talk to you. It's important." When she got him to their bedroom, she shut the door and turned around to look at him. If she had been a cartoon character, she would have had her hands on her hips. She would have been tapping her foot. He could tell she was that steamed up. "What's goin on here?" she said.

"Nothin. I wish somethin was, but you didn't give me no chance."

"Well, that's good."

"You won't think so when I tell you what Danny told me last night. When you hear it, you'll want me to beat up the bastard too."

"Not now, Sam. Right now you need to cool down."

"Bonnie, God damn it! There are some things you just can't be cool about."

She sat down on the bed with a big thump and motioned for him to sit beside her. "Look, Sam. Don't tell me about it now. It's Steve, ain't it?"

"Yeah. Of course it is."

"Well, I don't want to know until the reunion's over. Just stay away from him. Otherwise you could start a fight...."

"That's what I want to...."

She put her arm around his shoulders. "Let me finish, honey. If you start somethin, the first thing you know, all your hothead relatives will be pilin into it."

Sam liked that picture. He had to grin a little. Steve didn't have anyone on his side.

She pulled him toward her and kissed his cheek.

He put his arm around her back and leaned into her. "Hey, babe, you want to start somethin?"

She pulled away a little. "You know we can't. Promise me you'll stay away from Steve."

"Oh God. How can I...?"

She jiggled him back and forth, so he was off balance. "You have to," she said. "I won't let you go til you promise."

"That could be okay," he said. He patted the bed beside him.

"Sam. I mean it. Don't fool around. Your whole family is right outside the door here." She stood. "You got to promise. Okay?"

He looked up at her standing there. "Okay," he said. "I'll try, Bonnie. But I can't promise nothin. If he gets in my face, and I see him hurtin Marnie or Danny...well, I don't know what I'll do then." She was looking down at him. "Just so you know," he said.

"Thank you, Sam. You're a good man. I know you'll do what you say you'll do."

She opened the door, and they went back to the kitchen together. There were people getting food, and Bonnie immediately went to help them.

Sam went out. Junior and Alma were on the porch setting up. Sam went past them. There were people everywhere. He went out to the barn to check on the pigs, but mostly to be alone for a minute. He really hated it when Bonnie acted like she was his mother. He sat down on the pigpen fence and scratched the pigs with a stick. Nowdays it seemed like she was always telling him what to do and how to act. That's what she was doing now, and she didn't even know what that bastard did to Marnie. She ought to *want* him to beat up Steve.

At first he thought he would stay in the barn until the reunion was over, but after a while he began to wonder what was going on out there. He could hear Alma singing.

He went to the barn door and opened it a crack. There were people sitting all over the grass. But no one was looking in his direction. Alma was standing on the porch, and Junior was sitting at her feet playing his guitar. Alma was singing 'I'm So Lonesome I Could Cry.' She sounded like she was telling you about herself, like she always did.

Sam left the barn and walked to the garage to get a beer out of one of the coolers in there. The garage was crowded with people who wanted to stay in the shade and still have a good view of Alma.

Sam pushed his way past people to the back of the garage and got himself a beer. He popped it open and took a swig while he moved into the crowd to listen to Alma. Bonnie was in front of him. He was still smarting from the way she treated him, acting like he was a bad boy and she was his mother. Still, he was just about to edge closer to her when he saw Uncle Jimmy pushing toward her from the other direction.

Sam stayed where he was, a little behind them in the crowd. He was close enough to hear Uncle Jimmy say, "It was a terrible thing that Sam lost his job like he did. All of us Martels have been worried about him. And he ain't got another one yet. It's been quite a while now."

Even from behind, Sam could see that Bonnie was smiling her best company smile. "That's because he ain't lookin. You know Sam. He can always find work if he wants it." She turned away to listen to Alma.

Sam could tell that wasn't what Uncle Jimmy expected to hear. He leaned in closer to Bonnie and said something that Sam didn't catch, because just then Alma finished her song, and everyone was clapping.

Alma started another song, and it got quiet enough for Sam to hear Bonnie when she said, "You got it all wrong. It's a good thing. Sam's been tryin to start this butcher business for years now, only he ain't never had enough time to do it right. This was just the push he needed."

Uncle Jimmy opened his mouth to reply, but before he could get out a word, Bonnie patted him on the shoulder and gave him another of her best smiles. "I'll tell him you was askin." Then she moved away through the crowd.

Sam followed. She went around the outside of the house. She was trying to get inside without having to go by Junior and Alma. Good old Bonnie. That was the thing about her. She could get bossy, but then five minutes later, she had his back again. He caught up with her on the front porch. No one else was around.

"I heard what you said to Uncle Jim."

She was just opening the front door. She turned back in surprise. "Oh, Sam. It's you. I didn't know you was there. It was okay, wasn't it? I mean, you didn't mind, did you? He was askin me, and I had to say somethin."

Sam wrapped his arms around her and lifted her off the floor. The screen door swung shut. "Honey, you're the greatest."

"Put me down, Sam, before someone comes along. I'm too big to be slung around like this."

"You can't get too big for me. The more there is of you, the better I like it."

"Oh Sam, don't be ridiculous," she said, but she was laughing. "Was it okay what I said to Uncle Jim?"

"It was great. He was fishin to get you to say somethin bad about me, but you stuck up for me."

"He ought to know me better 'n that. He ought to know I ain't goin to bad mouth my husband in front of the whole Martel family." She took a deep breath. "Or any other time, for that matter."

"If he didn't know it before, he knows it now." He hugged her a little harder and then set her on her feet.

CHAPTER 27

Just past the head of the island, there was a sign for the campsite on the New Hampshire side of the river. It was late afternoon. The shadows were getting long, but the light was still good.

Richard turned the canoe into a cut in the bank. Alyssa looked back at him, and he gestured toward the sign. She nodded. There was a trail that went steeply up through the woods. The campsite must be at the top of the bank. He held the canoe steady so Alyssa could climb out.

"I think we ought to move everything up there to the camp so it's safe, don't you?"

"I guess so. It's quite secluded though. Maybe no one else will come along."

"We can't know that. Anyway, we don't have that much, and we need most of it for tonight."

He started to unload the packs onto the flat ground beside the canoe. When he looked around, Alyssa was gone. She must have started up the trail to the campsite. He hoped she had taken some of their gear with her. But when he got to the top with the pack of food and cooking utensils, she was sitting at the picnic table, looking out through the trees at the river. There was none of their gear with her.

He set the pack down on the table. "What a great place for a camp. That must be the Green Mountains over there."

She smiled at him, but she didn't say anything. He started to ask her if she had carried anything up, but he changed his mind. She looked tired. He didn't want to make her think he was reproaching her. He said, "I'm going down for another load. I'll be back."

"Okay. I want to sit here for a minute, and then I'll come and help. There's no hurry, is there?"

"No. There's plenty of time before dark. Take a rest."

She sighed.

"There's not that many loads, anyway. I'll be glad to do it."

When he got back with the next load, Alyssa was dragging some brush over to the fire ring. She said, "I got your hatchet out of the pack. There's lots of brush, but I don't see any big logs."

"We don't need logs. We've got a bag of charcoal."

When he got back with the last load, she had a small fire started with the brush she had collected. She was sitting beside the fire, breaking up little twigs to feed it. She still looked exhausted.

Richard took over. He worked the fire up to thicker branches, and then he began to put on lumps of charcoal. While he was waiting for the fire to burn down to coals, he set up the tent and made them a bed of spruce branches, with their air mattresses and sleeping bags on top.

By that time the fire was going well, so he began to cook. He didn't mind doing the work. He loved setting up camp. He just wondered if she noticed that he was doing everything, while she sat at the table, looking out at the sun setting across the river.

He put the potatoes in the embers to bake. Then he cooked each of them two hamburgers. There was nothing like being on the river to give you a good appetite. The hamburgers smelled delicious.

When everything was cooked, he carried the food over. He got the salad and dressing and the plates and forks and bread out of the pack. He arranged everything on the table.

Alyssa moved to the other side of the table. "Oh Richard, this looks so nice. I'm sorry you had to do all the work."

"That's okay. I didn't mind. Are you hungry?"

"It smells wonderful."

They sat facing each other. Behind her, Richard could see the bright outline of the mountains with the sun going down behind them. "What an incredible view," he said. "If I owned this land, I would build my house here."

"I know. I've been looking and looking." She took a bite of the ham-burger and set it down again. "This is so good. I wish I was hungry."

"Aren't you? I'm surprised. I was starving."

"I think I'm just too tired to be hungry. It's too much work to chew."

Richard didn't know what to say to that.

She sat there smiling at him in a wistful kind of way, and then she said, "Would you mind a lot if I went to bed? I can't seem to hold my head up. I'm sure I'll be fine in the morning."

"Of course I wouldn't mind," he said, although he couldn't help minding a little. He had hoped that the dinner and the beautiful view might lead to something romantic. They hadn't made love for such a long time. "The bed is all ready. Shall I bring you some water to wash with?"

"I don't think I'll bother. I'm not even going to brush my teeth." She smiled ruefully again. "Good night. I hope you don't mind my leaving all the mess for you."

"It's fine. I'll be along after a while."

He sat for a long time, watching the light fade behind the moun-tains. As the light seeped away, the mountains changed color, get-ting darker and flatter. Just before the light was completely gone, he stacked the dirty dishes and took them down the trail to rinse them in the river.

There was a canoe tied up beside his. Someone was sitting in it, a shadowy person, no more than a silhouette. Richard didn't even know whether it was a man or a woman until he heard the man's voice.

"I saw the light from your fire. I was tryin to decide if I should come up or not. Is the campsite full?"

"No. My wife and I are the only ones here. It's a small campsite, but there's supposed to be room for three tents, and we only have one."

"Is it okay with you if I come up?"

"Sure. I guess so. My wife's asleep."

"I'll be quiet."

"I was just going to rinse off my dishes. If you wait a minute, I'll help you carry up your gear."

"That's okay, man. I haven't got anythin but my day pack and a blanket."

"Don't you have a tent?"

"I don't need one. It's not goin to rain. Look at the stars."

"What about mosquitoes?" Richard was bending over, rinsing off the dishes.

"They won't bother me. I just put the blanket over my head."

"I guess that would work," Richard said doubtfully.

The man had taken his blanket and pack out of the canoe. He was standing at the base of the trail, waiting for Richard to finish his dishes. "If you keep a little fire goin, they tend to go there instead of to the people."

"Really?"

"It helps."

Richard stacked his dishes and stood up. "Okay," he said. "I'm ready to go."

It was full dark now, but enough light came through the trees to show the trail. When they got to the top, there was even more light. Richard still couldn't see enough to decide how old the man was. He had long dark hair tied back from his face, but lots of men, and not always young ones, had long hair these days.

"I'll get my gear off the table so you can have the space," Richard said.

"No problem, man. If you're done usin it, I might sleep on the table. Your dinner smells good."

"It was. Have you eaten?"

"No, man. I didn't bring anythin with me."

"You can have some of ours. We had a lot left over. My wife ate hardly anything."

"That would be great. The night can seem pretty long when you're hungry."

"I was planning to hang my food pack in a tree down the trail, so I wouldn't tempt bears or raccoons. I don't know about the New Hampshire side of the river, but there are lots of bears in Vermont. I don't want to leave my food in the camp here."

"I can help you with that problem, man. I'm always hungry."

Richard unpacked the leftover food. "There's the food for breakfast too. We'll still have to hang up the pack." He filled a plate with their dinner, potatoes, salad, and Alyssa's two hamburgers, one with a small bite out of it. "Here you go," he said, pushing the plate across the table to the side where the man was standing.

"Wow. This is a feast." He sat down at the table and pulled the plate closer. "Thank you, man."

Richard put some charcoal on the fire so they could see a little more. The lantern was in the tent, and he didn't want to wake Alyssa by going in. When he went back to the table, the man was just finishing the food.

"That was really good. I didn't realize how hungry I was." He went over to the fire and squatted down. "I got a little weed, if you want some." He stuck a twig into the fire and lit the joint with it.

Richard could see his face in the flare. He was probably in his late thirties. There was something Indian about the way he looked, even in that dim light. He took a long drag and held the joint out to Richard.

"No thanks," Richard said. He was packing up his pack again. He put the dirty plate in as it was. He left the pack on the table so he wouldn't forget to put it in a tree later.

Then he walked over to the fire and sat down on a stump. "By the way," he said. "My name is Richard, Richard Bradshaw."

The man reached across the fire. "Nice to meet you. Everyone calls me Rod." They shook hands. "Wow. That fire's kind of warm," he said, pulling his hand back.

"My wife's name is Alyssa, but you probably won't see her until morning. She was awfully tired, too tired to eat."

"If I said I was sorry about that, it would be phony. I mean, I benefitted. It was a good dinner."

Richard stirred the fire with a stick and put on a few lumps of charcoal. "I don't know what time it is, but I'm not sleepy yet."

"Me neither. I could sit here and talk for a while." He looked primitive, with the red firelight and black shadows on his face. "I wanted to ask you about your canoe. It was too dark to see much when I came in, but what I could see was beautiful."

"Thank you. I think so too."

"Where'd you get her. She looks old."

"I guess you could say that. She was made in 1962."

"That's not that old."

"I made her. I was in high school at the time."

"No way, man."

"I'll show you in the morning."

"Did you really make her? Did you do it from a kit?"

"No. I found some books that told how. My dad helped me. I built it in his woodshop in the basement of our house. I spent all my time working on it. I had no social life whatsoever."

"That's very cool."

"My parents were worried about me."

"You got a beautiful canoe out of it."

"Yes, and I guess they weren't too worried, because when I graduated, they gave me the money for a river trip."

Rod took a long drag on his joint and threw the stub into the fire. He looked like an ancient hunter crouching by his campfire. He held his breath in for a long beat and then blew it out. "What river, man?"

"This one. The Connecticut. I went with my best friend. My parents drove us up to the Canadian border. They got a motel room, and we stayed in the tent. We launched in the morning. Things were different then. There weren't campgrounds like there are now. We pitched our tent on the riverbank or else in cornfields."

Richard sat there thinking about those long ago days. Vermont seemed younger and more innocent, but then, so was he. The only boats they saw were rowboats with fishermen. "We would hitch a ride into the nearest town to buy groceries and to telephone our parents. I can't believe they were okay with not knowing where we were for days at a time."

"How long were you on the river?"

"We went from the Vermont border to Hartford. I think it took three weeks, but I know we didn't hurry that much, so I may be remembering it wrong. We had lots of adventures along the way."

"It sounds like it."

"And the canoe did really well. We had to fix a few things, but they were minor."

They sat there without talking for a while. The crickets filled the silence. Down by the river, there were frogs. Richard said, "You must be right about the mosquitoes. They aren't bothering me nearly as much as I thought they would."

"They're worse farther up. Did you come all the way down from Canada?"

"Not this trip," Richard said. "This is just an overnighter for us. We put in below St. J, and our car is only a few miles down the river from here."

"I started on the border. I thought I might have seen you before if you'd been on the river that long. But then, you never know. You can be just a few miles behind somebody and never see them. That's happened to me before."

"How far are you going?"

"All the way, man. From the Canadian border to Long Island Sound."

"I've always wanted to do that, but I never have. Alyssa's been sick. This is the first time we've had the canoe out this year." He thought about what he had just said, and then he went on. "The main thing is that she's going to be okay. She's in remission right now. She still has to do some chemo and maybe radiation, and then she'll be all done."

"Wow, man, that's heavy-duty. Was it cancer?"

"Lung cancer. But they caught it really early. We were lucky." He was going to say that he couldn't imagine life without her, but at the last minute, he changed his mind and didn't say anything.

An owl hooted up the river on the New Hampshire side. After a pause it was answered by an owl in Vermont. Behind the camp, away from the river, dogs were barking. All the sounds combined with the crickets and the frogs and the hissing of the fire to make the music of the summer night. Richard wished Alyssa could hear it.

"She's getting stronger since her operation, but I worry about her. She has to push herself to get her strength back. She needs to be in good shape when she starts the chemo. I know that's going to take her down again."

"You got to give her time, man. It takes a long time to recover from something like that."

"Time? What if she doesn't have much time?"

A silence opened up while they both listened to those words. The silence seemed to go on and on. The fire settled itself with tiny hisses. The owls were still calling across the river.

"I can't believe I said that. And I'm sure it isn't true. But she does have to be ready to fight. I know that. That's what I worry about."

"What does she worry about?"

At first Richard couldn't understand the question, but then almost right away, he did. "Well, I don't know the answer to that. We have never talked about it. I don't know what she would say."

"Maybe you should ask her."

"I don't think I could do that. She might think I was trying to take it over."

"Maybe she wants you to."

"Oh no, not her. You haven't met her yet. You'll see when you do. She's very independent." He stood up. "I guess I'd better get to bed. I'll take my pack down the trail."

He went part of the way down the hill to the river and hung the pack in a tree. He took a leak in the bushes and went back up to the camp.

Rod was already stretched out on the picnic table. He was rolled up in a blanket. His pack was under his head. "I banked the fire so we'll have some in the morning. Okay?"

"Sure," Richard said. "I'll show you my canoe then."

"Okay. See you in the morning, man."

Richard went through the mosquito netting in the doorway of the tent as quickly as he could, but some mosquitoes were certain to have come in. He hoped he wouldn't have to lie awake listening to them whine as they searched for him. He took off his shoes and his pants and climbed under the open sleeping bag on the bed he had made for them. He bumped into Alyssa clumsily several times before he got settled.

Alyssa groaned a little. Then she said, "Richard, is that you?"

"Of course. Who else would it be?"

"I had the strangest dream. In it you were showing someone around our house and telling him all about it."

"You must have heard me talking. There's another camper here. He came after you went to bed."

She didn't say anything, but she shifted around so that the spruce branches made a soft noise.

Richard felt like hugging her. "How do you feel now?" he asked.

"All right, I think, but I have to go to the bathroom. Is the camper a man by himself? Has he got his own tent?"

"It is a man. He's sleeping on the picnic table."

"Oh." She paused. "I was going to go to the bathroom in the woods."

"You'd better use the privy because of him."

"I looked in that privy. It's full of enormous spiders."

"Take the lantern."

She sat up. "I don't know which is worse—to see the spiders in the lantern light, or to be in the dark and know they're all around. I don't know what I'll do." She left the tent.

Richard was almost asleep when she came back. He didn't want to wake up, but she wanted to talk.

"Richard, I saw him on the table. I don't know whether he was awake or not. I went all the way down the trail to the river, so I wouldn't have to go into that privy. When I was coming up again, something was there in the woods near the trail. I heard it walking through the bushes, but I couldn't see anything."

"Could it have been a bear? I hung the food in a tree down there."

"Oh, I hope not. It did sound big though. Maybe it would have been safer to go into the privy." She shuddered. "But I'm glad I didn't."

"Alyssa, you'd really rather have an encounter with a bear than with a spider?"

"I didn't think about a bear being there, and I knew about the spiders. But, Richard, that man was lying on the picnic table. Can you believe it?"

"I told you so."

She settled herself deeper under the covers. Richard could hear the rustle of the sleeping bag, and he could feel the shifting of the spruce boughs as she moved around trying to get comfortable. "What's his name anyway?" She was whispering.

"Rod."

"Rod? That doesn't sound like a real name. There isn't enough of it."

"Maybe it's what he tells the people he meets on the trail. Lots of people do that." He was whispering too. "How do you feel now?" Lying so close to her in the darkness, he began to think about sex again.

She settled herself a little more before she answered. "I feel fine. I was just tired, I think. You made us such a cozy bed."

Richard gave up the idea of starting something. There were too many things against it. For one thing, he was tired himself, and she certainly wasn't thinking about anything but snuggling down so she could get back to sleep. And then there was Rod, lying on the table right outside their tent. He told himself that going to sleep beside her in the woods and so near the river was almost as nice as making love.

Richard woke up early in the morning. He put on his pants and left the tent carrying his sneakers. The light was cool and gray. There was fog behind the dark stems of the nearest trees. Rod was crouched over the coals of last night's fire. He was blowing it back to life. He looked as primitive in the daylight as he had in the firelight.

Richard went down the trail to pee and to get his pack. He left his sneakers by the tent. He thought he might see some tracks that would explain the sounds Alyssa heard in the night. But he didn't venture off the trail because he was barefoot. There were some marks on the trail, but it wasn't clear what had made them. Richard suspected either he or Alyssa might have been the cause.

He carried the pack up the trail to the table. The early morning air was full of damp scents from the river and aromatic smells left over from the night. Rod was still working on the fire.

"There's a bag of charcoal if you need some for the fire."

"Thanks, man. I already used some. I figured you wouldn't mind."

"Not at all," Richard said, but he did mind a little. It was his camp, and his fire, and his charcoal. That was silly, and he knew it, a pin-prick of discontent that lessened his pleasure in the beauty of the morning. He decided not to think about it. "I'll make some coffee when you get the fire going. I expect Alyssa will be up soon."

After they had all had some coffee and toast together, Richard went down to the river with Rod to show him the canoe. He was pleased when Alyssa followed them down. She sat down on the bank near them.

Rod tossed his pack and his blanket roll into his canoe and walked over to Richard, who was looking over his own canoe for possible scraped places.

"It's even more beautiful in the daylight, man. What's it made of?"

"Cedar—strips of red cedar and then a strip of white."

"I love those white stripes."

"Alyssa says they're too showy."

"No I don't, Richard. You know that's not true. You know I think it's the most beautiful boat I ever saw."

Richard felt a little embarrassed by the praise, but he liked it too. He was glad Alyssa was listening to the conversation. "It's the white cedar that makes the stripe."

"It wouldn't look nearly so good if it was painted on."

"The planing was the hard part. I had to get every strip exactly the same thickness. That took a long time."

"What do you do to preserve it?"

"I put fiberglass over the whole thing and then epoxy and UV varnish. I've never had to take off the old glass, but I've heard you can get into an awful mess with that. All I've ever had to do is patch places."

Alyssa said, "He works on it every spring, sanding it and painting it with epoxy and varnish. Right, Richard?"

"That's the reason it's lasted so long. I've been thinking of building a new one this winter."

"Would you use cedar again?"

"I don't know yet. I'll have to look around the internet to get some ideas. Maybe I would use cedar…it's so light."

Alyssa said, "But Richard, where would you work on it?"

"The garage. I think I could make it warm enough. We've got that place for a woodstove."

Alyssa started to say something but stopped. She looked worried.

Richard was talking to her, not Rod when he said, "It was just an idea I had when we were coming down the river yesterday. I've always wanted to build another one, maybe one that's smaller and lighter for when we get too old to maneuver this one up into the truck. Don't look so worried."

"I'm not worried. I'm just surprised. This one is so…I don't know… just right, I guess."

"It's getting awfully old. It can't last that much longer, even with me taking really good care of it, but that's not why I would be building a new one. It would be because I had such a good time doing it. I've always wanted to do it again."

"There you go, man. That's plenty enough of a reason."

Richard nodded an agreement with what Rod said, but he was glad that Rod was leaving because Alyssa still looked worried.

After Rod pushed off, they walked up the trail to get their gear and to break up the camp. Richard poured the rest of the coffee into their two cups, and they sat down beside each other on the same side of the table.

Alyssa still hadn't said anything. She sat with her hands wrapped around her coffee mug, taking little sips and looking down.

Richard waited for a while, and then he said, "What's bothering you, honey?"

"Nothing," she said in a low voice. They were both looking at the distant mountains instead of at each other. "You didn't tell *me* you wanted to build a new canoe. You told someone you never saw before."

He wasn't expecting that. "But it isn't the way you make it sound. I was planning to tell you last night. I just decided yesterday when we were on the river. I was thinking how if I really meant to do it, I had better get going. So I decided to do it this winter." He was looking at her now. She was still cradling her lukewarm coffee and staring straight ahead. "I was going to tell you at dinner last night, but you were so tired that you went to bed before I had a chance."

"So it's my fault you didn't tell me." Her bottom lip was trembling.

He wanted to put his arms around her, but she seemed so self-contained, so unapproachable. "I've always wanted to do it. You know that. Yesterday I thought I had better not keep putting it off, because then I never would do it. I thought I could cut back on my work and spend more time at home with you, and if I had the garage set up right, I could be working on the new canoe when I was home."

She nodded, but she still didn't look at him.

"Let's get going. We can talk about it while we're paddling down to where we left the car."

Alyssa nodded. She actually smiled a little.

Richard thought it would be easy to start the conversation again. But it wasn't. He didn't want Alyssa to have to turn around to face him, and he didn't want to shout at her. He sensed that being out on the river had cheered her and made her feel closer to him, and he didn't want to do anything that would spoil that feeling.

The sun was high enough now so that it sparkled on the water. The broad expanse of the river looked still and peaceful on the surface, but underneath it was moving fast. Trees on the riverbanks went sailing by.

A great blue heron was standing on the Vermont side in the reedy shallows. It stood like a statue on its long sticklike legs. It slowly turned its head to the side to watch them with a beady eye as they passed. Richard looked back and saw it spear the water with its long beak. By then they were too far away to see whether it caught a fish.

In the late morning, they got to the fishing access where they had left their car. Alyssa got out of the canoe, looking stiff but refreshed and happy.

They loaded their gear into the car and then put the canoe on the roof. Richard did most of it, but Alyssa tried to help. They talked while they worked. Alyssa said she had been worried that she wouldn't be able to keep up, but she was pleased that she had.

"I hope we'll have time for a lot of trips before winter."

Alyssa said, "Me too." Then she added, "I hope I won't feel too awful to do anything after the chemo starts."

"Let's wait and see. There will certainly be some bad days, but there are bound to be good ones too. The important thing is to not worry about it."

"I know," she said. "I'll try not to. We'll see what happens, like you say."

"We'll get through this together. You know?"

"I know, Richard."

CHAPTER 28

After lunch they all sat on the deck in the sunshine. It was hot, but then, Labor Day weekend was still summer. Monika had come to Vermont with Sonia and her family. Alix and Reuben were there too. She lay back in her chair with her eyes closed and let the sun bathe her face with its warmth, while the talk swirled around her. Richard had said he heard it might rain later, but there was no sign of it yet.

Monika was just thinking how peaceful it was, when Jack began to lobby his mother to take him up to the pool so he could go swimming. Sonia said she wanted to stay and talk to everybody, and Jack said everybody should come with them.

Monika was just about to tell Jack not to nag his mother. But before she had a chance to say a word, everyone chimed in with what a good idea it was to go up to the pool. Monika said she was going to stay right where she was, unless she went inside to take a nap. But no one would hear of leaving her behind. They overruled her objections about the difficulty of walking up there by saying it would be good for her. It was useless to protest. She consoled herself by thinking how fortunate she was that they wanted her company.

There was a delay while everyone hurried around getting their bathing suits and whatever else they wanted. Monika stayed in the chair with her face tilted to the sun. Long before she felt rested and ready for the trek, they were all gathered on the deck.

She stood up. "I'll come," she said. "But please don't wait for me. I'll go at my own speed." She flourished her cane to show them that she was prepared to go without assistance.

They set off across the yard and up the trail in a straggling group, everyone talking and carrying things. Monika held herself back a little so they would all see that she was going to be slower than they were. She would have felt that she had to hurry if anyone had stayed behind to keep her company.

When the trail went up into the woods, it got steeper, and she went even more slowly. It was cool under the tall trees, and it was quiet. She could hear them talking and laughing, but they were already too far ahead for her to make out the words. It was a pleasant murmur, like the chirping of the crickets or the gurgling of the brook down below.

She passed the little cabin. When she came out into the open above the pool, Jack shouted, "Look, there's Nana," and everyone cheered. That was nice. That made the walk worth it.

As she shuffled down the trail to the water, Richard jumped up from where he was sitting on the grass. He unfolded a chair. "I brought this for you, Monika. Where would you like to sit?"

"Anywhere," she said. He put the chair down near Alyssa, and Monika sat down with a thump. "Thank you, Richard. It feels good to sit down."

"The hike wasn't too hard for you, was it, Mom?"

"Oh no, I'm fine if I just take my time."

Jack was standing in the water, conscious that everyone was watching. He hit the water, making larger and larger splashes and laughing as he did so. It was bravado. He wasn't quite brave enough to go out deeper. Everyone kept an eye on him as they talked to each other, in case he decided to try something more adventurous.

Monika was looking for the right moment to bring up the subject she wanted to discuss with all of them. She was ready to start driving again. She knew it would be controversial when she brought it up. She didn't need their permission, but getting it would make it all easier. She had marshalled all the arguments she could think of, but she needed to wait for the right moment, and this wasn't it. Still, the whole holiday weekend was before them. She would find the time. It was so beautiful beside the pool, too beautiful for arguments.

Out loud she said, "I had forgotten what a lovely spot this is. The waterfall is spectacular, and that water is emerald green. It's so unusual. What do you suppose makes it that color?"

"I've often wondered that myself," Richard said. "It might be minerals in the water. Or it might be because it's so deep. It gets quite deep in the middle. I hope Jack is aware of that."

Jack must have heard his name because he turned around too fast, and his feet slipped out from under him. He sat down hard. That scared him, and he splashed, struggling to get to his feet again.

Sonia jumped up, but before she could rescue him, he was standing, trying bravely not to cry. Sonia sat down without going over to him. Monika thought that was wise of her. To comfort him would have made him think there was more to be afraid of.

"It's lucky he didn't slide out into the deep water," Alyssa said, but she spoke softly so he wouldn't hear.

No one said much after that. Monika paid more attention to the sound of the waterfall than she did to the conversation. A flock of crows flew over, calling to each other with noisy exclamations.

Jack got out of the water and went up the path. A few minutes later he came back with a handful of stones. He put them down on the bank and stood near them, throwing them into the water one by one.

After about an hour, Monika said she thought she would go back to the house and take a nap. She stressed that no one needed to come with her, that she would be fine by herself. "Besides," she said, smiling at them. "It's all downhill after the cabin. If I fall, I can just roll the rest of the way to the house." She waved her cane in the air, to show them she was joking.

Alyssa stood up. "I'll go with you, Mom. I need to check on the roast anyway. I put the oven on the timer, but it isn't all that reliable."

"All right," Monika said. "You are the one person I don't mind slowing down a little."

They started up the trail together. When they got to the cabin, Monika couldn't help saying, "When you decided to go to Vermont to be with Richard, I had no idea what your living conditions were going to be. It must have been so difficult to live there without running water or electricity. I don't know which I would miss the most."

"Yes, it was hard. But I loved it too."

"I guess I can picture Richard roughing it, but you, Alyssa, you couldn't even take a bath. I can't imagine it."

"Oh Mom. Don't be silly. Of course we took baths. We had a big tub. We heated water on the stove and filled the tub. It made a wonderful bath."

"It sounds so primitive."

"It was more trouble, but it was luxurious to take a bath in front of the fire in the candlelight, with the snow softly falling outside the windows, and the world so quiet and peaceful. I miss it actually."

"It must have been so much work—getting groceries, keeping warm, having enough light—I don't know how you did it. I'm glad I didn't know about it at the time."

"It wouldn't have been so nice if one of us had gotten sick. I was thinking about that after my operation. It would have been hard to recover if we still lived in the cabin."

"Oh dear, I don't like to think about it. Thank goodness you're more comfortable now."

"I am, Mom. Richard has been so good to me."

"I know. I used to think he didn't treat you right, but I know he's been doing much better lately."

They were on a part of the trail that ran under large pine trees. The ground was orange with fallen needles. It was soft underfoot. It would cushion her if she fell. The trail went steeply down the hill past a large stump.

"Phew," Monika said. "I'm going to sit down here for a minute. You go on ahead."

"I'll stay with you. I'm not in a hurry. When we lived in the cabin, Richard would sit at the table in the lamplight every evening and draw plans for our new house. He would show them to me, and we would decide what we wanted to build. It was so fun."

Monika sat down on the stump. "There's plenty of room for both of us to sit here." She sighed. "Everything is so hard when you get old. No one realizes how much work it is. Everything takes longer. And the worst part is that you don't trust yourself any more. I sat up there by the pool, worrying about how I was going to get back down to the house, and then we began talking, and I didn't think about it, and it was fine. It's the lack of trust that makes it so hard."

"I'm sorry, Mom. I know how you feel. I'll be glad when I'm done with this chemotherapy. I'm getting kind of scared about it."

"Poor little Alyssa," Monika thought. "Here I am complaining about getting old, and she is just hoping to be able to get old." She didn't even want to think about it. She patted Alyssa on the knee. Out loud she said, "I wish you didn't have to go through all that."

"I know. Me too. But the doctor thinks it's important. I hope it will be done by winter. Richard is going to cut way back on his work so he can spend more time at home with me."

"That's nice. He can take care of you for a change, instead of you always taking care of him."

"Oh Mom. I thought you were getting to like him better. Don't you think it's nice that he's going to be home a lot?"

"I guess so…if you do. And I do think he has treated you much better since you got sick. Maybe he's finally learning to appreciate what he's got."

"He's planning to winterize the garage so he can build a new canoe out there."

"What? What does he want to do that for?"

"He's always meant to build another canoe like the one he built when he was in high school. That one is getting awfully old. Come on. Let's go the rest of the way."

"All right," Monika said. She pushed herself up to standing. They started down the trail again. Gradually, Monika's legs loosened up.

But it was slow. It was always too slow.

Alyssa said, "Richard and I went on an overnight canoe trip down the Connecticut the other day. I was afraid I wouldn't be strong enough. Of course, I didn't say that to Richard. He would have worried too much."

"Oh Alyssa. Don't overdo it. You need to take care of yourself. Oh dear me."

"But Mom, that's what I'm telling you. I did fine. I got tired the first day. But Richard made us a wonderful bed of spruce boughs. I had a good sleep that night, and I was fine the next day. See. Isn't that good?"

"You slept on the ground?"

"We were camping, Mom." She was laughing, but Monika could hear a hint of exasperation in her voice.

They walked out into the yard. Alyssa looked up. Thunderclouds were boiling up in the sky above them.

Alyssa said, "I guess Richard was right. It *is* going to rain. I hope they come down before it starts. Let's hurry, Mom. There are a lot of windows that need to be closed."

They hurried across the yard, or rather, Alyssa hurried on ahead, and Monika followed as fast as she could. When she got to the house, she could smell the roast cooking. Alyssa was bustling around, making sure the windows were closed. Monika followed trying to help, but not being much use.

When they got to the room where Monika was sleeping, she sat down on the bed. "I didn't know how tired I was. I think I'll stay and take a nap, unless you need me to help you with something."

"No, I'm fine, Mom. Take a rest. I'm going to see about the roast and a few other things, and then I might go up to the pool again. I'll see you later."

"Good night dear." Monika kicked off her shoes and lay down on top of the bedspread. She thought she would read, but she fell asleep almost right away.

She must have slept for quite a while, because when she woke up, she could hear people talking in the other room. They had all come back from the pool. She lay still, feeling completely comfortable. She didn't want to move, so she didn't. After a time, she began to wonder if it was raining. She sat up and looked at the window, but it was closed. She couldn't tell what was happening outdoors, so she got up to look. The sky was full of piled clouds. They were dark and forbidding, but the ground was still dry.

Monika put on her shoes. She straightened her clothes and combed her hair. Then she went out to the living room. Sonia and Alix were setting the table. They had put the extra leaf in so it would be big enough. Alyssa was making a salad. They all looked up when she came in.

"Still no rain?" she said.

Alyssa smiled. "It's going to start any minute now. Did you have a good nap?"

"It was so nice I didn't want to get up."

"You could have stayed longer, Mom."

"Oh no, that was plenty. What can I do to help?"

"Sit down and talk to us. We have time. Richard took Brian and Reuben out to show them how he plans to heat the garage this winter. He wanted to ask their advice about it."

Monika sat down at the end of the table.

Alix said, "Do you really think Dad's going to build another canoe?"

Alyssa looked over the counter at them. "I don't know if he'll build a canoe, but I do know he's always wanted to. The table looks very nice. Thank you girls for setting it."

After a while Monika saw Richard at the glass door on the deck. Brian and Reuben were behind him. They all came in, followed by Jack, who was trying to be one of the guys.

Richard said, "I think it's finally beginning to rain a little. It was a good idea to set the table inside."

All through dinner the skies were dark and threatening, but there were only a few, scattered drops of rain. After dinner the western sky was a fiery red. The rain was over.

Alyssa insisted that Monika not help clean up. Since it looked as though it would stay dry after all, they decided to sit out on the deck.

Behind her Monika could hear Alyssa and the girls putting away the food and washing the dishes while they talked. In front of her, Brian and Reuben were asking Richard questions about building a canoe. She lay back in her chair and looked up. A transparent rainbow arched across the sky. She let the voices wash over her without trying to understand what they were saying. She was at peace.

She was surprised when she heard Alix and Sonia talking right behind her chair. Alyssa said, "Okay now. Let's all start together," and they began to sing happy birthday.

Monika sat up and turned around. She had almost forgotten about her birthday. The three of them were standing in the doorway. Alyssa was in the middle, holding a cake with lit candles. The candlelight shone golden on her face. She looked lovely and full of life as she sang.

"Oh goodness," Monika said. "You didn't need to go to all that trouble. I had almost forgotten that it was my birthday. I never meant to get so old. I'm not sure it's cause for celebration." Even as she said the words, she regretted them. Everyone was enjoying the festive occasion.

Alyssa set the cake down in front of her. "Now, Mom, make a wish on the candles. See, all the blue ones count for ten years, and the white ones count for one year."

"I hope you didn't put any to grow on. I don't want to grow any more." She took a deep breath and blew them out. Alyssa was all right now, and Monika felt free to wish something for herself. She wished that she would be able to drive again. She didn't have to have their approval, but it would be easier if she could get it. She decided to tell them her plans. She knew they would all be upset if she didn't let them know in advance what she was going to do.

She blew at the candles until she had no more breath. Then she looked around. Everyone was watching her. "Well," she said. "I guess I'll get my wish."

Jack was standing nearby. He leaned on her lap and looked solemnly into her face. "What did you ask for, Nan? It's okay to tell it when all the candles are out."

"I don't know, Jackie. I think it's safer not to tell anybody until the wish comes true. I'll tell you then, okay?"

He nodded.

She didn't want them to know that she wished for something for herself when she could have wished for something for Alyssa. And she wouldn't have done it either, unless she was sure that Alyssa was going to be all right.

She patted Jack on his little bony shoulder. "I was going to cut you a piece of cake, but maybe you don't want one."

"Don't tease me, Nana. You know how hungry I am."

Sonia said, "Jack, that's not possible. How could you be hungry when you just finished dinner?"

"I am, Mom. It's really true."

Monika didn't say anything. She sliced the cake and served them all, and she made sure Jack got a big piece.

When they were all comfortably settled eating birthday cake, Monika decided to chance it. "I was wondering what you all thought about my starting to drive again."

There was a little gasp of surprise from someone. Everyone looked at everyone else. No one said a word, but no one needed to. There wasn't anyone who thought it was a good idea. Monika could see that for herself.

"I still have my license," she said. "I was the one who decided it wasn't safe for me to drive. I stopped voluntarily. But now my eyes have improved so much that I think it's okay again. I have a valid driver's license, and there is a functional car in my garage. There's really nothing to stop me."

There was a short silence, and then Alix began, looking quite distressed. "But, Nana, you can't know your eyes are better. It could be wishful thinking. Any of us could convince ourselves that something was so, just by wishing for it so much."

"Look, I didn't say anything for a long while, because I wasn't sure. I was afraid I might be imagining it. But it's true. I verified it. I can tell how much my eyes have improved since I began to have the shots."

There was a general outburst when she said that. She certainly had their attention, but it wasn't altogether sympathetic. Brian wanted to know if the doctor had done specific tests to see if she should be driving, and she had to say no to that, although he did say her eyes were good enough for her to drive again.

"And I had my own test, just as good as the eye chart, better maybe. Remember last spring how I couldn't read the cards, and I was so embarrassed that I had to quit playing with my friends?"

"I remember," Sonia said. "Poor Nana, I felt so sorry for you. You loved your poker games."

Monika nodded. She had felt pretty sorry for herself last spring. "I've been playing solitaire to see if I could see the cards again, and I can. I told my friends I couldn't play during the summer, but summer's over. I'm going to start playing once more."

"I don't see what that has to do with driving. I think it's great if you can play cards again, but I don't believe you ought to be driving."

"You don't understand, Brian. My eyes are so much better than they were." She was hurt.

He was cross at her, impatient with her foolishness. "That's not what I'm talking about. I'm sure you can see well enough to drive if you say so. I think it was very wise of you to stop last spring when you were worried about it. Most people wouldn't have been so objective and sensible."

"Thank you," Monika said. His compliment made her feel a little better, but she could hear that something else was coming.

"But there's more to it than that." He paused and looked around to make sure he had everyone's attention. Then he said, "Insurance," as though he was saying something significant.

Monika was relieved. "That's okay, Brian," she said. "I kept on paying my insurance bill, even when I thought I probably wouldn't ever drive again. At the time, I thought I was being unrealistic, but now I'm glad I did."

"That's not what I meant. Think about it." He didn't have to look around now. He could probably sense that everyone's attention was on what he was going to say. "Suppose you get into an accident. The first thing they'll check is your health, and that includes your eyes. Even if the doctor said you could drive again, there would still be a question about your ability. You could have a little fender-bender, and someone could sue you for everything you've got."

"Oh," Monika said. "I didn't think of that."

"Suppose you bumped into a car while you were parking. The owner's insurance company would check on you and see that you had macular degeneration. They could take you to court and sue you. They could win. They could say that you weren't supposed to be driving, that you were endangering everyone on the road. It could be devastating."

Monika was crushed. She had thought of all the arguments she could make, like how she wouldn't drive at night, or outside town, how she would always take the train to Vermont, unless Alix or Sonia was driving up. But none of those restrictions would get around the fact that she could have a small, unimportant accident any time and any place, an accident that could mushroom into a huge liability.

Sonia could see how hurt she was. She said, "Nan, you could end up losing more independence that way than if you just gave up driving. Don't you see?"

"Yes," she said. "I do see." To herself she added, "But I don't want to." She lay back in her chair and looked at the sky. It was different now. The rainbow was gone. It must have faded while they were talking. The sky was dark, but the stars hadn't come out yet.

Monika felt unhappy and alone, so she was taken by surprise when Alyssa swooped down and wrapped her arms about her. "Don't feel bad, Mom. You'll find a way to live with it. After all, you've been doing fine all summer."

Monika felt like saying, "That's easy for you to say," but she kept quiet. It was just like Alyssa to notice that she was unhappy and to try to comfort her. And anyway, Alyssa had been through a lot worse this summer, and thank goodness, she would soon be well again. Alyssa's troubles made her own seem small by comparison.

She patted Alyssa on the back and said, "Thanks, sweetie, I don't mind that much. Nothing matters now that you are going to be all right."

Alyssa pulled a chair up beside Monika's and sat down close to her. She took Monika's hand in both of hers. "I still have the chemo to get through."

Alix said, "Don't worry, Mom. It's much better than it used to be. Everybody says so. It doesn't make people so sick any more."

"Some people smoke grass. Everyone says that makes a lot of difference."

Sonia and Alix started to laugh, but Alyssa said, "Oh good. It'll be like the '60s again. That'll be fun, won't it Richard?"

Richard nodded.

Monika was a bit shocked, but she didn't say anything. It was getting quite dark on the deck, and no one noticed. She was glad of that, because she wouldn't begrudge Alyssa anything, legal or illegal, that would make her more comfortable and better able to get through these treatments.

After a little while, everyone started talking about what they wanted to do tomorrow, and Monika yawned. She stood up slowly, balancing her weight on her stiff legs. "I think I'll turn in now," she said. "Thank you all for my birthday party."

She went inside and walked down the hall to her room. It was a great comfort to be able to see better, and even more of a comfort to have the state of her eyes out in the open and to have a doctor who was working on keeping what sight she had left. Things were so much better than they had been in the spring, when her main preoccupation was trying to keep anyone from finding out how blind she was getting.

She went into her bedroom and closed the door. It wasn't so important that she keep on driving. When you got old, one by one, things were taken from you, and you didn't get them back. You had to go on with your life in a diminished state, trying to be grateful for what you still had. And she had her family, and especially Alyssa. That should be enough.

CHAPTER 29

Sam didn't know what woke him up, but something did. He lay there in the dark, listening. Bonnie's breathing was soft and regular, almost a snore. Whatever he had heard, it wasn't enough to wake her.

He turned over and put his arm around her. She moaned a little in her sleep.

"Bonnie, what's that noise?"

"Just Minnie havin a bad dream."

There it was again, a clink of dishes and maybe a woman's voice. Minnie growled a little.

"It's not Minnie," he said. "Somebody's in the kitchen."

"I don't hear nothin. Colt would be barkin if there was anyone out there."

"I'm goin to see." Sam sat up and put his feet over the side of the bed. He grabbed his pants, pulled them on, and shoved his feet into his work boots.

"Bring me a glass of water when you come back, will you, Sam?"

"Okay." He stepped out into the hall. The door to the kitchen that they never closed was closed. There was a thin strip of light coming under it.

Sam went down the hall as quietly as he could. His boot laces clicked against the floor with every step. He opened the door stealthily, just far enough to look through. The light on the other side was so bright that for a minute he couldn't see anything. Then his eyes began to adjust.

Marnie and Danny were sitting at the kitchen table. Marnie was making a sandwich. She looked up and saw him standing in the doorway. "Hi, Pop," she said. "We was tryin not to wake you up."

"What time is it anyhow?"

When Danny heard his voice, he turned around. "Hi, Gramp," he said.

"Danny, do you want mayonnaise or mustard?"

"Both," Danny said.

Sam could feel the pressure building now that he knew who was out there. He stuffed the explosion down inside. "I'm goin to get some more clothes," he said. "And then, I want to know what's goin on."

He went back to the bedroom. He could hear the bed creak as Bonnie sat up. "What is it, Sam?"

"It's Marnie and Danny. I don't know what they're doin here, besides eatin, but I'm goin to find out."

When he sat down on the side of the bed to put on his socks, she said, "Where's my water?"

"Oh, I forgot all about it. I'll get it for you in a minute."

She threw back the covers. "Don't bother. I'm gettin up. What time is it?"

"I don't know that either. It's got to be after twelve at least."

"You go on," she said. "I'll be there in a minute."

When he got back to the kitchen, Marnie said, "I'm sorry, Pop. We were goin to leave you a note and explain everythin in the morning. We could of done it too, but Danny was hungry."

Sam looked down at the table. Her sandwich was just as big as Danny's. She must have been hungry too. He moved a chair up to the table for Bonnie and one for himself. After a few minutes Bonnie came in wearing her furry pink bathrobe that always made Sam think of the stuffed animals that people win as prizes at the fair.

Bonnie said hello. She started to sit down in the empty chair, but halfway down, she said, "Marnie, your eye. What happened to your eye?" She stayed there, not sitting, as though she couldn't move.

Danny said, "She's okay, Grammie. It's been like that for days."

Bonnie sighed and lowered herself into the chair.

Marnie looked at each of them in turn. "We had to leave. I couldn't take it, and it wasn't goin to get better."

Sam was still wondering why he hadn't noticed Marnie's eye until Bonnie did. It was a classic black eye. The bruised area was wide and dark. "How could you go to work like that?"

Marnie gave him a twisted smile that was full of pain. "I made up some story about it," she said. "But everybody knows the truth."

Sam could feel himself getting angry again. He could get in his truck right this minute and go down there and give that bastard what he deserved for treating Marnie that way. He said so.

"Oh, Pop," she said. She jumped up and put her arms around him. "I love you. I know I can always count on you, Pop." Her face was pressed against his shoulder, and the words came out muffled. "But I don't want you to do that. It would make everything worse, and besides, you might get hurt. Danny and I don't want to go back down there anyway. Can we stay with you for a while until we can get a little ahead?"

Sam could feel her look up, but she kept her arms around him. "What do you say, Ma? I was thinking Danny could go to school in West Severance like Junior and I did."

"Oh Marnie," Bonnie said. "Of course you can, baby."

Marnie went around to Bonnie's side of the table to hug her. "Thanks, Ma," she said.

"Damn that bastard. I should have done what I wanted to do to him when he was right here for the reunion. You shouldn't have stopped me, Bonnie."

"I was right, Sam, and you even knew it then."

He thought about that. He guessed he did know it, but he wasn't about to say so out loud. "God damn it, Marnie. Why don't you find yourself somebody who'll treat you right? You're a hard worker, and you're okay lookin. Why can't you find yourself a good guy, instead of always tyin up with these losers and mean bastards?"

Marnie was sitting down again now. "I don't know, Pop. Steve seemed so nice at first. It's hard to tell what someone's goin to be like when you know him better. I guess I don't know how to choose."

"You do too know how to choose, Marnie. Your track record's perfect. You choose a bastard every time."

"Hush, Pop. Don't talk like that in front of Danny."

"It's about time Danny knew the score, and anyway, he *does* know the score. I'm sure he knows his dad was bad to you."

Sam looked around at Danny who was finishing his sandwich with his eyes on his plate. "That ain't news to you, is it, Danny boy?"

Danny shook his head without looking up.

Bonnie went to the refrigerator. "You're not too full for some chocolate ice cream, are you, Danny?"

"Can I have some, Grammie?"

Bonnie got out a bowl and served him. "Anybody else?" she said, but Sam and Marnie shook their heads.

Bonnie sat down again. "What about all your stuff, your furniture and your clothes? What about the apartment?"

"I can't do anything about it as long as Steve's there, and if I try to get him kicked out, it could mess up his probation. Then he'd *really* be after me. I thought I'd just wait. He'll leave after a while. The rent ain't due for a while yet."

Bonnie said, "Well what about your job then?" That was just like Bonnie. She was always the sensible one. Sam was more interested in pounding somebody.

Marnie looked at both of them. "I told 'em a couple weeks ago that I was goin to have to leave. I been lookin for the right chance. Me and Danny packed our bags weeks ago. We been drivin around with our stuff in the trunk of the car." She smiled at him. "Ain't that right?"

He nodded. "I didn't tell any of my friends. They're goin to be surprised when I don't show up at school."

Marnie gave him a loving look. "I'm sorry, honey. But you can make new friends. And in a few days you can text Jason and Colin and tell 'em you had to move."

Sam said, "We haven't really talked about this."

"It's all right, ain't it, Pop? Could we stay for a while til I can get enough ahead to rent us a place?"

"I was thinkin how this might be more of a load for your ma to carry, and she's got to carry it single-handed, since I ain't got a job."

Marnie looked like she was about to cry. Bonnie reached out to her.

Sam wished he'd kept quiet. "I don't know," he said. "We have plenty of room, don't we? And there ain't nobody we'd rather do for than Marnie."

Bonnie was holding Marnie's hand. "Let's talk in the mornin about how we're goin to do it, but don't worry, honey. We want you to stay here as long as you want to."

"Oh Ma," Marnie said. She jumped up and put her arms around Bonnie again, burying her face in the pink fuzz of Bonnie's robe. "I love you, Ma."

Danny and Sam looked at each other, a guy look that said, "Women, they are always cryin and carryin on."

Sam picked up some dishes to put in the sink. Danny stood up too and began to put the food away in the refrigerator. They smiled at each other.

Sam said, "I guess we're goin to have to do all the women's work, Danny boy." That made Marnie and Bonnie both begin to help. After that they all started for bed.

Marnie said, "Don't come up, Ma. We can find what we need."

"Okay, honey. See you in the mornin."

As he was undressing in their bedroom, Sam said, "This could mean a lot of extra work for you, Bonnie. Don't you worry about that?"

Bonnie was already snuggled down in the bed with the covers up around her chin.

Sam lifted up the covers on his side so he could get under.

"Sam, hurry up. You're lettin in the cold."

Sam started to ask how he was supposed to get under without lifting the covers, but he kept his mouth tight shut. He climbed under and then reached up to turn off the light.

"You don't think this is goin to be too hard on you?" he said to the darkness.

"I don't want to even think about that part of it. It's Marnie, and she needs us. We'll make it work."

Sam turned over and put his arm around her. "You're the best, Bonnie."

"She's a good girl and a hard worker. I just wish she didn't have such bad luck all the time."

"I guess she plans to put Danny to school in West Severance."

"It sounds like it. Night, Sam."

Sam hugged her a little tighter. Then he turned over to go to sleep. He thought he was wide-awake. He thought he was going to lie there, thinking about what to do for Marnie, but the next thing he knew, it was morning.

Sam opened his eyes. The early light was pouring in the bedroom windows. Bonnie and Minnie were already up and gone. Sam could hear voices in the kitchen. He lay there remembering how Marnie and Danny came in during the night. He hoped Marnie had done the right thing by leaving. Steve could come after her. She wasn't that far away. Sam could and would do all he was able to do to protect her and Danny. Still, he couldn't be with them every second. She was definitely in danger, but she would have been in danger if she had stayed. Sam sighed and threw back the covers. He would love to eliminate the problem by eliminating Steve, but he could see that doing something like that would make a worse mess. The only thing was to hope that Steve would do something that would put him back in jail for a good long time.

Sam got dressed and went down the hall to the kitchen. Both women were sitting at the table. Colt was lying by the door. When he saw Sam, he beat his tail slowly against the floor. Sam leaned down and patted him on the head. He couldn't remember noticing Colt last night.

"Get yourself some coffee, Sam. There's a fresh pot on the stove."

When he sat down with his coffee, he said, "Did Colt bark at you last night?"

"He knew who we were. I said his name before I opened the door."

"That was smart. He's supposed to guard the place. Where's Danny anyhow?"

"I let him sleep. He was worn out last night. And, Pop, if you've thought it over and decided we shouldn't stay here...." she paused, searching his face. "Well, I wanted to give you a chance to say so, without Danny around."

Sam looked back at her, feeling so many different things at once. Could she possibly think he didn't want her or Danny to stay? Everything got so complicated and mixed up. She was so much like him, so emotional.

"Marnie, you didn't get what I was tryin to say to you. Of course we want you here, both of you. Your ma told you that last night. That ain't what I meant at all. I was thinkin about how your ma has to carry the whole place now that I ain't workin."

"I can help. I know how to work. And anyway, Pop, you are too workin. Your butcher business is really takin off, ain't it?"

"It might be. But it ain't like workin out for a regular paycheck you can count on. Your ma's the only one doin that."

Bonnie stood up. "You worry too much, Sam. It'll be fine with Marnie here. It's about time we had some young ones around again." She kissed Marnie on top of her head. "I'm goin to get dressed. I need to be in early today. You can get Pop some breakfast when he's ready."

"God damn it, Bonnie. You talk like I can't take care of myself." He looked at her over the top of Marnie's head. She was grinning at him.

When Bonnie left the room, Sam said, "You know she was just kiddin, don't you?"

"Oh sure, Pop, but you won't be sorry to have us here. I can help out a lot."

"I know that, honey." He stood up. "I'm goin out to smoke. You want to come?"

"Sure, if I can bum one of yours. Mine are upstairs."

"I been tryin to quit, or at least cut back, but I ain't havin much luck with it."

They stood side by side on the porch, blowing the smoke out into the wind. It was a beautiful morning, with a low mist over the field across the road. The maple trees were bright gold, and the sky behind them was deep blue.

Sam said, "It's goin to be a real pretty day, ain't it?"

"It makes me glad to be here."

"I'm glad you are too."

Bonnie came out the door in her pink uniform. They watched her get in her little car and drive away, and then they went back inside to fix breakfast.

A few days later Sam and Marnie were in the basement. Marnie was helping him cut and package a side of beef for a customer. The phone rang upstairs. Both Sam and Marnie had meat-covered hands.

Sam said, "Let's let it go."

But Marnie wiped her hands and ran up the stairs. "I'll get it, Pop. It might be Danny or the school."

Sam was sawing out some steaks. He didn't notice she was back until he turned off the saw. Then he saw her in her place, cutting up stew meat.

"Who was on the phone, Marnie?"

"Oh, Pop, you're not goin to believe this. It was Sherwood Manor. They've got work for me startin tomorrow."

"That's kinda short notice, ain't it?"

"I don't care. It's good for me. You won't need me here, will you?"

"No. I got two steers to do over on the other side of Severance." He was struggling with his feelings, trying to be glad for Marnie. He just wished someone would call *him* with a job offer. "What about Danny? Nobody won't be home when he gets off the bus."

"He'll be okay. He's a big boy."

"What if Steve comes around?"

"It ain't likely. If he was comin, he'd of been here already."

"I'm just sayin…."

"He likes Danny. He won't hurt Danny. I'm the one he's after."

"I could try to get done with the steers early so I'd be back when Danny gets home."

"Don't worry about it, Pop. It'll be fine."

"And that's another thing. We need to go down to Randolph and get your stuff out of the apartment before it gets stolen, or Steve sells it or gives it away, or somethin."

"You're right, and I hope you'll help me with that, but we don't have to deal with it for a while yet, at least until the rent is due. I don't want to have to pay another month's rent, and I hope I can get the deposit back, but right now I want to help you get this beef done up. I've finished all the stew meat. What do you want me to do next?"

"You might could wrap up these steaks. Put two in a package."

"Okay."

"It's great to have you workin with me, Marnie. I want you to know that." He had his back to her as he spoke. She didn't answer, and he thought she probably didn't hear what he said. He didn't look around to see. Part of him was relieved that she hadn't heard. It wasn't the kind of thing he felt comfortable saying, not even to Bonnie.

Then after a silence, she said, "I ain't goin nowhere, Pop, and it ain't a full-time job, although I could use the money. They want somebody to fill in. But that's good too, because then I'll have time to help you with your business some of the time."

"That could be good," he said, and he meant it too. She was a fast worker, but she wasn't sloppy. She did her work carefully and well.

A few minutes later, she had all the steaks packed up and in the cooler. "What's next, Pop?"

"We ain't got that much left. We got the roasts to wrap, and then we need to grind the hamburg and wrap it. That's all, I think. We'll get it done in good time."

"I can do the roasts now."

They stood side by side at the table. Sam trimmed the roasts, and Marnie packaged them. Without the meat saw running, they could hear the radio in the kitchen, playing one of the good country oldies, always Sam's first choice. Marnie said, "I forgot to tell you, Pop. When I went out to get the mail yesterday, there was a letter in the box for Richard and Alyssa."

"That happens all the time."

"I took it over to their house."

"You didn't need to do that. You could of just stuck it in their mailbox."

"I know. I guess I just wanted to say hello and tell 'em I was goin to be around for a while."

"Marnie, how're you goin to pay your bills? You didn't leave a forwardin address, did you? Steve could find it out."

"No, I didn't, Pop. I wasn't expectin any mail. I just felt like getting outdoors yesterday, I guess. I got my bills set so I can keep up online. That way it ain't a problem if I move around. But I need to tell you about Alyssa."

"Well, go ahead then."

"I walked up there. The glass door on the deck was shut, even though it was a beautiful day. I knocked several times, but no one came to the door."

"They go away a lot, Marnie."

"That's want I thought. I was goin to leave the letter on the table on the deck. I turned around to find something to put on top of it, so it wouldn't blow away."

"I hope you didn't leave it like that. Suppose they were goin to be away for a few days or even longer."

"I didn't leave it on the table, as it turned out. I heard the glass door open, and I looked around. Alyssa was standin there. I must have woken her up or somethin. I gave her the letter."

"Well, that's okay, then."

"No, Pop. It wasn't. She looked awful, real sick and real old, like she couldn't even stand up without holdin onto the door. I didn't know she was so sick."

"I didn't either. Richard said they got all the cancer, and she was goin to be okay."

"She sure didn't look okay yesterday. I gave her the letter, and I left as fast as I could. I didn't want her to have to stand there holdin onto the doorframe, tryin to be polite. I didn't even get a chance to tell her I was goin to be around for a while. Maybe I could catch Richard at the mailbox sometime."

"He don't need to know your business."

"But, Pop, if she's really bad, I could maybe…. I've got home health experience. And I *am* lookin for work."

"You might of just caught her at a bad time."

"That's true. Maybe she had to take some chemo or somethin. That can make you awful sick, but then you get better. I hope that's what it is."

They were both quiet for a while. Sam was thinking that he needed to keep in better touch with Richard and Alyssa. They were his only near neighbors. He got too caught up in what was going on around his own place.

They had just finished the beef and cleaned up the basement and were out on the porch having a smoke when the school bus arrived. Sam watched Danny get off. When he looked around at Marnie, there was no evidence of the cigarette she had been smoking. Sam opened his mouth to say something, but before he could get a word out, Marnie interrupted him.

"Shhh, Pop. Danny's been wantin me to quit, and I've been tryin. He don't need to know every time I slip up."

"God damn," Sam said. "Every time you turn around, somebody catches you doin somethin you ain't supposed to do."

"Well, that's the truth," Marnie said. And then Danny got to the porch. "Hey, buddy. How was your school day?"

They all went inside. Danny talked nonstop about his new school and the kids he met, while Marnie got him a snack. Sam left them together and went out to the barn to get his gear together for tomorrow.

CHAPTER 30

It was a little after noon. Alyssa was sitting on the couch in the living room reading New Yorker cartoons, when she looked up and saw Richard standing in the doorway. She had left the glass door to the deck wide open, because it was one of those warm late September days that seem like a gift from a benevolent universe.

"Oh, hi," Alyssa said. "I didn't know you were coming home so early."

"Alyssa," Richard said, and then he stopped.

"What?"

"You look…."

"What?"

"So much like your old self…and so beautiful, and…."

She was waiting for what he was going to say next.

"You look the same and different too."

"I feel like myself again, for the first time in weeks. I had such a pleasant morning. I didn't do much of anything, but I really enjoyed feeling well again, in my body, and in the world. Maybe you mean my hair. Does my hair look different? "

"No. I don't think so."

"A lot of it has been coming out. I keep hoping it's just my imagination, but the chemo is supposed to do that. You really haven't noticed?"

"It looks pretty. Is that red sweater new?"

"Alix and Sonia brought it when they came up for Labor Day weekend. Remember?"

"Oh, that's right. Now I remember."

"It was too hot to wear it then, and since I had the chemo, I haven't cared what I wore. Today's the first day I've felt like looking nice. Why are you home so early?"

"I finished the job I was working on for Tom Hartland, you know the one, and I wondered how you were and if you needed anything. I don't know really. I just wanted to be home to see how you were." He paused, still standing in the doorway. "You look fine. Maybe that's why I wanted to be home."

Alyssa was pleased, but a little shy too. She said, "Let's take a walk, Richard. It's been ages since we went farther than the pool. I was thinking of going by myself, but this will be much nicer."

"Do you feel well enough?"

"I really do. I feel like myself again. In a few days I have to have more chemo, so this is my one chance at the light, before I have to go back into the dark again."

"I'm so sorry you have to do it, but in the long run, I know you'll be glad."

"Don't be sorry. It makes me appreciate today. Let's go all the way to the top. Have you had lunch?"

"I had a sandwich in town. Do you really think you're well enough to go so far?"

"If I get tired, we can turn around."

"Okay."

So Alyssa got her shoes while Richard changed clothes. They took Richard's binoculars and started up the trail.

The sun was as warm on their heads as if it were still summer, but the air was crisp and dry, the way it is in the fall. When they got to where the path went uphill under the hemlocks, it was cooler.

Alyssa went slowly, not because she felt weak, but because she wanted to make the most of every moment. Each step was a fresh delight. She wanted to savor it all. In the weeks that were coming, she would have this day, this perfect day, to hold on to.

When she had the first chemo treatment, she didn't know what it was going to be like. She was worried and scared, but hopeful too— maybe it wouldn't be as bad as everyone said. But it was. She knew that now.

She'd had the first treatment, and some time off to recover, and now she was scheduled to have another treatment in a few days, and she knew how awful it would be. This one might even be worse than the last one. But she didn't want to think about it now. That would spoil the little time she had left.

Under the hemlocks, there was the smell of pine resin warmed by the sun. The thick layer of orange needles on the ground deadened the sound of their footsteps.

Alyssa reached for Richard's hand as they went by the cabin. He looked at her. She said, "I was just remembering the winter we spent there."

He smiled down at her and squeezed her hand. "That was a good time for us."

Up above the pool, crows were calling back and forth, and in a tree nearby, a blue jay was giving his sharp, warning cry.

Alyssa said, "Remember how quiet it was when the snow fell so softly. It was very romantic. That was our real honeymoon. When we first got married, we were in too much of a hurry to appreciate each other."

Richard said, "It was good for me because you were there. It was different when I was alone, before you came up to be with me."

They went on in silence, and then he squeezed her hand again. "You're right. It was a romantic time, but that was because you were willing to come live with me in a cabin in the woods, without electricity or running water. I don't know many women who would have done that."

"When I was still in Stamford and you were up here, after you lost your job, I realized that home was wherever you were. It was that simple."

They were up above the pool. The path was still going along the brook, but high now, so that they looked over a steep bank onto the trees and rocks below. They came to the place where the ravens had their nest. The remnants of the nest were there, but the ravens were gone.

Richard said, "What's that terrible smell?"

"That's Sam's animal dump. You haven't been up here since his business got going. It always smells like that now. I think he ought to bury all the guts and bones and stuff."

"That would be a lot of work."

"It isn't fair. That smell is coming over onto our property."

"If he buried everything, the wildlife wouldn't have the food. I'm sure the coyotes and foxes must get a lot of it. We benefit by having more wildlife around."

"You've always liked Sam. I think he takes advantage of the fact that his family has been here so long. This land is ours now. We paid for it. Dan Martel didn't have to sell it, or maybe he did, but that's not our fault."

Richard didn't say anything. They walked on in silence. Sam Martel was so big and full of bluster that Alyssa felt intimidated, but she knew Richard had always liked him, and liked him even more since he lost his job and confided in Richard about his worries and fears. She decided not to say any more to avoid arguments.

They left the brook trail and went through the woods to the field at the top of the hill, where Sam kept his sheep. Richard held down the strands of the electric fence with a stick, the way Sam had showed him.

Alyssa started to step over and hesitated. "Don't let the wires slip out from under the stick, Richard."

He looked up with a wicked smile. "Don't you trust me, sweetie?"

"Maybe I should hold it down for myself."

"If you want to, but it's harder. Give me your hand."

"I know how hard it is. I've had to do it before, when I've been up here alone." She took his outstretched hand and stepped quickly over. Richard handed her the stick, and she held it for him.

"This could be a metaphor for what marriage is about," he said, as he stepped over.

They walked across the field. The sheep raised their heads to look, and then they moved away, but they went slowly and nibbled as they went. They didn't seem alarmed.

The ancient hawthorn tree stood at the highest point in the field. They walked to it, the way they always did. They sat on the ground near it to look at the view. The hill was encircled by distant mountains; each farther ring was bluer and more pale.

Alyssa lay back and looked at the sky through the branches of the hawthorn. "I love this tree. I think it has magical properties—a sacred tree, a fairy tale tree."

"It's strange. I never heard of a hawthorn getting this big."

"You know they can. This one is living proof."

"Next time I come up here, I'm going to measure the trunk. It might set some kind of record."

"You can't measure magical properties. You shouldn't even try. It's just good to sit under its branches. I wish it was on our land."

"Sam doesn't mind if we come here."

"Suppose he decided to chop it down to make his pasture better? He could do that if he wanted to."

"The Martels have taken care of this tree for a long, long time."

"I know. I just worry about it. I'm glad I was strong enough to get up here. I can feel its healing power." She was silent as a new thought struck her. She sat up. Did Sam's mother come here when *she* had her cancer? If she had, it hadn't done any good, or at least it hadn't changed the final outcome. Alyssa decided she didn't want to think about it.

And she didn't want to say anything to Richard. She looked at him, lying beside her under the tree. His eyes were closed. Patches of light and shadow crossed his face as the light wind shifted the branches above him.

Richard opened his eyes and saw her looking at him. "What?" he said. "You look worried about something. What is it?"

"I was just thinking how we have been meaning to go visit Hank and Patty. I thought we would do it before I had to start the chemo, but we didn't."

"I know."

"It wouldn't be a big deal if we just went over to Ray Brook for the day."

Richard sat up beside her. Their shoulders were touching. He pulled up little tufts of grass and threw them out into the field beyond their feet. "I know we need to make that trip." He paused while he threw a handful of grass. "The truth is that I dread it."

Alyssa was surprised. "Richard," she said. "Why?"

"When we went over to Mom's funeral, it was so sad. Everyone from the family was gone, and the town was so different. And that was years ago. It's probably worse now. I don't know why Hank stays there."

"Don't you want to see him? I'd go anywhere in the world if I could see Aaron again."

"It's hard to talk to Hank. We don't have anything in common any more." He paused to think about it. "Maybe we never did. I can't remember."

She could see how it was for him. She had trouble thinking of what to say to them too. She always felt as though they thought she took Richard away. She hadn't thought about how it must have made him feel. She felt like putting her arms around him to comfort him, but at the same time, she knew he ought to keep in better touch with his family. So she said, "Well, I think we need to go...maybe after this next chemo, when I start to feel better. If I feel like I do today, I should be able to."

"All right. Let's try to do it while the leaves are still colorful."

"Okay, let's. And now, I wonder if there is anything in the house that I could cook for dinner. I've lost track of what's there."

"Do you feel like cooking?"

"I don't know. I feel like eating. Food tastes good again."

"Let's go out for dinner. Would you like that?" He was sitting up beside her now.

"I don't know. I hadn't thought about going out." She sat up too.

"I know. I'll go into town and get us a dinner and bring it out. We can eat on the deck, if it's still warm enough."

"I like that idea. I've gotten lazy these past few weeks." She moved a little closer. He was being so sweet. "No, not lazy. I felt too awful to even think about food. Everything tasted so queer and horrid. I hope, when all this chemo stuff is behind me, that I'll be able to be a good cook again."

"Oh you will. I'm sure of it. It will be like today, every day. But we won't have that feeling of dread about what tomorrow could bring."

Alyssa put her head on his shoulder, and they sat there, looking at the distant mountains and breathing in the spicy autumn air. Between the field they sat in and the mountains, the trees were turning into the bright reds and oranges of fall.

Richard said, "We're going to take some wonderful river trips when I get the new canoe finished. Just remember that's why you're going through all this chemo. I know it makes you feel awful. Keep trying to remember how glad you will be later on."

"I know, Richard. I've been telling myself that for the last three weeks."

"This is just temporary. Pretty soon we can go back to our lives again, and things will be better than ever."

He stood up and reached out his hand to help her to her feet. "Come on. Are you ready to go down?"

She took his hand and stood up beside him. "Yes, it's time to go home. Goodbye, hawthorn tree. We'll be back. Maybe after my next treatment."

CHAPTER 31

Sam rolled over in bed and bumped Bonnie. "What's that noise," he said. "It sounds like somebody shoutin. Honest to God, it's gettin so a guy can't ever get a decent night's sleep around here."

Bonnie whispered back. "Be quiet, Sam, and let me listen."

So they both lay without moving, not even breathing much, waiting for the next sound.

Then there was a man's voice, loud, right outside the window. "Marnie, I know you're in there. I can see your car in the drive. Let me in. I want to talk to you."

Bonnie's whisper was a hiss. "It's that Steve Louzone out there." She grabbed Sam's arm as he sat up on his side of the bed. "Sam, you don't even know does he have a gun. You're not goin out there, are you?"

"You're damn right I am. I want that bastard to stay away from Marnie. I knew he was goin to come up here."

"I'm comin with you. What if he's got a gun?"

"I don't care. I got my own guns."

"Now, Sam, that's just what I'm worryin about. You can go out there and stand by Marnie and see what he's doin up here. But don't do none of this cowboy stuff."

Sam grabbed his pants and shoved his feet in his work boots. He pulled on his shirt as he went down the hall.

When he got to the kitchen, Marnie was just ahead of him. She was dressed too, in blue jeans and a baggy sweatshirt. She was walking toward the kitchen door, but she stopped and looked back at him. "Oh, Pop, I'm sorry. I really hoped he wasn't goin to do this. Shall I let him in?"

"I'd like to say no, but he'd probably wake up everybody on the road. I guess you'll have to. Has he got a gun?"

"I don't know, Pop. He ain't supposed to go near 'em while he's on probation. I won't let him in if he's got one."

"Okay then. Go ahead. I'm right behind you, honey."

Bonnie was standing in the doorway in her fuzzy pink robe. When Sam looked around at her, she nodded her head.

Marnie went to the door and opened it slowly.

Steve was standing right outside. "Let me come in, Marnie."

"What do you think I opened the door for, Steve? But you've got to behave, or you'll have to leave."

"I'll behave, baby. I just want to see you. You look terrific. When're you comin home?"

She looked around at Sam and Bonnie with a twisted, disbelieving look on her face.

Steve reached out for her as he came through the door. She stepped back, avoiding his arms. "I wish I could say the same for you, Steve. You been drinkin, ain't you? Does your P.O. know you're up here?"

Steve looked past her at Sam and Bonnie. "Tell your parents they should go back to bed. Then you and me can have a nice, friendly talk. They don't need to stay up and watch us like we was little kids."

Sam could feel his temperature rising. He opened his mouth. He was going to let Steve have it, but just then he felt something on his arm. He looked down. Bonnie was beside him.

She said, "This is our house, Steve. We'll go where we want to, and we're stayin right here. You can say what you want to say in front of us, or not at all."

Marnie said, "Thanks, Ma."

Steve looked confused. He had probably pictured a romantic conversation alone with Marnie, convincing her to come back with him. He was drunk. He swayed back and forth on his feet, until he steadied himself by holding on to the doorframe. No one offered him a seat.

Everyone was waiting for Steve to speak, but the only one who said anything was Colt. He growled softly. He was standing beside Marnie, blocking Steve's path into the house.

Sam slapped his own thigh a couple of times, and Colt came and stood beside him.

Steve said, "What's the matter with you people? You gonna sic your dog on me just because I want to talk to your daughter? She's a grown-up, and she ain't always such a goody-goody neither. Come on, Marnie. We can leave if they won't."

"No, Steve."

"Come on, baby. Just come sit in the car with me, so we can talk without everybody listenin in. Come on. I need you."

Marnie said no again, but she was beginning to look like she might change her mind. She said, "What do you want, Steve? What are you doin here, anyhow?"

Sam watched closely. Steve had on a light jacket. He could have a handgun hidden underneath it. Sam's fingers itched for one of his own guns, but they were in their cabinet out in the front room. If he tried to go out there, Bonnie would try to stop him. But he might have to go for his guns. He certainly wasn't going to let the bastard lure Marnie out of the house. If he didn't have a gun on him right now, he probably had one in his car.

Bonnie went over to the coffeemaker. "Steve, I'm goin to make you some coffee. I can see you need it. You say what you have to say and drink your coffee, and then you get out of here and go back to Randolph before you get yourself in worse trouble than you're already in."

"Okay, Mrs. Martel." He said it like he planned to do exactly what she told him to do. Then he looked at Marnie. "I love you, baby. All I want to know is when are you comin home."

"I ain't, Steve. Danny and I are stayin here. He's in school, and I got a new job. We're startin over."

"But you can't...."

"Oh, but I can." She looked around at Sam and smiled a tight-lipped smile that made him want to hug her, his poor little girl who always fell for the wrong guy.

When the coffee was ready, Bonnie handed Steve a mug of it. The coffee was black. She didn't offer to put anything in it, and she didn't offer him a seat.

Steve stood there, leaning against the doorframe with the coffee mug in his unsteady hand, taking little sips. "This coffee is really hot. Thank you, Mrs. Martel."

Finally Marnie said, "So what did you come up here for, Steve?"

Steve began to cry. "I miss you, baby. Why won't you come home where you belong?"

Marnie opened her mouth to say something, but then she looked around at Sam and snapped her mouth shut again.

In his head Sam was saying, "Good girl." Out loud he said, "Okay, Steve, if there's anything else you have to say, spit it out and get goin. You got a long trip ahead of you."

Steve took a big gulp of coffee and said, "I love you, Marnie, and I always will." He handed her the coffee mug and left with tears running down his face.

None of them moved until they heard the car start and drive away. Then Marnie hugged each of them. "Good night, Ma. Goodnight, Pop. Thanks for standin by me. I'm sorry you had to." She went up the stairs.

Bonnie turned out the kitchen lights, and she and Sam went back to bed.

In Sam's dream he was watching one of Marnie's high school basketball games. Marnie had the ball, and everyone was shouting her name. She was just about to take a shot. Sam opened his eyes in the dark room. The sound of the dream was still going on. For a few minutes Sam didn't know where he was. Then he came to the surface enough to realize that he was in his bed, and someone was outside shouting Marnie's name. Steve. He must have come back.

Sam dragged himself into an upright position, sitting on the edge of the bed. His whole body was begging him not to get up. He shoved his feet into his boots and stood, feeling like an old man. He was trying to be quiet, in case Bonnie was lucky enough to still be asleep. When he picked up his pants, he realized that he had to take his boots off again to put his pants on.

He was standing in the hall, stupidly trying to think out his next move, when Marnie came down the stairs, heading for the kitchen. She saw him and stopped.

"Marnie," he said in a whisper. "Don't go out there. Maybe if we don't put on any lights, and we stay out of sight, he'll go away again. Who knows, we might eventually even be able to get a little sleep."

They stood close together in the dimly lit hallway. She was whispering too. "Oh, Pop, I'm so sorry. I didn't think he'd come up here. He's breakin his parole, and he ain't supposed to drink neither."

"He'd better get back down to Randolph before someone calls the cops."

"You think I ought to go out and talk to him?"

"You already tried that, and it didn't make no difference. Why would it work now?"

"I could go out to his car to talk, like he wanted me to do. Then maybe he'd leave."

Sam put his arm around her. "Marnie, honey, don't be crazy. He could hurt you. He has before. If you want to do something dangerous like that, I'm goin to call the state troopers right now and get 'em to take him outa here." He could feel his voice getting louder and louder. Part of him was hoping Steve would hear what he said.

Bonnie came stumbling out into the hall. They were all acting like they were on drugs. "What's goin on?" Bonnie said. "He's back, ain't he?"

Marnie hugged her. "I'm sorry he woke you up, Ma."

"She wants to go out and talk to him, Bonnie. Tell her it ain't a smart idea.'"

Bonnie did better than that. She hugged Marnie. Then she held her at arm's length and looked into her face. "You don't want to go back to him, do you, Marnie?"

"No, Ma. I made up my mind about that when I left. It's bad for me, and it's worse for Danny. I'm all done. I want to stay here until I can afford to get us a place of our own." She looked at Bonnie and then she turned a little to look at Sam. Her smile was hopeful and worried at the same time. "If that's okay with you and Pop."

Bonnie's answer was to hug her again.

Sam nodded his head. He didn't trust himself to speak. When he saw the pain on his little girl's face, his temperature began to rise. It was lucky Steve wasn't in the room right then, because Sam would have gone for him.

Just then the door to the stairs opened, and Danny stepped down into the hall. "What's happenin?" he said. "Why is everybody here in the hall?" He was speaking in his normal voice. It sounded very loud after their whispers.

Marnie hurried to his side. "What woke you up, Danny?"

"I don't know. I don't remember. How come everybody else is up?"

"Well, see, Steve came up here, and he was shoutin outside. We're waitin for him to go away."

"In here?"

"We don't want him to see us."

"But Ma, why doesn't Gramp go out and tell him to go away? Gramp's a lot bigger 'n Steve is."

Sam was nodding his head. "Just say the word, Marnie. I'll treat him gently, or I'll give him a little somethin to remember us by."

"Way to go, Gramp."

"No, it's not," Marnie said. "We don't want to hurt him. We just want him to go away."

Sam caught Danny's eye, and they grinned at each other.

"He'd go away in a hurry if Gramp got after him."

"Be quiet, Danny. We don't want him to hear. Maybe he'll leave if he thinks we're all asleep."

Danny and Sam looked at each other again.

Then Bonnie said, "If we're not goin to do nothin, we could get back in bed. I don't feel like standin around here in the dark. We can't even get coffee for ourselves."

"Okay, Ma. Go on up, Danny."

Sam and Bonnie went back to their bed. In almost no time, Sam could hear the breaths that Bonnie took getting longer and slower. After a short while, she began to snore, while Sam lay there in the dark with all his muscles tense, trying to listen past Bonnie's breathing to what was going on outside.

He couldn't hear anything. Steve might be gone, or he might be doing something he didn't want them to know about. Sam lay on his back, trying not to move, even though his legs felt restless and crawly. Sometimes he had to move, no matter how hard he tried to be still.

Steve could be messing up Marnie's brakes, or putting something in her gas tank. He could be out in the barn letting the pigs loose. He could be setting something on fire, either the house or the barn. There was no limit to the things he could do if he wanted revenge. They should have called the cops. But the women always wanted to hold a man down, even when he was just trying to keep them safe.

It was lucky that he didn't feel like going to sleep. He could lie there in the darkness, listening for where the trouble was going to break out. After a while, he got up and went to the bathroom in his Jockey shorts and bare feet. Then he went around to all the windows, trying to see what the bastard was up to. But he couldn't see anything. He couldn't even tell whether Steve's car was still there or not.

By the time he had finished the circuit of the house, he was cold. He hurried back under the covers and moved close to Bonnie's warm bulk. She didn't even stir. Gradually Sam began to get warm. He planned to lie on guard for the rest of the night, but the next thing he knew, it was morning. Bonnie was already up and gone.

Sam jumbled on his clothes as fast as he could and went out to the kitchen. It smelled of coffee. Bonnie was standing at the stove.

Sam said "Is everythin okay?"

Bonnie looked around. "Sure," she said. "What do you mean?"

"Well…." Sam said. "Did he do anythin to the place?"

"I ain't been out yet, but I don't think so. I think he just left when he thought we were all asleep."

"I'm goin out to have a look around."

"Don't you want some coffee first?"

"No. I'll be back. I need to check around."

"I'll have you some breakfast here in a few minutes."

Sam walked out to the barn. He was in a hurry to make sure Steve hadn't done any damage, so he didn't stop around the side of the barn for a quick smoke, the way he often did."

Everything in the barn seemed normal. He fed the pigs and chickens and opened the chickens' door, so they could go out into their yard. The sheep were up in their pasture at the top of the hill. He could check on them later. He knew there was no way Steve would go up the hill in the middle of the night.

He went all the way around the outside of the house, looking for any harm Steve might have done, but all he found were cigarette butts thrown in the bushes. When he got back to the kitchen door again, he noticed Marnie's car. He got in and started it and drove around the drive, testing the brakes. Then he went into the house. The kitchen smelled like bacon and coffee.

Marnie was sitting at the table. "Why'd you move my car, Pop?"

Sam washed his hands at the sink. He poured himself a mug of coffee and took it to the table. "I thought Steve might could of messed with it. I was checkin it out. But it was fine."

"You mean, like a car bomb?"

"It's possible. Or he could of done somethin to the brakes. I didn't want you to get out on the road and need 'em and not have 'em."

"Thanks, Pop, I appreciate it, but I don't think he'd do that. He don't want to hurt me. He wants me to go back with him."

Bonnie set a plate of bacon and eggs down in front of him. Sam looked up at her and smiled his thanks.

Bonnie said, "You don't know what he would do if he got mad enough, Marnie. He might of taken revenge because you said you wasn't goin back down there."

"He didn't hurt her car, anyhow," Sam said.

"You might ought to check out my car and your truck both."

"I'll do that after I eat. I looked around the house and the barn, but I didn't see nothin."

"What happened last night?" Bonnie said. "I went back to sleep."

Marnie said, "I watched out the upstairs window. He didn't stay too long. He walked back and forth a few times, and then he got in his car and left. I wonder if he made it all the way back to Randolph without gettin stopped. I guess I'll hear about it if he got in trouble."

Bonnie set a plate of eggs down in front of Marnie. "Where's Danny? I have his breakfast ready."

"If he ain't here in a minute, Ma, I'll go get 'im. Sit down with yours."

"Okay," Bonnie said. "But don't let Danny's get too cold." She sat down across from Sam. "If the cops didn't pick Steve up last night, he might come back and do somethin next time. What's to keep that from happenin?"

"Danny and I could move out if you worry about it."

Sam said, "He'd still come here, and *we* ain't movin. Naw, we'll just deal with it if we have to."

"There's not much we can do except call the cops," Marnie said. "Then he'd be back in jail, and we'd have to worry about what he was goin to do when he got out. The best protection is that he only does bad stuff when he's been drinkin, and he can't do much when he's been drinkin because he can't think straight."

"Well," Sam said. "There's always the shotgun. I got a natural right to defend my family and my property. If he comes around again, I might just not hear you girls when you tell me not to get out my guns."

"Okay, Pop. I hear you now, and that's fair enough. Let's just hope he don't come back."

CHAPTER 32

Richard was sitting out on the deck in the early afternoon sunshine when the mailman stopped at the mailbox. He shut his book and went inside to see if he could hear Alyssa upstairs. He stood at the bottom of the stairs listening, but he didn't hear anything. She was probably still asleep.

He walked down the drive. It was one of those October days that compel a person to live in the moment. Who could think about winter when the sky was such a deep, deep blue, and the air was warm and crisp, full of spicy smells. There was even a little breeze that brought down a rain of golden leaves. Richard walked to the mailbox, saying the poem 'Nothing Gold Can Stay' to himself, but he didn't believe what he was saying, not on a day such as this was. It was a poem for a sadder time.

He got his mail and stood by the box, flipping through the catalogues to see if there was anything of any importance. Then he heard someone walking toward him across Sam's yard. He looked up. It was Marnie walking through the leaves. She was smiling at him.

"Marnie," he said. "You seem like part of this beautiful day. How are you? I haven't seen you since that day last summer when the rain was coming, and we had to hurry to get your dad's hay under cover."

"I've been meanin to come over and see you and Alyssa. I wanted you to know that I'm goin to be stayin here for a while."

"Really? Is everything okay with your parents? They're not sick, are they?"

"No. It's not them. They're fine. Me and Danny had to move in with 'em until I can get us a place of our own."

"Oh, I see," Richard said. But he didn't see. He just didn't want to ask embarrassing questions.

"We had to get away from Steve, is what it was. I hated to take Danny out of school when he just started. He had to leave all his friends, and I had to quit my job. But we had to do it. Steve was gettin impossible." The smile was gone now. She turned around to open the Martels' mailbox. "Ma and Pop don't get that much except bills," she said, trying a little smile. "The bills keep comin no matter what, don't they?"

Richard tried to think of what he should say. Finally, he just blurted out what he was thinking. "I'm glad you left him, Marnie. I saw how he treated you last summer. I thought back then that you'd be a lot better off without him."

She swiped her hand roughly across her eyes and tried again to smile. "Thanks, Richard," she said. "Ma and Pop said the same thing. I've known for a long time that I would have to get away. It wasn't good for Danny. I don't want Danny to treat women the way Steve does. I knew I had to do it, but it's hard to start over, and hard to be alone."

"You can do a lot better than someone like Steve."

"That's what Pop always says."

Richard wondered about Sam, surprised that Sam, who was always ready for a fight, hadn't gone after the guy. But he didn't say anything to Marnie.

She said, "A couple weeks ago, Steve came up here in the middle of the night. There was quite the commotion. I hope it didn't bother you and Alyssa."

"Oh, was that what that was? I heard a lot of shouting. I got up and got dressed. I thought maybe your dad's pigs got out or something. I was planning to come over and see if I could help. But by the time I got outside, it was quiet again. I listened for a while, but I didn't hear any more, so I went back to bed."

"I'm sorry Steve woke you up."

"I had to get up anyway, to go to the bathroom." He rolled his eyes a little. "Old men, you know."

That made her smile. "*You're* not old," she said. "Don't be ridiculous."

"Alyssa never woke up at all."

"I've been wonderin about Alyssa. How is she?"

"She's up and down. After she has chemo, she feels awful." He paused for a minute, thinking. "The funny thing is that after the chemo, it takes a little while before she starts to feel bad. We always get our hopes up. We think maybe it won't be as bad as last time, but so far, it just keeps getting worse. She had another treatment two days ago. She's sleeping now. She'll probably sleep all day. If she wakes up, she'll be sick to her stomach."

"That's tough."

"She needs this chemo to keep the cancer from coming back. The doctors are pretty sure they got it all when they did the operation."

"How many more treatments has she got to have?"

"I'm not sure exactly. They say she'll be all done by Thanksgiving anyway."

"That's not too far off. You think she would like me to come visit?"

"I'm sure she would, when she's feeling better."

"You know, Richard, I'm a health care worker. I just got a job at Sherwood Manor, but it's not full-time. If you ever needed any help carin for Alyssa, I could give you a hand."

"Thanks, Marnie. She won't even let me help her much. She always wants to take care of it herself, but it's nice to know there's someone I can call on."

They were walking up the drive together to the place where Marnie would turn off to go to her own house.

Richard glanced at her sideways. She had Sam's tall, dark-haired good looks. Richard said, "Don't forget you can do a lot better than Steve. You don't need someone who treats you that way."

She whirled around and hugged him hard. He was so surprised, he couldn't do anything but pat her on the back. He could smell her shampoo, and under that, faintly, the smell of cigarette smoke. He was afraid she might be crying, but she wasn't.

She pulled back after a minute. "You're a good man, Richard. Alyssa is lucky."

"Well, thanks. I haven't always been so good to her, but I'm trying now. I try not to leave her alone when she feels awful."

They were standing at the place where their paths diverged. Was he talking so he could stay there in the golden sunshine with her? He knew how empty the house would feel when he went back to it. It was funny the way it seemed even emptier because Alyssa was sick. She was there, but in some strange way, she was more gone than if she had left.

Out loud Richard said, "Like this afternoon, for instance. I really ought to go to Burlington to get some materials I need for the canoe I'm building. I can't do any more work on it until I get the strips of cedar I'm putting on the sides. But I'll have to wait until she feels well enough again."

Marnie looked down. She drew in the dirt with the toe of her sneaker. "I'm workin at Sherwood Manor, but I'm hopin to get with the visitin nurses, or some other organization like that. I want to be able to go to people's homes and take care of them there. I'd love to be out on my own, goin places. Imagine bein stuck inside Sherwood Manor on a day like today." She looked up at Richard and smiled. "I mean, I could stay with Alyssa now, if you wanted me to."

"Thanks, Marnie, but I don't need to hire anybody. Alyssa just has to get through these chemo treatments, and then she'll be fine."

"I didn't mean you'd have to pay me. I just meant it's what I want to do anyway. I could stay with her this afternoon, so you could get the stuff you need. You wouldn't have to pay me."

Richard looked at her without saying anything. He wondered if she offered to stay with Alyssa to be nice, or because she needed the money, even though she said he didn't have to pay her. Maybe she thought they were going to need her even more later on. But that would mean that Marnie didn't realize that Alyssa was going to beat this disease. Marnie probably had a warped idea of people's chances of recovery since she worked mostly in nursing homes. But he hadn't said anything. She must be thinking that he doubted her ability as a caregiver.

"Marnie," he said. "That sounds like a wonderful idea, if you have time, but of course I would pay you."

She grinned at him. "Okay. Obviously I could use it. I'll go over to the house and leave a note for Danny, so he'll know where I'm at when he gets off the bus. I'll be right back, and you can tell me what you want me to do."

"Okay," Richard said. "I'll be at the house."

When he got there, he went upstairs to get some clean clothes. Alyssa was sleeping soundly. He didn't want to wake her to tell her where he was going. She might still be asleep when he got home.

When he went downstairs again, Marnie was on the deck. He invited her in. "Alyssa is upstairs in the bedroom at the end of the hall. She's sound asleep."

"Is it okay if I go up and look, so I'll know where she is?"

"That would be a good idea."

A few minutes later, she was back. Richard looked up and saw her standing by the counter in the kitchen. "She seems peaceful. I think she'll sleep for a long time, maybe the whole time you're gone. That would be good, wouldn't it?"

"If she does wake up, she'll probably call for me, and you can go up and see what she needs."

"Okay. I looked at the paintings hanging on the stairs. They are really beautiful."

"Those are Alyssa's."

Marnie looked puzzled.

"Alyssa painted them."

"Really?"

"Yes."

"I didn't know she was a painter."

"She didn't know it either until a few months ago. She painted them last summer. I think she always planned to try her hand at painting when she wasn't so busy with other things, but she never did until last summer. When she came home from visiting a friend on the Cape, she had some paintings to show me. I think she was as surprised as I was."

"You mean she did it without even takin any lessons?"

"The first one, yes. That's the one of trees at the top of the stairs."

"Oh, I like that one a lot."

"After that she took a few lessons. But this fall she missed a lot of time because of the chemo. When she gets all done with the treatments, she'll have more time for painting."

"She's really good. I hope she knows that."

"She's having a lot of fun with it."

Marnie looked surprised by that.

"No," Richard said. "I don't mean fun exactly, because she's serious. What I mean is that it's important to her."

"Well, it's wonderful. I wish I could paint."

"Alyssa didn't know she could do it until she tried."

"If she wakes up before you get home, I could ask her about it. She must have a lot of talent. I don't think I do. I've never done anything like that."

Richard was beginning to get restless. Now that he was actually going to go, he was eager to get on the road. "I won't be gone too long," he said. "It might take three hours, if you count driving time. I'll be back as soon as I can."

"Don't worry about it. I don't have anythin I have to do today. Danny knows where to find me. I'll just hang out and read your magazines unless Alyssa wakes up and needs somethin."

Richard drove away into the golden afternoon. He opened the windows and put on his favorite Miles Davis CD. He tried not to feel guilty. He felt so free, as though a heavy weight had been lifted off him. He didn't want to feel like that. Alyssa wasn't a burden. The difficult time she was having now would be over in a month or two, and of course he wanted to be by her side to help her through it.

It didn't take long to get what he needed for the canoe—red and white strips of cedar, some fasteners, and some good glue. He resisted the urge to browse. He could have spent a whole day wandering around the store, looking for different ways to do what he was planning to do.

He loaded all he had bought into his truck. It was when he was securing the long bundle of cedar strips with bungee cords, so that they wouldn't bounce out of the back of the truck, that he began to think about the lake. He couldn't see it from the parking lot, but he could feel how near it was. He hadn't spent much time in the store. He decided to reward himself with a quick drive to the waterfront, just for a glimpse of the lake before he went home to West Severance.

The traffic was light going down the hill, and all the way he could see the blue surface of the lake in its ring of mountains. When he got to Waterfront Park, there was a parking space right in front of him. It would have been crazy to pass up such a gift.

He walked across the pavement to the wall and looked down. Right below him was the beach, with little waves slapping onto the sand. He looked out at the sailboats like birds flying over the water. Then he went back to the truck, but when he opened the door, he happened to glance down the walk that ran along the edge of the water under the trees. No one was in sight at that moment. It looked so inviting. It would only take a few minutes to walk to where the land curved out toward the point.

He walked along beside the lake, remembering how Alyssa said it would be fun to canoe through the middle of town, looking into people's backyards. They could put the canoe in the water right there at the park. A jogger passed him going the opposite direction, but he didn't pay any attention. He was picturing how they would paddle along the shore and out around Rock Point, viewing Burlington from that new angle.

A woman's voice behind him said, "Richard? Is that really you? I don't believe it."

He turned around. It was the jogger who had just passed him. She looked familiar, but he couldn't place her.

She was hunched over with her hands on her thighs. "It's me," she said, still out of breath. "Sandy Ryelands."

Richard tried to look as though he recognized her, but he must not have been convincing.

She said, "From the Wilburs' party twelve years ago. Well, actually, it was twelve years and two months ago. That was the night Tom told me he wanted a divorce. He told me at the party, and you were so nice to me."

Now Richard was beginning to remember how she ran out into the rain, sobbing, and he went out to bring her back, only she wouldn't come inside, so they stayed out in the rain, while he held her and tried to comfort her until they were both soaking wet.

"You took me home, but you wouldn't stay with me. I tried to get you to stay. I didn't want to be alone. I used to fantasize about how different everything would have been if you had stayed with me that night."

Richard said, "I had to get back to the party. Alyssa was waiting for me."

"Oh Alyssa. I forgot about Alyssa. Are you still together? How is she?" Her skin was pale, with blotches of color. She had wrinkles on her face, and her upper arms were flabby.

"Alyssa's okay. And I really need...."

"Richard, I live so close—my apartment is right on the other side of the park. Come with me, and I'll make us some coffee, and we can catch up on old times. Don't say no, please. It has been so long."

"I wish I could, but I can't. I really need to get back as soon as I can." He was uncomfortably aware that strolling along the waterfront wasn't consistent with being in such a hurry. But he didn't care. He didn't want to say anything about Alyssa.

"Oh I wish.... It seems like I'm always begging you to stay with me, and you are always turning me down." She sighed and stood up straighter. "It's been great to see you, anyway. You don't know how important you were to me, Richard."

"I didn't do anything but give you a ride home." But even as he said the words, he knew they weren't true. When he put his arms around her to comfort her, and when he stayed outside in the rain with her in his arms, there was a lot more going on between them, and they both knew it.

"Yes," she said. "I always wished there had been more to remember. Still, you hold onto all you can. Maybe I ought to have tried harder to get you to stay. I knew at the time that you shouldn't."

"We both knew that."

"You're a good man, Richard. Alyssa is very lucky." She held out her hand. "Goodbye. Please tell Alyssa I said hello."

Richard said he would, although he already knew he wasn't going to say anything about it when he got home.

For a while, one of his worries had been that they would be walking in the same direction when he went toward his truck. But now to his relief, he saw that she had turned around also, and they were still going in opposite directions.

On the way home, Richard thought over the whole incident. He was surprised that he had been tempted to be unfaithful to Alyssa, although that wasn't the only time. In his memory Sandy was more attractive than she was today. Was it because she was crying in the rain?

Richard thought about the way it was when he got back to the party that night. He found Alyssa in the kitchen, talking to some people. He couldn't remember who the people were, probably because he couldn't pay attention to anyone but Alyssa. Her dark eyes blazed when she saw him, but she didn't let the others see that she was angry. She nodded to him with a tight little smile on her face. He was eager to tell her that she could be proud of him. Sandy tried to get him to stay with her, but he hadn't done it. He put his hand on Alyssa's shoulder, thinking how lucky he was to have her, and conscious of how grubby and wet he was by comparison.

The party was starting to break up. He asked Alyssa if she was ready to leave, and she said sweetly that she would do whatever he wanted. But she didn't look at him. She looked just slightly off to the side. In fact, she hadn't looked directly at him since the first blazing moment when he came back to the party. He remembered that quite plainly, because that was when he knew he was in for it.

Neither of them said anything on the drive home. Richard kept thinking that if he could just find the right way to tell her what happened, or rather what didn't happen, then she wouldn't be angry any more. All the way home he kept thinking of how to start the conversation, but he couldn't think of the right opening.

He remembered how cold he was by the time they got to the house. His clammy clothes were clinging to him. He went to take a shower, hoping the words would come to him there. Then they could have a good talk.

But when he came out of the bathroom, Alyssa had gone to bed, and the bedroom door was locked. So that was that. He had to spend the night in the guestroom.

They must have talked at some point, but Richard couldn't remember that part. What stayed fresh in his mind was how beautiful Alyssa was when she was angry, and how much he wanted to tell her what really happened, how much he wanted her to know it hadn't happened the way she thought. Did they talk about it? He didn't think she ever believed his version.

He thought about it some and decided he wouldn't mention Sandy when he got home, even if Alyssa was feeling well again. They had gone on to a different era in their lives, and the past was behind them

CHAPTER 33

Monika would never have heard the telephone if she hadn't turned off the vacuum cleaner just as it rang. It was Ira Dorfeld, Mabel's son.

When he told her who he was, she said, "What's happened to Mabel?"

"What makes you think something's wrong?"

"Tell me quick. How bad is it?"

He laughed, and his laugh made her feel better. "It's only her arm," he said. "She fell on Sunday and broke it."

"Thank God. I thought she might have had a heart attack or something."

"Nothing that serious. She's at home. She's going to be fine. But I wish I wasn't so far away. I'm hoping you'll go over and see if she has everything she needs."

"I'll go right away. I don't know why she didn't call me herself."

"She talked about it, but she didn't want to worry you, and she didn't want you to have to drop everything and hurry to help her. You're not too busy, are you? You wouldn't have to go right away, if you're busy."

"I'm not. I was running my vacuum cleaner, and I'm always glad to stop doing that."

"Will you call me if there's anything to worry about?"

"I will. I promise."

Monika put away the vacuum cleaner and changed her clothes. She had been meaning to call Mabel all fall, but she hadn't done it. She had stayed away from everyone in the summer because she didn't want to have to talk about her eyes. She could see now that Mabel and the others might have taken it wrong. They might have thought she was mad at them. She had been so embarrassed, so eager to keep them from knowing what was happening to her, that she had never thought of how they might misinterpret her disappearance. She could see that now.

She was in her kitchen, dressed and ready to leave, before she thought about how she was going to get there. If she called a cab, she would have to wait. Her car was right outside. Dr. Lali said she could see well enough to drive. Brian might think it was wrong, but Brian wouldn't know.

She decided just to see if the car would start. She couldn't remember when she had used it, but it had been a long time ago. She got in and tried it. It started the first try.

She drove down the drive and out onto the street. She felt nervous and unsure, so she went slowly. Several times people honked at her, but she knew she couldn't afford to make a mistake. She had to be cautious, and she got to Mabel's apartment building with no problem. She parked in the visitor's parking and went upstairs and rang Mabel's doorbell.

After a minute she heard Mabel fumbling at the door, and then it opened.

"Monika, what a surprise! What are you doing here?"

"Ira called me."

"He said he wasn't going to do that."

"I'm glad he did. I can't believe you didn't call me yourself."

Mabel looked down at her feet. "I thought…you know…I mean, we haven't talked since you stopped coming to the card games."

"Did you think I didn't want to be friends any more? We've been friends since high school. That's a long time."

"I know it. I didn't know what to think."

"Well," Monika said. "We can't have much of a conversation out here in the hall. Are you going to invite me in or what?"

Mabel swung open the door and stepped back. "I'm sorry. I really was going to call you." Her right arm was in a splint, held up by a cloth sling around her neck. When Monika stepped inside, Mabel fumbled to lock the door one-handed. Monika turned around and did it for her.

Mabel walked into the living room and turned off the television. "Everything's in a mess. It's hard to pick up with only one hand. I've let it all go. But I'm glad to see you. I really am. It's been too long."

"I know," Monika said. "How are you feeling? Does your arm hurt a lot?" She looked around the room. It didn't look that different. It was always crowded with furniture. Mabel had tried to squeeze all the contents of her house into her apartment.

"It doesn't hurt much. It's just a nuisance. Was Ira worried? Is that why he called you?"

"I guess so. He asked me to see if you needed anything."

"Oh Monika, you didn't need to stop whatever you were doing to check up on me."

"I wasn't doing anything but vacuuming my front room. I was glad to stop that."

"Would you like some coffee? Come out in the kitchen, and I'll make us some."

The kitchen was more of a mess. There were a lot of dirty dishes in the sink. After Mabel had fumbled, trying to make the coffee, Monika pushed her aside and took over.

While they were waiting for the coffee to brew, Monika started to wash the dishes, over Mabel's protests. Monika had been trying to think of how to explain why she had been so out of touch. It seemed easier to talk about it with her back to Mabel. "I'm actually glad of this chance to tell you what's been going on."

"Oh dear, I knew you were mad at me. I knew it. That was why you stopped playing cards, wasn't it?"

"Is that really what you thought?" Monika swung around and hugged her without even waiting to dry off her hands. "It wasn't you. It was me. It was my eyes. I couldn't see the cards. Didn't you notice how many stupid mistakes I was making? I even had to stop driving my car."

Mabel hugged her back with her good arm. "Really? It was your eyes? I didn't notice you making stupid mistakes. Everyone makes mistakes. I thought I'd done something that made you mad. Why didn't you tell us?"

"There was nothing you could do. I thought there was nothing anyone could do. And it was hard to talk about. I just wanted to stay in my house with my cats."

"Oh you poor thing. And here I am feeling sorry for myself." She hugged Monika to her with her good arm. But then she pushed her away and looked into her face sternly. "How did you get here today?"

"I drove my car."

Mabel looked shocked.

Monika said, "Don't look at me like that. I wouldn't have done it if it was dangerous. The doctor said I could."

Mabel stepped back a couple of steps until she was pressing against the kitchen counter. It was as though she didn't want Monika to get too close to her.

"It's different now. It's so much better. It turns out there *was* something to do—a new treatment—and it made my eyes better. I mean they're much better than they were at their worst. They're not better than they were before all this happened."

"Really?" Mabel said from where she stood, pressed against her kitchen counter.

Monika could see that she didn't believe it. Just then the coffee finished perking. Monika got out cups and saucers and some spoons. "I remember where everything is," she said.

Mabel got a bag of cookies and the milk out of the refrigerator.

When she saw Monika looking, she said, "I keep everything in the refrigerator these days. There are ants and mice, and I'm afraid there might be cockroaches too. Do you want some sugar? The sugar bowl's in there too."

Monika shook her head and poured coffee into their cups.

"Let's go out in the living room so we can be comfortable."

They carried their coffee cups out to the couch and sat down. Mabel had a handsome dining room table at the end of the room near the kitchen door, but it was piled with letters and business papers and cardboard boxes. There was only enough open space for one person.

Mabel said, "This is very nice. I haven't had any coffee for days. It's been too much trouble to make it one-handed."

"I wish you'd called me sooner."

"I should have, but I didn't know what was going on with you. Tell me more. Is it really okay for you to be driving now?"

"The doctor said it was. I had to have a series of shots in my eyes."

"Ooooo. I've heard of that. Did it hurt a lot?"

"Thinking about it before it happened was the worst part. And then afterwards, I felt as though someone had punched me in the face, but that part only lasted for a short while. It was definitely worth it. And I can see so much better. I was lucky about that. I should have told you."

"We all thought you were angry about something."

"Is the card game still going on every week?"

"No, it isn't. We gave up on it, I guess. We tried to keep it going after you left, but it faded. You were the center of it."

"Oh fiddle. I don't believe that."

"It wasn't your fault. I don't mean that. But you were the one who united us, and after you left, it all fell apart."

"Well, I'm back now. I've been playing a lot of solitaire, so I know I can see the cards again."

"The shots in the eye did that?"

"They say they don't always make it better, but they stop it from getting worse. I was one of the lucky ones. The shots actually made my vision better."

"You were brave. I don't think I would have the nerve to get those shots."

"Yes you would. You don't have a choice. But I'm going to go use your bathroom. I'll be right back." Monika stood up slowly and stiffly, getting her legs settled under her.

Mabel said, "Please don't notice the mess in there."

"I won't. If this were July, your secret would have been safe with me. I wouldn't have been able to see the mess."

Maybe she still couldn't see very well, because Mabel's bathroom looked as tidy as it always did.

She started talking on the way back to her seat. "It looks fine in there, Mabel. You don't need to worry." She sat down too hard on the plump cushions and bounced Mabel up. "I'm sorry for that clumsy descent," she said. "My legs aren't what they used to be. I guess I should be glad I can still walk. It's the ups and downs I have trouble with."

"I know what you mean," Mabel said. "It's embarrassing when you're out at a restaurant, and you have to use the table to haul yourself to your feet. I always hope no one will notice."

Monika laughed at that. "It's so good to be around someone my own age for a change."

"Wait a minute, Monika. I'm younger than you are. I was two years behind you in high school, you know."

"Okay. That's true. I'm just glad Ira called me."

"I wish he'd move back to Stamford. He wants me to go out to Arizona, but I'm not going to do it. I wouldn't have a life out there. All my friends are here."

"I know what you mean. I'm lucky to have Alix and Sonia near Stamford, and Alyssa isn't that far away in Vermont."

"How is Alyssa?"

"She's going to be all right, thank God."

"What do you mean, 'going to be'?"

"She still has a few more rounds of chemo to get through."

"Monika, what are you telling me? Surely not that Alyssa has cancer?"

"Lung cancer, yes, but she's going to be all right."

"I don't believe it. How long has she had it?"

"It all happened about the same time last spring. I was worrying about my eyes, and then Alyssa found out about her cancer. It just seemed like too much to deal with. I don't know why I didn't tell you. I suppose it was because I couldn't talk about it. It was hard even to *think* about it when I wasn't sure she was going to be all right. I couldn't even *see* her clearly, and I didn't want to say anything about my eyes because I didn't want everyone to have to worry about me too. Oh, it was an awful summer. I'm so glad it's over."

"You poor dear, and here I am feeling sorry for myself about a little thing like a broken arm. Is Alyssa really going to be all right?"

"Yes, thank God. They did an operation at the beginning of June, and they said they got all the cancer. This chemo is just to make sure." She drank the last of her coffee and set down the cup. "My eyes are better, and Alyssa's better, but I feel a little superstitious talking about it. I know it's silly, but I can't help being afraid that the powers of the universe or the fates might notice that Alyssa is going to be all right."

Mabel stood up. "I'm glad about Alyssa. What about Richard?"

"He's taking wonderful care of her. I must say I didn't expect him to be so good. She used to be the one who took care of him."

"Well, that's something then. Here, let me fill your cup for you."

"No thank you." Monika stood up too. "I need to go pretty soon, and I want to do your dishes before I go."

"You don't need to do that. I can do them."

"I know I don't, but I want to. It's so much easier with two hands."

They went to the kitchen. Mabel put things away, while Monika filled the sink with soapy water.

Mabel said, "Why don't you use my dishwasher? It works fine."

"I think it's easier to do them this way. I always do them like this at home. I never use my dishwasher any more."

When she finished all the dishes in the sink, she looked around the room, but there was nothing else to wash. "There," she said. She let the soapy water go down the drain. "That'll be a little easier for you."

Mabel handed her a towel, and she dried her hands. "I'm going to stop at the supermarket on the way home. Is there anything you need?"

"I'll tell you what I'd like," Mabel said, looking at Monika and hesitating a little.

"What? Whatever it is, I'll get it."

"No. What I'd really like is to ride to the store with you. I could walk home. But you'd have to wait while I changed my shoes and combed my hair." She looked at Monika again. "Would you mind waiting?"

"I'll be glad to. Take your time. I'll be able to tell Ira there was something I could do to help."

It didn't take long. When she was dressed, Mabel brought out a little cart on wheels that folded up.

Monika said, "You don't need that. I'll drive you back with your groceries."

"That would be nice, but I'll still need the cart to get up to my apartment."

She didn't say anything to Mabel because she hadn't made up her mind whether she was going to go back to driving or give it up. But she thought to herself that if she decided to stop driving, she would get herself one of those carts like Mabel's.

On the way to the car, Mabel asked her if she felt safe driving.

For a few minutes Monika had to struggle to keep from saying something mean. Was Mabel afraid to ride with her?

When they were both in the car, Monika said, "You can judge for yourself about my driving. There's only one worry that I have. Sonia's husband Brian says that even if I bumped someone lightly, even if it wasn't my fault, the insurance company could say I shouldn't be on the road at all, and I could get sued. He thinks I should never drive again just to be safe."

She started the car. Mabel didn't say anything. Monika was afraid to ask her what she thought, or even to look around at her. She waited impatiently.

After a few minutes, Mabel said, "I see what he means."

Monika was about to protest, when Mabel went on. "But it's not fair. They are using scare tactics. I can see why you don't want to give in to that kind of pressure."

"I was afraid you were going to be on their side. You don't think I need to give up driving, do you?"

"No, I don't. The younger generation is always trying put us in a box so we'll be safe and not cause them any extra work or trouble. It's just like Ira wanting me to move to Arizona."

Monika pulled into a parking spot at the supermarket and shut off the car. "Well," she said. "How'd I do?"

"I don't know," Mabel said. "I forgot to watch." That made them both laugh.

They sat in the car together. Neither of them made a move to get out. "Seriously," Monika said. "You're exactly right. They want to treat us like children. What do you think I ought to do?"

"I'm not sure, because, of course, Brian is right." She was staring out the window. "Look at that woman in the pink shirt. How do you suppose she ever let herself get so fat? She can hardly walk."

"Mabel, don't tease me. What were you saying about Brian?"

"You could have a little fender-bender, and the whole thing could turn into a nightmare."

"I know," Monika said, feeling miserable.

"But then, what's the sense of anything? No, Monika, this is what I think you should do—drive when you need to, and be extra careful when you do. You can cut down on the trips you make, and that will satisfy your children. And then, when you really need to drive, well, you still have a driver's license and a good car."

"I like that," Monika said. "And, you know, I think that's what I've been doing without even realizing it."

"There you go," Mabel said.

"I'll save the driving for when I really need it."

"Yes, for times like right now when you really needed to take me shopping." They were both laughing when they got out to get their groceries.

Monika thought about it while she shopped. What Mabel said

made her see that it didn't have to be so black and white, all or nothing. She could drive a little when she really needed to, and that would be pretty safe. It wouldn't be as safe as never driving at all, but safe enough, a small sacrifice, instead of the large one she thought she had to make. Just like with her eyes, and with Alyssa's cancer, she had been given a reprieve, at least for the time being.

CHAPTER 34

When Sam and Junior came around the corner of the barn, the school bus was just pulling away. Danny was walking to the house, kicking his feet in the dust of the drive.

He looked up and saw them, and of course he spotted their bows and arrows. "Hey, Gramp. What are you doin? Hi, Junior. Can I come with you?" He stopped by the back porch steps long enough to shrug his arms out of his backpack and leave it where it fell near the steps. "Where're you goin? Where've you been?"

Sam and Junior looked at each other and laughed. Sam felt great, and he was pretty sure Junior did too. Both their bows were sighted in, and most of their other gear was ready. It seemed like even the weather was going to cooperate.

"What's goin on with you guys?"

Junior said, "We're gettin ready for Opening Day, Danny. How was school?"

"When does it start? Can I come?"

Sam said, "It starts on Saturday, but you can't go with us."

"Why not?"

"Because you ain't ready, that's why."

"I can get ready, Gramp, just tell me what to bring."

"It ain't somethin like that, Danny. You got to learn how to shoot. You can't go huntin if you don't know how to shoot. That would be a waste of time."

"Oh," Danny said. For once he seemed to have nothing more to say. He looked at each of them. By this time they were all on the front porch, and their hunting gear was jumbled around.

Sam said, "Don't worry. We'll teach you how, and if you practice real hard, you might could be ready to go out with us next year."

"I have to wait a whole year?"

"Pop, where's that little bow I learned on? It's got to be around here some place."

Danny said, "Maybe Gramp could let me learn on his."

"Didn't you take it over to your place for your kids, Junior?"

"Nope. It's here. It's got to be upstairs some place. You ain't seen it up there, have you, Danny?"

"What's it look like?"

"It's smaller than these here. It looks like it's made out of light-colored wood, but it might be some kind of plastic."

"Can I go up and find it now?"

"You can," Sam said. "But don't leave stuff all over the place, or you'll have Grammie after us."

"Okay, Gramp."

When Danny was out of hearing, Sam said, "I made us some beef jerky the other day."

"Did you make it spicy?"

"I did. I know how you like it. You wanna try a piece?" He handed the bag to Junior.

"Wow," Junior said with his mouth full. "Nice job, Pop. That heats you right up." He pulled some arrows out of a bag that was lying on the porch swing. "I went to Stevens Archery to get myself some huntin arrows, and I got some for you too." He handed the arrows to Sam. Then he dug into the bag again. "I remembered that you broke your wrist protector last year, so I got you one of them too." He handed it to Sam.

"Thanks, Junior. I thought I could fix it, but I ain't done it yet. How much do I owe you?"

"Nothin. It's my treat."

"But…."

"Forget it, Pop. You're plannin to drive, ain't you?"

"I was thinkin I would."

"It'll even out in gas pretty fast."

"Well, thank you, Junior." He didn't say any more. It was complicated. He knew Junior just wanted to help him, and he *did* appreciate it. But at the same time, it made him feel small. Here he was out of work, so that his son had to buy his hunting supplies. What kind of a man gets himself into a place like that? Not the kind of guy he wanted to be, that was for sure.

Danny came back to the porch to tell them he couldn't find the bow. He spotted the new arrows right away. "Hey, Gramp, are those yours?"

"Junior got 'em for me."

Danny picked up one of the arrows and started waving it around.

"Watch out, Danny. Them things are razor sharp."

"Gramp, let's go up in back with your bow, so I can try it out. We can use the new arrows." He looked at Sam. He could tell the answer was going to be no. He said, "Please, please, please."

"You have to learn how to shoot, Danny. You can't just *do* it. See, you don't use huntin arrows. When you're shootin at a target, you use target arrows. And you can't use my bow. It's too big. You need to go find the one Junior was tellin you about."

Just then Marnie drove in. Sam said, "Here comes your ma. Maybe she knows where the bow is at."

Marnie got out of the car and walked up the porch steps. "Hi, Junior. What's everybody doin out in front? Hey, Danny. Did you have a good day at school?"

She tried to hug him, but he twitched himself out of her arms. "Ma, do you know where Junior's bow is? It's some place upstairs."

"No, I don't. Is there a bow upstairs?"

Junior said, "It was mine. The one I learned on. Remember?"

"No, I don't. And it's upstairs?"

"We think so."

"Come on, Ma," Danny said, pulling her toward the door. "Help me find it so Gramp can teach me how to shoot. They're goin out deer huntin on Saturday."

"Oh cool. If you're takin Danny, I get to go too."

Sam said, "We ain't takin Danny, not this time anyhow. He's got to learn how first."

"Come on, Ma. Help me find Junior's old bow, the one he learned on."

"Where is it, Junior?"

"It's got to be up there. I don't think Ma would of thrown it out. Did you look in my old room, Danny? It could be in the closet on one of them shelves. It's goin to be up there somewhere."

Danny said, "Come on," and ran toward the stairs.

"I'll be there in a minute. You get started," Marnie shouted after him. Then when she thought he was out of hearing, she said, "I know you ain't goin to take Danny this time, Pop. Can I go instead? I need to learn more about huntin, so I can teach him. His dad sure ain't goin to do nothin."

"We'll teach him, Marnie. You don't need to worry about it."

"Thanks, Pop, and you too, Junior. But I'd like to go with you anyways. It sounds like fun, and I have a day off on Saturday."

Sam was shocked. "You can't come. This is a huntin trip, not a fun time in the woods. You'd jinx us."

It was Marnie's turn to be shocked. She looked like he'd hit her. "I would not!" she said. "I'd do whatever you told me to do."

"That don't make no difference. You're a woman. That very thing would jinx it."

"Oh come on, Pop. People don't think like that about women nowdays. What about it, Junior?"

"I got to agree with Pop," he said, not really looking at her. "Women don't belong on a huntin trip. Besides, we ain't got that many chances to go out this year. Pop might could be too busy butcherin other people's deer when rifle season gets here. Why don't you help Danny learn to shoot a bow?" He looked at her and smiled. "You used to practice with me. You used to be pretty good."

Marnie wasn't having any of it. She went inside without saying a word, but she slammed the screen door as hard as she could.

They were both quiet for a minute, and then Junior said, "She wouldn't of liked it anyhow. She'd of wanted to use the flashlight on the way up."

Sam was thinking about how upset she would get if they killed a deer, and killing a deer was the whole point of the trip.

"I got a big rip in my camo pants, and I forgot to ask Alma to fix it. I was plannin to see if Marnie would do it, but now I guess I won't."

"Use duct tape," Sam said. "I got a roll around here some place. It'll work just as good, and you won't have to ask."

"Okay. I'm plannin to leave my clothes over here so you can bury 'em in the hay with yours. You can bring 'em when you come to get me on Saturday. They ought to smell like hay by that time."

"Okay. I'll do yours when I do mine. I've got a can of cover scent. We can use that too.

When Sam's alarm went off Saturday morning, his first thought was that it was a mistake. He had just gone to sleep a few minutes ago. He snuggled a little closer to Bonnie. She was so soft and warm. She moaned a little in her sleep.

He almost drifted off, and then suddenly, he was wide-awake. He had caught himself just in time. He jumped out of bed and grabbed his clothes and headed for the kitchen. The coffee was already perking when he got there.

By the time he was dressed enough to go to the barn for his camo, the coffee was ready. He poured himself a cup and filled the thermos. He kept one nervous eye on the door to the stairs, in case Marnie came out dressed and ready to go with them. She could be planning that move. Neither of them had mentioned her coming with them since the other day on the porch.

Colt was lying by the door. He looked relaxed, but Sam knew he was watching his every move. Colt knew he wasn't going to get to go. He was pretending he thought he was invited, since that might make Sam change his mind. Sam patted him and told him to stay. He had made some beef jerky without spices, the way Colt liked it, and he had a piece for him now. He held it out, but Colt wouldn't take it. Sam laid the treat on the floor beside him. He patted his head and went outside. He wanted to look back through the door to see if Colt took his treat, but he didn't. He'd already hurt Colt's feelings. He didn't want to insult him too.

He left the lights off in the barn, but he checked around with his flashlight. The sheep were still out back. The pigs grunted in their sleep. He had planned to ask Marnie to feed them, but he didn't do it. It wouldn't hurt them to miss a meal. He got their hunting clothes from the hayloft. He put his on and left the barn carrying Junior's.

Junior must have been watching out the window because he opened the kitchen door as soon as Sam turned the corner. When Sam stopped, Junior was right there. He opened the door and climbed in.

"Mornin, Pop. What time is it?"

"Three-twenty."

"That ain't bad. We'll be in our stand by five."

"There's some coffee in the thermos."

"I'm good. I had some at home."

After that they didn't talk until they were near the parking spot. Junior said, "I ain't seen any cars along in here. That's lucky. No competition."

"They might could be further along. Say down by the flats."

"They might not too. It could be we'd have the place to ourselves."

"I hope so."

"Me too."

Sam parked the truck, and they got out. He put Bonnie's lunch and the thermos out of sight behind the seat. Then he went to the back of the truck, where Junior was putting on his camo.

It was still night. There was no gray in the east yet, and the moon was down. There was a faint light from the stars, but Sam had to leave the headlights on while they got ready. It was warm enough for the crickets to chirp. People said you could tell what the temperature was by how fast the crickets chirped, but Sam had never tried to figure it out.

They strapped on their quivers and packed their pockets with their gear. They both had full camouflage suits and face masks. Junior had his pistol in a holster at his waist. Sam had his best hunting knife. They both had headlamps for emergencies, but they wouldn't use them to see the trail. They would wait for their eyes to adjust to the dark logging road under the trees.

Sam went first. Not far from the truck, the road began to climb steeply uphill. Behind him Sam could hear Junior's breathing get louder. Every so often, there was the crackling of leaves or the scuff of a pebble as he or Junior stepped down too hard.

The mysterious night was breathing around them. Off to the sides of the trail, there were rustlings and sometimes a squeak from a little creature, but near them all was silent, as though the business of the night was temporarily suspended while the humans went by. They moved in a wedge of silence. That little piece of the night was theirs and familiar. Beyond it was darkness full of alien life.

Soon there was a grayness in the air. The road was darker than the woods off to either side. Above the trees, the stars were fading. The air smelled of dawn and ozone.

Sam was looking for the place where two logging roads came together to make the one they had just walked up. One road went north along the side of the ridge, while the other continued straight uphill to the west. Their stand was where the two roads met. From that spot they could see anything that came along either trail. And the wind was from the northwest, so it blew their scent back down the way they had come.

Sam was getting more excited the closer they got. He could hear Junior plodding steadily behind him, and he couldn't slow down, for fear Junior would walk right into him in the dark. Just then Junior stumbled and caught himself. He didn't make a sound, but Sam could hear his arrows rattling against each other in their quiver as he lurched, trying to regain his balance.

Something small and fast crossed the road ahead. It left behind a faint ribbon of musky scent as it ran off through the trees to the north.

All of a sudden, Sam knew they were there. He had been worried that he might miss the spot, but when they arrived, it was obvious. The light was growing. He could see where the two roads came together. He could even make out the patch of bushes and small evergreens that they would use as a blind.

He turned and put his hand on Junior's shoulder. Junior said, "Huh," and then, "Oh," almost in one breath. He stopped short.

They moved stealthily into the cover at the side of the road. It was a good spot. There was enough room for them both to crouch without bumping into each other. Whoever was going to take a shot could stand and have a clear line of sight over the bushes.

The light was stronger now. The whole world was different shades of gray. There was no color yet, just a soft light everywhere. It was silent, except when a drop of water fell from a tree onto the leaves below. The birds would be noisy later, although a lot of them had already left for the south. And the insects would add to the noise when it got warm enough.

They hadn't been settled very long when there was a light shuffling in the leaves on the road uphill, a few soft steps and a pause, and then more light steps. Sam felt Junior's hand on his back, and he gave a slight nod of his head, meaning Junior should be the one to take this shot.

Sam's heart was pounding and his breath came short. Those feelings would vanish when it was his turn to shoot, but right now all he had to do was wait and be excited.

The footsteps got closer. Sam was pretty sure it was a deer. He could feel Junior tighten like a spring, ready to go, and then slowly he was rising up. There was a loud crash and the sound of running feet.

Sam felt Junior sag back into a crouch beside him. He could even see him now. The light was that much stronger. Junior would have been able to see to take his shot if he'd had a chance. As it was, they'd seen nothing because the deer had spooked before it came in sight.

They crouched, waiting. Colors were beginning to emerge from the grayness and the mist. Sam could hear Junior breathing. He looked around at him. Junior must be disappointed, but it didn't show on his face. Sam motioned for him to take the next shot. At first, Junior shook his head, but Sam made the motion again, and Junior gave him a small smile and a thumbs-up. Sam smiled back. He always loved it when Junior did something that reminded him of Bonnie.

They waited for a long while. Sam was stiff and cramped. He was just about to suggest that they head down to the truck for coffee and some of Bonnie's lunch when he heard a sound up the hill. He felt Junior tense beside him, so he knew Junior had heard it too.

They waited. For a while they heard nothing, and then there were tiny, crackling sounds coming from the road above. Something was definitely coming, something dainty, by the sound of it. After what seemed like forever, a doe came into sight, followed by two nearly grown fawns.

Junior was ready. He waited until she was almost abreast of him. Then, with his bow drawn, he rose up in one smooth motion and shot. It was pretty to watch. Junior was a big man, but he wasn't clumsy. It should have been a perfect shot, but he missed. When the arrow went by, all three deer exploded down the other fork of the road and off the trail into the woods.

Sam should have backed Junior up by taking a shot of his own when Junior missed, but he wasn't ready. He had been too involved watching how smoothly Junior rose into position to think about getting ready to take a shot himself. By the time he thought of it, there was nothing to be seen but disappearing rumps.

"Nice try," he said to Junior.

"Not nice enough. I should of had her."

"Let's go down to the truck and get some coffee. We can figure out what we're goin to do next. There ain't goin to be anythin happenin here for a while."

"Okay, Pop."

When they got down to the truck, Sam poured them each a cup of coffee. It was still early, and the air was still cool.

Junior said, "You should of left me at home and taken Marnie. She'd of done better'n I did this mornin."

They were sitting in the cab of the truck, cradling their mugs of coffee in their hands and looking ahead out the windshield instead of at each other.

Sam said, "Gimme a break. I'm sorry about that shot, but don't bring Marnie into it. Women ain't supposed to be in the woods in huntin season. It's against their nature. You ain't never seen your ma out there with a bow or a rifle. There ain't no good that can come outa that."

"I messed up good this mornin. What'll we do now, Pop?"

"You want some of your ma's lunch she packed for us?"

"I guess not. I ain't hungry yet. We should go back up the hill again first, unless you want somethin."

"No, I can wait. I ain't hungry either." He reached in the glove compartment for his cigarettes.

Junior said, "What's this, Pop? I thought you quit."

Sam shrugged and lit up. "Well, I did, only sometimes I cheat a little."

"What does Ma say about that?"

"Nothin. I don't cheat all that often, you know."

"The deer'll smell the smoke."

"I don't think so, but I'll put some more cover scent on. You want to go back to the same spot?"

"I thought we would."

"Because I have an idea I'd like to try that little meadow up there just where the road starts to get steep."

"Oh yeah," Junior said. "I know that meadow, but we didn't see nothin when we came down."

"This is true. I still want to try it. I just got this idea in my head about it."

"I think I want to go up to the old spot. How much time do you need?"

"An hour should be plenty. Let's see what time it is when we get to the meadow. We can do an hour from then. That'll give me plenty of time to check it out."

"Okay, Pop. Let's get goin then. We want to catch 'em while they're still feedin."

Sam said, "You're the boss." He took a long drag and dropped the cigarette in the dirt as he opened the door of the truck. He stepped on it as he got out.

They both sprayed themselves with cover scent and loaded up on the gear they had taken off. It was full daylight as they went up the logging road. When they came to the meadow, Sam stopped. They waved to each other, and Junior went on.

Sam walked along the east side of the meadow, looking in through the trees, until he found a spot behind a log where he could conceal himself. When he heard something, he could rise up and take a look, or maybe a shot, the way Junior had.

He sat with the sun on his back, warming him. He felt peaceful. If a deer stepped into the field, he would shoot, but if not, he would sit there and wait for Junior to come down from their stand. They could have some lunch at the truck and try the other side of the road for a change.

There was a whoosh and then a thud. He didn't know where he was or what he was doing. He must have dozed off, because when he looked over the log, he saw a deer take a couple of steps and stagger and fall. He hadn't even known there was a deer in the field. He stood up. His legs were cramped. It was a minute before he could use them. Then he stepped out into the meadow to see about the deer. He still didn't understand what was going on. When he saw Junior come out of the woods, it added to his confusion. He must have been asleep.

Junior said, "Pop, I didn't mean to get in ahead of you. I waited, but nothin happened. I figured one of us better shoot."

"It's good you did, Junior." They were both hurrying to the deer. It was a big doe. She wasn't dead, but it was clear she would be soon. She was lying on her right side. Her feet were twitching as though she was still trying to run.

"That's a beautiful shot, Junior. You must have hit her in the heart." Junior was taking out his pistol to finish her off, but her feet stopped twitching, and her eyes clouded over before he could point it.

They didn't say much while they opened her up and gutted her. Sam wondered if she was the doe Junior had missed before. Her two fawns were plenty old enough to take care of themselves. They might be nearby in the woods, watching.

After a while, Sam left Junior to finish the dressing, and he went down to bring the truck up as close as he could. The road was rough, but with the four-wheel-drive he was able to get all the way to where the road went past the meadow. She was big, but Sam couldn't remember ever dropping a deer in a more convenient place. He sure was right about that little meadow.

Junior tagged her, and they half-dragged, half-carried her to the pickup. When they reported her at the store, she weighed in at 120 pounds. It was too warm to hang her outside, so they decided to put her in Sam's cooler.

No one was home when they drove in. "This is lucky," Junior said. "I might want to brag about my deer, but not with Marnie givin me a hard time."

"It was a beautiful shot. I wouldn't mind braggin on you." Sam backed the truck up to the bulkhead door.

They were both out of the truck, working on getting the sinews in the hind legs opened up so they could put the hooks in place, when Junior said, "Watch out now."

Sam looked up just in time to see Marnie's little car swoop to a stop right in front of the pickup. Both doors opened, and Marnie and Danny got out.

Marnie said, "What's goin on?"

Danny climbed up on the back wheel so he could see in. "Cool," he said. "Who shot him?"

"Junior did."

"No way! Did you really kill him with a bow and arrow?"

Sam and Junior lifted the deer out of the pickup and hung it on the track. Sam ran it along the track into the cooler and shut the door. When he was walking back to the truck, he heard Marnie say, "That deer was a doe."

Junior said, "We had a permit."

"Pop said women ain't supposed to have nothin to do with huntin."

"Marnie, you got to move your car so I can get out. Junior would probably like a ride home. We've been up most of the night."

"Sure, Pop. I'll move. I was just foolin around anyhow. Me and Danny have been out lookin at a horse."

Sam and Junior looked at each other, but neither of them said anything.

"There's a woman at work who's gettin rid of her eleven-year-old gelding, because she can't afford to feed him." She got in her car and backed it up without saying any more.

When they were in the truck, Junior said, "You suppose Marnie's goin to want that horse?"

"She didn't say she did."

"I thought she was waitin for a chance to ask you."

"Sounds like kind of a nice horse, don't you think?"

"You're goin to do it then?"

"I don't know. I might."

"Do you have enough room?"

"We could always build him a stall. I been plannin to replace Daisy, but if I've got enough hay, I could do that too. It'd be nice for Danny."

"You never would get a horse when we was kids."

"Times were tougher in them days. I was workin all hours. I don't know—you could say I made a mistake long ago, and I'm goin to do better this time. I'll see what Marnie has to say about it and then decide."

"I know you, Pop. You're goin to have that horse over here before we get my deer cut up. You wanna bet?"

They were at Junior's house now. He opened the door. "Thanks for the ride. I'll get my gear outa the back."

Sam said, "We could go out again tomorrow mornin. I'd like to get one for myself."

"I'd like that," Junior said. "I'll call you later."

CHAPTER 35

It was late when Richard woke up to a faint scratching noise coming from out in the hall. He lay in bed listening, trying to think what could be making such a sound. When he whispered to Alyssa, she didn't answer, so he reached out to touch her. No one was there.

He threw back the covers and got to his feet to go out into the hall, but he stopped in the doorway. Alyssa was crouching on the floor by the bathroom. She was scrubbing at the hall rug with a washcloth.

He said, "Oh, Alyssa, what...?"

She looked up. "I didn't mean to wake you. Sorry."

"But what...?"

"I got sick again. I was hoping I could clean it up without you knowing."

"But I *want* to know. How can I take care of you if I don't know when something's wrong? And anyway, you shouldn't be cleaning the floor in the middle of the night. It's not good for you. I want you to get stronger, not weaker."

He went to her and helped her to her feet. "Poor little Alyssa. Come on back to bed now." He gently twisted the washcloth out of her hand and dropped it on the floor. "I can do that in the morning. You've got to help me take care of you. I'm not very good at it, but I'm trying to learn. Come on now."

He half-carried, half-supported her down the hall. She was very weak, hunched over, trembling so violently that she couldn't stand without his help. She was so fragile, it broke his heart.

When they got to her side of the bed, he eased her down and picked up her legs and arranged her so she was curled on her side. He tucked the covers around her. "Go to sleep now, my sweet."

She made a small noise, something between a sigh and a moan, but she didn't say anything.

He went around the bed and got under the covers on his side. Even without touching her, he could feel her shivering. He lay still, listening to her breathing. At first it was short and rasping, but gradually it got slower and smoother, and she stopped trembling, although every once in a while her body would give a jerk that rocked the bed. After a while, that stopped too.

He thought he would go to sleep himself as soon as he knew she was settled, but as he lay there beside her, he got more and more awake. He felt so helpless. All he could do was stand by and watch while she went through these bouts of nausea and all the other manifestations of the chemo—the rashes, the sores that wouldn't heal, the bowel problems that humiliated her, and the endless pain. His efforts to help her were useless. She was so dear to him, more than ever before. But what good did that do?

He had to keep reminding himself that all this suffering was necessary so that she could make a full recovery. And it was temporary. When the chemo treatments were over, they could take up their life together the way it used to be.

Richard kept shifting around, trying to get into the right position so that sleep would come to him, but it was no use. Alyssa was asleep, and he was afraid he would wake her with his restlessness. He got up and went to the bathroom, stepping carefully over the place on the rug where she had thrown up.

Then he went downstairs. The stove was still warm from last night's fire, and when he stirred the ashes, he found enough coals underneath to get the fire going again.

He sat down in the chair beside the stove. He didn't feel like reading. His mind kept circling back to Alyssa's small body, trembling with cold and sickness. It was too hard for her, but she had to go on. She needed the chemo treatments to beat this disease. And she had to beat it, no matter what the cost, because he couldn't bear to lose her.

After a few minutes, he went to the glass door and slid it open to the frosty night. He stepped out onto the deck. The boards were covered with a film of ice. It was so cold that it stung the bottoms of his bare feet. He stood there, feeling the pain and even liking it, because he knew that he could end it whenever he wanted to.

A dark shape slipped from the trees by the water's edge and went past the shed. When it crossed the yard, Richard could see it more clearly. It was a fox. It trotted silently up the trail by the cabin and disappeared into the darkness under the hemlocks. Richard went back inside to his warm floors and his fire.

A few days later, Alyssa was feeling well enough to cook a beef stew. They didn't talk much at dinner. Alyssa seemed preoccupied. When they were clearing the table, Richard mentioned that he had made an appointment for tomorrow morning to have the winter tires put on the car.

She was walking up the steps to the sink, and she swung around to look at him. "I can't believe you would make an appointment for tomorrow. You know I have to have chemotherapy. It's so unfair." She slammed down the dishes in the sink. "You're always so mean. I just don't believe it."

"I'm sorry. I only meant to say that I have to remember to call and cancel it before we leave for the hospital."

He was carrying his dishes to the sink. She snatched them out of his hands.

"Don't be angry," he said. "And please let me do the dishes."

"No. I'm going to clean up, and I want to do it, and I want to do it alone."

He knew she was dreading tomorrow. He put his hand on her shoulder, thinking to comfort her, but she twitched away from his touch.

He said, "All right, if that's what you want, I'll go upstairs and check my e-mail, and when you're done with the water, I'll take a shower."

She didn't answer or even look around. Her only response was to turn on the water.

He sighed and went upstairs to his computer. After a little while, he couldn't hear the water running or the clink of dishes, so he leaned over the railing and said, "I'll take my shower now. Okay?" He had to say it twice before she answered. She sounded just as angry as before.

He went into the bathroom and turned on the water. When he was partly undressed, he realized that he had forgotten to get out any clean clothes, so he shut off the water and walked down the hall to their room to get some clothes.

It was when he was on the way back to the bathroom that he heard the crash. He dropped the clothes and ran toward the balcony, but before he could get there, he heard another crash and then a third. He stood on the balcony listening. She was crying and swearing. There was another crash. It wasn't an accident. She was down there breaking her dishes on purpose.

He didn't know what to do. She must have thought he was in the shower and wouldn't hear anything. After a few indecisive minutes, he tiptoed back to the bathroom and turned on the water again. He undressed and got in and stood under the water, crying.

The next morning he wondered if he would see broken dishes. He looked around the kitchen. She must have cleared all the wreckage away. In the cupboard, her favorite pie dish was sitting in its usual spot. He was pleased to see it there. He reached for it and discovered that it was broken into little pieces that she had set carefully back into place. He didn't know what he could say to her, and she volunteered nothing, so they rode together in silence to the chemotherapy appointment, and that was the worst of all.

CHAPTER 36

Alyssa woke up when they were passing Brattleboro. She looked at Richard, but he didn't notice. His eyes were on the road. He was listening to a CD of jazz that he had turned down low. He must have lowered it when he saw she was sleeping.

"I didn't mean to fall asleep," she said. "I didn't even know I was tired. Shall I take a turn at driving? I suppose I'm rested by now."

Richard smiled at her. "Only if you want to. I'm fine. I'm glad you got some rest."

"But I *couldn't* need any more. I've been taking it easy for days, so I would be ready for this trip. What's the matter with me that it's taking so long for me to recover?"

"You'll get your strength back. It takes a long time to get over an operation, and then you had all the chemo to go through. Six months isn't a long time. Sleep is the best thing you can do. I just hope all the people and all the cooking and cleaning up at Thanksgiving aren't going to wear you out."

"I don't think it will. I want to see Sonia and Alix...and Mom too, of course."

"We've got to take good care of you so you'll be ready for next summer. We missed a lot of last summer, but we're going to make up for it when I finish the new canoe and you get your strength back."

There was a sign beside the road that said they were leaving Vermont. It gave Alyssa a twinge of homesickness, even though they were only going to Stamford, and they would only be gone for three days—really just two complete days and two partial ones.

Alyssa sighed and relaxed back into the seat. It was reassuring to hear that Richard was so sure the cancer was gone. Now that the chemo treatments were finally behind her, when she thought she ought to be stronger or more resilient, or when she noticed small pains or changes in herself, she couldn't help worrying. But Richard thought she was getting better, and maybe he was a better judge.

Alyssa wanted to ask him if he really thought she was going to be all right. Did he *believe* it, or did he say it because he wanted her to believe it? She didn't know how to ask. She didn't want him to think the aches and pains were worse than they were. And most of all she didn't want to add to his worries about her. It was unclear to her, and that made it much easier to say nothing.

Richard was so good to her while she was sick. She looked at his profile, dark against the landscape out the window. The bare trees and the gray sky went past behind him. She loved looking at the sharp outline of his face. She could see him the way he looked years ago. There had been times when she'd thought of leaving him. Now she was glad for whatever had caused her to stay. She reached out and put a hand on his shoulder.

He smiled at her again. "Are you hungry? We could stop in Greenfield. When's your mother expecting us?"

"I told her we might not get there until seven-thirty or eight. I said that so we wouldn't have to worry about her worrying."

"Good girl. And it isn't even two. Do you want to stop?

"Not unless you do. I'm not hungry."

He looked at her more seriously this time. "You need to get your appetite back."

"I know. It's happening, but it seems very slow."

"The girls are going to tell you how great you look, since you've lost some weight. I hope you don't listen to them."

"But, Richard, I've been trying to lose weight for years. It's the only good thing that's come out of all this. And I'm afraid they'll notice how skimpy and strange my hair has gotten. Do you think it's too noticeable?"

"It looks fine to me."

"You're just saying that. It comes out in clumps. Sometimes I think I ought to shave my head and be done with it."

"Oh no, Alyssa. Now that the chemo is over, you need to try to get back to normal life. You need to try to eat as much as you can, so your appetite will come back."

"I *am* trying, Richard. It's hard to eat when you don't feel hungry, and even worse when you feel sick."

They were both quiet for a little while, and then Alyssa said, "There's going to be an awful lot of food at Mom's because of Thanksgiving. They've all been telling me about what they were making for the dinner. I'm kind of worried about it, actually."

After that, she fell asleep again, but more restlessly this time, so that she often woke up and looked around and then slid back into sleep, while Richard went steadily on.

When they got to the Merritt Parkway, he woke her up. "I have a great idea," he said. "Let's go get your mother and take her out to dinner."

"Okay. But I'll have to call her and see what she says."

The first thing she wanted to know was where they were. Alyssa told her they were on the Merritt already and would be there soon, and that they would like to take her out to dinner.

After Alyssa hung up, Richard asked what she'd said.

"She wants us to go without her. She'll get something at home. Sonia's coming over to put the turkey in the oven, and she wants to be there so Sonia can tell her what to do."

"We could call Sonia."

"No. Let's not. She really doesn't want to go."

"Here's another idea. We can order a take-out dinner and bring it to her house."

"You mean, like Colonel Sanders or something?"

"No. I mean like a regular restaurant meal. We can take it to the house and eat it there. We can bring enough for her too."

"Oh, I like that idea. Then we'll get to see Sonia tonight."

So that's what they did. They surprised Mom when they drove up. She opened the kitchen door just as Alyssa was getting out of the car. "You," she said. "I was sure it was Sonia when I heard the car in the driveway." She hurried down the steps and hugged Alyssa, and then she pulled back so she could look at her. "Alyssa," she said. "You're too thin."

"Don't you think I look nice? I've been trying to lose weight for a long time."

She didn't take the bait. "You look hungry, maybe a little gaunt. I feel worried when I look at you. Are you really all right?"

Alyssa hugged her. Sometimes her worries were annoying, but right now they felt different. She was worrying about the possibility that Alyssa might not get better, that she might even be dying. Alyssa was worrying about the same thing, only she couldn't tell those worries to anyone.

The three of them walked up the steps and into the house. Richard set the boxes of dinner down on the kitchen table.

"What's all this?" Mom said.

"We thought we could have dinner here with you."

"You didn't need to do that. I don't need a big dinner."

Alyssa said, "We know, Mom, but we thought it would be nice. This way we'll get to see Sonia."

"I want to keep this table cleared off because Sonia will need some place to put everything down. Bring all those boxes out to the dining room, Richard. I have the extra leaves in the table. It's set up for tomorrow, but we'll have to use one end of it and fix it back later."

Richard started to pick up the boxes. "I'm sorry we're disrupting your plans, Monika. We thought you might be hungry."

She was stumping into the dining room ahead of them. It wasn't clear whether she heard him. He shrugged.

Alyssa hurried in front of him, so that she could move the tablecloth and clear a place for their dinner at the end of the table. "This looks beautiful, Mom. You must have spent a long time getting everything ready."

"I did." She gave Alyssa a quick smile that was almost a grimace. "We'll have to put it all back later."

Richard set the boxes of food on the end of the table. "I'd better go move my car, so Sonia can pull up to the back steps," he said. "I think I'll just put it in your garage. Then it'll be out of the way when she comes."

"My car's in the garage. You can park on the street. There's plenty of room there."

"Mom," Alyssa said. "I thought you stopped driving last summer."

"I did."

"Why didn't you get rid of your car?"

"I don't know. I will. Sit down. Let's lay everything out. It'll be ready when Richard gets back. You must be hungry. There are worlds of food here."

"Richard ordered it."

A few minutes later they could hear Richard talking to someone.

Mom said, "That's got to be Sonia. You go say hello and tell her I'll be right there. I just want to close up all these boxes so the cats don't get into them."

Alyssa left her and hurried out to the kitchen. Richard was just setting an enormous turkey down on the kitchen table.

Sonia was coming through the door with her arms full. She said, "Oh, I'm so glad you're here." She put what she was carrying down on the kitchen table and turned to hug Alyssa. "You look wonderful."

Richard said, "I told you the girls would think thin was better."

Just then Mom came into the room and said, "She's too thin, Sonia. Don't encourage her."

Richard said, "That's exactly what I've been telling her, Monika. She'll have more strength when she gets those pounds back."

Alyssa could have been annoyed, but she was so glad to be there and so glad to see them that she just laughed. "I wouldn't mind a few more pounds, if I could be sure they would end up in the right places, but all the extra pounds I get seem to gravitate to my waist."

They talked for a little while. Sonia put the turkey in the oven and set the timer. She put bowls of stuffing in the refrigerator with lots of instructions to all of them about what to do and what to look out for. She acted as though none of them had ever cooked anything before. Alyssa didn't mind the delay. She knew it was going to be a bit of a struggle when she had to eat. Both Richard and Mom would be watching every bite.

Richard was getting restless. He kept trying politely to get dinner underway, but something always seemed to thwart his efforts.

Alyssa said, "We brought some dinner from Sorrenta's, and it's getting cold out in the dining room. Come have some with us, Sonia. There's plenty."

But Sonia was in too much of a hurry.

After she left, the three of them sat down to the boxes of cold dinner. Alyssa wanted to heat the food up, but neither of the others wanted to wait, and Alyssa could see how hungry Richard was. It would have been cruel to put it off again.

Later, when they were getting ready for bed, Alyssa said, "I tried to ask Mom about her car, but I couldn't get anywhere. Why doesn't she sell it?"

"Maybe she hasn't gotten around to it."

"There's more to it than that. It's just sitting in her garage and deteriorating. That's the kind of thing that drives her crazy. She's got to be worrying about it."

"Let's ask her tomorrow."

"If we get the right opportunity. I don't want to put her on the spot in front of the girls, and especially not in front of Brian. He has such strong opinions about the insurance and everything."

Alyssa lay down and pulled the covers up. Then she reached out to turn off the light on her side of the bed. She lay quietly, thinking about the day and all the driving they had done. She could hear Richard brushing his teeth in the bathroom across the hall. Then he came back into their room and raised the covers to get under beside her.

All of a sudden, she was completely awake again. "You don't think she's driving with her eyes like they are, do you, Richard? That would be awful."

Richard settled himself under the covers before he spoke. "You worry too much. She wouldn't do anything so stupid. After all, she stopped driving when she couldn't see well enough. No one told her to. She was the one who made the decision."

Alyssa woke up early the next morning. She felt rested and ready for the day. She was looking forward to seeing Alix. Maybe the baby was beginning to show. She got dressed and went out to the kitchen. Richard was there, having coffee with Mom. The turkey was cooking, and the kitchen was full of delicious smells. Alyssa was surprised and pleased that the food smelled so good. It might taste good too.

She poured herself a cup of coffee and took it to the table. Richard smiled at her and asked her how she was feeling.

"Fine. I slept very well." She sat down at the table between them. "What were you talking about when I came in?"

"Monika was trying to convince me that we should move down here now that Alix is going to have a baby."

"How is Alix, Mom?"

"I think she's all right. I don't see much of her, the way I do Sonia. I think she's happy about the baby."

"We all are. And it's about time too. Is it making her sick?"

"No. I don't think so."

"That's good."

"You're too thin, Alyssa. You need to gain some weight."

"That's what Richard always says." She looked around the kitchen. Nothing had changed since the last time they were there, and that was a long time ago. The fourth chair at the table was taken by a large, orange cat.

Mom saw where she was looking. "You remember Marmalade,

don't you?"

"Is that Marmalade? He must be awfully old."

"Almost fifteen. He's out here now because the oven's on. He feels the cold. I can sympathize. Your circulation gets so poor when you get old."

Marmalade raised his head and looked solemnly at Alyssa. He narrowed his eyes and then widened them. He put his head down again.

"He's saying that he's glad you're here."

"So am I. The turkey smells good."

"I hope you'll eat a lot."

"I'll try to."

"I want you to gain weight so you'll get your strength back."

Richard said, "We haven't always seen eye to eye on things, Monika, but I agree with you about this. She would be stronger if she wasn't so thin."

"I want the two of you to come back to Stamford. Your whole family is here, and soon there'll be a new baby. We want you near us. And you can get such good medical care here."

Alyssa looked over at Richard, but he avoided her eyes.

Mom didn't notice. She was busy making her case. "You would be close to Sloan Kettering. They are even planning to open some new facilities outside the city. I know you think you don't need them because the cancer is gone, but it could come back."

"I think we know that, Monika." Richard spoke quietly, but Alyssa knew he was thinking that he wished she hadn't said anything in front of her.

"You ought to live in a more hospitable place. It's too cold in Vermont, too cold and too far away from everything, and you need good medical care."

"Monika," Richard said, in his patient voice. "Now we are going to disagree again. There are plenty of good doctors and hospitals in Vermont. You talk as though we lived on the arctic tundra or something. Alyssa has an oncologist that we think is very good, and he can always refer her to Dartmouth. That's the best in the country."

"I'm talking about Sloan Kettering, Richard."

Alyssa sipped her coffee while they argued about what was best for her. She didn't listen. The coffee was delicious. The smells of cooking turkey were wonderful. She pretended to be Marmalade, soaking in the warmth and the company without thinking. She loved Richard. She loved Mom. In fact, this morning she loved everything and everyone.

Mom said, "Don't you agree, Alyssa?"

Alyssa said, "Mmmm, I guess so," and then she looked at Richard and saw by his face that she had said the wrong thing.

She was wondering how to fix it, when the door burst open, and Sonia hurried in, surprising everybody. Marmalade jumped off his chair and slipped out of the room.

Sonia's cheeks were pink. She bustled into the room full of energy and importance. "I had to go to the store for some butter. I was going right by, so I thought I'd stop in and baste the turkey, in case you forgot. You didn't do it yet, did you, Nana?"

"No, I thought you said to do it at eleven."

"Well, it doesn't matter. I'll do it now, and then you won't have to." She went to the cupboard and got out a vase for the flowers she was carrying. She filled the vase at the sink and arranged the flowers in it while they all watched. "I thought these would look nice in the middle of the table." She carried the flowers out to the dining room, and in a minute she came back. "Nana, the table looks beautiful, but you set the wrong number of plates."

To Alyssa's surprise, Mom didn't say anything, but then Alyssa was always surprised by the relationship Sonia had with Mom. It should have been a disaster—they were both so strong-willed and stubborn—and yet they got along well.

"There are eight of us, Nana—Brian and Jack and me and Alix and Reuben. That makes five, and then the three of you makes eight."

"My friend Mabel is going to come."

"Oh no, Nana. It's supposed to be just family, celebrating Mom's recovery."

"Mabel won't get in the way."

"But she's not part of the family."

"What's the difference? She's an old friend."

By this time Sonia had the turkey out of the oven. She was basting it as she talked. "I haven't even heard you talk about Mabel recently."

"I didn't see her all summer, but that was my fault, not hers. Anyway, she has nowhere else to go for Thanksgiving. She won't be any trouble."

"It's not trouble I was worried about. I had this idea that it would be just our family."

"I'm going to...oh, I mean, Richard, would you drive me over to pick her up?"

"Sure," Richard said.

"Dad, really? Is that what you want?" Sonia shoved the turkey back into the oven and slammed the door.

"It's okay with me. It's your grandmother's house, after all."

"I thought this was going to be a celebration of family." She went to the kitchen door and opened it and turned to look at them where they sat around the kitchen table. "I'll be back later with Brian and Jack," she said. She went out without saying goodbye.

"Oh dear," Alyssa said. "What shall we do?"

"Don't worry about it," Mom said. "She'll be fine when she comes back. She just has to blow off steam."

And Mom was right. When Sonia got back with Jack and Brian a little after noon, Mabel was already there. Sonia put down the pie she was carrying and went around the table giving everyone a quick kiss hello. She included Mabel. Alyssa looked at Mom. She didn't look back, but she had a satisfied smile on her face.

Jack came in carrying another pie, and Richard jumped up to help him with it. Brian went out to move his car so Alix and Reuben could park in the driveway.

Sonia took off her coat and Jack's and carried them out to the front hall. She put the pies on the dining room sideboard and the stuffing in the oven with the turkey. She was everywhere doing everything while they all watched her work.

Brian came in with a large pot of mashed potatoes, and soon

afterward Alix and Reuben arrived. Alix was carrying a big salad bowl. There was food everywhere. It was going to be a feast. Alyssa began to feel uneasy. It didn't look and smell so good to her any more. She hoped no one could tell how she was feeling.

As soon as Alix stepped through the kitchen door with the bowl of salad in her hands, Sonia shrieked. Everyone stopped talking and looked at her. She was looking at Alix.

"What is it?" Mom said. "Sonia, you're scaring everybody. Come in Alix, and Reuben too. What's going on?"

Sonia said, "Your finger, your finger."

"What's she talking about?"

Alix set the bowl down on the table. "I haven't even had a chance to say hello to anyone. She's talking about our rings." She took a step back to stand beside Reuben. "We were going to tell you all when we were sitting at the table. We got married."

Alix looked so pretty, smiling shyly, pink in the face from telling her news. Maybe the baby was showing a little, but Alyssa couldn't be sure while Alix was wearing a coat.

"What do you think, everybody? Are you happy for us?"

Alyssa said, "I'm very happy. It's something else to be thankful for today." She stood and opened her arms, and Alix came over and hugged her. She felt strong and healthy in Alyssa's arms. She smelled of the cold, fresh, outside air. Alyssa was glad and pleased for her, and yet she couldn't help a twinge of envy. Alix was just beginning a new and exciting time of her life, so different from what Alyssa herself was going through. She looked at Richard to see what he was thinking.

He smiled and said, "Monika, I hope you have enough wine. We're going to have to make a lot of toasts."

Sonia said, "We brought some. Brian, those two bottles are on the floor of the car. Will you get them?" Then to Alix, she said, "Why didn't you tell me? I wouldn't have told anyone."

"We wanted it to be a surprise. We've been planning this for a long time, but we figured we'd better hurry up because of the baby." She took off her coat and went to the front hall to hang it up. She came back into the kitchen already talking. "The table looks beautiful,

Nana." She was wearing a sweater and slacks, but Alyssa thought the baby was beginning to show. To Sonia she said, "Okay, now I'm ready to go to work. What shall I do?"

Sonia was standing in front of the stove. She turned around with her hands on her hips. "The first thing is to get everyone out of here, so you and I have some room to work." She raised her voice a little. "Okay, everybody listen to me. Go out and sit in the living room and give us a chance to get the food on the table. We'll come and get you when we're ready. Brian, you stay with us so you can carve. We'll put the turkey on the kitchen table as soon as everybody's out of the way."

Alyssa stood and tapped Richard on the shoulder. "Come on, Mom and Mabel," she said, taking a few steps toward the door to encourage them.

Mabel went willingly, but Mom kept turning back to look at things in the kitchen and in the dining room. Finally, they were all settled in the living room. Alyssa tried not to mind that she had been moved to the group of nonworkers. Before she got sick, she would have been out in the kitchen with Sonia and Alix, bustling around, sharing the laughter and comradeship of work.

Mom had hardly settled into her chair when she was up again.

"Mom, where are you going?"

"To see if I can help."

"But they told us to stay out of the way."

Everyone was watching.

Mom paused in the doorway and looked back at her. "It's my house. I can go out in my kitchen whenever I want to. There are lots of things I can do to help." She disappeared around the corner.

After a minute, they could hear Sonia telling her that they had it under control, and they didn't need any help. Alyssa smiled at Mabel and tried to think of something she could say.

After a while, Sonia appeared in the doorway to tell them to come to the table. They filed into the dining room and stood around, waiting for Sonia to show them to their seats. Alyssa was told to sit at one end of the table. Mom was at the other end. The long table was loaded with food. Alyssa sat looking at it all, while everyone got settled. She didn't feel sick, but she wasn't hungry either. She hoped no one would notice how little she ate.

Alix was seated beside her. She reached out for Alix's hand and squeezed it. "I'm so glad about the baby, and about Reuben and everything."

"Thanks. Me too."

"I brought a present for you. I meant it for the baby, but now it can be a wedding present too."

Alix smiled at her. There wasn't a chance to say more. Bowls of vegetables and plates of turkey were being passed from hand to hand. Alyssa dutifully filled her plate. She could remember how it felt to be hungry, how you could long for food, and what a pleasure it was to eat. But that was just a memory now. Maybe those feelings would come back some day, but she didn't see how forcing herself could help.

She managed to keep up the pretense of eating, and she thought she was doing quite well, until Mom, who was on the other end of the table, said, "Alyssa, you're not eating." She said it so loudly that everyone at the table turned to look.

"Oh Mom, I am too. I'm just eating slowly and enjoying it."

Sonia said, "Leave her alone, Nana. She'll eat when she gets hungry. She looks great."

Alyssa smiled at her. "Thank you, Sonia, for defending me." Then to change the subject so people would stop watching her, she said, "Mabel, tell us how you came to break your arm." It was a good move. Even Mom stopped noticing how Alyssa wasn't eating.

The talk swirled around. Sometimes Alyssa paid attention, and sometimes she disappeared into her own thoughts. She heard Mabel tell how she fell in the garage of her own building, and how at first she thought it was just a sprain, but by the end of the day, it hurt so much she couldn't sleep.

When Mabel told how she had to take a taxi to the hospital, Sonia said, "Oh if only you had called Nana. You probably didn't think of it because she doesn't drive any more, but she would have called me, and I would have taken you."

Alyssa thought she saw an odd, conspiratorial look pass between her mother and Mabel, but it was quick, and she couldn't be sure. She looked around to see if Richard noticed, but he was looking down at his plate.

Later on, after toasts to her recovery, to the family, to Alix and Reuben, and to the coming baby, when everyone was slowing down, talking about how stuffed they were, how impossible it would be to find room for dessert, Alyssa went and got the present she brought for Alix.

When she handed the package to her, Alix said, "Oh Mom, I can already tell that it's a painting, and I know I'm going to love it."

Everyone got quiet and turned to watch Alix unwrap the painting. It was a small watercolor of the brook just above their house in Vermont, where the water came down the hill from the pool. It was done while the leaves were turning in the fall.

Alix said, "Oh," and turned the picture so Reuben could see it. He nodded and smiled. Everyone was watching. Alix held the picture high so they could all see it.

Sonia said, "Pass it around, Alix. We'd all like to see. If that's okay."

Alyssa nodded. She felt shy, but she was pleased too.

So the painting was passed from hand to hand around the table. When it came to Mom, she said, "I don't see how you can find time for painting right now, Alyssa. You need to be spending all your energy trying to get your health back."

"I have some time, maybe not very much, and painting is how I want to spend it."

There was a silence for a minute after Alyssa said that. She felt she had been too blunt, because implied in her statement was the idea, which she definitely had, that she might not have much time left.

When Sonia was handed the painting, she said, "I feel like I'm there right now. It's kind of like a window into that other place." She handed the painting to Brian, and then she said, "It's going to be so good for the baby to lie in her crib and look at this beautiful scene. It will probably influence her whole life."

"Her?" Mom said. "How do you know it's going to be a her? Alix, do you know?"

Alix reached for Reuben's hand. "We haven't decided whether we want to find out ahead of time or not. But Sonia is sure it's a girl."

Mabel said, "It's a wonderful painting, Alyssa. I didn't know you were a painter. Monika never told me."

"That's because I'm really not a painter. I only started last summer, and I had never had lessons when I began. There is so much I don't know how to do." She paused. "But I love it. I forget everything while I'm painting." She looked down the table. Everyone was looking and listening. She smiled at them all in a self-deprecating way. "Sometimes there's a lot I don't want to think about."

"Well," Mabel said, "I don't know about the rest of it, but that painting is certainly beautiful. I've always thought I'd like to try my hand at it, but somehow it's intimidating. I don't even know why. Could it be that I'm worried about what people would think of me if I messed up?"

Alyssa said, " I never think about that. I know I throw away an awful lot of paper, and I have to sit and look for a long, long time. I do a lot more looking than I do painting, but I think that's what I love about it. I see more than I ever saw before. I look at ordinary things, and they seem wonderful."

Alix reached for Alyssa's hand. "Thanks," she said. There were tears in her eyes.

No one spoke for a minute, and then Jack burst loudly into the silence. "What I want to know is when we're going to eat those pies."

Everyone laughed. Sonia said, "If you want some dessert, Jackie, you'll have to help me clear the table."

Alyssa jumped up to help too. The three of them carried the dinner plates out to the kitchen. Jack tried hard to help. Sometimes Sonia had to jump in to grab a plate that was tilting at a dangerous angle, but Sonia was good at being everywhere at once.

While Alyssa was picking up a bowl of vegetables, she heard her mother saying something about having a hobby. She was talking to Mabel. Alyssa felt a twinge of pain, knowing that her mother was talking about her. That's what it was, a hobby, a pastime, a diversion. Suddenly, the pleasure of helping to do the work, the pleasure of moving around after sitting still so long, all of that was gone. It was as though a cloud had unexpectedly covered the sun, turning the bright afternoon dull.

Much later, on the way home to Vermont, Alyssa talked to Richard about it. She said, "My painting looked okay in the baby's room, didn't it?"

"I thought so, and I could tell Alix and Reuben thought so too."

"That's all that matters," she said, but she couldn't help a sigh.

Richard heard her. "Everyone thought your painting was beautiful. What's wrong?"

"Oh Richard, I overheard Mom talking to Mabel about it. She said it was a hobby, and I suppose she's right."

"That's just Monika. You can't let what she says bother you. Take what you agree with and leave the rest. You know how bad her eyes are. She can't see much. How could she appreciate them when she can't see them?"

"I know you're right. It's just hard to ignore what your mother tells you."

"I learned how to do that with my mother. I wanted different things than my parents did. And you do too. This isn't a hobby for you. I don't know what you would call it, but it's important to you. That's what matters. A hobby is, by definition, something that's not important to you."

"I hadn't thought of it that way. Somehow when I'm painting, it seems like the most important thing in the world. I feel as though I'm looking right into the beating heart of the universe." She stopped and thought about what she had just said. "I guess that's kind of dumb of me."

"It's pretty amazing that you could do that without lessons."

"Looking is one part, but putting it on paper so someone else can see it is another. That's the part I have trouble with."

"When you get your health back again, you'll have more time for lessons."

"That's going to be wonderful."

It had been overcast when they left Stamford, a gray day, cold, with a cutting wind. The farther north they went, the worse the weather was. By the time they got to the Vermont border, the wind was blowing squalls of snow across the road in front of them. Richard had to concentrate to see, and they didn't say much for the rest of the journey.

It was almost dark when they got to their own drive. "Oh thank goodness we're here," Alyssa said. "Don't stop for the mail. We can get it later. I can't wait to get inside our own house."

"I feel the same way. There's no place like home."

CHAPTER 37

The weather was bad the Saturday after Thanksgiving. In the morning, it was windy and cold. By noon there were squalls of snow. Sam was coming out of the barn around two when Marnie's friend Andie drove into the dooryard in her truck. She was pulling a horse trailer. They must have got their signals crossed somehow. Sam had told Marnie that Andie should come over first to see if they even had a place to keep a horse. He planned to suggest that they needed to go over to Andie's to check out the horse before they agreed to anything. And here she was pulling in with a trailer. The timing was terrible. He already had six deer to process for customers, and hunting season wasn't over. He might even get a couple more.

He was feeling annoyed, and then the kitchen door slammed, and Marnie came down the porch steps two at a time, with her jacket only half on. Her face was bright with excitement, his own little Marnie who had wished for a horse her whole life.

They both got to the truck at the same time. Sam told Andie to pull into the front yard under the trees where it was level. She did what he said and then cut the engine and got out. She was a big woman with graying hair under a feedstore cap. She looked competent anyway. They could hear stomping inside the trailer. Marnie grinned at him and shivered with excitement.

Danny came out and stood beside Sam. He reached up for Sam's hand. His small hand was warm. The three of them watched while Andie undid the bolts at the back of the trailer.

She lowered the ramp and opened the door. Then she told the horse to back up. He came out obediently, but slowly, feeling his way behind him. Sam could feel Marnie trying to restrain herself.

When the horse had all his feet on the ground, Andie led him in a circle until he was facing them. "This is Moose," she said. He was large and brown and goofy-looking.

Sam hadn't planned to take an interest in this horse. It was Marnie's deal. But as soon as he saw him, he knew he wanted to ride him. He said, "Is Danny goin to be able to handle a horse that big?"

"Andie says he's real gentle, Pop."

"Yeah, but if Danny was up there, would the horse even know it?"

Marnie grinned. Danny was looking up at them. Marnie said, "I guess we're goin to find out, ain't we?"

Andie stood nearby, holding the line. Moose was already nibbling at the frozen grass. Andie looked at all of them. "He's a sweetie. You're goin to love him. I wish I didn't have to give him up."

Danny said, "I didn't know he was goin to be so big. How am I goin to get up there, Gramp?"

"I don't know. Maybe we'll have to get you a ladder."

"Don't kid me, Gramp. I really need to know."

"I can't tell you what I don't know myself. You'd better ask your ma."

Marnie laughed. "We'll have to get a saddle for him, Danny."

Andie said, "I can leave my saddle over here until you can find one of your own. I ain't goin to have anythin to put it on anyhow."

"It might be a while before we can find one we can afford. And we're goin to need a bridle too."

"I was goin to give you this one of Moose's. It fits him real good."

Danny said, "Is his name really Moose?"

"Don't you think it's a good name for him?"

"I guess so. Was he always this big?"

"When I got him, he was only a couple of years old. He wasn't big then, but you could tell he was goin to be."

They all watched Moose trying to find something to eat on the frozen lawn. The wind blew swirls of snow around him, but he didn't seem to feel it. Colt was lying on the porch with his front paws hanging over the top step. He was watching everything, but Sam could see he was skeptical. He must have been thinking, "We don't need this. We were doin fine before this big lunk came along. What do we need him for?" That's what Sam was thinking before he saw Moose, but now he'd changed his mind.

Andie was talking. "He didn't know nothin when I got him. I had to teach him everythin. He's good now. I wish I could keep him. I'm goin to miss him somethin awful."

Marnie said, "You can see him and ride him whenever you want to, Andie. We really appreciate you lettin us have him."

Sam said, "I should show you the barn. Maybe you can figure out where we could put him. I'm glad I didn't get started on a stall before you got here. I wouldn't of made it big enough."

"I'd like to see what you got for a setup, Mr. Martel."

"We don't got much yet. This is a cow barn, not a horse barn. But if you tell me what he needs, I can fix it up for him."

Andie handed the lead line to Marnie and followed Sam to the barn. They went in through the milk room, the way Sam always did. When they got to the main room, what used to be Dad's milking parlor, Andie said, "It's okay in here, but I don't know about that little front room there. I don't think Moose could get through that way. He's too big for that door. You got another way in?"

"I can show you around the back." He led the way down the aisle between the sheep and the pigs. The back door was larger, and there was a ramp down to a back room with a dirt floor and a big sliding door to the pasture behind the barn.

"This is better," Andie said. "Moose could live back here. He'll do okay on a dirt floor. That concrete would be pretty hard on his legs."

"Well," Sam said. "I can clean it up and build him a stall back here if you think this is the right place for him. It would be warmer in that other room."

"The cold never bothers him. He gets a good winter coat. All he needs is some way to get out of the weather and a fenced-in area, so he can get some exercise. If he's back here, you could leave the door open so he could go in and out. He'll do fine back here. He's an easy keeper."

When they came out of the barn, Danny was holding Moose's lead line, and Marnie was brushing him with her hairbrush.

Andie said, "So Danny, you think you want to try him out? We could put you up there."

"Can I, Ma? Is it okay?" Danny was shivering with the cold. Sam almost said something, but he decided not to.

Marnie said, "You can ride, if Andie will show us how to get him ready. I don't know how to do that yet."

"Sure. I want to show you that stuff. You'll have to know how."

They put the saddle and bridle on, or rather Andie did it, showing the steps to Marnie, while Sam and Danny watched.

Then Marnie lifted Danny up into the saddle, and Andie handed him the reins, but she kept on holding the lead line while she walked the horse in a circle around the yard.

Danny shouted at Sam. "Gramp, look at me. Do you believe it? He's so big. I didn't think he would be this big. Did you?"

Andie stopped in front of Sam. "You have to make sure he does what you say, Danny. Remember that. It's important."

"Okay," Danny said. "Now take the line off. I want to go around without you."

Marnie started to say something, but she stopped herself. Privately, Sam wondered why anyone thought something as big as Moose was going to pay any attention to someone as small as Danny, but he didn't say anything. If Danny was going to ride that horse, and he clearly was planning to, then he would have to be in control. Sam had been around animals all his life, and he knew that authority counted for a lot more than size.

Danny went around once by himself. Sometimes he looked a lot like Marnie. When Sam saw that look, his heart gave a lurch. He hadn't meant to get so attached to Danny. He hadn't meant to fear for him, the way he had always feared for Marnie. Out loud he said, "Do you think that horse even knows Danny's on his back? He might think it's a fly up there."

"He knows," Andie said. "He's bein good now, but sometime Danny'll have to show him who's boss. Marnie, why don't you take a turn?"

"I want to, if we can get Danny down."

After some coaxing, Danny got off, and Marnie had a turn. She went across the field to the brook before she came back, and then Danny wanted to go that far too.

They offered Sam a chance, but he turned it down. He said it was because he had to get a place set up in the barn and a yard fenced in, but the real reason was that he wanted to wait until he could be alone with Moose. He knew he was going to have to walk him over to something to climb on, and he didn't want a bunch of women around while he tried it out.

They took off Moose's tack and found a place for it in the old milk room. It was going to take a while to find a saddle big enough for Moose that they could afford to buy, but Andie said she didn't care how long it took.

Marnie led Moose to the back of the barn and gave him some hay and a bucket of water. He could get some shelter under the ramp that led up to the hayloft. At least he could get out of the snow and the wind.

Moose seemed satisfied. He immediately began eating the hay.

But Sam could see that Marnie wasn't going to be suited until Moose had a real stall. He knew he would have to get to that job before he did anything else. The deer would have to wait.

When Minnie heard them open the door of the house, she came out to greet them. When she smelled Moose's scent on their legs, she started barking her most high-pitched bark that was like a scream.

The more they tried to calm her down, the more hysterical she got.

Bonnie said, "She thinks the horse is dangerous, and she has to warn us."

Sam grinned at her. "Colt knows better."

"She thinks Colt's wrong too. She thinks it's all up to her. She's the only one who knows. She's the only one who can save the family."

Sam said, "Well, she'll have to get over it. He's stayin."

"She will. Just give her a little time. She's tryin to do her job."

Danny gave her a treat, and after that she got quieter, but every so often she'd burst out in a little series of barks, like she couldn't believe they weren't doing something about the problem.

Sunday morning Sam woke up a little before his alarm went off. He lay on his back, listening to Bonnie's soft breathing, while he tried to decide whether to get up or to enjoy the last ten minutes of sleep time. That was when the way to build Moose's stall showed up in his thoughts. It wasn't exactly a picture, but it wasn't an idea either. He just knew how he was going to do it, and he knew it would work. He didn't need to figure out the details. He knew they were all in place.

Yesterday he'd cleared a lot of junk out of the back room, trying to figure out how to build the stall. Last night he had gone to sleep with a lot of different ideas floating around in his head. He had felt as though they were all clashing with each other, so that he would never be able to come up with anything that would work. But this morning the right plan was there, fully formed. The only thing he had to do before he was ready to start building was to take out the old ramp, and that wouldn't take long.

He was wide-awake now. He shut off the alarm and got up quietly. In the kitchen, he poured himself some coffee and sat down at the table to think about what he was going to do.

Later on, when they were eating breakfast, Marnie said she had to go to work. "My shift ends at two. I'll be able to help you some this afternoon." She didn't ask Sam whether he was going to work on Moose's stall, so he didn't tell her his plan. He probably couldn't have put it into words anyway. She'd see it when it was done.

"Would you give Moose his hay and water this mornin, Pop? I meant to take care of it myself, but I'm runnin late."

"No trouble. I'll be glad to."

"Thanks, Pop."

Danny came downstairs while Marnie was putting on her jacket. She said, "You stay away from that horse unless Gramp is right with you. You hear me?"

"I will, Ma."

"We have to take it slow while we're learnin. When I come home, we can get him out and brush him. Okay?"

A few minutes after Marnie left, Sam headed for the barn. Before he even got the barn door open, Danny was by his side. "What do you say, Gramp? Shall we get him out and put his saddle on?"

"I got to work on a stall for 'im, and I thought you was plannin on helpin me."

"Well, sure, but we could ride first and work on the stall later."

"I think you got it backwards. We need to work first and play later. That's the way we do things around here."

"Okay, Gramp."

"Besides, Moose ain't even had his breakfast yet." He looked at Danny, walking beside him past the animal pens. "And what about you? You ain't had any breakfast either. I'm surprised Grammie let you out."

"Grammie was in the bathroom when I left."

"You better get back inside on the double then. She's goin to be out here on the warpath when she gets back to the kitchen and finds you ain't there."

"Okay, Gramp."

"And, Danny, when you come back, bring my alarm clock from the nightstand by my bed."

"Okay, Gramp."

When Danny got there with the clock, Sam set the alarm and put the clock down on one of the crosspieces of the barn wall, where Danny could see it. "Now you watch this clock all you want. You ain't goin to have to ask me how much longer we got to work. It's set for two hours, see. That alarm's goin to go off at twenty to eleven. That's when we'll take a break and spend some time with Moose for a payoff."

"Okay, Gramp."

They got the old ramp out and cleaned up before the alarm went off, and Sam got part of the new stall framed up.

Danny turned out to be a pretty good worker, but he worked in spurts. He would work hard for a while, and then, kid-like, he would slow down and fool around, watching the clock and not making any forward progress. Sam pretended not to notice, and after a little while, Danny would get back on the job again.

At one point Sam noticed that Danny was shivering. He sent him inside to warm up. He thought that would be the last he saw of him, but he was wrong. After about fifteen minutes, Danny was back, ready to work again. Sam liked that. He gave Danny the big magnet and had him go over the dirt floor, looking for nails.

When the alarm went off, they went inside to warm up. Then they went out to get Moose. The weather was better than yesterday. It was still cold, and there was a little snow on the ground, but the storm was over, and the wind was quiet. They walked Moose around to the yard in front of the barn and put on his saddle. It took a while to figure out, but finally Sam thought they had it right.

He lifted Danny into the saddle, and Moose set off at a steady walk across the field to the brook. When they came back, Danny wanted to go around again.

"Okay, but you need to be careful when you get to the road. You need to stop and look both ways, same as if you was on foot. You want him to know to do that."

"Okay, Gramp."

The next time they came back, Sam said he wanted a turn. He lifted Danny down and led Moose over to his pickup. From the back bumper, he was able to step into the stirrup and climb on.

Afterwards, he couldn't remember how it had happened. He must have given Moose some signal that meant he wanted some action, because Moose wheeled around and took off for the brook at a gallop. They were flying. Sam felt like he was in a cowboy movie. They galloped all the way to the water's edge. Moose wheeled around, and they came pounding back, screeching to a stop right in front of Danny.

"Wow, Gramp. I didn't know you could do that. Way to go! Can I try it?"

Sam was about to say he was going to take his second turn, when Danny said, "You forgot to stop and look both ways when you got to the road. Suppose there was a car comin."

Sam stopped himself from telling Danny not to tell his mother or grandmother. He climbed down and lifted Danny up into the saddle. Danny's feet didn't come near the stirrups. Sam started to try to figure out how to adjust them, but he saw that it could turn out to be a fairly big job. He'd have to bore new holes in the leather straps to get them short enough. Andie might not want him to do that. And Danny didn't seem to care.

"How do I make him go fast, Gramp?"

"I don't know."

"But you did it."

"I don't know what made him take off like that. I guess I did somethin, but I don't know what it was."

Danny and Moose started off slowly, but Danny must have figured out how to tell Moose to go fast, because they were galloping before they got across the field, and they came roaring back. Sam had misgivings about Danny riding like that without his feet in the stirrups, but he didn't know what to say, short of calling a halt to what they were doing, and he wanted another turn.

After that, there was no holding Moose back. He galloped back and forth at top speed, and nobody remembered to stop at the road. At the end of an hour, Moose was soaked in sweat. Sam said, "It's time for us to stop. I know we ought to do somethin about how wet he is."

"We could dry him off."

"With what?"

"We could get one of Grammie's big towels, couldn't we?"

"I guess so. But we don't want her to find out. I'll get one from way in the back. That way she won't miss it. You hold onto Moose while I go for it."

They dried him off as much as they could and walked him around for a while, because Sam thought he'd heard that it was bad to put a horse away when it was sweaty.

The towel was pretty wet. Sam hung it up in the barn in a place where he hoped Marnie wouldn't see it. Bonnie hardly ever went into the barn, so that should be all right.

They put Moose in his pasture behind the barn with some hay. Then they went into the house for some lunch before they went back to work on the stall.

When Marnie got home, she came out to see how they were coming along. Sam showed her how by opening the door at the back of the milking parlor, Moose's stall could be made part of the main room. But by closing that door, Moose could have an open door to the outside without letting the cold into the rest of the barn. Sam could tell Marnie liked the way he was setting it up. She gave him a quick kiss, something she hadn't done since she was little.

Danny said, "Ma, you said we could get Moose out when you got home."

"Yes, we can. Pop, you want to do it with us?"

Sam said, "Thanks, but I think I'll just keep on workin for a while." He very carefully did not look in Danny's direction.

Danny and Marnie left together while Sam went on framing up the stall. He was pleased with his design and pleased that Marnie saw how good it was. He was almost finished with the framing when Marnie burst in. She was out of breath and wild.

She startled Sam. He'd been listening to the radio and hadn't heard anything. He didn't even know how long they'd been gone. His first thought was that Danny had been hit by a car. "Is he goin to be all right?" he said.

"Who?" Marnie stopped in her tracks.

"Is Danny hurt?"

"No. But he could of been, Pop. What the hell did you do to Moose?"

"Honey, calm down, and tell me what's goin on."

She tried. "Danny said you did somethin to Moose to make him run like crazy, and you wouldn't tell him what it was."

"I must of given him some signal, I guess, but I don't know nothin about horses—you know that—so I don't know what I done. He just took off for the field. I didn't have no choice about it."

Marnie was a little calmer now, but when she began to tell what happened, she began to get excited and angry all over again. "That horse was a totally different animal from yesterday. I didn't even get settled in the saddle before he took off runnin. I almost fell off. I can't let Danny loose on him like that. It ain't safe."

Sam agreed with her, although privately he was thinking that it wouldn't be much fun to ride without that rush of speed. He wasn't interested in just walking around. That could get old for everybody, including Moose. He couldn't say that to Marnie, so he said, "Where's Danny now?"

"He's brushin him. We got him tied to the back of your pickup. The saddle's still on, but I ain't goin to let him up there." She paused and thought about it. "I hope he ain't goin to try it. I better get back outside."

A few minutes later, Danny showed up. "You might as well quit workin, Gramp. She's goin to get Andie to come over and take him back."

"I don't believe it. She's just upset. She got a scare."

Danny looked a little more hopeful, but he said, "Well, that's what she says anyhow."

"Let's us just wait awhile and see how it sugars down. I might take a break and go inside to warm up."

He was still in the house when Marnie came in. "Are you goin to be around home tomorrow, Pop?"

"I guess so. Why?"

"Andie's comin over to show us how to control Moose, and how to tell him what we want."

"That could help."

"She's comin around four, so Danny'll be home from school. I want him here too."

They were all in the kitchen when Minnie started barking and jumping in circles, the way she did when she thought something exciting was about to happen. Colt was stretched out by the door, but he only raised his head enough to cock one ear. He left the barking up to Minnie.

Danny looked out the window. "It's Andie," he said. "She's in her pickup, but she don't have the horse trailer on it."

They all grabbed their boots and jackets and hurried out. The sun had been shining all day, warming everything. It felt more like September than the end of November.

By the time they got to Andie's truck, she was standing beside it. "So, Marnie," she said. "What was he doin? We can straighten it out whatever it is."

"When I got on him yesterday, he ran away. I couldn't control him at all. What if he did that with Danny?"

Danny and Sam looked at each other, but neither of them said anything.

"All right," Andie said. "Let's see if he'll do it for me."

They got Moose out and saddled him. Andie got on while they all watched. "Okay, Moose," she said. "Let's see how you behave." She clicked to him, and he walked in a big circle around the drive and back to where they all stood. Sam could see she was keeping a tight grip on him, but he couldn't tell exactly how she did it.

When she and Moose got back to the others, she pulled back a little and he stopped. "Did you see his ears?" she said. "He was listening to what I wanted him to do. I think he's fine. Now, let's…."

She never finished what she was going to say because Moose wheeled around and headed across the road at a gallop. Andie was almost to the brook before she could stop him. She made him turn and walk back slowly. She was keeping him under such tight control that he was prancing as he came across the field.

Marnie said, "Look at that. Isn't he pretty. But I don't think you'll be able to keep him tamped down like that, Danny. He's so big. I don't think I can do it either."

Sam decided he shouldn't say what he was thinking, which was that he'd love to have the chance to try.

When Andie got back to them, she made Moose go across the field again at a sedate walk. Then she said, "Okay, Marnie, now it's your turn."

Marnie made faces and looked uneasy, but she climbed up and sat on Moose's back, while Andie gave her more instructions than anyone could have remembered. Sam noticed that Andie had a firm hand on Moose's bridle the whole time she was talking.

"Okay, Marnie, I want you to make him walk to the middle of the field and then ask him to turn slowly and walk back to us."

"I'll try," Marnie said. "But I don't think it's goin to work."

Andie let go of the bridle. Moose stood there for a minute. Maybe he was beginning to get the message that not everybody wanted him to do the galloping stuff. Anyway, he hesitated. But then he took off across the field. They could see that Marnie was trying out all of Andie's instructions, but Moose kept running. Sam thought he might be having a good time with it. It would be fun to let out all the stops and scare people.

In a minute, Marnie was back in front of them. "I tried everythin, Andie, but nothin worked. He just kept goin, no matter what."

Sam wished they would ask him to try it, and when he looked over at Danny, he could see Danny was thinking the same thing. But Andie wanted to teach Marnie, and Sam was already feeling guilty about his part in the whole thing, so he decided to go back to work on the stall. If Marnie gave up on this horse, she would probably want another one anyway.

Later on, they all three came back to where he was working.

Marnie was glowing. "Oh, Pop, it's so wonderful. Andie thinks I'm startin to get it, and Moose must think so too, because he started to do what I said. I wish you'd been out there to see us. But you will, because Andie thinks the best way is for you and me and Danny to get Moose out when we can all three be there together. Then we can all help each other.

Sam said, "If that's the way you want to do it." He was thinking that it didn't sound like much fun. He'd had a great time galloping around yesterday, but he guessed that wasn't going to happen again, and he wasn't sure he was interested in anything else. Still, it was good to see Marnie so happy. He would do a lot for that.

Marnie showed off all the good points of the new stall.

"Boy, Mr. Martel," Andie said. "It's goin to be a real nice place for him to live. I'm sure he'll be happy here. He'll have the other animals for company too. It's much nicer than what I had for him."

She went out to say goodbye to Moose, and then she left. Marnie and Danny walked out to the truck with her.

Sam said goodbye right there. It was tempting to go outside since the weather was so warm and sunny. How many more days like that would there be before the winter closed in? But he wanted to see how much he could get done before Bonnie got home. After that, it would be time for dinner and chores.

CHAPTER 38

Richard was sitting by the woodstove drinking his morning coffee, when Alyssa came down the steps into the room. She put her coffee cup on the table and sat in the chair at the end.

Richard went on reading the Times on his Kindle. After a few minutes, he looked up. It was snowing, and the ground outside was already covered. The room was filled with soft, white snowlight, the way it was only in winter. Alyssa was looking at him.

"What is it?" he said.

"I have an appointment with Dr. Girard today at eleven."

"Oh. I guess I forgot." He went back to reading the paper. He was skimming around, looking for a story that interested him. The next time he looked up, she was still watching him.

He said, "You're not worried about the roads, are you? I don't think we're supposed to get that much snow. It's just blowing around."

"I'm not worried about it."

"Do you want me to go with you? I don't have much I have to do today. I was planning to work on the canoe. Would you like me to go?"

"It would be nice."

"In that case, of course I'll go. We could stop for some groceries on the way in."

"Okay."

They got started later than they meant to, so they decided to do the grocery shopping on the way home. That made them early at the doctor's office. They sat in the waiting room. Richard wished he'd brought his Kindle. They couldn't talk much because there were other people sitting around them.

It was just a routine appointment, but Richard kept noticing that Alyssa seemed uneasy. She had one leg crossed over the other, and she kept swinging it back and forth in an energetic way. After a while, she uncrossed her legs, and the restless motion stopped. Then she began to tap one foot on the floor. Richard glanced around to see if any of the other patients thought it was strange, but no one was looking at them. They all seemed lost in their own thoughts. Richard couldn't think what to say to Alyssa, so he reached out and patted her hand. She smiled at him briefly and went on tapping her foot.

Finally, Dr. Girard called them into his office. He told them to sit down. He went through the usual polite remarks about the weather, and then he said how glad he was that Richard was there too.

Richard smiled and nodded. Dr. Girard was an important person. It was evident in his big, dark wood desk with all the silver and brass ornaments and the photographs of his family. But still, he was generous enough to be welcoming, to want Richard to be there to hear the good news about Alyssa's progress.

That was what Richard was thinking anyway. That was why he was completely unprepared for what he heard next. The doctor was apologetic as he said the chemo wasn't working. Tumors had reappeared in the past month.

After that, Richard tried to pay attention, but his brain was full of fog. He thought of it rising like a scene on the moors in an old horror movie.

Alyssa was taking it much better than he was. She was listening and nodding with a serious look on her face, while the doctor talked about other possible treatments.

Richard tried to listen. He needed to help Alyssa understand her condition, so she could decide what to do about it. She was the one who would have to make the final decision about what kind of treatment she wanted. He knew that. His job was to steady her and calm her so she could think clearly. His job was to pay attention to what the doctor told them to do.

But when they stood up to leave, Richard wasn't sure what he had heard. Alyssa took his arm as they left the room. At first, he thought she needed him to steady her, but then he realized that she was calm. She was trying to steady him.

Neither of them spoke on the drive home, until they were almost to West Severance. Then Alyssa said, "Hey, weren't we going to stop at the grocery store?"

"I forgot all about it."

"Should we go back?"

"I don't want to. Do you? I can't even remember what we were going for."

"I guess it wasn't anything important. I'm willing to skip it if you are."

When they got home, Richard stoked up the fire and sat down beside it. His brain was still fogged in.

Alyssa was her normal self. She acted as though nothing unusual had happened at the doctor's office. "Are you hungry? I thought I could heat up that chicken soup I made. We could have soup and some bread and cheese." She stood there looking at him until he answered.

"Fine. That'll be fine."

A little while later, she had everything laid out on the table. She told him to sit down, and he did as he was told. He felt like one of those men in an African tribe who goes through all the moaning and screaming of labor, while his wife is having the baby. He was as stunned as if he were the patient. Alyssa was acting the part of the caretaker.

After a silence he said, "I was really surprised by what Dr. Girard said."

"I know. I'm sorry."

"Weren't you surprised?"

"Not really. In some ways it was a relief when he actually said it. It was what I suspected."

"Alyssa. I can't believe it! Why didn't you tell me?"

If he hadn't been looking at her just then, he would have missed the quick flinch of pain that passed over her face. But when she answered, she was calm. "I thought about telling you. I played it over in my mind a lot of times."

Richard exploded. "Damn it, Alyssa. Whatever was going on in your head couldn't do *me* any good. I felt like a fool. I sat there in front of him, nodding and smiling, getting it entirely wrong." The more he said about what happened, the angrier he got. "I acted just like one of those animals Sam butchers, so eager for a stupid, little dish of grain, that he doesn't even see Sam standing there with his .22 at the ready. You should have told me what was going on." He was really furious now, outraged on his own behalf. But at the same time, he knew he was behaving like an asshole, and he wanted Alyssa to stop him.

Instead, she burst into tears. Instantly, his anger disappeared. He was horrified to see that he had been thinking about his own feelings, when he should have been thinking about hers. "You seemed so accepting," he said. "I don't understand how you could take that diagnosis so calmly."

"I don't understand it either. Maybe it's because I've been getting more and more convinced that the chemo wasn't working and wasn't going to work. What the doctor said didn't surprise me, and at least this settles it."

When he heard that, Richard stood up and walked to the wood-stove. Then he walked to the glass doors. "You can't have *known* it wasn't working," he said, looking outside at the deck, peaceful and quiet under the new snow.

"I could feel it, like a presence. It weighed me down."

He walked back to the table and sat facing her again. "Maybe we should get a different doctor. Maybe your mother is right. Maybe we should go to Sloan Kettering. There's a lot we can do."

"I don't know, Richard." She didn't look directly at him. "I don't know if I want to go through all that."

"But you've *got* to. You can't quit now, Alyssa."

"I'm not sure."

"What are you talking about? You don't have a choice. It's a life or death situation. You've got to fight."

She didn't answer. Richard thought of other arguments he could use, but she was getting upset, so he kept quiet. He didn't want to bully her, and at the same time, part of him wanted to shake her, to make her see what she had to do and how high the stakes were.

After a silence, Alyssa said she would make a pot of coffee if he wanted some but that she was feeling tired. She thought she would take a nap.

She left, and Richard stayed at the table. He thought about working on the canoe, but somehow, he didn't feel like it. He decided to go back to town for the groceries. He still had the list in his pocket. He left a note for Alyssa on the table.

At the grocery store, he decided to cook the most beautiful and nourishing meal he could manage. He would do it all himself. He needed to learn how to cook especially healthful meals, if he was going to take care of her while she fought this battle, the most serious battle of her life.

When he got back from the store, he set the groceries on the counter. Alyssa was still upstairs. He was putting some wood in the fire when she walked into the room. She stood by the counter, looking down at him.

"I hope I didn't wake you up."

"No, I was lying there already half-awake, when I heard you drive in. Where did you go?"

He told her, but she was looking at the bags of groceries, so she already knew.

"Two trips to town in a snowstorm. How were the roads?"

"They were fine. It isn't coming down that hard."

"I guess winter's really here."

"It looks that way."

Alyssa started taking things out of the grocery bags.

Richard shut the door of the stove and went up the steps to help. "I got everything on the list, and I also bought some salmon. I thought I would cook dinner for us tonight. Would peas and mashed potatoes look pretty with the pink of the salmon?"

Alyssa smiled. "Now you're thinking like a painter."

"I'm trying to think of what would please you."

"That's sweet of you, Richard, but I can do the cooking. I feel rested since I took a nap."

"No. I want to do it. You can sit and watch. I need…I mean, I want to learn how. It'll be fun. You can advise me when I do something wrong."

It was good to see her laughing. "Okay," she said. "If that's the way you want it."

"I want to do it for you." He didn't mention the future and neither did she, but it lay unspoken between them.

When it was time to start the dinner, Alyssa sat by the fire reading, or pretending to. If he didn't know what to do, Richard asked her what came next, and she always seemed to know.

The dinner turned out pretty well, considering. The potatoes were lumpy, and they had cooled off by the time the rest of the dinner was ready, but other than that, it was a success. He had a good time. He planned to try something more ambitious next time.

After dinner, Richard cleaned up. He insisted that Alyssa stay in her chair by the fire. When the work was done, he stood in front of the stove, warming his back. He was trying to decide whether to finish reading the newspaper or to read his book.

Alyssa said, "This fighting stuff, Richard…we need to talk about it."

"Don't worry. We'll do it together. I'll be right there by your side.

I'll be with you every step of the way." It felt good to say it.

And it should have pleased her. She always said she wished they could be more together. Here was just what she said she wanted, but she didn't look happy about it. She was leaning back in her chair, and she was frowning.

He waited, but when she didn't speak, he said, "You don't need to be afraid. I *know* we can beat this thing." He looked out the glass doors at the black night. It was so quiet. The wind had died down, and the snowstorm was over. The only sound was that of the melting snow dripping from the eaves, a ticking that was answered by the fire inside the stove.

Alyssa sighed and stood up, still without saying anything. She walked over to the couch and sat down so she was facing Richard where he stood in front of the woodstove. He thought she was going to speak, but she didn't. She lay back against the cushions, and now she closed her eyes.

Richard opened the door of the stove and got a chunk of wood to put on the fire, even though it didn't really need it. He sat down across from her. When she still didn't open her eyes or say anything, he began to think he misunderstood what she meant about fighting. He'd thought she meant fighting the cancer, but now he saw that she could have been talking about the way he got so angry at lunch when they came home from the doctor's office. He didn't think of that as a fight exactly, but they probably ought to talk about it.

He said, "I shouldn't have gotten so angry this morning. I was completely unprepared to hear that the tumors were back."

"I'm sorry. I have wanted to say something about it for a long time, but I didn't know what to say. I knew you wouldn't believe me."

"You *knew* what the doctor was going to say?" He felt profoundly disoriented.

"No, of course I didn't know. If I'd had facts, I could have told you, and I would have. I just suspected the tumors were back. Somehow they didn't feel...gone."

"I can't believe it."

"See. That was my problem. I didn't want to try to convince you. I didn't want to get in an argument, because I kept hoping I was wrong about it."

"I thought you were getting so much stronger. But it doesn't matter. We *will* succeed. There's a lot of things we haven't tried yet."

When Alyssa answered, she spoke so softly that he wasn't sure he heard her. There was a moment before he could take it in.

She said, "I'm not sure I want to fight any more."

So he got the second shock of the day when he realized what she was talking about. It must have been visible on his face.

"I'm sorry, Richard. You've been so good to me, so supportive and kind through all of this. I know it's got to be hard for you that we're not making this decision together."

"The choice is so stark."

"You mean, I will die if I don't fight it?"

"Yes, exactly."

"I guess I see it differently. I've been reading articles about lung cancer on the internet, articles about how to treat it, and the odds of surviving it. No matter what you do, no matter how much chemo, or radiation, or surgery you have, your best odds are still around fifty-fifty. They call that success. And even if you are one of the lucky ones, it's likely to come back in a few years. When you look at it that way, it seems that I am likely to die pretty soon, no matter what I do. And I would like to go out with dignity, peacefully accepting my fate, not struggling against the inevitable. Everyone has to die, after all." She paused and sighed. "I want to use the little time I have left to paint as much as I can. I wouldn't be able to do that if I was taking a whole lot of chemotherapy."

Now it was Richard's turn to lie back in his chair with his eyes closed. He couldn't think of anything to say, but she was waiting. Finally, he said, "What about your mother?" He knew it was lame.

"I was planning to call her tonight, only I needed to tell you first. I'll call her in the morning. There's Alix and Sonia too."

"You make it sound so final. You only went to the doctor this morning. It's too soon to make a decision. You need to think about it for a while."

"I *have* been. I've been thinking about it all fall."

"But I…." It was a pain that numbed his thinking, the way it had in the morning. But this was worse. This was an ache in his gut that spread to his whole body. His face felt swollen, and the swelling went down into his chest.

"Oh Richard. I'm sorry I left you out when I was trying to decide what to do. I didn't know how to talk to you about it. You would have argued with me. You would have tried to talk me out of my suspicions. I didn't want to have a conversation like that. I think I was scared to. I guess I didn't trust my own instincts enough. You would have convinced me, and I would have had to come to this hard realization all over again."

"We can fight this thing together."

"That's sweet of you, and I know you mean it because you have been so good to me ever since I got sick, but it's my cancer, not yours. I'm the one who has to make this decision. I thank you for being so good to me, but it's my life, and I have to do what's right for me."

"But you *can't* decide something like this by yourself. We're talking about my life too. What would I do if you weren't here any more? I wouldn't have anything to live for."

Alyssa stood up abruptly and left the room. Richard sat there, too numb to move. After a while, he wondered what time it was. It must be getting late. He was just about to go and look at the clock when she came back and sat down again. She had a handkerchief in her hand.

"This is such a difficult thing to talk about. I don't want to hurt you." She dabbed at her eyes. "I wish this wasn't happening."

"Me too."

"Did you hear Dr. Girard this morning? He said there were other kinds of chemo I could try. If you really wanted me to…." She looked at him, waiting.

At first he thought he would say yes, he did want her to take more chemo to try to beat the cancer any way she could.

But only for a minute did he think that way, because almost immediately, he was horrified by his own selfishness. She had been wrestling with these questions all fall. There was no one she could turn to for advice and help. She soldiered on, doing things for him, while she was trying to make sense of her difficult options, unable to talk to anyone who could give her an honest and unbiased answer, because whoever she turned to would want her to make the decision that was best for that person. He had just shown that was true for him too. And here she was, offering to put herself through a lot of suffering if it would make things easier for him.

So at the end of this long rumination, what he said out loud was, "I could never ask you to do such a thing for me. You should only do it if it's what you want for yourself, and it sounds as though you have already made the opposite choice. My heart will break, but I must accept that."

She stood up, and he did too. He put his arms around her, and they stood there together for a long time, like two people in the midst of a natural disaster. They clung to each other for support. She didn't cry, although she seemed close to it, and so was he. At first he hoped she wouldn't notice. But then he thought this was something new in their relationship—an openness, a frankness that they may never have had, even in the beginning when everything was rosy. So then he thought he would try to build on this new thing; he would try for honesty now at the end, to perhaps even let her see him cry if he felt like it. So what if there wasn't much time left to build something between them. They could have it now for this tiny bit of time, because all anyone ever had was a tiny bit of time.

CHAPTER 39

Monika was sitting in her kitchen, drinking her second cup of coffee and making a list of the Christmas gifts she was going to get today. It was already eight-thirty, but she wasn't dressed. She had decided not to add to the stress of the Christmas crowds by trying to drive herself. She could shop at stores that were close to each other and take a cab there and back.

The phone rang. She left her coffee and went to answer it.

"Oh you're there, Mom. It rang so many times, I thought you must be out somewhere."

"It takes me a while to get to the phone. I can't go very fast any more."

"You could move the phone to the kitchen. That's where you spend most of your time, isn't it?"

"I've thought about it. There's no place to plug it in. You know, one of those jack things."

"You could get a portable phone. That might be even better. Then you could have it nearby wherever you were."

"I don't want to. I hate all these new devices. Why can't they leave things alone? I'm too old to learn how to operate all these new things."

"Have you got all your Christmas shopping done?"

"Not yet. I'm planning to do a lot today."

"I'm going to try to do some too. What's the weather like?"

"It rained yesterday, but it's all right this morning. It's still kind of cloudy."

"We got a couple of inches of snow yesterday."

"Oh my heavens. I hope there won't be too much snow when we come up."

"You want a white Christmas, don't you?"

"Well yes, but it seems early."

"It's December, after all."

"Alyssa, do you think Sonia would like Aunt Sarah's cut-glass creamer and sugar bowl?"

"I'm sure she would."

"You don't mind if I give them to her, instead of to you, do you?"

"No, of course not. I think it's a lovely idea."

"I thought I could give Alix the big cut-glass bowl. What do you think?"

"Yes, do that. I was going to ask you about Alix. You're going to give them as Christmas presents?"

"I thought I would, if you don't want them yourself."

"No, Mom. That's just fine. I think the girls will be really pleased, and I wouldn't use them."

"I'll do that then."

"But, Mom, I have something to tell you."

Monika felt a sudden stab of fear. "That means it's bad, doesn't it?"

"Well...."

"That means it's really bad."

"Mom, don't make it harder than it already is. I went to the doctor yesterday. The tumors are back again."

Monika's thoughts were scurrying around in her head like squirrels in a cage.

"And they seem to be growing."

"Alyssa, you must come down here. I've been trying to get you to do that for a long time. I knew it was necessary. I wonder if I could get them to see you before Christmas. We could drive back to Vermont together. Would Richard come down so he could do the driving? That would be the best."

"Mom, dear Mom, I know this is hard to hear. I'm not going to get better. That's what this means. I've been doing a lot of reading about lung cancer on the internet, and…."

"You can't believe what you read on there. You know better than that." She had been feeling frightened, but this was something easy to dispute. She felt relieved by that. "People say all kinds of crazy things on the internet."

"There are serious studies too. That's what I've been reading."

"Alyssa, you've got to go to Sloan Kettering. They are the ones who know what's going on. That's the place to find serious studies."

"Mom, listen to me. I have a good doctor. I trust what he says, but I don't want to spend my last few days feeling awful. I don't want to try any more treatments, especially not chemotherapy treatments. I would like to do a few paintings while I still can. I would like to have some peaceful days. If I thought I could get better, I would do what you say, but I'm pretty sure I'm not going to get better."

Monika felt as though someone had struck her. She couldn't get her thoughts in order. "Thinking like that is going to make you sicker. You've got to *believe* you'll get better. You've got to *believe* in yourself. You've got to."

"I'm sorry Mom. I know this is so hard for you."

"You're not allowed to die. Do you hear me? You must not. You cannot. You're all I have."

"Oh Mom, I'm so sorry."

"What does Richard say? I want to talk to Richard. Put him on the phone, will you?"

"Mom, he's not here right now."

"Why isn't he with you? He ought to be with you." She could feel herself getting a little crazy, and she knew she was being annoying. She could hear it in Alyssa's voice.

"He has a life too, you know. He went into town to talk to a client about keeping his books for him. Do you want him to call you when he gets home?"

"No…yes…I don't know. Yes, I do, yes. Is that okay?"

"Sure, Mom. I'll tell him."

They said goodbye. Monika hung up the phone and went back to the kitchen, to her coffee and her Christmas list. She almost couldn't make sense of what she had written. She couldn't imagine going shopping now. She couldn't do anything until she'd had a chance to talk to Richard. She sat there doodling around the edges of her shopping list. She was only able to fidget. She was unable to concentrate on anything. She even turned on the television to one of those morning shows that she only turned on when she was feeling lonely and wanted to hear people talking, but they were so irritating that she turned it off again.

After a while, she decided to get dressed. She didn't want to dress for the shopping trip since she didn't know whether she would go or not. It all depended on when Richard called and what he said when he did.

It took her a long time to find something to wear. She kept thinking she heard the phone, and she would have to go out in the hall to listen. Finally, she carried her clothes out into the hall and put them on by the phone. When she was dressed, she went back to the kitchen and got out her playing cards for a game of solitaire. But it was no good. Even being able to see the cards again didn't please her. Alyssa's phone call had been so unexpected and so frightening.

She thought about it. Alyssa had looked a little too thin at Thanksgiving, and it was true that she didn't eat very much, but of course, she was still recovering. She had slept a lot too, but she had just made the trip down from Vermont, and Monika knew how tiring that could be. It was all explainable, or she had thought it was.

And now, less than two weeks later, the situation was suddenly so dire. It was hard even to think about it. Monika wanted to talk to Sonia, but she didn't know if Sonia knew, and anyway, she couldn't use the telephone, because Richard might call any minute. No, she couldn't do anything but wait. She laid the cards out for another game, even though her heart wasn't in it.

Richard didn't call until four-thirty. By then, she was so relieved the wait was over that for a minute she couldn't remember why she wanted him to call. Then it all came back to her.

"Oh Richard, I need to talk to you. This morning Alyssa said something so worrisome. I need to know what you think about it. She said she didn't think she was going to get better. What did she mean? You don't think she's just going to give up, do you?"

"I don't know."

"When she says something like that, what do you do? You've got to take charge of the situation. You can't let her talk or think like that."

"Monika, I don't see what I *can* do. She has a right to choose. It's her life we're talking about here."

"No, you're wrong. She doesn't have a right to choose. She's not making the right decisions. Maybe she's afraid. Anyway, you have to overrule her because she's not being rational."

"That's because you disagree with what she says. She says she doesn't want to spend her remaining time feeling awful. I can understand that, and I sympathize. I don't want to ask her to try more treatments and then watch her suffering through her last few days. We don't know whether her cancer can be put into remission or not. We have to make these choices blindly without knowing what's going to happen."

"But she can't die. She *must not* die. It would be too awful. I couldn't bear it."

"You haven't seen how hard the treatments are on her, how sick they make her feel."

"I don't want to hear about it. It doesn't matter. The fact that she says she doesn't want any more chemo shows that she's not in her right mind. She's wrong. So naturally, the people who love her must choose what's right for her. It's obvious."

"Monika, let's talk about this when we are all together at Christmas. We can include Alyssa in the conversation. It affects her more than anyone."

That upset Monika even more. Richard hadn't heard anything she'd been saying. She tried to stay calm. She bit her tongue and didn't reply. She didn't want it to turn into a fight, but the whole point was that Alyssa shouldn't have a voice in this discussion because she wasn't acting rationally. The people who loved her most needed to step in and do what was right for her. Richard hadn't always had Alyssa's best intentions at heart. There had been times when he had treated Alyssa badly. She had reservations about him because of those times, even though she knew he had been wonderful to Alyssa through this last, most recent trouble. She was still deciding what she should say when Richard spoke again.

"Monika, I know this is kind of sudden. It was to me too. It's only a few weeks until we'll all be together at Christmas. And I think after you've had a little time to digest this news, you'll feel more peaceful about it."

Monika was almost sputtering when she thanked him. She said goodbye. There wasn't any sense in going on with the conversation. Sooner or later she was certain to say something she shouldn't say.

After the phone call, she tried to go back to her card game, but she was too upset. She wanted to talk to Sonia, but she probably couldn't get her this time of day. She decided she would allow herself to telephone Sonia at seven o'clock, even though it meant more restless waiting after an entirely wasted day.

As it turned out, Sonia called her. She seemed to know what was going on. Maybe she had talked to Richard. Monika didn't ask. They talked for quite a while. Monika felt as though Sonia was on her side about it all.

But after the conversation was over, she couldn't recall exactly what Sonia had said that made her think so. She was just going to have to wait until they were all in Vermont for Christmas. Then they could all talk about it together. She would be able to convince them that Alyssa needed to keep fighting the cancer, and that she would be able to get well again if she persevered. Monika *knew* it. It *had* to be true. They could all help, and that way they could keep it from being too awful for Alyssa.

But the first and most important step would be for Alyssa to come down to Stamford, where she could go to Sloan Kettering, and where Monika could take proper care of her. She felt sure that when she had them all together, they would see that.

CHAPTER 40

Sam was hanging around the kitchen waiting for Bonnie to leave, so he could work on her Christmas present. It was Christmas Eve, and he was just about out of time.

A car pulled into the driveway and stopped in front of the back porch. Sam looked out the kitchen window. It was an old Subaru hatchback. It was pretty banged up. "Who the hell could this be?" he said.

Marnie was just coming down from upstairs. "It's Ray. Danny's goin over there for Christmas." She turned back and shouted up the stairs. "Hurry up, Danny. Your dad's already here."

Danny threw his bag down the stairs and came pounding after it. Marnie had his jacket ready to hand to him. She acted like she couldn't wait to get rid of him. Sam was surprised for a minute, and then he realized that it was Ray she was in a hurry to get rid of.

She helped Danny into his jacket. She kissed him on top of the head and then pulled on his toque. "Say goodbye to Gramp. Did you pack your toothbrush?"

"Aww, I forgot."

"Well, Danny, you go right back up there and get it. I *told* you to put it in."

"I've got it, Ma. I was just kiddin ya." He grinned at Sam. He hugged his mother, and then he put his arms around Sam's waist. "I'll see you tomorrow, Gramp. Keep my presents safe for me."

He opened the door and ran out and down the porch steps. Marnie followed with his bag.

By the time Sam stepped out onto the porch, they were all three standing by the car. It was still overcast, but there were breaks in the clouds. It was going to be sunny later. The sun would warm things up.

Ray opened the hatchback. He put Danny's bag in and took out a long, thin Christmas package. "Here, Danny," he said. "That's your Christmas gift from me. I don't want Lori and the girls to know what I'm givin you, and I especially don't want Eric to see it."

"Okay, Pop."

"Put it under your Christmas tree. You can open it tomorrow night after you get home."

When Danny took the package, he said, "Wow. It's heavy. What is it?"

"Don't worry. You're goin to like it."

Marnie said, "Give it here, Danny. I'll put it under the tree, so you and Ray can get goin."

"No, Ma, don't take it." He moved a few steps away from her. "Pop, is this what I think it is?"

Ray lit a cigarette off the one he had smoked down. He dropped the butt into the slush of the driveway and ground it out with his toe. He looked at Sam. He hadn't said hello, and Sam hadn't said hello either.

"Pop, it's a gun, ain't it? I mean, really."

"You'll find out. Come on. Let's go."

Danny asked his mother if he could open his present before he left, and she said he had to ask his dad.

Danny said, "I'm just goin to take a look, Pop, and then we'll go. Okay?"

Sam was standing on the porch, watching the whole thing. He

could see by Ray's smug smile that he wanted Danny to open the package, even though he didn't say so.

Danny didn't wait to find out. He ripped off the paper and set the box down on the steps.

Sam was looking down at him as he opened the box. "Whoa," Sam said. "That ain't a .300 Savage, is it?"

"Yeah." Ray blew out a stream of smoke. "I bought it off a buddy of mine. It's a good deer rifle for Danny. It's in real good shape."

Marnie didn't say anything. Her face looked hard and stiff. She picked the wrapping paper up off the ground and crumpled it into a ball.

Danny was sighting down the rifle barrel, waving it around and pointing it at everything.

Sam told him to come over to him, and Danny ran up the steps, waving the gun. "Look, Gramp. Look at it! Do you believe it? A real deer rifle!"

Ray said, "Give it to your granddad, Danny. We got to get goin. I told Lori I'd have you home before one. They're waitin for you to decorate the tree."

Sam took the gun and opened the chamber. He told Danny he should always check to see if a gun was loaded before he did anything else. He was thinking that Ray was the kind of dumb bastard who might actually give Danny a gun with bullets in the chamber. He didn't say any more to Danny. He could see that Danny was too excited to pay any attention.

Danny danced down the steps and over to Ray, who was still standing by the back of the car. He threw himself at his father. "Thank you, Pop, thank you. I love it! My own deer rifle."

"Okay. Come on. Turn loose. We got to get goin." He looked at Marnie. "I'll have him home tomorrow night."

"You do that, Ray."

"Hey, baby, ain't you even goin to wish me Merry Christmas?"

"You take good care of Danny, okay Ray?" She didn't even pause. She called Danny over to her. She lifted up his hat and kissed him on top of the head.

He gave her a quick pat on the shoulder. "See you tomorrow, Ma." He climbed in the car.

Ray tooted the horn, and they drove away.

Sam said, "Hand me up that box, Marnie. I'll put this under the tree. It's a real good rifle for Danny to start on."

"Oh Pop, don't tell me about it. Did you check to see was it loaded?"

"It wasn't loaded. Danny was a pretty excited boy, wasn't he?"

"Yeah, he was, but that damn Ray. He ain't goin to be the one to teach Danny how to hunt. He just acts like a big man with his fancy gift, so Danny thinks he's somethin. He never does any of the hard work."

They watched the car drive away. Danny was looking at his father and talking, and he didn't see them waving. Marnie walked up the porch steps, and they went into the kitchen together, with Sam carrying the rifle in its box.

He said, "I got out that bow that you and Junior used to have when you was kids. I got it fixed up for a Christmas present for Danny. I might as well of not done nothin. He ain't goin to see anythin but this one thing now." He went out to the front room and put the rifle under the tree.

When he got back to the kitchen, Marnie was standing right where she'd been when he left. He said, "Do you have to work today?"

"No, Pop. I got the day off. I'm goin in tomorrow morning, so Juliette can stay home with her family."

"Me and your ma'll be havin a quiet day, I guess, unless your ma has something planned with Junior and Alma." He was thinking he hoped not, because with Marnie gone to work, he could fix up a water system in Moose's stall. He had an idea of how he could get water to Moose without it freezing, so they wouldn't have to keep carrying it to him in buckets. He'd been worrying about getting it done before Christmas. This would give him a lot more time.

Marnie said, "That god damned Ray. I'd like to take that gun and shoot him with it."

"Whoa there, Marnie. What's got you goin? It ain't that bad."

"It's Ray. Did he think about who was goin to teach Danny how to use that damn rifle? No, of course not. He never thinks about the hard part. He leaves that for somebody else to do."

"I'll teach him, honey. Don't worry about that."

"I know, Pop. It just makes me mad. He don't never think about nobody but himself. He was showin off givin Danny that rifle. Now Danny's goin to think he's the best. You know what I got him for Christmas? A new jacket for school and socks and boots. And it came outa my paycheck cause Ray don't make his support payments. Why did you ever let me marry him, Pop?"

Sam was surprised. "Marnie," he said. "Don't you remember how it was? I didn't want you to do it, and your ma didn't neither. We couldn't stop you."

"You could of locked me in my room."

"I considered it. I really did. You'd of gone out the window."

She was laughing now, and that was just like Bonnie. The anger disappeared, turned into laughter. She flung herself at him and hugged him. "You're the best, Pop."

Bonnie came into the room, dressed for work. "What's goin on?" she said.

"Ray came to pick up Danny. He brought him a .300 Savage deer rifle as a Christmas gift."

Bonnie was putting on her jacket. "That's all right, ain't it? He's old enough."

Sam answered for Marnie. "Yeah, but you know how Ray operates. He didn't ask if it was okay, or who was goin to make sure Danny knew how to stay safe, or nothin. He just gave it to him. We ain't goin to be able to keep Danny away from it."

Bonnie had her hand on the door. "Well, that ain't nothin new. Ray's always been that way. I'll see you later. I hope it's goin to be quiet today."

After Bonnie drove out, Sam said, "Now I got to get to work. I ain't got much time left."

"What're you workin on, Pop?"

"Them cupboards down in the basement. For your ma to keep her canned goods in and the stuff she stocks up on when there's a sale."

"Does she know about it?"

"That's why I ain't got it finished. It's a surprise, so I couldn't work on it when she was around."

"She's goin to love it, Pop. I'll help you when I get home. I got to go downstreet for some last minute stuff."

He was working away, and he had the radio on, so he didn't hear Marnie when she came back, until she said, "That's real nice, Pop." She was right behind him.

He couldn't help jumping. "I didn't hear you come in. Did you get what you needed?" He was trying to sound calm.

"Yeah, I'm all set. What's Ma want done with the jars of raspberry jam sittin on the table?"

"I'm supposed to take 'em to Richard and Alyssa."

"There's a couple of out-a-state cars over there."

"I guess they're all up here for Christmas."

"I'll take Ma's jam over, and then I'll come back and help you."

"Okay, honey. Thank you."

It was quiet again. He was almost finished when Marnie got back. That was good. Bonnie might get home early if it was a slow day.

"The whole family was there, Pop. Alix is goin to have a baby in the spring. I met her husband. But, Pop, Alyssa is in kinda rough shape. Richard walked back with me so he could tell me what was goin on. The tumors have come back, or maybe they never left. Anyway, they're growin."

"The last I heard she was gettin better."

"Richard doesn't think she's goin to. It's pretty serious, I guess. I told him how I was workin over to the Manor. Later on, he's probably goin to need some help if she stays at home."

While she was talking, Sam put the final touches on the cupboards. He shut the doors. They fit pretty well, considering. "There," he said. "Do you think she'll like it?"

"I *know* she will. Are you goin to show her when she gets home?"

"I might. I don't know. What do you think?"

"Show her right away. I want to be here, and I won't be here tomorrow."

"Okay. I'll see what she says when she gets home."

"I'm goin out to see Moose. Don't show her without me. I was plannin to take a ride, but I don't have time. I want to clean out his stall real good and put in some fresh beddin."

CHAPTER 41

Alyssa carried Richard's coffee up the stairs and set it on the bedside table. She said, "Richard. Wake up."

He moaned and burrowed even deeper into the covers. All that showed in the dim light was the very top of his head.

Alyssa opened the curtains and shut the window. "It's going to be a lovely day. It's almost as warm as yesterday, and I think it might be sunny, at least some of the time."

Richard hauled himself up just enough to see out the window at the foot of the bed. Then he took a drink of coffee. "Thanks. This is good," he said. The sun wasn't up yet. The world was a soft gray in the dawn light.

Alyssa sat down on the end of the bed. "There were lots of stars in the sky when I first got up. I think it's going to be clear."

"How do you feel today?"

"I'm okay. I got awfully tired when everyone was here. I just don't have any stamina any more. But the tiredness didn't last. I think I'm back to where I was. It only took me a few days to recover."

"You probably ought to be careful not to let yourself get so tired."

"I *knew* you were going to say that. Don't you see that's one of the beauties of not doing any more chemo. I can do whatever I choose. I don't have to get myself ready for anything. I can let myself get extra tired if I want to. And also, I'm not counting the days, dreading when I have to go for the next treatment, knowing how sick I'm going to feel. Oh, that was awful."

"But, Alyssa...."

"I've been thinking. There *is* something I want to do while I'm still strong enough. I hope you'll be willing to help me."

"Of course I will. You know I will. What is it?"

"Don't you think it was good that everyone came up here at Christmas? It gave us a chance to talk about what was going on with me, and how I had decided to stop the treatments."

"Yes, it was good. But that's something that's already happened. I thought you were going to tell me about something you wanted to do."

"I'm getting to it. After we'd talked for a while, everyone understood what I wanted to do, don't you think?"

"The girls did. Sonia said to me that it was your life and you had a right to make your own choices. I think she really got it. I'm not sure your mother did. But she's in a tough place, and she always likes to be in control. I'm not sure she will ever accept it." After another sip of coffee, he said, "Hell, I'm not sure I ever will either. I just have to try."

"I'm sorry, Richard. I know it's hard." She moved farther onto the bed and leaned back against the bedpost. "I've been thinking about who else should know. I haven't seen much of anyone for a long time, since I got sick, really. Some of my friends are probably wondering what's going on with me, and I haven't known what to say to them. But it's beginning to get clear. I thought I could make a lunch and invite some friends—Karen and Suzanne and Bonnie, maybe...."

"Bonnie Martel?"

"No, not her. I'm talking about close friends who are going to be upset by all this. I meant Bonnie Schultz. She was the librarian in Severance for a long time. Don't you remember?"

"Okay, now I do."

"I haven't seen her for quite a while. I think she's retired. But I'd like her to hear it from me, and not because she hears some gossip from somebody else."

"It makes it so definite."

"But it is, isn't it?" She was pleased to be able to speak in such a matter-of-fact way. It had taken some doing to get to that place. "Oh, I forgot Carla Baird, and Cynthia. I couldn't leave them out."

"I still don't see where I come in—what you want me to do."

"I might not need help with this. I just don't know. I don't trust myself any more. Suppose I'm feeling awful on the day they're supposed to come. Suppose I can't get the lunch together. What I'm hoping is that you will hang around, in case I need help. I'll probably be fine if I do it soon. I'm really hoping they can all come some time this weekend."

"That's very soon."

"I know, but I don't know how much longer I'll be well enough. Could you be home? Not at the lunch—that might be uncomfortable—they'd all be watching you to see what you thought about it. Could you be in the garage, working on your canoe, but nearby, in case I needed you?"

"I could, if that's what you want. But are you sure? It would be so much easier to deal with one person at a time. That way it wouldn't be such a big production."

"Then I would have to say the same thing about how I was dying over and over again. Five different times? I don't think I could do that."

"Or Facebook. What about Facebook? You could tell everybody all at once like that."

"I hadn't thought of that, but I don't really like it. I guess I'm too old-fashioned. I think I want to tell my best friends face to face. And I need to do it before I get too sick. I don't think my looks have changed that much yet, do you? Except for my hair, I mean, and that's actually getting better."

Richard nodded and took another drink of his coffee. It was

daylight outside now. Alyssa could see the serious expression on his face.

"Besides," she said. "If they are all together when they hear it, they can support each other. I'm not saying I'm so important, but they *are* my friends. I know this will make them sad. This way they can talk to each other. What do you think?"

"Of course I'll be here, and I'll be glad to help you if you need it, but it seems so final."

"Death is final, isn't it?"

"Yes, that's true, but you're not leaving any room for other possibilities."

Alyssa couldn't help sighing. "I can't afford possibilities. That kind of thinking could tempt me into believing in a different outcome."

"You have such a strong mind, Alyssa. Aren't you afraid you'll influence what happens by being so sure you already know the outcome? You've heard the stories of people who died of no apparent cause because they thought they had been bewitched and that the outcome was certain."

"Maybe I have to take that chance. I'm afraid of tantalizing myself with false hope. I'm not sure I could bear that."

"I wish this wasn't so hard."

"Me too, but it is. We have to get through it the best way we can. Will next Saturday or Sunday work for you, if I can get them all to come so soon?"

"I'll make sure it does. You're the most important thing in my life right now, and in fact, I'm sorry for all the times in the past when I forgot that."

Alyssa didn't say anything. She had two thoughts at the same time. The first was a bitter thought that he should have thought of that years ago, not now, so close to the end. But she pushed that thought away and tried to dwell on the other thought, the fact that he felt that way now.

He said, "I'll be glad to help if you're sure you want to do this."

"Why wouldn't I?"

"Suppose you felt like changing your mind."

"I'd love to change my mind, but I don't think the cancer's going to change its mind. If I could convince the cancer to go away, I could have another party to celebrate, but I don't think that's going to happen, and there are a few things I'd like to settle while I'm still able to."

Richard got out of bed and left the room without speaking or looking at her. When he came back, Alyssa said, "You're not mad at me, are you?"

"Oh no," he said. "I'm not mad at you. I'm mad at the situation, I guess. I hate it that you need to do this. It breaks my heart to see you worrying about how your friends are going to take it. That's what I'm mad about."

"I think I was angry for a long time, and then at some point, I realized that it wasn't going to change anything. I've got a certain amount of time left. I can spend it being angry, or I can spend it savoring the time I have left. People don't talk about this stuff, and they don't even like to think about it. So there's no template for how to get through it in a good way. I want it to be out in the open. That's one of the reasons I want to have this lunch party."

"I'll help."

"But I'm scared about it too, because some of them might be offended by my being more open than they want me to be. It might be awful and embarrassing. That might be one of the reasons people don't talk about death and dying. Being scared about it makes me want to get it over with as soon as possible."

To Alyssa's surprise, everyone but Carla Baird was able to come. Alyssa decided to go ahead with her plan to have the lunch on Sunday at noon. A steady snow began in the morning, but it wasn't hard enough to block the roads, and no one called to cancel.

Alyssa spent the morning getting ready. She used her best dishes, the white ones with the gold rim around the edge. This might be the last time she would have a chance to use them. She put out bread and two platters of cheese. The pot of chicken soup was warming on top of the woodstove. After each addition, she stood back and looked at the table. The white, shadowless light made everything on the table look significant, like a still-life. Through the window she could see the trees. Even so early in January, the tips of the branches were reddening with the beginnings of buds, the promise of a new year and new growth. The light was already staying longer.

Everything but the salad was ready, and it wasn't even eleven-thirty. Alyssa was chopping vegetables for the salad when she looked up. Through the glass doors, she watched a little red car drive up. A woman got out and then leaned back in to get something. It took Alyssa a minute to recognize Suzanne, dressed flamboyantly as usual, in a black coat and beret with a large scarlet scarf draped across her shoulders. She carried a big dish covered with tinfoil.

Alyssa put down her knife. She grabbed a dish towel and hurried to the door, drying her hands while she walked. They met in the doorway.

"Suzanne. It's been too long." Alyssa wanted to hug her, but the dish was in the way.

"I thought if I came early, I could help you get ready." She handed Alyssa the platter.

"What is it?"

"I know you said I didn't need to bring anything, but I thought these might be good. Stuffed mushroom caps."

"Oh that's just what we need. I didn't get any appetizers. How did you know?" Alyssa stood holding the platter.

They were inside now. Suzanne took off her coat. "You always say the right thing. Where shall I put my coat?"

"I'll take it."

"No, you won't. You already have your hands full. I'll put it in the closet. I can put my boots there too."

Alyssa set the platter down on the table near the woodstove. She peeled back the tinfoil. A strong scent of garlic rose up. "Mmmm, that smells so good."

Suzanne had draped the red scarf around her neck over her black sweater. She had changed into shoes with little heels.

Alyssa said, "You look elegant. I don't know how you do it."

Suzanne hugged her. "I'm so glad to see you. You look great too.

I like your hair really short. It's very becoming." Her eyes went all around the room. "The table's ready, I see. Is there anything left for me to do?"

Alyssa walked up the steps into the kitchen. "The only thing left is the salad. That's what I was working on when you arrived."

Suzanne followed her. Alyssa got out another knife, and they stood side by side, chopping salad vegetables while they talked.

After a while, Suzanne said, "Retirement must really suit you. You look so fit. Have you lost some weight?"

"Well, actually, I have."

"Oh lucky you! What's your secret? I'm always looking for a new diet to try."

Alyssa went on chopping the pepper she was working on. She didn't look up. She could hear that Suzanne had gone back to her chopping too. What should she say? Should she tell Suzanne the real reason, or stick to her plan of telling everyone at the same time?

The chunks of pepper got smaller and smaller. After a few minutes of hesitation, she put down her knife and hugged Suzanne. She didn't want them to see each other's faces while she told it. "I have lung cancer," she said. "That's why I've lost weight and why my hair's so short. It's just beginning to grow back, since I stopped the chemo."

Suzanne gasped and pulled away and looked into Alyssa's eyes. "For a second I thought you were joking, but I can see that you're not. Oh my God, Alyssa."

"It's all right, Suzanne." She hugged her again and patted her on the back.

"Will it be? Really? Are you going to beat it? I don't even know what kind of cancer it is."

"I told you. It's lung cancer, and…." She was going to say that she wasn't going to beat it. But before she could speak, she glanced out the window. Over Suzanne's shoulder, she could see a car pulling up.

"But here comes someone." She could hear car doors slamming and women's voices. "More than one person. Let's go see who it is. I'm going to tell everyone at lunch, and you can hear the rest then."

It was Bonnie Schultz and Cynthia. They came into the house

laughing and stamping the snow off their feet, bringing with them a wave of icy air and snowflakes.

Alyssa went down the stairs to greet them. Behind her in the kitchen, she could feel Suzanne trying not to cry. Alyssa hoped she was working on the salad too, but she didn't dare look around to see.

Before they even had their coats and boots off, Karen drove up. The room seemed full of people milling around and talking to each other. Alyssa slipped away to help Suzanne finish the salad. When it was ready, she put the bowl on the table and coaxed Suzanne to join the group.

Everyone stood around the woodstove talking and eating Suzanne's stuffed mushrooms. Alyssa was enjoying herself. They all said how great she looked and how glad they were to see her and how they had missed her. Karen said it was such a good idea to get them all together, that they ought to make it a regular occurrence. Alyssa just smiled at that. The only thing she minded was that once in a while, she would catch a look of worry and sadness from Suzanne.

When they sat down at the table, Suzanne made sure she was sitting next to Alyssa. After everyone was served a bowl of soup, Alyssa sat down too. Along the table in the soft winter light, her friends were laughing and talking as they ate her food.

She was feeling satisfied and smiling when she looked at Suzanne. *She* looked stricken. She dropped her spoon and got up from the table abruptly and hurried out of the room. No one noticed but Alyssa.

When Suzanne sat down again, Alyssa reached out for her hand and squeezed it. She could see that Suzanne had been crying. No one seemed to notice that either.

Alyssa watched for the time when the eating and the talking slowed down. She felt, not nervous exactly, but on edge and excited. Pieces of what she wanted to say kept running through her head. Everything had been leading up to this point. She waited as long as she could, and then she stood and tapped her glass with a spoon to get everyone's attention. She said she was so glad they could all come on such short notice, and how fun it was to have them here. Then she said she had something she wanted to tell them.

She reached out for Suzanne's hand. "I told Suzanne a little of it because she got here early. You are all my dear friends, and I want you to know that I have lung cancer. They discovered it last spring."

There was a gasp of surprise and then silence. Alyssa looked down the table. All the faces were turned toward her, and they all had the same expression of sympathy and concern.

She said, "It's kind of like an AA meeting, isn't it? Hi, I'm Alyssa, and I have cancer." She thought it was funny, but nobody else did.

After another silence, Karen said, "Alyssa, I'm having a hard time believing this is true. You look so well."

Other people nodded and agreed.

"I can't believe you could be going through this so calmly. It's so sudden."

"I'm sorry it seems so sudden to you. It hasn't been for me. My calmness comes from a lot of soul searching."

Then everyone started talking at once. Cynthia and Bonnie and Karen all said they had heard rumors over the summer, but none of them had believed them.

Alyssa said, "No one would think I looked healthy right after I had chemo. You could ask Richard about that."

"What does Richard think about the cancer?"

"You should ask him. In fact, I'll go out and get him to come in."

Suzanne jumped up. "I can do that," she said. "Is he out in the garage? I saw the smoke when I came in." She hurried out without stopping for her coat.

Alyssa said, "Richard has been very supportive. He agrees that I should stop doing all these things to myself, so that I can live out the remainder of my life in peace."

"What about your daughters?"

"They do too. They were here for Christmas, and we all discussed my options. I think they understand why I want to stop these treatments."

Bonnie was sitting beside Cynthia. When she leaned back, Alyssa couldn't see her face, but she could tell that Bonnie was getting more and more irritated by the conversation. She was muttering that this wasn't something people ought to talk about, and especially not at a pleasant lunch party. Maybe other people agreed with her. Alyssa couldn't tell.

That was when Suzanne and Richard came in. Richard sat down at the end of the table. He said, "Alyssa, I would love some coffee if you're thinking of making a pot."

Alyssa went up to the kitchen, but she tried not to miss any of the conversation. She heard Richard telling someone that he thought she had decided to stop fighting the cancer too soon, that it was easier for him before she stopped. And even after that, he said, he realized that he secretly hoped she would change her mind and go back to fighting to stay alive. Then he had to amend what he said, because in some ways it was harder when she was still on the chemo. It was harder when he had to see her feeling so awful.

Alyssa listened while she got the coffee ready. She had thought she and Richard were in complete agreement about her cancer and its treatment, so she was surprised by what she heard.

When the coffee was ready, she set the pot on the table beside her chair and sat down again. People began passing cups to be filled, and as she served them, she looked down the table at Richard. She couldn't see his face, only a dark silhouette of his head with the white light from the window behind him. "Did you really think I was going to change my mind about the chemo?"

He said, "I don't know whether I thought it or hoped it. It took me by surprise when you decided to stop the treatments. I told myself it might be temporary, that after you had a rest and got your strength back, you would want to try again."

She looked at him past the faces of her friends. She couldn't tell what he was thinking. "No, Richard," she said. "I've made up my mind. I don't think I'll change it. I want to spend that time looking at the beautiful world around me and at the people I love. I'd rather spend my time saying goodbye."

Someone said, "But how do you know what it'll be like."

"I don't. But the doctors didn't tell me what the chemo would be like either. And they definitely didn't say that seventy to eighty percent of people with lung cancer die within two years. I'll probably be okay for a while, and then there will be hospice at the end." They were all looking at her. She smiled a wry smile. "One of the few perks of this disease is that you know a little more about the future than most people do. I mean, I know I don't have much time. I can plan for that. I'm being quite selfish about it. I could be putting all our papers in order and cleaning out the closets for Richard, and I'm not doing that. I'm painting and reading and listening to music and taking long walks. I'm trying to make every minute count."

During that long monologue, she could see her friends looking to see what Richard thought of it.

And later, after everyone was gone and Richard had helped her clean up, when they were both sitting by the woodstove, she asked him if what she said to everyone was all right with him.

"Sure," he said. "What do you mean?"

"I don't know. I guess I just want it to be all right with you."

"Alyssa, how you handle it is fine with me. I love your honesty about it all. But the *situation* can never be all right with me. I'm trying not to give in to my fantasies. I guess that's what I was doing when I was thinking you might go back to the chemo. I was fantasizing that things would be all right, that they would be like they were before you got sick."

"Oh Richard, I'm sorry."

"I need to grow up, I guess."

"I'm suddenly so very tired. And I'd love to snuggle down close to you. You were so good to me today, and I'm so glad it's over. Do you think it would be ridiculous to go to bed so early? I mean, it isn't even eight o'clock, and yet I'm exhausted. I'd love to be in bed now."

"That sounds good to me. Eight o'clock is only a number, after all. You could go ahead. I'll do the fire and then join you."

"Okay."

Alyssa was almost asleep when she felt Richard lift the covers and get under. She waited for him to put his arm around her. When he didn't, she woke up enough to ask him if everything was all right.

"Yes…I mean, no…I mean, I don't know."

She rolled over and raised up on her elbow. She was facing him, but she couldn't see him in the darkness. "What's the matter?"

"It's nothing, I don't want to talk about it."

"What?"

"Look, Alyssa, I'm trying. Okay? I just got to thinking it was like that day in the doctor's office when I couldn't get my head around what he was saying. I felt like an idiot. All your friends were looking at me like I was an idiot today."

"I don't understand."

"Oh never mind. Go back to sleep. I looked so stupid in front of all your friends. I started thinking about it downstairs, and I got more and more angry." He threw back the covers and got up.

"Richard," she said. "Where are you going?"

"Everyone thought you were so brave. No one even noticed what it was like for me. When I think about it, I can't stop being angry. I know I would just keep you awake if I stayed, and you need your sleep. I'm going to take a shower, so I can calm down enough to go to sleep. I'll be back in a while."

She meant to get up and follow him so she could understand what he was talking about. But before she could move, she sank back into sleep.

CHAPTER 42

It was snowing and blowing outside. Monika had thought she would walk to Joe's Market, but she dreaded going out, even though she had a good pair of ice grippers for her boots. It might be invigorating, if it wasn't for this awful, head-stopping cold. She'd had to tell Mabel not to come over because she was afraid Mabel might catch it. She'd had it ever since she got home from Vermont. Nothing seemed to make it better. She was depressed too, which didn't help. It was winter and nasty outside, and Christmas was over, and there wasn't much to look forward to. The crying jags weren't making it easier.

She sat down at the kitchen table, as another one came over her. She blew her nose, and that hurt her head. She hoped she was mistaken when she thought she heard a car door slamming in the driveway. Mabel might have decided to come over anyway. Her arm was out of the cast, and she was driving again.

Monika only had time to wipe her face with her sopping handkerchief and run her fingers through her hair, before someone was at the door. Sonia was looking through the glass. Monika went to the door and opened it.

Sonia had a grocery bag in each arm. "Hello, Nana. I thought you might not want to go out in this weather, so I brought you a few things." She set the bags down on the table. "But, Nana, you look awful. What's the matter?"

"It's just a cold."

"Are you sure? Have you been to the doctor?"

"I don't need to go to the doctor. It's getting better."

"I don't think it is, Nana. Something's been going on since we got back from Vermont. That's too long. And I feel really guilty. I should have checked on you long before this. I knew something was going on."

"This was so nice of you, Sonia," Monika said, trying to change the subject. "What did you bring me?"

They unpacked the bags together. Sonia always knew what she liked. They talked about the groceries while they put them away, and then Monika went to get her purse to pay Sonia back.

When she got to the kitchen with the money, Sonia said, "Nana, will you go to the doctor if you don't get better in the next few days?"

"I'm already getting better."

"But will you? Will you promise?"

"We'll see. Have you talked to your mother today?"

"I talked to her the day after her party. She was really pleased about it. She had a chance to see her friends and catch up with their news and give them hers."

"Oh yes, that's right. She told me about the party too."

"I think she's being awfully brave, don't you?"

"Well, I guess so. I don't really see why she thought she had to entertain all her friends. I mean, she needs to be resting so she can get her strength back."

"Nan, we don't know what's going to happen, of course, but she might not get her strength back. She thinks she's not going to anyway."

"She certainly won't if she doesn't start to take care of herself."

They had put most of the groceries away and were standing by the table. Sonia pulled out a chair. "Let's sit down for a minute, Nana.

I'm worried about you."

"It's just a cold. Don't worry. I'm surprised it has lasted so long, but it's getting better."

"No, Nana. It isn't that. This has been going on ever since we got back from Vermont. I don't think it's a cold at all. It's this whole thing with Mom's cancer. I think that's what's making you sick. And I can see why. It's worse for you than for anyone."

That almost made Monika cry. She blew her nose hard to cover up her watering eyes. She said, "Oh, this damn cold. I'm so sick of it."

"To know your child is going to die soon...."

"Stop it, Sonia! Don't talk in that negative way. I'm going to get her to come down here to Sloan Kettering. They're the best. They'll be able to do something to make her get well again."

"This is one of those terrible times when the best isn't good enough. We all have to accept that. You do too."

Monika stood up. She was furious. It came over her so suddenly that it surprised her as much as it surprised Sonia. "I will *never* accept such an idea," she said, feeling very righteous. She could see that she had scared Sonia, but she wasn't able to back down.

After a minute, Sonia stood and walked around the table to hug her. She hugged Sonia back, but both of them were stiff and uncomfortable.

Sonia said, "I guess I'd better go." She walked to the door and turned to look at her. "Goodbye, Nan. I'll call you soon. I hope your cold gets better." She left.

Monika sat there alone. She felt awful. Her head was so stopped up that her whole face hurt, and the fight with Sonia made her hurt in a whole new way. She sat at the table, cradling her head in her hands, trying to decide whether to pull herself together and get some supper, or to give up and go straight to bed. But if she did that, she would probably wake up in the middle of the night and not be able to go back to sleep again. Weary hours stretched before her with nothing to look forward to.

She got up and switched on the television for company. Perfectly groomed people sat behind their desks, talking about disasters. They

began to annoy her. She switched them off.

It was good of Sonia to bring her groceries, and it was awful of her to get so angry at Sonia. She wasn't even sure how it came about. She could only remember the feeling of fury that boiled up and out of her. It was because Sonia said she didn't think Alyssa was going to get well.

And then she was sobbing again. She had lied to Sonia, dear little Sonia, who was so good to her. She knew that she was playing a part when she acted as though she had never heard the conversations at Christmas. In truth, she believed what Alyssa had said, and didn't believe it at the same time. She was conscious that she chose to act indignant that anyone thought Alyssa would not recover. And maybe it wasn't a choice either, because how could she believe that Alyssa was going to die?

She could feel herself watching her own indignation. Maybe Sonia was right and it was harder for her than for anyone else. At the same time, if Alyssa's death was the reality, what could she do with that? She felt unable to bear the weight of such sorrow. How could she go on if Alyssa didn't recover? What would she do? How could she eat, sleep, take a bath, do anything ever again, if Alyssa wasn't all right?

And if she thought that way, someone else, some other member of the family, would have to take care of her, and that someone would probably have to be Sonia. The whole thing was too awful. She began to cry again. And that was when she saw that the crying, and the being depressed, and the bad cold were all ways she was able to protect herself from seeing the real issue, the issue of what was happening to Alyssa.

She saw it plainly, as though the scales had fallen from her eyes. She felt sure she could never go back to the comforting blindness. She could see now. There was a kind of cold clarity that gave her strength.

She blew her nose and called Sonia. The phone rang four times. Monika had already decided not to leave a message. She was preparing to hang up when Sonia answered.

Monika didn't even say hello. "Sonia," she said. "I apologize. I'm so sorry I got angry. I know you're right. I didn't think I could bear it, but it's worse trying to deny it. I'm making it harder for you, and I don't want to do that. I'm so sorry. You were a dear to bring me groceries so I wouldn't have to go out."

"Thank you, Nan. All of us are struggling to accept this."

"I'm ashamed of myself for making it harder for you."

"Oh Nana, you're doing the best you can. We all are. It's an awful situation, but if we can help each other.... I'm so glad you called me. When a person pretends it isn't happening, then that person is cut off too. Everyone is isolated and alone. That's what makes it harder."

"I'll try not to be so blind again. I feel as though I couldn't go back to that old way somehow," Monika said. Both she and Sonia were crying by the time they said goodbye.

Mabel came over to visit a few days later, and Monika told her about her breakthrough, and how she was beginning to be able to accept what was happening to Alyssa. They were having coffee at Monika's kitchen table.

Mabel said, "I really don't see how you could accept it. I couldn't accept something so awful about Ira." She paused for a minute, thinking. "I wouldn't want to either."

"You're lucky. It's not happening to Ira."

"It could be. I mean, I can't be sure that it isn't. He's so far away. But you said Alyssa looked very well at Christmas, didn't you?"

"She did. Everyone said so, and you remember what she was like at Thanksgiving too."

"So why can't you say to yourself that you know she's going to get well again? Because, I mean, you can see she is. Getting better, I mean."

"I've been doing just that since we came back from Vermont." Monika took a sip of her coffee. It was still too hot. "Can I get you anything? Would you like another cookie?"

Mabel shook her head. "I'm fine, thanks."

"I tried for weeks to believe that Alyssa was getting better. It just didn't work. I was trying to live a lie, I guess. I was miserable. I cried all the time, and my cold wouldn't get better. Finally, I realized I had to change the way I was thinking."

"I wouldn't know how to do that."

"I don't know how either. It just seemed to happen by itself. Sonia came over, and I got angry at her for saying that she thought Alyssa wasn't going to get better. After she left, I realized that my blindness was making it harder for everyone, and especially for Sonia, and I felt I couldn't do that any more."

"Really?" Mabel said. She was turning her coffee spoon over and over, and she didn't look up at Monika.

"Once I saw that my denial was hurting Sonia...well, I just couldn't keep on with it. And after that, my cold began to get better." She smiled at Mabel. She was embarrassed, but she wanted Mabel to see that she was doing the best she could with a difficult situation.

"For a couple of days I felt really good about it—not about Alyssa's cancer, of course—but at least, that I wasn't making things worse. And then this morning I was lying in bed thinking about getting up, and I saw that I was making a new kind of mistake. I was thinking like a person in a fairy tale or something. I realized that I had this idea that if I convinced myself thoroughly enough that Alyssa was not going to get well again, if I could really make myself believe that, it would be like a magic button."

"What?"

"I was secretly thinking that if I could truly believe Alyssa was not going to get well, that would trigger a miracle, and she *would* get well after all." She sat back and looked at Mabel. "See what I mean? I've fallen into a trap again."

"But what difference would it make? I can't see how thinking that way could hurt anyone. If it makes you feel better, why not just keep on thinking that she's going to get well again? What's the harm?"

"I want to respect Alyssa and her struggle. If I think that I can trick the universe into making her well again, then that seems disrespectful to Alyssa and her clear thinking about what's going to happen. Don't you see?"

"Not really."

"I get so confused between what I want to believe and what I can't help but believe. Every time I think I have it clear in my mind, I fall into another trap. I just hope I don't start that crying stuff again."

"You worry too much. You need to get out more and have some fun. I do too. My cast's off now. Let's get the card game started once more. Don't you want to?"

"I do want to. That's what we need. I miss those games, and who knows, it might help me take my mind off Alyssa's illness. Let's call everybody and see what we can do."

By the time Mabel left, they had made a list of people to call. Monika was feeling hopeful. At least, it was something to think about besides cancer and death.

As Monika cleared the dishes from the table and took them to the sink, she noticed that she was feeling excited about something for the first time in ages. Nothing had changed, and still she was looking at things differently.

CHAPTER 43

Sam had one workboot already on when the phone rang. He thought about not answering, and then he sighed and took his boot off again.

It was lucky he did. It was Bonnie calling. "Come get me, Sam. I'm hurt."

He hung up and grabbed the jacket and boots he wore to town. While he was putting them on, he realized that he didn't even know what happened or how bad it was.

Colt stood by the door, waiting to go with him. Sam pushed past him and told him to stay. He left him on the porch.

At the restaurant, Bonnie was sitting slumped in a booth with her back to the door. Sam touched her on the shoulder, and she jumped.

Janine came over. "It's her ankle, Sam. She was back there takin off her coat when we heard her scream. I don't believe she can put any weight on it. She's probably goin to be out for a while. But tell her not to worry. We can cover for her."

"Thanks, Janine," Sam said, and then, "Come on, Bonnie. Let's get you home."

Bonnie tried to stand, but when she put weight on her right leg, she collapsed back onto the seat. "Oh Sam, it hurts too bad."

"Okay, don't worry. I'll hold you." He pulled her up so he could get his arm around her waist, and then he half-carried her out the door that Janine held open for them. All the customers were watching.

They had a hard time getting Bonnie up into the truck seat. Sam had to get behind and boost her. When she put some weight on the bad leg, it made her cry.

Sam wanted to say that they ought to go to the ER, but it meant getting her in and out of the truck an extra time, so he kept quiet. She would have said no anyway.

They rode home in silence. Every time Sam looked at her, tears were rolling down the cheek he could see. He wanted to say something, but he couldn't think what it should be.

At home, it was easier to get her out of the truck, but the steps up to the porch were hard. Sam kept supporting her and walking her along until he got her to the couch in the TV room.

When they got there, Bonnie dropped heavily onto the cushions. "Oh my God, Sam. I never thought I'd get here."

Sam helped her out of her jacket. He pushed over the ottoman and lifted her feet up. She moaned in pain.

"Bonnie," he said. "We got to get that boot off."

"Oh no, it'll hurt too much."

"It don't matter, honey. It's got to come off."

"Let's wait for Marnie. She'll know how to do it."

"Okay," Sam said, even though it hurt his feelings. "You know what? You ain't even told me how it happened."

"There ain't much to tell." She was leaning back with her eyes closed, one boot on and one boot off. "I was out in the back, takin off my jacket, and I tripped over somebody's boots layin there on the floor. I guess I landed wrong. That's all. But it sure does hurt."

"Could you of broke somethin?"

"I don't see how. I think I just twisted it wrong. It got sprained or strained or somethin. It'll be all right tomorrow."

When Marnie came home, she got Bonnie's boot off and put an

ice pack on her ankle. She helped Bonnie into her nightclothes, and she got some blankets and pillows and made her comfortable on the couch. "Tomorrow I'll get you some crutches from the nursin home, Ma. Then you'll be able to get to the bathroom a lot easier."

Bonnie told Sam what to do, and he got together a supper of leftovers for them. Sam took his and Bonnie's into the TV room, while Marnie and Danny ate in the kitchen.

When the chores were done and the dishes cleaned up, Marnie and Sam went to get Bonnie's little car from Severance. They left Danny at the kitchen table with strict instructions not to bother Grammie unless it was an emergency.

On the way in, Marnie said she was worried about Bonnie's ankle. "Ma seems to think it's goin to be back to normal tomorrow, but, Pop, you saw how swollen it was. It's goin to be a week, maybe two, before it's down to normal, and that's just if she stays off it and does everythin right, and you know she probably ain't goin to do it that way. She's goin to want to get right back to work."

"We can try to keep her down," Sam said without really believing it.

"Yeah, we can try, but we both know she's goin to go crazy sittin there doin nothin. We ain't goin to be able to do it."

When they got to the parking lot, Sam pulled up beside Bonnie's car. Marnie opened the door and got out.

Sam leaned across the seat and looked at her. "I know you're right, Marnie. We ain't goin to be able to keep her quiet, but we still got to try. Be careful comin home."

"Thanks, Pop." She slammed the door of the truck.

Sam waited until he saw her start the engine, and then he took off for home. Bonnie wasn't going to get paid for the time she was laid up. Her salary wasn't that much, and she wouldn't get tips either. And here he was without any butchering jobs to do. It was always something. He should have been out applying for jobs last fall, but he'd been too busy with butchering to take the time, and then deer season came along, and he was swamped. And now that his work was caught up, he really ought to be at home, in case Bonnie needed something.

Still, he hated the fact that Marnie was the only person in the house who was bringing in any money.

A few days later, there was a thaw, the January thaw that they didn't get in January. The sun came out, and everything started dripping. After lunch Sam and Colt went out to check around the barn. Marnie was at work. Danny was in school, and Bonnie was asleep on the couch.

Little streams of water were running down the drive. There was water dripping everywhere, and once in a while there was a grating sound and a crash, as ice and snow slid off a roof.

When Sam stepped inside the barn, he couldn't see a thing. He had to stand in the doorway and wait for his eyes to adjust to the dim light after the bright sunshine outside.

When he could see again, he walked down the aisle between the pens. The sheep and pigs were all right. They had enough water. All of them were stretched out, enjoying the warm weather.

Sam went on toward the back of the barn with Colt following him. Moose wasn't in his stall, but Sam was sure he would find him out behind the barn sunning himself.

He ducked under the fence, planning to go out and pat Moose, but when he got out back, he couldn't see Moose anywhere. At first he thought he must be lying down behind a snow bank.

He was walking around the perimeter of the pasture, when he came to a break in the fence with Moose's slush-filled hoofprints going downhill around the other side of the barn. Sam followed far enough to see that the trail led through the strip of woods on the property border to Richard and Alyssa's place.

He went back to the barn for Moose's halter and lead line. Then he whistled for Colt to tell him to come too. They found Moose on the edge of Richard's driveway. He was pawing through the slush with his hoof to get at the few blades of grass underneath. He didn't try to run away when he saw Sam. He stood patiently while Sam put on the halter and tied the line to a nearby tree.

There was smoke coming out of the stovepipe on Richard's garage.

Sam could hear a machine running inside. There was a radio too. He waited until the machine shut off, and then he knocked on the door.

Richard shouted, "Come in." When he saw Sam, he said, "Oh hello. I thought it was Alyssa. I couldn't figure out why she bothered to knock. How are you, Sam?" He was standing beside the partly-built hull of a cedar-strip canoe. "What brings you over this way?"

Sam was always surprised by how quickly Richard got to the point. "Marnie's horse got out. I trailed him over here. I thought you might wonder what made the tracks in your drive."

"Do you want help catching him?"

"Naw. It was easy. I've got him tied to a little maple out there. Thanks, anyway."

"I didn't even know Marnie had a horse."

"A big one named Moose. He looks like a moose too."

"Alyssa told me she saw a horse out behind your barn. I didn't believe her. I said I was sure you got another cow."

"I've been plannin to. My pigs could use the milk, but I guess this big moose is goin to eat up all the hay. I might wait til spring."

"I'll have to tell Alyssa she was right."

"How is Alyssa?"

Richard walked to the back of his garage and turned off the radio and then walked back to Sam again before he said anything. "Well, she's feeling better."

"That's good, ain't it?" He could see that Richard didn't look altogether happy about it.

"It is and it isn't. She quit the chemo. It was making her feel awful. She's feeling a lot better now, except that she's still short of breath. She gets tired easily."

"What's the reason she quit takin the chemo?"

Richard hesitated. He looked past Sam into a dark corner of the garage. "She just decided she didn't want to put herself through the pain any more. I tried to change her mind about it."

There was a lot Sam thought about that, but he wasn't sure he knew Richard well enough to say anything. He said, "Man, how's she ever goin to get well if she don't do what the doctor says?"

"She says she knows she's not going to get well."

"She won't get well if she don't get treatment. Did you tell her that?"

"We talked about it."

"You're a good man, Richard. You helped me a lot last year when I had to tell Bonnie that I got laid off. I don't want to say more than I ought to, but I need to say this much. Sometimes you got to lay down the law to 'em, and this seems like one of them times. You got to tell her she's makin a mistake. You need to help her with that. Sometimes people don't know when they choose wrong. You're her husband. The man's supposed to be the boss."

Richard paced back and forth on the other side of the canoe. He didn't look at Sam. "Alyssa wouldn't agree with you. She pretty much makes up her own mind." He stopped pacing. "Does Bonnie let you make all the decisions?" He looked at Sam directly. "Even about her own stuff, like this is?"

Sam started to say yes, and then he couldn't help grinning. "I'd like to say she does, and I think most of the time she does, but right now we got a situation where she ain't listenin that good."

"I hope you're going to tell me about it."

"Okay, well, here's the thing. Bonnie sprained her ankle at work about three days ago, and it's still pretty bad. Marnie and I been tellin her she's got to stay off it. She acts like she hears what we say, but when she thinks we ain't watchin, she gets sneaky. She gets up and does stuff around the house."

That made Richard grin right back at him. "Well, Sam, I'd say you got a problem with who's the boss, wouldn't you?"

"True," Sam said. "Too true. But I still think Alyssa should be takin as much chemo as she can get. I wish Ma had been able to get more treatment when she had her cancer. But that was a long time ago. They can do a lot more nowdays."

"I had forgotten that your mother had cancer."

"She died of it. That was why my dad had to sell you this land that you're on right now. He needed the money for her medical bills. She was already gone, but he still had to pay all them bills."

"I never knew why your dad wanted to sell. I didn't ask, and he probably wouldn't have told me anyway. I always felt like he didn't like us."

"He didn't like anythin or anybody after Ma died. He was angry at me and Sondra because we didn't stay home and take care of Ma when she got sick, but he didn't stay home. He said he had to work out because he needed the money, and then on top of that, he had all the farm work. Sondra was down in Randolph already, and I was livin in town, tryin to take care of my own family."

Richard was looking down at the hull of the canoe he was working on. He ran his fingers over the strips of wood.

Sam said, "Is this goin to be for you?"

Richard nodded. "I wanted a small one, easier to load, one Alyssa and I could use for day trips. I've been planning to build one for years."

"It's beautiful work. You glue all these strips together, one by one? That's got to take some time."

"I really had a good time making the one I made when I was in high school. I've always meant to make another one. Besides, I want to stay around here in case Alyssa needs me, but I don't want her to think I'm hanging around just to take care of her."

"Alyssa's lucky. I hate to think of all the time Ma was alone. She was in a lot of pain, and she got too weak to make up the fires. When my dad would get home, the fires would be out, and the house would be cold, and Ma would be shiverin under a pile of blankets. He'd really be mad at us then."

"At least Alyssa won't be in that situation. But sometimes it's the opposite. She gets so cold that she cranks the stove up into the red zone. That's another reason I like to be around to keep an eye on things."

"There was a neighbor woman, a big, heavyset woman, who used to come and sit with Ma. She'd straighten up the house and cook and keep the fires goin. It was nice when she was there, but she couldn't come that much." It made him feel bad just to think about Ma's slow and lonely dying. "You know, Richard, Marnie works at Sherwood Manor these days, and she's trained as a nurse. I'm around a lot of the time too. We could give you a hand."

"Thanks, Sam. That's nice to know. Marnie stayed with Alyssa one time last fall when I needed to go to Burlington. You're good neighbors. But what about your butchering business? I thought you were getting a lot of work."

"I ain't had any for a while now. Here's Bonnie laid up, and the only one bringing in money is Marnie, and she needs hers for her and Danny."

"But, Sam, I remember asking you last fall, and you were really busy."

"That's the problem. It's seasonal. I tried to plan for that by puttin money away. We're okay for now. It just feels uncomfortable with nothin comin in."

"It sounds like you were ready for a slow down."

"I should of been. Maybe it's like when someone dies—you think you're ready, but you really ain't. It still takes you by surprise."

"I guess that's true," Richard said.

Sam could see he was thinking about Alyssa. He was sorry he'd said anything about dying. He wanted to take it back, but there wasn't a way to. So he said, "Well, I suppose I better get this horse back over there before Marnie comes home and wonders why he's tied to one of your trees."

Richard walked with him to the door. When he saw Moose, he said, "I don't believe it. He really is as big as a moose. He's huge, Sam."

"Yeah. Some woman Marnie knows from work gave him to her. When I saw him, I thought we'd have to feed out everythin in the barn to keep him goin, but he don't eat a extra lot. He's pretty much of a easy keeper."

Colt was lying on top of a snowbank, watching the door and waiting. Sam got Moose's lead line and whistled to Colt, and they went back home. Sam put Moose in his stall with some hay, while he fixed the fence, and then he and Colt went indoors. He thought he heard Bonnie hurrying for the couch when he opened the door, but he didn't say anything. He took off his jacket and boots to give her time to get back to the couch before he went into the TV room to say hello. He was thinking how glad he was that he wasn't in Richard's situation.

Later on, Sam cooked hamburgers while Bonnie sat at the kitchen table talking to him. Marnie came in and said hi and started to take off her jacket and boots.

Bonnie said, "Marnie, where'd that jacket come from?"

Marnie was hanging the jacket up. Over her shoulder she said, "It was a Christmas present, Ma."

"Bring it over here. Let me see it."

"I just hung it up."

"Well, bring it on the hanger then. I want to get a closer look at it."

"Aw, Ma."

"Bring it here."

Marnie carried the jacket over to where Bonnie was sitting.

Sam was busy at the stove. He didn't pay much attention until Bonnie said, "Marnie, this is fur. Where'd it come from? Who gave it to you?"

"Well, I guess it must of been Steve."

"Steve don't have that kind of money. This is real fur, Marnie. Where'd he get it?"

"I don't know, Ma. The box was left at the Manor for me. It was there Christmas day. I opened it and saw what it was, and I put it right back in the box. I figured I'd hear somethin about it, but I ain't heard nothin."

"I bet it's stolen."

"Maybe Steve won the lottery."

"Don't you have friends down there who tell you what he's doin?"

"They might. I guess somebody would of told me if Steve won the lottery."

"I don't think you ought to touch it. How long have you been wearin it?"

"A couple of days is all. Everyone on my shift has been sayin I'm crazy not to. It's right there in the box. It looks great, and it's warm. My old jacket is all ripped up. I ain't heard nothin from Steve. So why not?"

"It ain't yours, that's why not."

"*Somebody* gave it to me. The box had my name on it. It ain't doin nobody any good sittin in a storage closet at the Manor. I don't see what's the harm."

"Sam, tell Marnie why she can't keep that jacket."

Sam was standing at the stove, watching the hamburgers sizzle in the pan. They made enough noise so he could pretend he hadn't heard the conversation. He looked around at Bonnie and said, "Huh?"

"Oh for God's sakes. Didn't you hear any of what we were talking about?"

"A new jacket? I saw Marnie when she came in. She looked great." He smiled at her. "But then, she always does."

"Thanks, Pop." She was standing beside the table, holding the new jacket on a hanger.

"How do you know it's so expensive?"

Bonnie flashed a bad smile at Marnie. "There. I knew he was listenin. Show it to him, Marnie."

Marnie brought the jacket over so he could touch it. But when he reached out his hand, his fingers looked so big and dirty that he swiped it lightly with the back of his hand. It was so soft and white that it was like the downy underlayer of feathers on the breast of a partridge. He said, "I'm glad Marnie has somethin so soft and warm."

"See," Bonnie said. "You're just as bad as she is. She should stay away from anythin that has to do with that Steve."

The hamburgers were getting too done. Sam turned his attention back to the cooking.

Marnie hung up her jacket. She said, "You don't even know if it was Steve that gave me that jacket, and if it was, maybe he worked for the money. He owes me a lot more 'n a jacket, even if it is a fur one, plus it's the only way I'm likely to get anythin from him, not to mention that it's cold, and I need a jacket."

Bonnie said, "Marnie, the table still needs to be set, and you got to call Danny. Them hamburgs is about to burn up."

No one mentioned the jacket after Danny came downstairs.

The next day Sam noticed the jacket was still hanging in the closet, so Marnie must have worn her old one when she went to work.

CHAPTER 44

Richard said, "I can think of a lot of things I ought to do this afternoon, but look what a beautiful winter day it is."

"It's quite cold," Alyssa said from the kitchen. She was putting away the bread and cheese and cold cuts they'd had for lunch. "It isn't as nice out as it looks."

"I want to be outdoors anyway. Would you like to go skiing with me?" He opened the stove door and stuffed in another log.

Alyssa leaned over the counter and looked down at him. "Thanks, Richard. If I had more energy, I would love to, but as it is, I feel too weak for something so strenuous. I was thinking of taking a nap."

Richard straightened up and stood warming his back by the stove. He wanted to ask if she thought she might be getting sick, or if she thought something else was wrong, but he didn't want to act as though she was an invalid. He couldn't help the cold clutch at his heart, and the thought that maybe this was the beginning of the end, but he didn't want her to know what was going through his mind.

Alyssa hadn't noticed anything. She came down the steps to wipe off the table, smiling to herself.

"Oh damn it," he said. "I can't go skiing after all. I forgot. One of my bindings is broken."

"You could fix it and then go."

"It would take too long. By the time I got it fixed, the light would be gone. I can fix it later. I'm going to go on snowshoes instead. I'll go up the brook to the ravens' nest and just keep going. That's a better snowshoe trek anyway."

"It sounds lovely. I'll come with you next time." She smiled at him. "There. I'll leave the dishes for later. I'm going to take a nap. I'll see you when you get back. Have a nice walk."

Richard put on his outside clothes and went to the door. Should he take binoculars, or maybe the camera? He said no to both and went out. He got his snowshoes down from the wall in the garage, put them on, and started up the trail, along the black, ice-fringed waters of the stream. He went past the cabin, which looked forlorn surrounded by banks of snow. No one had been inside all winter. He continued up the trail without going down to the pool. It was covered with ice and snow, except for a small opening where the waterfall poured in. Even that had a shield of ice spray over it. The ice looked like lace with the sun glinting through it.

The trail stayed high above the water. When Richard got to the ravens' nest, he could see it plainly through the bare branches of the surrounding trees. The nest was in the top of a pine, almost at the level of the trail since the pine grew by the water below. The nest was made mostly of gray, weathered sticks, but Richard could see where new freshly broken twigs had been added. He wished he had his binoculars. He couldn't see if there were any eggs in the nest yet.

It was still February, probably too early for eggs, although the ravens were clearly getting ready. Ravens did their nesting early when the snow was just beginning to melt. The carcasses of animals that had died during the winter would be surfacing from under the snow when the female was sitting on the eggs and later when the chicks were small. At least, that was what Richard had read in the bird book.

He had only taken a few steps past the nest site when a huge, dark shadow slid across the trail in front of him. He looked up. A raven was circling in the air above. It began to make its raspy *quork, quork, quork*. Richard kept walking, but he was conscious that he was being watched. After a few minutes, he stopped. In the silence, he could hear the leathery whoosh and creak of the large wings. There were two birds circling above him now. He went on again.

The next time he stopped to look and listen, they were gone. Did they think he was a new and threatening stranger, or did they recognize him as their neighbor down the brook? His clothes were different, especially his feet. How would they know he was the same person?

The steep bank above the stream sloped down gradually until the trail went along the edge of the brook. The cascade of water over the boulders in the stream was so loud that it drowned out the crunching sound his snowshoes made when he took a step.

The wind was stronger now. He could feel it on the uncovered parts of his face. He felt more alone since the ravens stopped watching him. The sun was getting low. The shadows of the trees stretched in long, dark lines across the snow.

Richard turned around and headed down the trail over his own tracks, walking faster now because he was starting to feel the cold. He began to think how nice it would be in the warm house beside the fire, talking to Alyssa.

He came to a grove of softwood trees, where he frightened a little flock of chickadees. They swirled up into the air, like leaves in a whirlwind. Richard kept walking. The chickadees were fluttering around giving their little *dee, dee, dee* calls. But when he had gone farther and looked back, they were all settling onto the branches again.

As he went by the frozen pool, he noticed something bright red near the edge of the trail in an open place. There were tiny dark lines on the surface of the snow, radiating out from the bright spot. Richard was curious. There were no tracks in the surrounding snow. The bright thing was a drop of blood, and pointing toward it were slight depressions, which the slanting sun showed up as a row of tiny ridges with dark lines of shadow.

At first Richard was puzzled. Something came and went mysteriously. Then he knew. The radiating lines were made by large wings that lightly brushed the snow when the bird stooped to grab some small creature. There were no tracks, because the bird flew off with its catch.

Richard stood there for a minute and then went on toward home. One minute the tiny creature was alive, and the next minute it was gone. An easy death, if you thought about it. That made him think of Alyssa. But he didn't want *any* death for her. He wanted her to stay alive, in this world, and with him.

Then he thought of the bird. It had to kill to keep itself alive. It was a large bird, an owl, or a hawk, or maybe even one of the ravens, the kind of bird that he and Alyssa loved to watch. He looked forward to describing to her the story in the snow.

He hurried across the yard and took off his snowshoes before he went up the steps to the deck. When he stepped through the door, he stepped into a thick layer of warm air that wrapped around him like a blanket. He leaned his snowshoes against the wall behind the stove to dry and took off his outdoor clothes.

He had been expecting Alyssa to be there. He had pictured how he would come in from the walk and sit down beside her in the bright room to tell her what he saw. But the room was empty and full of dark shadows, and the fire had burned down to coals. He turned on all the lights and built up the fire, trying not to think that this was the way it would be when she was gone.

Upstairs, the door to their bedroom was partway open. The room seemed dark and stuffy after the bright, clean air outdoors. The mound of covers rustled a little, and Alyssa said, "Richard?"

"I'm back."

"Oh good. Was it nice?"

"Do you feel like getting up? Come downstairs by the fire, and I'll tell you all about it."

"All right. I think I feel better than I did before. What time is it?"

"It must be after five. It's starting to get dark out. I was going to make myself some hot chocolate. Would you like a cup?"

"No. I'll get up and come downstairs, but I don't think I want anything."

Richard went down to the kitchen, feeling full of energy and very much alive, glad to be in his warm house, and glad of the beautiful world on his doorstep. He made himself some hot chocolate and sat by the fire, savoring how delicious it was. While he waited for Alyssa, he thought over his walk and what he wanted to tell her about it.

Later, he got out his book, but he couldn't concentrate on the words. He kept expecting to see Alyssa coming down the stairs. Finally, around seven, he went up to see.

She heard him coming. "Oh Richard, I'm sorry. I knew you were waiting for me. I've been trying to get up, but I feel so awful, I just can't."

Richard said, "Don't get up. I'm hungry. I'll make myself some supper, and I'll bring you yours in bed. What would you like to have?"

"Nothing. I feel too sick. But it feels different than when I had the chemo. Maybe I have the flu."

"What about some tea and crackers?"

"I don't think I could eat anything. But you...can you get something for yourself?"

"Oh sure. Don't worry about me. I'm sorry I left you alone this afternoon. I didn't realize you were feeling sick."

"I didn't either. I thought I was just tired. It came on suddenly. I hope it leaves as fast."

"Maybe it will. Anyway, don't get up. I'll come back in a little while to see if you need anything."

Richard went back downstairs. He didn't understand why he felt so disappointed. There had been lots of times since the fall when Alyssa felt too sick to get up. He didn't know why he minded so much tonight, unless it was because she had been feeling so much better since she stopped the chemotherapy that he had allowed himself to believe in the possibility of a miracle.

He needed to sort out what he was feeling. He didn't see how he could do without her, and tonight was a bleak example of that. He saw that he had been so focused on the possibility of her being all right again, that he hadn't even pictured what it would be like if she wasn't. He was thinking that way even after she stopped the chemotherapy. Was that a kind of denial?

Alyssa had seen more clearly. She looked at the statistics and realized that even a remission would be a short-term reprieve. He saw how selfish it was of him to be so shortsighted.

At least he hadn't let her know what he was thinking. Several times he almost asked her how she thought she was doing, and if she thought the cancer was gone. She seemed so much more like her old self that he was tempted to start that conversation. But he remembered how she had said once that she didn't dare allow herself to hope for a miracle. When he thought of that statement, he had decided not to say anything, and each of them had remained separated by their own private thoughts.

He made himself a sandwich and sat down by the fire. The room was warm and bright, but it felt empty without her. There were a lot of hours that he had to get through before he could go to bed.

And that was another thing. He wanted to sleep beside her in his regular place, but he knew he shouldn't. If she had the flu, he could catch it. What would they do if they were both sick at the same time?

If he slept downstairs in the guest room, he wouldn't hear her if she needed him during the night. He decided to sleep in Alix's room, down the hall from his own. He could look in on Alyssa when he got up to go to the bathroom. And if he left the doors open, he would hear her, no matter how softly she spoke.

He came around a corner in his thinking, and there it was again. She would be here less and less, and then she would be gone, and the whole house, the whole world would be bleaker than the room was tonight.

Ought he to call Sonia and Alix, and maybe Monika? It could be the flu, even though both he and Alyssa got flu shots last fall. If it was the flu, she would get better, and he would have worried them all for nothing.

Or it could be the cancer moving to a new stage. If that was the case, he ought to let them know so that they could make plans to come and see her before it was too late.

It was impossible to know what to do. He decided to wait until morning to see how she was.

CHAPTER 45

When Alyssa opened her eyes, Richard was standing beside the bed looking down at her.

"I didn't mean to wake you up," he said. "How do you feel?"

"I think I'm much better. Is it morning?"

"Yes, it's about seven-thirty. It looks like it's going to be another pretty day. I could bring you something, unless you feel like getting up."

"I think I do. Open the curtains, will you? I want to see the morning."

Richard pulled back the curtains, and the pale, early morning sunlight streamed in.

Alyssa sat up. It didn't make her feel worse. She felt light and fragile, but a member of the world again. "Where were you last night, Richard? Every time I woke up, you were gone."

"I stayed in Alix's room, so I wouldn't bother you."

"You wouldn't have bothered me. I missed you. The bed doesn't feel right when you're not here with me."

Richard sat down on the end of the bed. "I know what you mean. I feel the same way, but you were sick last night. I didn't want to make it even harder for you to get the rest you needed." She could see that he was smiling, even though the light was coming from behind him. "And to be honest, if it was the flu, I didn't want to catch it from you."

She nodded.

"It worked out well for me to be in Alix's old room. I was able to check on you in the night, and I think I would have heard you if you had needed anything."

She nodded again. She knew he was right, but she didn't want to say so. All she really wanted was for it to be the way it used to be.

"And, Alyssa, if you get sicker, I may need to spend more time in Alix's room."

"I want you with me, Richard, now, even more than before."

"I'm here, and I will be here. I promise you that. But I want to take good care of you too."

She wanted to say more, but she could see he was getting kind of upset, so all she said was, "Thank you. I love you."

After a short silence, when he had better control of himself, he said, "Shall I bring you some breakfast?"

"Let me see how I feel when I get up. I'm hoping to feel well enough to come downstairs."

"All right. I'll go down and let you get dressed. Call me if you need me."

"Thank you," she said, because she wanted to be alone when she tried to get dressed.

When she got downstairs to the kitchen, full of morning light, she felt translucent, as though the light was pouring through her skin and filling her up. She sat down at the end of the table.

Richard said, "Would you like a cup of coffee?"

"I think so. My stomach might have a different idea, but I would like to try."

Later on, Richard decided to go out and work on the canoe. Alyssa was feeling fragile, but not sick. She knew she ought to call her mother. She made a cup of ginger and lemon tea for her stomach and sat down on the sofa in a nest of blankets and pillows. The late winter light came in through the glass doors. Spring was coming. Being alive was a luxury.

"How are you, Mom?"

"All right, I guess. Well, I'm good, except that I've been worrying about you. I haven't heard from you for so long."

"I called you Monday. I feel fine now, but I was sick yesterday."

"Oh Alyssa, I knew something was wrong. I worried all day."

"You could have called me."

"I didn't want to bother you. Oh dear, I knew it."

Alyssa was exasperated. She tried hard for sympathy. "It was nothing. I felt tired in the afternoon, so I took a nap, and when I woke up, I didn't feel well." She was conscious that she was concealing how bad she had felt. She always seemed to do that when she was talking to Mom. "I'm fine this morning. I'm up. I've had coffee. Whatever it was, it's over now."

"But what *was* it?"

"Maybe it was just the flu or a cold. That's what it felt like."

"Did you have a fever?"

"I didn't take my temperature, but it felt like it."

"Why didn't Richard take your temperature? Honestly...."

"Now, Mom, don't start on Richard." Alyssa was annoyed. Why couldn't she see that talking like that made Alyssa want to get away?

"We need to know what's going on with you."

"We do know, although all these dire predictions come from the doctors and their tests. I feel pretty well except for this cough, and that isn't as bad as it was." She didn't mention the strange aches she had been having in her hips lately. They didn't seem to be related to anything else. "I just want to go on living my life, even if it's not going to be very long."

"Oh don't, Alyssa. I can't bear it when you talk that way. I think you need to go to the doctor."

"But Mom, I did exactly what I felt like doing, and it turned out to be the right thing to do. I went to bed and slept, and now I'm better.

I'm taking good care of myself. You should be proud of me."

"Yes, you're taking good care of yourself in the short run, but not in the long run, and that leaves me to face some things I don't even know how to face."

Suddenly and without warning, the sympathy that she had been struggling to feel was there. Alyssa saw the situation from her mother's point of view. "I'm sorry, Mom. I'm doing the best I can. I know it's awful for you. Are you okay?"

"I am, although I wish I weren't. I ought to be the one who's dying. If only there was some way I could go instead of you. I really wouldn't mind not being alive any more. But you, your life isn't over yet. It's too soon. I can't bear it."

"I wish I could spare you, Mom, but I don't think I will be able to. You *will* survive it. You survived Daddy's death, and you survived Aaron's death too."

"Yes, I don't know how I did survive that. I certainly didn't want to. And now you...I think I'll have to do something to myself before that day."

"Mom, please don't talk like that." Alyssa paused and then went on to say things she hadn't ever said so directly before. "I need you to be strong. I need you to help me. I'm counting on you to stay alive in case I can't. Someone needs to be there for Richard and the girls. Someone needs to hold the family together."

"Don't say that, Alyssa. It's too much. It's impossible. I can't do it. I've got to get off the phone now." And she was gone without even saying goodbye.

Alyssa sat in her nest of blankets with the phone to her ear until the annoying voice came on to tell her to hang up and try again. The feeling of well being had dissipated. All she had left was sadness and the struggle to get through this ordeal however she could. It wasn't reasonable to feel abandoned. She had always been aware of Mom's limits. Richard had said that he didn't think she would ever be able to face what was happening.

She was actually in tears when Richard came in through the glass door to the deck. She picked up the corner of the blanket and wiped her eyes, but she wasn't quick enough, and he saw.

"Alyssa, what's wrong? Are you feeling sick again?" He didn't even take his boots off. He pushed the blanket over and sat down beside her. "Shall I help you back to bed?"

"No, Richard, thank you. It isn't that at all. It's Mom. I called her."

"Is she all right?"

"Yes, she was fine...until I upset her. And I shouldn't have said anything. I haven't before." Telling it made Alyssa begin to cry again.

Richard put his arm around her and patted her on the shoulder. "Don't tell me if it's going to make you feel bad."

"It does make me feel bad, but I want to tell you." She wiped her face on the corner of the blanket again. "Mom was talking about how she thought she would have to kill herself, so she wouldn't have to face me dying."

"She said that?"

Alyssa nodded. "But there's more, and I shouldn't have said what I said. I know that. I told her I needed her to be strong and to stay alive to hold the family together."

Richard said, "Well, that's true."

"She got so upset that she hung up on me. That's what made me cry."

"I'm sorry, but it's no surprise really. She's never going to be able to face what's happening to you. You've always known that. Remember how she was when Aaron died?"

"She stayed alive after Aaron died. I pointed that out to her."

"I guess I'm not surprised that she couldn't hear it and had to hang up."

"Oh Richard, don't make me feel any worse than I already do. I know I shouldn't have said anything."

Richard put his arm around her. They sat side by side in silence for a few minutes. It was kind of him to comfort her. He must have been hot. He hadn't taken off his jacket or his boots.

The phone rang. Alyssa looked at the caller ID. "It's Mom," she said.

Richard stood up. "I'll be back soon. There are some things I ought to check on." He went out.

Alyssa answered the phone. She was afraid Mom was going to repeat what she said before when she was so upset.

"Alyssa, can you ever forgive me? I was horrible on the phone, only thinking of myself. I'm so ashamed of how selfish I was."

"No Mom, you don't need to apologize. This is hard for all of us."

"Yes, I know, but you needed me to be strong, and I failed."

"Don't say that. It's strong of you to call me back like this. I *do* need you to help me."

"I'll try to do better. You know how much I love you, don't you? This selfish behavior came out because I love you so much that I can hardly bear the thought that you might not be all right."

"I know, Mom."

"What is it they say in AA—give me the strength to change what can be changed, the courage to accept what can't be changed, and the wisdom to know the difference."

"Something like that."

"That's what I need right now."

"They also say to take one day at a time. I feel fine today. I'm trying to be satisfied with that."

"I promise I'll do better, Alyssa."

"Oh Mom, you're doing fine. Just remember I need you to be strong in case I can't be."

"I will. And, Alyssa, you know how much I love you, don't you? I would gladly go in your place if I could."

"Sometimes it can be an act of love to let someone go."

Mom didn't say anything. She just made a little moaning noise.

They were both in tears when they said goodbye, but it was different for Alyssa this time. She felt closer to her mother than she had for a long while. She sat on the sofa in the nest of blankets, warm and happy inside. It was surprising how different everything seemed. She wished Richard would come back so she could tell him about the conversation.

The room was filled with soft light. It was most lovely where it fell across the end of the table. Alyssa moved the bowl of narcissus into the shaft of light. The narcissus was just beginning to blossom.

Richard had brought it home a few days ago. Alyssa had managed to suppress the bitter thought that Richard might have bought the flowers because he was afraid she wouldn't be here in April when they blossomed outdoors. She told herself she had no time to waste on such thoughts.

She put her empty teacup down beside the bowl of flowers. She liked the way it looked. She pushed the bowl and the cup around a little and stood back to see the effect. Then she got out her paints and tried to begin. She put marks on the paper, but awkwardly. She was impatient not to waste the little time she had, so impatient that she was forcing herself to try, but nothing was happening. The magic wasn't there. For a while she kept on in the hope it would come, but by the time Richard looked in the glass door, she had given up. She was just sitting with the paintbrush in her hand and tears rolling down her cheeks.

As he came through the door, Richard said, "Alyssa, you're painting. That's wonderful." He slid the glass shut. When he turned around, he took a closer look, "But what's wrong? Did Monika say something that upset you again?"

"No, it's not that." She wiped her eyes. "She apologized to me. We actually had a wonderful talk. I wanted to tell you about it, but you were outside."

"What's wrong then? Something's bothering you." He sat down beside her. "You don't feel sick, and you had a good talk with your mother, and you are sitting in front of a bowl of flowers with your paint box, and you're crying?"

"I know. It's stupid. I just can't do it. I guess you have to be part of the world to be able to paint it. There's a relationship between you and the thing you're painting. And I'm leaving that world behind now."

"You can't know that."

"No, I suppose not, and yet that's what it feels like. It's not my world any more. I'm not part of it, so how can I paint it? The marks I put on the paper have no meaning. They're just scribbles."

"Don't say that, even if you can't do it today. There will be other chances. Today's just a bad day."

He didn't understand anything, and it made her angry. She turned on him. "But when?" Can't you see I have no time? This was my chance. I'm feeling all right for a change, and look what happens." She threw the paintbrush across the table. "This is what happens—I can't do it. It's the thing I want the most of all, and now I'll probably never get another chance." She paused to gulp some air. "And I loved it. It made me feel whole. So of course I can't do it. I'll probably never be able to do it again." She pushed the paint box aside and laid her head in her arms on the table and sobbed.

She was aware that she was unfairly dumping her pain on Richard, but when he tried to pat her on the back, she twitched her shoulders until he took his hand away. She didn't care that she was being unfair. She could feel his dismay as it all came pouring out, everything she had tried to keep under control all these months, the unfairness of the looming deadline, the fear and the uncertainty and the worry that she wouldn't be able to get through it without it being too awful, too painful or embarrassing—it was hard to know what. She was putting all of them, all the people she loved, through the worst thing she could do to them, and she didn't have a choice. And that wasn't even the worst part, because it was over. She'd had her chance, had her turn, and she'd wasted it.

Finally, the crying slowed down. She lifted her head and looked at Richard. He was sitting beside her, but he wasn't looking at her, and he didn't seem to realize that the crying had stopped. He was hunched over, looking at his hands in his lap. And of course, the pain on his face was her doing and her fault too.

"I'm sorry, Richard. I didn't mean to dump it on you the way I did." She wiped her face. "Mom apologized to me for being selfish, and now I have to apologize to you for being selfish. What a mess this cancer is making." She stood up. "I didn't think it was going to be this way. I thought I would be taking care of you someday. What a mess I am. I'm going to go and wash my face."

Before she could leave, Richard stood up beside her. She wrapped her arms around him. They stood like that for a long time, hugging each other, because what else was there to do?

CHAPTER 46

Sam sat at the kitchen table for a while after Bonnie went to bed. They'd been playing Yahtzee until she got too tired. Now that she was back at work, she got tired pretty early. Sam had to check the barn before he could go to bed. He needed to take another look at the sheep that might be ready to go tonight.

When he got his jacket and boots, Colt must have thought he was going out for a smoke. He didn't lift his head. He just thumped his tail on the floor a few times in a friendly way, like he was saying it was okay with him if Sam went out, but he felt lazy and was going to stay in the warm kitchen.

Sam stopped on the porch to sniff the air. It was a wintery night, but the change was coming. There was a smell of water and earth in the icy air. It wouldn't be long before the sap started to run. Sam didn't know whether he was going to try to sugar this year or not. Bonnie's injury had put him behind in everything. It would be a job to get geared up in time.

He went into the barn through the old milk room and stood in the doorway of Dad's milking parlor without turning on the lights. There was a lot going on in the quiet room. He could hear the animals sighing and chewing and moving around. Moose stamped his foot, and the pigs grunted to each other.

He hated to turn on the lights and startle them, but he had to check on the sheep. He had moved her to a separate pen with a heat lamp, but he hadn't turned it on yet. He flipped the switch and walked down the aisle to the pen where he'd put her. She was lying in the hay and chewing her cud. She looked peaceful. Maybe nothing would happen tonight.

Sam thought he would watch her for a while, so he climbed into the pen. She looked surprised when he came over the fence, but she didn't stand up. He settled himself into the corner across from her.

The next thing he knew something woke him up. The sheep was lying on her side now with her legs stretched out stiffly toward him. She was grunting. While he watched, she tensed all over for a few breaths, and then she relaxed. She was pushing. He could see the motion of it in her side. He sat there half-asleep, wondering what time it was, wondering what was going on in the house.

After a while, he woke up enough to check on the sheep's progress. He stood and raised her tail and looked under it. She was so intent on what was happening to her, that she didn't pay any attention to what he was doing. There was a watery discharge coming out, and as he watched, she gave a push. Something came into view and then slid back inside. It was so quick that he couldn't see what it was, but he knew it wouldn't be long now.

He climbed out of the pen and got the jar of iodine and climbed back in. After a few minutes, he looked under her tail again. This time when she pushed, he could see a little bit of the nose and a mouth with the tongue sticking out. He thought he saw the tips of the front hooves before everything slid back inside again. He sat down to wait until he needed to do something. So far she was doing fine without him.

He sat back in the corner, waiting to see what would happen next.

She was groaning now, straining so hard that her legs raised with each push. She seemed to be making no progress and suffering more and more. She stood up and turned around and lay down in a new position, but she didn't stay there. Before she was even settled, she got up and lay down again with a groan.

Sam resisted the urge to interfere, only because he wasn't sure what he ought to do at that point, although it was tempting to think of getting a grip on the head or the feet and pulling the lamb until it came out. Then the sheep gave a loud *blat* of pain as she pushed, and the lamb in its sack slid out onto the hay.

Suddenly, everything was still. The sheep lay on her side, exhausted. She was panting a little. The lamb didn't move. It was still partly inside the sack. Sam peeled the sack away, but the lamb lay limp and apparently lifeless. It wasn't breathing. All that work for nothing.

Sam joggled the body where it lay in the wet hay. A tremor shook the little pile of skin and bones, as though Sam's rough hands had flipped a switch. It began kicking its legs and swinging its head around, trying to figure out how to stand up. At first, it seemed impossible, unachievable, but each try went a little further, until there it was, with its legs splayed out, wobbling back and forth, but standing. As often as Sam had seen it happen, he never stopped thinking that those first moments of life were impossible, that this time the electric charge would fail, the magic wouldn't work. Once in a while, he was right, and then the little creature lay still, getting colder and colder. But that only made the moment when life took hold more amazing and magical.

This lamb was a female. Sam dipped her umbilical cord in the iodine jar while she stood swaying, trying to figure out what to do with her long legs. She bleated a few times, and the mother raised her head and answered.

Sam got a dish of grain for the sheep. When he put it on the hay beside her head, she tried to eat lying down. But then she heaved herself up onto her feet. The afterbirth slid out. She wasn't having twins.

Sam gave the baby a push. She took a few steps toward her mother on stiff legs. When she bleated again, the mother answered with her mouth full. At first the lamb looked in all the wrong places, sucking on bits of wool, but finally she found a teat, and after some fumbling, she began to get it right. The mother turned to watch. She shifted around a little, but she didn't push the baby away. The lamb was getting stronger with each swallow. The mother began to clean the baby's backend, and that made the baby drink more vigorously, wagging her tail as she sucked.

Sam was wide-awake now. No matter how often he saw a birth, it was always exciting and new. He got the mother some hay and fresh water and waited until the lamb was full and lay down to rest. Then he turned out the lights and left the barn.

While he was shutting the outside door, he looked over at Richard's house. He didn't know what time it was, but it felt late, too late for there to be a lot of lights on, unless something was wrong. He hoped Alyssa wasn't worse, but then he remembered how he hoped for Ma to be all right, even when nothing could slow the pace of the disease, as though an alien force had gained control of her body and was riding it down to destruction. He shook his head to clear it out. He didn't want to think about that time ever again, now that it was over.

Before he even touched the handle of the kitchen door, he saw Colt through the glass. He was on his feet, looking anxious and wagging his tail just a little. He acted like he wasn't sure who was coming in.

When Sam opened the door and spoke to him, he got very excited, jumping around and wagging his tail much faster. Sam patted him and let him smell his hands. Then he took off his jacket and boots.

It was ten past one by the clock. He felt too wide-awake to go to bed. He made himself a thick sandwich and sat down at the table to eat it.

The door opened, and Marnie came in. "Hey, Pop, how come you're still up? Is everythin okay?"

"Yeah, fine. I could ask you the same question."

She took off her outside clothes and came over to the table, stopping to pat Colt on the way. "I had the late shift, and I stayed after work for a little while, talking to Andie. What's in your sandwich? It looks good. I want one just like it."

"Now you sound like you used to when you were little. You always wanted to do what I was doin."

She was over at the refrigerator, getting things out. "I still do. What's in there? I'm always starvin when I get home from work."

"Ham and Swiss and tomatoes and lettuce, mustard and mayo." He opened up the sandwich and looked inside. "There's pickles in here too, and some onions."

She was setting the ingredients out on the table. "Boy, Pop, how do you get it all to stay in the bread?"

"You got to stack it up just right and then kinda press it down so it stays together."

"Okay. I'll try to do it like you do. How come you're up so late anyhow?"

"We had a lamb tonight, a nice big one, a single. I thought she was goin to go. I been watchin her."

"Was it okay?"

"Yeah, it went fine. I didn't need to be there, but it's great when it goes okay. I'm glad I was there."

"I remember we used to lamb in warmer weather when I was a kid."

"Easter's late this year. I thought I'd try for the Easter market. It pays good, and you can get rid of 'em fast if you time it right."

"They kill 'em so young."

"Yeah, well, what're you goin to do? I don't like it either, but it's business. It's all about money. Nobody wouldn't raise lambs if there wasn't a market."

Marnie was assembling all her ingredients, trying to stack it all on the bread. She didn't look up. "It's always money, ain't it, Pop?"

Sam watched her while he took a bite of his sandwich. "How come you ain't wearin your new coat?"

She looked at him then. "Ma gets so upset about it. It ain't worth it."

"She'd get used to it after a while."

"I know, Pop, but what's the point? I don't particularly want to look good. I *definitely* don't want no more relationships." She was sitting at the table across from him now. "How do you get your mouth around a sandwich like this?"

"Your ma always said I have a big mouth." He was grinning at her. "I guess you'll have to take little bites around the edges, unless you have a big mouth like mine."

She smiled at him and then took a bite. After a minute she said, "Did you see Moose when you was out in the barn?"

"I didn't go down there, but I could hear him stompin around."

"I can't wait until the snow is gone and I can ride him again. It smelled like spring out there tonight."

"I know. I thought so too."

"I don't need fancy clothes...or relationships. I got Moose and Danny...and you and Ma, as long as you'll have us."

"That'll be for a long time. It feels good havin you and Danny here." He looked at her, sitting there, with her black hair around her face. She was still young, still good-looking. "But, Marnie, you might meet somebody, you know."

"Don't wish that on me, Pop. I've had enough of that kind of pain to last me for a lifetime."

"There's the good times too," Sam said, thinking of Bonnie, the big warm bulk of her in their bed, sleeping and probably snoring a little.

"I know, Pop. You and Ma have good times and bad times. It's different for me. I don't get the ups, only the downs."

"Maybe if you picked a different kind of guy...."

"And that's another thing. I don't want to expose Danny to guys like Steve and Ray. I have to let him see Ray, but luckily Ray don't make time for him that often. I want you to be the one to teach Danny how to act right. I want you to teach him how to hunt and how to shoot. You can teach him how to be a man, not like those creeps."

That gave Sam a warm feeling of pride. It even embarrassed him a little. "What do you hear about Steve?" he said, to change the subject.

"Nothin, thank God. He left town some time in January, and if there's anybody that knows where he's at, I ain't heard about it. I don't ever want to see him again, and if it wasn't for Danny, I wouldn't ever see Ray again neither."

Sam didn't say anything. He was glad she wanted him to spend time with Danny.

They put their dishes in the sink. Marnie hugged him and went upstairs. When he opened the door to the bedroom, Bonnie was snoring. He sat down on the edge of the bed, and Bonnie woke up enough to ask him where he'd been so long.

"Out in the barn. There's a new lamb."

When he got under the covers, she rolled over and put her arms around him. "I missed you," she said, and then she was snoring again.

CHAPTER 47

From where she was lying on the couch, Alyssa could see the night sky. Sometimes it glittered with icy stars, and sometimes the stars hid behind the little clouds that went racing by. The wind prowled around the house, trying to get in, but Richard had made the house too tight. There were no openings for it.

Richard was sitting beside the woodstove, reading. When he looked up and saw her watching him, he smiled and said, "What is it?" He closed the book on his finger to keep his place.

"Don't stop reading. I was just thinking how cozy we are on this winter night. It's gone back to being winter, hasn't it?"

Richard set the book down on the floor. "Can I get you anything?"

"No thanks. I don't need a thing. Keep on reading. I'd be reading too, except that I want to pay attention to how happy I feel. I want to remember this lovely night."

"I can read later. I'd rather talk to you if you feel like talking."

They were both quiet for a minute. Neither of them wanted to say what they were both thinking, that there would be plenty of time for reading after she was gone.

"Alyssa, if only…."

"Hush. Don't say it. Don't spoil this moment. Most people never have such moments of harmony, no matter how long they live."

"That winter we spent together in the cabin was like this," Richard said. "But after that we drifted apart again."

"I know. I've often wondered why."

"I suppose we both got too busy with our own work."

"I'm sorry we wasted that time. I wish we could do it over."

Richard said, "I've always wondered why you were willing to give up everything and come to the cabin in Vermont."

"Have you forgotten the little birch-bark box you made me with the poem hidden inside? 'Come live with me and be my love.' How could I resist?"

"It wasn't a very good poem."

"It was very romantic, and anyway, when you came down to be with us that Christmas, I realized that for me, home was wherever you were."

"It was a brave thing for you to do."

"The girls didn't really need me, and besides, they had Mom."

"That might have been our best time together, even better than the beginning."

"Except for now. Now might be the best of all. I'm glad we can have this time together, just the two of us."

Richard sighed. He stood and put another log in the stove. Then he came over and sat on the edge of the couch beside her. Alyssa moved over to make room for him.

He looked down at her and said, "You know Marnie is a practical nurse. She's working at the Manor. We could get her to come in and help if there are things you need that I can't do."

"We could, but maybe we won't have to. Maybe I'll be able to take care of myself—the cleaning-up kind of things that I don't want you to do. Maybe I'll be able to do those things with just the help of the visiting nurse, until…well, until the end." She tried to smile, but she could feel that she wasn't doing a very good job of it. "Let's not talk about that now. We'll deal with it if we have to, and maybe we'll get lucky."

Richard nodded. "All right," he said. "Just remember that we could easily do that. Are you getting tired? Shall I help you upstairs?"

"In a minute. There's something else I'd like to talk about first. It's something that I've been thinking about ever since the party. I would like to say goodbye to Hank. I know I've never had much to do with him, or with his family, but he is your brother, and your only close relative any more. It's something I think I need to do. We always meant to go to visit him in Ray Brook, but I don't think that's going to happen. At least, I don't think I'm strong enough any more."

Richard stood up and reached his hand down to her. "Come on," he said. "I'll help you get ready for bed. And I'll call Hank tomorrow and then give the phone to you, and you can say whatever you need to say."

"Okay, I guess that will do. I guess it will have to. Thanks, Richard."

It was the next afternoon before Richard talked to Hank. Alyssa was in bed when Richard brought the phone to her. She had always felt shy of Hank, mostly because he was Richard's big brother, and Richard had always looked up to him.

She said hello, and then she couldn't think of anything else to say. When he asked her how she was, she said she was fine, and then she realized that wasn't what she meant.

"Hank," she said, "I wanted to say goodbye. I was hoping we would get over to see you and Patty in Ray Brook, but I don't think that's going to happen now."

Hank made kind of a gurgling noise, and that confused her even more. There was an uncomfortable silence, and then he said, "Alyssa, thank you, but could I talk to Ritchie now, please."

She gave the phone to Richard and lay back to listen to his end of the conversation. She could tell that he was trying to explain the situation to Hank, and that Hank didn't want to accept the idea that there was nothing to be done.

When Richard finally got off the phone, he said, "I think you really upset him."

"I'm sorry. It seemed like I ought to say goodbye. Maybe he'll worry about you and try to stay in touch with you when I'm gone."

Richard sat down on the edge of the bed and took her hand. He said, "Hank wanted me to promise I would take you to the hospital. Of course, I had to say I wouldn't. That was probably what upset him the most. I hope he won't hold onto the idea that I'm not taking good care of you, but if he does, he does. I know I'm doing my best to do what I know you want."

"Thank you, Richard. We're doing this together. Thank you for helping me."

CHAPTER 48

The television was on. Monika was in the kitchen, drinking her third cup of coffee, while she played one more game of solitaire. When she looked up, there was Mabel, smiling through the glass of the kitchen door. It was so unexpected that Monika jumped and dropped the cards. Then she recovered herself and called to Mabel to come in.

Mabel opened the door. "I'm sorry I startled you."

"I didn't hear you drive up. Is everything all right?"

"Yes, it's fine. I'm pretty much back to normal." She took off her coat and laid it across one of the kitchen chairs. Then she held up her arm. "See, the cast's off. It aches sometimes, but I can use it again."

"Sit down. Shall I make you some coffee?"

"No thanks. I've been out getting groceries. I was driving by your street, so I thought I'd look in and see how you were feeling. I'm not going to stay."

"I'm feeling okay," Monika said. She was glad she didn't have to get up to make coffee. She was embarrassed that she wasn't dressed when it was almost noon. "I've been lazy this morning. It's such a treat to be able to play cards again."

Mabel sat down across the table. "We've got to get that game going now that winter's practically over."

"Yes, we do." Monika almost said she was afraid she would be in Vermont, spending time with Alyssa at the end. She started to say something, but then she decided not to.

Mabel said, "How is Alyssa getting along?" It was as though she heard the words Monika was thinking.

"She *says* she's all right. I haven't seen her since Christmas, so I can't really tell. We were going to go up one time in February, when Sonia had a few days off, but there was a snowstorm, and we had to cancel the trip."

"You should go."

"Yes, I should. I could take the train. I really need to see her." She thought for a minute. "I'm almost afraid to. Suppose she's much thinner, or sick, or weak? I think that's why I haven't gone. I'm scared of what I'll find."

"You can imagine all sorts of awful things. It's better to go and see what's really going on."

Monika got up and shut off the television. When she turned around, she remembered her nightclothes. She said, "I'm sorry I'm not dressed. I'm really not sick any more. I was just being lazy."

"No need to apologize. You didn't know I was coming, and anyway, I don't care."

"I could make you some coffee, or something."

"Don't bother. I've got to get going. I have groceries to get home. I just stopped in to see how you were."

"I'm all right. I wish I wasn't. I can't stop thinking about poor, little Alyssa."

"I wish I could drive you up there, but I don't think I could do it. It's too far. I hope she's all right. She's such a dear person."

"It's awful, isn't it? I was on the phone to her the other day, and I just lost it. I said I thought I'd have to do something to myself so I would be the first to go."

"You said that to her?"

"Yes, I did. I'm not proud of it. I was feeling sorry for myself."

"I don't blame you," Mabel said. She stood up and started to put on her coat. "It's awful to have to watch your child going through something like that, especially when there's nothing you can do to help." She was looking down as she buttoned her coat. "The thing is, you don't want to make it harder for her."

"I know. I felt so bad that I called her back and apologized. We had a good talk after that." She didn't mention to Mabel that she had hung up on Alyssa, and she felt guilty about that, but really, she didn't have to tell Mabel every single thing. "Alyssa said that sometimes it was an act of love to let someone go."

"I think she's right about that."

"I've been thinking about it ever since she said it. I hope it isn't going to come to that." She didn't want to hear what Mabel would say, so she hurried on. "I'm pretty sure it will come to that, and I don't think I'm going to be strong enough to bear it." She wasn't crying, but she was close to it.

Mabel must have thought she was asking for sympathy because she walked around the table and kissed Monika on the top of the head, in the messy tangle of hair that she hadn't even combed for the day.

"You'll be plenty strong enough when you need to be, Monika. Don't ever forget that." She went to the door and turned to look at Monika. "It'll be easier when you can see her. I hope you can go soon."

"Thanks, Mabel. I'll let you know."

After Mabel left, Monika picked up her cards and got dressed. She tried to call Sonia, but she didn't get her. She was pretty sure Sonia wasn't going to be able to go, and she would have to take the train, because Mabel was right. She needed to see Alyssa and to be with her for a while.

But Sonia did want to go. They decided that the two of them would make a flying trip over the weekend, when Brian could take care of Jack.

On Saturday morning, quite early, she and Sonia put their overnight bags in Sonia's car and started for Vermont. It was a beautiful, sunny morning. There was spring and hope in the air. Everything was dripping, and all the drops sparkled in the sunlight.

"I was sure you wouldn't be able to get away on such short notice, Sonia."

"I really need to see Mom. It's just luck that Brian was planning to be around all weekend. How often does that happen? I'm only sorry that it has to be such a quick trip."

"That's okay. We don't want her to get too tired. We don't want her to feel she has to entertain us or take care of us."

Sonia said, "I just want to see her, you know?" She looked around, and Monika could see the worry on her face. "We'll know right off when we see her. Don't you think so?"

"I hope we will." She thought a little more. "But no, I'm not sure if I want to know."

"Oh Nana, I'm *counting* on us knowing when we see her. I think we will."

Monika didn't know what to say.

Sonia looked at her again, and then she said, "I've got to know if she's close to...close to...close to anything happening."

Monika said, "I don't know what I want. I just have to see her, and yet, I'm scared to. Suppose she's sicker and weaker than we expect? When we see her she'll know we're watching her to see how she is, and she'll see that we think she's worse. It'll be right there in our faces."

"Oh God, it's so hard to know what to do."

Monika saw she had to pull herself together. She was in danger of dragging Sonia down with her. "Listen, Sonia, we do know this— both of us want to see her and be near her, and we both need to find out firsthand how she is. That's all we can do. I don't know how to help her. In fact, I feel like whatever I do will make it worse. I worried and worried about my children, and I did everything I could do to keep them safe, and now something like this comes along, and I can't do anything right. There's no way to make it okay. It's so ironic. But somehow, in spite of everything, I need to be with her."

"It's so confusing. We just have to do it and see what happens, don't we?"

When they drove up, Alyssa came down the steps to greet them. Maybe she was a little thinner, but she looked pretty well. She was standing by the car door when Monika opened it.

Monika said, "Alyssa, you ought to have your coat on. You'll get sick." She was instantly sorry. She said it before she thought.

Alyssa hugged her and patted her on the back. "It's all right, Mom. I'm fine. Did you have a good trip?" She went around to Sonia's side.

Sonia got out of the car. "Oh Mom, you look beautiful. You don't look sick at all."

Alyssa kissed her and smiled a sweet smile that was full of such sadness that Monika, who was walking by her, felt her heart breaking. She turned away and hurried up the steps to the deck.

Richard was standing in the open doorway. Monika put her arms around him. It took him by surprise. She was always reserved around him. She couldn't explain that she did it because she was very close to tears, and she didn't want him to see her face.

Sonia and Alyssa followed them into the house. They were carrying the overnight bags and talking about Jack's nursery school.

Sonia put their bags in their rooms, while Alyssa made a pot of coffee. They all sat down around the table.

"It isn't even three o'clock," Richard said. "You made very good time."

"We started at eight-thirty, and we only stopped once, for breakfast and some gas. There wasn't much traffic either. I hope we won't have more trouble on the way home."

Monika said, "Now, Alyssa, I hope you'll let Sonia and me make dinner. We can do it without any help. Can't we, Sonia?"

"Don't worry about it, Mom." Alyssa reached across the table and gave her hand a squeeze. "It's all settled. Richard has been learning how to cook this winter." She smiled at him. "He's getting pretty good at it."

He said, "I hope you like salmon, Monika. I know Sonia does. It's something Alyssa can always eat, even if she's not feeling well."

"Dad, I don't believe it. You never used to cook anything."

"I'm learning. There are a few things I can do now. But I always used to cook when we were on camping trips. Don't you remember?"

"That's different."

"I don't see why."

"Everyone's always so hungry that no one notices if things are burned."

After a while, Alyssa went off to lie down, and Monika decided she would like a rest too. When she got up, Sonia was helping Richard in the kitchen. They had laid out the best dishes and put candles on the table. It looked like a celebration. When Alyssa came down, she seemed pleased by the arrangements.

But during dinner, Monika noticed that Alyssa ate very little. She spent most of the time moving the food around on her plate with her fork. Monika was careful not to look at Sonia. She didn't want to know if Sonia saw what she saw.

Alyssa didn't stay with them very long after dinner was over. She went back upstairs while they were still sitting around the table talking.

Monika waited until she was sure Alyssa was gone, and then she asked Richard how he thought she was doing.

He said, "Didn't you think she looked well?"

"Yes, she looked lovely, but I don't trust appearances. I'm sure she tried hard to look her best for us. You see her every day. How do you think she is?"

Richard sat forward and looked steadily at her. "She has good days and bad days. That's the truth. She's not taking much medicine, not even much for pain, so maybe it's possible to get a clear reading of what's going on, or at least, as much as you can tell without doing a lot of tests." He paused and looked at each of them in turn. "But I might not be the right person to ask. I might be too close to see the changes." He stopped again. Monika thought he had said all he was going to say, but she was wrong. "Look," he said. "This is terribly flaky and based on nothing, but it's my sense that the end is approaching."

Monika felt as though someone had punched her. She said, "Oooo," and reached out blindly for Sonia.

In a voice that trembled, Sonia said, "Has she been to a doctor, Dad?"

"No. She won't go. She says there's no need to go."

"Maybe she thinks it would take too much effort—to go all the way in to town and have to wait in the doctor's office and all."

"Maybe, but I don't think so. And her doctor is really kind. He told us he would come out here if we needed him to."

Monika opened her eyes. Everything looked the same, and that was surprising, since she felt so different.

"A woman from hospice was here a few days ago. Someone from there comes every week to see how Alyssa is and if she needs anything. She hasn't needed anything yet, but I'm glad they keep checking on us."

"You could ask them what they thought."

"Well, I did. I waited until she left the room, and then I asked her how long she thought Alyssa had left."

Monika was watching him closely now. He seemed uncomfortable, and she was glad. For that second before he spoke, she hated him, hated that he was strong and alive, when her lovely Alyssa was dying.

He said, "I didn't learn much. She said everyone was different. Alyssa might be here for quite a while, or she might go soon. She said that at some point Alyssa would start to actively die, and that she hadn't started that part of the process yet. She said the only person who would really know what was happening was Alyssa, but she might not want to talk about it."

No one spoke. They sat there in the candlelight and thought about Alyssa, or at least Monika did. After a while, she felt she had to get away. She said, "I'd like to help you with the dishes, Richard, and after that, I think I'll go to bed."

"Go ahead, Monika. You don't need to stay up for the dishes. I can clean up. There isn't that much."

"Don't worry, Nana. I'll help him. I'm not sleepy yet. You go ahead."

"Okay, I will. I'll see you in the morning. Thank you for the dinner, Richard. It was very good."

She left and went to her room. She thought she would get into bed quickly, but instead, she sat on the edge of the bed for a long time before she even got undressed. She felt too exhausted to get herself ready for the night.

It was another long time before she took out her toothbrush and her pills and went down the hall to the bathroom. She could hear water running in the kitchen, and the voices of Richard and Sonia, but she couldn't tell what they were saying, and she didn't have the energy to stop and try to listen.

When she came out of the bathroom, she was eager to get to bed, and she didn't stop then either. She got right into bed and turned out the light. She thought she would be asleep in minutes. Instead, she lay there in the dark wide-awake. She thought of Alyssa and how much she loved her. She thought of how she was upstairs, lying asleep in the darkness, or maybe, awake up there, thinking of dying and being afraid. Would she slip out of life soon, some day when Richard was out in the garage, working on his new canoe and she was all alone? The pain of that thought was intense. If only she could get away from it by falling asleep, but she couldn't manage it.

The covers pressed down on her legs. She threw them off. And then she was cold. She pulled the covers back over her again. She thought about getting up to see if Richard and Sonia were still in the kitchen, but she didn't do it. It would have taken too much effort. Instead, she lay on her back, looking at the ceiling and thinking about getting up.

Some time much later, she did fall asleep, but not for long. She kept waking up, picturing Alyssa now as a grown-up, now as a child. She couldn't remember what her life had been like before Alyssa was a part of it. And now she was lying upstairs, maybe alone, maybe afraid and dying. Monika's restless mind wandered all night long through the barren wasteland of her thoughts, where everything hurt, and there was no comfort to be had.

In the morning, before she opened her eyes, she thought, "I'm going home today." And immediately, she thought, "I can't leave Alyssa."

She got up, got dressed, and went to the kitchen. Everyone else was already up. It was eight forty-five. Alyssa jumped up to get her a cup of coffee.

When she sat down at the table with her coffee, Sonia said, "Mom was just saying I ought to go and wake you up. I think we need to be on the road by ten o'clock. Otherwise, it'll be so late when we get home."

"I know," Monika said vaguely. She was wondering how she could get a chance to talk to Sonia privately. Alyssa seemed so well that for a brief minute, Monika considered leaving with Sonia. But it was only for a minute. She couldn't leave Alyssa. She just couldn't do it.

She let the talk swirl around her for a little while, and then she said, "Sonia, could you help me with my overnight bag, please?"

Sonia immediately jumped to her feet. "Sure, Nana," she said.

When they got to Monika's room, she said, "Please shut the door, Sonia." Her voice sounded sterner than she meant it to.

"What is it, Nana? You're scaring me."

Monika sat down on the bed and looked at Sonia still standing by the closed door. "I can't go, Sonia."

"I don't understand," Sonia said. She sounded frightened. "What's wrong?"

"I'm sorry, my dear. I know this is a surprise. It is to me too."

Sonia sat down beside her on the bed. "But what is it, Nana? You're not sick, are you?"

"Oh no, it's not me. I just can't leave her, not now. I stayed awake all night last night, thinking about it, and when I woke up this morning, I knew I couldn't leave. I know it's not what we planned, and I'm sorry."

Sonia began to cry. "I can't stay. I have to go home. There's my job and Jack…she's not that close to the end, is she?"

"No one knows that. I can call you every day and tell you what I know. That will be a help, won't it?"

Sonia wiped her eyes. "But, Nana, what will you do? How long will you stay? You don't have any clothes with you."

"That doesn't matter. I can wash things out at night or else borrow something from Alyssa. I don't suppose I'll be able to help much, but that's not why I'm staying. I just want to be where she is. I don't know how long I'll stay. I can always come home on the train if they want me to leave."

"What did they say when you told them you were going to stay?"

"I haven't had a chance to tell them yet. Maybe I should say I haven't asked them, but I don't think they'll say they don't want me."

"When are you going to talk to them about it?"

"Right away, if it's all right with you. I wanted to talk to you first." Sonia wiped her eyes. "Thank you, Nana."

They went back to the kitchen, holding hands.

Richard and Alyssa were sitting in the same places at the kitchen table. They looked up with curiosity when Monika and Sonia came in.

Monika felt that she was making a formal statement. She stopped at the top of the steps, looking down at Richard and Alyssa. Sonia stopped beside her, still holding her hand.

"Would it be all right with the two of you if I stayed on for a while? Somehow, I just feel that I don't want to leave just yet. What do you both think? I'll try not to be in the way."

There was a silence. She saw them look at each other across the table. She gave a nervous laugh and said, "You could always put me on the train if I got to be a nuisance."

Alyssa turned in her chair so she was looking up at her. "Of course, Mom, we'd love to have you stay, but what about your house, your cats, everything at home?"

Monika squeezed Sonia's hand. "I haven't even asked her, but I know Sonia will keep up with things. I know I can count on Sonia."

Sonia was nodding in agreement.

"So do you think it would be all right if I stayed? Somehow, Alyssa, I just can't bear to leave you now, even though you look as though nothing is wrong." It was as close as she could come to uttering the idea that Alyssa could die soon.

Richard and Alyssa nodded their heads, and Sonia went to gather her things to go home alone. It didn't take long.

They all three walked out on the deck with Sonia. Monika went all the way to the car to hug her goodbye. When she turned around, both

Richard and Alyssa were watching her. She couldn't wipe her face without making it even more obvious that she was crying. How was she to explain that she was crying because Sonia was leaving without her, but that she was staying because she wanted to stay?

She walked up the steps to stand beside them. She didn't have boots on. There was snow melting in her shoes. They were looking at her with concern.

She said, "I can always go home on the train." It was all she could think to say.

CHAPTER 49

Alyssa looked at her mother's face as she walked up the steps to the deck after kissing Sonia goodbye. She had tears running down her cheeks. Why didn't she go home if she wanted to? No one was making her stay. It was annoying.

But Alyssa didn't say anything as the three of them went inside, back to the kitchen table and their cups of coffee. Alyssa was reading the Sunday Sentinel, and Richard had the Times on his Kindle. Mom just sat there, looking into her coffee cup. She had wiped the tears away. After a while, Richard stood and picked up his coffee cup.

Alyssa said, "I hope you're getting yourself another cup of coffee." It was difficult enough to concentrate on the newspaper when Mom was just sitting there. Without Richard, Alyssa didn't think she would be able to do it, and she had hardly started on the Sunday paper.

Richard took his cup to the sink. He walked down the steps and stopped by her chair. "I thought I'd make a fire in the garage, so I could get a little work done on the canoe." He patted her on the shoulder, and she understood that he was silently asking her if she was all right with the situation. Out loud he said, "Do you need me to stay in the house?"

"We'll be fine," she said, when what she wanted to say was, "Don't leave me alone. What am I going to do with her?"

As if he were reading her mind, he said, "Monika, would you like to see my new, half-finished canoe?"

She smiled up at him. "Thank you for inviting me, Richard. I'd like to see it sometime, but it's too cold out now. I'll have plenty of other chances."

Richard patted Alyssa's shoulder again, meaning, "There. I've done what I can." He said, "Okay. I'll be in after a while." He grabbed his jacket and left without his boots.

Alyssa sighed. "What do you want to do while you're here, Mom?"

"I don't know. Just be here, I guess. I really haven't thought about it." She looked directly at Alyssa. Her eyes were full of love. "I just want to be with you."

Alyssa looked away. She didn't want to see that expression. It made her feel guilty for thinking that having Mom here was going to change everything. She felt too old to be told what to do all the time. And this time it wasn't going to be for just a couple of days. Mom might be planning to stay until the end. What that meant was that all her chances to do what she wanted to do were behind her.

"Would you like something to read, Mom? You can read again, can't you?"

"Yes, I can, unless the light is bad or the print is small. But don't worry about me. I can read the Sunday paper. And I brought a pack of cards in my suitcase. I don't know why, but I'm glad I did."

"Okay. If you really don't need anything, I thought I might go and take a bath."

"I want you to go, Alyssa. I'll be fine. I don't want you to change anything."

"Okay, I will then." She went up the stairs thinking about Mom. She said she didn't want to change anything, but how could she not know that everything was different now that she was here?

Alyssa got out some clean clothes and went into the bathroom. She turned on the water and started to undress, feeling angry. Here she was, supposedly the center of all this concern, and she felt ignored or not considered. She was being run over and left out.

She made the bath very hot, and she had to get in a little bit at a time. It was a while before she could lie back in the hot water. It felt lovely. She didn't hurt anywhere. She lay back in a drowsy peace. She might just as well stay where she was. There was nothing she had to do. One of the perks of being a sick person is that no one expected much of you. Busy people went past you as though you were a rock sticking out of the river. The current flowed around you and went on its way.

The irritation that she felt about Mom staying on and by that, changing her life, that annoying realization began to fade as she lay in the warm water.

After a while, she began to see that it wasn't Mom who was changing her life. It was the cancer that did that. Mom just acknowledged it before she did. Mom saw that everything had changed. Maybe she even saw that it was time to put all petty squabbles aside because they were facing something much larger.

All of a sudden Alyssa was crying hard. She knew that Mom's staying was the next step in a process that she herself had set in motion, the process of accepting what was inevitable, so that she could live what life was left as peacefully as possible. Peaceful didn't exactly describe living with Mom, or it never had before. Still, Alyssa felt she had chosen what seemed like the best of the few options she had. She had worked to make everyone she cared about understand what she was doing, and she had succeeded with Mom. Everyone, including Mom, was trying to do what she wanted them to do. Even though Richard had said that Mom would never be able to realize that her child was dying, here she was, adapting to that idea and even accepting it. Her own mother was accepting the fact that she was going to be dead soon. That's why she was crying. Of course, Mom would want to be here at the end. But calm and accepting? That was the part that threw Alyssa, even though she realized that Mom had had to struggle to get there, and that she would grieve when Alyssa was gone. But Mom would still be here, able to go on with life. And Alyssa would not be.

She wanted to shout, "Wait a minute. This is *me* you're talking about. This is *my* life that's being tossed aside so casually. Am I going to go out like a candle when it gets to the end of its wick? And that will be that?"

She was trying to keep Mom and Richard from knowing that she was crying. But at the same time, she wanted to scream, "Stop! I want to stop this. It *must not* happen."

She turned off the water. It had been pouring out the overflow drain for quite a while. Maybe she had cried all she needed to. She sat in the cooling water. She could think or say that her death must not happen, but at the same time, she knew it was exactly what was going to happen. It had to happen. It happened to everyone sooner or later. She knew all that. She had argued with her family until they knew it too.

So what was going on? Why did she have to come to these realizations all over again? She thought she was out in front, and all of a sudden, she was at the back of the pack, and out in front was—guess who—Mom. That took getting used to.

She got out of the tub and dressed. But instead of hurrying downstairs to see what Mom was doing to entertain herself, Alyssa went to her room and sat on the bed. She felt weak, drained of energy by the hot water. She saw that she was coming to a new realization of what was happening to her. Before today, she knew she was going to die, of course. But she knew it with her head. She had to learn it again, until she knew it with all of herself, with her heart, her soul, and even with her body.

She was sitting on the edge of the bed, trying to take in that idea and make it her own, when Richard sat down beside her. It startled her. She had been concentrating so hard that she hadn't known he was nearby.

He put his arm around her shoulders. "Are you all right, Alyssa?"

"I was taking a bath."

"Your mom said that's where you were, but she said you'd been up here for several hours. She was wondering if you were all right, but she didn't want to intrude."

"Is *she* all right? What's she doing?"

"She's sitting at the kitchen table playing cards with herself. Are you sure you're okay?"

"I'm fine, Richard. I just needed a little space, so I took a bath, and the hot water made me feel sleepy. Have you had lunch?"

"I came in because I was hungry. Your mom said she was hungry too. What about you? Are you going to come downstairs and have some lunch with us?"

"Yes, I will. You go down. I'll be there in a minute, okay?"

After he left, she sat there, wondering why she hadn't told him what she had been thinking. For some reason, when he was sitting beside her, she felt that it was important to spare him. She wasn't sure what she didn't want him to know, and she didn't trust her motives, but maybe she would understand more after a while.

CHAPTER 50

Richard tramped around behind the house. There were places where the snow was still deep enough to pull at his unlaced boots. But there were other spots where the ground was already bare. He was on a voyage of discovery to see what had made it through the winter. The path up the brook under the hemlocks was still deep in snow, but the garden was bare. By the shed, the tips of the daylilies were poking through last year's dead leaves. There were snowdrops along the edge of Alyssa's flower garden.

Monika was out on the deck. When he went by, she said, "Are you hungry, Richard? I thought I would heat some soup and make sandwiches to go with it."

"That sounds good to me."

"I wonder if Alyssa would like some lunch."

"I'll go up and see. She might want to sit outdoors in the sun this afternoon."

"It'd be good for her. She hasn't been down in days."

"I'll go up and see if she's awake. We could wrap her up in blankets if she felt strong enough to be outside."

Monika said, "She's not making enough of an effort any more. She has to try harder."

"I don't agree with you, Monika. This is Alyssa's show. She has a right to do it her way. Unless she asks you or me to take over, the kindest thing we can do for her is to let her be in charge of her own situation. I have to ask you to agree to that."

Monika turned away without speaking. Both he and Monika were more alive, more part of the awakening world than Alyssa was now. Monika must be struggling with that. He felt sorry for her. It was bad enough for him, but it must be worse for her.

He went inside and kicked off his boots in the corner before he climbed the spiral staircase. He walked down the hall in his sock feet to their bedroom, which was Alyssa's room now. He peeked silently through the open door.

She was lying on her back with her eyes closed. She was breathing softly. He was just about to slip away, when she looked at him and smiled. Her eyes were dark and enormous in her pale face.

He said, "Your mom is making soup for lunch. I forgot to ask what kind."

"I've been lying here thinking how much I love you, Richard."

It took him by surprise. He said, "Oh," and then, "Your snowdrops are up and flowering. We were hoping you would feel like coming downstairs for some soup. It's a beautiful day outside. You could sit on the deck and soak up some sunshine."

"Thanks, Richard. It sounds nice, but it's a long way to go, and I feel too peaceful to move. Stay with me for a little while."

"All right." He sat down on the chair beside the bed. "Are you hungry?"

"Not at all, but thank Mom for me. I don't want anything." She closed her eyes.

He sat there thinking she had gone back to sleep. He had decided to slip away without saying any more when her eyes opened, and she reached out toward him.

He took her hand in his own, but he couldn't help thinking of how

Hansel fooled the witch by sticking a chicken bone out for her to feel. He couldn't help wishing it was a trick and Alyssa's hand wasn't so painfully thin that her rings jangled loose on her fingers.

She squeezed his hand and said, "What are you going to do after, Richard?"

"I'll probably go back to work on the canoe, although it's so beautiful out. I might rake the leaves off your flower beds."

She smiled. "No, silly. I don't mean today. I mean after all this is over. What are you going to do then?"

"I don't know. I don't want to think about it."

Her dark eyes were fixed on his face. "In time you'll want to find someone else."

"Don't, Alyssa. I can't talk about this."

"I've been thinking about how strange it is. I used to think that you felt trapped and you resented me for it, and now, when my sickness has really trapped you, I don't think you feel resentful at all. But I want you to know what I've been thinking. Can I tell you my idea?"

"I don't know. I guess…if you want to."

"I might not get another chance. There's Suzanne, you know. She's beautiful, and she doesn't have anybody in her life right now."

"Don't Alyssa. There's nobody for me, except you."

She smiled a wicked, little smile. "That hasn't always been true, Richard."

"If you only knew how much I regret that foolishness, and that's all it was, although I know I hurt you a lot. You could have left me. I'm so glad you didn't."

"That's the past. But what I'm talking about is the future. You're going to be alone soon. I don't want you to be unhappy. I don't want you to spend whatever time you have left in a memorial to me."

Richard didn't answer. He was struggling to keep from crying. He felt like putting his hands over his ears, but he was still holding hers.

She said, "I want you to be happy." When she smiled, her teeth seemed enormous in her skeletal face. "You could have a lot of years left. You could do a lot of interesting things. Don't waste your time thinking it's over when it isn't."

He almost said, "If you want me to be happy, don't leave me." But that would have been cruel. Luckily, he stopped himself in time. He didn't know what he *could* say. He didn't want to cry. He was going to have to go downstairs pretty soon, and he didn't want to upset Monika. He wasn't sure he believed in Monika's calm acceptance.

Alyssa squeezed his hand. "I love you, Richard. Just remember this conversation later, okay?"

He nodded his head, feeling miserable.

"Promise?"

"Of course I promise, and I don't have to promise not to forget you. You're my whole life, Alyssa. I feel so lonely because I know our paths are separating, and you're going where I can't follow." He was very near tears again.

"We are companions right now, and that's something. You need to concentrate on what we have, not on what we're losing."

He nodded. He hesitated for a minute, before he said, "You are so brave, Alyssa. Aren't you afraid?"

"I used to be. I used to think about dying a lot, but lately I've forgotten about it. It just doesn't seem to matter. Something is different now. Maybe it's because I know I can't change what's going to happen. There was a time when I wanted desperately to stay alive, but now I know it's not my world any more. I used to hate the idea of being burned up, and I hated the idea of being shut in a box even more. Now I don't care. You can do whatever is the easiest for you."

Before he had time to say anything, a woman's voice called from the bottom of the stairs, asking if she could come up.

Richard and Alyssa looked at each other. Then Alyssa said, "Oh, that's the hospice woman. Tell her it's okay."

In a minute she was in the doorway, bringing with her a sense of health and fresh air. Richard recognized her face, even though he couldn't remember her name. He stood up.

She walked over to the bed. "It's Kathy Morrisette, Alyssa. How are you today?"

Alyssa said, "Fine." They all three looked at each other, and then they all laughed.

"My husband used to say the same thing—no matter how bad he was, he'd say he was fine."

Richard said, "Here, Kathy, have a seat."

"Thanks. I will." She looked at Richard more carefully. "And how are you? Are you fine too?"

"I'm not sure. I think Alyssa is a lot braver than I am."

Kathy sat down. "Stairs don't get any easier as you get older. What do you think, Alyssa? Is he all right too?"

"I hope so."

"It's a beautiful day outside. What about sitting out on that nice deck of yours?"

"Richard already asked me that. I'm so comfortable right here, or I would."

"That's okay. It's all good. I'm going to put a comfort pack in your refrigerator, unless you object. I always like to ask. We don't want to leave it, if you really don't want us to."

"What is it?"

"It's a packet of medications in case there are any problems. We find they are medicines it's convenient for people to have on hand in these situations."

Richard was standing in the doorway, watching. He could see that the conversation was making Alyssa uneasy. She had mastered her feelings about what was happening to her—she was brave about that. But this was something new, something she hadn't factored in yet, and Richard could tell that it scared her.

He watched her face it. "What kind of things are the medications for?"

He could see Kathy being careful too. "Some people have trouble breathing, and some have trouble with nausea and pain. Some people get very restless. They just can't get comfortable."

"Oh," Alyssa said. "I'm not having any of those problems."

"I think you're already getting a low dose of morphine to keep everything stable. We'll just stick this in your fridge and pick it up later. Lots of people never use it at all."

"Okay," Alyssa said. "You can put it in there. But I don't want to use it. I've thought about this a lot while I've been lying here. I know it's going to happen soon, and I think I can face that, and accept it. But I would like to be conscious when the time comes. I want to see what happens."

"Hmmm," Kathy said. "You're looking at it like it's an adventure. I like that." She bent over her bag on the floor, rummaging around in the contents.

Richard and Alyssa looked at each other over her bent back, and Alyssa smiled at him.

Kathy straightened up. "My bag is always such a mess. I can't ever find things. Could I take your vitals now?"

"All right, and then I think I'll go to sleep for a while. I feel so sleepy these days."

Richard slipped away without saying anything. He went downstairs. The sandwiches were sitting on plates on the counter. Monika was standing in front of the stove. She had one hand on her hip while she stirred the soup. She looked at him curiously when he walked in.

At first he thought she was wondering if the hospice worker was with him. But then he realized that she was probably seeing on his face how close he had come to crying. He said, "Alyssa is being wonderful. I'm in awe of her bravery."

Monika turned off the stove. "The soup's more than ready, and our sandwiches are getting dried out. Shall we ask that woman if she wants to have some lunch with us?"

"Okay."

"I'll have to make another sandwich. I knew Alyssa wasn't going to want any lunch."

"She says she feels too peaceful to move. She doesn't want anything. I think she'll go to sleep. Having that hospice worker to talk to has made her kind of tired. The woman's name is Kathy, by the way."

"I'll ask her to stay for lunch when she comes down."

"That should happen pretty soon. She was going to check Alyssa's blood pressure and other vital signs. I don't know why they need to do that, but they always do." He stopped, wondering what Monika would think.

She didn't seem to notice. After that, there was an uncomfortable silence while they both listened for any sound from upstairs. They heard Kathy say goodbye, and then they heard her walking down the hall to the stairs. Monika turned around and tried to look busy stirring the soup.

When Kathy walked into the kitchen, Monika said, "We're hoping you'll join us for some soup and sandwiches." Monika was using her best company manners.

"Thank you. I wish I could stay, but I'm already running late. Maybe next time. I'm going to be checking in every day now."

Monika said, "Oh," but it was almost a moan.

Kathy asked Monika if she could put the comfort pack in the fridge, and Monika looked startled.

"Don't look worried. You probably won't need it at all, but it'll be handy if you do. I'm going to leave the instructions on top of the fridge."

"But I thought a nurse would come if we needed one."

"That's true," she said. She walked past Monika and put the medications in the refrigerator.

Richard went down the steps to be out of the way.

Kathy said, "Alyssa was okay with my leaving it here." She turned toward Richard. "It looked like you two were having a good conversation when I barged in. I'm sorry I interrupted you."

"That's okay," Richard said. Monika looked at him with curiosity, but he didn't want to tell either of them that Alyssa was worrying about him being lonely when she was gone. He picked up Kathy's jacket from the couch and held it out for her. As he walked her to the door, he asked how she thought Alyssa was doing.

"She seems at peace. It's beautiful to see."

"Does that mean she's close to the end?" He opened the door onto the deck, and they stepped outside. He could see Monika up above in the kitchen, trying to look busy.

"Everyone is different, so of course we really don't know, but yes, it will be soon. You should probably tell anyone who would like to see her again that they should come as soon as possible." She got in her car and waved goodbye.

Richard went back inside, trying to think of how to tell Monika what he'd just heard.

She was putting their lunch on the table. She looked older and more bent than he ever remembered seeing her.

They sat down. Richard said, "I'm going to ask Sonia and Alix to come up."

Monika dropped her spoon, and soup splashed across the table. "I'm sorry, Richard. I didn't mean to be so clumsy."

They both sat still, looking down at their plates. After a while, Monika said, "Eat, Richard."

"I'm not that hungry any more."

"I know. I'm not either."

They sat there for a while longer, trying to get used to the new way things were, because every time they began to get used to the way it was, everything changed.

CHAPTER 51

When Sam came in from the barn, they were all at the breakfast table. Marnie jumped up and came over while he was taking off his boots.

"How's Moose this mornin, Pop? I been meanin to get out there to spend some time with him."

"He's doin good," Sam said. "He eats a lot, I know that."

"I could pay for his feed, you know."

"I'm just kiddin, Marnie. It's no problem."

She sat back down at the table. "You let me know, Pop. I can pay for him, if you want."

Sam went over to the sink to wash his hands, conscious of Bonnie watching. He knew she thought he ought to wash up in the bathroom, but she didn't say anything. Over his shoulder he said, "You need to brush him, Marnie. He's startin to lose his winter coat, and it's all over the place. It's comin out in handfuls."

Bonnie got up and served his breakfast. "Do you want some coffee, Sam?"

"I can get it, honey," he said. But she brought it to him anyway.

Danny said, "When I went by on the bus, I saw a whole bunch of cars in the drive next door. What's that all about?"

Bonnie and Marnie looked at each other, and then Marnie said, "It's because Alyssa is so sick."

"I saw out-of-state plates too."

"That could be her daughters."

"Oh," Danny said. "Hey Gramp, when are we goin to shoot my .300 Savage? We should set up a target. There's a good place across the road."

"Eat your breakfast, Danny. It's time for the bus."

I can talk 'n eat at the same time, Ma."

"You can talk later too. Hurry up."

They went out together to wait for the bus. Bonnie had to get dressed for work. Sam sat at the table, drinking his coffee and thinking about what he needed to do. He had some time since he wasn't sugaring. Soon enough he would need to start the garden and get the animals out on pasture, but it was still too early for those jobs. The beauty of sugaring was that it fit right in between winter and spring. He ought to have had time for it this year, since he wasn't working out, but somehow he didn't get ready in time. He would plan better next year.

Marnie came back in and sat down at the table. "Pop, I'm countin on you to teach Danny to shoot, but his grades ain't that good right now. What do you think if we said he couldn't use his gun until all his homework was done?"

"We could try that, I guess."

Bonnie came into the room. "I guess I'll get goin," she said.

"How's your ankle today, honey?"

"I can't tell yet. It's okay if we ain't too busy and I can sit down and rest it once in a while. If I don't, it aches somethin awful."

"You got to take care of it, Ma."

"I know. I try to. I'm goin to the supermarket, Marnie. Do you want me to pick up anythin for you?"

"No, Ma, thank you. I'm goin in later. My shift starts at four today."

"I'll see you then. Bye, Sam."

After Bonnie left, Marnie poured them each another cup of coffee. She sat down at the table again and said, "Last night at work, there was a woman who does some work for hospice. She was talkin about Alyssa. She said Alyssa was gettin close to the end."

"I guess I ain't surprised. I been noticin all the comin and goin over there recently."

"I could of helped them if they'd wanted me to."

"Maybe Richard didn't need help. I think her mother's been stayin over for a while now."

"Danny said out-of-state plates. Maybe Sonia or Alix is there too."

"I wish Ma had more company when she was dyin. It's hard to have to die alone. I always felt bad about that."

"You couldn't help it, Pop. You had too much goin on right then."

"My dad never really forgave me." He thought for a minute. "But he wasn't there either. He came home one day, and she was gone. And then he had all them hospital bills that he still had to pay, even though they didn't do her no good."

"It's so sad. I wonder what'll happen when Alyssa's gone. Do you think Richard'll sell the place?"

"He's had it for a long time. I expect he'll stay where he is."

"It's different for us. We got family here. His family's all down-country. Don't you think he'll want to go down where his girls are? He's goin to want to be near his grandkids."

"Maybe," Sam said. "All I know is I felt awful bad when Dad sold that land. But that was a long time ago, and they been good neighbors. Who knows who we'd get if he sold it. And it won't be us, now that house is there. We won't ever have *that* kind of money."

"You never know, Pop. Maybe I'll win the lottery one of these days." She stood up. "I do know one thing—it's time I cleaned up this kitchen."

"I'll help you."

"Okay. I was thinkin I might walk over next door. I'd like to know what's happenin. You want to come?"

"Sure. I'll walk over with you."

When they got the kitchen cleaned up and the dishes washed, they went out on the porch together. They stopped for a smoke, even though they were both trying to quit. Then they walked over to Richard's house.

It was still early and still cold, but the sun was out. Everything would start to melt later. You could smell earth and moss and water in the air, and when they stepped in the snow between their property and Richard's, it was just a dry husk that crunched under their boots. The sun would make short work of that.

When they got to the tree line, Marnie said, "Look Pop, the bloodroot is up already."

Spears of pale green, still folded around the flower, were just poking above the leaf litter under the trees.

"When everythin is comin to life again, it makes you happy, don't it, Pop?"

"It makes me worry about how much I got to do. I do know that."

"Oh Pop, you're the best."

They were both grinning when they got to Richard's deck. Sam knocked on the door, trying to look solemn. He could see shadowy people at the table inside.

It was Richard who opened the door. "Hello Sam, Marnie. Come in."

Marnie kicked off her boots outside the door, so Sam did too, even though Richard said not to worry about it.

Sam might have preferred to stay on the deck, but Marnie went in, and he followed her.

Alyssa's mother was sitting at the table. There was a man Sam had never seen before and a young woman.

Marnie said, "Alix, is that you? It's been so long since I've seen you."

It was Alix. She jumped up to hug Marnie. She was very pregnant. She said, "Oh Marnie."

"We came over to see how your mom was doin."

Alix's face crumpled a little. Sam was afraid she might cry. "She's peaceful. She's gone down a lot in the last couple of weeks. She sleeps most of the time now. She breathes very slowly. Sometimes there's kind of a raspy sound. Would you like to see her?"

"Yes, I would, if I won't get in the way." She looked around at Sam, but he shook his head. "I'll look in on her for a minute, if you don't mind waitin, Pop."

"I'll stay here. You go ahead."

Alix said, "Sonia's up there with Mom's friend Suzanne."

"Okay." She went up the iron staircase in her sock feet.

Richard said, "Come over and sit at the table, Sam. I'll bring you some coffee."

"That's okay. I just had some to home."

"Well sit down, anyway. This is Reuben, Alix's husband. You know Monika and Alix."

Sam nodded hello and sat down across from Alix and her husband, who stood and reached his hand out to Sam. They shook. Sam looked around at all of them. He couldn't think of a thing to say. Alyssa's old mother looked miserable. She was hunched over her coffee cup, not noticing anyone. Sam thought about Marnie and how hard it is to see your child in trouble.

Richard sat down beside him with some coffee for himself. "You sure you won't change your mind, Sam?"

"No, I'm good."

"We were hoping Alix and Reuben's baby would get here in time for Alyssa to meet her. But it looks like they'll just pass each other on the road."

Alix said, "The baby's due in a few weeks." She was looking at Sam. "We already found out that it's a girl."

"Congratulations," Sam said. "That's great news." He wondered if Alyssa knew, but he didn't like to ask. He thought for a minute, and then he said, "Maybe the baby will come early." Right away he realized that was the wrong thing to say.

Alix looked around at her husband. He said, "She needs to be in Connecticut, where her doctor and midwife are."

Sam didn't have to reply because just then Marnie came through the kitchen. She stopped at the top of the steps, and everyone looked at her, waiting to hear what she would say.

She stood there for a minute, looking at them all below her, and then she wiped her eyes. She said, "I work as a nurse, but it's always hard."

Richard had turned in his chair so he was looking up at her. "How do you think she is?" he said.

"She's peaceful. I think she's very close to the end now."

Alyssa's mother made a low moan, but nobody said anything.

Marnie said, "You have all done such a good job of making her comfortable." She looked at Richard. "It's not that easy to take care of a person at home like this. If there's any way I can help, please let me know. I can always change my schedule around."

Sam stood up. "I could help too. I wish there had been more people around to help my mother in her last days."

Richard got up too and walked with them to the door. While they were putting on their boots, he carefully closed the door. Then he said, "Thank you both for your offer of help. I haven't always been the best husband, but I'm trying to make up for it now. I know I'm going to lose her in just a few days, and I want to spend every minute I can with her. But thank you. I'll remember your offer, and if I need a hand, I'll ask you. It's good to have such good neighbors." He shook hands with each of them and went back inside.

As they were going down the steps, Marnie took Sam's hand, and they walked home the way they had so often when she was little.

When they got to the tree line, Marnie said, "It's so sad she has to die when it's finally gettin to be spring and the whole world is wakin up. I hope I die when it's twenty below and everything is buried under snow and ice."

Sam squeezed her hand. "You better not die for a long time after I do, and that's an order. I felt sorry for Alyssa's mother. She looked like what was happenin to Alyssa was goin to kill her. She looked so old."

"She's in her eighties, I think, Pop."

"Well, she looked ten years older than when I saw her last, and it wasn't that long ago."

When they got to their porch, Sam said, "Want to stop for a smoke?"

"Oh Pop. That's really bad of you. I'm tryin to quit."

He grinned at her. "So amn't I."

"Okay," she said. "But just remember it's your fault."

"I'm okay with that. So tell me about Alyssa."

They sat on the porch railings, one on each side facing each other and lit up.

Marnie blew out her match, took a deep drag and looked at him. She wasn't smiling any more. "It was so sad. Alyssa used to be so beautiful and full of life. Now she's tiny, nothing but bones. She hardly makes a bump in the covers. There's no flesh on her face. You can see her skull so plainly. I know I see it all the time at the Manor, but the people are usually a lot older, or maybe it's because I didn't know what they were like before they got sick. This is so sad."

Sam didn't say anything. He was thinking that she could have been describing how Ma was at the end.

"Sonia was there. She was tryin not to cry. I don't think I could stand seein my mother shrunk down to nothin but bones."

"It'd take some doin to get your ma's bones to show." He wanted to cheer her up, and she did smile a little. "What're you doin today, Marnie?"

"I'm goin to brush Moose for sure. I ought to have a look at his fence. I don't want you to have to track him down, like you did before."

"Yeah, as the weather gets warmer, he's goin to be lookin for greener pastures."

"What about you, Pop?"

"Do I look like a guy who's lookin for greener pastures?"

She laughed. "That ain't what I meant, and you know it. What're you goin to do today?"

"I don't know yet." He ground out his cigarette on the sole of his boot and stomped out the sparks that fell to the floor. "I got cleanin to do in the house and more to do in the barn."

"I can help, and then you'll get done faster."

"You don't need to. You work plenty hard already."

"I know what we can do, Pop. You clean the barn, and I'll clean the house. When we both get done, we'll get out Moose and brush him together."

"Okay, honey. You got yourself a deal."

That was what they did. While Sam was cleaning the barn, he thought about how they came back from visiting Alyssa, who was dying of lung cancer, and sat down on the porch to smoke. And they didn't even notice what they were doing.

CHAPTER 52

He heard a voice saying, "Richard, wake up." It was Alyssa with his morning coffee.

He said, "In a minute. You can put it down beside the bed." He almost said, "Come back to bed with me," but something felt different, and he didn't say it. Instead, he opened his eyes. He wasn't where he thought he was. It was night and dark. He was in Alix's room. The door was open. By the light in the hall, he could see Monika standing in the doorway.

"Richard, please come. Something is different. I don't know what it is, but I'm scared."

The present came back to him in a rush. He threw back the covers and jumped to his feet. Monika was already on her way back to Alyssa's bedside. Richard followed her. At the door of Alyssa's room, she stood aside, so he could be first.

Alyssa was lying on her back with her eyes closed. She was breathing slowly. Every few breaths, there was a rattle in her throat. But she had been like that for a long time—several days that seemed like forever. And there had been a couple of terrible nights when she was so restless and uncomfortable that she couldn't be still, when they all took turns holding her in their arms to comfort her. She was much quieter now.

Richard looked around at Monika behind him.

"I was sitting beside her, and I think I must have dozed off. Suddenly I was awake again. I don't know what waked me up, but there was a change in the room, or I thought there was. That's why I came for you. Maybe it was a mistake."

Richard put his hand on her shoulder. "I'm glad you did. Sit down. You must be tired." He patted her shoulder. "Well, we all are. If there *is* a change, it would be worse for me to sleep through it."

Monika sat down in the chair, and Richard sat on the foot of the bed. He leaned back against the footboard and watched Alyssa's chest slowly rising and falling.

"I think I'll stay with her for a couple of hours anyway, so I can take over. Would you like to go to bed for a while?"

"No thanks, Richard. I want to be here. I still feel that something is different. I want to be here if anything happens, but I'm glad you're going to be here with me."

They both sat there without saying any more. It was hard for Richard to stay sitting up on the bed. He longed to lie down across the foot of it and close his eyes, but he knew if he did, he would fall asleep. When Alyssa made a soft moaning sound, he was instantly wide-awake, waiting for what would happen next.

Gradually, he began to realize that Monika was right. There *was* some subtle change. Did things feel more resolved? For days, even when Alyssa was still conscious, when he looked at her, he would think of a butterfly, struggling to break out of its chrysalis. He would see it thrashing, as it worked to get out of its hard, confining case, so it could spread its beautiful new wings and begin its new life. Why did he always see that image?

Monika interrupted his thoughts. "What do you think, Richard? Was it just my nervous imagination?"

"No," he said. "You're right. There is a change. We need to wake up

Sonia and Alix."

"Oh goodness," she said. "I don't know whether to be glad or sorry. I'll go get them. You stay here."

"Okay. That would be good." He was glad she was willing to go. He didn't think he would have been able to leave Alyssa right now. And he was full of pity for Monika. He could see that she was so afraid of Alyssa dying that she was afraid to be alone with her. But it was what was going to happen, what had to happen. It was going to happen soon, and Monika knew it and couldn't bear that knowledge.

Sonia came in first, and Alix followed soon after. They were both in their nightgowns. Monika was behind them.

Sonia moved the bedside table over and put the chair close to the head of the bed. She sat down and took Alyssa's hand and began to speak softly to her.

When Richard stood up to get chairs for Alix and Monika, he noticed for the first time that he was wearing the long underwear he slept in and nothing else. He was embarrassed, but he didn't want to take the time to get dressed. He hurried down the hall to the balcony at the other end to get the two small chairs that he knew were there. He put them down for the others, and then he sat on the foot of the bed.

Sonia stood up to give her seat to Alix. "Talk to her," she said. "That hospice woman named Kathy said that a person's hearing is the last sense to go. She can probably still hear us."

"What should I say?" Alix looked close to tears.

Sonia hugged her. "Tell her you love her. It doesn't matter what you say, just so she hears your voice."

Alix nodded and sat down. When she began to talk, Alyssa's eyelids fluttered, but she didn't open her eyes. There was a long time between her breaths, and when she took in air, she drew it in with a gasp, as though she was going to say something.

The only light was the one on the bureau at the far end of the room. Someone had draped Alyssa's red scarf over it. The room was full of shadows, and the soft light was tinted pink, but even in that light, Alyssa's skin was gray.

Monika sat in the chair that had been brought for her, but she was too restless to stay. She got up and stood behind the chair. She walked out into the hall, but in a few minutes she was back, sitting in the chair again. After a while, Sonia grabbed her hand and led her over to the chair beside the bed to talk to Alyssa, but she was crying so hard, she could hardly speak. She just sat beside Alyssa, looking at her and crying.

Richard waited for her to have some time beside Alyssa, and then he stood up. When she looked at him, he said, "Monika, I would like a chance to say goodbye."

"Oh, of course." She jumped up and stood wiping her eyes, as he took his turn in the seat beside Alyssa. They all acted as though Alyssa was going to die in the next few minutes. They seemed to be in agreement about it, although no one had said anything. There was a difference, and all of them felt it, even though they wouldn't have been able to put it into words.

Richard took Alyssa's hand in both of his large, clumsy ones. Her hand was like a small, dead bird—an arrangement of delicate bones under the thin, cold skin. "Oh Alyssa, what can I say to you? I love you, and I'm glad you will soon be at rest, in spite of my breaking heart. Goodbye my love."

When he said that, she gave a little sigh. So maybe Sonia was right, and she could hear what they were saying. He sat there while he thought that thought, and then he looked at Alyssa's face. There was a new kind of stillness there.

He looked at the others, but they hadn't noticed yet. "She's stopped breathing," he said softly. "It's over."

No one moved. They didn't come closer to see for themselves. The stillness told all.

Then Monika, who was sitting on the end of the bed, collapsed sideways until she was lying across Alyssa's feet. She buried her face in the covers. She didn't move, and she didn't make any noise. Richard wondered bleakly if she had fainted, and if he ought to do something about it. But he didn't move. He sat where he was, still holding Alyssa's hand in both of his. It seemed too final to put it down.

The silence in the room was a huge presence. Was it that Alyssa's spirit was still there with them?

Sonia stood, and then Alix did. They fell into each other's arms and stayed that way, until Alix disentangled herself and said, "I've got to go tell Reuben."

Sonia turned toward Monika. "Are you okay, Nana?"

Monika looked up. Her face was dry. She sat up. She didn't speak and she didn't move. She just sat on the end of the bed.

Richard was still holding Alyssa's hand. When he realized it, he laid her hand on her own breast and smoothed out her cold fingers. Every word and action fell into the pool of silence.

Sonia said, "Can I help you to bed, Nana?"

"I don't want to go back to bed as though everything is the same, when nothing will ever be the same again." She sat, hunched over with misery.

"Let me help you back to bed."

"I don't *want* to go to bed. I know I couldn't sleep."

"I'm going to make you some chamomile tea. That'll help."

Monika nodded, and Sonia left the room before she had a chance to change her mind.

Monika sat staring into her own lap, and then she rose stiffly and slowly to her feet, holding on to the footboard of the bed. She said, "I think I'll go down and see how Sonia is coming with the tea."

Richard nodded. He didn't feel like going back to bed either. He was wide-awake now, but he didn't feel like doing anything, and he hated to leave Alyssa.

He stayed beside her until he needed to go to the bathroom, and then he got his pants and a sweater from Alix's room and went downstairs in his sock feet.

The light over the stove was the only light in the kitchen. Sonia stood under it, making some tea for Monika. Richard patted her back as he walked past her. The glass door of the woodstove was glowing red, and the firelight flickered in the dark room. Richard went down the steps. Alix and Reuben were sitting together on the couch. Alix had her head on his shoulder. Monika was beside the woodstove.

Richard walked over to the glass doors and stood looking out. The sky was full of stars. There was no hint of morning yet. Richard thought of all the nights he and Alyssa had sat on the deck, looking up at the night sky. Now they never would again. Part of him wished he were alone with his sorrow, so he could break down if he wanted to. But another part of him was glad the others were there, behind him in the room. The emptiness of being alone without Alyssa was too big. He couldn't bear it.

Where was she now? Would she have a difficult journey? Would it be a journey at all? He felt the immensity of it. He shivered and retreated into the room to stand with his back to the fire.

Sonia had made tea for herself and Alix, as well as for Monika. She carried their cups to them and then sat down at the table with her own. Richard watched. He felt separated from everyone else by a huge distance.

He looked around at them, and then he said, "I wonder if we are supposed to wake up the hospice people. Didn't they say we were supposed to call as soon as she died? Does that mean even if it's in the middle of the night? Are they going to come as soon as we call to take her body away?"

Sonia said, "Let's wait until morning. I'm not ready to let her go just yet."

"I agree. When we call them, everything will be different. Is that all right with you, Alix?"

She nodded.

"And Monika?"

"Yes," she said. "If we could only stop time so easily. I can't imagine moving on."

Richard said, "We can't stop time, so we'll all have to find a way to live with it, but we can grant ourselves a little grace. Let's wait until morning."

They sat together in the shadowy room. They were silent most of the time. Richard didn't know about the others, but he sat without thinking, feeling the warmth of the fire and watching it make odd shadows that flickered across the walls and ceiling. Time had slowed to a crawl.

They sat together until the first few streaks of morning light came into the room. Then, one by one, they left to get dressed. When the morning arrived, everything would be different. There would be so many things that had to be done.

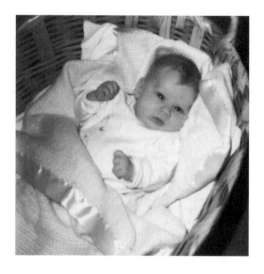

CHAPTER 53

When they got near Stamford, Monika began to get excited, even though everything looked ugly and dirty. It was a cloudy day. The ground was bare of snow, but nothing was growing yet. Still, it was home. She had been away for more than three weeks.

When the car turned onto her street, Sonia smiled at her. "Almost home, Nana."

They hadn't said much on the drive from Vermont. There were long silences. During some of them, Monika thought about Alyssa and how she would never see her again. But there were other times of silence when Monika didn't think at all. She just sat, holding up the weight of her sadness.

Sonia turned in the driveway. The house looked shabbier than Monika remembered it. The yard looked awful.

Monika opened the car door and stretched out her legs slowly, one by one. It took a while to get them straight, and it hurt a lot. They had been folded for too long. She stood, holding onto the car door, trying to find her balance. It felt as though she had to get everything stacked up just right before she could take a step.

Sonia opened the trunk. "Don't hurry, Nana. I'll take your things into the house. I have a key. And I'll check on the cats. Brian said they were fine when he and Jack checked them this morning."

Monika took a few stiff steps toward the house. By that time Sonia had been inside and was already on her way back to the car. The next time she went by, she was carrying one of Alyssa's jewelry boxes.

Monika said, "Don't bring that in. That's yours."

Sonia said, "I know," but she kept right on going up the steps into the kitchen.

Monika started slowly up the steps after her, bracing herself on the railing. She was loosening up as she went. She stopped in the doorway. The jewelry box was sitting on the kitchen table. It was open. Sonia was bent over it, looking inside.

Monika said, "Sonia, your mother wanted you girls to have her jewelry. What are you doing? You divided it so nicely last night. Your dad thought it was lovely the way you two were so generous to each other."

"I know, Nana, but just a minute. I'm looking for something. Oh, here it is." She held up the little crystal star by its chain.

"I gave that to your mother when she was twelve or thirteen."

"She always loved it. She wore it a lot."

"Yes, I know she did. Isn't it funny? When I gave it to her, I never thought it would be so important—just an ordinary, five-pointed star, not even a Jewish one."

"Alix and I thought you ought to keep it to remember her. We have all the rest."

"Oh," Monika said, feeling the tears pooling behind her eyes. "How could I not remember her every minute of every day?"

"I know, Nana. Me too. But we want you to have this." She fastened the chain around Monika's neck and kissed her on the cheek. "It looks nice, a little piece of Mom to stay with you."

"Thank you, dear," she said. She was swollen with sadness. On the one hand, nothing could ever be all right again, and on the other hand, she still had Sonia and Alix. She touched the sharp points of the tiny star. "Yes, it *will* remind me of her." How confusing life was.

Embedded in the pain of losing Alyssa was the sweetness of these girls.

She put her arms around Sonia. She would have liked to hold her there, but she could feel that Sonia was eager to leave, so she gave her a little push and said, "You'd better get home. They'll be wondering where you are."

"There's nothing you need tonight, is there?" Sonia went over to the refrigerator and looked inside. "I asked Brian to get you milk and fruit and bagels, and I see he did, but I forgot about tonight. Is there anything you would like for tonight? I could bring it over later."

"No, dear, thank you. You've done too much as it is. I'll be fine with bagels and fruit."

Sonia gave her a quick kiss. She picked up Alyssa's jewelry box and hurried to her car.

Monika watched the car back out to the street and drive away. Then she sat down heavily at the kitchen table. The house was musty and unfamiliar. She felt too unsettled even to cry. She was numb. She couldn't think, and she couldn't feel. Making herself comfortable seemed like an enormous and pointless task. She felt as if she were coming down with the flu.

After a while she carried her bags up to her bedroom. Marmalade was lying in the middle of the bed. She lay down beside him and stroked his fur. It was a softer orange now than it had been when he was young, but it was still bright and beautiful after all these years. He began to purr.

"Did you miss me?" she said. "I'm so glad to be back home." It hurt to be glad about anything, when Alyssa was gone forever.

Her tears fell onto Marmalade's back. She stroked them away, but that wasn't good enough. He stood and stretched and then jumped off the bed. She lay still, curved around the empty hollow where he had been. She was alone.

She got up and went downstairs again. Her legs were stiff. She needed to lean a lot of weight on the banister. She knew she ought to eat, even though she wasn't hungry. She opened the refrigerator. There were apples and grapes and plain bagels. She shut the door.

At the table she picked up the pack of cards and began to lay out a game of solitaire, but even before she had all the cards out, she had lost interest in the game. The only thing that could make a dent in her loneliness and sadness was a phone call from Alyssa, wanting to know that they got home safely. Monika pushed the cards across the table. She cradled her head in her folded arms and lay on the table and cried.

Days passed in the same numb way. She walked to Joe's Market for food a couple of times, and Sonia brought her some groceries. She knew she needed to call Mabel, but she kept putting it off. She would have to tell her about Alyssa's last days and her death, and she wasn't ready to talk about it yet. The weather stayed cloudy and cold, the perfect weather for her mood. She lost track of how many days went by, since they were all so dull and gray.

If she had the flu, it was strange, because she wasn't getting worse or better. She supposed she was grieving, but it was unlike anything she had ever experienced or read about. It certainly wasn't the way people experienced sadness in the movies. She was too lazy to do anything, weighed down by the heaviness of her grief.

It was about nine in the morning when Sonia called. She sounded excited. She didn't even say hello. She just asked if Monika was dressed. Monika hesitated. She didn't like to tell Sonia that she had slumped so badly that she was wearing a mixture of day and night clothes all the time. Getting dressed was another thing that had fallen victim to her gray fog of numbness.

"I guess I'm partly dressed. Why?"

"Hurry. Get ready. I'm on my way over to pick you up. Alix is already at the hospital."

Monika's heart gave a lurch. More bad news was what she instantly thought, ignoring the delight in Sonia's voice. But she didn't have time to say anything before Sonia rushed on.

"She and Reuben got there at six this morning, and I'm on the way over there now. Reuben called to say everything was going fine, and that it wouldn't be long before the baby arrived. I'm taking the day off, and Jack's at the babysitter's. I'll be over in a few minutes to pick you up."

Monika had just time to say she'd be ready before Sonia was gone. If she'd had more time, she might have said she didn't want to go, but Sonia had hung up. She grabbed some clothes and combed her hair. She thought she might say something when Sonia arrived, but Sonia was so excited and in such a hurry that Monika felt overwhelmed by her enthusiasm and said nothing.

At the hospital Sonia let her out at the door and went to park. Monika stood there passively waiting until Sonia came hurrying up. Then she followed her across the lobby to the elevators. The fluorescent lights were blinding, and the noise and bustle and the hurrying people confused her. She had no time to think about Alix or about the baby coming. She really had no time to think at all. The elevator came, and Sonia gave her a little push to move her into it.

She followed Sonia out of the elevator and down the hall and stood waiting while Sonia asked the nurses about Alix. They were told to wait in the room across the hall. Alix had just had her baby. Someone would come and get them when they could see her.

They sat down together to wait, but almost right away, Sonia jumped up again. "Stay here, Nana, in case they come for us. I'm going to look around and see what I can find out. I'll be right back." She hurried out of the room. Monika could hear her voice in the hall.

There were magazines on a table, but she couldn't reach them without getting up. A television high up on the wall was tuned to a morning news show. Monika sat there, waiting for what would happen next, listening to the unintelligible mix of voices, not thinking, just waiting. Then Sonia was there in the doorway. "Come on, Nana. I found out where they are."

Monika stood up slowly, trying not to look as old as she felt. She followed Sonia down the corridor and into a room where Alix was lying in a bed with the baby beside her, protected by her encircling arm. Reuben was standing near the bed.

Sonia went up close, talking away. She was bubbling over with excitement. Monika stood back behind her. After a little while,

Reuben got a chair and pushed it near Monika, so she could sit down. She was grateful for that.

Sonia said, "Tell Nana what you want to name her."

Alix smiled her shy smile and said, "Nana, Reuben and I were thinking about naming her after Mom, but we wanted to make sure it was all right with you first."

Monika didn't know what they wanted her to say.

"Won't it be wonderful to have a new Alyssa to take the place of the one we lost?" Sonia said. She picked up the baby and carried her over to Monika and set her, all wrapped in her blankets, on Monika's lap.

Monika looked down. The baby was staring up at her with her deep blue eyes. Everyone says that babies can't see when they're first born. Monika didn't know if that was true, and she didn't care. When she looked into the baby's huge, dark eyes, something passed between them. Sometimes on a cloudy day, a shaft of sunlight streams toward earth from a hole in the clouds. That was what the baby's gaze made Monika think of.

The baby stared without blinking. Monika's heart exploded with love. She said, "Alyssa, yes, that's her name."

The baby opened her tiny mouth into a pink yawn. She smacked her lips and shut her eyes.

Monika looked up at Alix. "Yes," she said. "Her name has got to be Alyssa."

CHAPTER 54

Danny and his friend Timmy sat on the fence, talking to Sam while he cleaned the pigpens. Sam thought they might feel like doing some of the work, but he wasn't surprised that they didn't want to. It was a smelly, dirty job.

After a little while Danny said they were going to go to the house. It was late morning. Sam figured they must be getting hungry. Danny was hungry pretty much all the time these days anyway.

"Fine with me," Sam said. "Just don't leave a mess in the kitchen. Okay?" He thought they were going to make themselves sandwiches and turn on the TV.

But when he went in to get his own lunch about an hour later, they weren't there. It looked as though they'd had some lunch, and they hadn't left a mess for him to clean up. There was a note on the table that said they were going to take a walk, maybe up the road into the woods. The note said they wouldn't go far. Sam got himself a sandwich and some coffee. He listened to the weather report and then went out to do some more work in the barn.

By the middle of the afternoon, he had done everything he meant to do. The boys hadn't come by the barn. He went to the house to see if they were inside. He took off his barn clothes and walked into the kitchen.

He was standing there, trying to decide whether to reward himself with a beer or not, when he looked out the window and saw them walking down the road toward the house. They were walking side by side and laughing. Danny was carrying his deer rifle.

Sam's first thought was that if he could get out of the house without them seeing him, Danny would have time to put the gun back in the gun cabinet, and nobody would have to deal with it.

The whole thing was a surprise. He didn't even know that Danny knew where the key to the gun cabinet was kept. It wasn't hidden, but he hadn't told Danny where it was either, and the top drawer of the chest of drawers in his bedroom wasn't a place Danny would have had any reason to explore on his own. Up until that moment Sam had assumed, even though no one had actually said it, that Danny would only be handling his rifle when he and Sam were together.

By then the boys were in the yard, and it was too late. Sam just had time to get himself a beer. He wanted to be doing something when they came in.

Danny took off his boots and jacket and walked into the kitchen, carrying the gun. He said hello and walked through the room to put the gun away. He was cool. Sam couldn't tell whether he knew he was breaking the rules or not.

When Danny came back, he and Timmy went upstairs, and Sam went down to the basement to give the place a good cleaning, since he had finished all his butchering jobs. The cooler was empty, and the table was bare. There wasn't anything on the schedule either, but he hoped that would change, and he wanted to be ready when it did.

Bonnie fixed macaroni and cheese for supper. Timmy asked to stay over, but his mother wouldn't let him. After Sam got done with the chores, they sat down to eat. It was just the three of them, since Marnie was working a double shift.

Toward the end of the meal, Bonnie said, "I wonder how Richard is gettin along. I feel sorry for him over there all by himself."

Sam said, "You didn't see him when you walked by his house, did you, Danny?"

"No, but I wasn't really lookin for him either."

Bonnie said, "I wonder what he'll do."

"I don't believe he'll sell out. He's been there for a long time. He built that house, and he lived in the cabin for a while before she came up to join him. I always liked her for bein willin to live there."

"That used to be your cabin, didn't it, Gramp?"

"That's right. I built it when I came home from 'Nam. I had nightmares. I needed to be some place where I wouldn't wake everybody up. I didn't want anyone to know. I thought I was mental. Nobody knew about PTSD in them days."

"What about you, Grammie? Did you live in the cabin?"

Sam said, "A little while after me and Grammie got married, I moved into town. We got an apartment."

"I couldn't live out there with no runnin water. I had a waitress job in town. I had to go to work lookin clean."

"Did Gramp wake you up at night?"

"I got used to it. It don't happen that much any more, but you might hear him yellin one of these nights."

"Can I have seconds?" Danny handed his plate to Bonnie.

She got up and filled it and set it down in front of him. "You're hungry tonight."

"Thanks, Grammie. It's good. I wish Timmy could of stayed. He would like this."

"Maybe next time," she said. She looked at Sam. "You might go over to Richard's and see how he's doin."

"I don't want to go over without a reason. I wouldn't want him to think I was snoopin. He might think I was tryin to find out if he was goin to sell the place."

"I don't see what's wrong with a neighborly visit. I suppose I'm goin to have to bake a pie for you to take over to him."

Danny said, "That's a great idea. You can make one for us too. We like pie, don't we, Gramp?"

"That's for sure."

After they finished supper, Sam and Danny cleaned up the kitchen. They tried to get Bonnie to go into the other room and watch television, but she stayed in the kitchen, trying to help. When the dishes were done, Danny went upstairs to his room.

Sam shouted up from the bottom of the stairs. "Hey Danny, is it all right if I come up? I got somethin I want to talk to you about."

There was a pause, and then Danny said, "Sure, Gramp. Come on up."

Sam stopped in the doorway of the room that used to be Junior's. Danny was lying on the bed, looking worried, or maybe scared. He sat up and moved his feet so Sam would have room to sit. He'd been holding his cell phone. He set it beside him on the bed. He tried to keep his eyes on Sam, but he kept sneaking looks at the phone.

Sam sat down. He said, "Where'd you and Timmy go this afternoon?"

"Up the road and into the woods above Richard's. That's still your land up there, ain't it?"

"Yeah. You could of got there faster by goin up behind the barn."

Danny looked down at his phone. "It was easier walkin on the road."

Sam knew they didn't want him to see them going by the barn with Danny's rifle, but he didn't say so.

They sat there in silence. Sam could see that Danny was waiting for him to make the next move. After a while, he said, "I saw you boys took your deer rifle."

Danny didn't look up. "I wasn't tryin to *sneak* it," he said.

"You didn't ask permission."

Danny looked him in the face then. "It's my gun. My dad bought it for me."

"I know that."

"You don't need permission to take what's yours."

"A gun is different. It's like a car. You have to learn how to operate it first."

Danny sat forward. "That's just exactly what I was tryin to do! Timmy was teachin me."

"Timmy?"

"He's got his license and everythin. He took the hunter safety course last year."

"I don't care what he's got. I'm the one who's goin to teach you."

"But Gramp, you don't have time. That's what you always say when I ask you. Ma don't know how, and my dad ain't around. What am I supposed to do?"

"Well, you can't just ask some little kid. We don't even know his parents."

"He ain't just some little kid. He's the best hunter in the class, maybe in the whole school."

"How do you know?"

"Everybody knows that, Gramp."

"Well, all right. It don't make no difference anyhow, because I'm the guy who's goin to teach you about guns and huntin. That's what your ma wants, and that's what I want. That way it stays in the family."

"I'd like that, Gramp, if you have the time. I was tryin to save you some trouble."

"You're a good boy, Danny. I know you weren't bein bad. It's kind of enterprisin of you to find a way to get what you need. I appreciate that."

"Who taught you to hunt, Gramp?"

"My dad took me out a few times, but he was busy. He had a dairy operation." He stopped, listening to what he had just said. "I suppose the grown-ups are always too busy."

Danny grinned at him. "So what did you do when your dad was too busy to teach you?"

Sam thought back about the way he had learned. He hadn't ever looked at it that way before. "I guess I did pretty much what you did. I went up in the woods and figured out how to do it."

Danny started bouncing up and down when he heard that. "See, Gramp, that's what I was tryin to do. You always say a guy's got to be able to take care of himself."

"Hold your horses, Danny. *I* did it that way, but that don't make it right for *you*. This is a whole different place than when I was a kid. All these new people have moved in and brought their downcountry ways with them. There ain't near as much woods as there used to be, and there's a lot more rules and restrictions. There wasn't even a hunter safety course in them days. So don't get the idea you can do it the way I done it, because you can't.

Danny picked up his phone and looked at it and put it down again. He sighed.

"So what did you boys do up in the woods?" He still hadn't decided whether to say anything to Marnie or not. If he told her, it would take the situation to a whole new level.

"Timmy showed me how to shoot. I shot at a tree. I only hit it one time. I need a whole lot more practice." He paused, studying Sam's face. "Then Timmy shot a porcupine. We thought you'd want us to. I know how much you hate 'em, so I thought you'd be glad if he killed it."

"What'd you do with it?"

"We left it where it was. It was definitely dead. If you want to see it, I can go get it tomorrow."

"Naw. That's all right." He stood up. Maybe he'd better tell Marnie. He thought they were just walking through the woods, pretending to be hunters, but if they were going up there and actually killing things…."

Maybe Danny figured out what he was thinking, because he said, "Gramp?"

Sam was walking toward the door, but he stopped and turned to look at Danny. "What?"

"I was just thinkin that we wouldn't need to bother Ma with this." His eyes scanned Sam's face, trying to see the answer there. "I mean if you think we could handle this without her. It's really up to you."

Sam sat back down on the end of the bed. "That's the very thing I was tryin to decide."

"See, Gramp, this is between you and me, but I got a plan for us." He sat up straighter. "Suppose you give me some jobs? Then you can get your work done sooner, and you'll have some time to teach me how to shoot." He was grinning now. "The more work I do, the more you can teach me."

Sam was grinning back. "I like it, Danny. I like it a lot." He thought that even if Marnie minded them keeping a secret from her, she would be pleased that Danny was being so grown up, finding a way to get what he needed.

"I can work hard, Gramp. You'll see."

Sam stood up again. "All right. Let's give it a try. I'll think up some jobs you can do for me." He took a few steps and stopped in the doorway. "I just thought of somethin," he said.

"What is it?"

"You fired your rifle quite a few times. Did Timmy tell you to clean it after you fire it?"

"No. He didn't say nothin about cleanin it. I didn't know, Gramp."

"Well, okay. That's our first lesson right there. You got to learn to take care of your rifle."

"I want to, Gramp. I'm really glad you're goin to teach me. It won't hurt it not to clean it today, will it? I don't want to hurt it."

"Naw. We'll do it soon. Good night now."

"Night, Gramp. See you tomorrow."

Sam went downstairs, feeling good about the situation. He was glad he didn't have to say anything to Marnie. He decided not to mention it to Bonnie either. It wasn't something women could understand anyhow.

A few days later, when Bonnie was getting ready to leave for work, she said, "I made a pie for Richard last night."

For the first time, Sam remembered the conversation. "Why don't we eat it? Richard can get his own pie."

"I made one for us too, and I want you to take Richard's over to him. I want to find our how he's doin. That's the whole point."

"I didn't know you was makin pies."

"You was doin somethin outdoors. I made 'em after supper. It didn't take long. You could of smelled 'em cookin. They're out on the table in the front room. I set 'em out there to cool. Take Richard's over while it's fresh, okay?"

"I got to get some work done out to the barn first, and then I will."

"All right. See you later."

When Sam came back indoors, everyone had gone. He got himself some coffee and took it out to the porch, so he could smoke. It was warm in the sun. The white-throated sparrows were back. Sam could hear them singing. Their call always meant that spring was finally here.

But spring meant a lot of work too. Sam thought about not going over to Richard's. He could tell Bonnie that he forgot. Then he thought how she had put some work into making the pie, and he would like to know how Richard was getting along. It wouldn't take that much time to go and see.

A little while later, he walked up Richard's drive, carrying the pie. He was heading for the house, but when he passed the garage, he heard a radio playing, so he stopped and knocked on the door.

There was no response. After a minute, he opened the door and looked in. Richard was standing with his back to the door. He was sanding the bottom of his canoe by hand. He didn't realize Sam was behind him.

Sam was tempted to shut the door. He could take the pie up to the house and leave it on the deck for Richard to find later. But Bonnie would question him, and he hadn't seen enough of Richard to be able to tell her anything.

He stepped inside and around the canoe so Richard could see him. He thought Richard might jump, but he didn't. He just looked up and smiled. "Hello, Sam. What can I do for you?" He didn't look as good as he sounded. Sam had never seen him look so disheveled.

"Bonnie sent you a pie." He held the pie up so Richard could see it. "Where shall I put it down?"

Richard gestured to a shelf by the stairs. "Over there with those dishes. I'll take it up to the house later. It looks good. Thank Bonnie for me. That was thoughtful of her."

There were a lot of dirty dishes on the shelf. Sam had to pile them up to make room for the pie. He looked around the garage. Richard's dirty clothes were piled on the stairs. His sleeping bag was spread out in the back of the pickup.

Sam walked over to where Richard was working. He wondered if he ought to say anything, and then, before he made up his mind, he said, "You're not livin out here, are you, man?"

Richard smiled, a twisted, little smile. "No, not really. I've been spending a lot of time working on the canoe, and sometimes it's easier...." His voice trailed off, and he started sanding again.

"How can I help you, man?"

"It's okay. It's okay. The pie is nice."

"I'll tell Bonnie you said so."

"Yes, please do. What kind is it?"

"I don't even know. I was just the delivery boy." He walked over to the shelf and smelled the pie. "It's apple," he said, walking back to where Richard was working. "She made one for us too. It smells good."

He stood there, watching Richard work. Richard's hair was straggling over his collar, and he hadn't shaved for a while. Plenty of guys looked that way these days with long hair and the beginning of a beard, but you could tell when they did it on purpose. With Richard it seemed like he had forgotten how to take care of himself.

Sam took a chance and said, "Are you sure you're doin okay since...." He didn't know how to finish the sentence.

Richard stopped sanding and looked at him. For a second, Sam thought he had gone too far and offended Richard, but when he started to speak, Sam realized that wasn't true. "I guess so. It's a lot different than I thought it would be, but I guess when I used to think about what it would be like, she was still here, and my thinking was skewed by that. You know what I mean?"

Sam nodded. He saw so much pain in Richard's eyes that he had to look away. Richard had helped him a lot when he lost his job. He really wanted to return the favor now that Richard was having a hard time. He said, "I'm sorry, man. What can I do?" He knew it was lame and that it wouldn't get anywhere, and it didn't.

"Thanks, Sam. I appreciate it. But, you know, there's nothing anybody can do. I keep thinking of things I want to tell her, but I can't. She's gone." He started sanding again.

"I'm goin to be turnin over my garden pretty soon now, and I can do yours at the same time, like I usually do."

"I don't know," Richard said. "I don't think I'll have a garden this year. There's only me to feed. If I was working in the garden, I think I'd miss her even more than I already do. That's something we always did together. I don't think I could take any pleasure in growing things this year." Richard was sanding while he talked, so all Sam could see was the top of his head.

Sam stood there watching. He couldn't think of anything to say. He felt sorry for Richard, but there was nothing he could do.

He was just about to say he was leaving, when Richard said, "Besides, I really need to get this canoe finished. I planned to get it done before warm weather got here. We were going to use it for day trips this summer. I had it all planned—how she would be recovering, and we could spend a lot of time out on the water. I thought it would be so good for her." He stopped, thinking about what he had just said. "I'm all mixed up. I can't get it out of my head that I need to finish this canoe, even though I know there isn't any reason to hurry anymore."

"That ain't true, man. You're still here. You can take some river trips. Get it finished so you can see how it'll do in the water."

Richard looked up at Sam then, and gave him a sad smile. Sam wasn't sure whether Richard liked what he said, or whether he thought he was foolish to say it. But he didn't have anything left to offer, so he said goodbye and went out the door.

On the way back to his own place, Sam thought about getting Danny to set up a target behind the house against the hillside. They might as well do a little shooting every day. Since he had taught

Danny how to clean his gun, Danny had been cleaning it over and over. He might as well fire it so he would have a reason for all that cleaning. Bonnie might complain, but if they set up the target fairly close to the house, they ought to be able to get out there almost every day. Sam thought it might make him a better shot too. There was no way to get too good.

CHAPTER 55

After Sam left, Richard went back to work again, but his tears kept falling into the sawdust and gumming it up. Talking to Sam had brought up a lot of things that he had been trying not to think about.

He walked to the shelf where Sam put the pie and sorted through the dirty dishes, trying to find one that was clean enough. All the dishes were pretty bad. He wiped off a fork and started to eat the pie out of the pan. It was delicious. He only took a few bites because he could feel Alyssa watching him and disapproving. It made him too uncomfortable. He had told Sam that he was all right, but he wasn't. Sam didn't notice, but Sonia and Alix would. Suppose one of them came for a surprise visit to see how he was doing? One of Alyssa's friends could happen along to check on him.

He needed to pull himself together, and he needed to straighten the place up. He found a cardboard box and loaded all the dirty dishes into it. He set the pie on top and carried the box to the house. When he stepped inside, he noticed a musty smell, as though no one was living there. He put on a Coltrane CD and went around the house opening all the windows, even though it wasn't that warm outside, and the fire was out.

He had to force himself to go into their bedroom, the room where she died. He pushed back the heavy drapes and opened the windows. The light poured in. The spring air smelled of mud and water and moss. It was hard to open up that room. He felt as though her spirit had been hovering there in the dark. He didn't want it to move on, and he didn't want to move on himself, but he knew it was better for both of them. He hoped she would understand.

He looked around the room. Nothing had been moved since she died. Her red scarf was still draped over the lamp on the bureau, and the bed was still rumpled and unmade. He would have to get to all that soon. He wouldn't want the girls to see it like this.

And at some point he would have to go through Alyssa's things. But it was still too soon. He felt as though there was a thin crust of earth beneath his feet and under that was a seething volcano of boiling emotion. He had to step lightly. It was possible to function, but only if he was very careful.

Downstairs, he put all the dirty dishes into a sinkful of hot, soapy water. A dishwasher would have come in handy. He remembered how he had tried to convince Alyssa that they should put one in when they were building the house. She wouldn't have it. She said the kitchen was too small, and she needed the space for cupboards. So Richard washed and washed.

When the dishes were done, he cut himself a slab of pie, put it on a clean plate, and took it out on the deck to eat it. He sat down on the steps. It was cool, but no colder than it was inside with all the windows open and the fire out.

Now there were two things to regret. The first, the most painful, was the loss of Alyssa. But there was another loss to be sad about. That was the loss of solitude, the weeks alone, grieving while he worked on the canoe, because Sam was just the first. Richard could feel the world seeping back into his life. Before Sam came over, he hadn't thought of anything but the canoe and his grief and sadness. Now he saw that he had to take care of himself or people would notice.

He spent the rest of the day straightening up the house, cleaning and putting things away. He went to the garage for his dirty clothes and his sleeping bag. He did several loads of laundry. By dark he had made the house comfortable, even though it felt empty without her.

Sonia called, as she often did at night. He surprised her by answering the phone.

"Oh Dad, I was expecting to get your message machine. Is everything all right?"

"Fine. I mean as fine as it can be. How are you?"

"Okay. I talked to Alix a little while ago. Dad, you haven't even been down to see the baby."

"I know. I've been busy."

"Busy? I thought you pretty much stopped working when Mom got sick."

"I had to clean up the house today."

"I wish I'd been there to help you."

"I could've used some help. There was quite a lot to do."

"How did you let it get so bad? I wish you had someone there to help you."

"It's okay. I was just too busy to keep up with it. I've been working on the new canoe."

"Your canoe? That's crazy, Dad. You don't need to do that now. You need to come down and see Alix's baby, the new Alyssa."

"I'll do that soon. I can come as soon as I finish my canoe."

"Dad, listen to me. The canoe isn't that important. It doesn't matter when you finish it."

He wanted to say, "It matters to me," but he refrained. He knew she was thinking that he cared more about the canoe than he cared about Alyssa. How could he explain that the thought of Alyssa's death was so painful that he had to block it out by working on something. He didn't know what to say.

Luckily, Sonia didn't wait. She went on without noticing the silence. "Dad, Alix and I were wondering what kind of ceremony we are going to have for Mom's memorial. Where are we going to scatter her ashes? We need to invite all her friends."

"I thought that when I got the canoe finished, I would go out in it and sprinkle her ashes in the Connecticut River."

"But what about us? We want to be there too. Nana couldn't go out in your canoe."

Richard couldn't speak. This is what his sadness had done to him. He was so absorbed by his own grief that he had forgotten everyone else's. He never thought that Sonia and Alix had lost their mother. Finally he said, "Please forgive me, Sonia. That was so selfish. Of course you need to be there. Everyone who loved her should be there to say goodbye."

And Sonia, who always bustled in to tell everybody what to do, was silent herself. Then she said, "Thank you, Dad."

"Let's think of another place."

"What about the pool above the cabin? Mom loved it there."

"That would be a good spot."

"And Nana could get there."

"Yes."

"Or the waterfall. What do you think about that, Dad? That would be a beautiful spot too, and it isn't that much farther."

"Wait a minute. I just had an idea. Do you know that hawthorn tree at the top of the hill in the Martels' sheep pasture?"

"I don't think I remember it. I never went up there when I was little. We always played in the brook."

"It's a strange tree. It's huge. It must be very old. Hawthorns almost never get that big. Your mom said it had magical powers. She called it a fairy-tale tree. And it does look as though it belongs in a fairy tale."

"Could we scatter her ashes under that tree, do you think?"

"We walked up there last fall. It was when we still thought she would get well again." In his head he saw that lovely, hopeful, autumn day. "When we left to go down the hill, she said goodbye to the tree, and she said we would come back again, but we never did. Winter came, and by then she was too weak."

They hung up soon after that. Richard thought he could tell that Sonia was in tears and couldn't talk. Thinking about that day was hard for him too.

A few minutes later, Sonia called back. When he answered the phone, she said, "Do you think Nana could get to that hawthorn tree?"

"Sure. I could drive her up in my truck. I'll have to ask Sam, but I'm positive he won't mind."

"I'll call Alix and see what she thinks. I love you, Dad."

After he hung up, he realized that neither of them had said they wanted that tree to be the place for Alyssa's ashes. They didn't need to. Both of them knew it was the right spot.

Richard felt more peaceful than he had for a long time, even though life and the world were drawing him farther and farther away from Alyssa. It made him sad, although he knew it was inevitable. It was what had to happen. It would have taken a tremendous and futile effort to hold onto his grief and isolation, and it wouldn't do any good.

CHAPTER 56

Monika knew she must have been very soundly asleep because she didn't remember driving through Severance. She woke up when the car stopped in front of Alyssa's. The afternoon sun was shining so brightly that it made her squint. Richard was standing on the deck. He was alone. She said, "Richard is there. Where is Alyssa?" Right away she realized her mistake. She wasn't fully awake yet.

She looked around. Either the others hadn't heard what she said, or they were politely pretending that they hadn't. Sonia was taking a sleepy Jack out of his car seat, and Brian was turning off the car. She hoped they hadn't heard, but there was nothing to be done about it except to hope.

She got out of the car and stood by the open door, giving her legs a moment to gather their strength. Then she started to walk toward the steps. Richard was coming down to help them with their bags. He hugged her and patted her on the back. She stood there at the bottom of the steps, waiting to see if they needed help bringing their things in.

Jack was subdued, clinging to Sonia's legs. He must be aware of the tension that all the grown-ups were feeling. None of them had been to Vermont since the beginning of April when Alyssa died. It was hard for all of them. Maybe Jack couldn't understand why everything was different, but he must have felt that it was.

When they went inside, the house seemed full of Alyssa's presence, as though she might walk into the room any minute. The house was clean, but everything was the same. Richard hadn't changed anything. She wondered what he had been doing. She supposed he could have asked her the same question. What had she done in those three months? Very little, except to be sad.

Sonia may have been grieving, but she bustled around the way she always did. She had brought a lot of food for the buffet they were going to serve tomorrow after the trip to the top of the hill. Monika couldn't understand why they wanted to scatter Alyssa's ashes in someone else's sheep pasture in Vermont, but Sonia and Alix were so positive about it that she hadn't even tried to discuss it with Richard. Alyssa would have been just as stubborn. She remembered how she had tried to get Alyssa to go to Sloan Kettering for treatment. Everyone knew they were the best, but Alyssa wouldn't hear of it. So there you are. She had to swallow down any bitterness she felt. Life goes on, and the world belongs to the young. The old have to keep quiet. Their ideas have passed their expiration date. No one wants to hear them any more.

The next morning, Alix and Reuben arrived with the baby. They surprised everyone by being so early. They had left home about five o'clock while little Alyssa was still asleep. She was awake by the time they arrived, but she was rested and in a mellow mood.

Monika sat on the couch, and Alix brought little Alyssa to her. She held her so she could see the commotion in the room, as everyone went back and forth, carrying dishes and food and making last minute decisions. Monika was glad to sit with Alyssa and be an observer. Alyssa watched everything seriously, studying the grown-ups with her wide, deep-blue eyes.

They covered the table with Alyssa's best tablecloth and got out her good china. Monika was expecting that they would have to send Richard or someone else to the store for things they had forgotten, but she was wrong. Sonia, in her bustling way, had remembered everything.

Late in the morning, Alyssa got fussy. Alix sat down to nurse her. Sonia brought Monika a sandwich and some tea. Everyone sat around having lunch, while Alix changed Alyssa and put her down for a nap. Monika was sorry to see her go. They had shared the time together, watching the others work. Monika was able to sit still and feel that she was making a contribution.

Alyssa's friend Suzanne walked in about twelve-thirty. She looked lovely. Monika struggled not to be jealous on her Alyssa's behalf. Why should Suzanne be so very much alive when her beloved Alyssa was dead? It was so unfair.

After Suzanne, other friends of Alyssa's began to arrive. Richard went out to organize the parking. He needed to be able to get his truck out. A little before two o'clock, Sam Martel drove in backwards. He came to pick up anyone who wanted a ride to the top of the hill, but Monika and Karen Baird were the only ones, and they chose to ride with Richard. Sam drove away, and they got in Richard's truck and followed.

It was happening, the final event of Alyssa's life. Monika felt that she was being pulled along. She had to be there as a witness, even though she felt like saying, "Stop. Let's not do this. Alyssa's too-brief life should not be over. Let's not go forward with this ceremony." But she said nothing. She just sat impassively in the truck between Richard and Karen.

Sam stopped in front of his back door. Bonnie Martel came out and hoisted herself up into Sam's truck.

Karen said, "I guess it's lucky I came with you, Richard. There isn't going to be any extra room in *that* truck."

Monika said, "I haven't seen Bonnie for a long time. She's put on a lot of weight, hasn't she? I mean, she's always been heavy, but this is a lot more."

Richard said, "She hurt her ankle last winter and was laid up for a while. I guess that's what did it. She's heavier than when I saw her last, and it wasn't that long ago."

Sam's truck started up the hill past his barn, and Richard followed him. The dirt road was steep and bumpy. There were trees lining both sides. When they got above the barn, they passed the first of the people who were walking up from Richard's house.

Karen said, "I didn't see those people go by."

Richard said, "There's a shortcut through the woods above the pool."

Sonia waved when they went past.

Monika said, "It's funny. It doesn't seem like a funeral because everyone is wearing bright colors." She looked down at her own gray skirt. But her blouse was white. It would have been too uncomfortable to wear black in the July sunshine.

Karen said, "It's not a funeral anyway. It's really a celebration of Alyssa's life. Don't you like that better?"

Monika thought about that. "I guess I do. It's hard to stop thinking it ought to be the way it's always been, even though I can see that Alyssa would like it to be like this."

At the top of the hill, Sam drove into the field along a wide, fenced corridor that led to the hawthorn tree where they were going to have the memorial ceremony.

Richard turned into the field too. "Sam did a lot of fencing up here. When I asked him if we could do this, I didn't realize what he'd have to do to get ready for us. I should have helped him." He parked his truck beside Sam's. "I'm going over to thank him. I had no idea."

Bonnie Martel was sitting in Sam's truck with the door open. Monika waved to her.

"Do you think we should get out?" Karen said.

"Let's not hurry. No one is here yet. Let's sit down while we can. I wish we'd thought to put some lawn chairs in the back of Richard's truck."

"Yes, we should have. There's nowhere to sit but on the ground."

"I don't think I could do that," Monika said. "I'd never get up again."

"I might try it anyway, if I get tired enough. I'm still not over my surgery yet."

The walkers were beginning to come along the corridor. They gathered under the tree's spreading branches. The tree was just at the end of its flowering. A few white blossoms shone like stars among the green leaves, and there were white petals strewn by the wind across the grass.

Monika said, "Well, I guess it's time for us to go."

Karen got out and walked over to the others. Monika slid off the seat until she was standing on the ground beside the truck. She put on the straw hat she was carrying. She hoped that if anyone were watching, it would look as if she were standing there to adjust her hat, but really she was giving her legs time to straighten out and find their strength.

Sonia came over and hugged her. "Nana, that's such a cool hat."

"It's your dad's."

"Well, you ought to get him to give it to you. You look better in it than he does."

While they were standing beside Richard's truck, another one pulled up beside Sam's. A heavy man and woman got out.

Monika looked at Sonia with a silent question. Sonia said, "I think that's Junior Martel and his wife. Dad said they were going to play some music for us."

Monika watched them walk by. The woman was wearing a tank top and a long, flowery skirt that clung tightly to her wide hips. The man was carrying a guitar case. Monika could see it was going to be some kind of hillbilly music. What was Richard thinking?

Bonnie Martel was standing alone, halfway between the trucks and the tree. While she was standing there, looking as though she wondered what she was going to do next, a boy ran over to her.

Sonia said, "That must be Marnie's little boy. Jack is going to be so interested. There aren't any other children here except for Alyssa, and she's too little to count—in Jack's eyes anyway." She hugged Monika. "You look so nice, Nana, and you're wearing Mom's little crystal star."

Monika put her hand up to her throat and touched the star. "I wear it all the time," she said. "It makes me feel that she's not so far away."

Sonia hugged her again.

They walked over to join the group of people under the tree. It was difficult walking. The ground was uneven. Tufts of coarse grass stuck up in places. From a distance it looked like a lawn, but when you tried to walk across it, it was unexpectedly rough. Monika was already wishing she could sit down.

Richard stepped out into the field where everyone could see him. Behind his back, beyond the green curve of the field, rows of blue mountains ringed the horizon, each row paler than the one in front of it. Reluctantly, Monika admitted to herself that the view was breathtaking.

Richard was holding the little wooden box that contained Alyssa's ashes. Monika had seen it sitting on the side table in the kitchen. She knew what was inside, even though she didn't want to know. It was such a little box, and it was all that was left of Alyssa. All that was left, and soon that would be gone too.

Richard said, "Can I have everyone's attention, please?" He had to say it several times before the talking stopped.

Monika looked around the group. Some people were still standing, but most of them were sitting on the ground. Monika saw that Karen Baird was one of the ones sitting down. She wished again that she had brought something to sit on. Richard should have thought to provide some chairs.

Brian and Jack sat near where Sonia was standing, and a few minutes later Alix and Reuben were there with the baby.

Sonia whispered, "Come on, Nana. Let's sit down with them."

"I can't. I won't be able to get up. There isn't anything to hold onto."

Sonia sat and pulled on Monika's hand. "Don't worry. I'll get you up. Come on."

Against her better judgment, Monika allowed herself to be pulled down onto the grass. It was a relief for her weary legs.

Richard had been telling everyone why they chose this spot for Alyssa's ashes, and now he said, "We are all going to take a turn in the scattering, but first…" and here he put the box on the ground at his feet. "Several people have told me that they would like an opportunity to share their memories of Alyssa." He stopped talking and looked around at the crowd of people. Two large black birds were circling high in the sky overhead.

For a long moment, no one said anything. Then Suzanne stood up. She walked to where Richard was standing, talking as she stepped around people. "Okay. I'm the one who said that to you, Richard, although I'm not sure what I meant by it." She turned around to face the others. "There's too much to say, and there's really nothing to say. I miss Alyssa terribly, even though I didn't see her that often. But the world is definitely not the same now that she's gone." She stopped and stood there looking around. "And if I try to say any more, I'm just going to break down crying. So thank you." She walked back to her seat under the tree.

There was a silence while everybody looked at everybody else, trying to encourage, or maybe to embarrass each other into taking a turn at saying something. Then a small woman with white hair stood up and began talking without introducing herself. Monika hadn't ever seen her before.

The woman said, "I don't think I've ever told anyone about the time Alyssa and I went to the Modern together. We drove down from Vermont. Alyssa seemed comfortable driving into Manhattan. I couldn't have done it."

She spoke softly. Monika had to strain to hear her. She looked at Sonia. Sonia was listening intently too.

"The other day when I was thinking about Alyssa and what a wonderful person she was, I tried to think of how to describe what she was like, and I remembered this incident where she was so brave and didn't think a thing about it. She probably never told the story to anyone. She probably didn't ever think of it again. I'm going to tell you all, so the story won't be lost. This is how it happened. We both wanted to see this art show, and we agreed we would drive down to New York together.

"We left the car in a parking garage and were walking toward the museum when we passed two boys shouting angrily at each other.

Just as we walked past them, the biggest boy pulled out a knife and started toward the little one. I stopped in my tracks. I'm sure my mouth was open. I was paralyzed. But not Alyssa. She didn't hesitate. In her best schoolteacher voice, she said, '*What* do you think you are doing? Give me that knife this instant.'"

Everyone laughed with delight at this picture of Alyssa, but Monika couldn't help fearing for her and thinking she might have been stabbed right there on the street. How strange to fear something that was over so long ago and couldn't matter now that Alyssa was gone. And still, she was afraid to hear what happened next.

"When she told the boy to give her the knife, she held out her hand for it. She surprised him so much that he handed it to her quite politely and ran away. The little boy's mouth was wide open, but he didn't say a word, he just ran off in the opposite direction.

"We went on walking. When we were just about to the doors of the museum, Alyssa looked down and saw that she was still carrying the boy's knife. She opened her handbag and dropped it in. I was afraid that someone in the museum would check our bags and find it, but no one did.

"We had a nice time looking at the paintings, and then we had dinner together and drove home. I don't think either of us mentioned that incident then or later. I don't know what happened to the knife. Maybe she threw it away. I don't even remember what it looked like. It all happened so fast." She sat down.

Beautiful, brave Alyssa. How could she be gone, when her old mother was still here, an old woman who couldn't even get up, sitting in the grass in this field she never imagined she would ever come to. She hated herself for being here when Alyssa wasn't. If there was such a thing as God, He was making some very poor decisions.

Several more people stood up to speak, but Monika was so full of her own thoughts that she wasn't listening. If they had had something new to say, she might have paid attention.

When it got quiet, and no one else seemed to be going to stand up and speak, Richard said he thought it was time to move on. He was out in the field with the wooden box of ashes at his feet. Now he squatted to open the box and the plastic inside it. He fumbled at the plastic, trying to get it to stay out of the way. Monika couldn't watch. She had to look down at her hands.

Finally, Richard stood, and, taking a spoon out of his pocket, he flung a spoonful of ashes out into the field. The air was still. Against the light, a graceful arc of ash fell to the earth.

Just then the guitar began to play, and then the woman started to sing 'Amazing Grace.' It was beautiful and haunting, full of pain and loss, as though the woman felt exactly what Monika was going through. It was strange too. Monika would not have been able to put that voice together with that heavyset woman she had seen walking past.

Richard handed the box to Alix. She threw a spoonful and gave the box to Sonia.

Sonia threw some ashes and reached out to Monika. "Here, Nana, it's your turn."

Monika shook her head. She couldn't stand up. She knew she would be too slow and clumsy, and everyone would be watching.

"Nana, you've got to."

Monika was almost in tears. It was too much, too hard. She didn't want to be here. She didn't want to listen to that music. She didn't want to throw the little bit that was left of Alyssa out onto this lonely hilltop.

But Sonia kept holding out the box, and she had to do something. She managed to get to her knees. She took the box and the spoon and flung a spoonful the way the others had. Then she sank back down to the rough grass of the field. She held up the box and spoon and felt them being taken out of her hands by someone. She didn't know who. She couldn't see anything but a blur.

She sat for a long time, trying not to think, while verse after verse of 'Amazing Grace' flowed around her. The woman's voice was full of longing and sadness. It was just what Monika was feeling. Richard had been right after all.

People were taking turns throwing Alyssa's ashes, until finally someone handed the box to Richard. He looked inside. Then he looked slowly around at everyone and said, "It's done." He put the lid on the box and started walking slowly toward his truck.

People began to get up. The music stopped. Monika saw Sam's son and the heavyset woman walking toward their truck. Everyone was moving. Pretty soon Monika was the only one still sitting on the ground. She could get onto her knees, but she knew she couldn't get all the way to her feet without something to hold on to. Everyone seemed to have forgotten about her. She saw Sonia not too far off talking to Jack. She called to her.

"What is it, Nana?"

"You said you'd help me up. I need you. I can't stand up without some help."

"I'm here, Nana." She held out her hand.

Monika grabbed it and pulled hard and managed to get to her feet, although she almost pulled Sonia over in the process.

"Oh thank goodness," she said. She was a bit out of breath. "I thought everyone was going to leave, and I would still be here, looking at that hawthorn tree, two ancient relics alone on the hilltop together."

"I wouldn't have left you, Nana."

Monika was busy straightening her clothes. "That was difficult," she said. "We should have brought some lawn chairs. I'm going to get in your father's truck." She patted Sonia on the shoulder. "I'll see you back at the house."

When she got to the truck, Richard and Karen Baird were waiting for her. Monika climbed in, and they drove down the hill, passing the people who were walking. Richard said, "Did you see the ravens circling in the sky as we scattered the ashes? Alyssa would have loved that flyover."

At the Martels' house, Sam was helping Bonnie out of his truck. Monika said, "Richard, did you invite Sam and Bonnie to come over for some food?"

"I told Sam about it. He didn't say what they were going to do." Richard drove over to his house and let them out.

Monika climbed the steps and collapsed on the deck in the nearest chair. "Suddenly, I feel exhausted. I hope there's nothing I ought to do, because I don't think I could move."

Karen Baird walked by. "Don't worry, Monika. I'm sure there's nothing. Alyssa's girls are so efficient." She went on into the house.

Monika was alone for the moment. She wanted to just sit and not think. Soon the walkers would be arriving, and she would have to make polite conversation.

Then Sonia sat down beside her. "Nana, are you all right?"

"I think so. I just feel very tired. I don't know why."

"We've been through a lot this afternoon. I feel tired too."

"I was planning to work on your mother's flower gardens. They need weeding desperately."

"You can't do that while everyone is here."

"I know. And I feel too tired anyway."

"Why don't you go lie down for a while? Alix and I can handle everything that needs to be done." She paused. "Unless you feel like staying and talking to everyone."

"No. I don't. But don't you think it would be rude to leave?"

"I can explain. Everyone will understand. They were all Mom's friends."

"Okay, Sonia dear. I'd like to do that."

She walked past the people on the deck and in the house. She shut the door of her room, muting the sound of voices. She kicked off her shoes and lay down in her clothes. After a few minutes, she opened the waistband of her skirt. She planned to lie there and think about all that had happened, but she fell asleep almost immediately and slept so soundly that she didn't even dream.

She was woken up by Alix knocking on her door. "Nana, can we come in?"

"Of course," she said, and she sat up, trying to straighten her twisted clothes.

Alix opened the door. She had little Alyssa in her arms. "We needed a quiet place to nurse, but we could go upstairs, only there are people all over the house, looking at Mom's paintings."

"Don't go. I want to get up anyway. I had a good sleep."

Alix sat down on the end of the bed and began to nurse. Alyssa made little moans and smacks as she drank.

"I remember those gurgling sounds," Monika said. "My babies made the same noises when they had their bottles."

"You didn't breastfeed Mom and Aaron?"

"No, I didn't. Nobody did in those days. We all thought we were too modern to do something like that. How silly we were. I wish I'd done it now. It looks so cozy."

Alix smiled at her. "I love it. I'm worried about what I'll do when my maternity leave is over."

"Why don't you stay home with her?"

Alix said, "I don't know if we could handle that." She was quiet for a minute, smoothing Alyssa's hair away from her forehead as she thought. "That might be hard for us financially. And I love my job. Maybe I could work from home some of the time." She sat Alyssa up and patted her on the back to get her to burp.

Monika stood and fastened her skirt. "I probably should go out and talk to everyone."

"Can I put Alyssa down for a nap on your bed?"

"Of course. Will she be safe?"

"She can't roll over yet, and I can put pillows on both sides of her. It's the quietest spot in the house, and I can look in on her every little while."

Monika smoothed her skirt and combed her hair. When she left the room, Alix was changing the baby's diapers. Monika tiptoed away.

There were still a lot of people around. Monika went out on the deck and sat down in an empty chair. It had cooled off some, but it was still hot. Monika was glad the chair was in the shade. She looked around. Everyone else was standing. Richard was talking to Suzanne.

Jack walked around the corner and sat down on the steps. Sonia was right behind him. She sat down beside him and turned to look at the people on the deck. "Oh Nana, you're up. Did you have a good sleep?"

"Yes, thank you. I feel much better."

Suzanne asked Richard what he was going to do now. "Do you think you'll move?"

"No," Richard said. "Definitely not. I want to stay right where I am. I feel closer to Alyssa here than I would anywhere else."

Sonia looked around. "We've been trying to talk him into moving closer to us. Actually, Dad, the perfect thing would be for you to move in with Nana."

Richard laughed. "What do *you* have to say about that, Monika?"

"You know you would be welcome, Richard." She tried to sound as though she really meant it, but she couldn't help thinking that it would be a big adjustment for her to have someone in the house with her all the time. She had been alone since Sonia moved out.

Richard said, "Thank you, Monika. I'm glad you're willing to take me in, but I can't imagine leaving this place. I love it here. Nothing could make me leave. You'll have to carry me out feet first, Sonia."

"Oh, Dad, don't say stuff like that. I can't even get used to Mom being gone. I want you to live to be a hundred, at least."

"All right, if you say so. But I'm going to stay right here for whatever time I have left."

"I guess we'll have to visit a lot then. Won't we, Jack?"

Jack said, "I like it here. We can go fishing every day."

"Nana, have you seen Alix?"

"She was in my room, feeding the baby. She was going to put her down for a nap there."

"Okay, thanks. Come on, Jack. Let's go find them."

As they were going inside, a man Monika didn't recognize passed them coming out. "Richard," he said. "That's an incredible box."

Richard smiled. "Thank you. I made it for Alyssa's ashes."

"It's cedar, isn't it?"

"It's some of the red and white cedar I had for my new canoe."

"You're building a canoe?"

"I worked on it all last winter. I wanted to be nearby in case Alyssa needed me. I finished it not long ago. Would you like to see it?"

"I'd love to."

"Come on then. It's in my garage." They went down the steps

together, already deep in a conversation about canoe building.

Suzanne came over and sat on the railing near Monika. "We won't see those two for a while," she said. "Are you hungry, Monika? I could bring you something."

Monika stood up slowly. "Thank you, Suzanne. I *am* hungry, but I can get myself something. I need to move around anyway." She walked toward the glass doors. "I'll see you again before you leave, won't I?"

"Oh yes, Monika. I wouldn't leave without giving you a goodbye hug. Alyssa was my most important friend."

"Mine too," Monika said. She went into the house.

There was still quite a bit of food. She found a plate and got herself some potato salad and a glass of iced tea that wasn't really cold any more. She thought it was good of Alix and Sonia to honor their mother's memory by using the best china, but they would have a lot of dishes to wash later, and they would have to do them in the sink, because Alyssa refused to have a dishwasher.

She took her food to the living room couch and sat down to eat. She hadn't realized how hungry she was.

A few minutes later, a woman sat down beside her. Monika didn't know her. She looked to be about Alyssa's age. She said, "You must be Alyssa's mother. I'm so glad to meet you. My name is Cynthia, Cynthia Shepherd. Alyssa and I worked at the same school. She was a good friend. I'm so sorry she's gone."

Monika nodded. Her mouth was full.

"I've just been looking at Alyssa's paintings. I thought I knew her well. We often talked about art. But I didn't even know she was a painter."

"She really wasn't. She always cared a lot about art, but she only began to paint at the end of her life. I think it took her mind off her cancer."

"She had such a talent."

Monika smiled. "I wish she was here so you could say that to her in person. It was important to her." She cringed when she remembered how she herself had called it a hobby, implying that it wasn't serious.

It must have hurt Alyssa to hear her say that. And now there would never be a way to make it better.

She had been so upset to hear Alyssa say that she wanted to devote the time she had left to painting. *She* wanted Alyssa to do everything she could to stay alive, even if it made her feel awful, even if it proved to be of no use. Did she want that because she couldn't face the knowledge that Alyssa was going to die? Or did Alyssa give up too soon and cause the prediction to come true?

Cynthia said, "I always admired Alyssa for being so feminine and lovely. And I knew she was smart and thoughtful, but I never realized how strong she was. Had you ever heard that story about how she took the knife away from the boy in New York?"

"No. Alyssa never told me that."

"It was a brave thing to do, and so was deciding to end the treatments when the doctors realized that the cancer couldn't be stopped. I don't believe I would have been strong enough to do that. And you all supported her. That's so wonderful."

Monika nodded and smiled and took the undeserved credit because it was easier than trying to justify herself.

Late in the afternoon, when all the guests had gone and Alix and Sonia were helping Richard clean up, Monika went outside to walk through the yard and look at Alyssa's flowers. All the beds needed weeding, and there wasn't enough time to do much of anything. She strolled around, looking, trying to decide where to begin. She pulled a few weeds here and there, and then she gave up and went back to the house.

Richard was on the deck.

She said, "Alyssa's flowers are a mess. I was planning to weed the beds while I was here, but I'm sure they're going to want to leave in the morning."

"That's all right, Monika. I'll work on them. Now that the memorial is over and I've finished my canoe, I'm sure I'll have time."

"Maybe we'll get back again before the summer is over. We came up last year for Labor Day weekend. Maybe they'll want to do that again."

"You could always come by yourself on the train."

"Thank you, Richard. I'll think about that. Alyssa loved her flower gardens. I'd like them to be in good shape." She paused. "So you could enjoy them and think of her."

He smiled, but he didn't say anything in reply.

CHAPTER 57

"Hey, Gramp."

Sam looked up from his shoveling. Danny was standing right outside the pigpen. "Hey yourself, Danny," he said.

Danny climbed onto the railing and sat there. "What're you doin, Gramp?"

"What's it look like?"

"Are you goin to be cleanin the barn all day?"

"Naw. Just this pen. I'll be done before long. I'm planning to skid down some firewood."

"Can I help?"

Sam took a big shovelful. Then he said, "You can come. You can't drive while we're skiddin. It's too tricky. You ain't ready for that yet."

"I can learn. You can teach me when I'm ridin along."

"That's right."

Danny jumped down and started for the barn door. He was running. Sam went on with the shoveling.

In a few minutes, Danny was back. He was out of breath. He

climbed over the fence into the pen. "I had to get my boots, so I could help. What should I do?"

Sam handed him the manure fork. "Take out the wet beddin. Throw it into the wheelbarrow." Sam didn't need to say he was glad to have some help, because Danny knew. It reminded him of what Marnie was like when she was little.

The first forkful Danny took was so big he couldn't lift it off the floor. Sam was curious to see how Danny was going to handle it. He watched while he did his own shoveling.

Danny pulled back the fork until he was only lifting half as much. From then on, he was able to move the pile into the wheelbarrow, and he worked steadily.

After a while Sam said, "Okay, that's good enough. They're just goin to mess it up again, and we'll have to do it all over in a few days. You get some fresh beddin from over by Moose's stall while I take this out and dump it. Then we can get ready to skid down them logs."

When he had dumped the wheelbarrow, Sam gave the pigs fresh water and opened the gate so they could go back into their pen. They came in snuffling and grunting. Sam and Danny leaned on the rail to laugh as the pigs rooted around, inspecting the new arrangements and grunting their comments. Then they went up to the house to change out of their boots.

It wasn't raining for a change. The ground was soggy, but the sun would dry it out later. The logging chains and the ax and peavey were already in the tractor. They gassed it up and loaded the chainsaw, and they were ready to go.

When they got to the gate into Moose's pasture, Sam stopped the tractor. Before he could say anything, Danny jumped out and opened the gate. He waited for Sam to drive through, and then he closed the gate again. When he climbed back to his seat, Sam said, "Good man," and Danny grinned.

They went up the hill past the log lengths laid out by the road. Sam pointed them out to Danny. "There's three left to go down. I did two of 'em yesterday when you were over at your friend's house."

"Oh yeah. I saw the drag marks where you went across the road. I meant to ask about 'em, but I forgot."

Sam drove to the top, turned around, and came down to the first log. He pulled in front of it on the downhill side and turned off the engine.

"You didn't need to do that, Gramp. I could of stayed on the brakes while you hitched up."

"This is safer. I'm goin to chock the tires too. I brought some rocks for that."

"I wondered why you was carryin rocks around."

"It's slower, but it's better. Accidents can happen. We don't want to take no chances." He wanted Danny to learn the best way to do the job, so he didn't mention that he'd been sloppier yesterday when he was working alone.

They got out the chains. Sam showed Danny how to put a chain under the log and fasten it to itself.

"Ain't you supposed to put that hook through one of them links?"

"You don't do it that way. It ain't a piece a jewelry. It goes over both sides of the link. It's stronger like that. Now when I back up, you hitch this other chain to the drawbar, and do it like I said. Okay?"

Danny nodded. He looked serious. Sam backed up, and Danny hooked on. Sam raised the end of the log enough so it wouldn't drag in the mud."

He shouted, "Okay. Let's go."

Danny climbed into the cab. It was always tricky starting out, but when they got rolling, the log went along fine.

When they were on the way down the hill with the last log, Danny said, "Gramp, are you all done gettin hay outa the meadow?"

"For this year, I am."

"So, what if we pulled all them logs out into the field?"

"What would we want to do that for?"

"I don't know. We might could make a obstacle course for Moose, like they do on TV. We could teach him to do tricks, or we could train him to jump over a log."

"We got to have them logs for firewood."

"I know that, but they're goin to be sittin around until you got time to cut 'em up, ain't they?"

"Well, yeah."

"They might even dry better out in the open, and we could have some fun til you got to 'em."

They were sitting in the tractor at the landing now. "Okay," Sam said. "Suppose we was goin to make this obstacle course of yours, how do you say we ought to lay down the logs?" He could see the excitement in Danny's face. "I'm not sayin we're goin to do it. I'm just askin. Okay?"

"I know, Gramp. I was thinkin we could lay them out like a big H, two on each side and one across the middle. We walk him in, see, and he's in a box. He has to jump over the one in the middle. So that's the way we teach him."

"Would you be on his back when he walked in?"

"That's the whole point, ain't it?"

"We could do that."

"Really, Gramp?"

"Sure. Why not? I was hopin we'd have time to get Moose out later anyhow." He got out of the tractor seat and sat on the fender.

"What're you doin?"

"I thought you could skid them logs. You know how they're supposed to go. It's a good place to learn. It's flat. There's less to go wrong."

"Oh wow," Danny said. He sat in the seat and put his hands on the steering wheel, but he didn't do anything else for so long that Sam began to wonder what was going on. Then he looked around and smiled. "I was tryin to figure out how to do it. Now I think I know."

"Good man. Try it out. I can take over if you want me to."

Sam hitched for him, but Danny did all the skidding. Sam liked how he worked slowly and seriously, figuring out how to drag the logs into position and not asking for help. It took a couple of hours before he had the logs laid out the way he wanted them. He made an H shape, with two logs angling in toward the crossbar and the two on the other side of the crossbar angling out.

They walked around the H, shifting the logs with the peavey until they were both satisfied. Then they put the tractor and the tools away and got Moose out. They brushed him and put on his tack.

Sam boosted Danny up. "Hold him here until I get over there. I want to see him go over that log." He ran across the road.

"Here we come, Gramp."

"Okay. Let 'im rip."

Moose trotted over to the opening in the H. Then he balked. He stopped so suddenly that he sat down on his haunches. He wasn't going to go into what he saw as a trap. Danny kicked him and slapped him with the end of the reins. He moved up and down in the saddle, trying to give Moose the idea of going forward. But all Moose did was step around a little. He wouldn't go in between the logs.

"Do you want me to lead him in?"

"No, I want to do it myself." He kicked and slapped, until Moose turned around and walked over to the picnic table.

"Here," Sam said. "Let me take a turn."

Danny got down, and Sam climbed up. He could feel Moose stepping around nervously under him. "Okay, now. Watch this." He kicked Moose hard and turned him. He kept a tight grip on the reins.

Moose walked toward the H. For a minute, Sam was sure he was going to do it. But when he got just inside the logs, he stopped and reared.

Sam wasn't even surprised until it was over. Then he had time to wish that Danny had taken a picture. It would have been a good one.

"Wow," Danny said. "That looked cool. Do it again, Gramp."

"I can't. I didn't do it. Moose did."

"Try to make him do it again."

But when Sam tried, Moose turned around and hurried back to the picnic table.

Sam got off while they tried to figure out what to do next. They couldn't talk to Marnie about it, because she might nix the whole idea. She could say they weren't treating Moose right, or some such thing.

They led Moose through the H with nobody on his back. They each took a turn at that. Then Danny got on, and Sam led him through.

Moose stepped delicately over the log, one foot at a time. They didn't know how to tell him to go over with both feet at once. Finally, in exasperation, they put him back in his pasture.

That night, as he was falling asleep, Sam thought he had it figured out. He would lead Moose over the log again and again, until he got used to it. Then he would put something on top of the log to make it higher. Eventually, Moose would have to jump. It was a good plan, and it didn't matter how long it took, because it would be fun.

CHAPTER 58

Late in the afternoon, Richard went outside to look around again. It had been a dark day, with lots of wind and a hard rain. It was one of those days that come sometimes at the end of August and give a preview of the weather coming later in the fall. Richard had spent the whole day upstairs on the couch at the end of the hall. He'd been reading and listening to music to drown out the sound of the wind and rain.

He was also keeping up with the weather reports on his computer. Hurricane Irene had come ashore in North Carolina yesterday, and this morning it had landed again, first in New Jersey and then in Brooklyn. It was supposed to be heading for Boston, but by the middle of the afternoon, it was clear that it was going straight north toward Vermont.

Richard had talked to Sonia twice and Monika once. They were all safe, but without power. Sonia tried to bring Monika over to her house, but Monika wouldn't leave her cats. The last time Sonia called, she said she thought the worst was over for them. The storm was moving north. Now she was worrying about Richard.

After he talked to Sonia, Richard put on his rain parka and went outside. The roar of the water was deafening. It was raining even harder than before. He thought about putting on his boots and walking up the trail to the pool, but he didn't do it. It was damp and cold out in the weather. He didn't think he had much to worry about. His house was quite high. He felt sorry for people who lived down in the floodplains near rivers. They were the ones who needed to worry about flooding. He went back to his cozy spot on the upstairs couch.

About an hour later, he went to the glass door to look outside again. This time he got a shock. There was a thin layer of water flowing over his lawn and down his drive. It was lapping at the tires of his truck. He decided he needed to move it to higher ground. He put on his boots and rain gear and went out. The truck started right away.

The water ran down the drive, crossed the road, and spread over Sam's meadow. Richard drove through it and along the road to Sam's drive. That had no water on it. He parked beside a beat-up little car in front of the barn. He looked for Sam's truck, but it wasn't there. When he knocked on the kitchen door, Sam's big dog began to bark.

Marnie opened the door right away. "Richard," she said. "Is everythin okay at your place?"

"Yes. I don't think I'm going to have a problem, but the water is coming up on my lawn, and I thought I ought to move my truck. Can I leave it here?"

"Oh sure. I think it'll be fine where it is, but leave the keys in it, in case we need to move it."

"I put them over the visor. Is your dad home?"

"He went downstreet to pick Ma up. He didn't think she ought to be drivin in that little car of hers. There are places where the roads are flooded."

'Is everything all right over here?"

"I think so. The sheep are up in the high pasture. I didn't go up there, but they're probably all right. Moose's stall has some puddles in it. The pigs are dry. I shut the chickens up, so they're dry too. We'll be fine. We're up a little higher than you are."

"I never noticed that before, but I can see it now."

Marnie was standing in the open door. "Would you like to come in? Pop's been gone most of the day tryin to help people, but he'll be bringin Ma home soon."

"Thanks, but I want to get back over there. Tell your dad I think it's okay. He'll see my truck. Tell him I moved it just to be safe."

"I'll tell him."

Richard went back to his house through the trees on the property line, instead of going through the water on his drive. He hadn't been back on his couch for very long when he heard someone knocking. He hurried downstairs and slid open the glass door.

Sam was standing on the deck. He had his fishing waders on. "Richard, this looks serious. Get your gear. I'm here to evacuate you."

"I think I'll be fine, Sam. Look, it's not raining as hard as it was. You've got enough to worry about without adding me to your list. You saw I moved my truck over to your place?"

"That's good, but you need to think about yourself too. What're you stayin here for, anyhow?"

"I thought I'd move some stuff out of this room, in case it gets as high as the deck, but I don't think it will."

Sam looked in through the open door. "You want some help movin the couch and the table? Them are too big for one person."

"Thanks, but I wasn't going to move the big stuff, only some books and lamps."

Sam took off his hat and banged it on his leg and put it back on again. "There's a awful lot of water goin by."

"I know. It's flowing down my drive and across your meadow."

"Right over them log lengths I got laid out to dry. They ain't goin to do no good like that."

"I had three cords delivered just last week. The pile is sitting in the water behind the drive. I haven't even stacked it yet."

"You might come over to our place after you get your stuff moved. It can come up pretty fast. I helped evacuate one place where the water was gettin a foot deeper every fifteen minutes."

"It's not going to do that here. At least, I can't imagine it. But thanks. I'll be over if I get worried."

"Marnie's goin to be there if you need a hand with anythin. I'm headin back in to Severance to see what I can do to help. There's a lot of people in trouble. I know that. You take care of yourself." Sam clapped him on the back and gave him a half-hug, which was a lot for Sam to do. Then he walked down the steps and back toward his own house.

Richard watched him sloshing away through the water. The water seemed deeper than it had a few minutes ago. Richard hoped that was only his imagination. He was glad he hadn't noticed it when Sam was with him. It gave him kind of a jolt, and he was glad Sam wasn't there to see it.

He closed the door. The living room was the lowest room in the house, on the same level as the deck. If he was going to move anything, it should be what was in that room. He sat on the couch and looked around, trying to think what to do. After a while, he decided he had better do something. He took armfuls of coats out of the closet and piled them on the bed in the downstairs room where Monika always stayed. He took all the boots and dumped them on the floor in Monika's room. Most of the coats and boots were Alyssa's. He was glad she wasn't here to see him make such a mess. She would hate it.

He rolled up the small rug that was in front of the couch and put it along the wall in the hall. He put the dining room chairs up on the table and unplugged the lamps and set them on the kitchen counter. He took all the books out of the lower shelves of the bookcase and set them in piles in the hall with the rug.

Just after he moved the books, while he was trying to figure out what to do next, the lights flickered and went off. For a minute he stood still, stunned by the blackness. Then he shuffled across the room, feeling his way to the closet shelf where he kept his headlamp. Before he turned it on, he went to the glass doors and looked out. Beyond the deck, there was nothing but water. It caught glints of the fading daylight as it moved. It was almost full dark now. He turned his headlamp on and shone a beam out across the yard. Black water was rolling past. He could hear it slapping the walls of the house.

He shut the door and shone his light around the room. He'd been trying to decide what he needed to move when the lights went out. It would be so much harder to do in the dark. He decided to give up and let it happen.

He got some cheese and crackers and a cup of tea and went up to the couch on the balcony. He sat down, but then he remembered the candles Alyssa used to set on the table at dinner. He remembered how the little flames would be reflected over and over in the glass of the windows and doors until there were little lights dancing everywhere, and Alyssa sat there in the midst of them, looking lovely, ready to give him some delicious food she had made just for him.

He sat for a minute, thinking of that time, gone now and never to come again. There was a pain in his stomach, in his heart, in all his insides, when he thought of how he had wasted those times, not appreciating, not savoring what he had while he had it. He almost couldn't bear to think how often he had been resentful and angry, irritated by Alyssa's ceremonies. He would give anything to have another chance to have what he had then. Maybe he ought to appreciate what he had now, but he didn't even want to think about that.

He ran downstairs and found the candles and candlesticks in one of the kitchen cupboards, where they had been sitting ever since Alyssa got too sick to bother with them. He carried them up to the table in front of the couch. With the eight candles lit, and the headlamp to read by, he felt quite cozy. The golden light flickered across the ceiling. It was warm and dry in the upstairs. He could hardly hear the roar of the brook. He thought of trying to get out the portable radio that he took on canoe trips, but he decided that he didn't want to hear what was happening to anyone else. There was nothing he could do about it anyway. All of that could wait until morning.

He was reading the jokes in the most recent edition of The New Yorker and enjoying his snug lair, when he heard a strange gurgle. He looked over the balcony railing. His headlamp shone into the room below. A layer of water was creeping across the living room floor. He hurried downstairs and walked through the water so he could look out the glass door.

There was water where the deck was supposed to be. At first he couldn't believe what he was seeing. He thought it was impossible for the water to cover the floor of the deck because it would run through the cracks between the boards. Then he realized that the water that covered his yard had gotten so deep that the deck was submerged.

He slid open the glass door. All he could see was water, and all he could hear was the roar of it. His first thought was that he had to get out of there right away. But after a few moments of panic, he calmed down enough to see that he wasn't in immediate danger. His house was being flooded, but it wasn't going to be swept away. He thought of all the people in New Orleans who had stayed in the upstairs of their houses for days until the water went down. What he needed to do was to go back to the comfortable place he had made for himself and wait until morning, when he could see how much damage had been done. He thought again how glad he was that Alyssa didn't have to go through this, but he also realized that if she had been here, it would have forced him into the role of the calm one. It was harder for him to calm himself when there was no one there to be calm for.

Later on he got the quilt from his bed and put out the candles. He lay on the couch in the dark, listening to the water. At first he hated to hear it sloshing and gurgling downstairs. It was a living creature, an alien invasion. That was frightening. Then he pretended he was camping beside a beautiful waterfall, and the water sounded calming and peaceful.

He meant to stay awake so he could keep track of what was happening, but he must have been more tired than he realized because he fell asleep. Sometime in the middle of the night he woke up. He didn't know where he was. He really thought he was on a camping trip, until he remembered the flood. He got up, put on his headlamp, and went to the bathroom. Then he started down the stairs. He had only gone down a few steps when his headlamp lit up the water below. It looked black and oily, gleaming and sinister in the dim light. It was in the hall, rocking gently to its own rhythm, making a sucking sound. He couldn't tell from above how deep it was, but if it was in the hall, the whole downstairs was flooded. It slapped slowly and calmly against the stairs. He sat down where he was. It was a monster, and it was toying with him. He was scared and almost in tears. He was so alone that he wished Alyssa was here with him, but no, he didn't really wish that. Whatever happened, he could be glad that she didn't have to be here now to see what was happening to the house she loved so much.

He retreated upstairs and went to look at the clock in his bedroom. It was only a little past two o'clock, and that meant at least three and maybe four hours until daylight. He went back to the couch and wrapped the quilt around his shoulders. He sat there for a long time, listening to the water sloshing through the house and roaring past outside. He didn't want to call for help, either 911 or Sam. The telephone probably wasn't working anyway, and there was never cell service at his house. He concentrated on waiting for daylight.

After a while, he lay down, still wrapped in the quilt, and sometime after that he fell asleep. When he woke up, he thought everything was the same, but as he lay there in the dark, he realized that the sound of the water outside wasn't as loud as it had been. Was the light on the ceiling more gray than black? He lay there, not daring to get up. If he looked out the window or down the stairs, he might destroy his lovely, fragile hope.

Finally he had to get up to go to the bathroom. Then he went down the hall to the room he used to share with Alyssa in that other life that he had lost forever. He opened the drapes and looked out. There *was* a hint of gray in the sky. He didn't know what time it was, but it had to be close to morning. He could see faint gleams of light on the dark water. The water was everywhere. His house sat like a rock in the middle of a stream, but it wasn't a raging torrent any more. It was still, almost peaceful. It looked like a lake. There was a little hope after the dark despair of the night.

He went back to the couch on the balcony and got the rest of his clothes. If only he had brought his rubber boots upstairs. They were on the floor in Monika's room, where he dumped all the boots from the closet when he emptied it last night.

He went down the stairs in his shoes. The hall had no water in it, but the floor was covered with a slimy layer of gray mud. He tried not to look at the rolled rug or the piles of books, a wasted effort. The kitchen floor was covered with mud too. He went down the steps into the living room. The water was gone, but the mud was deeper and wetter on the steps and on the floor. He walked across the room to the sliding glass door, opened it, and looked out.

There was more light in the sky. It shone on the rippling water. He looked down below his feet in the open doorway. The water was there too, nothing but water, no floorboards, nothing. The deck was gone, all of it. The water flowed peacefully across the yard and down the drive. It lapped against the house, and it was chuckling.

He went down the hall to Monika's room and found his rubber boots on the floor. They looked all right on the outside, but inside they were wet and covered with the gray mud. In the kitchen cupboard he found some plastic bags on a high shelf that hadn't been flooded. He put the plastic bags over his sock feet and then put on the wet boots.

He went to the front door, the door no one ever used, and opened it. He had been standing in a dark, mucky place that smelled of damp and dirt, an atmosphere of ruined possessions and wasted work. But when he opened the door, he was in another world. The sun was rising. Everything smelled clean-washed and new. Irene had brushed him with one swipe of her gigantic hand, showing him just how insignificant he was. But he was still here. His house was still here, and it was going to be a beautiful day.

He went down the front steps. They were made of large blocks of granite, and the water had not dislodged them. The bottom two were still submerged. When he stepped onto the ground, the water came halfway up his boots. It was about a foot and a half deep, and it was going down.

He waded through the shallow water to the garage. That was when he realized that he hadn't even thought to close the garage door. Alyssa's car was there. He wondered if it would start. There was no water in the garage now, but he could see by the marks on the walls that it had been more than three feet deep at some point during the night.

He looked around. Irene had cleaned out the garage the way Alyssa had always wanted him to do. All his cans of paint and varnish, the small tools, all the debris of building the canoe had been swept away. The garage was bare, except for a thick layer of mud and some piles of debris caught in the corners. He would have to replace all the tools and supplies that had been taken, but he didn't mind. He had weathered the storm. That was a cliché, but he didn't care.

His feeling of triumph only lasted until he realized that the new canoe, the beauty of his heart, was gone. Now the garage didn't seem swept clean. It seemed empty. He stepped out the door and looked down the drive, afraid he would see pieces of her caught in the branches of the trees. But there was nothing. She had sailed away with the storm. He could hope that she rode the storm crest downstream, and that she had been left on a bank, as the water went down. If she were damaged, he could fix her.

He splashed down the drive through the shallow water and across the road to Sam's meadow. The water was gone from the road. The meadow had wide puddles in it, but there were large sections that were dry. Richard could tell exactly how high the water had been by the gray mud on the grass. He walked across the meadow to the stream. It was tumbling along with boils of white water, but it was back within its banks. It looked the way it did in spring when it was full of snowmelt. The evidence of its rampage was in the debris hanging on the tree limbs and the bushes and piled high up the banks.

He looked down the steam where it made a wide curve around the edge of the field. The bank had been gouged away. Fresh-dug dirt showed all around the curve. Richard walked downstream beside the water. At every bend his heart beat faster. He was so sure he would find the canoe. But he found nothing. He went as far as the bridge, and then he decided to turn back. He climbed up to the road and walked toward home.

When Richard saw Sam standing on his back porch, he turned in Sam's drive and stopped at the back steps. Sam stood there, looking down at him. He was in his sock feet. He had a cup of coffee in his hand.

"Richard," he said. "What are you doin down there in the meadow?

I was on my way over to check on you. I been worried."

"I'm okay. The water was in my downstairs last night, so there's some damage. And it took my deck. But the worst part is that I can't find my new canoe. It must have floated out of the garage when the water was deep. I've been down the stream looking for it."

"Them log lengths I had in the meadow is gone, every one of 'em. You didn't see them down there, did you?"

"No, but I wasn't looking for them either."

"Somebody's goin to get his firewood brought right to him."

"Mine's gone too, the whole pile. There are a few chunks sprinkled down my drive, but not very many. Most of it went down the stream with yours."

"I been out all night on emergencies. It's pretty bad out there. You want some coffee?"

"No thanks. I'm good. I want to get back to my house and take another look around. How deep did it get over here? Did it get in your barn?"

"It didn't. It went over your property and down your drive to the meadow. It took the log lengths and my picnic table, but the house was spared. I ain't been up to check my sheep yet, but I expect they're fine."

"That's good news."

"I'll be over later to see how you made out. I'm beat. I'm goin to get a little sleep first, now that I've seen you made it."

"Thanks, Sam. I'm coming back soon to get my truck. I'd like to see dry ground over there before I move it back."

"Okay. See you later. Come back if you run into problems."

"I will," Richard said. He walked to his house. The water had gone down a lot since he left.

CHAPTER 59

When he went back into the kitchen, Bonnie was there in her pink uniform.

"I got to have a ride, Sam. My car's in town."

"Glad to do it, sweetheart. Just let me get my boots and another cup of coffee."

"You ain't had no breakfast."

"I'll get something later. Everythin's goin to be mixed up today."

"You think we can make it?"

"Sure. We might have to take a few detours. I came out a little while ago, and I didn't have no trouble, and the water's goin down."

"Are you okay? You ain't slept all night."

"I'm beat. That's for sure. After I take you in, I can come back out and go to bed."

"Don't find no more people to help, Sam. I know you—you'll kill yourself tryin to help everyone else and not take care of yourself."

He put his arms around her. "That's your job, sweetheart." He was smiling. He felt really good about himself. He'd done some things that she didn't even know about yet. He hoped they would impress her. He wanted her to see he was a hero.

But she was thinking about herself. She ducked out of his arms. "I got to get goin, Sam. I don't know what kind of a situation I'll find when I get in there. It might be crazy."

"Where's Marnie and Danny gone?"

"They went over to Timmy's. Danny couldn't get him on his cell phone. I guess it'll be a while before we get our power back."

"I forgot about that. How'd you make coffee?"

Now she smiled. "I did it the old-fashioned way, like we use to do before we got the coffee maker. Remember?"

"Are you ready? I need to get in and back, so I can feed the pigs."

When he got home later, he checked around and fed the pigs, and then he went into the house. It was so quiet that it was spooky without the electricity. He stripped down and got under the covers and lay there wide-awake. The room was full of daylight. He pulled Bonnie's pillow on top of his face to shut it out.

Behind his eyes was everything that had happened in the night— the flashing lights, the white, boiling water, the terrified faces. He imagined he could hear the shouts, and the sirens, and the roar of the water.

There was so much action in his head that he couldn't stay still. He threw back the covers and sat up on the side of the bed. He walked to the kitchen in his bare feet to get himself some water and went back to his bed and lay down to give it another try, but it was no use. He lay there for a while, stuck on the idea that he needed to catch up the sleep he had missed. It was pretty obvious that no matter what he thought about it, his body was not going to cooperate. It was wide-awake and ready to get on with the day.

He threw back the covers and stood up. After he'd put on clean clothes, he felt more like himself. He walked through the kitchen, got his boots and whistled to Colt. He didn't feel like stopping for coffee or breakfast.

The first thing was to make sure the sheep were all right. He loaded his chainsaw and Colt into the back of the pickup and started up the hill. After that, he would go next door and check on Richard's situation. The brook was still very high. He could hear the roar of it even in the truck.

He hadn't gone very far up the hill before he came to the first downed tree. He could thank the storm for replacing the firewood it took. He got his saw and cut out a section of the trunk so he could drive on. There were three more trees across the road before he got to the sheep pasture, but they were all smaller than the first one.

The sheep were grazing peacefully, looking bright white in the sunshine, washed clean by the rain. The fence was another matter. He would have to walk the whole thing. He took the wires off the battery and grabbed his chainsaw just in case there was something bigger than branches on the line. He told Colt to stay in the truck, so he wouldn't spook the sheep, and he started walking along the fence just inside the line.

Sheep raised their heads from time to time to watch him, but they knew him, and he wasn't walking directly toward them, so they stayed calm. A few would look up and then go back to eating. He was able to count them. All fifteen were there. It was a sunny summer morning, a different world from yesterday and last night. It was hard to believe he was in the same place. He went all the way around, clearing the line, and then he hitched the wires to the battery again. When he put the tester on it, he was getting a good charge.

He would have to dig a new place for the sheep to get their water. The water had rampaged through the channel he'd made in the brook, taking the tub and filling the hole it sat in. He searched for the old tub and for the salt block, but the water had taken them both. He would have to come back later with another salt block and another tub, and he would have to dig a new hole and a new diversion channel for the water to fill the tub. He could do that later today when the water had gone down.

He got in his truck and drove down the hill. He planned to leave Colt at the house when he went to Richard's, but Colt looked disappointed when he told him to stay. "Oh, what the hell," he thought, and whistled for Colt to follow him.

They walked through the tree line and stopped dead to look around. The water was gone, but it had left a layer of gray mud everywhere. Sam could see that the water had covered the whole of Richard's yard, surrounding his house and garage and going right up to the trees on the property line. He couldn't see the other side of the yard or where the deck had been, because the house was in the way.

Richard came out his front door with his arms full. He saw Sam and smiled. He looked pretty cheerful, considering. "Well, Sam, you were right." He threw down a bundle of soggy clothes. "I never thought it could get so high. It just goes to show how wrong a person can be."

"When I came over here yesterday," Sam said, "I didn't think it was goin this high either. I was tryin to make sure you didn't get into trouble and get hurt."

"I appreciate that, Sam. It was neighborly of you." He started toward the door again.

"Did it get the whole downstairs?"

Richard went up the steps and turned to look back at him. "I'm afraid it did. It's a mess in here. Come and see for yourself."

Sam told Colt to stay and went inside. Richard was right about it being a mess. The gray mud was everywhere. It smelled wet and sour. It wouldn't be long before everything started to mold, and then the smell would be even worse.

Richard said, "I guess I'll have to gut the whole downstairs."

"Looks like it," Sam said. He walked along the hall to the kitchen and looked down the stairs into the ruined living room. "We should of moved your couch yesterday."

Richard was right behind him. "It wouldn't have mattered. We wouldn't have moved it far enough. I took a lot of stuff out of this room, but I put it in the bedroom, and the water got it there. We would have done the same thing with the couch."

Sam walked over to the sliding glass door and looked out. Richard said, "It took the whole deck, stairs and all."

"It looks like it took a lot more than that. Everything's different. It took your whole yard."

"I haven't been back there yet, but when I was looking for my canoe, I saw how it changed the banks downstream." He was standing beside Sam, looking out at where the yard used to be. "Remember all those loads of fill we brought in before we built the house? That's all gone, isn't it?"

Sam jumped down to the ground. It was a soft landing because of the mud. Richard followed him. They stood together looking at what used to be Richard's yard.

Sam thought the land was the way it was when he was a boy—a long curved bank by the water, low and flat. In ancient times the river must have carved it out. When he was a kid, it was covered with bushes, alders and shrubby willows. Now it was bare of everything but a layer of gray mud. The high water was flowing past right below the bank, chuckling a little.

Richard's face was blank, and his mouth was open. He looked like he was in shock. He said, "It's all gone, all of it, the gardens, the trees, everything. I can't believe it."

"Your house is still standin.'"

They both turned to look at the house. That was when they saw how the water had dug all the gravel out from under the foundation. The slab was cantilevered out over empty space.

After a silence, Richard said, "I thought it had spared my house. Now I'm not so sure."

"You need to get someone to look at it to see if the structure's been damaged."

Richard said, "It's a lot worse than I thought at first." Then he started to laugh.

That surprised Sam. His first thought was that Richard might be losing it. "What's so funny?" he said.

"Did you ever see that Charlie Chaplin movie called *The Gold Rush*?"

"No. I don't think I did."

"He's in this cabin that slides until half of it is hanging over a cliff. He doesn't know it, but every time he walks across the floor, the whole cabin tilts and he has to run back to the high side. It's very funny. You should see it sometime. I'm going to have to be careful how I walk in my house, so it doesn't tilt over empty space. That's what I was laughing about."

"You might want to move out until you can get some work done on that foundation."

"Yes, I could do that. Maybe I will. It would be a lot less depressing if I moved up to the cabin you built up by the pool." He was quiet for a minute. "Alyssa always loved the winter we spent in that cabin. I'm glad she isn't here to see this. It would break her heart. All her flowers gone, and maybe her house too." He looked at Sam. "If I could just find my canoe. But I've got to look some more. I only went as far as the bridge this morning."

Sam put a hand on his shoulder. "I'll ask around. Someone could of found it. You could put up some signs around town." He felt sorry for Richard. He didn't know if Richard had enough money or not. He probably didn't have flood insurance anyway. No one could have expected this little stream to go crazy the way it had.

"Thanks, Sam. I'm going to go out looking again pretty soon. Maybe it's further downstream. I haven't gone very far yet."

"I'm headin into Severance now to see what I can do, but I'll check on you when I get back to see if you found anythin."

"Thanks, Sam."

"Take it easy, man." He whistled to Colt and walked back to his house. No one was home. He left Colt on the porch and drove into Severance.

He got as far as the edge of town, where Spaulding Brook comes down the hill. At the house on the corner, there was stuff spread out on the lawn, and people were coming out the front door with their arms full. Sam didn't know the people who lived in that house, and he hadn't noticed that they were in trouble when he went by last night.

He parked his truck on the road and walked up the walk. He smiled and said hello to everyone he met, but he couldn't tell whose house it was or who was in charge.

Inside it was a shambles. Things were overturned. Everything was wet. There was mud covering the floor. Sam joined the lines of people working to clear out the rooms. It was fun for a while. Everyone was cheerful. People made jokes as they passed each other going in and out. If some of them were the owners of the house, they were certainly taking it well. Sam worked for almost an hour before he began to get restless. He wondered if there were other people in town who needed his help more than these people did.

When he finished the next load, instead of going back inside for more, he walked to his truck and got in. He waved to the people outside as he drove off toward the downtown. He stopped at several other houses and helped for short periods and then went on. There didn't seem to be any organization, just neighbors helping neighbors.

The whole city was filled with the sound of big machines. They rumbled past—bucket loaders and bulldozers and dump trucks full of mud and tree branches that the machines had picked up. It was amazing how much debris there was.

People were coming out of City Hall with armloads of boxes and piles of papers. Sam stopped long enough to ask someone what that was about. He was told that all the basement offices had been flooded and all the records were soaked.

There was lots of noise and bustle and plenty of work, but there weren't any more life-and-death situations like the ones Sam had participated in during the night. He felt disappointed. It might have been because he hadn't had any sleep that he felt so let down, but whatever it was, he didn't feel like participating in this new part of the disaster right now. He decided to go back home.

CHAPTER 60

Monika had been sitting in the kitchen playing solitaire all afternoon while she waited for the electricity to come back on again. The storm must have taken down a lot of wires. The rain had finally stopped, and the wind wasn't blowing so hard, but the daylight was fading. Soon it would be too dark to see the cards. Monika had to save her batteries. She would need the flashlight later if they didn't get the electricity fixed before night.

She realized that she hadn't seen Marmalade all day. That was unusual for him. He always seemed to make a point of walking through whatever room she was in. She didn't know whether he was checking on her, or giving her a chance to check on him, but whichever it was, he hadn't done it today.

She decided to check the whole house before it got darker. She went into each room and looked around. By the time she got to the front bedroom upstairs, she had seen all the other cats. And there was Marmalade sleeping on the guest bed. She must have forgotten to close the door. Marmalade looked up, blinking sleepily, when she shone the flashlight into the room. They both knew he was breaking the rules, but he didn't even look guilty.

She decided not to deal with it. She went back to the stairs and started down, holding onto the banister. It was dark, but she had the banister to guide her. She turned off the flashlight to save the batteries. A few steps further down, her foot landed wrong. She stumbled. She grabbed the banister with both hands to keep from falling, and the flashlight clattered down the remaining stairs. She heard it smash at the bottom, and she heard the batteries rolling across the floor of the hall.

She limped the rest of the way down and sat on the bottom step. Her ankle hurt so much it made her cry, and when she tried to put some weight on it, it hurt more. She couldn't even look at it, because the flashlight was broken. She sat there for what seemed like a long time, feeling sorry for herself. Then she got on her knees and pushed all the pieces of flashlight into the corner and limped down the hall to the downstairs bedroom.

She meant to rest for a little while, but the next thing she knew, it was eleven o'clock. She was surprised that she had been able to sleep with her ankle the way it was, but she was glad. It was definitely better when she woke up.

At least, it was better until she stood up to go to the bathroom. When she tried to put some weight on it, it started to hurt again. She went to the bathroom and then hobbled back to bed without even trying to clean her teeth in the dark.

When she finally fell asleep again, she dreamed that Alyssa was a little girl. She wanted to ride her bike to a new department store on the edge of town. She was eager to go there, and for some reason, Monika couldn't take her in the car. They were standing on the front lawn. Monika knew that's where they were, even though in the dream, the house and the lawn were different. Alyssa was holding her bike, ready to get on. Monika said she couldn't go. The traffic on the highway made it too dangerous. Alyssa got angry. She started to cry, and she flung down her bike. It hit Monika in the ankle, and she woke up with her ankle hurting. When she was awake, she felt the added pain of knowing that the days were gone when it was possible to keep Alyssa safe.

The rest of the night she slept fitfully, but she didn't allow herself to get up until the windows turned gray with daylight. Soon after that the phone rang. She hobbled out into the hall and answered it. It was Sonia.

"Nana," she said. "It took you so long to answer."

"This old plug-in phone in the hall is the only one that works without electricity. And it's early. Is something wrong?"

"We need to get you a new cell phone. You could carry it in your pocket."

"That's okay. I didn't like the one I used to have. It wasn't shaped like a phone. I never knew how to hold it."

"Is everything all right? Did you sleep well?"

"Pretty much. I twisted my ankle last night, just at dark."

"Oh damn it! I knew you took too long to get to the phone."

"It's better this morning."

"Why didn't you call me last night?"

"I didn't want you to worry. I thought it would be better this morning, and it is."

"But you're still limping. I can tell it's not all right. Could something be broken? I think you ought to go to the doctor."

"I will if it doesn't get better soon."

"I'm coming over to take a look. It's probably worse than you're telling me."

"No it's not. There's not much to see. Well, I haven't really looked. I broke the flashlight when I fell, so I couldn't take a look last night."

"Oh, Nan, I'll be right over."

Monika finished getting dressed and went to the kitchen to make herself some tea. That was easier than making coffee without electricity. She had just put the kettle on to boil when Sonia burst in.

"Nana, I want to talk to you about something. It's important. I've been thinking about it as I drove over here."

"Oh dear," Monika said. She sat down at the kitchen table. "It's not bad news about your dad, is it? Mabel called yesterday. She heard that the storm was devastating Vermont."

"We heard about flooding. That's all over Vermont, and lots of roads are washed out, but Dad doesn't have to worry about that. He's up quite high."

"His house is right beside the stream that comes down from that pool. That might be a cause for worry."

"I don't think it is, but I'm planning to call him in a little while. It's still too early. Right now I'd like to see you walk across the room. I can't tell anything while you're sitting down."

"All right, but it's really nothing, Sonia." She stood, leaning on the table. "My balance isn't so good any more. I must have twisted something in my ankle. I'm going to be careful of it today." She walked to the stove, slowly, trying as hard as she could not to favor the hurt ankle. She turned off the kettle. "I'm having some tea. Would you like a cup?"

Sonia was standing just inside the door. "No thanks," she said. "I can't stay. I just ran over to see how you were." She looked worried. "I can see that you're trying not to limp, but you're still limping a little. Is it swollen?"

"I don't think so. Don't worry so much, Sonia dear. It'll be okay by tomorrow."

"I hope so, but here's the thing, Nana, I think it's time for you to move. This is something I've been thinking about ever since you had all that trouble with your eyes."

Monika poured some hot water into her cup and carried it and the tea bag to the table so she could sit down. "It's very sweet of you, Sonia, and I appreciate it, but I'm fine. I don't need to be taken care of. I don't need it yet, anyway." She paused. "I hope I won't ever need it. I hear the distant rumblings, but maybe I'll get out before the train gets here, before you have to take care of me. That's what everyone hopes for, isn't it?"

"But, Nana, it's getting too hard for you living here alone. I mean you can't drive…."

"You don't understand. If I lose my independence, I won't ever get it back."

"I want you to be *safe*, Nana. You got hurt last night, and I didn't even know."

"But it was okay. I did all right on my own. A person wants to stay on their own as long as they can. You understand that. Once I get put into some system that takes care of me, I won't get out again. I'll get weaker, and after a while I won't be able to do anything for myself. I probably won't even be able to go to the bathroom on my own. That's a horrible thought."

"Nana, Brian and I want you to come and live with us. It would make us so happy."

"What would Jack say?"

"He loves you, Nana, and he knows if you were at our house, I could take much better care of you."

"And my cats? What about the cats?"

"Oh Nana, I don't know. I've thought about them. We could find them homes." She looked distressed.

Monika was sorry, but Sonia wasn't as distressed as *she* felt at the idea of abandoning her cats. She said, "They trust me. I couldn't betray them. Luckily, I don't need to. I'm doing just fine. You worry too much, Sonia. The day may come when I have to leave my home… and my cats…but it isn't here yet, thank goodness."

After Sonia left, Monika had such a sudden bout of diarrhea that she couldn't get to the bathroom in time. She had to spend a lot of time cleaning up after herself, and all the while she was thinking how fortunate she was to be living in her own home, taking care of herself. Maybe it was difficult as Sonia said, but she was glad she could take her time cleaning up, and that no one had to know about it. These accidents were happening more frequently the older she got, but she was able to keep them as her own little secrets.

Around noon, Sonia called. She had finally managed to get Richard on the phone. "You were right," she said. "It's much worse than we thought. That little stream turned into a monster torrent. It burst over its banks and took their whole yard, all the gardens, the tool shed, and part of the driveway. It ripped the deck off the house and took every board. Nothing was left. And it dug all the gravel from under the foundation of the house, so that the cement slab is sticking out in the air. Dad doesn't even know if it can be fixed. Can you believe it? And Dad was there the whole time. He was upstairs. I guess he's lucky the house wasn't swept away with him inside it. The whole downstairs got flooded. And you know what? The Martels' house right next door didn't even get touched. It's unbelievable, isn't it?"

All that came out in a rush. Finally, she had to stop for breath, and Monika was able to ask a question. "Is your dad all right?"

"He says he is, but you can't be sure. He was talking about how he had to go find his canoe. I guess it got swept away too. He sounded like he was more upset about the canoe than he was about the house. That makes me worry about him. I mean, maybe he's in shock or something."

"What's he going to do?"

"He says he's going to clean up the downstairs and rebuild the foundation, but he doesn't even know if it's possible. He has to get someone who knows about stuff like that to look at it and tell him what needs to be done. I guess we're pretty lucky. He could have been killed."

"If he does rebuild, where's he going to live in the meantime?"

"He says he's going to move up to the cabin while he's getting the house fixed, but he can't stay there very long. In a few months it'll be too cold."

"He and your mother stayed there for the winter once."

"That was a long time ago. They were much younger, and he had her for company. But that's what he's saying now."

"Oh Sonia, this is the first time I have had a reason to be glad that your mother isn't here any more, but I am so grateful that she didn't have to see all her care and hard work for her house and her gardens wiped out in one night."

"Me too," Sonia said. "I'll call you back if I hear any more."

CHAPTER 61

Richard woke up with his face buried under the covers. As soon as he stuck his nose out, he knew why he was sleeping the way he was. The fire must have gone out some time during the night. The air was icy.

He burrowed deeper into the warm covers. He was in the cabin. It was the day before Thanksgiving, the day he was planning to drive to Stamford for the holiday weekend.

Last year he and Alyssa went together. She had been sick all summer and fall, but everyone thought the cancer had gone into remission. Everyone was grateful that she would get better. Now that he thought about it, he could see that perhaps Alyssa had known that she wouldn't recover, but no one knew that then. Was it really only a year ago? It all seemed to have taken place in a different life and to different people.

He felt the way he had felt long ago when he lost his job and moved into the cabin from Stamford, like a wounded animal going to its burrow. Here he was living in the cabin again, with no idea what he was going to do next. That other time he thought he had lost everything, but he'd been wrong. Alyssa joined him in the cabin, and it turned out that they were beginning something, not ending it. But this time really was the end. Alyssa was gone, and so was the life and the home they'd built together in Vermont.

He stayed in the warm bed for as long as he could, but eventually, he had to throw back the covers and pull on his icy clothes. When he went out to the outhouse, he noticed that the temperature was the same outside as it was inside. The fire must have gone out early, and it must have snowed all night. A fresh, puffy blanket lay over everything. In the dawn light, it was almost blue. The trunks and branches were black lines etched against it. Slow flakes were still coming down.

Richard considered stuffing what he needed for the weekend into his knapsack and heading for Stamford without making a fire, but he didn't want to leave that way. Instead, he made a quick hot fire with a lot of kindling and small pieces of wood, so that in half an hour the cabin was beginning to get warm and he had a kettle of hot water for coffee and a wash-up.

It wasn't the way it used to be when Alyssa brought him coffee in bed, but then, nothing was the way it used to be. The whole landscape changed when Alyssa left it, and nothing would ever be the same again. Sometimes he thought it was getting harder for him to be without her. He didn't seem able to get used to the new reality. He missed her more than ever.

Around noon, he let the fire go down and got ready to leave. He had spent the morning in the soft silence of the new snow. Even the animals and the winter birds weren't moving around yet. It was the right way to say farewell. And anyway, he didn't know how much time he wanted to spend with Monika, now that Alyssa wasn't there for a buffer. What he did know for sure was that he planned to make good use of her running water.

It was snowing lightly when he started out, but the roads were good. He got to Monika's a little before five o'clock, after an uneventful trip. Everything at the house looked just the same as last year. Monika even seemed glad to see him.

He offered to take her out to dinner, but she didn't want to go, so they sat at her kitchen table and talked for a while. Finally, Richard found a chance to ask if he could take a shower. Monika seemed surprised.

"If you would rather I waited until later, that's fine," Richard said.

"Oh no, of course not. You go ahead. I put some clean bath towels in your room. It's the room where you always used to stay..." she paused, looking distressed, "...with Alyssa," she finished in a whisper.

"I'm sorry, Monika," he said. "It's hard for us all." Now it was his turn to pause. "And I don't think it will get any easier. I think it might even be getting harder." He reached out and patted her hand.

She smiled a sad, little smile and pulled her hand away so that she could take off her glasses and wipe her eyes. "Thank you, Richard. Now go take a shower."

"I will." He stood up. "It's been almost three months since I've had a real shower. I've been fantasizing about your plumbing the whole way down. I'm eager to know if it feels as wonderful as I expect it to."

She smiled.

He took his knapsack upstairs to the front bedroom, got some clean clothes, and his toothbrush and hairbrush, and went across the hall to Monika's unfashionable bathroom.

Her shower was in an old claw-footed bathtub. The shower curtain hung in a circle over the tub. Richard didn't care what kind of arrangement she had, as long as he could stand under hot water and get clean all at once, instead of washing a little section of himself at a time with a washcloth dipped in a bowl of warm water.

He got undressed, adjusted the water temperature, and stepped inside the circle of shower curtain. It was even more wonderful than he had imagined. He had forgotten what a pleasure a hot shower could be. Or maybe he had taken the pleasure for granted in those days when he could take a shower whenever he wanted. Maybe he should stay in his cabin in the woods and come down every month or two to visit the family and indulge in the luxury of their plumbing.

He stayed under the water as long as he decently could. He didn't want to use all her hot water. Finally, reluctantly, he turned it off and stepped out into the steam-filled room.

In the kitchen Monika had laid out some crackers and cheese. There was a bowl of chopped vegetables and some sauce to dip them in.

"I wasn't sure how hungry you would be, Richard."

"This looks fine to me. I had a big breakfast at home."

She looked surprised.

"In the cabin in the woods. That's where I've been staying." He sat down and took some food.

When he looked up, he saw that she was frowning at him. For a minute he was afraid he had done something wrong, but then she said, "But have you been warm enough? It's been getting cold lately."

"There's a nice little woodstove in that cabin. It's plenty warm enough when the fire's going well. Thank you for the supper. What's the plan for tomorrow?"

"Sonia's cooking the turkey at her house this year. I told her I would be glad to do it, but she had something new she wanted to try. She has a new oven. Maybe it's that."

Richard said, "Is there any way I can help?"

"Well, actually, there is. I'm counting on you to pick up Mabel. She's coming again. Sonia doesn't seem to mind this year."

"I can certainly do that, but I could do some cooking too."

"Sonia and Alix have divided it all between them. I offered to help, of course, but they said all they wanted us to do is to set the table." She looked down for a minute. Then she said, "It will be just like last year, except we have traded one Alyssa for another." She looked at him then and tried to smile, but it was a small attempt, and it wavered and died away as she looked down again.

Richard opened his mouth to say something comforting, but what was there? They would always bump against the cold reality that Alyssa was gone. Finally, Richard said, "Sometimes I feel as though she isn't really gone. She's just somewhere else, and some time sooner or later, I'll see her again. I even feel that she's keeping up with us and knows what's happening to all of us. Do you ever feel that way?"

She looked up with a real smile this time. "Oh Richard, you said it so well. That's just the way I feel." Then a shadow passed over her face. "I think I used to feel that way about Harry and about Aaron too, but maybe not as often. Alyssa was so much a part of our lives. And Aaron was on the other side of the world when he died."

Neither of them said anything more for a long time, and they didn't look at each other, but Richard felt closer to Monika than he ever had before. They sat there in silence, until they both stood up at once and hugged each other. Richard didn't even know which of them moved first. Then Richard went upstairs to his room, leaving Monika to turn out the lights and lock the doors for the night.

The next morning when Richard went downstairs, Monika was in the dining room struggling to put the extra leaf in the table.

"Here, Monika, let me help you with that." He took the other end of the leaf and helped her to slide it into place. They stood at opposite ends of the table and pushed it together. "That does it," Richard said. "It looks nice. Will it be big enough?"

"There will be nine of us, just like last year, but Alyssa is going to be sitting in her high chair. Alix and Reuben are bringing it. So we only need to set eight places." She was pushing chairs around as she talked. "See—three on each side, and one at each end—doesn't it look nice? We can put Alyssa's high chair on the corner beside her mother. Thank you for helping me."

"You could have called me. I was just being lazy. I had another shower, which I didn't need. It wasn't as amazing as last night's, but it was pleasant."

"Good. Did you sleep all right?"

"Yes, thank you." He didn't tell her that he had woken several times during the night reaching for Alyssa, before he remembered she was gone.

In the kitchen Monika poured him some coffee and then started back toward the dining room.

"Aren't you going to join me?" he said.

"I'm too nervous, Richard. Once I get everything on the table, I'll be able to relax. I want everything to look as nice as it did last year. I don't know why, but it seems important."

"I can understand why you feel that way, but I don't think anyone will notice."

"I suppose I feel that I'm doing it for Alyssa." She paused and thought about what she had said. "I know that doesn't make sense. Forget I said it." She went out of the room.

Richard stood in the kitchen, sipping his coffee and thinking about what she had said. Then he carried his cup to the dining room, and they set the table together. They worked out a system without saying anything. Monika put a pile of plates on the table, and Richard spread them out to all the places. They did that with the silver and everything else. They didn't talk, but they didn't need to. When it was all in place, they stood back and admired their work.

"I think we're ready, don't you, Richard?"

"It looks ready to me. It looks better than last year. That's what I think. I'm going to pour myself another cup of coffee, and then I'm going to go pick up Mabel. Will she be ready?"

"I'll call her and tell her to meet you out front."

"That would make it easy. Shall I pour you some coffee?"

"Yes, please. I can relax now."

Soon after Richard returned with Mabel, the others began to arrive. Suddenly the kitchen was full of people, taking off coats and bringing in pots and bowls of food. Sonia staggered in carrying a huge turkey in a roasting pan. She was the center of importance. Richard could see how she liked that position.

He sat at the kitchen table with Monika and Mabel. He expected he would be given orders to help, but he wasn't. Alix and Sonia and their husbands put the food on the table. Jack hovered near the food getting in everyone's way, and Baby Alyssa sat on Monika's lap. She was cheerful and curious until her mother walked past, and then she looked as though she was going to cry.

Finally, everything was in order, and they were told to go to the dining room. Richard was directed to sit at one end of the table and Monika at the other with Mabel beside her.

Richard looked down the table. Everyone was serving food while they talked. Richard thought about last year, when Alyssa, the real Alyssa, sat beside him. She was trying to eat, but mostly she was trying to disguise the fact that she wasn't eating by pushing food around on her plate.

"Dad, you're not listening. I asked you a question."

"I'm sorry. What was it?"

"We were all wondering what your plans are."

"Plans for what?"

"What are you going to do next?"

"I'm not sure. I don't have much in mind. I thought I would stay here for a few days." He looked down the table. "That is, I'd like to stay, if Monika will put up with me. I expect she has some things that need fixing. I thought I'd probably stay through the weekend."

"Oh Nana, show him the back door, the way all the cold comes in."

"And the television aerial," Brian said. "She doesn't need it any more. It's come loose, and it's banging around up there. I've been meaning to take it down. I could bring my ladder over on Saturday, and we could do it together."

"Let's do that," Richard said. "What about it, Monika?"

"I'd like that. The television aerial has been much worse since that storm that ruined your house. And there are a couple of other things I want fixed. I can't think what they are right now because I'm trying to remember. They'll come back in a minute."

Mabel asked Richard what he was going to do when he went back to Vermont.

"There won't be much I can do until spring. I spent all fall trying to find out what I needed to do to repair the house and who I could find to do it, and I didn't get very far. Everyone is so busy. I hardly ever see Sam Martel any more. I don't know when he does his barn chores or his butchering."

Brian said, "I should think you would at least be able to get an estimate."

"I know," Richard said. "It's very frustrating. There was an awful lot of damage, so there's a lot that needs to be rebuilt. Everyone is trying to get done before winter really gets here, and maybe I haven't been persistent enough. I haven't been sure what I wanted to do."

Suddenly Alix jumped up from the table and hurried out of the room. No one said anything, and in a few minutes she came back and sat down again.

Richard asked her what was the matter.

"I couldn't help it," she said, trying to get control of herself. "All of a sudden, it seemed so awful that everyone wanted to know what you were going to do, and no one mentioned Mom at all."

"But of course not," Sonia said. "She isn't here."

Alix looked at her and wiped her eyes. "That's what made me cry. It seemed so awful to leave her out, when she used to be the center of everything. And then I remembered how she brought us one of her paintings last Thanksgiving. I look at that painting every day in Alyssa's room, and I think about how amazing it is that Alyssa is here, and then I think how Mom isn't here, and it's all so strange. Sometimes I get overwhelmed by it."

Richard would have liked to put his arms around her to comfort her, but little Alyssa was in the way, so he did nothing but look at her, knowing just how she felt.

She was wiping Alyssa's face. She looked up at him and said, "Dad, why are you going back to Vermont now? Why don't you stay down here for the winter?"

It caught him by surprise. His first thought was that he really needed to get a couple of cords of wood delivered while a truck could still get up to the cabin, but he didn't say it out loud because that was one more thing he wouldn't need to do if he wasn't there.

Sonia said, "Oh Dad, that's such a great idea. You could stay right here with Nana."

Richard looked down the table at Monika, but she was talking to Mabel and hadn't heard what they were saying. "She might not want a permanent houseguest for the whole winter," he said.

"Dad, we've all been so worried about her. I wanted her to move in with us, but she won't leave her cats. She really shouldn't try to live alone any more. This could be the perfect solution."

Brian said, "Wait a minute, honey. Don't rush him. He's got his own life up there, and his own business. He's got to think about whether it's possible. He knows we want him."

"Thanks, Brian. I actually don't have much business right now. I cut way back on clients when Alyssa got sick, and I haven't really built back up again."

Alix said, "It would be wonderful if you were here this winter, Dad. Alyssa is changing so fast. She does something new almost every day. I don't want you to miss seeing all the things she's learning to do."

Richard looked down the table. Monika was listening now. "I want to think about this, and Monika and I will need to talk it over and see if we can work it out. What do you think, Monika?"

She nodded and smiled at him. "We'll figure it out. Don't worry."

CHAPTER 62

Sam had to leave the job site early to fix his chainsaw. For the first time in a long while, he got home before Bonnie did. He could have worked on the saw in the basement, but he decided to spread out some newspapers and take the saw apart in the corner of the kitchen floor near the woodstove. That way he could spend a little time with Bonnie while she cooked dinner.

They were talking about Richard when Marnie got home. Bonnie said she saw his truck in his driveway.

Marnie took off her jacket and boots and sat down at the kitchen table. "I've seen his truck a couple of times in the last few days. He must be back from wherever he went. Have you talked to him, Pop?"

"Not yet. I ain't even seen his truck. I'll get over there one of these days."

"You think he's really goin to stay in that cabin all winter?"

"That's what he said."

There was a crash and then Danny came into the room.

Marnie said, "Danny, I told you not to do that."

"It's okay, Ma. I was just practicing my long jump. I can do six stairs now."

"Well, don't do it any more. I've told you before."

"Good old Ma," he said, sitting down beside her. "What're you doin, Gramp?"

"Fixin my saw. It's clogged with sawdust. I have to take it apart." He was hoping Danny would take an interest. He planned to show him how to keep a saw running.

But all Danny said was, "Cool." He had his phone with him, and it interested him much more than the saw did.

There was a knock on the door. Bonnie's little dog started barking so hard that every bark shook her whole body and drove her back a step. Colt raised his head and looked at the door, but he didn't stand up.

Bonnie said, "I wonder who that could be."

"I'll get it." Marnie jumped up and went to the door. "Hello, Richard. Come in. Speak of the devil. We were just talking about you."

"That doesn't sound good," Richard said. He stepped inside and kicked off his boots by the door.

Sam stood and brushed the sawdust off his pant legs. "How you been, Richard? We ain't seen you for a while."

"I've been in Stamford. I went down for Thanksgiving, but I stayed on for a couple of weeks."

Sam pulled a chair out for Richard and sat down at the table himself. "Have you been livin in the cabin?"

"I have. I was up there until Thanksgiving, and I've been there since I got back a few days ago, but I haven't got much wood left."

"We can help you out, man. Don't worry about that."

"Thanks, Sam. I knew I could ask. I appreciate it. I would have bought a couple of cords, but I've pretty much decided not to stay up there this winter after all."

Sam could tell Bonnie was listening. She asked Richard if he wanted her to make him a cup of coffee.

"Thanks. I'd love some, but I need to get on the road. I'm heading down to Stamford tonight." He looked at Sam and shrugged his shoulders. "Alyssa's mom wants me to stay with her this winter, and there's not much I can do on my house until spring."

Sam said, "I've had so much work myself that I ain't had a chance to get over to see how you were makin out."

"That's okay, Sam. I knew you were busy. Not that much has changed since the storm anyway. I cleaned out the ground floor, but that's about it. I'm taking a load of stuff down to Stamford, and I guess I'll be down there until spring, and after that...I don't know."

"I ought to be able to find you somebody good in the spring if you decide to rebuild."

"Here's my problem, and I really think it's why I haven't gotten anywhere all fall. I'm not sure I know what I want to do. Does it make any sense to spend the kind of money I'd have to spend to fix that foundation?"

When Sam looked at Marnie, he was surprised to see how intently she was listening.

Richard stood up. "Anyhow," he said, "I put a padlock on the door, and I want you to have a key in case you need to go in there for any reason." He took an envelope out of his pocket and handed it to Sam. "I put down my cell phone number and Monika's phone number and address. That's where I'll be staying. The key to the padlock is in there."

Sam stood up and walked to the door with Richard. "I'm sorry to see you go, man."

"Maybe in the spring, I'll have a better idea of what I ought to do." He bent down to put on his boots.

"Have you ever thought about sellin the place?"

Richard stood up and looked him in the eye. "I have, yes. I'm beginning to think the Vermont part of my life might be over—first Alyssa and now the house...."

Sam didn't know what to say to that.

Marnie was standing there with him now. She said, "We're real sorry, Richard."

"I'm confused about it. If I try to sell it without putting a lot of money into it, I won't get much, even assuming I could find someone who wanted it."

"Richard," Sam said. "You know my dad sold you that property to pay for Ma's hospital bills. He thought he had to do it. He didn't tell me until it was a done deal, and I guess that's because he was ashamed of it, but if there's any way we could work out a deal to buy it back... well, I don't want to rush you, and I know you ain't made up your mind yet, but...well, just remember that it might be that we could work it out." He could feel Marnie's hand on his shoulder.

Richard was studying his face. "I won't forget that, Sam. We've never talked about this, and I guess I wasn't sure how you felt, but of course, we never had a reason to talk about it before. I'm really glad to know." He held out his hand, and they shook on it. "I'll be in touch. I have to think about all this. Goodbye, Marnie." He waved to Bonnie and went out the door.

After the door shut, Marnie said, "Wow. I didn't see that comin."

"Me neither," Sam said. "I been too busy to think about what he was goin to do."

Marnie looked out the window. "He ain't goin back to his place. He's goin the other way."

"He must be leavin for downcountry, like he said."

Sam looked around at Bonnie, and the next thing he knew, Marnie had him by the waist and was waltzing him around the kitchen table.

Danny looked up. "Hey, what's goin on? What's all this about?"

"Richard's goin to sell his land, and we might be able to buy it. Just think, Danny, we could get Gramp's land back." She kissed the top of Danny's head and sat down at the table. She was out of breath.

Bonnie turned around to look at them. "He didn't say he was goin to sell his place. He said he'd think about it."

Sam went back to the saw and lowered himself down to the floor beside it. He'd finished clearing out the lumps of sawdust and was ready to put it back together. He couldn't see Bonnie from his spot on the floor. "He's goin to sell, honey. You heard him say the Vermont part of his life was over."

"You and Marnie better not get your hopes up. Where would you get that kind of money anyhow? You don't know what he's goin to ask for it, but you can bet it'll be more than your dad got when he sold it."

"You're probably right, Ma, but we never thought we'd even get this close. And who knows. It might could happen."

"Set the table for me, will you, Marnie? The spaghetti's just about cooked. Danny, you can help too."

"In a minute, Grammie."

Sam had his saw back together. He set it in the mudroom and carefully folded the newspapers around the piles of sawdust. He put the papers in the woodstove and went to wash his hands.

When he walked into the kitchen again, Bonnie was saying it could happen.

"What're you talkin about?"

"Richard's house. It wouldn't make any sense to rebuild it because another storm could come along and take it out again."

When they were all sitting down at the table with their plates of spaghetti, Marnie said, "I wouldn't build down there so close to the water. You can see how the water is always goin to go over that low place on its way to the meadow across the road. But look at this house. It wasn't in danger. Those old-time people knew what they were doin."

"They probably wouldn't let you build in a place like that nowdays. The regulations'd get you."

Bonnie said, "How come Richard got to build there then?"

"That was a while ago. They didn't have all that floodplain stuff when Richard was buildin. And they couldn't stop him if he wanted to rebuild because it's grandfathered. If we bought the land, we could repair the house if we wanted to, and they couldn't stop us."

"Maybe," Marnie said. "But it wouldn't make sense. If it was mine, I'd use the utility lines and septic that's already there, and I'd put a doublewide up in the tree line. It'd be safe there."

"Really, Ma? We could do that?"

"Who knows? We'll have to wait and see. We'll be okay either way, but it would be great if we could pull it off."

Sam looked over at Bonnie. She was smiling.

CHAPTER 63

Monika said, "It was a wonderful idea of yours to open up this fire-place, Richard. I would never have done it without you."

"I realized that the thing I missed most from Vermont was a wood fire. A fire makes you feel at home wherever you are."

"What do you think you'll do when spring comes?"

They had rearranged Monika's living room so that they each had an easy chair pulled close to the fireplace.

Richard got up to put another log on the fire. He looked down at Monika as she sat looking into the flames. He remembered how she was always trying to boss Alyssa around and how it drove Alyssa crazy. For some reason, he didn't have that problem. When she tried to tell him what to do, he laughed as though it was meant to be a joke, and that was the end of it.

He shut the fire screen and sat down again. He looked into the fire when he spoke. It was easier to be honest that way. "I don't know what I'll do. I kind of dread going back. It didn't seem so far away when Alyssa was alive, but now.... Somehow I would like to stay closer to the girls and their children." He paused. "I say I don't know what I'm going to do, but I have taken on a few clients in the last couple of months, as though I was planning to start a new life in Stamford. I did that without really making a decision." He kept his eyes on the fire. "And then there's living here. You and I have gotten comfortable with each other this winter. At least, I know I have.... So, I guess I wouldn't mind staying on, if you'd have me." He didn't look at her, but he could hear her shifting in her seat.

Then she sighed. "I would love to have you stay on. When Sonia suggested that you move in, I wasn't sure. It seemed like another way to lose my independence...and maybe it is. But it has also been very comfortable. There are so many things, like getting to the grocery store, that I don't have to worry about now. But what about your house?"

"I've been thinking about it, and I think I might sell it as it is. I could clean out what's salvageable and just let it go."

She looked at him then. "But, Richard, what about Alyssa's ashes?"

"They're on the Martels' land, and besides, the Martels would love to buy my land back. I've been thinking that I might be able to make that possible without having to take a big loss myself. After all, I made my living as a tax accountant." He smiled at her, but she looked away into the fire.

They were both silent for a while, and then Richard said, "She isn't there anyway. She's in our hearts. She'll always be in our hearts."

"It's so hard."

"I know. It will always be hard, but we have to go on."

"Yes," she said. "We have to go on, and we have to take little pleasures where we find them. Alyssa taught me that. It *will* be hard, but there are always little pleasures."

ACKNOWLEDGMENTS

Thanks to everyone who helped me with this book:

John Mahoney for the cover photograph.
Molly Porter for the watercolor still life on the frontispiece.
Ceres Porter for her beautiful poem, *Night Time at Noon.*
Molly Porter for hours and hours of copyediting and recommendations for changes that made the book much better and deeper.
Glenn Suokko for his beautiful design.

I had a lot of help with the photographs for this book, and I would like to thank all the people who contributed. First of all, Bill Porter drove with me all over central Vermont looking for the right photographs. We went to lots of places trying unsuccessfully to find ravens. Then Jane Culp gave me permission to use five of her wonderful raven drawings. Her drawings are at the beginnings of Chapters 4, 10, 12, and 56. There is another drawing at the end of the book.

Dave Bulow gave me the raven photograph for Chapter 1. Art Knox gave me a photograph of his band for Chapter 16. Katie Decker took two pictures of her cat for Chapters 42 and 60. Peter Macfarlane let me photograph a canoe he made for Chapter 20, and he gave me a photograph of a canoe he was building for Chapter 43. Bill and I went to his home in Vergennes where he builds his cedar strip canoes for his business, Otter Creek Smallcraft.

At the beginning of Chapter 45 is a photograph of a pastel still life done by Anita Morreale near the end of her life. Chapter 51 has a photograph of two ravens by Tom Stuwe. Chapter 52 has Molly Porter's watercolor of a butterfly, and Chapters 58 and 59 have photographs of Hurricane Irene that I found on the internet.

Thank you all for your help.

Ruth Porter was born in New York City and grew up in Alliance, Ohio, where her father was a doctor. She graduated from Laurel School in Cleveland, and from St. John's College in Annapolis, Maryland. She did a year of secretarial school in Boston and then got married to Bill Porter. In 1964, they went to Vermont, to Clarendon Springs, near Rutland. After eight years they moved to a hill farm in Adamant, near Montpelier, where they have lived ever since.

Ruth raised four children and took care of the farm. (One of the children said that she and Bill learned everything they knew about farming from books, and most of those books were novels.) They had varying numbers of sheep, cows, pigs and chickens, and a big garden. Altogether, they raised most of their food.

Ruth spent her whole life reading and writing, but she began working on serious fiction during those hectic years. She has published three novels, as well as a book about her grandfather, Maxwell Perkins, one of America's most widely respected editors. Bill and Ruth started the publishing company, Bar Nothing Books, in 2005.

For more information about Ruth Porter and Bar Nothing Books go to: www.ruthkingporter.com and www.barnothingbooks.com.